RADON DAUGHTERS

Iain Sinclair has lived in London for thirty years. In the 1970s he ran Albion Village Press, publishing Brian Catling, Chris Torrance and several volumes of his own poetry. He is the author of two other novels: *Downriver*, which won the 1992 Encore Award for the year's best second novel, and the James Tait Black Memorial Prize; and *White Chappell Scarlet Tracings*. He has also published several books of poetry, including *Lud Heat* and *Suicide Bridge*. His most recent books are the critically acclaimed *Lights Out for the Territory*, a record of journeys on foot around London, and *Slow Chocolate Autopsy*, a collection of linked stories illustrated by Dave McKean.

Also by Iain Sinclair

FICTION

White Chappell Scarlet Tracings
Downriver
Slow Chocolate Autopsy (with Dave McKean)

NON-FICTION

Lights Out for the Territory

DOCUMENTARY

The Kodak Mantra Diaries (Allen Ginsberg in London)

POETRY

Black Garden Poems
Muscat's Würm
The Birth Rug
Lud Heat/Suicide Bridge
Flesh Eggs & Scalp Metal: Selected Poetry
Jack Elam's Other Eye
Penguin Modern Poets 10
The Ebbing of the Kraft
Conductors of Chaos (Editor)

Iain Sinclair

RADON DAUGHTERS

A voyage, between art and terror,
from the Mound of Whitechapel to the
limestone pavements of the Burren

Granta Books
London

Granta Publications, 2/3 Hanover Yard, London N1 8BE

First published in Great Britain by Jonathan Cape 1994
This edition published by Granta Books 1998

A CIP catalogue record for this book is
available from the British Library.

1 3 5 7 9 10 8 6 4 2

Printed and bound in Great Britain by
Mackays of Chatham PLC

For
Nick Austin
who let the hare from the gate.

And
Christopher Petit
who valiantly attempted to shoot the thing
(before it got away).

A commonplace event, it belonged in another book. A headless body recovered from the foreshore of the Thames at Wapping. Male. Caucasian. Age unknown. A returned floater.

Bare legs. Waistcoat. Buttons removed from the shapeless coat.

No ID. No personal jewellery. No cash. No plastic.

A shard of pottery, the colour of dried blood, screwed into the fist. The fingers had to be cracked to remove it. An animal, panther or jaguar. Broken off at the neck.

A sodden pellet of paper and wool was extracted from the lining of the coat. Tweezered, smoothed, fed into the image intensifier. A satisfying puzzle for the technicians. Curse? Or coded instruction?

TWO THOUSAND YEARS AGO PERU DEATH.

The man, DB461, was subsequently identified as Emanuel Swedenborg.

BOOK ONE

SWEDENBORG'S ORCHARD

Let me tell you, my friend, that there are things done to-day in electrical science which would have been deemed unholy by the very men who discovered electricity — who would themselves not so very long before have been burned as wizards.

Bram Stoker, *Dracula*

ONE

The Roebuck (where else?) was not Sileen's kind of boozer. *I don't want this*. He limped over the cobbles, his maliciously polished boots kicking sparks from their irregular contours. A snarling, unlicensed killer dog buckled the mesh fence of the car auction yard, its chisel teeth exposed in wistful savagery. Sileen convulsed, serrated fingernails clawed at an impacted gut. Grimly, he advanced on his rendez-vous, blind to the feral distractions of the night: a pre-arson warehouse, rubbled tenements, things that crept beneath a smoky and defiled moon (a cigarette stub fizzing in a saucer of yellow milk).

I can still change my mind. He smiled a warning. Unconvinced ghosts backed off, revenants drew up their knees, huddled deeper into their pits, bolstered the webbed and furry shadows. It was all a painterly sham. A fraud with hair. The walls of the pub trembled in anticipation. Sileen's ruthlessly cultivated tunnel vision eliminated any other way out. *It is written*. Mortality sucks. *I will pay the price*.

Sileen had been troubled by the house again, the grey rock landscape, the tower. He had seen them here. Seen them floating above the hospital like a dark conspiracy, like clouds cut from corrugated fencing. Remote, fantastic, a vision that did not concern him – his life. He was a dead man on parole. He knew how the story ended. Digressions, he abhorred.

Used light, eager to escape, revived the heraldic beast that had been etched into a panel of frosted glass, blooded its eye. The Roe-Buck. Sileen spurned the omen and stepped inside. Askead was late. The dingy bar was solid with lowlife, too stupid to hang themselves at home. Homeless. This was their home. Meaningless draff cut loose by the rationalization of the brewery. The pesthole was their last oasis before an eternity of streets, cardboard coffins, piss-lacquered doorways.

Sileen elbowed his way to the plank, brushing aside slack spinneret tongues, nylon thigh exchanges, the suck of fat stockings, tweed burs, mouths moist and dark as dentated armpits. He waited, he endured. An elongated agony of flat time, while the curate decapitated a pint of the black stuff with a tineless comb. Sump oil iced with idiot spittle.

He swayed, balancing his brew. The only resting place was on a wooden bench, between a one-eyed tinker and an old biddy who was clearing the deck for her next half by letting the dregs of her previous one run out from her shoe. *This is no use to me. It belongs to a lesser mind.*

'I can take *you* anytime. Two fingers. The stump of me tongue.'

An old feller sparred his way out of a mossy jacket, revealing thin white arms, deformed by clusters of blue-veined muscle.

'Sit down now will yer, for Jasus' sake. Sit down, Pater.' The woman in the mulberry coat plucked at his sleeve. 'Sit down and I'll fetch you a drink over.'

'Old man, am I? Watch me dance then. I'll paddle your mug to custard, I will.' Creaking, he tried to pull back his shoulders, heaving, stalk-eyed, on an imaginary chest-expander. He jabbed and spun, pounded at the defenceless air. Fell back, white-lipped, whistling like a kettle, onto the bench.

Sileen was ready to jack it in, give the whole business up. It was all too familiar – the cycle of challenge and counter-challenge, the sorry rituals of violence glissading into a show of blood and tears.

A silver-dipped vagrant with the ineffectually faxed version of a handsome face looked hard at Sileen, and would not drop his gaze.

'Two things, Sligo. Two things, am I right?' He smiled, generously, dangerously, this countryman. 'The music . . . and the drink. The booze and the song.' He began to tap his foot, to rock back on the high stool. And, immediately, others joined with him. Ancient enemies, feuding brothers, condemned traitors – arms around one another's shoulders, slapping, laughing; salty droplets trickling from pale blue liars' eyes.

'You ould divil, you shite icicle. Any dacent man'd lay you on the boards 'fore you'd so much as gob in his pocket.' A previously silent presence, percolating in a thunderhead of suppressed grievances, stepped forward from the obscurity of the bar's outer darkness, the Maltese quarter. His shoes were soft and clean, always a bad sign. And his target, the old feller, was gone, out of it; sunk into the peaty torpor of racial melancholy, Atlantic weather. It was the Sligo man was revenged

8

himself against future insults. Hollow, clubbing blows skidded from the victim's head and shoulders – the bandaged futility of a blackthorn thrashing a dead donkey.

The ill-matched pair locked faces; geriatric adulterers sick with remembered lust. They cooed with hate, spitting into their partner's throat. The floor tilted on them in a shatter of plywood, broken chairs. They rolled and writhed through puddles of ash and ullage, poultices of reeking mud. To yelps and loud halloos, one of the combatants would gain an edge, straddle his chum, crunch bone until gouty knuckles peeled and split. Then he would obligingly withdraw, roll off, soak up his own dole of punishment. Streaked with gore, the men groaned and gasped in furious cloacal absorption. The work was grim, merciless, carried out, so it was understood, on behalf of all the drinkers. On behalf of the room itself. The bricks demanded it. The paper was dying on the walls for want of a lick of plasma. It did not matter who the celebrants were. One night was as good as another. All nights were the same.

It ended as suddenly as it had begun. The spiteful aggressor slipped back into the shadows to claim his perch among the pimps. The Sligo man vigorously french kissed the mulberry coat, easing the sting from his fist beneath her trailing skirts.

Inevitably, at the post-coital lull, Ian Askead manifested himself – fists balled in pocket, shouldering the door, pug head rolling from side to side, checking the mugshots, weighing his chances, death or glory in a roll-up drag. Lupine (on a cadet scale), urgent, blasphemous, he picked at chainsaw teeth with a blunted matchend. The horizontal tails of his nicotine-tanned labcoat swished, as he bounced towards what remained of the action. There were skulls to stomp. Women to be violated as part of the general amnesty. He polished his crotch in undisguised excitement, placing an ankle with mischievous precision to tumble the largest of the professional alcoholics, a genial and brain-burnt horsebutcher, into the lap of a Valletta razorman. Who happened to be gobbing on his palm, prior to highfiving an arrangement, whereby he would trade a brace of hot Sierras (1600L, D reg, MoT 9 months, 2 months tax) against some underage gash from Bootle, who had already served eighteen months on the kiddieporn circuit. You can't wind the clock back when thirteen year olds develop that laboratory monkey look.

An anachronistic switchblade upped the ante. Spectacular on a Sexton

Blake paperback wrapper, useless among this mob. Damage was trivial and confined to the Mediterranean corner, a zone without status. Puncture wounds, a spilled malt. Which Askead, on his knees, lapped like a dog from the table's formica rim. Disgusted, the venerable curate waddled around the L of his bar to turn up the sound on the overhead television set: an act which perversely affected the colour balance. Louder was brighter. A limegreen apologist in burgundy chalkstripes suffered a riptide embolism. His lies were screams. The scarlet worm of the Jubilee Line was a random leucotomy, disconnecting nothing and nothing. Countering depression, chronic anxiety, fucking the circuitry. The spokesman worried an outflow of irradiated mildew from the purple spiral of his ear. Betrayed his unease, a karma of hypocrisy. He denied everything. Lacking a remote, the curate hopped channels with a broomhandle. Contrails of bloodsmoke, hepatitic gutter lights, winking police-eyes. Mustard tapes sponsoring the bombed vehicle, making it an exhibit. No people. Rain haemorrhage. Erratic pans across a border landscape from which the chlorophyll has been drained. Car suicide. The machine has killed itself by spontaneous dismemberment. Crowds, flags, banners. Skinless tanks, pink as body-stockings.

Askead insinuated himself against Sileen. On the otherwise deserted bench. He tapped imperiously on his client's tin leg. Frankenstein's handservant. A pander. A necessary instrument.

'Got the dosh, Baron?'

Without disturbing his television fix, Sileen backhanded a brown envelope. Greedy fingers squeezed comfort from layers of soiled banknotes. The bar was rapidly becoming an untenable fiction. The luridly overscored newsdrip was tarnishing the innocent petulance of the drinkers. *Save me.* They were scorched by a vitriol of bent statistics, emasculated catastrophe. Their flesh was corrupt, lymphoblasted, pustular with psychotic strobes. *Show me the path.* Vein channels agitated by electrical impulses. You could see through them. The furniture. The bricks and plaster. They were mapped by chosen diseases, lit from inside by angel fire. They were dying.

Any price.

A sympathetic loop fed the rash acts on the floor of the Roebuck into the cosmetic mayhem of the TV. One of the Maltese villains watched himself on the screen making a confession. 'I don't like the word gangster. It's not like that, it embarrasses me.' The horsebutcher chomped at the last fibres of the pornographer's ear. A thin blade skewered his hand to the table.

Revenge. Sileen hauled Askead towards the door, before the Glaswegian dwarf could reach for his first wet one. Night air hit their shamed, flushed faces like a cerebral insult. Rumours of tyre smoke and wet leaves. The smells by which Sileen navigated, the stink peculiar to this locality: a shed of maggots bred for fishermen, badly cured leather, forgotten dead things left on the hook. The cobbles glistened. Stone spawn. A frog plague about to hatch. The limping man led the other, who was still mourning the waste of a pint, for which he had foolishly laid down his own money. Wistfully, Askead glanced back: somebody would pay for this.

But Sileen was remorseless. Dues delivered, the victim called the shots. They tunnelled through shadowlands, cancelled dwellings, their shabby history. Over the railway, the secret alley, the gap in the buildings. Until they achieved the winged figure, the green hermaphrodite who stood across the boulevard from the hospital. Rectangles of blazing light. An ocean liner eager to crush them in its wake.

This was Askead's territory. Vaults, underground passages, locked rooms. He jangled his keys, his authority. He pressed the bribe, a small shield, against the diminishing warmth of his heart. Now it was his turn. The condemned machine, unstable, unsatisfied, concealed in its polished walnut cabinet, was waiting for Todd Sileen.

TWO

Self-surveillance.

'He' becomes 'I', that is what a dream is. He/I: a horror shared is a horror doubled. He can't hold it together, the plot, the arbitrary shifts in narrative. Friable pages of text reeling across the cobbles. Loose signatures pasted to oil-slicked walls. Late pedestrians scraping deleted paragraphs from the soles of their boots. A book edited by weather, blown to pieces. Spasms of language ameliorated by the random collisions of the city. The binding fails, cheap glue on the fingers. The silver wrapper sliding from his hands, a broken necklace of mercury beads. Pink lettering of the partially-obscured title. *OUSE ON ORDERLAND.*

Open the door, and listen!

The book is the dream. Prosecuted by its own rhythms. Words become images. The voice of the dead man, the author, in its awful persistence. Nothing can be forgotten. Nothing left out. Too late for revisions.

The house again. The house from the horror story. Windows like eyes burnt with a poker. Unkept gardens. Wilderness beyond. A lunar landscape in which nothing grows. Rock, thorn: future fire. A landscape that does not solicit attention. A landscape that requires blood.

An old man, Sileen, is inside the house. Inside the book. Watching himself at the window of the tower. Excited, passionate – fated. A cold wind frisks him, probes and worries. No ceiling, no sky, no visible guidance from the stars. Coercive darkness weighing on limestone. Sileen runs.

Away from the house, the gardens, the chasm. The voices trapped in crumbling stone. Sand gushing from the walls. Running, his leg was restored. He slithered on a ramp of slime, porkmash, rue. Down towards the mouth of the pit. Fingers spread, lichen filling his nails, skin tearing. The noise. A cataract. A vertical river. It took his breath. Bad news racing gratefully through the body cavities. Ulcers. Epilation. The stench of human shit. Death fear. Loneliness. Sick ripeness, abundance. Growth without form or function. The chasm. A vegetal gash in this sterile plateau.

Where?

Surfacing, trying now to wake from the nightmare. Waking, each time, deeper into terror; layer beneath layer, the impacted dreamlife of a dying city. The sickness had its own intelligence. He *was* the sickness, or he was nothing. He gave it all his trust. A slurry of mud slowed him. He was slipping closer to the edge of the pit. That which remained undescribed. Indescribable. Unfinished business. Earth scorched him. Any movement was a loss of will, a retreat. Keep still. Play dead. He had to escape before the creatures returned.

An unclean, half-animal face, that looked out, vilely, from somewhere about its middle. And then, I saw others – there were hundreds of them. They seemed to grow out of the shadows.

The words were not his. They lesioned from the melting house. He disowned them. Pinched the wound, kept running; stitched the sea into his side. Adjusted to the harsher light.

In wartime X-ray machines picked up premonitions of death, splintered auras, spirit doubles on the razzle. Sileen suffered this transfusion, a rapid ionization of atoms, backscattering. Crookes' dark space: cathode glow, grey seepage from ex-rental TV sets. The fog of uncatalogued nitrate films, rusted into their cans. Light fetishism. Obsession of folds and creases. Orgasmic moans postsynched onto costume dramas. Newsreels incubating cruelty.

Sileen ran beside a dead sea; pulpy, carcinogenic. A tideline of fungal photographs, frame-numbers reviving specific pain memories. The sky was assembled from contradictory recipes for smoke. Breathing hurt. Blue, when he tried to summon it, was orange – grainy, abrasive. The house had vanished, he had no further use for it. Sharper fears replaced the pit. His skin was wood, dusted with chalk. He forced himself to go back, stage by stage, over the narrative connections.

How did it begin? The padding steps on the stairs, the fumbling at the doorhandle. The key that turns once only is fated to turn forever. After extinction, what knowledge?

Stone fields cut into terraces. He gasps. The land sucks him in. Now the idea of the sea sickens him, that fulgent emptiness. *Keep moving*. He had to absorb light while it was still within his reach, devour its worms and darts. *DON'T STOP!* There was – he had to acknowledge it – a shadow, another self, tracking him. Among the dunes, a contoured projection. A black replica, folded like a shirt. Crouching when he crouches. In the scrub. Miming the warp of his mood.

Sileen at the centre of a triangular field. Seen from above, as he does see it, the apex of a pyramid. A persecution of shadows closes on him, the lines necessary to his calculation – they crush his thorax. *That sound?* horses. The stone breath of riderless equestrian statues. Displacement. Columns of cold air heralding their arrival.

The figure has not moved. *I can't move*. Sileen might as well be strapped to a table – the field a torch fitted to the surgeon's head. He's lost among trenches of horse statues. A necropolis. He wants to touch, to feel. To brush against their sides. Metal or polished stone? Veins transplanted into black glass. Disbelief. His faith in his own story falters. No logic. Not even the logic of a dream. The field cannot exist. It is too far from the house. *What house?*

The great animals are toppling over, toppling onto him. He will be stopped, smashed. Printed into mud. Weight, weightless, falling. He resists. Flesh loses its milk. Flesh is no obstacle to sight. The horses are X-rays of themselves. Bone tents. Anti-sculpture. Peeled. All jaw. Lizard-heads on an armature of wooden clothes-pegs. He tries to fend them off. His hand slides into the basket of a ribcage. He goes down.

Bruised, breathless, he crawls between the rigid legs of the horses, a bronchial tree. Uphill. His fingers scratch at the ground. His nails peel. He drags himself on. Sweat blinds him. Something catches and holds him back. The leg. Leave it behind. The earth shudders as the horses tumble at the perimeter of the field. Is he advancing, or digging himself deeper into the mire? Starlight cannot penetrate this maze of tunnels, brambles, flints and skulls.

He must use his elbows, shuffle and gouge, inch by sorry inch. A maggot in earthmeat. Through shellholes filled with putrid water. An officer's glove shrunken by mustard gas to the size of a bellflower. Sileen is excavating a military graveyard. This is where all paths intersect. This is where he ceases.

A faint glow of whitish light. I am free. Sodium haloes. Beads of wet light fermenting on high poles. Lanterns seen through a rain filter. Light breaking up. Yellow and scarlet. Razor wire. Feathers, bird-shreds, tattered cloth: they flap and flutter in a perpetual wind. A wind from the past. A wind excited by its own mendacity. The field is behind him. The field and the sea. The border fence stretches from horizon to horizon, telegraphing Sileen's most private fears to remote and unknown watchers. His movements are mapped and recorded in distant rooms.

Which is the safe side? Which side is ours?

An observation tower: its broad concrete steps. Sileen climbs. In darkness. Panting and resting. Wind drives him back from the slits in the wall, squeezes his face. He is unrecognizable. Even to himself. Another I. He loses his footing, Water and blood. They flood the steps.

The head of the stairs . . . a sound . . . the rattle of bolts being unshot.

This is all he needs to know. It's not too much to ask. Who is waiting for him up there? What form does the evil take?

Hefting the drag of his game leg, he went on. Twisting at the tower's bore, butting against the dark. His hearing, always keen, was inventive now, anticipating dread before it could be given a name. Something was moving ahead of him. Moving when he moved. He was enraged. He climbed faster, closed on himself. He had been here so many times, been this far. A crack of light under an iron door. Hand reaching out for the knob. Must look back, see what lies beyond the ruined house.

I won't have the strength to reach this place again. Almost two hundred steps. *Almost?* Did he forget to count? Did he hell. I can hear the light.

Film rips like Egyptian linen. Chars, burns. FX: the blast of a shotgun recorded in a confined space, in a parked car. Sound reversed. Guilt sucked back into the barrel. There is no guilt. Only the shape of it. A man strapped to a table. Random objects left in the room have been solarized. Leave them alone. Sileen in negative. Wild light pulsing against a foam pillow.

Ian Askead's spittle-flecked grin, and then the rest of him. Smoke leaking from his spidery nostrils. 'Oi, Sweeney.' The beard like a bad pubic graft, the foxy teeth. Askead's childlike hand leaves a raw print on the curve of Sileen's naked shoulder. Sepia goggles and a red rubber apron, into which pouches of flat lead weights had been sewn. Sileen reeled before the evocative, sick bay smell. He wanted to wet himself. The technician's weird Masonic outfit was a drowning kit, a suit for suicide swimmers. It creaked with self-gratification.

'Finger out, Baron. We'z gotta get ourselves outta here sharpish.' Askead was unfastening the thick leather straps. They have shared a secret. Nothing else could have kept them in the same room.

Slowly, Sileen inhaled the grey corruptions, centred himself in the windowless cellar room. Sweat varnished his thick torso. He experienced an unaccustomed tenderness for the frailties of the self to which he was returning, a flood of sympathy for the condemned husk he was about to reoccupy. Let blisters of brown paint settle on the clapboard wall. Let fever speckle the stone flags of the floor. He could raise the low ceiling by the expansion of his chest.

Askead slid the plate out from under the cripple, wheeled back the rickety contraption, its funnel and trailing wires. The Glaswegian was active in real time, shooting for the next score, dragging on a dying roach. He was hot to sluice Sileen from the premises. A surplus radio faulted between the bands, cutting pill-popper anthems with storms of granite rhetoric from the east.

There was nothing precious about Sileen's secret: he was addicted to X-rays. They fed him, and they fed on him. Anxiety pictographs. An intercept, at the high energy end of the electromagnetic radiation spectrum, releasing a chain of negative hallucinations. It was why he had become involved with the malevolent dwarf: a conspiracy to flatter their mutual distrust, to thrive on cunning, deceit, greed, sadism, all the vices – except hypocrisy. Askead would lead the one-legged man, late at night, deep into the bowels of the London Hospital. Soft floors, smells of carbolic and confinement. Autistic watercolours, forced flowers. Heat that would soak a shirt without steaming the apprehension from your fingertips.

They had both taken a drop too much. They tended to stumble, kick open the wrong door. The place was built on concealment, occultation, lies. They skidded down a ramp into a basement that existed nowhere on the hospital charts, a black hole struck from the records. They ghosted freely among path labs, mortuary trays, accidents. They circum-navigated floes of Californian refrigerators that concealed reject tissue, urine samples that defied analysis, Polish lager, green bacon, bottles of infected blood.

A raw and naked animal, Todd Sileen reclined on the padded Barium platino-cyanide bed, under the insect hum of the machine; the green eye whose soft luminescence probed the mantle of damp flesh. Beneath trivial sinew, bloodrace, prospecting for unregistered electrical deposits. Future memories were unmade. Premonitions of death. Alternative paths. What could be imagined was also true. Fractal gardens that branched and dazzled in tropic profundity. Ferns erupting from clogged veins. Light cannibalism. Those who have eaten human flesh are said to glow like Byzantine saints. Featherless Sileen was cooked on a rubber mat.

The hospital was the only route back into the landscape that obsessed him: the ill-favoured house, the unkept gardens, the chasm, the sea of photographs, the triangular field, the borderland tower. Criminally prolonged X-ray séances were his fix, his serial novel. He knew it ended on the concrete steps. But that was not enough. He wanted to force open the iron door, step onto the platform, view the other side, accept the dictation of the stars. Some extraordinary concentration of evil awaited his intervention.

Naturally, the bribed Askead was happy to leave him basting for longer and longer periods. *It doesn't work. The persistence of rational consciousness. Always a loss of nerve at the final step*. Cheese culture skin, hair loss, stomach cramps: Sileen stumbled out of there like deposed Royalty. A scalp ornamented with scabs, white at the crown, greasy mane fouling his collar. Safety thresholds were scorned. The erythema dose jumped the critical stage and caused all the fruit-machines in all the spielers from Smithfield to Forest Gate to spit forth a jaundiced multiplicity of lemons.

The rays were his only salvation. The only way to rewrite his destiny. Dying Sileen had read the tale before, another country, another order; he was not yet ready to leave his calling card with the author.

THREE

Sly Street suited Sileen. The current state of Wapping and the riverside induced in stray humans that form of panic that expresses itself most effectively as traumatized silence. It was the hour of the grey ones, softly-spoken ghouls, whisperers in mouseskin. Disbelief hung over the dead hamlets like a fog of congenital embarrassment. Sileen was there before them: a growler, a beetling monoped, a cripple's cripple. His huge fists hammered at mustard-plaster brickwork, rusticated facades. He was a good hater. His true life was submerged, his work hidden from prying eyes. He was delighted to retreat into a territory that had erased all traces of its previous identity, a territory that matriculated in obscurity. The more he discovered the less there was. Wapping was the carpet under which all the worst mistakes had been swept. After Sly Street there was nowhere else to go.

He advanced like a cold front, a cloud charged with iron filings. He bullocked through flocks of chattering Bengali sweatshop girls. A sharp hit of toxic scent to counter synapse-destroying diesel fumes, wet newspaper, tandoori, cured leather. Released onto the streets, deliriously made-up, crackling and crinkling in sculpted black jackets over thin bright robes, they rattled their bangles in defensive magic. Tiny wooden heels tapped enquiringly over badly-fitted paving stones. Their voices were speedy and gay.

A wedge of Mecca souvenirs – spiritual shortcuts, gimcrack Paradise games, windows raffish with beads and compasses – was rapidly spreading over the washed-out fantasies of pinkeye architects. The game was up. Immigrant energies rushed hungrily into the culture vacuum. Traffic light strobes left Sileen sick and dizzy, ardent to puke a stream of electron-bombarded green bile into the next 'enervated Neo-Classical' doorway, the latest spread of Rancho Notorious cattle pelts. It was like trolling through a transferred Marbella nightclub, a hell disco. He ducked, he dodged; he flinched, cursing, from the mindless 24 hour madness of Cannon Street Road. He disavowed every sight that met his disbelieving gaze.

Nowhere left. Nowhere was best. The intervals between X-ray sessions were so much dead time, satin time, time to kill. His blood was stagnant and slow, his brain clagging into silt. He scratched fresh clinker from his cheeks. X-ray séances, Roentgen visions, dreams that were true. They were the only truth. Sentences burnt from his stalled body.

His room was at the top of what appeared to be a derelict building, a definitively spurned 'riverside opportunity'. The bottom lefthand corner where the coffee had spilled onto the town planner's blueprint. Therefore Sileen was safe. Progress was retrospective. Decay could proceed according to its own dignity. Mortgages in Shadwell were as unfamiliar as abortionists making housecalls.

Sileen possessed the only unboarded window in the block, the only sheet of glass. His room, a voyeur's delight, guarded the corner: he could anticipate danger in its infancy. Tracking in, he checked the window to be sure it was unoccupied. He had to confirm that his outing was not an aberration and he was already at home.

A master of urban cuneiform, Sileen registered the latest slogans, the ones that had appeared in the few hours he'd been away. HANG MAGGIE. A GUZMAN ESTA AQUI. BOYCOT EVERYTHING. Traditional values: the red suns and black flags of Anarchy. A fetching pink horse of the neolithic tendency, bounding on two legs across the breeze blocks. Its affiliations were lost on Sileen. Spray-on plagues accessed the wounds in the masonry, the grazes in mortar. The fabulous brickskin scintillated, pathogenic, crimson in the evening light.

He hopped up the creaking stairs, using the strength of his arms, working the viscid banister. He unchained the padlock from a door which was protected by strips of corrugated sheeting. Dust salaamed a welcome, as the door closed, then settled again on bare unsanded boards. Unsanded? Ridged with splinters, knotholes, linoleum spatulae with jutting nailheads. A few books in irregular heaps. Unsold rather than unread. A room defined by its negatives. A monster tub that stood in for the deleted bathhouse (Ensign Street) from which it had been liberated.

Sileen called his woman's name, and, not trusting the silence, stomped around the corner to jerk back the tartan rug that gentrified the chemical toilet. Nothing. A lifestyle may be purged to these fragments, but existence is still a choker.

'Cunt.'

He spun on his heel, soliciting confrontation, the exchange of blows. She was gone, at work, out of it. The bitch. Asserting her other identity. A hex on her womb.

Ferociously, Sileen crumples a book into the grate; cracks a chairleg, guts a cushion. He starts a fire, heats a bucket of water, then another; fills the tub. A slow business, shadows lengthening, time to brood. He needs to wash off the afterburn of the machine that is eating him alive.

Rolls into his white enamel cauldron, an absurdist cartoon. Water cascading over the side, he wallows: part sacrifice, part charlatan. The uncookable in a mat of hair. Lukewarm water, and plenty of it, distorting the planes of his over-developed musculature. Muscles that were needed to compensate for a loss of will, the stolen limb. A warrior's cladding bolted over the heart of a spoiled priest.

Floating, Sileen felt the missing leg return, felt an ache in the tendons, a twitch in the toes. The membrane of his maimed consciousness was soothed and healed. He lacked nothing. It was the uncut flesh that hung heavy on his bones. Lose it all: that must be the longterm plan. Dreams should drift and flow without bodily inhibition. Invigorated, fired by obscure spiritual exercises, he withdrew, watched himself from above: a pale violet light trembled above the knot of his belly. The X-rays had not broken him.

He would not breathe. He sunk beneath the water – all the room was water now – shut his eyes on the distractions of the ceiling, the interesting moulds that took the form of islands that never were; Redonda (which *does* exist, but not like this), Treasure Island, the islets of Langerhans; fatty cells dividing and reforming to the splash of passing cars. Exoticisms that flourish in any fault.

An inch under and the cripple's face was a snuff shot, shuddering in the photographer's dish. Bruises gave him definition. His eyes bulged. Water was liquid glass, gelling in his throat. *Take a breath*. His skin was scaled and scorched, streaked with silver. He was losing his body hair. Rusty clumps swam to the surface. Balls of the stuff. The tub was a soup of thatch. The man was plucked. He could have pulled his teeth with a twist of the fingers. He wriggled them on his tongue. He could feel the fractures in his bones like a nest of arguing voices. His bones were flaking to paste.

Breathe. Seconds, minutes ticking away. Water absorbed him, absorbed all of him. He slowed. He let it go. A rich mud percipience enveloped the flickering irritations of mortality, the premature rigor. No contest. Sileen and the water were of one mind.

The celluloid sea. Curls of restricted film caught on the wire. Pit-intimations creeping across a dappled lawn. The hurt green of borderland fields. The solitary observation tower. Water gushing down broad concrete steps. Forces himself. Crawls. A painful rush of light. One more step and he will discover the secret of reversed sound.

How long had Houdini lasted? Arse-up in a milk churn? In milk. Manacled, restrained. Longer than this. This was a breeze. A non-decision, a sample of Majorite positive thinking – do nothing, don't breathe. Feed from the water, develop gills. Halibut had done it, why not Sileen? Time expands in any vacuum. It's yours to manipulate. Sileen finds himself eavesdropping on conversations at the corner of the street, horses' names, the click of cards in the hospital canteen, febrile leaves in Itchy Park, dull weather on the river pilot's radio. All the drowned voices of London, accumulations that audition for – *now*. He listens to death.

He is standing over the bathtub, pressing crossed hands against the chill of its curved rim. He is watching himself die. It's not much to write home about. The prim infibulated mouth about to come unstitched, burst horribly open, scream for air. Sileen will marry water. They can do what they like with him – with it, the lump, the thing. Toss it, as a sop, to rats in a stormdrain.

A red pulse at the stairhead. Those legs. The intertextured rasp of stocking on stocking, silk on skin. Bliss in sound. Sileen, on the far side of the bath, penetrates the panels of the door, the metal shield, the chains. *Don't open it!* He's floating in the water, on it, through it, a sleep of marvels, a dreamer's dream. Every cell is coming alive, sentient and self-aware. Each solitary hair an independent intelligence. Each pore. Each diamond web of grey scurf skin. The water's cooling.

Don't open your mouth.

Sileen can taste the scarlet movement on the stairs. The door opening before it does. Opening like a fan, a stutter of progressive stills. What's the big deal? What could be more natural, opening is what doors do?

Why should this act expect a significance outside its presumed mimetic range? (For Sileen that is.) The doorness of the door was an affront. He was the only witness. Ever. He didn't count. He was a corpse in a cylinder of ice.

Her perfume. The one she rations for working days. It had a name. He knew the name. It was the woman he didn't know. Helen/Isabel, a vermilion goddess, breaking the spell. Fingernails. Big hair brushed from her eyes. Leg tensing on the last step. Heels. Cobweb stockings. Imagine. Seeing what he wants to see.

Not now. Isabel. The name flashed for a nanosecond across her chest. The credit. White over red. Catch it if you can, you Breakfast TV insomniacs, mad to fang every public female. Dawn raiders with trembling, punch-drunk hands. Isabel belongs to you. The weather vamp with the startling carmine lips. Lips like sofas. Wide-set eyes that read you like an autocue. Magazine hair. Charmer of isobars, soother of depressions, synoptic muse. Helen was snuffed by the suit, the Wonder Woman respray. Isabel achieved. Sileen's life.

On the stairs. Spiked footfall. Louder. Fumbling at the door. The red suit. What there was of it. Legs, heels. The rasp of stockings. That culchie. The provincial, the scholarship girl – stupid enough to try living with Taylor. Jesus Christ! The bullshit she had to swallow. Caravan on Howth Head. Garden flat in the lee of Joyce's Tower. Under the flags of Merrion Square. Anglo-Irish decay by the swampload. A white piano half-submerged in a duckpond. Table-sized steaks. Cod opera. Nights of mutual masturbation. *NOT NOW*.

From her arms Isabel is dropping packages, slippery silver cartons, hot food bullion. They float for a helium instant, burst. 'Kidney dishes,' Sileen thought. He choked. 'The butchers are coming for me. To force a living heart into my chest. Pack me with infected tissue.' The woman is spilling her bundle of meat confectionary. Tandoori seepage. Saffron rice escaping into the grooves between the boards. She is pulling him upright, out of the water, this standing cadaver: ex-Sileen.

His mouth opened, his lungs heaved, soliciting an implosion of the room's sour breath. London's dust. A gasp, a fit, a spluttering wetmouthed cough of despair. Beaten, sinking, damp: against her breast. Soaking the red cloth. She was slapping his cheek. His ragball head rocking backwards and forwards. Heaving the body, letting slip, manhandling him over the side of the tub; kissing, penetrating. Their tongues. Damning his soul, his unborn children. Biting his neck. Dragging him naked across the splintered floor. Inflicting heat, her anger: clawing language from his sullen leadblue lips.

Through the smeared ruin of the Commercial Road takeaway, he pulled himself on top of her. A walrus, battle-punctured, host to parasites, scabby, scaled, Parmesan scalped, stinking of fishmush. He fell on her. Sodden. She pushed him off, shoved against the brute weight. Her suit, the television suit. Her stockings laddered and her shoes were lost. Did it have to be like this? He held her arms. He wouldn't allow her to remove the suit, fold it, hang it away. He had torn off her pants and was crushing them in his hand, sniffing at his fingers.

'No,' she said. 'Wait. It'll be better later. Let me . . .' Later? That was a concept he couldn't acknowledge. There was nothing to wait for. Nothing. This was the only time there would ever be, unrepeatable. It had never happened before. 'No, *please*.' An absolute, sick exhaustion. It came to her in waves. The aftershock of performance. Getting herself up for the job. Concentration. Anticipated disaster. A bluescreen map. An England that was invisible to her alone. Holding all that detail: the fixed smile, the rolling autocue, speeding as she speeds, slowing if she slows. Weather orchestrated by the movements of her arm. Thumb on the button. Coffee nerves. Dry mouth. Prison light. Sleep. Sleep was sweeter than anything else. 'Stop it.'

Fat fingered, awkward, he unbuttons the jacket and kisses the slopes of her breasts, pushes his head between them, rubs against their smooth warmth. He searches hungrily for deposits of bitter talcum. He can only feel what she is feeling. He has nothing to give. He is insane, sweating, to make her feel something he can steal back from her. Fake gentle kisses. Urgent and slow. He teases her nipples. She hardens by reflex. She must. Sleep. Let it finish. Share this stupid hunger, so he will tire of it, spurt, spend. Shut my eyes. Fake it. Fake sleep. Pretend. Feel what he feels. Believe the pretence. She acts, bites. Returns his kiss. Pulls back. Scratches. Strokes him fiercely. Rolls him. Straddles. Staring into his face. Hot. That *he* should feel and not pretend. She doesn't care. Not now. It could be anyone.

He's stopped, it's lost. He's lying back. He sees her as she is, another being. No. She falls across him, smothers him, breasts in his mouth, must bring him on before it passes for her too. His engorgement has nothing to do with it. He has withdrawn from her. He's watching. She pounds him, punches him, takes him with her lips, her tongue, licking, nipping, enfolding. He's lost all sense of who she is. He's feeling what she feels. He's letting it happen. Hold back. An enveloping, corrupting softness. Those female things: light, colour, texture, sense. He wants no part of them. Why doesn't she fuck him? Pretend. Pretend she has the power, because that surely is what she wants. To fake excitement. Choking noises coming from his throat. Trust him? She was so very tired.

Sileen had raised her skirt up around her waist, his hands under her buttocks, lifting her towards him. He loved the sight of her. It shocked him. He licked and slobbered between her legs. In the wound, the gristle. He nuzzled and pecked, sobbing endearments. So tired. I'm out. She was alarmed, detached; unable to stop herself, the mewling sounds. A moist walnut darkness, honeyed, rotten. He no longer knew what he wanted. Or who he was. The hurt growl of his voice soothed her. The fathering calm, the firmness of his shoulders. She knew that he understood, and did not fear, her power over him.

Now he must wait, blood racing in the throat. It was her time, Night, the black density of it, bending the panes of the window. The fire banked down in the grate, a dim orange glow. Water soaking into the dusty boards. Isabel stood up, walked away, brushing herself down, smoothing the creases in her suit. She knelt to lift a fallen chair, turned, glanced back to be certain he was watching. She undressed slowly, privately, folding the suit and hanging it over the chairback.

Domesticity had entered the set. Furniture was furniture and clothes were clothes. A gentler, more considerate expenditure of time. Isabel, quietly naked, retrieved her patent black shoes, and began the ritual of preparing them for the next day's show. She found the tie-bag, fished out the Meltonian solution and the yellow cloth. She sat on the edge of the tub. The water behind her was turbid, chill with Sileen's unfinished suicide. The shoe was a bondage glove. She worked it until it shone. And then the other. Both together. Nothing was more important in the world. She crossed her legs, put the shoes back on. She held out a hand. Sileen came to her, taking the chair, as she gestured for him to do. Smiling, she sat astride him, and it started again.

24

FOUR

Nobody over forty years of age enjoys opening a letter. Experience has long since triumphed over false optimism. They know today is the day when they've been found out, received the greeting card from the other side. Join us.

Sileen was first to the bucket, pissing out the night's frenzy in a boastful deluge, a golden shower with a head on it. He sat forward, as he had to do, on the ring of cold metal. He spotted the brown envelope. An iris shot in a silent melodrama. His bowels constricted. THE LETTER. Its sick tongue edging out from beneath the triple-bolted door.

Impossible. Not a living soul knew he was here. No postie would risk the Sly Street chicken-run: chancers would tap the packages for valuables and heave the rest into the river. The blokes with the sacks were all retards, subs, retro-hippies in gymshoes and no socks, dope-smokers who thought they'd done a good job if they found the right street, or anything that sounded like it. Numbers were a drag, man. They had a meet every morning in Mary's caff to sort the dreck aimed in the general direction of Cable Street into heaps of estimated worth. They were pretty good. They could smell currency. Finger pads would moisten and quiver for knuckles of resin. Mary's kettle kept up a constant head of steam to unpeel adhesive lips, slide out cheques, giros, negotiables. All fillers – sentimental maunderings, news from abroad, miscomputed bills – were consigned to the bald patch that fronted St-George-in-the-East. Dues paid, they could get on with fiddling their karmic returns and talking hyper-obscure pirate videos. No points if anyone else had heard of them. *The Electric Leg. Zombies of the Stratosphere. The X-Ray Fiend.* Anything by Mike Sarne.

Isabel must have blabbed to the girls in the winebar. Pillow talk among the chattering classes had put a noose around Sileen's neck. It couldn't get much worse. A letter! His meticulously signalled trail led to the States, a new life. All his creditors, and most of his friends, had fallen for the play. He'd cabbed it, ostentatiously, to Heathrow, bought a bottle of scotch, a gangland paperback – shouting the odds all the way – then vanished. Removed himself from the screen. The bounty hunters had written him off. America was too heavy; forget it, guy. The dealers he had shafted didn't belong to the families who went in for honour or any of that stuff, ancestral grudges. It was screw or get screwed on a daily basis. Wages. Cash money. Memory was a runner in the previous race. This morning's *Sun* was an antiquarian fantasy. Sileen was clear. Even Askead had no notion where the gimp kipped. When Sileen needed the technician's services he turned up at the Roebuck with fifty in readies.

Someone was writing secretly to the bitch. Who could afford the time? The postage? It *had* to be her letter. She was cheating on him. How could she? They had a gentleman's agreement. Out of sight was out of mind. You couldn't cheat on absolute indifference. He hopped, crouching, towards the door. Keep low, back to the window. They might be watching. What would they see? Charles Laughton with a bad case of tinnitus. It was nothing to them. They could smash in whenever they fancied it. His hand. The brown envelope. He overbalanced, went down snarling.

The scribble was familiar: block capitals agitated by a crude stab at joined-up sophistication. An illiterate stuffed with bad literature. Rocky Graziano coming on as Algernon Swinburne. All irony abandoned while counting his teeth on the floor of some North Side grogshop. It had to be Taylor. But Taylor was dead. Or banished to the Gaeltacht, the swine fields. Which came to the same thing. Samuel Coleridge Taylor. Sad Sam. He should have been eaten by his pigs. There wasn't much juice in his brain by the time he got out of Dublin. They strapped him, delirious and hallucinating, into an Aer Lingus stand-by, and plugged his mouth with a miniature brandy. London had done the rest.

Helen, seeing him in the city – exposed, paranoid, wet-haired – had called his bluff. She saw herself also, as for the first time. Phenomenological panic. She rushed to Leonard's for a geometric cut and a copper rinse. Job on *Time Out*, new moniker. Taylor had made a big splash in a small basin. 'The man who turned Trinity College on to linctus.' A generation of cough medicine addicts misquoting Wittgenstein. Misquoting? They couldn't spell his name. Where are they now? Fast hearts watching slow turnips. Mahayana travellers treading silage.

In London Taylor was a joke: a public blur feeding on private impurities. That had been Sileen's chance. To be around, a fixture, an unavoidable presence nursing his Rioja at the end of the table. Always there. Seat by the door, tapping his ash into his neighbour's yogurt. An abstainer, a dark puritan. His moustache spoke of stability, gravitas. *Tin Drum*. He stuck with it beyond fashion, even when it became the favoured lip-tickler for clones and fairies. He was in pain, he hurt. The limp preceded the wound. He might take a couple of draws in the evening, or a snort – if somebody was offering. Which they weren't. Not after '75. Sileen was straight. He even impressed Taylor. A published author, an amateur gentleman. The next best thing to breakfast with Doctor Johnson.

Without noticing it, Helen/Isabel had come into Sileen's orbit: encircled, stung with soft poisons, flattered by inattention. *Slit it*. He had fastened on her heat, the crab. *Touch it*. *Split the seal*. Taylor had fucked first, fucked for days at a time, without satisfaction. With choler. Henry Miller, Kerouac, de Sade, *The Story of O*. Pretentious bastard. Two weeks in Paris. He thought of himself as a prophet, a desert father: sand in the shirt, flies drinking from the milky corners of his eyes, a hot pebble on the tongue. Taylor cooking, talking, yapping while he stirred, splashing a yard of prime red steak into a black pan, tearing a strip with his teeth to hurl at his mad hound. Taylor, a wet green cigar wedged in his mouth, chopping wood. Rage in his wrists. Reading aloud every flighted nuance of a five-hundred page unpunctuated novel (some fool had left a Gertrude Stein lying around) at a single, allnight session, dosing his greedy parasites (the catatonic audience) on bottles of best Irish – Nepalese gold, opium, speed to keep them awake. Rodents. Sneering Brits (shirt-lifters), the occasional semi-housetrained Celt – some thirsty bog philosopher sharp enough to sniff out a Yank and bleed him to the bone. Taylor with his thinning hair scratched back into a rubber-banded ponytail. Wrist chains like the Count of Monte Cristo. Waistcoat hacked from a saddle. Steel spectacles. Roaring and whispering his demented prose. Blasting both barrels at the moon's halo. A booted nude.

Open it.

Was Isabel asleep? Sileen raked the fire. She didn't move on the mattress. Her mouth slightly open, curled like a chrysalis, needing nothing from him, the warm imprint of where he had lain. They buried each other last night, wantonly squandering their future ration of good times. They would pay for it. He wanted to wake her, so that the argument could begin again. He couldn't think without her. She had become his sense of pleasure. He relished the clarity with which she identified his flaws. He came close to tolerating himself in her magnificent independence. It was his way of knowing the world. Moving, risking, doing. Street noises, cloud shifts, embryonic shapes taking form against the darkened window.

He must start a new fire, ball a few leaves from some book he could no longer bear to open. Driftwood, paraffin. Handle it, turn it, *Slit the fucking envelope*.

Taylor had sworn to kill Sileen, sworn it publicly, and often. Stalked white gallery spaces – John Dunbar, Robert Fraser – with a bowie knife tucked into his boot. He sat on the floor of the Arts Lab, the Roundhouse, the ICA, communing with demons. He unpicked Richard Long's Silbury spiral, vowing vengeance. But he didn't know where to look. His London extended no further than the culture listings. The sites wouldn't connect. Every lighted restaurant was a book launch. They were laughing at him. Helen was a lost possession, an investment that had turned sour. The best screw he'd ever bragged about. He'd trained her from scratch, the scrawny streak of piss. Olive Oyl from the borderlands, the pebbledash bungalows. Little Miss Nobody from Nowhere, Monaghan or Cavan. She knew him, knew all about him, and it wasn't enough. It was nothing. Taylor didn't travel well. He'd never shaken off the East Village, had dragged it everywhere from Lagos to Goa. He talked too much. She had no regrets. No sentimental insights to confide to her diary. The men said it all in those days, hogged the bar. But it was the women who did the business, finished the courses; smiled, got what they wanted. Survived. Made it into television.

Now, apparently, all was forgiven. Maybe Taylor had O.D'd on an Alzheimer's serum. Sileen was impressed by the man holding himself in check long enough to scrawl an address. It was spooky that he'd been able to finger Sly Street. That was hard graft for those born on the parish. Taylor must have employed a psychic, a skiptracer. The envelope was franked in red. SAVE THE STARVING GIVE UP ART. Sileen grimaced and spat into the fire. He wanted the madman's liver on the end of a roasting fork.

FELLOW ARTIST ITS ALLREDY LATER THAN YOU THINK. ALL ART HURTS BUT SO DOES HUNGER. OUR IDEAS ARE NOT ORIGINAL THAT IS THERE ORIGINALITY. PLAGIARISM COMES FREE. ANYONE CAN PLAY. RIP OFF A RICH WRITER. HE HAS EXPLOITED THE VALIDITY OF YOUR SUFFERING. SUPPORT THE GLOBAL STRUGGLE INITIATED BY GUSTAV METZGER IN LONDON'S INSTITUTE OF CONTEMPORARY ARTS (ICA). 'ALL CULTURAL WORKERS TO PUT DOWN THEIR TOOLS & CESE TO MAKE, DISTRIBUTE, SELL, EXHIBIT THEIR WORKS FROM 1ST JANUARY.' RAISE THE LEVEL OF DEBATE & CONSCIOUSNESS BY DONATING 0.7 pc OF ALL INCOME FROM ARTISTIC ACTIVITIES . . .

'*Income* from art?' Sileen crushed the noxious whimper and was about to lob it onto the flames when he noticed an obscure holographic defacement on the verso.

this is yr last chance captain youre with us or you go under. whitechapel is fucking your humanity. ripper karma. literary cocktail parties will wither yr dick & fill yr seed with hate. whosoever dont kill power is kilt by it. bomb art is the most dramatic way of stating the case. BURN BABY BURN. liberate the transcendental man the original adam. just this morning i sat alone on the beach out by the rocks smoking & watched the waves comit harakiri momentous cloud continents rolling in like chicago on fire. i can smell the END the finale. niggers spicks sliteye gooks its there time now. but we still have the moss the fields fresh warm milk from the longhair goat. go where the sun goes or stick in the dirt like the chalk outline of a butchered hoar. yr enemy & onlie pal, SAM.

First light and he was beaten. He wanted to fall back on the mattress. *He* shouldn't be the first one up. There was no sweeter arousal than watching Isabel dress – better, more provocative, than any strip, Eyes shut, nursing a bowl of coffee, he could picture what was happening. The slither and scrape of her stockings. The rush, the preoccupation; detached from any notice of display. He could scarcely contain himself. The way she sniffed at yesterday's underwear. The contortionist's skill with which she fastened her bra strap behind her back. He adored her casual agility. His own fingers were useless: Cumberland sausages burst in the pan.

Isabel had left him: she was preparing herself, perfecting the day's mask, making those tiny, final adjustments. Blue strokes of eyeliner. Hiss of hair mousse. Full lips pouting against pink tissue. He had to grip the cup, force himself not to climb out after her, fuck her on the floor. And that, of course, only served to heighten his excitement.

Torch it. The alternate self: lover, partner, sensualist. Get real. Eyes peeled. Out there. Do a Bertie. Nark a few deals, pick up some change from the local filth. Their budget was the only one still on stream. Fight crime by paying the criminals to stay off the streets. Things looked rosy for the back-of-the-hand boys, the whisperers. Grassing was a growth area, a career with prospects. We have to decide our own destinies: villains or informers, participants or voyeurs. Change and change about. Bogus confessions in the snug, parkbench narratives. Nothing else remained of oral history. Telling tales to Drage-Bell was Sileen's last punt at fiction.

He pulled on a black shirt, deconstructed jacket, skullcap. He powdered the nagging stump and strapped himself together, deftly harnessing the prosthetic sections. It was like transvesting a resistant manikin, corsetting a side of beef. In sweat, he clumped towards the stairs, a bionic centaur. His flesh was corrupt, wood-hard, suppurating against the tired clothes.

But Isabel was also capable of watching, and watching the watcher. To-day, Sileen's wardrobe fantasies were just that. Naked, the weather girl had hidden herself behind the tartan rug. She crouched at the side of the window until the limping cripple reached Kinder Street's junction with Commercial Road. Then she squatted, smoothing out Taylor's letter on her thigh. She extracted the cigarette she had hidden down the spine of a book, and lit it from the last embers of the fire. Exulting in her solitude, she nestled beside the clinkered grate, smoking – relishing each longheld, delighted drag. The wickedness! She waited. She hugged herself. She wanted to be perfectly ready to concentrate on her former patron's words.

Not now. Not yet. The room was settling slowly, reforming, becoming her own. She laughed aloud. And clapped her hands.

FIVE

Eight thousand feet? Perhaps even higher. Ragged mammae on the underside of the stratocumulus. White growth, a morphology of addition and division; shape-shifting moisture. Beyond conceit, these puffball pillows, slated with threat, offer us an intelligent ceiling. Without them we are lost, trapped inside the cave of our eyes.

Helen/Isabel holds to the centre of Abbey Lane. Out early. One of the damaged sisterhood who perambulate some small particular zone of the city; remote-controlled, clinging to the apex of the sliproad's camber. Dawn and dusk. Confirming the white lines, unviolated by traffic – repulsing it with the vigour of their force-field, the conviction of their folly. Tappers who mark out the borders we must all obey.

Massive ironwork gates. An agitation of leaves: ovate, deltoid, elliptic. Promiscuously mingled. The house at the end of the drive, hidden in foliage, a redundant municipal extravagance. A humming in the wires, pylon music. Drooping curves of interference. Industrial cicadas. She looked up at the mud elevation of the Outfall, the sky. Cumulus. Prophetic anvils thinning, reforming into parallel lines. Cloud streets. Shabby, anonymous. Transitional. Hands in pockets. Hair tied back.

Helen breaking from Isabel, her twin. It fades: the red suit, the fingernails, the blue screen on which they backproject a diagrammatic Britain. Suzanne Charlton had to stand on a six-inch platform to reach Cromer, a petulant toss of the hair might wipe out Aldershot. Sweet Suzanne, the nation's favourite niece, her blazer – the ideal stand-in for Patrick McGoohan in *The Prisoner*. The airfixed smile. The compulsive cocktail-shake of her hand gestures. But Isabel fitted that 5′9″ slot to perfection. An audible docking of eyelashes. A fasten-your-seatbelts wink. Straight into her act: jaunty self-fulfilling promises, weather babble. A demonstrator. An Avon lady of the airwaves. Hiss of a million electric kettles, lavatories flushing, newspaper consultations, aether fractured by jolts of channel-hopping anxiety. Cold fronts. Severe depressions. Her specialist audience blues with oxygen deprivation: the concentrated frenzy of their two minute koan.

Isabel sees herself in the fat black trumpet of the lens. They see her seeing herself. The fixed duration quickens their lust. Her left arm lifts to chide a rogue spiral over Aberdeen. Subtle movement under her tight jacket, the shifting of her body mass. They freeze-frame, rub noses up against the screen. A single bead of moisture, a visible darkening of the cloth, will suffice. A communal groan and it's over.

To disperse self, become what she saw. Helen's hand tightened on the cheap circular mirror in her raincoat pocket. A wind from the east, visible only in the rapidly shunted sky, clanked and jingled the line of metal prongs that hung from a gantry to deter the HGV cowboys. A melancholy complaint of rusted chains. Beyond the gantry the road curved into a dark brick tunnel. Helen took to the pavement. Followed a pier of steps as they twisted back, away from an onion-soup gasometer, and on to the high track of the Northern Sewage Outfall – London's spurned Ridgeway.

She climbed quickly, suppressing all remembrances of last night's discomfort, Sileen's savagery – the sweats and leaking mucus. A not unpleasant chaffing sensation where the pubic arch tugged against the coarse material of her jeans. She was comfortable in borrowed woollen socks and loose fitting trainers. At the summit she hesitated, before turning south, alive suddenly to the porterage of her own microclimate. Her warm breath bringing the wasteground to life. Vetch and campion. Danewort and celery-leafed crowfoot. An articulate movement in the air. She was closer to it than ever before, the uncluttered dome of the lost hamlets, the lid of the tent. The whole sky: her mirror. Walking, she knew the rush of all the extinguished hopes, pumped beneath her feet, through darkness to the river. 600 million gallons of sewage controlled and directed from Joseph Bazalgette's grandiose mosque, the pumping station behind the iron gates, the red queen of this post-industrial desert.

Inosculate exhalations, breath fibres, a layering of smoke blocks; overblown immensities wheeling out from the past, that which is least known. A viewing platform, this embankment. Helen wanted the open skies of Luke Howard. Howard of Plaistow. Quaker, pedestrian, retail chemist, meteorologist. He was addicted, this prim, neat, cowlicked Londoner, addicted to study. 'Skying', he called it. 'Keeping a daily record of the Phenoenomena, regarded as passing occurrences, extending our knowledge of the Oeconomy of the seasons.' Careful, exact, modest. Luke Howard. His *Essay on the Modification of Clouds*, 1804. His pamphlet *Against Profane Swearing*. The groundbreaking achievement of *The Climate of London, Deduced from Meteorological Observations*. 2 vols, London, 1818–1820. Goethe called him 'Master'. His reply to an autobiographical sketch sent by the Cockney chemist was the poem, *Howard's Ehrengedächtniss*. A taxonomy of clouds in verse. Constable annotated his own copy of Thomas Foster's *Researches About Atmospheric Phaenomena*, 2nd edn, 1815, taking a lively interest in the first chapter, *Of Mr. Howard's Theory of the Origin and Modifications of Clouds*. Shelley translated Howard's classifications into a demonology of celestial forces: cirrus, stratus, cumulus, nimbus. The man of business had pressed his fingers against the pulse of the transient. His skying-dish: the cupola over West Ham, Plashet Park, Plaistow, Bromley-By-Bow. A suspended ocean.

Luke Howard with his sketchbook, rehearsing the unattainable; recalling the spectacle of the instant, synaptic epiphanies, time-lapse erasures. Light in his eye. Worship by analysis. The revelation of God's hand stirring the waters. Helen stands on the same ground, solicits a connection. To remember what lay ahead, to redeem the past. And let it go forever. Her fingers white against the rim of her circular mirror.

Suddenly exhausted, her legs shaking, she clung to the balustrade, the ornate teardrop ironwork of the bridge overlooking Abbey Creek and Channelsea, with its flotilla of floating islands – hair mounds, polluted deltas. Helen gave herself up. What she saw was all there was. Clouds skimming the smoothed nitrate water, vanishing among sluggish counter-currents. The rosined surface concentrated the sky's essence. These unpeopled scrublands couldn't touch her.

She sank to the ground, the gravel – fractured mud crusts with a green varnish. She knelt, her cheek accepting the cool print of the ironwork. She wanted something more than Luke Howard, his maleness: his thirst to name, differentiate, describe, control. She wanted loss. She wanted to renege on the envelope of identity. A quality beyond the insufficient sex moment, a conjunction with cloud form. She wanted to be directly affected by the procession of light, growing moist and expectant. To mark the migration of stratocumulus tribes by the electrical intensity of her orgasms. To take light into her blood. Exchange and release. Scarlet rages, sun cycles filtered through red glass. The blackberry sickness of incipient thunder.

Defenceless, open: her shadow painted on the stone path, the bed that ran alongside the Channelsea bridge. Lying there, face down, she was hidden from the sight of other walkers. Roughcast blocks shaped a rudimentary submarine pen. The whole area was nudged by military detritus: pillboxes, peepholes, obstacles to prevent the passage of any vehicle thicker than a bicycle. Her shadow was the shadow of a victim. She wanted to leave it behind, have it surgically removed.

Too weak to raise herself, Helen took out the mirror. A magical device. A property. A cloud trap. It weighs time. Oceanic repositories of sleep. Dreams from the west. Snatches of conversation. Threats. Luke Howard delving into the Apocrypha, annotating the margins of Ezekiel. 'Then said he unto me, Prophesy unto the wind . . . breathe upon these slain, that they may live.' Sammy Taylor's malignancy ascending into the Atlantic cloud quilt, Dursey Islands, the Slieve Miskish Mountains, his mastic foreskin stretched over the glass. Helen shivers, suffers the occlusions of that remote headland.

The wired grin. He knows. Taylor knows. Complacent in a rocking-chair, bollock naked, white as a leper, shotgun lying cocked in his lap: he's got the viral trace on her. She smells the gun oil. The dirt worked into the cracks of his fingers. Polishing the stock with a filthy rag. The rumble of Taylor's laughter: a shuttle of silver trains, overground commuters on the District Line. Folded reflections traversing the blind windows of terraced houses. She touches the mirror with her tongue.

There is a sheet behind the horizon. The red building stands in stark relief. Helen needs nothing else to confirm her identity. The pumping-station is truth. A freak, a fantasy of turrets, spikes, parentheses. A too rational folly. Any trick to disguise its function as the Cathedral of Shit.

Beneath her, on the east side, in the yard of a discount warehouse, a man was hosing himself down. Stripped to the waist, longhaired, contagious: a future better left unvisited. A liaison, one of ten thousand possibilities, to be permanently postponed. He liked himself. She moved down the steps towards him, down to the platform where she could hesitate, feign an interest in the wide-angle panorama, take a harder look at him. She could read the flat belly, the black ace of body hair, the procured musculature. All the stages whereby this man had worked over his own portrait. On his left bicep, and brought to life by the venom with which he directed the jet of water, was the blue algae tattoo of a snail, its exaggerated prongs. Enough. Helen turned, retreated to the Outfall track. She took the steps two at a time. She jogged.

Nobody followed her. She pushed it, she sprinted. Soon she was dwarfed by the skeletal elegance of the electricity pylons: an X-ray forest, a place of enchantment. Cradles of limp wire transmitted her advent along the invisible line of zero longitude, in the direction of the *Financial Times* complex on East India Dock Road, flicking intimations of panic into the already paranoid markets

SIX

A deeply unfashionable place, its population subdued, quiescent –
untroubled by the fret of traffic. Helen strolled among the tombs of the
East London Cemetery, not craving a smoke, not craving anything. One
of nature's metaphysicals, she previewed her mortality, balanced her
bodily warmth against the imagined clutch of skeletons. Can these
bones live, the sinews and the dehydrated flesh? Her loose coat became a
designer shroud. Complacent in its icy folds, she travestied the playful
Doctor Donne. A star-field of white crosses. Helen was in humour: with
herself and with the setting.

The dream of death. She had never knowingly been here before, but
everything was joyously secondhand. The best surrealism is that which
is most expected. One crucifix, out by the wooden fringe, is a Méliès
levitation, film reversed. The martyred Christ is a sunbather wrapped in
a towel, yawning on a granite tree. Helen browsed. There was nothing
to remember, no detail to log.

The charm of these pretty pretensions: monuments faking it as
temples, gates, archways. Marble ovens opened to release the parboiled
dead. Plaster doves flapping under cellophane. The wings of angels
lacerating their bridal trains. Stone libraries quite innocent of text.
Lecterned pages defaced by sanctimonious doggerel.

A man was following her. Or: a man was taking the path she was
taking, an eccentric traverse, lacking resolution. He anticipated
decisions she was not conscious of having made. 'Anthony.' She knew
his name. Said it out loud. Without having seen him before. Without
looking at him now. Without laughing.

Anthony, heavyshouldered, clayfooted, stepped up the pace. A
shaggy wetlands creature ringing steam from his tight, checkered
overcoat. Benevolently martial, a disincentived minder, he wallowed in

the wake of a spectral self, a fleet double. Overfilling two mirrors, he saw himself as a sleek, Ray Danton hood, a well'ard bastard. But fair with it. Heart of gold. He drew alongside the young woman, breathing heavily, a lamentable asthmatic whistle.

Helen turned. They faced each other. Anthony wiped his nose on his sleeve. He was visibly struggling. Conversation was not really his line. The woman was smiling at him. He was game for a bit of ad hoc surgery, foot-in-the-gob, freelance grin extensions. But not this. Expectant, alert, up on her toes. As if she'd been waiting for him. He dropped his gaze. At their feet, tethering them, was a massive iron anchor. He gasped for air. They were in this together, going down for the third time, a marine keepsake: man, woman, anchor. A scrimshaw fragment of time – never to be annulled.

'My brother. He's got a picture of the disaster, HMS Albion. Thames Ironworks, June 1898. Near enough six foot, he is, an educated man.'

Helen wanted to take his hand and pat it. The strain of linking consecutive phrases was doing him in. His eyes bulged, a thick vein-worm wriggled in his neck. 'Two hundred in the water.' The story was familiar: the launch, a ten foot wave, staging swept away. Women and children waving and drowning. A local tragedy earthed by the solidity of this obscure memorial. A white-washed anchor, the roll call of the dead: Ann Dives, Leah Dearl, Eliza Eleanor Tarbox, Mary Anne Eve. Wives, mothers. Spectators became the spectacle. The inspiration for civic art. The Albion, its guns and chains, is forgotten, scrap. The ghost anchor lives on.

Had he finished, exhausted his repertoire of anecdotes? Anthony scuffed the oaty gravel with his boots. Helen was ready for a savage initiation. The words of Alice James, Henry's tormented sister, came to her. 'The unholy granite substance in my breast.' She spurned them. She was beyond spiritual torment, red suits, bachelors. Bottled lightning was in her blood. She could incinerate Anthony at a touch. Side by side, they contemplated the marine memorial, rehearsing and rejecting future roles as sexual partners. In circumspect silence they walked back through the graveyard, fuelled by the promise of Anthony's alpha brother.

Between the lady florist and Ossi's Doner Shack was a smoke-windowed monumental mason, Tarten's Marble Co. All the necessities peculiar to this neck of the woods had been taken care of, and yet, ungrateful world, business was slack. Behind curdled net curtains the street leaked a non-specific menace.

Black glass hinted at a death/pornography enterprise. Helen moved closer, bending her reflection among the angels, the unrented plaster virgins stacked on Tarten's shelves. Fastfood lights winked at her presumption: a purple and red rosary for the madonna of the revolving lamb. Was this *it*? Was this the flower of freemarket invention? Could Plaistow service so many virgins? A flag floor logjammed with Disney princesses, a dwarf brothel. So much piety, Helen thought, could only be kept in balance by some spectacularly corrosive humans.

Nicholas Tarten sprawled in a deckchair, rolling a tight ciggy. His arrogant self-possession (cologne and spearmint) countered Anthony's steelshod innocence – by this distribution of humours they remained brothers. Nicholas eyed the girl, swiftly unlayering her body disguise; shifted in his chair, made as if to rise (too deep). His cancelled gesture alluded to rules of etiquette (man/woman stuff), known but suspended. The chair's base squeaked like chalk on slate. Anthony backed off to trundle a kneehigh angel, by the wing tips, to a favoured position near the door. Then to return it to the precise spot from which it had embarked on its flight.

Nicholas hit her with a sort of smile. She feared the whiteness of teeth that zippered that tightly ironed face. His left forefinger cruised suggestively down a scar that ran from the crown of his razorcropped skull to within an inch of the winklepicker jaw. A textbook cleaver shot, full-frontal, the kind that gave the exotic traveller, Sir Richard Burton, his *farouche* appeal. Tarten was a street dandy, a culture killer.

'That old Albion, gel says she's interested. Wants a gander at your pictures.' Anthony offered, scuttling across the flags to locate a pool of darkness in which to lose himself.

'*Au contraire*. Correct me if I'm wrong, Anthony. Reading between the lines, I'd guess she'd go more for clouds. Clouds would be her thing. Know what I'm saying, Tone? Fallstreaks, crepuscular rays, spouts. She's got the hots, it's only my opinion, for our local celeb. And, hello, all of a sudden, out of a clear blue sky, she's trolling down Howards Road.'

The dominant brother was on the toot. His nylon (New York/London) accent so weirdly, abrasively camp: a blast of apostrophes –

like an upwardly-mobile dogcatcher, or Sir Alf Ramsey on laughing gas. 'Beautiful mover, Anthony. Floats like a dancer. Air sign, take my word. Gemini.' Nicholas had an eye for a face. He watched television at times when honest folk were abed.

The strength had gone from her legs. Helen needed to sit down. There was only Nicholas Tarten's lap. She was nudged by hooded albinos of restricted growth, hard-edged sexless things. She shivered, knowing he knew her, anticipating his grip on Isabel's black silk knee.

'My brother, he spends a lot of time up the cemetery, helping out. Quiet word with old pals he's laid to rest. Keen to point a punter, such as yourself, in the right direction. Fond of a chinwag is Anthony. Me, I'm more of a lone wolf. Been away a lot. Know what I'm saying? Sit in my chair now, roll a fag, wait to see who'll walk through the door. Done much in the ring?'

The scar on Tarten's cheek was alert, independent, a rind of alien intelligence. It divided the plains of his face into an aborted cubist portrait. On the shelf above his head was a cloud shrine, a collection of weather postcards, storms, downpours, that threatened to connect into a single diorama, the ultimate millennial night. Helen dreaded that Tarten's lies, once spoken, would become the only available truth, definitive as a work of published fiction.

'A hobby of mine, blood sports. Nothing heavy. No cause for Frank Warren to get iffy. Bump into Mickey Duff in Bloom's, don't drop me in it. Private affairs between consenting adults. I thought, as soon as I clapped eyes on you, Anthony's come up trumps. He's found a live one here. It's all in the shoulders. Then again the calves. Do a lot of walking? Not all poundage, see. More a question of temperament. Take Paddy Dinnear. One of the wickedest cobble-fighters north of the river. Worked on the buses, my life. 149, Liverpool Street to Edmonton. Take my card. Anthony'll run you home. He'd be delighted.'

Tarten offered a pasteboard rectangle. Helen did not – could not – respond. The card was too civilized an intimacy. The chainlink identity bracelet on his hairy wrist said it all. Too much. The scabby tattoo lost in the thicket: a jungle animal with an attitude. An anaconda swallowing its own tail. Memento of some Colombian knocking-shop. She had to cut loose.

A rush of warm air from the street: cut flowers, sizzling onions, condemned horse. She could hear Anthony panting significantly after her. Feel his panic on the back of her neck. Posing, momentarily, for a window check among the buckets of guillotined carnations, she released her hair, turned up the collar of her coat. Anthony's persistence was endearing, but it was going to earn him a poke in the eye.

'Nicky's right, love. The area's gone down. Once upon a time you could poodle about with impunity. Nowadays you can't shift for Turks lurking.'

Helen ached for the high ground, the uncontaminated land, history on the hoof. The curse of winter sunlight illuminating silted tributaries and overgrown paths. One more word of cod Pinter and she'd slap his face.

'You read books and that, darlin', you'd know.' He couldn't help himself. The disinterested pursuit of knowledge. 'I never can work it out. This Howards Road caper. Did they call it after the bloke then? Or was it like one of those things . . . wait up . . . where you live in a gaff what's already got your name? I would take you, honest to God, but there ain't no motor. And I never had no licence. He's got his own sense of humour, my brother.'

SEVEN

In the umbrella shade of an elderly sycamore: Drage-Bell, a book resting on his lap, perched on the edge of one of the green diamond-shaped lozenges, beside the memorial font to the old Swedish Church in Swedenborg Gardens. The sea-planks of this rickety structure were alive, resurrected, slippery with lichen. Their colour was the colour of Drage-Bell's skin. Exposed to sunlight he manufactured a coating of protective starch to disguise his endemic mycosis, the network of parasitical fungi snacking upon his humanity. The man was condemned timber. He moved in his corruptions. He was at home here on this raised platform, this catafalque. Unburied, he smelt of damp soft bark. A sudden break in the cloud cover dressed him in a carpet of shivering leaf shapes. He was invisible. He made no pretence at reading. He ran his curved finger-quill up and down the book's edges – as if to discover what was inside by touch alone. As if he had vestigial eyes in the tips of his fingers. The book was no book. It was a bookdealer's catalogue.

Sileen had never been able to decide if Drage-Bell invariably sat upon this bench in the mornings, or only at certain periods of the morning, or only on certain mornings: or if he was able by hermetic means to anticipate the occasions when Sileen needed to find him. It was an unvisited place, arcane and domestic. One that had volunteered to step outside the notice of the quotidian world. It suited the policeman. Like Howard Hughes he had settled for permanent mufti; a gaudy state of mourning, his brittle phalanges crammed into ruined plimsolls. His emaciated form wrapped in anything that was grey and discounted. Irradiated shellsuit pantaloons mixed and matched with a *Naked Lunch* T-shirt and a clubbable (blackballed) jacket. He made the Oxfam army look like posturing fashion victims. His lank chip-pan hair hidden in a charcoal sock. At night the man could pass for a Rastafarian exterminator.

Money. Sileen could smell the notes folded inside a brown envelope in the policeman's pocket. *Was* he a policeman? Who could confirm it? Did such creatures still exist? They were harder to identify than the oblique hiatuses of waste ground that Drage-Bell haunted. Up West it was a bandaged city, buildings shrouded in green gauze, hospitals of sleepers cut off from their life-support systems. The Eastern Sector was a confederacy of open wounds, undressed rubble, the boarded windows of crack precincts. Where did they hide themselves, the enforcers, those watchers who never intervened? They were apart. They fancied themselves as cinematographers of chaos, logging gangland misdemeanors, taxing the players, provoking the climate of potential terror. It was all on tape. The surveillance agencies had better archives than the news channels. And they were liquid.

Blood money. X-ray afterburns licked spitefully at Sileen's follicles, bussed the redundant flesh. Recapitulated dreamsleep blanked out the policeman's transitory reality. The borderland story had to be concluded. Sileen had to get back, reach the head of the stairs, step out into the light. He could sell anything, anyone. There was nothing. He had nothing to offer.

'Don't start on Kinder Street. We know everything there is to know about Kinder Street. Tell me about the Gasman. Lie to me.' Drage-Bell didn't bother to look at him. He toyed with the laces of his plimsolls. Sileen stood behind his paymaster – deferential, bent, mooning into the water of the cold stone font. Black clouds transgressed a subterranean ocean. HERE STOOD / ULRICA ELEONORA / THE FIRST SWEDISH CHURCH / IN LONDON / 1728–1911.

'Right, boss. It's going to happen. Definitely. Any day now, the Gasman.' Sileen was bluffing. He knew nothing about Kinder Street. The Gasman was a name sprayed on a wall. There were so many others. Directories of them. He memorized the haiku, the secret books of the city. Debrett's for nonentities. A lamppost on Crowder Street: TEMPO / THE HARDEST MUTHAFUCKA / IN THE WORLD. All of two feet off the ground. Scripted by a dwarf. The door at the entrance to the gardens: YOUR MUM / IS A COCK / SUCKING BITCH / BY YOUR FATHER / DOPE 9T3.

Drage-Bell read him and leered: turned to enjoy the sullen amputee twisting and jerking in his pathetic attempts to earn mandatory gratitude.

'You're dead stock, kaffir, obit column. Along with all the melanin-enhanced brothers, the non-traditional shoppers, kerb creepers, dole dopers, bum bandits trying to nick a living off of my patch.' Drage-Bell lifted his catalogue to his lips in a gesture of dismissal. 'You know, I might just stroll down the Dolphin, make a few calls. I might have been premature in spurning the commonplace Hodgsons. This geek's a bookdealer like the Krogers were bookdealers. He can usually be relied upon to seriously underdescribe condition and provenance. What's your opinion?'

The burn. The forgotten taste of tobacco. Anything to scorch his dry mouth. Tar in the lungs. The flavour, however distant, of extinction. He wouldn't try to restrain this man. He would go for him. Teeth in the throat. Rip out his pocket. Grab the cash. Do a runner. Go underground. It was there. Fifty. Five crisp tenners. The wad, the lettuce. Enough to subvert Askead.

'Wait.' His hand on Drage-Bell's shoulder, forcing the rozzer back down onto the bench. 'There've been whispers going the rounds, left-footers on the manor.'

'Yes?'

'I don't have the details, as such. Not yet. A big one, Mr Bell.'

'Bollocks.'

'Takes time to soak the bung in. I swear it, boss, a political dimension. God's truth. A woman I know works for one of the TV franchises. An insider. Give her a pull, lean on her. She'd never cross you. You're good with women, Mr Bell. You'd get the truth from her.'

Cheap tinted glasses masked the copper's parrot eyes. He was up and out, chasing his shadow in the direction of Cannon Street Road, with the incontinent Sileen worrying at his heels. He stopped, waited, laid a finger against his snout's heaving chest.

'Con the conner and you're horsemeat. Put up, or crawl back under your stone. What's the Provo code for a bomb warning?'

'P. O'Neill.' An easy one that. Any mug drinking in the Roebuck could have told him. 'P. O'Neill. Then the message. I know what I'm talking about, Mr Bell. But I have to show my face around their boozers, stand my round. Christ, those Taigs can put it back. Sweat more into their shirts than we'd swallow in a month. Empty a pint pot by looking at it. I've got to melt into the scene. I need a little something in my hand.'

'That's your trouble, you blaspheming turd, you've had a little something in your hand too often. You stink of it. You're two shakes from a straitjacket. "O'Neill" is years out of date. It was when "Francis Stuart" came in that I started to get twitchy. Planning had passed to a superior breed of lowlife – evening class lecturers, beards, articulate teeth. The bastards have moved so far upmarket they have to be dubbed by Stephen Rea. Ambitious? I tell you, son, it won't be long before we're disinterring Michael MacLiammoir.'

'The Gasman, Mr Bell. I'll put the word out in the Roebuck, Queen's Head, Widow's Son, the Maurice, the Seven Stars. Detail here, end of a yarn there. Cash. That's all it takes to paste these fragments together. I must have a few quid to stay on the story.'

'Story? What story? Maltese ponces on a pension. Piss artists, old boilers, tunnel visionaries, cellar scum. *Story?* It's an apocalypse, chum, a freaks' carnival. You wouldn't survive to the last chapter if they put you on wheels. A maggot is what you are, Sileen, you belong on a corpse.'

The amputee was immovable, a tree trunk. He kept his hand out. The spook did not drop his forensic gaze – fanning himself with his catalogue. Neither man spoke. A Mexican standoff. A woman brushed past them, swatting at a thin, neatly dressed child with one hand, while dragging another, rigid, behind her. The children were mute. The woman's rage was irreversible, escalating in quantum leaps from the incident that triggered it. She looped her accusations into a venomous mantra. Every ten or twenty yards she boiled over, drumming her blows against an undefended head. The procession moved fitfully across the tired yellow grass in the direction of the tower blocks, the younger child's delinquent feet scorching a double track in the dust.

'There's a basement club.' Sileen improvised, anticipating a scratchy infusion of banknotes, stuffed like dry leaves down his shirt front. 'Meetings late at night on the full moon. Goings on, ceremonies. Cars from outside. Serious motors, Mr Bell. Mercs. Daimlers. Polished black numbers, drivers in caps and gloves. Diplomatic plates, complimentaries.'

'History, comrade.' Drage-Bell withdrew a dentiflex snot-thread from his spidery nostril. 'You can clock that old cobblers in the *Hackney Gazette*. Turks, Kurds, Blood and Honour, Tamil Tigers, Shining Path. We've got the lot. A growth industry, boy. Boom time. We encourage the fuckers – to keep up our level of funding. All surfed. Time-coded on tape. Kinder Street? We built that place.'

'Fifty, Mr Bell. I'll earn it. I swear to you.' Sileen was gone. Only the money mattered. 'Put it on the slate, a favour.'

The policeman flinched. An ugly word, favour. 'There *is* something. Not worth that kind of money. A lowlife neighbourhood scallywag. He's been taking it from both ends. We want him clipped.'

The brown envelope! Sileen grabbed for it, bit, gouged, tore it open; slicing his lip on the paper's edge. Blood-beads dripped onto the photograph, the polaroid. An unknown. A longhair; sullen, bruised. Under interrogation. Asking for it. A nobody in a string vest. Sileen shook his head.

'An irritant, an antigen. Been soliciting a slap on the wrist from the day he was born. Turning up at the right time in the wrong company. Name of O'Hagan. Imar O'Hagan. A left-footer, definitely. Anything that goes down, he's on the end of it. Used to live in a hole in the ground, a bunker over in Bow. Went ex-directory three months back. Disappeared. Get a fix on the slag and we'll talk again.'

'I'll track him, boss. Bolthole to belltower, I'll tread on his shadow. But I must have cash, cash money. Be reasonable. If I can't eat, I can't chase. He's nailed.'

The rogue bureaucrat slashed open another, identical, envelope with a horn talon. Slowly, deliberately, he extracted the fifty pounds, note by note. 'Kill a man, Sileen, and he's yours for eternity. Women don't count. They're a different species. No credits for women. Remember that.'

He fondled the bounty, snorting each individual note – licking as lasciviously as any snowbird. Forty-five pounds were returned to the envelope. A solitary Dickens was laid flat on the surround of the grey font. Where a playful zephyr caught it and lifted it over the flagstones towards a hedge of thorns. Sileen, creaking to bend, snarling like a dog, scrambled after it.

EIGHT

Arcana Caelestia, or Heavenly Secrets, which are in the Sacred Scripture, or Word of the Lord, laid open; as they are found in the sixteenth chapter of Genesis, together with the wonderful things that have been seen in the world of spirits and in the heaven of angels.

Emanuel Swedenborg, a young man, twenty-two years old in 1710, takes passage from Göteborg to the port of London. A sorry sequence of annoyances, delays, mental trials. Traditional picaresque colouring: Danish privateers, sandbanks, fog. A bad novel. Plague warnings, quarantine: Wapping Old Stairs. He comes in on the tide like an ugly rumour. This sheep-head scientist, holy fool. A celibate enquirer. The youngest of the dead. A walking corpse with peach-fuzz on his cheeks. He hunts the soul to the innermost recesses of the body. Place: an undefined riverside geography has its hooks in his chest. He is fetched. As they are all fetched, these madmen – necessary, an ingredient; humid, vegetable menstrum. Potential fossils, future deposits, we must scratch their darkness in order to see. They lay down memory-traces in the clay of our city. Strange communings, reveries, visions. Their posthumous sleep poisons our weather.

Swedenborg, a talkative skull, is frantic to be buried alive. He must die. Only God lives. Creation is death, a game of shadows and correspondences. The prophetic books are literal truth. Adam *is* the church. Man has become a building, a repository of white secrets. The building stands. Studying it, we release the possibility of the archetypal man. Tide-locked, midriver, Swedenborg scrys Nicholas Hawksmoor's unbuilt church, St George-in-the-East: its subsequent history visible only from the deck of that stalled ship. The visionary's first burial site.

A band of spirits arose. He clutched at his head, choked with sudden pain, anxious to snap the thong. The spirits were deceitful, making their way behind him, and above. He saw what they saw; saw *through* his eyes and not with them. He was standing upon the parapet of the church tower looking at the river. Mark that. Freeze the moment. He turned, walked the circuit of the available space, dizzy, memorizing what he had never seen, section after section, views of the city. On the deck of the boat these views became separate cards fanning his hand. He could lay the cards out on a table, small progressions in time. They would knit into a panorama: white buildings, scrubby groves, the highway, the river. No section fitted smoothly against its neighbour. The scars were awkward. Window refused to lock on window. Masonry overwhelmed masonry. The angles were wrong. It was all approximate, botched. But here is the mystery: the clouds above formed a seemless transcendent whole. They moved as he watched them, summoning a wind that carried the plague-ship to shore. Jagged constructions, urban scree, scaffolds, ropes, ladders, pyramids of Portland stone: the clouds were another river. Divided, Swedenborg saw all things as narrative.

A New Church, Jerusalem, to be launched on this meadow. Realized, earthed, fitted with towers, lanterns, octagons, domes, urns. He was anchored, trapped: 'Samson shorn by the churches.' Where else would they find their homeland, the legions of the English dead? Two large cities Swedenborg saw. London. He burnt to test what he already knew. 'Where do I meet people?' Flamsteed, Halley. The weight of Newton's speculations left him heartsore and reckless.

Landfall.

The sour river fog was romance, mere fiction. He slipped ashore, a man forbidden. The plague-ship tied up at Wapping Old Stairs, under a six week prohibition. He was caught. He should have been fed on gin, hung on chains while the tides washed over him, modelled in mud. A gull's perch. Privileged connections: his brother-in-law, Erik Benzelius, the bishop. He was saved, condemned to live.

Salty, engorged. On the lam. An 'immoderate desire' for knowledge, the pressure of libraries, skills to master: lens grinding, clock making, book binding. Machines to develop or to invent: submarines, blast furnaces, fire extinguishers, maps of the brain. Men who were unwritten books. Oxford always. Scholars who were channels, who appeared as the written word. Naked men bound in calf and morocco. He must speak with them all.

Conventional, shrewd, affable, damned: the young man was a fugitive in the streets, the close alleyways, the chasms between warehouses. That time in his life is expunged. It cannot be recovered. From the instant he stepped ashore to the instant he was captured: in suspension. A preview of some future tape.

What he discovered survives to this day, secreted beyond the fallout of development: a wild orchard. A thatch of white blossom, a tangle of broken boughs – thorns, couch grass, berries. Between Cable Street and the Highway, to the south of Wellclose Square: a green tunnel. Apple, whitebeam, sycamore, plane tree, black poplar. A grove sequestered from the open ground in which is buried the rubble of the Swedish Church, Ulrica Eleonora. Persistent exploration locates a grey stone font on which the church is pictured as a black ark, something abandoned, hostage to the furies.

Here. Invigilated by the gun turrets of St George, Emanuel Swedenborg was buried in a vault beneath the altar. In 1908 his body was exhumed and returned to Uppsala, out once more upon the river. The skull, famously, was mislaid. Disputed. Did it wink beneath the bar of the Crown & Dolphin with other contraband trophies: the caput of John Williams (the Ratcliffe Highway scapegoat), bone lanterns of defaulting gangsters, twicers on a definitive losing streak? Or was it fated to endure as a masonic resource, boxed in black velvet in the depths of Queen Street?

Swedenborg lay on the coarse grass, resting his back against a tree. Dappled sunlight. Shadowplay on the vellum of his outstretched hands. His soul resolved into discrete points of motion. It was of one substance with the sun. He was diffused, lost, estranged from himself. No longer did he converse with the dead. He died and became one of them. He remembered what was not yet known.

NINE

Sofya Court showed the others an apparently random selection of her photographs. She gave them coffee, strong, slow to percolate in an old pewter device that looked as if it belonged in the cupboard of a synagogue. She gave them wine that was purposefully dry, dry as chalk. Restless, determined, she glided between the curtained kitchen and the studio. Barefoot, she approached them; touched their arms, jumped back, filled the glasses, laughed as she turned, snatched up some portrait whose flaws had become unbearably obvious to her. A social solitary, she could not live alone. Night hurt her.

Wresting a print from Andi Kuschka was tricky, not because Andi resented the intervention, rather because these light-infected cards were, so it appeared to her, a product of a unique artistic sensibility – to be handled with pantomimed deliberation and tact. Helen, accepting them, in her turn, from the Canadian girl, looked with a less inhibited eye; rapidly balancing the design – as she scanned the fabrics, textures, perfumes of the room, Sofya's nervy migration through it. From time to time, with studied spontaneity, she isolated a telling detail; asserting her membership of the curious sisterhood. The PMT posse, as she thought of them. Buoyant survivors – Post Margaret Thatcher.

Sofya passed the bottle Helen had brought, without comment, to Andi. A strong, clockwise twist. Andi, laughing, speared the liberated cork at the retreating Sofya, wanting to know if she wasn't taking a chance, pushing too hard in pursuit of her latest project. Andi knew these streets, they were lethal. And getting worse. A rage culture: skinheads provoking violence to seduce the camera crews, vigilante narcissism. Spit gestures, simulated sodomy. Tributaries of risk. She walked them incessantly with her tight flocks of whitecoat Japanese murder buffs, leasing them the sacrificial sites, coaxing them to sniff the

49

stones, place their palms against the heat retained in the walls. Click/click/click. They activated instant memory triggers, *fumetti;* converting their grubby trek into a viable photo-romance. Dr Jack was an honorary Samurai. The visiting Americans were heavier, talking loudly to ward off ghosts they refused to acknowledge. For them, Whitechapel existed in dry ice and cheap yellow paper. *A Study in Terror.* Reality did not travel beyond their own shores. To service these fee-paying predators Andi traced and absorbed all the relevant texts; she swallowed facts, regurgitated the statistics of horror. This relationship with her temporary sponsors was a metaphor for the precise transaction – coin/semen/alcohol/blood – her ghouls had paid to celebrate.

Helen told about the Tarten brothers and boxing. The other women shrieked.

'Boxing? What do you *wear*?'

Helen didn't want to imagine. Anthony as her bucket-carrying sponge man. 'Go on, gel. Nut 'im, my son.' Nicholas, proud of fellating a black cigar and chewing gum at the same time. A wet mouth in a camelhair coat. Patronizing endearments, slapped silk buttocks. It was preposterous. She loved it.

Laughter: they sprawl across the tan sofa, commingled, loose jointed, faint. Sofya falls with them. Gashes of red light in the window panels. Street sounds. Racing feet. The busy silence returns. They are calm. Green plants, seascapes, prints of unvisited places. They pick up their drinks. Andi admires the sleeve length of Sofya's blouse. Helen amuses them: the game of pencil skirts in open plan offices. Bitchery of weather princesses competing for fan mail, the jump into legitimate variety. They trawl the heavens for attention-grabbing manifestations of the millennium: water-spouts, mock suns, frogs, earthquakes, cataracts and hurricanoes.

Helen lights a cigarette. A small violation. The gesture suits her. The lifted shoulder. The decorative movement away from her scarlet lips. With no mere male present to be heartstruck. The transformation: Helen to Isabel. Appreciated, not envied. Andi also succumbs to the spirit of occasion. A few rapid puffs and the butt burns her fingers. Tucking their heels beneath them, they occupy opposite wings of the sofa.

The photographs. Sofya had forced an entry, infiltrated a corner of the imaginary past. She had nominated her ancestors and come to live amongst them. The unphotographed are the forgotten. The faces Sofya interrogated were potential cousins. Future generations would honour them with invented titles. To walk these streets, even with an empty camera-case, was enough. Recognition in every doorway. The comfortable risk of belonging.

But how to enlist the genuine contenders? Now all the vagrants were performance artists. Do you want the upraised Special Brew shtick, the squeeze-box, the scars, the Equity card? Cellar dives and backstairs spielers touted for American Express. Whores shadowed by their own documentary crews. Sofya's heavy gold hair was cropped. Watchful, over-alert, the flame of her charm adjusted like a blowtorch: she prepared herself for a journey. It was more demanding than her West African odyssey. In Ghana *she* had been the exotic. Corruption was exuberant and undisguised. The smell of blood on a warm wind. She was primed for a new adventure. She clumped in steel-capped boots. Getting serious was an exercise in style: the cut of her khaki, the number of buttons on her denim jacket. She followed old men home, shooting their backs, the buildings that swallowed them.

At first she could not bring herself to squeeze the shutter. A tautology. The act would confirm her failure. The brief theft of light would drain her chakra. There was a forfeit to pay. Better to be an unnoticed value in the scene she was observing. She stayed defiantly within the shady backdrop that gave weight to her unachieved compositions. In bondage to a reality that had long since decamped.

Where were Israel Zangwill's proud Sephardi, with their attendant parasites, the shnorrers and shysters? Dissolved. The lens magnified her eye into a dead moon. She saw nothing. Hair trapped in mortar, wasp husks colonizing autumn bricks, wilderness gardens. Soup-kitchens given over to shvartzers. Where were the dispersed hoards of the Ashkenazi? Their tenements captured, bagels devoured by vulgar taxis. Where were the faces of the prophets? She demanded a territory beyond the sentiment of ribboned albums. Where were the blackhats scuffling in hallways, the schleppers of brown paper parcels? Where were the glistening butterball heavyweights, hauling themselves aboard muddy Volvos? Arrogant zhlubs hefting her into gutters? Where could she trace the runnels of cold sweat, the pain she solicited?

Oxford, that's where. Out of season. The decorous lawns of Christ Church, the Memorial Garden. Splash of water. The foul-breathed war dead are too timid to haunt this sanctuary. Pre-menstrual, ungenerous, Sofya stooped to read John Bunyan's words, set in copper letters into the pavement. 'My sword I give to him that shall succeed me in my pilgrimage.' She rejected them. Through the viewfinder they were spoiled, a mindless homily. She was here to observe, but she could not bring herself to commit a single image to film.

They babbled and seethed over the gravel paths, arms semaphoring in racial caricature like a Yiddish version of *Alice In Wonderland*. The commission was killed. How could she offer these stereotypes to *New Society*? She was about to walk out through the gates, hit the streets, return to the station. Why dignify this babel with the title 'Symposium'? Put any three Jews together and you've got a conference. Thirty of them and it's a revolution. Crows and rabbis. Plump, sleek, feathers waxed; they hopped over the manicured verges, the incipient meadowland. Beaks greasy with worm, bloody with argument in a dozen languages, they pecked and nodded. Her Leica stayed in its canvas satchel. She was a woman, unmarried, without status.

Then she saw him, her ideal. He belonged at the heart of her pet project, a man who *had* to be followed. He had even anticipated her urge to escape – but, instead of rushing for St Aldates, he slouched, solitary, contracted, into the narrow path that led towards Merton College.

She stuck to him like a shadow. Hurt radiated from his hunched shoulders in an aura of bronchial purple. An angel, burdened with wings of steel, fished from a sewer. A gargoyle searching for a ledge from which to hang himself. The man turned, held out a hand, withdrew it. 'Donar. Mordecai Donar.' A good head of silvery vaselined hair. A deep crease between tufty eyebrows. Round smooth cheeks. Lips working convulsively before the sentences could be formed. Wide, sloping shoulders. No neck.

She had done it. She had walked into the trap. She could neither move nor speak. Now she was the one who is watched. It was as if a door had opened in one of her photographs and the contained darkness had flooded the world.

Fatherly, respectful, he continued at her side; his hand always on her elbow. There was no destination, their path ambled beneath high walls: a gentle circuit that carried them back towards the point from which they had set out. Mordecai Donar talked. He told Sofya they were in Deadman's Walk, a route taken by Jewish funeral processions to the burial ground on the site of the Botanic Garden. He crowded her silence with tales of violence, suffering, urban terror – the Polish partisans, the Haggannah. He carved deep trenches in the ruled lawns; he poisoned the Bhutan Pine. English light failed him. Waves of tender air scorched Sofya's throat.

She did not believe his stories. The lies were so exactly what she expected to hear. He was telling her nothing. The relationship was impossible. She would not allow him to conceal himself inside her instrument. There must be a distance. She would handle his shoebox of photographs – and, while she stared at the alien faces, listen to what he had to say. Donar's family avoided the camera's eye. They were in profile, or half-turned towards the stranger in the window. Sofya held grimly to her duty. This man must never be included in her secret portfolio.

Mordecai, for his part, with his foolish tilted grin, slipped focus: a liquid vessel. His voice was a constant, a drone of saccharine and horror. Dry crumbling biscuits, sweet wine. They were grave goods. He posed, head above the lampshade, fated – freedom fighter or victim? He shrugged: an invertebrate, a creature recently knitted. He nibbled at things that looked like raisins, but weren't. Saucer to mouth: his congenital restlessness freezing for 1/250th of a second. Engaged in some secondary activity – tea-brewing, marquetry, brass polishing – he would sneak a glance at her, call her 'Cantor'. She directed his worship, he said. Nodding, loose as wool, he waited for her reaction. He smirked at her unease.

Breaking away from her tormentor, back in her own room, arms outstretched – the freedom – she plunges delicate hands into the marzipan pile of the heavy velvet curtains. She feeds a CD into the newly-purchased system, runs a bath. The phone rings. Donar. It is always Donar. He has her wired. He is there when she is too tired to imitate herself, when she is desperate for sleep, shutdown, the pit. She closes out Whitechapel and he intrudes. He is the clink of milkbottles. The elbow on the car horn. He sours her first cup of coffee. He takes up residence in her cupboards. She is never free of him. The guilt trigger, black smoke over pine forests. He has invented her.

In Oxford Mordecai Donar was tolerable, an exotic, a man to be followed. He muddied the benign complacency of established privilege, aggressively conserved beauty. He spat on polished floors, gobbed tubercular phlegm into herbaceous borders. He used memorial gardens as a means of forgetting: he transposed their formal rigour onto the multi-ethnic chaos of Tower Hamlets. He was a beggar at the gates, lecturing to ganefs in their own redoubt. Returned, and on his home patch, he was an unreconstructed disaster, bad noise, a yelping meshuggener. There was no shaking him off. His story was unfinished. He begged Sofya to visit him in Grace's Alley, off Wellclose Square, so that she could commit his portrait. A space was waiting on the walls. He sent her dead roses macerated in aftershave.

She submitted. It was the only way to finish with the man. A bargain was struck with the squad of spectres she had been pursuing. Donar consumed them. After this there would be no more spying, no lurking; nothing concealed, nothing furtive. She would willingly collaborate. She would photograph those who asked it of her. She would be the handmaid of place, filing anonymous images for future enquirers. Mordecai had made a request she couldn't refuse. A big mistake, but it was no longer her decision. She had been summoned.

There's not much left of Wellclose Square. Vestiges of historical record caught in the trees. A conspiratorial diminuendo in the jar of light. Wind scudding off the river, worrying the green canvas drapes the builders left behind when they abandoned their speculation. Hard to believe anyone can pretend to live here.

Donar was ready for her, for her hesitant footsteps on the wooden stairs, her knock on the open door. He had been ready for a long time. His room was a set, a scene-of-the-crime polaroid. No camera was needed to record it. The few books on display represented the sum total of Mordecai's knowledge. All the notable synagogues of the eradicated Jewish East End had been preserved as marquetry panels: Spital Square, Fournier Street, Cannon Street Road, Princelet Street, Heneage Street. Photographs discovered inside a condemned tree.

Donar guided a plate of pastries across the table, lumps of sugared bone-dust. He raised a treacle of brown sherry to her dry lips. She waited, her satchel at her feet. She looked away from him, watching the spankers of the treeheads shake out their cargo of darkness. Her mouth had been stitched. She zipped and unzipped the pockets of her bag.

The phone rang. Its shrill, asexual insistence splitting the moment beyond repair. Sofya's mother. In Cambridge. Andi and Helen could overhear the familiar litanies. Warnings, instructions, spools of impenetrable gossip. Yes, Sofya was eating properly. No, she would never go back to the classroom. The psychotic infants with their dangling shoelaces and snotty noses could conduct their mayhem without her. Yes, she wore gloves and socks and scarfs, and clean knickers, to go out taking her photographs of *those* streets. No, she wouldn't leave Whitechapel and come home where she could be looked after for a few months. No, she didn't want her mother to speak to the woman she had met at the Cambridge Darkroom about an exhibition in the new year. Love, yes, always. Helen heard it from a distance. She was warm, comfortable, a little drunk; nobody outside this room knew where she was. Andi was safe too. Her mother was on the far side of the Atlantic.

The fiery redness that had lit up the window was extinguished. And replaced by a carbon solidity in which nothing lived. Andi was leaning forward, roseate with the heat of the room, the rush of drink and smoke and confession. She tried to pull herself up out of the sofa, to cross the floor, breathe the night air. Sofya was filling her glass. A bottle of bourbon had been found. A story about the man who had left it behind. It was too early to break up the party.

'I am the Ice Queen.' Andi said it aloud, stressing the capitals; relishing, rejoicing in, the qualities that kept her apart from the others, the two young women who were rocking back, helpless with laughter. They were all childless. The biological clock was tapping out its doom. Night lurked behind the curtains. Andi was built on a different scale. She had the strength of the pioneers, the colonists. These were girls, sheltered, untested. Andi's becoming feyness, her whispering, hesitant speech was an attempt to disguise competitiveness and a driving sensuality, to avoid giving offence to delicate European sensibilities. There was nothing more to say. It was unreal: the studio, the talk, the art spiel, the flirtations – powder room gossip. These dilettantes knew nothing of landscape, cold, distance. Sofya's project would never work. It was too rational. It lacked spontaneity. It didn't cost her enough.

The booze was beginning to take over, take possession of Andi: submerged longings, overbright eyes, a quickening of the breath. She allowed herself to subside into the stream of memory, sensation, fantasy: the street. A public demeanor (assertively modest, startlingly drab) as she rode herd on her tame pilgrims, the shrine-hopping murder trippers. Andi was their guide, a soubrette of bad karma, gaily traipsing the somnambulist's circuit of sweatshops, weavers' lofts, decommissioned synagogues, anarchist craters.

Andi nursemaided the cameras through Blood Alley, gave suck to telephoto excesses. She became the inevitable conclusion of their scenario. Courteous Japanese industrialists, with surgically implanted smiles, forced her to pose against butchered walls. They bowed and touched her arm. Video pulses blink in scarlet excitement. Camcorders race over the topography of her standing figure. She is multiplied: so many simultaneous versions of herself. She is faint. She leans against the sated bricks. Each movement is divided into its constituent parts. She shields her face. A grotesque close-up: lips, tongue, teeth. Lifting a hand in protest. Shaking her head: murderously tight reverse angle. Surrounded. They kneel at her feet or climb onto boundary walls and the bonnets of cars. They become a single swollen eye, assaulting her.

She conceals her shape beneath long winter coats, loose, men's shirts. She wears ugly fingerless gloves. But somehow the punters sniff out her secret history. Camera-faces feed on her, on that generous unmilked bosom. Useless to protest. She is not the same woman. The name has changed. The skinmag model was a child, fresh off the boat, hungry for the courage of bohemian life. She had been willingly airbrushed, a cellophane nude: monochrome, glossy, incapable of response. Prized for her tits, acorn nipples grown hard in draughty studios. Glancing down, between sessions, at the nocturnal comings and goings of Goslett Yard. Earning the money to define her art. Ateliers of Paddington and Camden Town. Gaggia coffee-bars of Old Compton Street. Red formica, cups like ashtrays. New Wave at the Academy, the Paris Pullman. Bergman in Hampstead. Spaghetti and candlelight. Meatballs. Floor fucks. The Pretty Things

The Soho photographers were a joke. From pimps to property developers overnight. Fleshy, chain-smoking, medallion men; bearded, wheezy with chat. Necklaces, bangles, hairy as gorillas. Those open-necked black Italian shirts, splitting at the seams, dank sweat stains ringing the armpits. She was impenetrable, blood-denying – a tool of the eye. Andi soldiered on, stupid and brave. It was the world that changed.

Sober with too much whisky, growing calmer and more centred with every sip, the women descended into a companionable silence. They had bypassed the decencies of self-censoring language and gesture. Sofya became that thing which is forbidden by the arbitrators of political correctness, a blonde. Not a blonde photographer, nor a blonde supervisor of infants – a blonde glorifying in her blondness; sassy, hand on hip, unrepentant. A fright wig dressed her cropped head. She swayed and wriggled. She was Monroe in *Bus Stop*. Only the burning, firecoal eyes denied the performance, kept Helen's wolf-whistles and boy-hoots in check.

Without exhibitionism, Andi pulled off her sweater. This was no premeditated theatrical effect. She hugged herself, then stood up, stretching out her arms above her head. She subdued the urge to give a cowboy yell. Once her breasts had been better known than her face. Covered, she was anonymous. Turn up the volume, girls. Glorious display: she revolves, twirling her tassels, to imaginary stamps and cheers. The women are the three white witches, percolating the fate of the city. Together they can do anything. Their sense of power is tangible. They show themselves. They are inviolate.

Men are forbidden, absurd. Drink up. Andi and Sofya, talking at the same time, over each other, in and out of synch, garbling one story. Both have been involved, often on the same day, the same afternoon, without previous knowledge, to their mutual satisfaction and pleasure, with the painter Imar O'Hagan.

'*Who*?' Helen has never heard of him, cannot believe that name.

Andi was first, sees him still, greets him in the Lane, odd hours of the night, slouching home drunk from some dubious assignation. His oblique charm, the unlaced boots, the paint-smeared overalls. The rat!

The thing with Sofya was more dramatic: tears, telephones, anathemas. Libidinous secrecy is O'Hagan's métier, juggling appointments behind the locked doors of a tumbledown house. The weasel. They were both fond of him. So boyish and unashamed in his narcissism. Mirrors, drawn blinds, self-portrait on the easel. He was his only subject. Under a single bulb, repeatedly painting himself, naked. Cocksure. Never satisfied.

'Who *is* this man?' Helen is intrigued. What stud could appeal so forcefully to such contrary temperaments? 'What what *what* did I say?'

The others are hysterical. Think about it and it's impossible. Sofya hugs the bare-breasted Andi. Andi puts an arm around Sofya's shoulder, imagines the photograph of Mordecai Donar. *Now* it makes sense. Another male self-portrait, manipulated by Donar – through the medium of Sofya's confused compliance. There's something mock-innocent and unmade about this old hermit, with his objects, his toys and icons. He cheats death. He's trying to put the fix on his obituary.

Touching hands, they share each other. Difficult to comprehend, they share O'Hagan. Share the singularity of the painter's vision. The hours in that ravaged house have been stolen from their biographies. Hours that were complex, mysterious, infuriating to recall. They can't be recalled. They've been snuffed, censored. A taste of lukewarm coffee; stale air; the overwhelming imminence of squalor. Step outside O'Hagan's door and it doesn't hold. It cannot be borne. They thought, both of them, for that brief interval, while it was happening, while he made love to them, that it all made perfect sense. The world could be recovered from a still point.

It was the hour of least resistance, when children are born, when old people die, go out on the tide. The city pleasures itself, freed from human frets: a dreadful lucidity. The women withdrew, but the conversation went on. Sofya found that she was stroking the skin of her shoe, fingering the thread, caressing a loose cuticle of hide. There was a subdued fetishism in her fascination with the person and habits of Imar O'Hagan. It was not serious, so could it be true? Was a fetishism – of objects, texture, scent – the trigger for her haywire response, her liminal addiction?

'The vest.' Andi spoke, knowing just what Sofya was thinking. 'That terrible string vest. Taking his shirt off in a restaurant. Oh God.' Was it the vest itself or the elegant gradient of his clavicles?

The others roared. Collapsing into furniture catalogue poses, they passed judgement on O'Hagan's pouting profile – the Rank Charm School coshboy. Dirk Bogarde with a padded jockstrap. An overhead fan processed the delicious beads of sweat that dripped from his cowlick.

They were quieter, slower, more obviously tired. Talk was reduced to single phrases. 'City Airport? She *couldn't*! Hand luggage?' They yawned. Sofya and Andi took themselves to bed. Helen arranged some cushions on the floor. 'The tattoo.' She lay back with her eyes open. Reflected light from passing cars, bifurcations on the ceiling. Andi and Sofya had confessed. The snail on his left bicep, that was *it*. So weirdly apposite, the faggoty awfulness of his taste. Oh yes. Imar was undoubtedly the man Helen had seen, stripped to the waist, washing himself in the yard of the discount warehouse, beneath the North Sewage Outfall.

TEN

Sileen found it agonizingly difficult to hobble past the marmoreal bulk of the London Hospital. He sweated with desire. He sucked at air vents, wanting to channel the warm used breath into his failing lungs. He drooled over moss islands colonizing the silver foil of the building's intestinal ducts. Broken skin – peeling, wounded; a fur of asbestos and heat-sanctioned conglomerate. The very ground was blessed. He endured that tendresse a wrongly accused man experiences walking away from a night of furious interrogation.

A swaying conga of Watchers, as these nurse-substitutes were now known, reeled down the hospital steps, attempting ineffectually to hold each other up. They were totalled; gloriously, helplessly rat-arsed. A full-blooded return to pre-Victorian values, to the days when nurses who attended the mixed wards were perceived as the lowest of the low. Honest streetwalkers sneered at them. Drink wasn't consolation, it was a necessity. Their sole qualification lay in not being Irish. About which they lied. All the Irish lied. Therefore they *were* Irish. Nobody else had the stomach for the job. The cycle of history had limped gratefully back to its point of departure. The Watchers catcalled after Sileen's retreating form. He belonged inside. He belonged in a cage.

'Sweeney, come back, darling. We'll give you a shave you'll never forget.' They whistled and screamed as he dodged into the traffic. 'You'd be safe with that one, girls. Can't get his leg over till he takes it off.'

If only the rest of his condemned meat, that hell of sinew, brainmess, bloodflow, was as biddable as his tin leg. Mere thought, an order from upstairs, was enough to kick this borrowed limb towards responsible action. Sileen flinched to follow, some rind of ethical consciousness held him back. Creature of twilight, his chalk face and feral eyes scorched through the rusty nape of evening light. He was trapped, midstream, punching at vans, slapping at the reflected sodium puddles on the roofs of over-revving escapees. Another casualty, another care-of-the-community maniac. They barely noticed him, sealed into their Dagenham capsules, lithium-fixed by anodyne intercuts of news and bad noise. Disaster raps. Blamblamblam rhythms. Headache-inducing repetitions of traffic control. The thudding down-draught of surveillance helicopters.

Whitechapel Road poured its illuminated rage-caravan from horizon to horizon, tilting like a wave game, a tropic of obscenity. Sileen held resolutely to his ground, in the thick of it, fists aloft: an involuntary exile. Let them rush to perdition. He could wait until London was a paradise of wild palms, strollers, pavement cafés, conversation. He hallucinated the silence of the X-ray cabinet, the melting basement. He'd stoop to anything to recover that state. He'd even talk to a journalist.

Gray Hood was that exception; a disgrace to his craft, a pariah – he did not drink. Neither did he smoke (sniff/snort/ingest/gobble/lick/inject/inhale/pinch/rub/passively blast). He was clean. Hideous to behold, his hand did not tremble. His breath was like the perfume counter at Harrod's. His eye was not the traditional suicided leech in a net of broken veins. His nose was moist. His tongue pink as dressed ham. With a dash more vanity he could have been a Democrat, a candidate. But he was further disadvantaged by not possessing a repertoire of criminally sexist jokes and cheesy smoking-room anecdotes. Fuck him, Hood was a paragon. If he'd been able to rub two sentences together and produce the feeblest spark, he might have risen higher than legman for the *Hackney Gazette*.

Hood was an unimpeachable anorak, stepping daintily, peg on snout, through fastbreeding mayhem. He was incapable of blowing pepper up a pit bull's nostrils. Everyday rapes and mutilations were effortlessly neutralized by his formulaic prose. Get the victim's age right and the rest will be forgiven. He processed gothic outreaches of malignancy into acceptably flavourless paras. Analysis was not his bag. Confronted by the manifold defaults of the flesh, he muttered: 'I pass.' But, worse than his other shortcomings, he loved literature. Say no more. The fiend. Beyond and above literature, he worshipped writers.

Writers? Scum! Hood ogled them from afar. Or edged up to PR tables, standing mute, eavesdropping on their peevish chat of royalty fiddles, game shows, agents out of Frankenstein's workshop. Pristine hardback pressed to bosom, he waited in line at Old Broad Street signings. Biographers, fruit fly celebrities flushed with scandal, ghosted gangsters: it was all one. Peter Ackroyd or the bloke who broke into the Queen's bedroom. There was magic in the transformation of naked words into book-objects. Books had their own life. They survived the embarrassment of authorship. The writer was holy. Even Sileen. Even the noisome cripple must be tolerated. He had published – once. Once was enough. For Sileen it had been rather too much, an aberration. He stamped on this jejune urge to confess, to shape the seething muckball on which he jigged into his own image. All forgotten. The world had forgiven him. His obscurity was such that he could expect a two-column obituary in *The Independent*. A single question remained on the journo's lips. 'Why *you?*'

As with Catholics, there are no ex-authors: Sileen, lapsed scribbler, shouldered his way through the crush of hawkers who blocked his access to the Grave Maurice. His event horizon was the distance that kept him from the bar. The stereophonic gehenna, occurring behind his back, was wiped. Revolving blue-pulse beams, a downsweep of searchlights, horns, hoops of agitated air. At the railings: chaos voyeurs, their faces betel-leaf scarlet, gawping at the terrified patients who gurnied against the glass. The line of windows was a neutral interface between seers and seen. Deep-trauma surgical misadventures oscillated from the wards to inspect the incoming trawl of casualties.

Just another bomb outrage – a pumping station, a litter bin. The hospital shuddered as the helicopter-ambulance subsided on its roof. Even when the blades had stopped the machine trembled like a captured greyhound. Dust columns flighted a spectral trap, behind which the violet stumps of the city hovered in the haze, waiting their turn to fly. Inmates responded; raging against their restraints, to shake the walls. Beading tranquillized sleep with cold fear. The street rabble read the bandaged waifs as future cartoons, offcuts from the ambulance's cargo.

Mutilés de guerre. Maimed, shocked, palsied, dumb: the experience was spreading like a stain. The perimeter of the city was defined by those targets worth detonating. Furniture warehouses, golf clubs, suburban recruiting offices. Trash alped where potentially incendiary receptacles had been removed. Letter-boxes were nailed up and parcels prohibited. Communication was left to the mercy of the privateers. Cut wires trailed in the wind, sparking over canal banks and dry reservoirs. A state of war had come into existence, which was not worth reporting. Hood couldn't sell the tabloids a picture of Silvertown in flames. Not if it was painted by John Martin. Yawn. Seen it. Done that one, son.

The legman was as legless as Sileen when it came to investigative reporting. Not for him the tedious transcription of names, injuries, birth dates. Get the mortuary attendants to phone in a tally. He wants to talk literature, give Sileen the third degree, winnow fact from fiction. Must a writer first experience what he will later exploit?

Not so fast, squire. The Grave Maurice prides itself on stocking the most expensive bad cigars in London. The trepid guv'nor reaches suspiciously into a yellow Cuban box, intended to flatter inebriated medics, and retrieves a crumbling tube of dust, quite innocent of lubricious sweat from the thighs of Negresses. This publican's worth a couple of sentences of local colour to any aspiring hack. Bored to the borders of catalepsy, his complexion is ashy with shingles of necrotic tissue. He's beaked like an albatross: an ill-advised dandy who's been talked into having hair-extensions grafted up his nostrils. The bags under his eyes would cost him a serious excess tariff. Hood, completely missing this opportunity to beef up his similes, counted out the coins from a pentagonal dispenser. Sileen chewed greedily on the foul stalk. It gave him an excuse to remain silent while the journo rehearsed yet again favoured passages from the book Sileen had repudiated forever. He dreamt it, another life – he can dream no more.

A steady precipitation of grey plaster scurfed Sileen's skullcap. A labouring overhead fan was making conceited allusion to the ambulance-helicopter: as Sileen's leg made allusion to the rest of him. He never thought of it as a limb that had gone missing, but as a role model, a forerunner, for the clinging skinwrap which had not yet achieved its higher state. Why could he not be pure silver to the touch, an aluminium robot, sleek and immaculate? Oil his tracks with Pils and whisky: he snatched them from the journalist's hands. The room was cold as an abattoir. Fire those motors: he tossed back the liquid fire and demanded a refill. Where had they all gone, the Grave Morries, the revenants? His chums, his gossips, the circle of dedicated boozers – why had they all fled the city? Sileen was tired of making conversation with policemen and jaded mercenaries.

Hood, primed for his next bar run, occulted Sileen's sightline on the street, the windows of the hospital. Worse – he was keeping him from the cabinet of prophetic light, the soothing torment of the Finsen baths. Ancient selves waited in the cellars to pass on their narrative infections. This aniseed clown was his *best* hope? A yarn he could flog to Drage-Bell for cash? Was it worth the tedium? The game was up; he might as well simulate masonic semaphore with a cut-throat razor. Check the freak out. Hood's nobody-at-home benevolence was an insult. He would always be too young, too fresh. He looked like the geek who couldn't say 'when' to a liposuction pump. The fat was gone, the gristle and the brains with it. Even the journo's clothes were offensive – distressed, but radically laundered. His grin, an unnerving flash of the natural, had Sileen gumming in impotent fury: his own hollow-cheeked mug shot returned in duplicate from the dazzling lenses of Hood's rimless spectacles. Poverty can be repulsive when it is so effectively husbanded.

Sileen took a whisky flashback – a previous informant, dead now, dismissing Hood. 'The kind of slack cunt who's heard all you need to shift the prints is the rhetoric of Lady Thatcher and the bristols of Sam Fox. Cocks it up, don't he? Smacks 'em with 27 million units of Sam's thoughts on the hard ecu and a centrespread of Lady T's tits.'

'What have you got?' The impatient amputee glugs on his brew, enduring a ripple of painful contractions in the throat, as his hand locks on Hood's collar, drawing the pale nark to within a few inches of his interrogator's bubonic breath.

The usual melancholy recitation, the city plagiarizing its ruin: abuse of children, council chamber conspiracies, sequestration of tower blocks by privateers, the absolutely final and definitive account of the murder of Jack the Hat. Yes yes yes. Conscience on autopilot, Sileen needs more, much more than this. There's no percentage in human misery.

The tarts. The Spitalfields girls have been at him again. Apparently a new breed of client has evolved: Pevsner in one hand, bloody pliers in the other. The punters want to be serviced on the exact sites of the Whitechapel murders, and will pay a premium for the full set. Polite sadists, offering Diners Club cards, they 'collect' the shrines of infamy – like mountain peaks to be ticked off. They indulge in perverse athleticism, spiced by a heritaged whiff of the underskirts of Victorian squalor. If no toothless mouths are available for hire, they will create them.

The girls are jumpy. They complain to the *Gazette*, to the bored legman. Hood listens, phone cradled between clavicle and chinstrap, fishing congealed milk-powder from his coffee with a paperclip. He offers them none of the sympathy he lavishes so wantonly on Sileen, that published man. He wishes now he *had* followed up on their incoherent diatribe – if only to supply an accredited author with the raw material of literature.

Picaresque, but useless. Drage-Bell would sneer at the mention of such antics. A third whisky anchors Sileen to his stool. It was going straight through his skin, bloodsweat. The palm of his hand was sticking to his jaw. He chewed on the dead cigar for sustenance, hadn't eaten in days. Needed to push the world back. Switch off all sensory input: Hood is talking and he's out of synch. He reaches into his shoulder-bag, fumbles for a book. At *this* time? He is actually asking Sileen to autograph a copy of that novel. The pen is a midget's unconvinced erection. It spurts black semen onto the title-page – as Sileen scrapes away all traces of his original nom de plume.

'Kinder Street.'

Again: Kinder Street. Journalist and filth have been wired to the same source. What do they want with a middleman, with Sileen? Let them have Kinder Street. To hell with Kinder Street. Give me whisky. Rumours. Hood said. Whispers out of kiosks in abandoned precincts. A delirious razorhead. Name of Seabrook. Something curious happening down there.

The liquid steadies, the glass rotates. Sileen is hypnotizing himself. Lighter fluid washes against the rim, subsides, leaving a lickable stain. Lick then. Lungs rinsed in warm suds. Toss it back: a rusty screwdriver into the tongue. Kinder Street. SUPPORT PEOPLES WAR IN PERU (R.C. Maoists). The Gasman. O'Hara? O'Hagan. Sileen's target. Wasn't he webbed up in a kidnapping score? Sheltering a wife-beater? Political dimension? Stay with Kinder Street.

Seabrook's a name to be instantly deleted. Seabrook doesn't matter. A registered nutcase, Hood reckons, always touting for space. Claims to have heard goings on in the basement, the flats behind the London Hospital, down by the river. Mysterious internal floodings. High Rise turned into a submariners' training tank. We checked. Dry as a bone. Suspicious in itself. Given the neighbourhood. Proximity of sewers. Walbrook, Fleet. Lost rivers.

The out-patient insisted. Called in every time he found an un-vandalized dog. Another meet, more drinks. Limousines. Late at night.

Swears it. Mother's life. Names invoked, granite faces. Impossible. Suspects you'd never suspect. Not of this. Club queens, ministers who'd never have made it into Dr Caligari's cabinet, public gangsters. You can't tell me that men used to eight course lunches in Brussels are going to break bread with backstreet barbers, legbreakers, piss-artists in Old Etonian ties? That's the yarn Seabrook's trying to stiff me with. Dinner jackets, black candle orgies, Clerkenwell rent boys. Flooded cellars. A desert by morning.

Forget it. Sileen refuses to sift these insane accumulations of horror. He can't shape a coherent narrative from the mess, nominate a single strand from this quantum chaos. The punctuation had gone. Sleeping/ waking, death/memory, inventing/reporting. Cold Pils to temper the false inspiration of whisky. Whisky to ignite the nordic gloom of the lager. No finer place on earth. The automated limb measuring its length on the red plastic banquette. Doors wide to the evening, a soothing thud of Casablanca fans.

The couch creaks and Sileen's prosthesis is lifted into the air as that well-respected local canker, Joblard the sculptor, uninvited, joins them: bulky in layers of stolen coat, freshly-minted head, thirsty grin. Sileen shot out a reflex arm to protect his untapped bottle. Joblard is attended by some gaunt acolyte, a ceiling-scraper. Introduced as 'Axel Turner'. Another bonehead: a Futurist whose future is all used up. Left ear tagged like a sheep, livid with secondary infections. A demonic partnership. It was bound to end in tears. They're hot to swill away the latest performance art freak show, some tame crypt they've polluted. Memory is their scam. Empty factories, discontinued industry. The art of the Eighties: the proposal. Fliers, ponderous explanations of unachieved events. Without a pot to piss in, these paupers travel the globe, dowsing native energies – clay and cake, mud and ice. They roger the complacent culture wives. This is all Sileen needs. A stubble-chinned team of unrented assassins.

'Anybody you know?' Hood queried, before trotting to the bar for a bigger tray: not trusting his luck, an authenticated haul of boho artists.

'They're *everybody* I know,' Sileen growled.

Sawn-off anecdotes; overactive, sclerous tongues – like scarlet pokers dipping the stout. Halting fragments, demented laughter. They sicken the aesthetic journalist. They sicken Sileen. These booze-hounds will stretch their stuff until the lights are killed. The leech of radium is further than ever from Sileen's grasp.

Reyjavik, Tel Aviv, Prague, Aachen. Meaningless names. Turner is improvising a shaggy fable. 'A Norwegian novelist.' He waits for the jeers to stop. A Norwegian novelist, it seems, opted to live in Hackney. Without coercion, his own choice. Stoke Newington. Clapton ponds. What does it matter where? This Norwegian, the writer, published a book in his native language, impossible to obtain, hugely popular in and around Bergen, sold about a dozen copies. Work of fiction, a mystery. Dealing with Swedenborg, Emanuel Swedenborg's career in Whitechapel.

The bar darkened. The landlord was calling time. Sileen, at last, was awake. Calm enough to kill. He was about to invade his own synopsis. Turner was confirming what he already knew. The loop was completed.

Joblard was prompting Turner, keep it going, a chance to grope in the murk for misplaced glasses. The crucial vision, Swedenborg's breakthrough of consciousness, the initial communication with the spirits of the dead, occurred in what is now (he didn't frequent such places) a public-house in the vicinity of the London Hospital. A cellar or basement.

At the height of his abilities, the call to renounce worldly ambition. His sight was cleansed. He spoke with angels. He passed among the dead. They touched him on the stairs. The entrance to hell was concealed beneath the floor of an East London hostelry. Not as a metaphor, a conceit – an exact location. Stones melted. Brick was sand. Pent-up fires from the concupiscence of evil consumed the interior of his mind. He was there, he saw it. Evil cannot be removed until it appears. Swedenborg, the agent provocateur. He caused its manifestation, solely to annihilate its power. Hell had fixed its gate.

This is what Axel Turner, sitting in the deserted bar of the Grave Maurice, remembered. This was his account. An absurdity that left Sileen breathless, primed for an act of violence. Turner's gloss was irrelevant. He spoke with Sileen's voice. The script he had dreaded. It was all true.

The reeling cripple heaved back the table, sending a residue of bottles clinking and plummeting towards the floor. He knew now the extent of his fall, the depravity of his present condition. He had *almost* – it was the nadir in a belly-crawling vocation – tried to bum a temporary sub from Joblard, King of Schnorrers. He was ready to trade all the visions for a oncer, a quid in the hand. Combat fatigue! He peddled streetwards, herded by the taunts of the performance mercenaries.

ELEVEN

Carbon-starved, parched for the drench of ionizing radiation, Sileen embraced the green angel plinth, and gazed across the Whitechapel Road at the soft focus hospital. He enjoyed, from the inside, the afterglow of his alcohol rub. A scatter of late pedestrians clotted like scarlet PVC on cheap video. Orange beams puddled like a melt of coloured ice. Movement smeared the phosphorescent slipstreams. The hospital was still one of the sights of London: imperiously democratic, a ghost ship. Its floodlit grandeur mocking the sullen warrens that wallowed in its wake.

He submerged himself in the purple hour, the twilight velvet. Edible light. Sileen caressed it. The arrogance of the building comforted him. That such things had once been possible: benevolence, fortitude, hope, nurturing, charity. Good words. They dissolved into thin windows that kept him from sleep. He was banished, an outsider – prohibited from the machinery that could transport him to his remedial nightmare, the landscape of fear.

The arches of the main entrance were dimly illuminated, so that the dead could be carried discreetly down to the tall-sided furniture vans: disciples of cholera, septicaemic afficionados, internationalists game enough to sample legionnaires' disease. Incineration was out of the question. Too many had enlisted and too suddenly. The burning chimney threw up a perpetual column of black smoke, bone fragments, unseasonal snow on the sweatshops and formica-tabled curry caves. The burial ground on the south side of the hospital, once known as the 'Garden of Eden', was choked with compacted stiffs; their bones poking through the wretched soil in a leafless harvest. Even the sheep that grazed the gravel were evolving into carnivores. Grass was a troublesome memory. Staggering on rickety legs, they jostled like a pack of snaggle-toothed Augustans, touting for patronage. It was feed yourself or starve.

A mothglow of gas mantles. The promiscuous torches of the Watchers plying their trade among the terminal wards. Dowsing for a live one, tapping the sheets for concealed bottles. Sileen watched too, and was released: his own pain cast in a grander form, a lambent surge to ravish the dull walls and make treaty with the speeding clouds.

His arm tightened around the neck of the bronze angel. It struck him, hard, the true nature of this monadnock rearing over a featureless peneplain. The hospital, like Ayers' Rock, hid the greater part of its sulking strength beneath the ground: tunnels, caverns, railway systems, sideline experiments. It anchored the entire district. Roots burrowing through unresistant clay. Sealed storage units, locked rooms, films, photographs, documents: a Brunoesque house of memory. A honeycomb of secrets.

The drink was burning out, Sileen flared like a dying match. The hunger, the fever to be inside: he glowed. His exclusion was an irritant, no more. This latest X-ray martyr hobbled into the traffic, turning neither to east, nor west – a muscled gear of will driving him on, up the ramp, into the anthill.

He was unchallenged. The uniforms are elsewhere, doubling as bouncers, night security. They are propping up card schools, collecting debts, dispatching minicabs. For the first time, Sileen's prosthetic limb signals a reluctance, forewarns. The empty hall, the deserted receiving rooms: it is all too easy.

Where is his benefactor, Askead? Sileen's rigid heel brushes the waxy linoleum like a broom swaddled in corduroy, an uninvited follower. He advances into a territory where all permissions are suspended. A feral scrabbling of ward squatters, an uproar of amateur medicals, banished from the taproom, and looking for action. Paramedics in defoliant flying-suits, who run everywhere, channel-hopping disaster tapes, bounce him. He blunders against uncomplaining vagrants. They retreat into deeper recesses of darkness. The hospital draws them all: generalized terrors are made specific. All present – the quick and the stumblers, operators and premature cadavers. All except the vulture in the nicotine housecoat. All except Askead.

Don't risk the lift, concuss the metal-ruled stairs. Sileen scorches his palms on the banisters, corners in haste. Was that a saturnine portrait in oils? Or was it a Dominican friar, getting the last rites in while he still had breath in his bugle? The edict of 1163 had been revoked, as a privatization sweetener, and the clergy cleared to shed blood once more: it was no longer the privilege of barbers. An ancient schism was healed, surgeons and priests were one. The dying could be comforted by their executioners. Blue-lipped victims make confession as they go under, babble of sins committed in future lives. Frock coats are crossed with pus. Soutanes are trespassed with wine dribble and crumbs of dry bread. The gospels are invoked as instruments of surgical intervention. The sword is taken down and the skull pierced with a nail.

'Askead?'

The friar is dumb, sheltering behind an admonitory finger. Sileen sinks deeper into his cloud of unknowing. Where cash money is absent, so also is Askead. There is no percentage in chasing a broken flush. The weasel is abroad – ear at counter, lurking in doorways.

Arriving exhausted at the Marie Celeste Ward, once a haven for nursing mothers, now a vanishing point in a corridor of shocks, Sileen threw himself down on the frame of a bed, twisting against the naked springs, pleasuring in pain. He shuts his eyes. Sees nothing. Is nothing. Darkness like a plank. An intake of breath scalds his throat with clinker. His strength has gone. He tosses and mewls.

One of the Watchers is stroking his cheek. The cool scrape of a celluloid cuff, a mothering jangle of keys. She can have him, hang him from the bedpost, this wardress of the night. A press of sour warmth: hop-mash, body odour, carbolic. He gags and stiffens – an alpine floret trapped between the pages of an elephant folio. Sileen would love to yield himself entirely to the eros of matronly persuasion.

She is soothing him, squeezing his pockets for cigarettes. Too long for a bottle, too firm for flesh – she navigates the tin leg. And is recalled to duty. She must sit at the bedside, or climb in with him, watch the window for the first dawn spurt.

'I'll pay you.' Sileen rolls out from under. 'Take me at once to the old X-ray department.'

'The X-rays, is it? Bit late for that, dear. Your stump no fresher than yesterday's lambchop. Sleep's what you'll be wanting.'

Alive, but past exploiting, this one. Turning her back on him, she sighed, and slid decisively into the surrounding gloom. The scratch of her long black gown scattering the spiders. She abandoned him to his fate.

'Wait. I've got money. Wads of it.' Sileen lied with rare conviction. Unaided he'd never find his way back to the street.

The Watcher teased the beam of her torch over the cracked linoleum to showcase a cruel glissade of swollen ankles. Ankles as shapeless as an umbrella stand. Bed-springs yelped adulterously as Sileen pulled himself upright. Hold her! Unmanly panic was overridden by the titillation he derived from observing the subtle dispersion of light at the base of the cone. Sashaying across the floor was this spectral egg: sharp at its centre, then dim, then bright again with a double circumference. Instant nostalgia: Sileen crawled after it, stretching out helplessly to clutch at the Watcher's invisible hem. The retreating cone became a wand with which his guide sounded her retreat. It swept the skirting, the tiles of the wall, and was lost.

'Wait. For Mercy's sake.' Sileen begged, fumbling his pockets for surviving coins. He clinked, he rattled, attempting to lure the woman by sound alone. He inched into the darkness – deserted, prey to all the terrors of the mind. Cold sweat, or some glutinous quality in the paint, held him. Nocturnal voices rose shrieking through the pipes: unweaned babes denied the breast, old ones flinching from the wing of death. The worst of nightmares confirmed by touch.

Blind. He was blind. Pierced by white light. Assaulted by the Watcher's abrupt renewal of interest. He tried to shape a reassuring grin. The torch was an eye. An eye in a cup. He knows the impression he makes: something on a slab, exsanguinated by shock, one of Weegee's pavement specimens. Stunned by a dustbin-lid flashbulb. Deboned. Eyebrows like campy exclamations of black paint. He's walked into it, become the nameless subject of discussion, the memento from the scene-of-the-crime.

'Fancy some business, dearie?' He tasted her spit. It stung like salt. 'X-rays is too hard a road for those pins.' She pushed her argument with a pinch at his thigh. 'Let's find ourselves a nice quiet ward, lie down, let Nanna inflate your tyre. This'll do.'

She released him from the beam. They stood together in the shaming darkness, unseeing, each savouring the other's breath. He could move again. He could follow the wand of light – and the Watcher's industrial-strength perfume: strong drink and stronger soap. He was pricked, alert.

The beam frolicked over a quilted door, an eiderdown nailed to its panels.

'Ever so peaceful in here, duck. The Luke Howard, the weather ward. Lovely gentle souls, all of 'em – thunder phobics, summoners of storms.' As she talked, she worked a hand between his legs, whispering, blowing in his ear. He responded, he was aroused by what she told him. Taut, ready to spill, he concentrated on the pitch and timbre of her voice. He must not lose the connection. If he could imitate her, he would know everything that she knew.

'We keeps a double layer of drapes over the windows, boards 'em up from outside. Like the blackout come again. Nice layer of lead on the walls, asbestos cladding overhead. Cheap stuff, dear, there's plenty about. Don't know they're born, the lambs. Can't tell night from day. Not a squeak out of 'em till the wind gets up on the marshes, pressure drops like drawers in an orgy, the river begins to stir. Sweet Jesus! Trouble? Takes a strongarm squad and a quiver of chlorpromazine to strap 'em to their boards. Gibbering like monkeys, they are. Crawling in corners, pissing theirselves, biting off their tongues. Bedlam, dear!'

'I'll give you the lot, the mazooma. All of it.' Sileen held out a wretched scoop of coins.

'Quick. Not a breath tonight. They won't watch, bless 'em. Black as the insect house in there. Two quid, cash, we'll say no more.' She forcepped his wrist, rifled her toll, stuffed his hand deep between the swelling mounds of her imprisoned bosom.

'No. You don't understand. Every penny, it's yours. *After* you take me down. The X-ray cabinet.' He was caught. Fingers in the till, micro-waved, brought to life – mindlessly teasing the thermometer-head of her nipple.

They descended: through labyrinthine corridors in the more public zones of the hospital, corridors whose immaculate darkness was despoiled by hissing intervals of gaslight. Down spongy slopes; Sileen skated, fell, clung to the aromatic traces of his guide. His Virgil. He was a fool. She wanted to be done with him. They wrestled on clammy iron ladders. They shivered across courtyards and assaulted storerooms. The twinned solitaries, the only sentient beings in a kingdom of sleepers. The quest hero, maimed in the heel, and the earth mother, keeper of keys.

She would go no further. She had run to the limits of her fictive reality. And beyond. She faded – in sympathy with the wilting beam of her torch. The first streaks of daylight undid them both. Sileen could no longer convince himself of her legitimacy. She snatched up the last of the coins and was gone. Sodium chloride, urea, exocrine secretions: a whiff on the breeze and she was history.

It was the wolfing hour; a washed stone greyness infected by shows of pulmonary blood. Steel fins slicing an aquarium sky. Shadowless, Sileen confronted the final door. Alone in the universe. Dwarfed by the hospital's dissonate mass. Outside. Folded into a city of corridors. Interior streets. He charged. He burst the lock. Raced from switch to switch. Fate: back to the borderland or toasted to a cinder.

The yard. Sileen had not moved. This was not the right place. Even Askead would blush to demand fifty notes as key money for a shed, an outhouse. Sileen shook to the syncopation of buried generators. Conned again. The Watcher had dumped him with the laundry.

Rotten wood splintered under his blows. He shot the bolt. Wrong, hopelessly wrong. The room would not conform to his account of it. Some anonymous ironist had defaced the wall with a pious exhortation. NOTHING LIKE PERSEVERANCE. The bleakness of Lear. Words to hold the fretful eye through the slow hours of treatment. This was no X-ray refuge, no coils of predatory light sparked the damp air. A Finsen chamber, a Danish charity, abandoned when the deformed ones took their hurt into the market place. This was a shack for out-patients: unsatisfied machines hung from the roof like spiders from Mars. Spiders whose legs were telescopes – playing a steady drip of ultraviolet rays onto empty couches. Lances to scour *lupus vulgaris,* to heal tuberculosis of the skin, where no skin remained. The couches themselves were cured; volatile, repulsing any human approach.

Sleep. He was weakening. Let him slide into any trap but these exhausted urban sentimentalities. Once the masked ones, the children, had crept from their dark corners to be restored in baths of light, sandpapered visions of a brighter self. They collaborated in the abdication of their singularity, the fabulous uniqueness with which they had been blessed.

Sileen abhorred cure. He thirsted for the wisdom of monsters. The satori of cut-throats. He would pay any price. Truth. He *solicited* the oracle of cancer. He had glimpsed the wound at the end of the tunnel's bore; he would pass through. Damn this pandering to the sturdy poor –

benevolent butchery. Let them drown and cheer as they choke. We are botched, all of us, and should learn to relish our flaws.

I am the face of pestilence. I will poultice my wounds with dung.

Rejoicing, Sileen slunk back to the warren – seeking sanctuary, a nest of blooded feathers.

TWELVE

They came together, the bulldozers close behind them – the work gang sloping off to Mary's to line their bellies with grease, before demolishing their quota of Late Victorian terraces. Isabel posed against the breeze blocks; retro Godard, arm outstretched – spun to greet Sileen's dusty incarnation with a mocking gesture of the thumb. Her key became a pistol. She winked.

The red suit – slashed in a generous V. Preoccupied as he was, isolated from events, he noticed her, she was unmistakable, swinging long legs out of a cab. All stockinged elegance; the holes in the black mesh artfully camouflaged by dabs of eye shadow. Teeth and hair. She looks good, even to Sileen. He shares her pleasure in the taste of the morning. Over-emphasized eyes, cardinal lips: a robust exotic.

Isabel's job was done. Breakfast weather was a winning game. She could shimmy with the best of them, the Tanias, Trishes, Ulrikas, Riannas. The Sians and the Sallys. Feelgood demonstrators. Give the punters their ration of armlifts to show how close the jacket was cut. Close to what? To living flesh. Let them speculate on what lay beneath the polyester. The forecast was over. An anodyne flash of brightness, a terminology massage. Reduce the unpredictable to infantile diagrams. Sway the shoulder: a rain pout, a mercurial smile. Each day the same as the last. Slicker than a blowjob. Two minutes and it's over.

Never forget. Disguise from the video surfers all knowledge of Sileen's existence. The beast. The Ravisher. No trace of this man. The preservation, or diurnal renewal, of a special virginity: a disengaged empathy between Isabel and the autocue. Simple words, precise gestures. Nothing to connect her with Sileen's remorseless invective. No homages to Luke Howard.

They went inside. The amputee heaved himself up the stairs in the

wake of her clacking heels. Salsa rhythms – her swift movements were
the play of sunlight over gloomy boards. She could not stop, she danced,
a blur of celebratory exuberance. Throws off the jacket, boils water, a
dozen heavy-skinned oranges rolling from a brown paper sack. Sileen is
an old man in the corner, eyelids wedged with toothpicks. He glimpses
her breasts, she is pulling on a baggy black shirt. Helical sunshafts on the
knife's edge. Juice spurting over her hands. Steam peeling the silver
from the glass. She props open the window with a book. He is tense,
unaroused. The length of the morning still in his throat: roof slopes,
pigeons, sphagnum dressing the cracks. Helen/Isabel unwraps
croissants; bites – buttery flakes cling to her wet lips. She sways and
sings, effortlessly navigating the field of Sileen's humped inertia.

He will not catch her eye, nor be caught by it. She puts down her cup,
wipes her mouth on her sleeve, sits on the mattress to unroll the
stockings. It's not a show, but he watches – tormented by the rasping,
slithering sounds. He is implicated, willing her to act, not guessing what
form that action might take. She rummages beneath the sheets, down
the back of the chair: other stockings. Laddered, unwashed. She knots
them together, constructs a rope, which – with a sharp tug – she tests.
One end is trapped by the window, the other is drawn to the wall above
Sileen's head, a hook. She has triangulated, sealed off, this area of the
room. Sileen does not understand. An untouched croissant perches on
his knee like a cottonwool lobster.

'I want you to show me the moves. I want to fight you.' Isabel
unzipped her skirt, kicked off her shoes. She feinted, flapped in delight;
puffed, boxed shadows, chased her reflection across the smeared
window panes. 'Come on, stumblebum. Try me.'

Her man growled at this perversity, such premature exhilaration. He
wanted a gin. He shut his eyes, but the sound stayed with him – her feet
tapping and sliding, the Ali shuffle revived. 'Come on, big boy, show me
what you've got.' Sileen forgave the flattery. The delicate arch of her
naked foot, sweaty with leather, was against his heart. Her mischievous
toes infiltrated his shirt, forcing it open, tearing off the two surviving
buttons. She kicked him. Hard. His head cracked against the wall.

Choleric Sileen swatted and missed. His dander, what remained of it,
was critically provoked. She kicked again, a venomous tease – he gasped.
The pain was sharp but not serious. When she balanced, leg retracted,
sunbeams sluiced along the leading edge. There were dark, intimate

creases where the knee folded, a subcutaneous gearing of thigh. He grabbed an ankle. She tumbled. He was on his feet and primed for the next assault. He panted like an overmatched lurcher.

They circled warily in a sawdust saloon. Isabel's laughter was ominously laced with hysteria. Sileen touched her cheek with his left, then followed over the top with a naughty cross. A lacklustre blow, it pitched her on the deck. No chance to admire the timing, she was in his face, slapping and gouging. He bit her thumb. She dug an elbow in his eye.

Sileen's head was ringing like a chocolate bell. An aspirin fog fired his sluggish blood: he could die with his boots on. Rebellious platelets drummed their warning. Fists raised, he waited for the kill. Let her scratch. A black karma of childhood sleights enveloped him: beatings, sermons, indigestible food, buggery, observed or experienced, he could never remember – and cold, the eternal cold. He tracked out, away from that monstrous building (a priest in every window), into rainswept playing-fields. Exiled by anger, damaged. He swung, drove her into the corner; cut her off; hammered blows at the softness of her shoulders.

She was faster, she could move; her wild swings sustained him. Discomfort was nothing to Sileen. Life. He smirked and cut a sharp right into Isabel's ribs. She was unschooled in violence of the formal kind. She tried to kick between his legs. A mistake. He caught her foot and twisted. She rolled as she fell, only speed could keep her safe. Sileen did not notice pain. She could tear off his eyelids and use them for stamps. He worshipped whatever hurt him most. She could not win. Submissive, she held up her open palms, kittened to his side – bit through his cheek. His hand closed around her throat, he walked her back, legs cycling off the ground. No room to weave or dodge. He dropped her like a bag of string. Lefts, rights, feints, jabs – stinging combinations, a scuttle of snakes.

She cannot stand. No shame in that. On her knees. Floor rising to bear her up. Sileen lowers himself, solicitously, to get a better shot. His knuckles are blooded and bruised. It's his blood trickling from the corner of her mouth. Her lips are swollen. Her eyes closed. A weary tipping into the dark. He's on her, smothering her, his weight. She claws. Peels the fiercely abraded skin. Clings. The teeth meet, clinking – a collision of tin cups. Her mouth is wide. His tongue samples salt blood. Rips off the black shirt. Head lost between her breasts.

She pulls, turns, signals him to turn; roll over, old dog. She sits astride, kneeling on her heels, guiding him, playing him in. She writhes, shows, lets him see her pleasure – as he retreats, allows all that is living to attend upon this heavenly conjunction. Moaning, unfinished, she requests his better side; face down; the graceful fury on his back. Once more she masters him.

THIRTEEN

She was suspect, and she knew it, walking rapidly through such a place – and without a dog. Dark glasses, fists clenched in raincoat pocket, a solitary. It didn't add up. The cerebrally disadvantaged loungers, snouts in steaming mugs, planted on the steps of the Cockney Hideout (EAT IN OR TAKE AWAY), tracked her gaunt silhouette – as she strode southwards down the Outfall trail. 'Oi darlin', what's yer game?'

They picked wool from their navels, jerked bacon rind through the gaps in their teeth. Where was the pit bull, the crossbreed? Where was the german shepherd tugging on her chain?

Helen, back in a theatre of clouds, Luke Howard's dolly, retraced her steps to Plaistow. The hauliers in the valley, trading their illicits, copped the best view. Tasty scrubber! Quality trim! What they wouldn't do, given the green light. Her dogless pilgrimage through the rubbish stacks set the scale for a Wagnerian diorama: ominous backlighting like the sound of a giant gong, cumuliform lungs of smoke processing from the west. A battle of the air masses: all the lineaments of a climactic that responded to her present confusion. She saw what she felt. She chased the aerial correlatives of a mood of ecstatic despair.

But it was trickier than that: local corruptions added their pigmentation to the mix. The spokesman for a wickedly parked Ibiza 1.2 holds a stanley knife to the throat of a forecourt salesman – who reaches blind for the .38 Smith and Wesson he conveniently discovered in the glove compartment of a trade-in Montego 2.0 SL. A white youth (with three previous convictions to his name) puts his hammer through the quarterlight of a BMW (Bob Marley Wagon). The radio-cassette is already missing. He settles for the tapes. Within sight of Tower Bridge, a woman who is something in publishing blows an unfiltered Gitanes rinse into the face of a severely ulcerated diner whose hour is running to a close before the arrival of the cappuccino. A ticket-inspector is punched in the face on the Tilbury Line, then flung from the train. A Kenyan Asian counter clerk refuses payment to an incensed African-Caribbean female with dubious paperwork. Multiplying episodes pollute the cloud membrane. Helen reads the microclimate and is part of it also. She knows that her brief transit will float a crucible of doom across the lower reaches of the River Lea's industrial corridor. The serrated culmination of her grapple with Sileen modifies the ground temperature, causing eddies of a dangerous complexity. She is sucked into her own slipstream.

The Outfall is withdrawn, reserved – elevated above the congeries of ruin. Cloudland has an immediacy the street lacks. It responds to Helen's advent: a panoramic generosity indifferent to the triumphs and terminations of the earthworms below. Nothing sustains life but this dream of escape. Clusters of silted tributaries, islands like geometrical figures, altocumulus drifting through sluggish tide channels. Wind-flurries temper abandoned allotments: the eye nervously traverses meads and water-meadows, picking on knotweed, tansy, hairy willow – whipping over the light-deflecting speculations of the southern horizon. There must be some way out. Listen. Shuddering rails. An amplification of tunnels. Look down. The train is gone before it can be appreciated. That is the essence of pleasure, whispers of elsewhere.

O'Hagan? What has happened to him? Helen can't resist a glance at the yard, a tremor of disappointment. O'Hagan's absence is palpable. A chill touches her side. He means most when he is furthest from reach. Could he be hidden by the parked van? She climbs down the steps. The pressure hiss of a hosepipe. Water splattering convulsively on stone. Her trainers pad stealthily over the wet ground; she hides her actions, even from herself. The absurdity. Her face pressed against the grid of the fence. An Asian, his lightweight jacket daintily held by an attendant youth, was sloshing the travel dirt from a company car. Outlandish, this notion of Sileen's. Imar O'Hagan a terrorist? An INLA bagman? The fellow she had seen was far too good-looking, too deeply implicated in servicing his own affairs.

As Helen climbed back to the Outfall, the Abbey Lane steps became a treadmill, a wheel of fate – propelling Todd Sileen over the cobbles. The stink of flyblown meat. The howling dog. Entering the Roebuck was like guesting on the Late Show. His movements were her movements. He swayed and floated. He was sheathed in silk. Her perfume was on his skin. His clothes had no weight. Cash money fanned his heart.

That confirmed pedestrian, Ian Askead, trading moody log books with the used car fraternity, watched the door, muttering under his breath the phrases of cod Maltese that might tickle the humour of Felix Muscat, retired pimp. 'Grazzi grazzi, timpana, lampuki, iva iva, Marsovin, Cola, Comino, Mdina, Tott-en-'am 'Ot-spur.' Meditatively grooming a sparse beard, he licked his empty glass, and sniffed: Sileen was windward of the brewery.

The cripple had conned fifty notes from his lover, from Helen/Isabel, to kit her for the fight. Scarlet gloves, head-guard, shorts, vest, lace-up boots, chest protector, leather cup, bandages, adrenaline solution, cotton buds: he bluffed and ran. Fifty was a down payment. On an X-ray séance. Fifty notes for Askead

'I can feel it in my water.' His man secured, Askead was firing like a donkey engine. 'A pony on the nose, Baron, half the wedge on *Carnacki* in the 3.15. Ask any of the paisanos, a racing certainty.' The diminutive Glaswegian darted among the Micks like an orange flame in a green powder-barrel. Professional drinkers, incubating slow pints, were forced to protect their liquidity by a constant realignment of the shoulder buttress. The first spill and Askead would be booking in to his own deepfreeze.

Sileen lumbered after him, unsuccessfully reaching out for the hem of his labcoat; anything to nail the scuffler – who rapped as he dodged, disposing of his loot before he had laid hands on the first kopeck. 'A clean split, Baron. Leave you plenty for a basement trip. Fancy something novel, a venograph? The chicks're all after me. Souvenir of the vein system. Quick jab with a clean needle and it's showtime – the radio-opaque compound boogies towards the old pump. A map of your mortality! A real buzz, baby. Hipper than colonic irrigation. And you won't need the nappy.'

Peevish, interrupted in his contemplation of the Four Doctrines, the publican slid their nourishment across the counter, straight churns of doom. A thick blob of creamy foam leapt at the angry bulb of Askead's nose. A long hard swallow soothed the X-ray irregular's grief. All this was nothing to the patron, vanity and foolishness. He conversed, after his own style, with the angels. 'There is nothing concealed that shall not be uncovered, and nothing secret that shall not be known.' No human folly could mitigate the oblique cynicism of his world-weary grimace. He looked away, dropping no more than the minimal provocations required to keep conversation alive among his flock of complacent deadbeats. He was a most subtle impresario of chaos, winking an adjustment here, a warning digit there. His son, congenital hernia spilling outside his weightlifter's belt, was the enforcer. His fearsome bulk undisguised by a slippery gameshow suit. His backcombed hair sweating with lard. Drunk beyond drunkenness, obnoxiously cheerful, he tapped his broken nails on a glass of yellow milk – primed, on the nod, to sledgehammer defaulters. Or anyone else who took the da's fancy.

Even to the preoccupied Sileen, this venerable fake, the guv'nor, was one of the treasures of the city; a Baggot Street transplant, he should have been made to wear a blue plaque around his neck. He was a sawdust immortal, rumours connected him to the dynamitings of the Eighties: Victoria Station, Praed Street, Mansion House, Junior Carlton. Jack the Ripper's contemporary, he was behind them all. A hundred years on and the boyos were operating with the same charts.

'Time, gents.' He shot a Tullamore varnish into a fresh glass, as his ox son nudged and worried the motor-traders back to their caravans. Even pagans must observe the holy hour. The stunted Maltese were decanted into afternoon grease caffs, where they curled and withered under a brazen flicker of TV serials. Only Muscat, Felix Muscat, remained in place. Some special relationship was evident, which allowed him to use the Roebuck as a front.

Muscat – chauffeur to the not-so-grateful dead. He was a bodybag out on licence, an associate of killers. Prison had sucked him dry. The eyes had died first, the rest was visibly catching up. A time-lapse Dorian Gray – his coarse hair teased into a crooner's nightsock. He had more lines than Pound's *Cantos*. He modelled a goldleaf deathmask. His chin rested on a trestle of clasped hands, while he perfected the Look – his patented version of the laser stungun. He needed the chainlink identity bracelet about as much as Jimmy Savile – to quantify the me-ness of me. Muscat's touch absorbed money in any of its disguises. It could not warm the ice in his blood. No trick would resurrect him.

Cash in hand, Askead was all business. He bullied Sileen through the bleats of pavement philosophers, inebriated savants. The hospital was slumped in post-prandial torpor – waiting for the next shuttle of helicopters, the clockwork goldfish in the sky. The technician was lightfooted, reckless: shoot the wad on a whim, burn the lot. Pelt it at condemned horseflesh. Bundle this pest, the amateur somnambulist, onto the slab. Cook him. Torch him with radon daughters. An unsightly bulge of notes in Askead's pocket, snug as a colostomy pouch.

The charm of migrating depressions is that they *do* migrate. The transformation, worked by Helen's fevered scrying, was a predictable delight. The Mare Tranquillitatis after a lunar storm. Sulphurous smoke bands lost conviction, and dropped, to graze the pylons, decompose among wilderness embankments. She experienced a quiet, post-coital clarity in the rapid expansion of the sky's dome. Milky cataracts scraped from the lens. Curved whites, shortwave blues – they implicated her in their ecstatic charge.

The purity of Luke Howard's obsessions, those realms of punctilious observations: such optimism. Mankind, though fated, *could* live usefully upon the earth. Wherever she touched the meteorologist's conscious-ness, over these abused settlements, there was light. He proposed a treaty. He saw light, and all its divisions, as a direct manifestation of God's purpose. Daily study – darkness and storm, sweet streaming waves of moisture – would temper the man, bring him to understand-ing. Resolute silence.

Helen, sinking to her knees on the path, allows Sammy Taylor's inscape of rage to suggest an alternative vortex. Cruelty. Hurt. Electrically charged curtains of bad faith. Rain that bites. Schisms, lacerations: lightning forked on the tooth. Exported melancholy from a weather system he manages to lock by ego to the Beara peninsula. A downpour of melted Devonian rocks. Discharges of obtuse revenge.

They had to exist, and exist within her, these contraries. The restless perambulations of Luke Howard, neck twisted, cataloguing the heavens – and the mania of the other one, Samuel Coleridge Taylor, her first lover, immobilized, gestating revenge on the clockwork of the cosmos.

She lay on the damp ground, all strength gone, giving herself over to a uniform darkness, the palpable absence of light. The sky thickened and pressed on the water. Channelsea shone, bright as liquid lead. She wept.

Into the rubber, face down. Amnesia-stimulating fumes. He heard the cabinet door shudder, then slide reluctantly on its groove. He had become an exhibit, hidden from sight – a skeleton trophy cased in disposable skin. *Get on with it*. He struggled against the straps. Useless. Askead adjusted a pair of blackened goggles over his eyes. Otherwise, he was naked. He must train himself to navigate by sound alone.

The operative was a disbarred alchemist, dividing his attention between a mimeographed list of Hackney dogs and a Danish wank mag. The pornography (anal, penetrative) had acquired a pathogenic colour balance from its long hours doubling as a pillow to Sileen's X-ray slumbers: bad 3-D without the green and red specs. Askead was no closet aesthete. He was a meat and two veg man, gravy thick as treacled sand. He calculated, sharpened his nails with a prodigious underbite, made his decisions. His system was a post-functional hybrid of calculus and onanism. Sufficiently aroused, he would stab his pen into the sheet of runners; act where the blob fell. A serpentine path, a kundalini yoga that did not permit him to spill his seed. He fertilized winners on the cosmic oval. He was the Edward Kelley (ears cropped in season) to Sileen's Doctor Dee.

Why the stretchy, elbow-length, pink gloves, the helmet, the gonad-protecting pouches in his latex apron? An innocent whim, a love of ritual. Sacrifice demands gravitas of its hierophants. Dress, Askead considered, was the better part of medicine. He was immune, behind glass, guarded from the fluroscope's unpredictable surges.

Sileen was no obstacle. His bones were losing their opacity – feathers of dirty water. Roentgen's mysterious current fed on what lay beyond the matrix of collagen fibres. Where would it stop? Would the rays carry Sileen's torment out among the parks and sepulchres, the leaf-filled troughs – fretting the dossers who kipped at the back of the sorting office? He began to yield. The naked man was a photographic plate. Hyperpolarized, his outline blocked the passage of intelligent light. He was forced to return, not to the borderland, but to the limits of this cell. He was imprisoned in a gothic fable, some fictional splinter culled from William Hope Hodgson's marvellous tale *The Hog*.

Askead's machine, his dungeon-of-horror veteran, stole its power from the accumulator of the People's Picture Palace in Whitechapel Road: the power to process Sileen, print his repressed negatives. The patient blinked, scorched lashes fluttered against restraining goggles, the night glass – centipedes in a killing jar. A switch had been thrown.

Optimum voltage. Nothing less would serve. Askead was well aware of safety limits; he ignored them. Manuals were for pedants. A capsule of barium platino-cyanide placed between the victim and the activated tube was sufficient warning. There was a sexual (brain suck) charge as the trapped colour mutated from torrential green to dull orange: the critical level was effortlessly achieved, and Sileen wired to the tremble in the universe. The epilation dose could no longer be adequately described as 'uncomfortable'. Clumps of hair were dropping from Sileen's sweating scalp, his dry leaf skin flinched and blistered.

The first movement concluded as the Glaswegian geek, with burning ulcer eyes, superimposed one of his rebarbative Viking leather boys across the defenceless Sileen. Then shot his wad down his trouser leg.

The X-ray machine learnt greed from its operative: a taste for blood which Sileen's landscape nightmares did not satisfy. It made withdrawals from the accumulator of the failed Bengali cinema. Sileen, transported, saw cropped squares twitch within the glass of the cabinet – Askead's bestial face. A Hindu pageant of dancers and banyan trees. Thickets of thorn, hairs in the gate. Flower garlands, fakirs, swords. The stink of frying acetate, as the technician jockeys the knobs – to unplug a sorry flood of Picture Palace memories.

The Kiss, that archivist's fragment, 1896, the eyes of the lovers shut, fixed. The smudged hands of John C. Rice, pestling darkness into May Irwin's cheek, become the hands of Ian Askead, the London Hospital's X-ray martyr. Sticks of calcified bone. Black fingernails varnished for the camera.

Sileen leers and feasts on this gallery of weathered film. The lips of the lovers never meet. May Irwin's hair is cropped as close as the hair of Andi Kuschka, Helen's friend. Or is she a man in a woman's nightgown? Not quite submitting to the starched collar and rapist's moustache. The obscenity of that tumid thumb. Not Andi, Sofya. Sofya Court. A man. On the floor, they are eating each other. Not Sofya, Helen. Assaulted by Sammy Taylor. On a bridge. A room. The pleasure of it burnishing cups, boards, empty shelves: dust frosting to diamonds.

Askead wanted to cook his client, not kill him; not yet. Bast the gimp through a dozen sessions, milk him to the final drop. But it's no simple matter to hit the right switches when you're more stoned than a Saudi legover merchant. His hands shook. He couldn't focus. Even his monkey was looking for alternative employment. He undid *all* the

84

straps, bolts, bulbs. Fusing one scarlet-tipped bomber from the last, he tapdanced up the walls.

Blinded, the electrical translation did not work for the naked man. The goggles bit like a tourniquet into his skull. He was getting flashes of Helen, not the gardens and the ruined house. The girl – before he had taken possession of her fate. Helen working on Taylor. The grinning American tied to a bed. Thick oils puddling in the palm of her hand. Sileen refuted these cartoons. Taylor was nothing. An idiot in a community of starving hogs and drooling kids. The peasants would put him to the torch. The landscape would be revenged – the rocks and stones he had mangled in his excessive prose.

Sileen fought his bonds; the floor beneath his trestle was riparian tar. Fetid as Channelsea's grimpen quag. Helen, in torment, writhes on the ground, scattering gravel seeds over the basement's melting floor. An irritating hail on the cabinet's roof aborts Askead's business call. He cradles the phone, strokes it, praying for mug's luck – as he lays his treble off with Nicky Tarten. The dwarf's nap is overheard by a chorus of white plaster angels. Tarten thumbs his scar, doodles on a yellow pad the rough draft for the promotional bill on which Helen/Isabel will be featured as the 'Wapping Wildcat'.

Askead can catch the rapid movement of Tarten's pencil, but no voice. He's forced to cut the generator, reprieve Sileen – who savours the salt wind in the observation tower. Lacking the pain to make it stick.

Brushing the earth from her raincoat, Helen takes the diagonal path through the graveyard. She walks faster, and with more purpose, than before. There are fewer distractions: Arthur E. Pope's icing-sugar folio, Samuel Bullard's wedding dove, Wally's valentine arch. Tarten's marble has colonized the entire field. It's the only possible destination. Helen is ready to close a deal with the deckchair, shake hands with the scabby, South American tattoo.

FOURTEEN

This thing with Andi Kuschka, it troubled Sofya. The message on the
kitchen table. 'Send me your dreams.' Verboten. Not to be recalled.
Dreams ease hurt. *Give* them away? Andi was mad, interesting, so
blatantly hung up on O'Hagan's purple dick. Like Yeats' *Crazy Jane*.
She'd do anything.

> *I know, although when looks meet*
> *I tremble to the bone,*
> *The more I leave the door unlatched*
> *The sooner love is gone.*

That's what Andi was after, the taste of O'Hagan, the salt of him on
Sofya's skin. His fingerprints on the curve of her shoulder. She was
pushing too hard. She wanted too much.

A cold fever, Andi's passion disturbed Sofya. The intensity of it. But
that didn't mean she was going to obey such a perverse demand. The
tiny blue envelope hidden beneath the butter-dish. 'Send me your
dreams.'

In her earlier incarnation – after college, supply teaching, Africa –
almost all Sofya's male friends were gay. She joked about it. Her cover.
Enjoyed their company, the stories they told. And the others, less easy,
the solitaries. Laid back, sure of themselves, tempering their rage – her
father. That's why she was here, back in the ghetto. A fag hag.
Rumoured to be. She started the rumour. Don't fall for appearances –
lightweights, neat on their feet, tidy about the house, discreet in poplin,
minimalist moustaches. Killers in drag. Cannibals. Users. She loves the
chat, the gossip; barely drinks. Sends them home in the morning.
Restlessness, bad nerves – the brave assumptions of a risk culture.

Daddy's mouth. She can't. The dream of the house on the river. The avenger with no face. Had it happened yet? Write it down. Make it go away.

The camera was her salvation. She gave it her trust: the weight of the canvas satchel swinging against her hips. The mechanical ritual of lenses, exposure, release. A satisfying solidity of sound. It was so cold, this mock science. Sofya knew this obsession for what it was – the insanity of the edge. Living by taking life. Living in death. She must heat the danger, push it, make it impossible – justify it by suffering.

Sofya would strap a lens, cold, to the flesh of her arm. A phylactery, a wordless amulet. It would hold her soul. She would be redeemed – that mistaken exposure, Mordecai Donar's openeye portrait, forgiven. Blasphemously, a female, she relished this conceit. The phylactery was bondage: a thong bound the lens to her arm, a soft suede pouch. The defiled square of film, the perforated window with Donar's quizzical pout, it was on the table. Locked inside the camera.

She posed, looked back at herself, over the shoulder: boyish, well fleeced, young. Naked in O'Hagan's long mirror. Her armband. The workman's boots. The painter's shoulders. As he worked.

Imar O'Hagan splattered and dashed at the raw canvas; unthinking, thinking with gesture. Great cheekbones. Generous mouth. The grin of a psycho. 'Out on the piss last night.' He scraped and scratched, he smoked. Knifework, carmine revisions. O'Hagan was a window-cleaner muddying his reflection with ovengloves. He wanted to be shot, wanted Sofya to shoot him while he painted. The real thing – like you never see for Bacon. Like the Freud self-portrait – without self. He would ignore her entirely.

She had come, she had accepted his commission. 'A snap of me working. With no me in it.' This was her only rule: refuse nobody. Her life would be reorganized to accommodate this peculiar challenge. Avoid situations where the question could be put, but deny nothing. Rapists, chartered accountants, performers. Abdicate self-interest.

O'Hagan was fast. In close, like a shiv specialist, then out – two or three hard drags – and back to it. He refused to acknowledge Sofya's company. An irrelevance. He transcribed the flakes and distortions of chipped glass within the texture of the skin. He was good at skin. Skin was his thing. Lawrence Gowing had commented on it. 'Embarrassment was his ally.' Skin like a plum on an ice tray. That was the word, the received wisdom of the Colony Room. That's what the soaks, the colonic irrigators, gabbled at him, as they poked or punched. 'Lov-ely sheen, dear. Nipples like coprolites. But no armature. Walk and you'll fall flat on your face.' French kisses, dribble, vodka.

He took an impression of the surface of the mirror, not the man who stood in front of it – scratching his scalp with the point of his brush, rubbing his genitals. The photographs were a further dimension, the proof that he had played some part in the transaction. Mirror, canvas, contact sheet: he would shift between them. Impossible to pin him down. He would vanish.

Which was, for Sofya, the paradox. This thirst for transcendant versions of himself, canvas after canvas stacked against the wall, or removed to other boltholes, storage vaults, garages, lock-ups. Buried in the ground, in woodland. Hidden under potatoes. The frenzy for photographs, articles, exhibitions. O'Hagan would show anywhere: slaughterhouses, synagogues, bomb bunkers, cathedral crypts. Enclosed space, off the map, difficult to find, beyond the reach of public transport. His ideal show was comprehensive – but unattended. The Heneage Street door was bolted, chained. He had ripped out all the electricals. Mere knocking, he ignored. There was no telephone. The blinds were permanently drawn. He would not sleep more than one night under the same roof.

Thirty-six – now thirty-five – exposures to nail the ghetto: makers, mendicants, meditative silent presences. A shimmering nimbus of light behind O'Hagan; the street shut off; a soft greyness, a filtered persistence. It engaged her. Why did she always fall for the faces on the contact sheet – and shudder to meet the people who had posed for them? She reached out to touch the camera. A transitory revelation – the grain of the floorboards protected by dust, a chipped mug, a rinse of whisky in which floated five cigarette butts. A thin crust of white emulsion on the back pocket of O'Hagan's dungarees. She watched it crack.

He was stretching his eyelids between first finger and thumb, capturing the shock effect with his other hand – in what Sofya took to be an act of ocular masturbation. Hooked and vitreous: Imar lovingly detailed the veins, ciliary muscles, radial ridges. The eye was all colour and brushwork, it saw nothing. It was decorative, it refused light. The painter's concentration was brutal. He needed Sofya's nakedness to sustain it. The nakedness of an available woman. The excitement of a potential crisis, bad faith, aroused him, kept him to the speed of his task. Shunting darkness, he had what he wanted. His left hand was busy in his pocket. He would get it done before they took him out. When he was whacked by the flak jackets, hung upsidedown on a butcher's hook, dumped from a chopper, the world would be loud with his ghosts. Skin tracings in every burrow. Mugshots secure in all the unmarked cavities. An army of phantoms.

He stopped. He lay down, stretched his length on the floor; stared unblinking, at the carbon rings deposited on the ceiling. Swiftly, Sofya picked up the Leica. O'Hagan was swallowing smoke as if it was due to be rationed. The knuckle of ash was critical, bending, about to detach. He shut his eyes. Not daring to breathe, Sofya released the shutter. He was captured, fated. He belonged to her.

A hammering at the street door; a coded sequence of knocks giving way to some peevish bootwork. O'Hagan did not stir. Smoke linked him to the light bulb in an umbilical twist. The knocks were reinforced by shouts. 'Imar. Imar the Rima.' Instinctively, Sofya stretched for her shirt, her underclothes. O'Hagan threw out an arm, stopped her. The knocking continued. Keeping low, beneath the level of the window, they crawled to the couch. He penetrated her immediately, withdrew. She stroked him, admired him; was amused. He settled for this. Tried to enter her again. They compromised, plea-bargained, exhibited. They held off, mock-sulked, began afresh. Until both were, separately, pleasured; indecently sated. Their time in remission.

When Sofya went through into the dingy kitchen to search out something to eat, a bowl of cereal, a round of buttery toast, her hand could not discover the light switch. She fumbled: spiky surfaces of wood, cold metal, bowls of foul-smelling water. A fridge. Rubber gone, faulty door. Miraculously, the bulb still worked. The ammoniac cave was lit like a roadside shrine, the commemoration of an obscure tragedy. The racks were heaped with money. Banknotes bound in icy prophylactic wads. No food. Not even the traditional carton of shrivelled-gonad olives. In desperation, Sofya felt behind the money, found a cloth bundle, retrieved it. She was starving. Kosher standards would have to be relaxed. She bit the string, unrolled the rag. A large black handgun – oily and alien. Fitted with a silencer.

FIFTEEN

Eyes closed, life-support system in shutdown – a camouflage of apple blossom was projected on the policeman's alabaster face. A mortuary lizard, he absorbed his healing dose of sunlight. One Roman mile to the north-east a door creaked, a slow foot dragged in the dirt. Drage-Bell's lids flickered, he collated the skirts of the trees. A yellow and green bowl. He counted the leaves, footnoting the swift shadowplay of a high sun. An aquarium of predators, paper fish spinning on threads.

The intelligencer sprawled upon the ground in his secret Wellclose orchard and drank the sun's unfranchised benevolence. Swedenborg spoke to him through the bark of trees, the black light trapped in leaf banks, sequestered places the world could not reach. 'Evils cannot be removed unless they appear' – Drage-Bell's code. The removal business. Clear the deck. Set vermin to devour vermin. The dead whisper only to the dead. He husbanded his seed. Swedenborg died in life to eavesdrop on those who had gone before, the ones who would not learn silence, the gabby sacks of bone.

He listened; he tracked the halting footfall, the hesitation at the crossroads. Truth is its contrary. Focus on evil and you will sing in the light. Without night's interminable blackness, the sun has no validity. No joy without shame – without cellars of pain, libraries where knowledge can be chained. His disinterested acquisition of the works of William Hope Hodgson (1877–1918) is philanthropic, benign, performed without expectation of praise or glory. Duty. Thief-taking in its highest form. Psi/Surv as a fine art. A torture aesthete, Drage-Bell focused on images of beauty – to capture and destroy them. Agent Orange among the green shoots. He would take into his mind all the flickering, flowering, living things – so that suspects, put to the question, should not have them. Cut the escape routes. Block the tunnels. Defuse the subversive karma of Green Books: interrogators are homosexuals with the protection of the Establishment, sadists through repression. Drage-Bell repressed nothing. If it could be thought, he was game, he'd give it a try. A Virtual Reality buff. As chess is to war, the copper's bibliomania was to his purging of infamy. Turn a page thoughtlessly and you destroy a city.

A very gentle wavelike influx, a zephyr of well-disposed spirits: the intelligencer basked. Powder-puffs of dandelion seed broadcast a petrol-scented breeze. A bitter river-taste on the tongue's papillae, the distant wash of launches. The nark was coming. Swedenborg Gardens. An uneven distribution of weight on wobbly flagstones; the ardent, leading stride and the tin heel hauled after it. A compulsive finger breaking the surface of the grey Swedish font, stirring the cloud soup. No balm of summer orchards without an equal displacement of fear. Arrest them all: the first editions, variants, proofs, revisions, reprints with new introductions. Bag them and seal them – before others are infected by these renegade fantasies; before the Borderland becomes a universal condition. He fought, the spook, to bury all transcripts of Hodgson's words. The ruined house, the dog of ash, those ebullient creatures from the pit — Paddies in hair suits. Forget them, before they escape. Barricade the deepwater docks before all trading vessels are invaded by Hodgson's phantasmagoric weather. Sharpen the horror. Leave no book at liberty.

The thrashing and cursing in the undergrowth was a mild irritant, the only kind Drage-Bell permitted. Blanket ennui was the price for vatic playback – scooping the headlines in advance of the action. 'The voice of honest indignation is the voice of God.' The intelligencer was deaf. Knowing what lay ahead might be divine, but it made for tedium. Prophecy is written in letters of fire – after the event. Sileen, his shiny, retread mug punctured by thorns, pumped into the clearing, mopping sweat. His black suit was sprayed to his back. His kapel had slid down his head like a dodgy syrup. He was as greasy as a rook, and stank of pep-permints and carrion.

'Do you ever consider,' Drage-Bell began – in a severely bowdlerized version of his interior monologue, 'the extraordinary privileges enjoyed by the private citizen of this realm? An element, as insignificant as yourself, allowed to breathe the same air, frolic in the same English sunlight, as the best of us; the taxpaying, equity holding, godfearing sodality – is it reasonable?'

Sileen could wait; he scuffed at the ground, tearing up bindweed and mallow. Let the rozzer blow himself out. Sarcasm was a good omen. Better than silent contempt.

'A leech, a twicer, a dysfunctional pedestrian. Think about it. The same fucking sky.' He mimed disdain, fanned himself with a black notebook. 'The figure, as of this moment, stands at £307. Without the VAT. Which, I'll admit, would be the icing on the cake. That's what you've pimped, kaffir. Stolen, filched. You've had the run of my pocket. And all you can offer is – what?'

Drage-Bell uncurled an arborescent forefinger and jabbed Sileen, hard, at the point where the sternum interacts with the costal cartilage. Mere pain was bypassed by curiosity – those anthropoid phalanges! The spook was clearly an interspecies heretic, the formal proof of a direct bloodline to pond slime.

'Names, locations, dates, times. Or it's over. You'll cop for the lot. We'll fit you up for everything on the books from the Mad Axeman to the West Ham Vanishings of 1881.'

'I've *got* names, Mr Bell.'

'Who, for instance?'

'The Gasman. O'Hagan. Sliema Felix.'

'And?'

'Le Fanu, Fitz-James O'Brien, Stoker.'

He improvised, white-lipped.

'They're all in it, Mr Bell. Webbed up.'

'Pathetic.'

This lambent morning was an unrepeatable offer; the intelligencer basked. He was frisky, knotting hair-strands into barbed wire. Sileen's choice was stark – stomp the spook, crush him underfoot, take off. Or creep, bellydown, in the dirt. Crawl for cash. He crawled.

'Stoker and O'Hagan are getting into bed with the Peruvians, winding up the Kurds (PKK). They'll turn your patch into bandit country, Mr Bell. Heavy stuff. Connections with the Arifs, Yardies, over the water. Cash 'n' Carry armourers. Transits. Under the railway, back of Vallance Road. A slaughter in Stoke Newington. Poetry mob. Lock-up down Leytonstone. Russian RPG-7 rockets. M60 machine guns, Nato issue. Semtex. Not Provos. Not INLA. Worse. Pure madness. No respect, could hit anywhere. St Paul's, the War Museum. Even, God forgive me, Canary Wharf. You can't cut me loose, not now. Think of England, Mr Bell.'

The policeman screamed. He coughed up a gold watch. The man was priceless. 'Canary Wharf? Nothing would give us more pleasure. We'd pay them to flatten it. We *do* pay them. We've had Micks on the payroll for years. Without your Celtic bogeyman who's going to fork out to keep Six and the Branch in the style to which they've grown accustomed? Who's going to prod Paisley and his melonheads into line? The government depends on those fundamentalist bastards. Get real, pegleg. Without regular doses of terror, there's no justification for security. Read the news backwards. Worse is better. Snuff a brace of royals and we'll be arsedeep in expenses.'

'You *want* them to succeed?'

'Why else would I carry a disaster like you? To blunder, provoke, stir shit nobody else would touch with a flagpole. Even as a failure, you're a failure. You're pressing shadows. Surely you've got there by now. My only interest, kaffir, is in you.'

Sileen was done with conversation. Where was the gelt? The plates of his skull were drowning in alluvial slop. He trenched a clabbered groin. But nothing, on such a morning, could discomfort his patron. The filth had lived outside society too long to be affected by personal mannerisms that would have reduced lesser mortals to belling an exterminator.

'Last chance, Long John. One final pop at the coconut. Then it's the bullet. No warnings, no kiss-off. Good-night and good riddance. The screech of expensive radials when you're shlepping home, pissed in the gutter. A pinprick from an upraised umbrella on Waterloo Bridge. Blackfriars hanging party at dawn. One ill-judged sexual conjunction. Those tired, hophead fantasies. All true, my friend. Can you feel it, the chill? You're dying already.'

The city of Oxford. Drage-Bell smoothes out the map, a street plan, as if it was the cloth for a picnic. Sileen is lost. Jumpy to reconnect, step westward at his sponsor's bidding. Follow Swedenborg? His meeting with Halley? Not Sileen's territory, Oxford. Black letters planted on the white blank of Christ Church Meadow. Can't see it. Doesn't travel well. The inhabitable world is the half-mile circumference around the London Hospital: Roebuck, Blind Beggar, Kinder Street, Monster Doss House. The rest is excess baggage.

Anticipate. Get there before he says it. Edmond Halley – born Haggerston, 1656. One of the Queensbridge boys. Like Maltese Felix. *It hurts*. Fragments of recall, cigarette-cards. Age twenty: St Helena, the transit of Mercury. Discussions with Newton, the law of force under which the planets move in elliptical orbits. *Principia* printed at Halley's expense. Voyage to determine the variations of the compass. Improved the diving bell. Savilian professor of geometry at Oxford. An emerging synaesthesia: East London/Oxford. The policeman's man – an acid burn in the grass. Swedenborg: the quest. A dangerous leap. Don't trust it. *Concentrate*.

Too late – the rozzer has palmed him. Sileen finds himself clutching a blue-paper copy of *Alden's Guide*, 1936. Sepia photographs. Why is the town only visible from the summit of towers? Spiked warnings, thunderclouds over low hills. *Here it comes*.

'Further your education and clear the slate at the same time. You've earwigged the rumours, my little weakness, haven't you?'

'No, Mr Bell, I swear. Nothing. Not a word.'

'Hodgson? The collection? Public knowledge. Like any other fashion, it began in the streets, on the barrows, in the coffee-houses. Test any of your academics with that name – William Hope Hodgson. Ask them what he wrote. You'll draw a blank. The alternative Conrad, and they've never clocked him. Too lazy. Waiting for the word from F. R. Leavis. The nod from George Steiner. Not one of Anthony Burgess' *Ninety-Nine Novels*, no chance. Not in the reference books, outside the Bradbury canon. They'll wait till hell freezes over before Hodgson is accepted. He's *mine*. I invented him. Skimmed the cream from the Dennis Wheatley stash when the old Satanist pegged it. All safely battened down. That's what I thought. Now I discover a couple of desiderata still out there. Oxford. You're going to collar them.'

'Hodgson? Name definitely rings a bell. Sorry, I didn't mean . . .' Sileen was one of the few; he'd scuffled a narcotic track through *The House on the Borderland* while his known associates were wowing with *Gormenghast*, paddling in Hobbitry. *Borderland* was shorter, a paperback. Those wankers. He had to play dumb to keep Drage-Bell running. Put promises on indefinite hold. 'Is he worth reading, Mr Bell?'

'*Reading*? What a curious question.' The intelligencer considered. 'Can't say I've ever read one. No, you miss the point entirely. Reading is for the great unwashed, spotty scrotes in self-supporting anoraks. Asperger's syndrome in all its galloping glory. A cover story for incontinent vagrants, an excuse to keep worthless libraries open. A bad habit. The kind of solitary practice to which I assume you are criminally addicted.'

'Not me, Mr Bell. In the clear. Dyslexic. Look at my name and I read "Silence". A rent-book is the only blot on my bibliography.'

'Collecting is the antidote to reading. Those who read can't afford to collect. Reading is a social misfortune, collection is a vocation – the essence of postmodernism. The drudgery of plodding through all those self-important words is no longer required. Collecting allows no time off for good behaviour. You must pillage *every* catalogue, not miss a single Saturday morning at Farringdon Road. Stick to the dealers like rubber knickers. They'll come, in the end, to believe they work only for you. Haunt them like a vampire. Suck until there's not a drop left.'

A simple choice: Oxford or death. Any sane man would shoot his arms straight up – to be measured for the wooden jacket. Not Sileen. The monoped was in hock to destiny. He *had* to know what happened at the head of the stairs; how it went after he launched himself among the stars. He was touting for custom, begging the intelligencer to throw the book at him. He'd creep the length of the Thames, ram his tin leg willingly into Drage-Bell's mantrap.

Here's how it worked. The spook would advance Sileen five notes (of the Dickens persuasion), and our disadvantaged quest hero would take himself off to Oxford. (Should that be 'up'?) Talk about *Jude the Obscure*. Sileen was obsidian at midnight, a total eclipse. But he would stick, he'd burrow like a tapeworm. Seek out Drage-Bell's target: T. C. P. Hinton, hedge-scholar, poet, barnacle at the Bodleian. He would ingratiate himself, rub against this gull in blasphemous familiarity. He'd play the ingle, the ganymede. It was as good as done.

His patron fed him the full S.P., marked his card. Slowly, mesmerically, step by step. Like the stages of the transmutation of gold into dung. Sileen tugged so hard at his master's lips it was a virtual clitoridectomy. This Hinton was a basket case, habitué of the soft cell, lounger on cardboard furniture. He'd been hit by so much electricity, he only needed a bulb in his mouth to double for the Eddystone Lighthouse. His hair was seriously distrait, late period John the Baptist; backcombed – like Medea in a wind tunnel. Bugeyed, the nebbish foamed, twitched, extemporised. And was generally considered one of the best, a diamond.

Poor Hinton was under the doctors (like the posh dead are under Kensal Rise) – ever since his unfortunate attempt to bring bibliographic order to the great Moorcock's literary archive. (Early days then – only a hundred or so novels, with three hundred titles. Revisions that preceded their originals. Holograph inscriptions dated a year before publication. Contemporary presentations from other fantastic masters, steampunks, who had been in the ground for half a century.) Hinton had flipped, pulled back, changed direction – taken to frequenting country house auctions, rummaging through barns, turning over the wastepaper of bent provincial solicitors. His grapewhite, zipped to the neck, golfing jacket was on nodding terms with all the Nigels, and half the villains in England. He could be relied upon to run up prices on unsaleable detritus. Until – it happens, even to the least deserving – the day he stumbled, by a pure fluke, on something interesting. That was the claim promoted by the lunatic fringe, the publishers of samizdat Hodgson fanzines. Hinton had laid hands on a sequel to *The House on the Borderland*.

'*Sequel?*' Sileen yelped, a reflex critic. 'Insane. The recluse has witnessed the death of the universe, the solar system – life, love, time. Plague has infected all living forms. Swine creatures from the pit have climbed the stairs and are straining at his door. He hasn't touched food for six days, his doggy chum is a pillow of cinders, the green pox is eating him alive – and you demand an encore?'

'An authenticated manuscript or a clumsy fake cobbled together by an indigent hack, it's of no consequence. Get it. Bring it in. Don't let the scum publish a single line. They're all Asps, pedants, button-counters. They'll whine through eternity chasing a misplaced comma. Snatch Hinton's bundle or don't come back.'

There was more to this apocryphal haul. A shoebox of photographic plates. Hodgson was apparently the first man to capture stalk lightning on film. Tripod set on a pitching deck. Weather visions. Prophetic fugues. Weather that must not be allowed to contaminate Oxford's provincial sandstone. Grab the lot. Fifty notes would be useless as a bribe. (They'd be in Askead's slimy pocket before the sun set over Itchy Park.) Persuasion might be attempted, but theft was more pragmatic. And quicker. Murder inclusive at no extra charge. By Sileen's own hand, or by the rented malignancy of assassins. They were plentiful. The public-houses were awash with auditioning hitmen. Yours for a pint of Special Brew and a packet of pork-scratchings.

Sileen was encouraged. The story was hotting up. Its complexity was skin deep, its crudity kosher. The sun was directly overhead, a pungent whiff of violence was in the air. Double-dealing, terrorism, lies, threats: London was Sileen's kind of town.

Shadows were blackleaded on the lush ground; triangulations, Poussin resonances. Drage-Bell's back was stiff against the apple tree; his legs splayed in an act of occult geometry. There was a freeze on the moment. Neither man dared to shift. Sileen, arms at his side, stood behind the policeman. Erase them both and their shadows would remain.

A higher consciousness, call it Swedenborg, was present to carry them away, spin the globe. An emblematic pern, wings outspread, to sink a beak in the nape; lift them, breathless, above the three-mast weathervane in Wellclose Square. Out – through the screen of branches, across the wasteground, where grassy knolls had swallowed the residue of the Swedish Church. A dizzying track around the Eucharistic font. Black water splashing on the mildewed flags.

This was the inauspicious locale – neutral, reserved – where whatever was incomplete, whatever Swedenborg left behind, would reach towards the hunger of another seeker (painter, pedestrian, schizo). His name? Rhab Adnam. Believe it or not. The psychic health, the covert history of the city, hung on this conjunction.

It never happened. Adnam was elsewhere. He was dowsing the fringes of the London Hospital, trying to make contact with the residual traces of the legend of the White Mount.

SIXTEEN

'The Soul's motion is, according to its essence, to be ever moving.' Rhab Adnam drifted England: pilgrim routes, weather anomalies. Serpentine energy currents swept him from St Michael's Mount to the Wash. And back – by ridgeways, dew-ponds, hill forts, springs and caverns. His pockets sagging with feldspar, limestone pebbles, roadside salt crystals. Chalk was his thing, the touch of it; the taste – a wafer dissolving on the tongue. Whiteness enveloped him. Dust on his Doc Martens, sedimentary flakes trapped by rusty eyebrows. His skull shone with internal fire. Rhab flitted – not restless; weary, smiling.

His travels were analogical, not literal. The dirt was there, the blisters, the hard miles of downland track – but they had another meaning, a parallel life. They opened him up; integrated and reintegrated dream selves, expanded and unfolded his latent power. Wessex was big enough to lose him in. He had too much weather on his face for Aldgate. He stood out like one of the bright-buttoned positive discrimination coppers.

Crinkled, squinting, shuddering against the blast of diesel traffic: Adnam's body language was all wrong. In fear and dread he confronted the absence of the White Mount.

What Mount? There was nothing to see, nothing missing, no hole in the pavement. Why fret when so many other monuments had been pillaged? What of the real stuff, doss houses, lunch-counters, schools? Sentimental ephemera. A mere hundred years. Not enough time to engage Adnam's attention. The visionary had returned to the city to pay his respects to the blunt cone of the Saxon earthwork that had once been the district's salvation. Its eastern gate. The mound defined the limits of the city. A tracery of paths, cut into its side, exalted the soul, and guided its circuits – upwards to a grove of trees. Taller than the hospital which stood uneasily beside it, the earthwork was not found out until 1830. A displacement of truths better left alone, the soil was removed by a procession of handcarts. Like unpicking the rigour of the pyramids. From its indefinite summit, tourists and scryers could trace the horizon, the sun rising above the masts and spires of Ratcliffe and Poplar.

Carried away, Rhab groaned at the loss. An equal depth of infamy was required to restore the balance, heal the gash. A project born in obscurity. To reassert the dispersed pyramid of soil by carrying its memory on a pilgrimage. To walk for as long as the legend stayed in his mind. West. He frowns in concentration, trying to resolve the nature of the quest, the shape that it required.

His eyes are slits. He's creased against the thinning light. A heavy scoring of lines in innocent flesh. Optimism measured with a pumice stone. His is a grander rage, a rage that does not slight, but swells and roars – where centuries are instants, black pepper on a grape. For him, the speculative destruction of the Mount, this crime, was news. Unrevenged, he circled and squalled. The paces winding out the harsh ascent would, by his will, restore the tattered dome.

One drawback: like Kit Smart, held in Mr Potter's madhouse at Bethnal Green, Rhab Adnam was given to public prayer. Compulsive, celebratory: we must all die. Corruption follows generation, we wither and shrink. But the unimpeded soul is free from death, self-activated – it moves, not towards something, nor because of it; motion is its essence. Rhab sang. Precocious in middle-age, a stalled child – brilliant and troubled. Frost in the red beard. Cleaning green threads from his teeth with a claspknife, he chorused on pavements. *Jubilate Agno*. The careful, slow, countryman's eye. Buffeted, spun; oblivious to the race of business. Outworkers clocked him. Brown girls fluttered.

Rhab Adnam and Todd Sileen were ghosts who had supped. When Sileen wrote, Adnam painted – and William Rees-Mogg pondered the wit and wisdom of Mick Jagger. A Wonderland padlocked by the official receiver. A pipedream. The smoke was real: torched cities, forests on fire, occulting the TV set, leaking burnt liquid flesh on the Moroccan rug. Sileen kicked his notebook under the bed, and bolted. Rhab persisted in his folly. Pursuit became flight, exile was his natural state. The road went everywhere, returning him to places he had never been. Whitechapel was a garden. He abstained. He starved to give praise: the claws of the black eagle, red fleas upon the fur of a cat.

It was troubling, Rhab back in the labyrinth – meaning, by the law of contraries, the microclimate was pure poison. Sileen glimpsed the ruin of the once-familiar housemate, shook himself, and blocked it out. Dipped his face in a rain-filled marble trough. Adnam in town, forerunner of apocalypse – spectre at the feast. The anguish must be palpable to conjure this messenger from the aether. Trapped in a downriver crowd, an unruly surge of drunks cut Sileen's sightline. Rival football firms? A public execution? Another AIDS gig? Three or four days without food and he was seeing visions. Another week and Askead's X-rays would be redundant.

Sileen made a positive ID – it *had* to be Rhab – as the bristling scarecrow went over the wall and into the park which once contained the parish church of St Mary Matfellon. Adnam was bent like a brownnoser, fingering the tilth of the soil, honouring the removed church's brick perimeter: an outline left in the grass to provoke a proper sense of bereavement. He stopped, squatted; scratched at a sketchpad. His arms waved as he aligned sepulchre and dry fountain. The decent vagrants withdrew into the sheltering shade of a tree stump. Head in the clouds, Adnam reassembled the White Mount.

The Feast. The Day of Licensed Riot. Sileen wrestled to keep Adnam in sight; elbowing windpipes, driving his tin hoof against defenceless ankles. (It only needed a steam of hot piss down the wellie to duplicate the Cold Blow Lane experience.) Sileen heaved to a crisis: cash on the hip and no way forward, the Whitechapel Road solid with demented plebs – a rooftop pigeon's view of the entire social spectrum; tophats to flat caps, skinheads, berets, Mohicans, Rastas, Goths, bikers, ballgowns. The shlemozzel. City Marshal, a swish of Bishops, the President and Vice-President of the hospital, physicians, surgeons, beadles, Watchers, waiters, urchins, sewage-toshers. The bells! Ring-a-ding. Oranges and lemons. The Hospital Feast. Like the Mexican Day of the Dead – on meths and cola. Rum and speed and shag. Freerange zombies flaunting thalamotomy scars – health service brain-cuts to chill anxiety. Caries in the community. Ensor pathologies. Trauma by drumbeat. Hysterical marchers. Doctors and victims shuffling together in an inebriated conga. A cakewalk of the damned. Sileen's everyday waking vision revealed as a general condition. Angst-ridden, he raked the tadpole faces for a CU of Askead. A thief to relieve him of his fiscal embarrassment, this wad in his pocket.

Hopeless. They cascaded from every manhole, hammering on brass trays, blitzing kazoos. A spiked tongue of discontent, a resentful giro-queue: that the food should vanish before the tailenders reached the hospital. Those who slalomed down the steps of Christ Church were the worst, lips purple from a dip at the communion wine; their saviour's flesh, in the form of a ricepaper badge, sticking to their palates. They wanted more. More of the same. Olympian conveyor belts of processed god substitutes. The cannibalistic symbols were not enough: they wanted meat that barked. Bloody wedges on the plate, pints of sack, potato buckets. They petitioned loudly for rivers of fish, estuaries of snipe, woodcock, widgeon, pheasant, quail. Pelt and claw. Feather and scale. They'd force it down while the wings beat in their faces. They hustled the surgeon-priests in their high stiff collars, their ermine trims. They rattled saws and scalpels. They dodged among porters struggling to maintain an equilibrium of palanquins on which rode the most prized of the pathological specimens – mummified bundles, prime abortions, bottled relics. A golden throne for the Elephant Man. A bell jar for the hairball stomach. Make way for the portrait of Sir Frederick Treves. Ring out St Leonard's, Christ Church, the great bell of Truman's Brewery in Brick Lane.

Bells bells bells. Bells everywhere. The word was a curse in which Sileen's intelligencer could hide. Bells deflowered the district's charm. A bell with grossly swollen clappers engraved in the glass of a pub. The Ten Bells! At the corner of Fieldgate Street, a bistre-panelled foundry in league with the churches. Bells like abandoned African brides haunt the yard. BELL / FOUN / DRY in the divided window panels. Bell hoppers on the street to collect broken bottles. No escape. Ring out. Sileen is gumshoed by a name.

Every chancer in town. Every dip, fop, welsher, spiv, sot, rake, ganef, shark, fence, slag, quack. Hydra-headed, multifaced. Sileen panned for Askead, one drunk among so many. He could take his pick of deformities, the definitive encyclopedia of corruption was on display. But not the snout he lusted for. Money burnt. He couldn't hold on to it. One more séance and he'd never return. The borderland was universal, true, but there were no gates, no bridges, not without Askead. It was the bite of radon daughters, or it was nothing.

A red beard swept along in a minyan of severe blackcoat worshippers: blood on the file. Rhab again. The cripple was too absorbed in his own delinquencies to rescue his mate. All that was not Askead was dross. Sileen was a voyeur, Adnam a participant. Their powers were equal but opposite. Put them together and the mantle of the city would tremble. Body and antibody in a race to perdition. The chalk traveller sang out, pitching his voice against the calypso of chaos.

'For I bless God in the behalf of TRINITY COLLEGE in / CAMBRIDGE and the society of PURPLES in / LONDON – / Let Ahio rejoice with the Merlin who is a cousin german of / the hawk.'

Stone crazy, the old hippie was rapping in tongues. Sileen caught him by the elbow. Let each decay in the other's dream. There was no way but – on. Adnam skipped and clapped, a village fool, and Sileen clapped with him. He joined the dance – to hobble it, pluck Askead from the currents of folly.

Clerks, dressers, virtuosi of the wineskin – they pursed their lips like a coven of apprentice fellators to catch the beaded, scarlet arcs. Claret, pumped in arterial jets, splashed their hot faces. Night-scrubbers and wardmaids joshed the pretensions of uniformed porters. Whistles, mimed obscenities, offers of wet-nursing. Storage jars tumbled from their uncertain mounts, crashed into the street. Formaldehyde, flesh wounds. The procession, with Sileen and Adnam clamped in its informal embrace, passed mosque, bell foundry, doss house – Commercial Street, Whitechapel Road, Fieldgate Street, Stepney Way – in a swaying outflow of benevolence. Those riding point could smell the bullocks turning on spits. They had beaten the bounds, no contest. The short journey from Spitalfields blessed them with the thirst of heroes.

The sick, the walking wounded, picketed the hospital windows, scanning the arrival of an invading army: it meant nothing to them but they waved. Turbaned Sikhs on the march, Yardies flashing Uzis (with optional bottle-openers on the magazine), the matted aprons of the Guild of Chicken Butchers. Out-patients, overlockers, ponces, nonces, squaddies tambourining bedpans. Urchins with contraband fire-crackers. Unsponsored performance artists milking the biggest audience they were ever going to mystify. The mob was getting dangerously high on its own secretions. It retrospected the great half-forgotten festivals of old. Saints' days. The Foundation of the Infirmary in 1740. The battle of Cable Street. King Lud. Luddite hammers. Wat Tyler. Brick Lane. Paki bashing. Petrol bombs. Class War. Nobble a toff's motor. Scapegoats and super-grasses. Hang John Williams, the Ratcliffe vampire. Hang the dead men. The condemned on hurdles. Papists, disembowelled Jocks. Rattles, bottles, blades. The crowd. The lads. Our own. A mounted escort gives form to the mob, a carapace of polished boots and glistening horse muscle. Victoria Park cavalry with Los Angeles nightsticks. Ghetto prods. Cossack sabres. A rumble, a riot – a shotgun liaison between tradition and nightmare. Frock coats, beavers, soutanes. Ganja, hardhats, trainers. The beat. The lion's roar. The trumpet. An overground sewer, a lost river returning to its borehole.

The whole thrust – the sizzling meat, ladles of fat poured over rotating capons – breaks on the stubborn vegetarian, on Rhab Adnam. Adnam has frozen where he stands, dipped into a cryogenic mode. A thin strip of traffic-light green moss. Ground fur – where rainwater has dripped, month after month, from a metal fence. He is in awe. Rejoice! Sileen tries to drag him away. No solitary detail must halt the rabble's flow. Nothing must disrupt the morphic resonance of yob consciousness. The moss is doomed to attempt transcendence without Rhab's blissful acknowledgement.

Hesitation works like a needle inserted in the back of the hand. This tiny contemplative incident, questioning time, invokes frenzy. Askead *is* out there – palming betting slips, cadging ciggies, rattling his cap at the spectators. Sileen has his man; but, in reaching out, unprepared, sees himself. A reflection in the showroom window of a Porsche dealer. Hungry ghosts soiling a resplendent parade of motors: blind beggars, grave morries, the dead reporting to barracks.

Askead netted, they abdicate individual identity, go with the flow. Sileen and his co-conspirators, the double A of Askead and Adnam – anonymously surfing the bore of directed anarchy. Tossing like corks, arm in arm to the steps of the Medical College.

The great dining hall has the dignity of a bookless library. A relic sustained by light; low sun expressing an end window. The other windows, tall and arched, fling back a constellation of winking candles. Even in its pillaged, threadbare state, the room is magnificent. Its panels have been sold as salvage and its cornices chipped. Dust falls from the galleries, catching the light-stream, filtering the ranks of bituminous portraits. Ancestors passing judgement on present folly. It's the inhuman scale that excites Rhab, baroque dream channels revealing a procession of sorcerers and surgeons. Sileen is beyond excitement. How can he feed his face within *touching* distance of the X-ray cellars? How can he detach

Ian Askead from the dropsical orgy? He refuses to grant credence to this remaindered Versailles, this boardroom for all the Reichs of hell. This Tara sound stage demolished by Potemkin mongols. The chandeliers are paste, the portraits are copies. Only the food lives. Trout flopping on beds of unwashed lettuce. Feral pigeons cooing in shortcrust.

The table is as long as a street, and the street possesses it. The rabble are seated according to status – and strength. The worthy poor wrestle for precedence. Canny veterans put solid distance between themselves and the dignitaries, drown out the speeches, relish the toasts. A flowing cup to the prosperity of the London Hospital. A health to the bishops of England. A health to the Nobility. Charge your glasses for the Lord Mayor. A health to the stewards, city, trade, our merchant adventurers. All rise.

'Let Shuni rejoice with the Gull, who is happy in not being good for food,' drones Rhab Adnam.

Not a yard from the corridor, a full furlong from the kitchen, they were banished: Askead at the table's end, flanked by Adnam and Sileen. The Glaswegian's carnivorous eye squinted for more exploitable prey. Pointless. They were trapped among the dogends; well-placed to do a runner, if – as expected – the library went up in flames, fisticuffs, serial fornication. Otherwise, business as usual. He took a shot from a flat bottle and sussed out the competition. Ganefs to the last man: the bastards were already loading their pillowcases. A rabblement in suspension. Askead fretted to light the touchpaper, detonate the underclass mutants. Look at them! He shuddered. Black and Decker prefrontals, knitters of haemorrhoids, junkie dentists addicted to their own sniffmasks, colostomy bagpipers. The port. It didn't exactly circulate, it coagulated – until snatched, liberated. Mouths as wet as a trollop's muff. They glugged, wiped off, glugged again. Askead was comfortable. He was amongst his own.

The boys could smell it, the charcoal meats, the charred fish armour, but they had to wait. Endure the speeches. Some palsied anatomist, strangled in chains, wheezing, assisted up the ladder to the musician's gallery; shoved from behind by one of the hospital's muscular Christians – a Greenlander, back from the whaling fleet, clanking with icicles; bible in one fist, bonesaw in the other. A tedious progress: the audience beat upon the table with their tankards.

'Prostate man,' whispered Askead, the insider. 'One of the best. He's fast but he shakes. Parkinsonism or some other wreckage of the basal ganglia. Been known to do the whole set – circumcision, vasectomy, castration – inside a minute, before he even locates the troublesome gland.'

'Let Dodo rejoice with the purple Worm,' responded Adnam, crossing himself.

'Your Royal Highness, Mylordsladiesangenlemun pray silence . . .' roared the MC, helplessly. The plebs were elbow deep in gravy. Trenchers of beast, cullings from the defunct Mudchute Farm, rustled victuals from abandoned inner city paddocks: Pedley Street, Weaver Street, Buxton Street, Stepney Green, the tenter grounds. Horse steaks ribbed with mustard. Donkey cutlets. Broth of tiger's testicles. You wondered who picked up the London Zoo contract? Wonder no more. Sledges and post-operative trolleys buckling under rhino ribs, baboon giblets, snake stew, grasshopper side salads. Bison skulls peppered with buckshot. Penguins boiled in their own oil. Paprika parrot's tongue. Armadillo kebab. Chienne en Daube. Extinct tree-rats knotted tail-to-tail around a polished bin lid.

Trumpeting and drooling, the starveling horde of subs fell upon the ex-inmates, their animal cousins. Lovingly, they plundered marinaded entrails and oozy cranial cups. The register of endangered species was washed down in complimentary madeira. The event couldn't fail to pass muster with the Goldsmiths: some space had been cleared upon the earth's over-infested crust. Sound ecology. Belching, they gave praise. They were prepared to swallow the sermon along with the feathers.

Even Askead lent an ear to the green babble, he was gutted. Rhab communed with bread and spurned the rest. Sileen would only drink. He undercoated Askead, waiting his chance to drag him out. Some hope. The little Scot spiked an eye winking in a mound of muddy rice, hacked into a steaming landfill of tripes and lights; spooned up a dribble of iced brain *consommé*. Lymphocytes sluiced from his prim mouth and were rinsed in brown sherry, Burgundy, poker-dipped stout. He loosened his belt, the neat paunch spilled. Scars from the dark kirk clamped him: hellfire as a chaser. The blast of pleasure/pain. Free Presbyterian guilt. Wooo. He rolled a fat one, an aid to contemplation, a mental suppository. Askead's head was an angry boil lanced in grassy smoke.

Sileen watched and waited. His social graces did not run to nudging the port or sharing his jug of Murphy's. Listlessly, he dipped a paw into a bucket of prawns, winkles, other gritty, pinkogrey inedibles. Rhab was stunned, after months of solitary walking – the frenzy, the discourteous cacophony. He picked at a cottage loaf, slowly dissecting a rectangle of coarse bread into smaller and smaller segments, building Mayan codices with brickbats of sweating Roquefort. His consciousness fused with the cheese dice, the crumbling counters of bread, a wine bruise soaking into the table linen. Rocks appeared to him, craggy peninsulas, mood-induced locations in the far west: the psychic spectra of shale, slate, sandstone. What he feared most became his destiny. And he embraced it – the *silence des artistes* proposed by Samuel Coleridge Taylor, that pacifist hitman, *rentier* pauper, celibate father of a tribe. GIVE UP ART. Rhab flinched. The stupidity. A choice open to those who are not cursed – the rest of the human race, the civilians.

'Taylor?' Sileen, the compulsive trace-artist, swooped. He *saw* the crazed American exile in Rhab's unsuspecting face – rubbery, monkey cunning, squeezing and tugging to gain control. Sammy Taylor was Sileen's death wish, his crow. A shapeshifter, he stretched Adnam's exhausted grin. Damned himself, his energies thwarted, the Yank strained to live within the minds of those who thought of him. It was the highest form of fiction: writing himself out, coaxing others to enact his suicide.

'Taylor?'

The name forced Adnam back to his epic pilgrimage: Hackney to West Cork, on foot. Things were difficult – ictus, vision, poverty. Star splinters wheeling overhead. An agony of uncurtained light. Paintings aborted on the easel; never-to-be-completed portraits, celestial mappings. Disintegrated, split, hurt, high – he fled, chased himself down the rocky road to Taylor's redoubt. End of the line, gate of the sea. Cross-section skies; Nordic twilight sliced like an onion filled with blood.

He must have dreamt the walk. Thames Valley, Cotswolds, Forest of Dean, Black Mountains, Brecon Beacons, Mynydd Prescelly. Into the Silurian, the mudstones. Sleeping in ditches, cold clear nights among the conifers. 'See, see, where Christ's blood streams in the firmament!' The channel crossing, hooked over the rails, ironing out the fretful waves. Kinsale, the Templebryan Stone Circle, Skibbereen. The Caha Mountains floating in the mist. New light undid him with its shifts. His paintings had arrived first – hung on rough stone walls, white powder encrustations. The works had outdistanced Rhab, struck their treaty with a rain-slashed landscape.

It wasn't easy getting Rhab to talk in plain language, separating him from the predatory Taylor. But Sileen needed news from the frontier – fast. Was Taylor out of it? Or might he reappear, pregnant with revenge? Might he act *through* Adnam? Or even the girl? Had he acted already – Helen's assault, her boxing fetish?

Rhab could say 'Yes' slower than any Londoner; 'ummm'. His eyes narrowed, cardiac arrest shockwaves creased his brow. But he struggled like a good 'un. Taylor? News? Pigs. Like some Jehovah-cursed wilderness-dwelling nomad forced to settle, Taylor had, against all temperament, taken to the cultivation of porkers. And they to him. Nuzzling against impacted layers of their own shit. He had the John Huston cap, the blackthorn. He tickled their furry bellies. He delivered their young. Fungus-plastered rocks, a jigsaw of vertical fields: the truffling swine honked at his door. They shared what he had.

Taylor went strictly by the book. *Productive Swine Husbandry* by G. E. Day. Lippincott's Farm Manuals; 4th edition, revised and reset. Chicago, 1924. 89 illustrations in text. The book came with the house. It was the only one. Long winter evenings of study by firelight; joint after joint of weak homegrown herb. He caressed the heavy paper, monochrome snaps sticking to each other like bombsite pornography. What beasts! Love at first spurt. Chester Whites, Poland-Chinas, Victoria boars with immaculate rungs of evenly spaced teats. He shuddered over the smooth, tapering hams of the lard hogs: the jazzy, shaggy-jacketed wealth of them. He doted and he counted his kill.

The sacred snouts went where they would; waddling and snuffling, they blocked off the lanes. They battered down fences. They stripped the land. Bristle-hided tanks against an entrenched peasantry. The bogfolk blasted back – without effect. The herd shook off the lead pellets and swallowed them as roughage. Taylor was king of the pigmen, a Pope in his own midden. It was only a matter of days before they burnt him out, torched him, his kin and his animals. But they'd have to hurry, before his peer group, the rest of the bohemian white trash, the deregulated hippies, blew him away. Mail-order Sufis, tofu importers, non-tenured lecturers: they were saving their grubby punts to take out a contract. Taylor was the Antichrist. Only Rhab visited him, for old times' sake, to catch the dragon line where it emerged from the Atlantic, to align himself with chthonic energies. His dreams: a speculative froth of geology and Jungian shadowshows. Closer to the truth than any newspaper. William Hope Hodgson's transcosmic visions were a cartoon to Adnam. Taylor was in far worse shtuk than the besieged recluse. He was in league with the swine-creatures. He was their spokesman.

The backwash of Rhab's travelogue affronted the other diners. Sileen twisted. Pig masks were de rigueur. Hogs, dragged from the horizontal, puffed on cheroots; stamped, swilled brandy, broke into song. A slaughterhouse caterwauling.

Sileen's money was radioactive in his pocket. Drage-Bell might – *would* – be having him watched. Check the cigars. One of these swine is a pig. He must break for Oxford or, immediately, hoist some other scam: bail himself out of this madhouse. Oxford was an unknown, beyond his range, a cluster of strangers, privileged enclosures. Scrub it. He needed Askead at his side. He must secure the dwarf, ream him with filthy lucre.

A start was made by lifting the Scotsman's face out of the chocolate pudding. His eyes were unattached, bungee-jumping; his beard garnished with sugar. He grinned at his rescuer and slid back under the table. It proved necessary to hold his collar, talk man to man, nose to nose – like a comedy two-shot. The boxing match, Helen and the other girl. Askead, a gamecock, woke up. 'Don't tell me.' He was in there, up to speed on the instant. This voyant of mayhem. Accessory before *and* after the fact.

'*Me*? You talking to me, son, about unlicensed shows?' Ian Askead, it seems, had practically invented them; scholar of form, talent spotter, tout, bagman, 'Pretty Boy' Roy Shaw, Leonard 'Mean Machine' MacLean, 'Pineapple' Pete Mancini, Harry the Jewboy, the Gambini Brothers from Hoxton. Like *that*. Closer than catamites. Askead was the archivist of the bareknuckle fraternity. He hobnobbed with body-builders, passing out the steroid milkshakes. In the sweatbox at Ironmonger Row, he polished pectorals, kneaded the tension from hawsered necks. Assessed the meatrack sparrers down the Royal Oak, Canning Town. Nodding terms with Jimmy Tibbs. Nudge and a wink in the Becket. Yarned about the Dai Dower fix. When the word came through from Johnny Bos ('Call the gravedigger. Get me some bodies.'), he was straight on the blower.

Pit bulls, bearbaiting, cockfighting: anything worth a flutter. Male or female. Sileen couldn't go wrong. 'Trust me.' Trust a man who's got to stand on a chair to put his arm around your shoulder? Safer to butter the notes and eat them with strawberry jam. Choke himself before Drage-Bell's heavies got their chance to finish the job.

'No messing. Do the packet, son. With Sliema Felix Muscat, down the Roebuck. Stick it on your judy.' Askead was purring, holding his bottle to Sileen's lips, babying him. 'How can you go wrong? You're sleeping with your investment. Take my word, birds are stand-up geezers. They don't care, no concept of honour. Won't take a dive for fear of pissing their outfit.'

What did Askead know about the suborning of women? His mistresses were one-dimensional with staples through their navels. Living bitches scrap for the love of it. Sileen had personal experience. Hysteria technicians, the whole bent sorority of them. Who did the rabbity midget think he was? One of those transsexual romancers who infuse you in sensitive monologues about the time of the month and sunset over Lake Geneva? There was no choice. He had to go for it, a bit of insider dealing.

Askead was in Sileen's pocket, measuring the wedge. Sileen might be holding but he was no mug punter. The whole fifty would ride on Helen's rival. Bet on failure, that was more his style. The Devil's Party. Always favour the hairiest one, the hunchback. Look for the lass who can't cram her hooves into a pair of ballet pumps. Box clever for once. Risk everything on a single throw. Then welsh it. He'd shaft Helen and fuck Isabel. Sacrifice his seed in a good cause. Another form of affection. His way of doing her a favour, putting her in the frame when the moon was in its awkward phase. She was much too classy a bint to make a career among the flatnoses.

SEVENTEEN

The Roebuck, in its glass forest, quivered – as Ian Askead hammered at the pub's bolted door. Never rely on a Glasgow pistol, not since Scotch Jack Dickson went queer. The nutter's horns were down, ready for the charge, when Sileen grabbed his coat. Softly softly. These were serious men, psychos in heavy equity suits.

'Hey, Muscat, you pimper of jailbait, get your arse out here.' Askead was fox crazy, he knew that Sliema Felix, the renowned shifter of corpses, flawed wheelman, was a lifer, released on licence; the wolf was muzzled. The legless technician, and the monoped Sileen, stood shoulder-to-shoulder in the night, howling. Their back-up, Rhab Adnam, was scanning a low sky; a millrace of iron clouds, proletarian smoke, bad script, warnings. The beauty of horror chilled him. Destitute buildings with insurance-mascara windows, bricked entrances. A shifty, local moon with acid-erased features.

They were outside fear. They had come too far and had nothing to lose. They could safely rattle Muscat's chain. That was the theory: when a Euston Films minder presented himself at the door's slit, and peered out in disbelief. Violence by proxy. Askead was too wrecked to have considered that option. The rental for a screwdriver in the eyeball, some nifty secateur work on the tendons, might still be within Muscat's means. Tread easy, lads, force an ingratiating leer.

This unstriped amateur, his shirt buttons popping, gawped in honest confusion. He was torn between conflicting impulses: nut the mouthy aberration, or offer him a craftsman's handshake? Who *were* these freaks? Winos, vagrants, tossers? Or David Bailey and a couple of mates come to pay their respects? The minder, sweating, slackened the knot of his tie – more Windsor than the castle – and checked out the cul-de-sac for a roller. Nothing. A night of mischief and shadows. He'd be happier back on the forecourt, in the ullage cellars, painting white lines on Hackney Marshes. He was Felix's nephew. No chance of genteel obscurity. Blood was thicker than vodka. Families made the East End what it is to-day.

A dog growled. The mutt was happy, so was Felix. He called the minder to heel and the trio of subterraneans dodged into the darkened sanctuary. Red flock walls and a red ceiling, redecorated by the yellow phlegm of horizontal consumptives. The Swedenborgian guv'nor and his corseletted son at opposite ends of the bar. The TV with its sound off. Some hairdresser's model doing a Sharon Stone on a high stool. An ugly white boxer, whose face had been flattened by a tray, snuffling at Muscat's feet. Then the famous suit itself: crisp, austere, Tory conference blue, tight silk tie, white triangle in breast pocket – a tiny yacht sailing to oblivion. An expensive mummification to boost the old lag's punctuated self-esteem.

The legend had a bad case of institutional jaundice – waxy nicotine skin. Cheese microwaved in its wrapper. Powder burns elongated his hollow cheeks. The geezer found it convenient to leave a virtual reality account of himself lying around the pub – freeing him to relive, yet again, the events of that fateful night.

What was the story? In his period as an apprentice wiseguy, Felix had tried to customize a shotgun at his kitchen table. He sawed off the wrong end, the stock. Did himself quite a mischief on the post-office job in Haggerston Road, went down for a seven. Now the skin was tight on the bone, it pinched. As did the shoes, chiselled affairs with elevator heels and Mexican silver toecaps. Felix was built-up all over, from the walnut whirl hair to the coat-hanger shoulders. A cork-tipped cigarette burned inside his hooked-back fist: an incense stick in a contraband Buddha.

What the lads were seeing was a cleverly contrived gangland memento: Felix was whatever his ghost (female) said he was. Muscat, the ultimate footnote, would replay, on request (cash upfront), the party line. His biography was an 'as told to' – which the pensioned pimp accepted as gospel.

The man's head tipped forward as the trio approached, ready to receive the lifegiving words from the court ventriloquist. He was the last of the Maltese faces, the dishonoured immigrants. He got his start on the door of a speakeasy in The Gut, Valletta, when Frankie Vaughan was topping the bill. Now it had come to this. The man who broke bones for 'Big Frank' Mifsud, ran messages for Bernie Silver. Who had drunk with the Micallef brothers in the Lane and watched out for Philip Ellul's girls in Berner Street. Who'd been a shaky alibi for Joe Grech. His ring record (12-2-7) was more comprehensive than Ronnie Kray's (4-2) but no more distinguished. His honours were all ceremonial: a fetcher of drinks, a drowner of car keys. He never progressed beyond introducing up and coming brothers to the Twins, remembering what he was supposed to forget. The only time they included him in a group photo was from the back of the prison van.

'Sorry about the formalities, gents,' Felix glossed, as the minder did his best to avoid contamination while patting the trio down for concealed weapons. 'You got to appreciate, it ain't – it's not – an easy job. Not nowadays. With all them videos. You take my old mum, God bless 'er, darsen't set foot outside the 'ouse.' Unblinking, cod-eyed, he laughed; gestured to acknowledge the fragrant presence of the status piece on the stool. 'My Julie. Saved my life, she did.'

Julie lit a very long white cigarette, tipped her head back to drag deep, squeezing the thin tube for warmth and comfort in a world of conflicting signals. She blanked these scruffs, shook down the dark glasses that were nesting in her hair; lifted a viridian fingertip for another hit of Bacardi. The Swedenborgian didn't move. He was in urgent conference with the Vegetable Kingdom. His firstborn, arms across belly, struggled the length of the bar to oblige: parked himself stolidly within Julie's heady ambience.

'These days, we do business with scum you wouldn't feed to a dog.' The boxer belched in agreement. 'Say what you like about the Twins, they wouldn't set foot in my motor with shit on their shoes. Ronnie *never* failed to offer me a compliment. "Felix, my son, you're all front." Immaculate gentlemen, they were. The heights of fashion.'

Felix was a tired man, a selective amnesiac, wired to ineradicable aggravations. However much the lads wanted to get down to it, bung the wad on the table, they had to respect the niceties of Muscat's tea ceremony. Or turn away – and suffer the hound's leaking methane. There was no putting the lid on this serial sentimentalist.

'You take this boozer, look at it now, then go back twenty-five years. A Friday or a Saturday night. You couldn't get near the bar. It was a totally different era.' He pronounced it 'error'. 'Motors? There wasn't a slot between here and the graveyard. Gave me a very special feeling to see them lined up – like Albert Dimes' funeral. I was proud to be a part of it. We had London in the palm of our hands. None of your Jap rubbish. Proper Yank stuff. Big black Buicks, Mustang 500's, Ford Galaxys. Put up the readies and Dukie Osborne would fetch you any shooter in the catalogue: Colts, Smith and Wessons, 12-bore Browning self-loading shotguns! Conspicuous class!'

The monologue left Sileen cold, but Felix's scent made his eyes water. Stand-up villains like Jack Spot swore by a quick splash of Dettol, anything fancier was for irons. Muscat showered in civet to kill the secretions of solitary confinement. 'After ten years inside, you die.' Sileen ruffled his fan of banknotes under the recidivist's nose – without eliciting a flicker of interest. The rudyard was happiest talking to himself in a darkened room.

'The women dressed up in their corner. Celebrities, welterweight champions, photographers having a pop. Ron – he had his own sense of humour – would walk through the door with some old tramp he's picked out of the gutter in Vallance Road. My life. Wrap his best cashmere round his shoulders, put a drink in his hand, shove him in the seat of honour. Introduce him to Judy Garland. That's the sort of man he was.'

The pause was so theatrical even Sileen noticed it. Should he applaud – or wait for the end of the first act? He was saved by Felix extending an open hand for a nicotine reload. No joy. The hapless minder was feeding pork-scratchings to the dog.

'Look at 'im, my Tone's youngest. What a streak of piss! 'E'll never amount to nothing. God's truth, I've seen 'im take six shots to chin some old slag of forty. You wouldn't credit his dad designed telephone kiosks. Straight as the Old Kent Road, got 'imself a lovely little gaff down the country, 'Ornchurch. Never once been away since 'e come out of Borstal. You ain't got brothers, you got fuck all. Who's gonna watch your back? "Be a mug then," I told 'im, "work for a poxy living." '

'Any chance of a wet one, Colonel?' demanded Askead – who had discovered that his credit with the publican didn't run to a ladle of Thames water. 'Before we get down to the nitty-gritty.'

A distributor of small favours, Felix gave the nod, and the old revolutionary waddled out with a bottle for their table. He favoured this temporary alliance of chancers with a magnificently supercilious sneer.

He might *choose* to pander to these parasites, he didn't have to see them as anything grander than they were: inbreeds, knuckle-draggers whose evolutionary tree achieved no tributary.

The temperature plunged. Felix took his spectacles from their case, and gave his clients the Look. It was what he was famous for – this alarming concussion of eyebrows, this fish-on-a-slab stare. More effective than a short jab to the solar plexus. In Muscat's pomp, the Look had disarmed mischief-making axemen. They fled the club wishing they'd settled on the old brown corduroys. The gimmick was wasted on these ingrates. Askead actually had the bad manners – Frankie Fraser would have chopped his hands off for it – to start laying out filthy banknotes on the table. Right alongside Felix's shotglass tumbler! Every sheet Sileen had, his plunge on Gothic futures, and then some. Coins fished from the lining of Sileen's jacket. They jingled onto the laminate like a ravished poorbox. Milk tokens, foreign alloys, the rubbish Askead had nicked from the charity plate at the hospital feast.

The vulgarity of it, the invocation of kitchen slaughters, hit Felix hard. The enterprise capitalist blanched. His olivegreen Asiatic mask put the twitch into Sileen, who was not notoriously sensitive. Sympathy pains flayed his stump. The silence that followed was filled with anxiety replays: swift, heterodox amputations. Like a dowager, Muscat would never admit to having laid eyes on the stuff, this grab of shekels. Like royalty, he claimed tax exempt status. Mere counting was left to bent briefs and pikers. The damage it would inflict on his pockets, the drape of his hopsack. Askead might as well have unwrapped a scarf of dog excrement. The minder, blushing, swooped to remove the last traces of the impertinence.

Rhab had wisely detached himself, to explore the pub's uncharted arcana: heraldic mirrors, medieval plumbing. He was engaging Julie in conversation, bravely copping a lungful of not-so-passive smoke. Julie had developed a refined version of the Look – an enigmatic, unseeing stare. Hypermetropic, she was saved from the worst excesses of the insistently local: dark glasses helped. Rhab was a pleasantly remote blur, an unformed dot matrix. She smiled. Put him in chocky mohair with a lemon silk cutaway shirt and he'd be halfway presentable. Nicely spoken lad. She drew deep, feigning attention. What *was* he on about? The roebuck as one of the sacred beasts of Britain? Roebuck, lapwing, and – dog? Julie, with her anachronistic shoulder-length hair, was a definite votive presence. Priestess. White Goddess.

The bloke was a nutcase. She stuck with what she did best – smoking; deep, rib-shuddering drags. It was her life. She was lost, this boy brought it home to her: in exile – a mile and half from her birthplace. Muscat had carried her over the water. Goodbye to Bermondsey; goodbye, Freddie Foreman. Her mum, the girls, the salon. Thrown among strangers, foreign habits. Too cruel. She snuffled.

'Right, gents.' Muscat's velvet base – that profoundly masculine, midnight rumble, drew Julie, skipping, to him. 'Time to get serious.' Hands pressed flat to the table: Look, no weapons. They looked. Short spade mitts, close-cropped cuticles. (Thank you, Julie, part-trained beautician.) Plenty of knuckle; square ring, a dazzler, on the pinkie – size of a magnum razor-blade. Passes as discreet in present company, avoiding the solecism of the gold sovereign number. Excellent for splitting cheeks but a dead giveaway: badge of the didicoi, the market-trader.

'Let's be clear. You gentlemen want a punt on a female prizefight, venue unspecified until three hours before the off – agreed?'

Agreed. They shook on it. Askead winked at Julie.

'How d'you fancy midgets? Amputee tag teams?' Muscat nudged Sileen invitingly. 'Give you choice odds on man against mastiff. Man's tooled up with a yard of chain, blindfolded – and the dog's got no eyes. In the brochure. I'll put a call through to my associates, see how the market's shaping.'

The gangland broker, thumb and little finger spread, gestured to the help – while Askead threw back the last of the complimentary booze and discussed head gaskets with the minder. A subject about which Sileen and Adnam, confirmed pedestrians, knew nothing. Julie, meanwhile, had draped herself behind Muscat, to massage his over-tense neck, and release those knots of frustration. She nibbled his lobe, waxing him, as he repeated his curious hand gesture. The jumpy minder, misinterpreting the semaphore once again, scuffled to his employer's side with an almost empty bottle.

'Cunt, you reckon I drink outta my ear'ole?' snarled the company director. 'The dog the dog!' More inter-generational confusion. The Elizabethan richness of sub-cultural argot lost: back slang, rhyming slang, Yiddish, the Gypsy codes that protected the ghetto – vanished. The minder relied on *Minder* for his heritage. And still he cocked it up, the literalist. Drink splashed into the white boxer's ashtray. A greedy, lapping tongue. Canine hysteria; yelps, farts, pseudo attacks, the ravishment of Sileen's good leg.

Felix banged the table. 'The phone, twatface. Or fuck off down the labour.' He worked his shoulders, shot his cuffs; objectified his discontent. It simmered. The licensed man could risk no domestics here: he tugged on his socks, flicked an imaginary mote from the daggered tip of his silver toecap.

Askead wheedled a mean measure of Irish from the publican's son, ostensibly to scour Sileen's befouled trousers. One scrub at the pug's genetically coded goo, then the rest goes down his throat. The trio huddled at the bar, backs to Muscat's dubious transactions – social deafness.

°'Allo, Nicky. 'Arright, son? Listen, mate, nothing to climb out of your pit for, but . . .' The deal was set, the odds fixed. Not the fights. No percentage in it. Market forces, primitive Darwinianism. The interesting dampness of the patch where the soaked cloth stuck to Sileen's calf. An epiphany. It flowed and spread. *Both* legs shared the pleasure of that overwhelmingly particular sensation. The disadvantaged quest hero saw himself as he was, the whole man. If Helen lost, he was reborn, granted a second chance. Bundles of loot, squits of mazooma; his panic alchemised into gold. Askead would be greased and the visionary chamber opened. The house, the sea, the triangular field. His hand was trembling on the bar. He was alive, condemned, on the cusp of fate. A simple defeat for his mistress and he was out of it for good. A victory – not to be thought on – and he was offal. Drage-Bell, Muscat, the Gasman's invisible insurrectionists, they could squabble over the pieces.

Returned to penury, the lowlife were surplus to the clubbable bonhomie of the Roebuck. The minder held the door. Felix had an arm around Sileen's shoulder, while he pumped Askead's hand. Losing them was like losing something precious, a microchip from the sum of human possibilities. He was genuinely moved, diminished by the speed with which he shot the bolts. The pub photographer, unfortunately, was off duty; there would be no snaps to pin to the wall. The meeting might never have occurred. Julie blinked a final identikit hazard at Rhab's possible future attractions. And they were out, penniless, under the stars – floating a mercury-bubble moon by an act of spontaneous communal willpower.

'A little way within the gloom,' sang Adnam, 'a roebuck raised his eyes/

Brimful of starlight, and he said: *The Stamper of the Skies.*' The Stamper of the Skies.

They were lightheaded, unscripted, without direction. They allowed themselves to be carried along by the pull of underground rivulets, the contradictory guidance of discontinued ley lines. Their steps became the steps of fictional ancestors, killers out of time, dream wraiths: they predicted routes the unborn would be obliged to follow. They were incapable of writing themselves back into a verifiably Cartesian city. Rhab wanted to suckle the cobbles. Sileen was weeping, soot and cinders.

The hospital. Gas-lamps softly fluting the darkness. The smoke of songs: as the feast declines into off-key flatulence. A brave remnant of Born Again hippies, New Agers, had formed a circle around the building, hand-in-hand, New Road, Stepney Way, Cavell Street, and back to the Whitechapel Road: a touch of warmth to preserve the monster, or to exorcise its demons. They were chanting in a fashion pitched somewhere between the Fugs and a John Ford burial party; as they attempted – the conceit of it – to levitate the barnacled hulk. A shamanism of intent. A millimetre would suffice, any distance by which the visible portion could be separated from its terrible igneous strata. All the names were invoked, listings of angelhood unheard since the Congress for the Dialectics of Liberation: Andonai, El, Elohim, Zebaoth, Jah, Sadai, Hamaliel, The Eagle, Raphael, John, Attis, Osiris, Ginsberg, Guevara, the God in the form of a Scarab, the Wolf, the Raven, Dylan, Madonna, the Mother of Battles. A wailing. One breath expelled into the damp night; a ring of carbon dioxide to smother the E of the hospital's site plan.

Did the foundations trepidate? Was there a momentary lurch in the pesthouse's arrogant self-belief? Plates jumping from shelves? Candle-flames oscillating? Spoons spilling thick syrups into the open necks of winceyette pyjamas? Yes, almost certainly. It's possible. Perhaps. The Asps, the Quakers, the orange tie-dyes: they thought so. Out-patients clutched at the more enlightened medics; Rhab Adnam was in the thick of them.

'Let Ohad rejoice with Byturos who eateth the vine and is a master of temperance.' What Rhab saw was a sequence of diminishing hoops, contours of smokebreath – *resurrecting the White Mount*. The hospital did not move, it was buried in ignorance.

Sileen stood back from this dance of death. 'Come up, brother.' The salvationist's benefaction was wasted – too general an invitation for such an elitist. Enraged clouds, the ectoplasm of idiots, raced through the windows. The cripple's head was a malfunctioning gyroscope. It was time to spit on the boots, march south, back to the hutch. And Helen. His trumpcard.

Not the dwarf, the canny Jock. Ian Askead floated down the daisychain of blissed-out Divine Lighters, dipping and patting, fishing purses from unprotected pockets. Their arms were wrapped in tribal futility. The unfortunate utopians were defenceless. Om. All one, all contributing. The rubble rat was solvent once more, bankrolled for incipient mischief.

BOOK TWO

THE TRIANGULATION

Adders and serpents, let me breathe a while!

Christopher Marlowe,
The Tragical History of Doctor Faustus

ONE

Escape: as essence. Helen's high-coloured cheeks. The momentum forcing her head back against the pillow in its grey towelette slipcase. Her spirits, and theirs – lifted above the pluck of London clay. Carried westward.

Daylight thins, a mute city: beads, eyes, smeared haloes. Victoria's begrimed pomp, her palaces and secrets. The luxury of paupers. They were authentic ticket-holders, sharing their freedom with a dole of students, a lone crophead nursing a six-pack, a weekend parent. Lost soul travellers.

So they enter the stream of traffic, bloodred brake lights. London is wet slate: greys, subdued blues, pedestrians abraded by grit. Slack faces, brainstems coated in lead. To be moving was a modest rush of pleasure.

Barelegged, Helen anticipates small adventures. A stagnant cloud-mass, ill-defined layers peeling from a dark base. She gave herself over to the ritual of observation, interpreting her mood by what she could describe. Magenta windows framing a sequence of time-lapse memories: weather from the past, noticed but ignored.

An outing, the three of them, flying, spiting fate – city of sleepwalkers. Helen watches, affectionately, jealously, checks the others out: what they are wearing, how they carry themselves, clothes, hair. Profiles in the darkening glass imposed upon inky buildings. Lives in suspension, the truce between doing and dreaming. The weight of traffic stalls them. Helen leans across Andi, strains for a glimpse of the river. Hammersmith. The ramp ahead of them. A mechanical conga, stopping, starting, Chelsea to High Wycombe – pitching its trust at the illusion of 'elsewhere'.

Sileen licked a finger to run it over Helen's note. 'I'm dumping the boxing fantasy. Keep the gear, especially those boots!! We might find a use for them later!!! Shooting down to Oxford with Sofya for a few days. Check out LUKE HOWARD show at MOMA the cloud paintings. Love.'

Then the letters of her name, the power of them, bringing tears to his eyes. Letters terminated by a warning row of Xs. A barbed wire kiss-off. A cancelled insult. He crushed the offending paper, he would teach her better manners. He was still human. Her absence hurt. He clawed at the stale air for some trace of his woman. Shame. She had reneged on instinct, the best part of her, to be at his side when he needed her. The strength to humour his weakness.

The room spurned him. His Sly Street den was a trap. Sileen marched through feathers, wall to wall, stairhead to grate. He tipped out the black bags in which Helen had deposited her dirty clothes. He nuzzled and sniffed. He drew a stocking across the roughness of his chin, straining to abrade its gossamer resilience. He discovered a suede and leather ankleboot, and tasted its mud to track her wanderings. Canal banks, graveyards, all the caprices of a free and independent spirit: he groaned. He choked on grass blades that spoke of obscure municipal assignations. Whimpering, he licked and sucked at the boot's limp tongue. A cold sweat drenched him. Were *they* watching?

The brutal wedge of Kinder Street. The pepperpot turrets of St George-in-the-East. They solved nothing. The trull! To ditch him, leave him potless while she promenaded England with her compliant bitches. Staring at the street, denying the potency of Helen's lingering sensors, he willed movement: bleached pink curtains fluttered in abandoned properties. Sileen's discomfort was a sirocco prickling the fur of rabid dogs, pitching vagrants from their doorways. They were hot on his trail. Wolf-eyes needling him from market caffs, video surf winking behind the walls of secure compounds.

A leper, he ripped off his stiff and stinking suit, the rags of his underwear. Unhooked the prosthetic limb. Incomplete, he would return to himself. Dysfunctional, he could map a blistered future. Sileen rolled into the tub of scummy water Helen had left behind: a uniform soup of skinflakes and baby powder, hairballs, splinters of enamel. The beginning of life: he submerged, desperate to think, to calculate, make his blood pound, fire the concussed channels of the thalamus. He masturbated – feverishly and without inspiration. Imageless. Spuming crusts of gush, they foamed to the surface. A yolky spawn, newts in cold slime: a weave he could safely ignore. He yawned and suffered.

One of those incidents that define urban life. Faces. In the half-dark, up against the window of the coach, seen from outside; the threat of rain. A small seizure, an unfulfilled expectation. The woman, looking out, sees nothing. Nothing she did not expect.

Helen leans across Andi Kuschka to search for the river. Their faces. Sofya Court, on the seat in front of them, is reading: the drudgery of London's impacted villages bores her. This nightscape was an involuntary dream – the drift of anonymous housing continued, even when the coach was at a standstill. Oxford remained the most fantastic of destinations.

Through a swarm of static, the driver broadcast his incoherent apologia for the eccentricity of the route they were obliged to endure. Road works, bomb warnings, burst water mains, leaves sticking to wet tarmac. The coach twisted after that mythical redness in the west. Hammersmith, Chiswick, back to Shepherd's Bush; Uxbridge Road, Hanger Lane – rehearsing chaos, achieving a worst case scenario by the act of anticipating it. A Grand Tour of entropy: exhaust fume addicts, purchasers of single milkbottles. Greenwich Mean Time was specific to Greenwich, other cantons had their own ideas. Shepherd's Bush was a whirling vortex of repeats and instant feedback. Drug shootouts occurring in the next street. The river was never *quite* there. It teased and leaked away.

Helen's perfume, an office freebie, was of a pungency suitable only for travel. It left a wake like a minesweeper. The better part of her would haunt that seat for generations. Her essence would bother Peruvian guerillas – as they stormed aboard to execute the coach's penultimate incarnation. The scent reminded Andi of leather gloves and theatre cloakrooms.

Below a mass of cloud this evening / a faintly orange light / slides on your lifting smile.

Andi relished the eros of tedium; narcoleptic suburbs, the sensory confusion of being separated from all that was predictable. She floated deliriously, giving herself over to the hum of tyres on the wet road. Occasionally some dream building would interrupt the flow by being more interesting than it deserved to be. Andi wanted nothing that lived outside her body. She was untouchable. The Hoover factory, shrouded in loose plastic, puffed by changing velocities of traffic, appeared to breathe. A birthing tent. Ground-level floodlights flattered its exoticism. Place names were glimpsed, not as possible destinations but as diagnoses. Perivale, Harrow, Northolt. Streetlamps curving at the windows – as if the bus had strayed onto an airport runway. They were peeling London so swiftly now; toying with expectation, chasing the last green rays of sunlight.

The cinnabar flush paled to a lemon-gold; Andi submerged, an unpursued fugitive. She was leaving no evidence behind her. Helen sat at her side, abetting her folly. To imagine the horizon's arch enhanced by the smoke of burning boats was a forgivable indulgence. A sword of light lifted above the dissolving sun and coupled with a portion of the parhelic circle to form a cross. The speeding coach had to stretch to maintain its inertia. Andi tolerated an unresolved landscape, resisting any detail that might represent progress towards a specific destination. Amersham. The word conjured a false memory of Arthur Machen in retirement. (How did she know that MACHEN was the angel name for Sunday's 4th Heaven?) A footnote to her guided London walks. The fault in them was that she walked to a purpose, exploiting a fraudulent past – she did not wander. Machen the Sage, white hair hanging over his mossy collar, accepting gin and I.P.A from blushing disciples: his words, half-forgotten, bent the lightstream. A pine wood, a small farm. Figures from the toy box. Where were the pink candles? The English landscape is taffeta and icing sugar.

Andi closed her thighs on the black holdall, ran the leather shoulder strap nervously through her fingers. The dread. Dodging the traffic in Victoria Coach Station – carbon monoxide fumes in an enclosed space, ticket in her mouth. WARNING. DO NOT LEAVE ANY BAG UNATTENDED. The sprayed addendum: IT MIGHT BELONG TO JEFFREY ARCHER. Sofya already aboard, waving from a high window.

The bag. She had come to accept the fact that it contained a living baby. Her child. She would never be parted from it. The bag had that weight. She felt its sides move against her legs; the kicking of something powerful, not yet ready to be born. Imar O'Hagan's gift.

He had been more than usually preoccupied, withdrawn. Which excited her profoundly. It was cold that afternoon. Her breath came fast.

She had brought a bottle, cognac, an air terminal afterthought from one of her punters. They drank, no time to search for glasses amongst the chaos of paint pots and coffee-lid ashtrays. It was disturbing; O'Hagan sprawled on his rug-covered sofa. Andi knew him in movement, staring hard, then back behind his canvas; ordering her to make a sandwich, or shocking her by having a fish soup ready on the table.

Now he did not trouble to disguise his indifference. He rolled cigarette after cigarette. He hummed – which unnerved Andi, but did not abjure her purpose. She undressed, sensing, with no annoyance, the hidden presence of others within the house. (O'Hagan had never permitted her to explore. She was confined to the studio and the kitchen. Too often, he did not allow her time to remove her coat. He had her, standing, in the hallway. Against the wall or among the boxes. Saw her back out into the street before she could push through the curtain which divided the studio from the living area.)

Joyously, to an audience of spectres, those others she would never meet, and who would never meet her, Andi stripped. O'Hagan was incidental, a prop. The cognac was delicate fire. It was like tonguing liquid air. She held her left breast in her right hand, swaying. She probed O'Hagan's groin with her shoe. His obvious interest, kindled by this performance, was an irrelevance. She walked over to the curtains and opened them. She wanted sunlight. She wanted an audience. The old O'Hagan would have laid her out, smashed her face. Not this one. Legs stiff, that absurd bulge in his overalls. Andi undressed in the window. She wanted to make the event public – before she took her pleasure with him.

He was sitting up when she came back. Slack, damp hair hung across one eye: not melancholy, subdued choler. A sullen, rent boy cynicism. The butt of immodest fantasies, a creature of the streets pleased to cozen his talent in exchange for a stream of double vodkas at the bar of the Colony Room. Andi's instincts were predatory, male. The ruin of O'Hagan's beauty had to be admired like a distressed first edition. The attraction was sentimental, nostalgia for something that had never existed. Andi saw herself as he saw her, excited by his excitement. She possessed some vital part of his attention; whatever darkness he had been brooding upon was charmed by the immediacy and the heat of her nakedness. A film of moisture on fine skin. Sweet rich country odours. Committed to the excitement of deceit, it hurt him, while – at the same time – he thirsted for her furry split, the sporran of curls, the thickening lips. He pouted. She turned away, hiding the extent of her titillation.

The peeling glass – drained by so many self-portraits. The strangeness of encountering her own face. Not to be borne. She took the offending object from the wall and manoeuvred it, so that a beam of sunlight exposed the dusty boards, emphasizing the texture of the grain, turning knots into eyes. The edges were sharp. She brought the beam across the sofa and onto O'Hagan, blinding him. He refused to blink, or drop his gaze. Andi moved closer, holding the mirror up, covering her face.

O'Hagan, instantly alert to risks of a new order, jumped at her. He saw the mirror shatter, splinters powdering the floor; saw the pitted surface form a mutated self that would be unrecognizable and corrupt. She pushed him. He went down; the mirror safe, wrenched from her grip. He tilted it, tilted the room. The flaking of the glass absorbed by his skin.

She was kneeling, releasing him, taking him in her mouth; then splashing him timidly with cognac. Sampling. Drinking from the bottle. Tasting again. 'Apples.' Rinsing and swallowing. She heard footsteps on the stairs. The sharp insistence of a child's voice in the room above. She knew everything there was to know about this house. Someone was knocking. They ignored it. Andi was ready to do whatever he wanted. Carry the black holdall to Oxford. Travel by the coach he designated. Leave the holdall in a certain public-house. At a specified time. What could any of this matter? She was tired, sated; too weak to stand. The darkening landscape of the Chilterns had been present in O'Hagan's studio, in the depths of the glass. The light she had manipulated was dying over these dim fields, stretching to accommodate her inertia. Andi was no fool. She knew exactly what O'Hagan was asking of her.

Rain. Beads tracking the grease. Weekend cottages and solitary farmhouses. Blue window TV clusters: war news, reported fire infiltrating the damp fields, the rooky copses. Quantum terrors. The women rode the night in truant ecstasy. They were frivolous, on tour. The modest storm brought them together. Protected, they listened to the hiss of heavy tyres. They were passive, shifting effortlessly between quiet observation and libidinal reverie. Their flight had become an epic of erasure. They prepared themselves, without confessing it, for riotous indiscretions.

Oxfordshire. It was too sharp a transition. The name, flashing out of the darkness, alarmed Sofya. She returned to her book, trusting that their eccentric route would return them, before long, to the outskirts of London. Life beyond Gerrards Cross was unthinkable. Some awful eavesdropping tower, satellite-barnacled, blinked at the roadside. They rushed on, going nowhere. A gash in the chalk, lime cliffs, the hint of a lost oceanic plain. Shapes muffled. Low cloud masking the star grid. They were not moving. The coach was stalled again – red tail-lights snaking to the horizon. Through the companionable snorts of sleepers, Sofya attended to the mesmeric whoosh of windscreen-wipers. Her paperback clutched tightly, she checked out her double, the unknown Jew who travelled beside her.

The unexplained interruption, which forcibly inducted them into a chain of frustrated migrants, did nothing to modify the swift passage of trees, escarpments, ribbed bridges. The experience of travel was too rare and valuable to be aborted by the inevitability of an overturned juggernaut. The nightland continued to flow eastwards. Earth energies were in turmoil. The coach was held at the point where the Icknield Way is amputated by the western surge of the M40.

The journey was superimposed on other journeys, times she would rather forget – being incapable of possessing them completely. She humoured the pain of involuntary recollection. She had no special use for former lovers. The affection remained – localized, nagging, not to be activated. Weekends. Rehearsals for this ride. The same canvas satchel, the same novel. She pretended to travel on impulse, a whim of the moment, but maintained a comprehensive wardrobe, a modest library, in her friend's house. It was never to be talked about, this converted stable at Little Wittenham. The name was too ridiculous. The yew in the churchyard. That Paul Nash hill-clump infested by amateurs. So respectful. Walking down the lane to the river, or up to take the view. No other choices. A log fire. A research scientist faking it as a painter. She felt safe with him – even as he choked her. She was almost ready to take communion, sign the roster for flower arranging. Every muddy stroll, complete with golden retriever and green wellies, reasserted the primacy of Whitechapel. Pus ran down the groins of ancient oaks. She needed the squawk of soup-kitchens, men talking on street corners.

In Wittenham she was always a few hours ahead of herself, anticipating the return to reality. She began to dream her man's dream, to resolve problems he had put aside so that he might promiscuously enjoy her company. His eternal present tense was excessive. Sofya remained a masochist: without the salt of hurt, these weekends were poisonous in their sweetness. She savoured the trappings of the affair – meals, country clothes, lovemaking – altogether too much. There was no other option. She ended it. Looking ahead, she chose to provoke that which could not be avoided.

The curse of intelligence, self-knowledge; the peripheral vision of the good photographer. Old blood. Minerva owl-eyes: she felt cold as the coach shuddered. Either the engine had died or they were testing the hydraulics. Rain obliterated the external world. She didn't want to come to terms with this place where they had stopped. Sirens, ambulances. Everything between Victoria Coach Station and Gloucester Green, Oxford, was dirt to be washed from the headlamps. Her dream was revoked. She must invent something richer and stranger.

Andi, sleeping, leant against her shoulder. She had moved beside Sofya, giving Helen her turn at the window, including Sofya in their alliance. Extraordinary events were possible if the three of them stayed together. They would sack cities. Andi's hair, an orthodox marriage wig, brushed Sofya's neck. Sofya reached up to turn off the overhead light. The black bag Andi was cradling slid across the seat. It was heavy, threatening. But it must not be moved. Nothing should disturb the peculiar pitch of Andi's sleep.

Sofya glanced back, a smile. Now it was Helen who was reading, in a spill of thin light – a white novice, in a cloistered niche, sustaining the doctrine through an age of darkness.

The sky was clearing – Andi's warm breath – miles of glittering emptiness above them. Hadn't Sofya's great hero, Ford Madox Ford, speculating in 1909 on the future of London, proposed setting his compasses in Threadneedle Street, with the pencil point at Oxford, to construct an outer circuit, 'round by way of Cambridge'? A moving chain to drive the starry dynamo. 'Think of all the buildings that would fall.'

Sofya knew in that instant what her mistake had been. Her restless mind compulsively working – obliterating, postponing or provoking the horror she wills herself to suffer. Too late. Mordecai Donar has undone the elegance of the solution she has just conceived. The numerology was botched. The first of those thirty-six exposures – his dead eyes open, staring directly at her. It was not enough, if she wanted to map the psychosis of Whitechapel, to shoot only those who requested her services. There was no purity in simply focusing on the eyes of her subjects. She would insist upon obedient, *conscious* masks. If she could doctor Donar, that false start, all was not lost. She wanted accidents, frames where her victims blinked in reflex sympathy: signals she must prime herself to receive. Shuttered faces. Six rows, six frames per row. Ilford FP4 Plus. Immaculate rectangles divided by thin black borders. Number codes running along the base. A single unit. The subjects in choosing to shut their eyes concede the discretion of the image – that was the forfeit, that was how the alchemy would work. Imar O'Hagan on the floor: broken concentration, a momentary detachment from his task, aroused. The perfect opening.

Mordecai Donar was the flaw, the immodesty with which he had revealed himself – cringing persistence. Unless Donar was rectified, all future exposures would be tainted. His look, in the top lefthand corner of the contact sheet, would dominate the others. The craftsman at his table, gabbing as he challenged her, forcing her to shoot as he shrugged with bogus resignation. She could treat him with acid, burn him with light, bleach his face to a featureless blob. Obliterate him in tempera. She could smother the wet print in hair, scratch it with sand. Donar would be lost in a maze of symbols, unpicked like the entrails of one of his clocks. Chopped apart, broken down into a heap of useless springs and cogs.

'. . . in her search for the Isabels. The group could not be made out . . .' Helen curled the hair at the nape of her neck tightly around her finger. *Nostromo*. Reading again what she had never read before. The best loved. A disinterested intimacy. She was an occasional reader, but an obsessive one. Childlike, thumb sneaked into mouth. One sentence could provide the sustenance for a compulsive daydream – which would surely return her to a previously unvisited point in the narrative. Names meant nothing. She would contentedly read the same paragraph over and over. '. . . supreme sinners, objects of hate, abhorrence, and fear, as heretics used to be to a convinced Inquisitor.'

Joseph Conrad belonged to her association with Sileen. It was his book. He read no other author. The last of his collection, it must have been mislaid when the rest were shipped out. Fondly, she sniffed the tanned pages, recovering her lover's exhalations: coarse shag, vindaloo, paranoia – his interminable progress through the one writer he admired without reservation. Taking the grand view of the thing, it was why he had given up fiction.

The tired blue of the calico cloth binding was the colour of Sileen's eyes, a sky innocent of cloud cover, bereft of drama. Perhaps that was why she had chosen to handle this object. Call it affection, at a safe distance, for a familiar monster. The book was in three parts, with *The Isabels* at its centre. The author's initial quotation, a Shakespearean tag, clinched it. 'So foul a sky clears not without a storm.'

She paid no attention to the stuff about Conrad being the 'godfather of magic realism'; the kind of gossip designed to promote an argument, or demonstrate that the perpetrator could pick his way through the *New York Times Book Review* without laughing, belonged to Sammy Taylor. Fuck Taylor. She flicked the pages, skipping fantastical congeries of quotation to find the good bits. The bit about weather. Conrad's weather was worth a thousand nautical miles of hobbled prose. 'In this foretaste of eternal peace they floated vivid and light, like unearthly clear dreams of earthly things that may haunt the souls freed by death from the misty atmosphere of regrets and hopes.' Necrophile meteorology. Nacreous cloudscapes of despair.

Lifting a lustrous nap of hair, Helen ran her hand from the base of her skull to the bony spur at the apex of her cervical vertebrae; half-aware, she stroked the slenderness of her neck – while projecting the anomalies of Conrad's barometer onto the featureless fields of Oxfordshire. That proud Pole, in downriver dejection, in some dank farmhouse, imposing baroque flourishes of South American light – memory and invention. Andi was asleep, her weight pressing on Sofya, who stared out at an agitated sky.

They moved. The coach moved. Helen caressing her own neck, shoulder, arm; no longer reading, the book open, reflected in the sombre glass.

She accedes to a fantasy that would not be possible without the mediating presence of the Conrad novel, the night, the drowsy passengers. The six-pack solitary is snoring heavily. One of his cans, dropped from his hand, is rolling up and down the aisle – like a bubble in the ether of a spirit level. Helen wants her head shaven, closer than the silver of this heavyweight boozer with his artillery of cans. She wants the thin stroke of a razor on her neck. The brutish buzz of a sheep-shearing instrument. The snip of long bladed scissors. All that cultivated, shoulderlength bulk of hair, all the hours in girly salons, cappuccino and gossip, all that exhilaration butchered – a sweep of curls on a checkerboard floor. Culling Helen's modesty. A new being, futuristic and formidable.

The dialogue, out of frame, should be obscene: weekend rubber goods, blue smoke, cheap cologne. 'Was your old man a barber?' The customers, deep chested, welded into three-pieces by Woods of Kingsland Road, growl out their mongrel anecdotes. Fight talk, women stripped on the bone like numbered Smithfield carcasses. The mysteries of the city. Industrial lighting preserves their masculine cave from the twilight street. Helen stretches long legs, a white bib around her neck.

'Three-handed, we were, didn't have a pot to piss in. Lovely feller, my mate, beautiful shoulders, slim hips, Hoxton boy, had the look of Edmund Purdom. I come back from giving one to this Norwegian slag, don't I, find him bunked up with the landlord, on his bleedin' knees, fifteen-to-eighting the bastard. He was dead straight, Jewish boy. Had to chin him. Spark out. Went the full four with Al Phillips, my life.'

MENS HAIRDRESSING. Helen was hurrying down Cambridge Heath Road, neutral territory, making her way back to the safety of the labyrinth: she noticed the sign. Dressing with hair, it appealed to her. If it could be reversed. The door closed with an hydraulic sigh. The men in suits walked out, pumping hands, faking jabs on the pavement. The Turk was shutting up shop, pulling down the blinds. Brushing off the framed Galatasary poster. They were alone. That's how she saw it. That's how she directed this playlet. She shocked herself. A delight.

It demanded a mordantly perverse sensibility to conjure up, and sustain, the barber. To let him approach from behind, an open razor in his paw, was deviant folly. The man spoke no English. His grin of complicity was a carmine slash across sweating suet. He dabbed and blotted. Helen had taken a furtive glance, passing the shop, then quickened her pace. Now she developed her John with transfusions of Akim Tamiroff in *Touch of Evil*. Pomaded, chewing benzedrine and cloves of garlic, he was lecherous and timid in his cruelty. A mail-order greaser whose wig, stitched from pubic clippings, slid erratically across a drenched scalp. The cashewed sweetness was anaesthetic, cold fingers fumbling with the strings of her bib. Unlanguaged flattery. Gold rings pinching the fat of his fingers.

Now it was Helen's turn to flush, drip, stick to the leather of the surgical throne: tilted to meet a new self in the mirror above the washbasin. Running water. Dark patches at her armpits. He circles, clipping and chopping, the blade cool against her cheek. Goose pimples of fearful pleasure. Forced to submit, allowing him whatever he wants to attempt. He grunts. If he gestures at the mirror, she will not look. She fixes on the pencil line above his upper lip and avoids the damage he has inflicted with his sharp tools. She cannot escape, but squirms in the chair, soaked, hungry for any detail to outlast this irreversible event.

Taps, bottles, empty chairs, fan photos. Kemal Atatürk, Martin Bormann. The posters are shrines to the Joseph Mengele Football Club. A dozen heavily-moustached street killers, arms folded, thighs bulging from tiny shorts. Her head was being shaved by a Turkish fascist. Hackney was awash with Turks, Kurds, political renegades. Coffee-houses packed with expelled and proscribed Marxists, landless victims, dislocated activists. Serious cases with sheaths of documents waiting patiently for a Kenyan Asian to feed them into his stuttering photocopy machine. Sad men in lunchtime restaurants making their selection from trays of nostalgic meat. Fly-posting fanatics. Collectors of non-voluntary tributes. And she nominates a retired torture mechanic, a monster too extreme even for a culture of extremity.

The hair curled as it fell; the thickness of it, damp and clinging, inside the open neck of her blouse, into her lap. He worked so fast. She was defenceless. She kept her eyes on the floor. The salsa of his pimp shoes, cream and black, over the marked squares. He whisked away the worst of it, the clammy twists that clung to her shoulders. It was piling horribly around her chair.

The barber handheld a small mirror. Her blouse: it was transparent. She might have stepped straight from the shower. The clearly visible outline of her breasts, the violent bruises of her nipples. Shame. He passes no judgement. Sprays her with puffball scent. Nowhere to set her gaze. The recall of Nicholas Tarten, the same lilac sweetness inside corrupt marble. Perfumed wounds, villainy bandaged in mohair. Above the mirrors, a collection of quiffed and campy portraits. James Dean S/M clones, pompadoured beachboys, pouting oralists. She shuts her eyes.

The swish of a broom, as the Turk shapes her fallen hair into respectable mounds. Who would have believed she had so much?

Mattresses, pillows of the stuff. Cloaks of pelt. Waistcoats of down. That scent. Stronger than ever. In the mirror, grinning, between the boychick pin-ups: Nicholas Tarten. He must have emerged from a backroom. Perhaps he has watched the whole show. The shop flips to mono-chrome. Guilt shadows – crepe de Chine and marsupial felt. Tarten's anaconda on the back of her chair.

We do not escape our ghosts so easily. She is fetched. Helen's flight into Oxfordshire dissolves at Tarten's touch. The posts in the drowned fields are graveyard sculpture, angels and crucifixions. Tarten undresses. His T-shirt and jeans meticulously folded, placed on the red leather. He selects an ivory-handled razor. His head is already shaved: a condemned man previewing his execution. A few swift strokes at the temple, a sweep of the neck, and Tarten's tense curls mingle with her own. The smocked Turk – infinitely calm, infinitely resigned – brushes the clippings. He could be mingling their ashes.

With hideous scrapes and violent abrasions, Tarten works over his body – beneath the arms, along the thighs, his firm flat belly. He flexes, parades, excites himself: prison muscles, the hard sweat of burnouts. A narcissism of hate. The Turk eased his clippers, with a low hum, down the curve of Tarten's spine. The mortician's pale body on a black rubber tile.

Then it is Helen's turn. The bride. Bought and paid for. She stands beside Tarten, not touching him, as the Turk unbuttons her, soaps her nakedness, lifts her arms, spreads her legs. Smooth strokes of the thin-bladed razor. Like stiff paper. Her protection is willingly sacrificed. Eyebrows, wrists, calves. She flinches involuntarily as he moves between her thighs. His indifference, the deftness of his touch. A flicker of pedestrians outside, shredded between the headlights and the slats of the blinds.

She submits. To her own fantasy. The seduction of Tarten's contempt. This scar man, this rumour killer. The arrogance of his lethargy. No choice. There never was. She must accept at once her engagement as an unlicensed boxer.

A gradual intrusion of suburbs. Sofya did not glance up from her book. Helen could not see what her friend was reading. Hospitals and charities. Park and Drive. Streetlamps forcing their tread over Andi's sleeping face, deforming her. The obsession Andi had with the recovery of dreams. Her dream book. Helen wondered if she carried it with her in the holdall. Had she invented the barbershop to tease the interest of this generous Canadian – who lacked the seasoning of irony? Or had Andi, wherever she was, instigated the performance? The wide, reasonable streets choked her. Their madness was so easily contained. Helen was fretting against privileges that had barely been asserted. Oxford was under a curfew of repression. The coach driver obeyed traffic signals where there were no signals to be encountered.

As they juddered forward yet again, Helen looked down on the only creatures left on their feet – a mud-spattered, filthy, staggering duo. One limped heavily, the other was burdened with a preposterous rucksack. Tinkers of fortune. Heads bent. The road their only constant, they were reluctant to foreswear its petty indignities. Beyond charity, they portered their resentments towards the place best suited to receive them. Legends of bread and small beer, warm broth, a coin in the hand. The insanity of a quest exhausted by its execution.

Helen knew them and turned, blushing, away. They were the past she was escaping, the future her sensual mooning had induced. She witnessed the last remnants of the Poor Law out on the trot. Soaking wet, they had paid their dues, and were primed for slaughter. Todd Sileen and his ghastly companion, Rhab Adnam.

TWO

Angels do not know what time is, although with them there is a successive progression of all things.

The head of Emanuel Swedenborg was preserved in a suede slipcover, laced with thongs. His amethyst eyes were open. The powdered wig sent taproots wriggling into his skull. Peppered horsehair had seeded and grafted onto bone. Life-in-Death. Unextinguished. Flesh soft as a girl at her first communion. Sweet as hay. So it was rumoured. By those who guarded the relic. Those who carried it, at night, by secret passageways, from the fridge of the Crown & Dolphin to the Kinder Street basement.

In eternity *all* eyes are open. Abimael Guzman, philosopher of terror, had published *On the Kantian Theory of Space*. Knowledge in advance of experience. Space and Time as non-sensible intuitions valid for all sensory appearances. Those who carried the caput of Swedenborg followed the Sendero Luminoso, also known as the Line of Force, the True Path, the track across an urban wilderness. Honouring that path to-day, we encounter the Invisible Ones – and are ourselves unnoticed. It shines like snail-paint and is found by those who have learnt to trust their *a priori* instincts. The inside and the outside of the world-mind. No demonstrations are necessary. Call it fate. Call it dialectical materialism. Call it converse with intelligent ancestors. There was lodged in Wapping a form of New Age terrorism. Marx, Lenin, Mao, the Panther. *Pachacuti* – when one millennium gives way to another. GUZMAN ESTA AQUI. His arrest was black propaganda.

Hearts are clocks to be torn from their envelopes of flesh. The red sun of the Incas; mountain dwellers who believed that white men would melt down their bodies to extract the grease. Strange fusions: terror cells and the myths of the Andes. Kinder Street, a forgotten tributary, is the storm pool. A ruined laboratory in which these spores can mate.

Carboniferous mist from the river. Articulate smoke from the hospital chimney. Possession of Swedenborg's mantic skull conferred power. To see with his eyes: the bright chain of correspondences. As above, so below. Indestructible atoms. The poor and the destitute, a resource in their abundant anonymity. Faceless numbers to be sacrificed. The already-dead who can die no more.

The bagged trophy was set on the table. Swedenborg talked freely with the ghosts who were now his keepers. This was a System of Hell he had not foreseen in his nights of wandering, when he slipped ashore from the plague-ship. The apples of his orchard were bitter with worms. His church was a careless dispersal of landfill. The black water in the memorial font took the fingernails from anyone foolish enough to risk the sign of the cross.

By these attentions, the false disciples suckled upon Swedenborg's holy visions. They would caress the occipital condyle, soothing the seat of his affections. They wanted entry to hell's earthworks. They would burrow like sand-moles to undermine the foundations of a besieged city. They pressed, this circle of expectant faces – black suits reinforced by hooded sweatshirts. White scalps. Bone ridges glistening in candlelight. The unsheathed head alert on the altar. Interrogators surrounding it, straining to interpret: a crystal set stitched from exposed meat.

Always closer. This thing they needed to know. The precise location of hell's gate.

Swedenborg had no sense of *who* was putting the question. His rhetoric – like Dr Paisley's – was available on demand: a seamless monologue, a loop with no end and no beginning.

'Some hells present an appearance like the ruins of houses and cities after conflagrations, in which infernal spirits dwell and hide themselves. In some cases contiguous in the form of a city with lanes and streets, and within the houses are infernal spirits engaged in unceasing quarrels, enmities, fighting, brutalities. There are underground tunnels into which those flee who are pursued by others.'

'Can these entrances be discovered?' The chief interrogator ran his thumb down a scimitar-scar. The attentive bureaucrats leaned forward in their chairs. Recording devices hummed like birds-of-paradise.

'As to the positions of the hells, it is something wholly unknown even to the angels in heaven.'

'But you, Great Seer, who are neither in heaven nor hell, know both. You can aid us.'

'The position in general is known from the quarters in which they are. There are also hells beneath hells. Some communicate with others by transits. How great the number is of the hells I have been permitted to realize from knowing that there are hells under *every* mountain, hill, and rock, and that they stretch out beneath these in length and in breadth and in depth. In a word, the entire heaven and the entire world of spirits are, as it were, excavated beneath, and under them is a continuous hell.'

'It is this continuous hell that we wish to penetrate.' Swedenborg was the lantern by which they could navigate. Remote-control cameras, bolted to dollys, had already penetrated to the limits of the sewer system, branching through stores of abandoned military hardware, decommissioned platforms, buried files, earthed-in rivers. Nothing. Every inch of the tape, played and replayed, had been analysed; rewound and frozen until the monochrome procession of tile and flood had entered the very souls of the programmers.

The lost rivers of London – Black Ditch, Walbrook, Neckinger, Effra, Tyburn – affected all surface life; our moods swung to their unpredictable subterranean tides. They were our unconscious. Somewhere in that drifting unfocused world the link was to be found. A door would open on the mysteries of life and death, being and non-being, good and evil. That was Swedenborg's benediction, his curse. That was why they tormented his exhausted skull. The visionary had passed beyond inhibition, touched his tongue to the spectre in the flame.

Todd Sileen sat up on his mattress, rigid with fear. Sleep was impossible, but the dreams still came, uninvited, one after another, or in pairs, competing for his attention. His single sheet was soaked. He wrapped up his nakedness and whimpered. Without her mediating presence, Helen's room was unbearable. Her absence let in all the others: Drage-Bell, Askead, O'Hagan, Sliema Felix. High-collar gangsters, company men, spooks, exterminators. The cripple could not decide which fiction to avoid. He twisted and rolled, spreading his hand to search beneath the pillow for Helen's nightdress. It was time for flight.

They had sealed his exits. Oxford was the only option. He must gather Adnam and trust to the demented pilgrim's psychic compass. A penniless road was better than the alternative, a city shrinking by every hour he remained in it. He would brush off his demons and bring Helen back. At the end of a rope, if necessary. He was checkmated, but it wasn't over yet.

He punched out the nearest window, to let in the night air. He drew a long breath. Keep moving. That was the answer. Things were never so bad if you stayed on your feet (or what was left of them). If you chased the sun, walked until the blood ran out from your shoes.

The street was deserted. None of Sileen's self-inflicted vessels of wrath had the courage to declare themselves. A few days of Adnam's ramblings was a small price to pay for a healthy slice of English landscape. Something was out there. No point in fooling himself. He felt it before he saw it. Hanging from the streetlight, swinging in the quiet breeze of the world's motion – a decapitated dog, smeared with red paint. Dripping a Pollockian circumference onto the pavement. Sileen knew, at once, what *that* meant.

THREE

Extracts from the Journals of Rhab Adnam
*(Edited with his permission, and somewhat revised,
by the present author.)*

DAY ONE. The triangulation burns like a brand. A shape in the stars. All night, in Vicky Park, watching, waiting. No revelation.

Finally, at first light, the wind spoke – gave me a direction. The pistils of the mid-lake fountain dispersed in a fine mist. Natural arcanum. A compass made from water.

'Rejoice,' as Kit Smart instructs, 'with the Water-Rail, who takes delight in the river.' As we must. Run to Oxford, City of Secrets.

There *is* a plan, a necessity. I am nervous of premature articulation. It's better unspoken. I'll speak. Obey the triangle, honour the mounds: Whitechapel, Oxford, Cambridge. Only by stamping its weight into the ground will we recover the meaning of Whitechapel's stolen pyramid. They removed it, carted it away. CURSE their stupidity, their sugarloaf hats and silver buttons. East London lost its gate, the solitary elevation that licensed all those subterranean rat-runs.

It is my duty to seek confirmation of the surviving earthworks. Oxford – does it still stand? The grassy breast at New Road, its deep well and sacred grove. Then Cambridge, once familiar, a small summit, a Castle, granting views of King's College Chapel and the Gog Magog hills.

Connect these beacons, return that connection to London, the source and origin. Knit the triangle. Affirm it in blood and blisters.

On Vallance Road I make the first entry: a damp newspaper wraps itself around my leg. The omen is evil, but I am obliged to check for subliminal messages, before folding the remnant as many times as it will stand, hammering it into a slit in the crumbling brickwork of the bridge. Let ink bleed into mortar.

'ON THIS DAY: the Campbells murdered the Macdonalds at the Glencoe Massacre, 1692; Asiatic cholera first appeared in Limehouse and Rotherhithe, London, 1832; Strauss's waltz The Blue Danube was first played in Vienna, 1867.'

Clearing the hospital, Cannon Street Road, I saw him ahead of me. The furious Sileen. Flinching from a presumption of buildings; hunched, bombasine, heavy in shoulder. He moves fast. His walk is a form of punting, the stiff limb repels the stone flags, drives him on. He detours around the human traces – caffs, open windows, the domesticity of slap and scream. Suspicious, he sniffs the foul air, hesitates. Turns, recognizes me. No surprise. Doesn't slacken his pace. Contraction of brows, a mime of rage. He's sick, horribly pale – face set in plaster of Paris.

The jetty. We had not exchanged a word, St Katherine's Dock; we both understood what lay ahead. The obvious drama of Tower Bridge, upstream, sheathed in polythene: Sileen had no time for this debased icon. His eyes, as I followed them, went downriver. A reflex of sentiment. The tincture of redgold in the East. A green lantern on a pole. Low wharves, smelted and foul. Thin rashers of cloud, inches above the horizon. Old water, pitted, rippling. Sweet Thames, colourless as used plasticene. We would have stayed there forever, time on hold, if a riverboat had not churned alongside, manoeuvring, backing in towards the shuddering boards, fracturing our meditation. Not for us, this luxury. Expelled paupers, we took to our heels.

A turbid morning, no shatter of sunbursts. No light, but what our boots can strike from the pavement. Hooked over embankment walls, gasping under bridges: the triangulation is our ballast. We must endure the long drudgery of shaking free from Whitechapel (where the bitch, URBAN TIME, has whelped). The further from the centre, the faster we must travel to maintain the same momentum. But faster *is* faster. The time-spiral relents as we strain against its antiquated bonds.

I pleaded again for Waterloo or Westminster Bridge: homage to William Blake, Bedlam's illuminated dome, Elias Ashmole at rest in the church of St Mary ('durante Musaeo Ashmoleano Oxon. nunquam moriturus'). The energy nexus Sileen refuses to celebrate. Neither would he yield to the garden beside Lambeth Palace, a cursory tribute to the herbalist and scavenger, John Tradescant the Younger. I carry his postcard in my pocket, the portrait attributed to Emmanuel de Critz. A marvel! Woolly skull at the great gardener's elbow, mulched by his secret formula. Driftwood bone carpeted in ginger curls. Tradescant's collar and the hem of his shirt blooming with lace daisies. A living man in affectionate company with Brother Death, observing, in amazement, the daffodils that burst forth between the sticks of his ribs.

O Sileen, so stubborn, now you'll never know Lambeth, lamb of the river, unspoilt pasture. Tradescant (the Elder) built his Ark here, his storehouse of curiosities, London's first museum. He exhibited (entry 6d) Powhatan's Mantle, the shamanistic deerskin of Pocahontas' father. A forked man at the centre of four stitched sections, bombarded with shells, spirals of wild light. Sufficiently arcane to fix the attention of the alchemist, Ashmole. Who acquired the house and land adjoining the property. His part in the suicide of Mrs Tradescant, the collector's relict, remains obscure. The grave goods, the Virginian rarities, the botanical specimens (along with the surviving papers of Dr John Dee), passed into his hands and were carted off to Oxford. Understand this fable and our journey is validated before it begins.

Sileen will have nothing to do with it. 'Didn't sign on for a spook's tour,' he grunts, opening out his stride. The Peace Pagoda, gold as an instrument of pure thought, has to be viewed from a distance. 'Om,' I chanted, 'rejoice with Buteo who hath three testicles.'

Beyond Battersea Bridge, we slogged, heads down. A mushroom crop of fresh blisters had us stuttering like platform-heeled fashion victims, the placement of each foot an ecstasy of spiritual torment. Something describing itself as 'Chelsea Harbour' (neither in Chelsea, nor a harbour) hid within a pall of black smoke from the Power Station. A prison of the soul. 'The modesty of Cardinal Wolsey and the good taste of Donald Trump,' Sileen muttered.

Bad faith drove us from the sight of the river: we were edgy, snapping, tired. Private sports grounds, builders' merchants, leafy streets where every lamppost advertises a lost dog.

An avenue of moulting plane trees, Bishop's Park. We can breathe again, the river our lung. Protected, ecclesiastical land. The lavender drench of the herb garden. We sprawl at the edge of a circular pond in the gravelled courtyard of Fulham Palace.

Refreshed by the spray from the small fountains, Sileen scoops a slimy pawful. Fat goldfish easing through their syncopated dance. A cloistered, collegiate atmosphere (such as can only be delineated by a foreigner: Pasolini, his *Canterbury Tales*). I flash to Cambridge. These fish are the colour of Simon Undark's tie. Undark, hermit and scribe, the conscience of England (retired). His one vanity, the virulence of his neckware.

Sileen plunges. Surely he can't be as desperate as that? His fist unclenches, he grins. A trawl of dull coins. Paydirt! Boots off, we paddle and scoop – till soaked pockets can hold no more. Sileen, recovered, sitting on the brick rim, caressing his stump. 'Affirm one leg,' he challenges, 'and I'll grant you the rest.'

Hammersmith. This time Sileen *must* cross the water, or I'll be forced to abandon him. There's too much at stake, the project in balance. Our voyage has been sanctioned as a three-legged race. Failing, he hangs on to me. The pain he suffers is a pain that's shared. My tears in his eyes. He knows he must quit the North shore. But the other bank is worse than Europe, it's a country of the dead.

I kiss him full on the lips. He responds, a reflex, forces his tongue down my throat. What a freakshow! Traffic swerving to give us a wide berth. Hoots and whistles from a stalled coach. We cling together, each daring the other to be the first to step onto the bridge.

We can't have it all. Chiswick Eyot at low tide, a tufty islet in a bath of mustard. Sacrifices have to be made. The houses of William Morris and Hogarth the Painter, the obelisk (*Imitatio Ruris*) in the grounds of Lord Burlington's villa.

Sileen rattles his coins, gesturing to the parade of waterside pubs. We'd never get through the door. Blue plaque territory, gourmands in distressed corduroy. Yellow and red Labour Party endorsements in the windows of wisteria-enveloped Georgian mansions.

A face, high above us, hidden behind the blue-tint of the coach's glass, witnesses our embrace. 'Helen!' Sileen yells. 'Isabel!' An understandable fantasy, as the light fails, our long day's exhaustion. His desire stalls the traffic. Pressed against the window, staring, blind, into the darkness – a woman. The brass rule of his lust falters, he refutes the evidence of his own eyes. Sunshine on our backs, rain in our faces. The bus is released from its psychic stranglehold. The sun, an angry boil, sizzles into the river. Sileen, howling, storms onto the flapping jaw of the bridge.

NIGHT. Ensconced, steaming, in the windowseat of the White Hart. Our black spirit-doubles outside, hovering enviously over the waters of Mortlake. Autographed oars hung above the bar. The guv'nor flaunts a limegreen bowtie. The lid of the piano is nailed down, a small mercy. The barman, working the pump, pronounces 'pianist' as 'penis'.

Pacing our coins, we share a pint of Guinness. Taking our turn at sipping the cream. Sileen is all heat: cinnabar, indignation. He excavates, from the depths of his jacket, a small blue twist of salt. He licks the sticky pyramid from his open palm. Eyes like a starving wolf. Growls at the portrait on the wall. It could be his hand-mirror. The same anger, vanity as a penance. A spoiled intelligence. Sir Richard Burton (1821–1890): 'Some thousand miles up river with an infinitesimal prospect of returning! I ask myself "Why?" and the only echo is "damned fool . . . the Devil drives." '

A compulsive annotator, Sileen should never have thrown down his pen. By refusing to write, he has lost command of his fictions, inflicting them on the rest of us. Now Burton will torment us, the unfinished manuscript his wife cast into the flames.

The diversion is unwelcome. I confess it, I coaxed Sileen to this place for another reason entirely. It was the benevolent mathematician, Dr John Dee, I presumed to contact. Could we not solicit the blessing of the Magus and his enigmatic legman, Edward Kelly (or Kelley)? The angel magick, the crystal, the Welsh tinctures. Was it permitted – that the scholar's upstream retreat should be invaded by future mountebanks?

Looking around the bar, I could see that nothing had changed. The locals were the same dismal crew that ransacked Dee's library (one of the great Elizabethan resources – 4,000 books, 700 choice manuscripts), as soon as he was safely out of the way. Like jabbing a fire-hardened stick into his brain jelly. They smashed his laboratory: retorts, matrasses, flasks, crucibles. Made a Beltane bonfire of the maps, star charts, hieroglyphs.

Sileen refuses to give credence to my tale. Turns his back on the relevant postcard from my collection: John Dee (anonymous, British School) in the Ashmolean, Oxford, displayed alongside the entrance to the Tradescant room. I try to explain how the painting has to be viewed while standing on your head: the ruff becomes a set of coral shoulder-wings, the poignard beard transforms itself into the vertical coif of a fire-beast. A revenging demon, eyeless in a dunce's cap. Lacking hands, yet able to fly. Suth, Maguth, Gutrix: names that provoke horror in all who summon them.

A dreadful hunger. Fish or meat. We'd eat anything, alive or dead. They've pitched us out onto the foreshore, Dee's estate, between river and church. The Queen, riding out from Richmond, to consult him. Sir Philip Sidney coming by water. I dowsed the claggy towpath for omens, holding Sileen back. He was ready to finish it, throw himself in, take his chances. I agonized over small sharp stones. A shard, curiously faceted, green glass: I tested it against the moon's lucidity. Could it be? Dee's crystal? Or the neck of a wine bottle, impossibly cold? Trust it, Rhab. Follow its prompting.

Up the slippery steps and away from the river, hurdling our shadows; warmer, ever warmer, the crystal burning in my fist. The High Street, then, abruptly, by a transit of alleys, close passages, to the church of St Mary the Virgin. Oleander, pine, clouts of lavender: the burial place of the Magus, of John Dee. We are obliged to walk under a stone collar, a solitary arch that requires no supporting edifice. Whoever searches among these tombstones finds his own name.

We've done it, we're lost. The bottletop scorching my skin. Night is on us, and a great weariness. Outside the churchyard it's the same desolation. Domestic enclosures glimpsed by the blue flicker of TV candles: pot plants, museum quality telephones, considered grids of paperbacks. Moonlight polishing the silver tracks. Utterly confounded. We climb onto the footbridge over the railway. Nothing left. Prospects hopeless. Must rest. A place to crash out. The headlights of passing cars preview the dereliction. Another church? Mary Magdalen?

But sanctuary is not on offer, not for us, the doors bolted against invaders. Broken, we circumnavigate the building, skulk into the undergrowth, the graveyard.

Hacking through the brambles in that unreal light (the wattage of liquid stone), I felt that my thorn-wounds belonged to someone else. No pain. Blood like honey. Sileen halts, refuses to move, overcome by a name he has discovered on the righthand page of a marble book: ISABEL. CAPTAIN on the facing slab. I scan his excitement too rapidly: CAIN/ABEL. A shrine in the half-woods. Caught in the moonlight reflected from frosty leaves. The tomb of Isabel Burton, a good Catholic. PRAY FOR HER. The justified wife (née Arundell) of Ruffian Dick, river pirate, journal-keeper, glutton for dark meat. ('I have got to live with him night and day.')

What a memorial! Memories, true and false, breeding on the shelves of this maggot hatchery. Sir Richard Burton, KCMG., FRGS., died Trieste. THE ENGLISH SCHOLAR AND THE ARAB SHEIK. A family-sized sepulchre, 18 foot high, sculpted in Forest of Dean stone and white Carrara marble. A Bedouin tent pegged out in Mortlake; wind-ruffled, the creases frozen in eternity. Room for their bones to stretch out. Lady Isabel swore it: I would rather be killed by an embalmer's needle than recover consciousness underground. Where better to bivouac our first night on the road? Who else should we honour?

Isabel: the obedient helpmate, tireless widow. 'I would like us both to lie in a tent, side by side,' Dick had said. And it was so. Secure in this jousting shed, he would never again escape her influence, plunge into jungles and forbidden cities. His manuscripts and private journals, she torched. He worked until his last breath on a 'manual of erotology', considering it the 'crown of his life.' A pillow of ashes. From his failing grip into the flames.

Our tent, lacked nothing – except a door. Unable to control my excitement, I seized Sileen's wrist and led him in a voyage of discovery. Lady Burton held séances on hubby's coffin, boiled tea on a spirit-burner, nibbled seedcake. His deathbed voice: 'Quick Puss! Chloroform, ether . . .' She refused him all medicines without the presence of a doctor. The jingle of camel bells on a faulty line.

Sileen mounted a ship's ladder, hidden at the rear of the stone tent, and, finding a glass panel, elbowed it. Headbutted the splinters. He swung himself down into the tomb. A sacrilege of dust and bone flakes. Agitated particles dampened by the spray of his arterial blood. He was reclaiming a vacant identity.

There was oil still in the lamp. Coagulated book objects to be examined. We lit the lamp, and waited.

Lying in the filtered yellow darkness, the strangest of sensations. Sileen, his Merv Hughes moustache rising and falling as he lolls on Burton's gilded box, sucking at his wounds. Eyes open, unblinking.

Stone furniture. The small library reduced to rodent powder. Black smoke. Cherubs, crucifixes, bell-pulls, a good firm mattress: the sepulchre is better equipped than a villa on the Algarve. I am shelved, without impropriety, on top of Isabel.

The desert of nocturnal London. Owls, ambulances. A strong start.

DAY TWO. Sundance on water – molecules and corpuscles and jewels in the blood revive; they fire and connect. Walk becomes song. Wind pipes in the reeds. Alexander Pope's *Pastoral*. 'Blest Thames's shores the brightest beauties yield, / Feed here my lambs, I'll seek no distant field.'

For the interim, striding out along the towpath, we must snack upon the sorrows of Mortlake, the Crematorium, smoke plumes and a building of Californian weirdness. Out early: it was still as quiet as the day they incinerated poor Stephen Ward. The black glasses that wouldn't melt.

A rush of wind through sycamore and willow. Morning is our shot at bliss. Step for step: hell or Richmond. Sileen walks in silence, powdered in dust like a Hindoo mendicant – Burton's bone talcum. He leans on a thorn stick torn from the graveyard. The river tolerates us. Kew Gardens: cult of 'Chinese irregularity.'

Syon House: a rooftop of basking lions. We're on the cusp, pulling free; the weave of PRESENT TIME is unspooling. The Whitechapel Vortex (and the storms that gambol around the absence of the White Mount) are dissipated. Obelisks, darts of the Empyrean, are needles puncturing entropy. They channel ropes of energy, keep the land alive.

Are we far enough out? Hard to tell. There's the irrational wish for some new system of belief to announce its advent. Intimations of a less frenzied life. Retirement, meditation – giving rise to a landscape of gardens, grottoes, follies.

A low sky, feathery and fast: effortlessly, we achieve the momentum of sewage flow. 3 mph. Sileen is revived, pivoting, throwing out his stiff leg. Brandishing his thorn. Fencing at wasps. Driven: an alpha male glorying in his horn. We've made all the right moves. The floating vision of bridge and hill confirms it. The grandest sweep in our sacred land. A truce with nature, wilderness tamed and shaped. A promenade of angels: Isleworth to Twickenham. The glory of Richmond Hill. Woods, herds, palaces. No permissions to be purchased.

We find ourselves entering 'view' and becoming part of it. The width of the sky colludes with man's nervous revisions of the landscape. A balance – whereby earth and air and water (interchangeable elements) swivel and spin. It is almost time. We must cross back over the river, but not yet. I don't want to disturb Sileen's high. He was tired, limping out of Old Deer Park and up to Richmond Bridge, a sleepwalker. Gradually, the effects of the *plein-air* acupuncture (and the escape from White-chapel) induce a ruralist buzz. Hat in hand. Thorn raised like a wand. 'Bonjour, Monsieur Courbet!' Matutinal, hearty, he salutes wired joggers, leashed dog-women. Holy Sileen, lovely man! He recaptures the ebullience with which, last night, he greeted the Stag Brewery and all its cock-red banners.

We saunter broad terraces, significant fakes, boathouses; barbecued chicken on the breeze, skiffs riding the swell. But there is a squalor mortgaging the Palladian, lice in the periwig. This notion of the Thamesside village as a retreat. Horatian exile for poets, Catholics, the mistresses of princelings. Caves and shrines. A steady drift from the corrupted centre.

'Smooth flow the waves, the Zephyrs gently play.' The ferryboat is summoned on a yell. Outboard chugging. Sileen can't believe his luck – just two days on the tramp and he's copping his first ride. Thames like a spill of liquid lead. Between worlds, between weather.

Now the pressure really bites; to cover (honour/activate) *all* the points of interest, the deposits of aboriginal virtue (Marble Hill, the fountains and statues of York House, Pope's gardens and grotto, Strawberry Hill, the birthplace of Gerald Kersh in Teddington), without diverting us from the narrative quest, the miles that must be knocked off before the sun sets.

Caffeine. Grit in milkscum, a sluggish clockwise spin. We are not comfortable outside the sandwich-bar in Marble Hill Park. A chill runs under the arriviste splendour of the eighteenth century. Sash windows cannot open on fine prospects, shadow-dappled lawns, without the accompanying signifiers of doom: fever, slavery, gin, the lash. Scalding coffee blisters our lips. A wasp paddles in Sileen's grungy wounds. A sting on the tongue would enliven him. He laps the slop from his saucer as if it was something rare and difficult to describe, a taste to hold in the memory.

———

St Mary's Church, Twickenham, is locked, but Pope's tribute to his nurse and 'faithful old servant', Mary Beach, is visible, cleanly carved. Sileen pays homage, after a fashion, by gnawing on a compressed ball of raisins, chocolate, peanuts, and herbs, that he has dug out from my pouch. Any sop to plug his terror. He confesses: he has lost faith in my ability to guide him. Too many Sions (signs).

'Popes Villa'. The missing apostrophe converts this redbrick mansion – an atrocity of tower and tile – into a retirement home for nuns. We hammered at the door, unnerved by an excess of blind windows. Sanctuary! The silence screamed madness: repression, lithium, mepro-bamate, Horlicks, approved radio. The poet's retreat torn down. A villa is anything that lacks a sense of the absurd.

I bundle the convulsive Sileen, jacket streaked with paint from the blitzing traffic, into Pope's Grotto. Pope's Grotto? That's a pub. Signboard of the savage wit resting on an elbow, book open, faking contemplation. A pose that Sileen mimics. The poet to the life (the one they called 'ape', 'monkey', 'crookback', 'little virulent Papist'). The boiling urgency has been leeched from our quest. Oxford is now as remote as London. There are leftovers on greasy plates, crusts and cheese rinds, olive pits with traces of green flesh. Sileen sucks, chilli sauce blooding his fog moustache. Surely an afternoon for drinking the last of our currency.

EVENING. We woke under a leaking sky, our bones cushioned on the soft riverside paddy. An infantryman tilted to challenge us from the plinth of a war memorial. His heavy coat, blown open, is a triangle of invitation. His Lee Enfield points at the stars. So innocent, boyish, vain – the camaraderie of pipe and mouth-organ. The flirtation with mud and horror.

Willows to the waterline. Melancholy. A lost hour between dusk and darkness. Shadows of the advancing dead. We press our swollen ears to the ground to catch the thunder of marching battalions, the legions of hell.

It was Sileen's idea. Give him credit for unexpected enterprise. (He'd just finished peeing into a turning tide.) That we should slip over the wall into Pope's garden and crash the *real* grotto. If it still existed. After Burton's funerary tent, where better? Or let us drown in the attempt.

Be sure, I was prepared: photocopies, pages and pages of grotto plans.

Pope's sketches, annotated, of January and December 1740 (a surfeit of allusions). John Serle's draft of 1745 – with the nine chambers. Sam Lewis' engraving of 1785: cave, statue, dark cavern, mirror in the roof.

A splendid notion, this creation of original ruins. Imported statuary, ballast, rock, shells. The scheme refined as it was executed. A dwarf waiting for his cave. A beast for his labyrinth.

I can't believe we're doing this. I can see the pair of us, as if from a distant point on the opposite bank, as we drip across the lawn to the house. We approach the iron gates, and freeze: a smear of light is tracking us from behind the dirty groundfloor windows. A throwing of bolts. A torch-beam sweeps the bushes, the shrubs in which we crouch.

The beam moves on. Now the figure is leading us. Hooded, dressed in a loose black bag – a woman. Struggling, she frees the padlock. The gate scrapes against the stone, granting entrance to the grotto.

We trace the amplified clatter of her footfall. A high-heeled nun sweeping along a low, rough-walled passage. Her slithery cloak billows out, shorting against a tangle of wires. Where has she gone? According to my chart, the 'Cave of Pope' is away to our left, while the narrower bore, leading to the 'Dark Cavern', is to our right.

We hold back while I puzzle over Pope's holograph addendum: '. . . from hence into the River under ground.' Are we lodged in the bore of a sewage outlet? A water-course? Beams of showband light, reflected from the mirror-glass fragments in the cave's roof, trap us within a spectral pyramid. The nun's torch. She turns. The death mask of Alexander Pope. Her teeth are black stones. Her eyes are feathers. There is no back to her head.

She vanishes. And the pitted grin with her. Darkness.

One consciousness, Adnam and Sileen, must be divided, split like the median lobe. Batteries of skin. The salt of fear. We are divorced by a discretion of terror. While I survey Pope's Cave, Sileen must be banished to the nympheum. I bid him crawl, by touch, down the flinty trench: to make his peace with the surviving statues.

Keep it simple, comprehensible. And the MEANING of the event will be comprehensible also. Allow the prose to run away and we're lost. We'll never get out, ghosts among ghosts. If I can describe it, it *must* happen. Pope's mineshaft reconstructed by desire. WHY, out of such an apparently ordered life, did the poet labour like a mole on this subversive folly? This annex of the Gothick.

FACT: under instruction from William Borlase, Pope ransacked R. Allen's Bath quarries. In a kind of delirium, he acquired the fruits of Cornish excavations. 'Spur, Mundick, Copper and Tin': illegitimate cargoes. He trembled over a fine Piece of Marble from the Grotto of Egeria. He imitated natural strata; spar effects, glitter, pebbledash. Infusions of tin ore, copper ore, lead ore, soap rock, white lead. All the degrees and conditions of transparency. They surrounded me now. Eclectic, insane. Hell's catheter. The walls of the tunnel bubbling with unhatched life-forms.

Doubled over, spasms in the gut – hunger or the vanity of starvation. Pope's mocking words: 'Broccoli and Mutton round the year . . . The Devil's in you if you cannot dine.' I can't move, can't breathe. Airless air.

Fissures, angular breaches, a variety of flints. The chamber is contracting. A voice in the stone: 'Dying is just a change of tense.' Sileen, blind as a mustard gas victim, worms his way along the trench; skins his knuckles on fossil shells. The source and engine of his present dream – WAR! X-ray flashback casualties. Direct translation to Passchendaele. All the regiments of Great War statuary brought to life. Bayonets, loud halloos. Helmets and howitzers. X-ray faces, grey as rain. Glass flesh. Our tunnel flooding with transparencies out of the past. Colours that don't belong: *the choir of greys between violet and copper*.

Sileen sinks to his knees, his arms raised above his head. Warding off the superimposed portraits of dead soldiers. The phantom water accessing through the walls. If his heart slows to mud, he'll be drawn into that poem: 1915, Saturday night, June 12. Wilfred Owen and Isaac Rosenberg, *both*, walking the streets of Whitechapel. Before embarkation, before France. Mapping that territory and hardly knowing why. 'I thought a little ugliness would be refreshing; and striking east . . . walked into Whitechapel High Street, and the Whitechapel Road. Ugliness! I never saw so much beauty . . .'

The London Hospital, even then, insisted on its toll, a scrape of memory plasm. Doomed poets on the leash of fate. Owen and Rosenberg, the same night, the same streets. In silence. The Whitechapel Warren branching into the Ypres Salient. Owen and Rosenberg. Adnam and Sileen. *Strange Meeting*. Not known to each other. The poem's necrophile spin, its reaming of unpliant nakedness. 'Scooped'. 'Groined.' 'Groaned'. 'Bestirred'. 'Probed'. 'Made moan'. 'Spoiled'. 'Jabbed'. An erotology of verbs.

'Loath and cold', shivering, sweating, Sileen gagged on limestone smegma: a tunnel that was contracting around his ribs. He beat his head against the flints. I suffered the reverberations. A shuffle of rats on yellow newspapers. A concert party called 'The Splints'. I draw myself into a defensive ball.

The eyes of the statue of the Virgin are painted red, critically so. They swivel and wink. We are being watched! Surveyed. Upstairs, a kitchen-cabinet of nuns are using us as bedtime entertainment. Cocoa and horse-blanket dressing-gowns. We are blobs on a monochrome screen. Fear has us mugging in a spastic tarantella.

We flee from the red eye, the lens. It leeches our heat. Back towards the river. Ammonites lacerate my lungs. Whose nightmare, his or mine? Memory soldiers tramping behind us. Sileen's face imprinted by the locked iron gate.

All of our terror is decanted into the furred domesticity of the nun's kitchen. A whistling kettle. Steam from the neck of a rubber bottle. Condensation on the TV screen masks the finish. Scourges, bells. Brilliant blades sewn into the hem of an underskirt.

DAY FIVE. Forgiven is forgotten. An avenue of poplars, bordering woodland, reflected in calmly racing water. Balance in nature. Quiet colours: ochres, greens, golds. The blood of berries. We move as the world moves, as the river flows. To the murmur of morning. The leathery jeer of rooks, a sardonic umbrella. Light is sacred. We cannot corrupt it. The fluvial rush floods our lifestream.

Le Pauvre Sileen. My knees have gone, I walk in splints. With him it's blisters. His boots haven't come off in days – not since the incident in the pub at Henley, the thing with the water bailiff. The sole of his foot, a pad of squelching puffballs. And that was *then*. Each step amplifies the agony. He audibly creaks. Stump raw as prime beef. Clings to his staff as to the mast of a sinking schooner. Bless his folly. Without pain he would have nothing. It's his lodestone, his motor. I must not wean him with consolations, promises of future reward. If each advance were not a fresh torture, his essential being would hook itself over a thornbush and cry out, 'No mas!' He'd quit on his stool like Roberto Duran.

We slept last night in a woodpile at Wallingford, crawled in amongst a creaking stack of pallet-boards. Snored loud enough to drown the crunching of beetles.

I woke to the stench of sodden paper smouldering in a pathetic bonfire. Sileen warming his hands. He'd managed a few puffs on a cigar stub flung from a passing motor. The journals, filched from my coat, were all he could contrive in the way of kindling.

I recover a few early pages, the rest is smoke. Let it disperse over the drowned fields. Sileen's generosity, in destroying our recent past, has freed us. All journeys, one journey, catch the earth current, the serpentine weave of the Michael and Mary ley lines. Was yesterday's vision at Medmenham, St Mary's Abbey? Or was that on the walk to Ireland? The jaunt with Tom Blaker and Morrie Goldstein, battling down the Ridgeway? It couldn't matter less. Absorb all revelation into this reality of clear light, distance, larksong. This preternatural awareness of sound: a single leaf sawing at the trembling air, a worm pinched in the beak of a bird.

Dorchester-on-Thames (more properly, Thame) is worth a detour: holy ground. Birinius, missionary monk, dipped Cynegils, the first Christian King of Wessex, in the willow stream. Oswald, King of Northumbria, standing godfather. Greensand and Gault clay of the Cretaceous. The Sinodun Hills are beacons on the floodplain. Chalk pilgrims must still pay their dues, pace out the network of burial sites, mounds grazed by glossy cattle. An alluvial island. Abbeys and ancient inns no longer distribute crusts, they charge a premium for their continued survival.

In passing down Watling Lane we scrump a few sour apples – and are then tracked along the otherwise deserted High Street by an affectionate swarm of mongols in reversed baseball caps. They stick to Sileen like multicolour burs. At his heels, attempting no deeper an intimacy. We process in a ragged file to the Abbey. They quit at the door. Wait outside in an expectant semicircle.

Wall-paintings in the People's Chapel. A 14th century crucifixion in earthy reds: the crosstree, sun and moon. Invoking Paul Nash's *Landscape of the Vernal Equinox*; the same deities hovering over the Wittenham Clumps. Waxy tomb-sleepers in the rictus of death. Battle honours, bits of flags. Fire windows: ruby splashes, blue robes, shadow patterns fibrillating on the north wall. Through light, its infusion, the dream is made manifest. The dreamer is released.

Sileen staggers over the road to the timber-framed George, and down the yard to the Gents. The speed of his exit catches me on the hop. I trace him by scouting the tail of the Down's syndrome crocodile. He's done, excavated and abluted, hair plastered to skull, by the time I reach the street. He has enjoyed, so he reports, the mother of bowel movements – the first since London. He howled as he filled the pan, passing soot, coal, curry, and a bolus shaped like a horseshoe, *in memoriam* the London Hospital. He's a new man, loose as Dean Martin. He slaps my palm. 'Adnam, you want my definition of a visionary? Someone who's always talking and never asks a question.'

High above the speeding water, the bridge at Day's Lock: *glad* that Sileen destroyed those pages of my journal, my paranoid eclectic masterpiece. He has absolved me of the complexities of the past. I float. *Here* and nowhere else. We must hymn the emptiness of the landscape: corduroy mud, pylons, private orchards. An aching, non-specific lust. Loss of dates, facts, the names of friends. A voluntary embrace of 'diffuse degeneration'. Least known, most favoured.

There's a table set outside the lock-keeper's cottage, a tray of interesting twigs: '2 for a Penny'. Sileen takes them at their word. He tears off an overhanging branch and strips it with his blade, hacks it into fingerlength portions – which he then deposits on the table. He stamps on the cashbox, reduces it to splinters. Another weighty haul of coins. Sileen: the charity ward ram-raider.

It's my fancy that these twigs are messages; the tray a maildrop for initiated travellers. Each nick a warning. Tip them all into the millrace, let them form an arrowhead aimed at the heart of the Clump.

We must ascend the Sinodun Hills, passing through the cruel V of a larchwood stile. I titillate Sileen with promises of Oxford, spires poking through a crust of cow pats. It is our last pan across these diffident fields. Heads down in the pews; we're coming in, boys.

Sileen, arm about my neck, wheezes on a sharpening slope. His stiff leg ploughs a furrow in the dew. I *see* the energy move along and beneath the surface of the earth. Dry cornheads – loud as locusts. The Michael and Mary currents cross (and fuse) at this gap in the chalk. The clumps defend a node point.

Sileen's arm tightens. He's flashing back to an earlier hierophant, Paul Nash at Boar's Hill: a sick man clutching field-glasses. The fever climactic. The alchemy of repetition, repeated viewings. The clumps and nothing else, the foreshortened *Landscape of the Summer Solstice*. Twelve miles across country, the painter dying. The sun sinks as the moon rises. Cobalt blue tunnels excavating the hillside.

Great sadness, *our* mortality. Sileen carried in a fireman's lift. Can't speak, expel breath; achieving the summit, I hold John Dee's crystal aloft to catch and interpret the singular condition of light. So much undescribed land: Thames and Thame, the Chilterns, the Valley of the White Horse, the smoke pall of Didcot's power station demonstrating the direction of the breeze.

The first Clump is melancholy, fenced off; an anchor to the panorama over which we levitate. The second Clump, with its earthworks, is the soul of our journey – its meaning. I am out there above the greyblue hills, one with the clouds. Not him, not Sileen. His legs stick in the turdy earth. He goes down, rolling in it. The stuff of England. Such strange compost, the green excrement of centaurs.

He can't rise up, turn his face to the sky. His skin is red, tight, a rash of melanomic bar-coding. The sun has cured the gimp like bacon. Five days of exposure: a peeling scalp, a dog-fringe of hair threads. It's my fault. I've blown it, burdened his tragic consciousness with histories, legends, lies. He's farctate. Now I must bear his weight.

I stand over him, his back rests against an ancient tree. Leafprints. His complexion, pellucid beneath its honeycomb of pustules, is the texture of bark. He is wood, protected, impervious to harm. All the remembrances carved in the oak trunk are transferred to his meat. The sun winks through a shimmering thatch of hornbeam and birch. The shadows are cool, dark passageways. Caves beneath the waters of Twickenham.

We sing, old men together. I agitate his lips with my fingers. He grooms the silver of my beard. Where did our lives go? The sound of thin voices.

'Rejoice with the Shag-green a beast from which the skin so called is taken.'

'Rejoice with The Beardmanica a curious bird.'

'Rejoice with the Book-Spider.'

We descant on the illustrious light of England. With the painter Paul Nash dying in his window. With Sileen, so bravely, advancing on his extinction. With all who ascend, or have ever ascended, or will in the future ascend, this hill.

I see the multitudes, especially in their absence. You, sir! Threadbare, solitary wraith with your camcorder. Good tailoring gone to seed. Witness without whose notice we have no existence. Take care where you point that thing. All evidence is dangerous. To the one who possesses it.

AMEN. HUZZA. SELAH.

FOUR

Mutually drained, individually elated, Todd Sileen and Rhab Adnam, husks warmed by sunlight lingering in old stones, stood silhouetted in the doorway of the church of St Michael at Clifton Hampden; high upon the mound, looking ahead to the delicate pink bridge, the river advancing on Long Wittenham. The last green rays of the setting sun presented a transitional landscape. At the death, it would all vanish – outlasting, outliving, them. They were nothing. The excesses of their route march were done with: the London to Oxford coach, with its cargo of women, could be safely released from its time warp. A new morning would carry them all into the city.

Hands over ears, hearing more than they were able to see, they shuffled under the bypass – that furious traffic-belt, its concrete piers. The amplified rage of tyres. Sileen, Y-fronts bulging, flogs on. Now Adnam strains to hold him. Those careless miles after Abingdon (weirs, nettles, prospect of Nuneham House) take their toll. The natural world no longer reveals itself like a leaf uncurling on a June morning. Their actions are goal-orientated, hideous. Adnam's knees click like a Geiger counter. His feet flinch from the touch of leather. His neck stiffens. The pilgrims violate the city's perimeter: ring roads, railway embankments, locks, back channels. All that stimulates Sileen, hobbles Adnam.

It was with the third jogger – black-vested, grim-visaged – that they knew they had made it. Close-cropped, elastoplast-nipped, she pistoned to the beat of a hissing Walkman. Out on the river, eight giants – heads in laps – were tongue-lashed by a squeaking midget.

Donnington Bridge. Thames or Isis. That's what the map says. A nice distinction wasted on Sileen. He had walked enough, he plunged. Sink or swim, it couldn't matter less. He must wash off the dust of the road.

Rhab followed, game to the last – a clean dive, headlong into the welcoming murk. Eyes wide open to the wonders of quag and silt, stirred by Sileen: his single leg thrashing like a propeller. A cold fall, white, under weight of water; Rhab surfaced, midstream, gasping. Sileen, prosthetic limb held overhead, recreated the *Deliverance* poster. Duckweed dripped from the griseous shell of his skull.

Going down once more, drowning in cold tea, he found Helen, naked, swimming towards him. Smiling, untrustworthy – he still reached out for her. Tumbling and tangling, Sileen meshed with the slippery hallucination. It could have finished him. This was no time for a lyric interlude.

Chastened, he tugged on the chain of air bubbles, readied himself to accept the guidance of Isis, drift with the tide. Oxford is water first, then parkland. Fulsome trees to the river's edge, boathouses with balconies and empty flagpoles, landing platforms; spurn them. The ceremony of initiation is not yet complete. Swimming is their homage to the elegance of the goddess with the moon trapped in her horns; wife to the ruler of the dead, mother of the falcon. Sileen's wits had been scattered like the fourteen segments of Osiris. With each laboured stroke, he was recovering the field of his intelligence. Old limper, what portion of his humanity had been abandoned with the hacksawed bone? What knowledge in the parcel of incinerated skin? Butting head towards Folly Bridge, dark imaginings oozed like tallow from Sileen's overworked abductors.

The oaf wallowed, pleasuring himself in tannin Thames; rolled on his back to let a weak sun tinker with gurgling belly tubes. Rhab was ashore, towelling himself briskly on an oarsman's shed sweatsuit. He offered Sileen a hand, gaffed him, reeled him in. What more to say? Time to fix a face for parting. Shrug of shoulder. Playful dig in ribs. There were mounds to measure, wells to dip, fetishes to prod. Roger Bacon, Duns Scotus, William of Ockham. Libraries, museums, quadrangles. Scorch marks where Christian martyrs had been toasted. Oxford gave respite to temporary migrants, lulled them, drained their speed, cut them loose. Sandstone shone. Light winds scoured the unanchored slack. The boys would have to learn fast; sharpen their claws or wash out to Kelmscott, Lechlade, and utter obscurity.

A pursuit mode clothed Sileen (black), his nostrils flared: his rags were tumble-dried in the scorch of his excitement. Knuckles to eyeballs, a sharper set of phosphenes. Fresh scents. T.C.P. (Germy) Hinton was afoot, hopping across paddocks, snorting tripe, snug in possession of his Hope Hodgson pastiche. Garrulous within the tiny realm of his pleroma, his fool's paradise. Sileen gobbed in the river. He was refreshed, shriven by the masochism of the road, sapient, expansive – tooled to garrotte the intramural bibliophile in the crook of his elbow.

Where to begin the search? With Lady Montacute's benevolence, the meadow of Christ Church? Too vast and ill-defined, infested by picture book cattle of a shaggy kind. There were too many faces peeping among Dean Liddell's poplars; poursuivants, psychic snoops reporting back to base. Drage-Bell's corvine associates. Furies on day release. Circuits of counter-terror: the watcher watched. And Helen too, madonna of the buses. Anguish and desire, lovers' needles: he shook out slime puddles, reversing to a standstill in a hail of grit.

One Judas peck on Adnam's cheek, a fumble in his chum's pocket. Their paths divided. Pilgrim and hitman. No middle way. It had been the best of times. They were glad to see the back of each other.

A prodigious and unseemly slapping of the water forced Sileen to turn his head, grant Isis her fond farewell. A swan, straining out of somewhere beyond Iffley, hogged the centre of the stream, beating its wings in frustration. It lifted, fell back, climbed above Folly Bridge, and away. The episode touched a splinter to Sileen's heart: deep nostalgia for scenes he had never known. His man, Adnam, had evaporated.

Where now? A wilderness of polished grass behind him, the river ahead. Do nothing. That was his infallible method. Sit still, dig in. Find the right hostelry (any hostelry). Get yourself wrapped around a jar of the dark stuff, and wait for it. Command any fixed point and the world will rupture itself in its haste to trample you down.

St Aldate was an undistinguished ascent, institutional brickwork giving way to distressed medieval splendour; vagrants rubbing humps with bemused trippers. There were correspondence colleges for near students who wore striped scarfs and called them 'wraps' – nightschools exposed to daylight. Police barracks, a memorial garden. Sileen steered compulsively to the left, away from all this. The coach station was more his mark, a morbid percussion of six packs. The Calvinist in him rose in his gorge against the fumy stink of Jesuits, Campion Hall. Speedwell, Rose, Albion Place, Brewer Street – a run of gargoyles and alleys. He was beginning to feel at home.

Sanctuary. Any sufficiently dim saloon-bar would do. There were several basic rules, tried and tested, in discovering such a place. He would clearly give a wide berth to the Blenheim, with its mock-Tudor bonhomie, its ominous proximity to the Museum of Modern Art. The last thing Sileen needed was a clatch of yattering art buffs – concrete poets who could barely heft a paperback, performance artists photophilic with narcissism, professional masochists busking for studio space in which to nail their foreskins to the wall. Even passing the door gave Sileen the runs. High decibel bitchery, bluster, sinecure-snivelling: it assaulted the public highway. The soft and deadly voices of serious women.

That was his other edict: no distaffs. *Any* female was bad news in a public-house. The odd, waiflike, half-cut slag he would tolerate – on the remote promise of a Clinton in a phonebox. Even those scarlet-mouthed, mummified tombcrows on their high stools served a purpose, memento mori. They were quite acceptable – as furniture – if they kept their own counsel, reminisced only on request. But the others, chirpy or abrasive, the ones with conversation, he abominated. Limp on, brother.

Sileen's tastes, and he was not ashamed to admit it, were not unlike those of the old Aragonian, the deaf one, Luis Buñuel. His motives were, of course, less exalted. (No publisher would fork out cash money for *his* martini recipes.) Bunuel required that his chosen bar should represent 'an exercise in solitude . . . quiet, dark, and comfortable . . . no music of any kind . . . and a clientele that doesn't like to talk.' Quite so. But such a mausoleum is rarely available to the underfunded grass. Sileen thrived on compromise. The Pennyfarthing was its paradigm.

It belonged on a Wimpey estate in Ilford. There was a punt at respectability, overwhelmed in a blizzard of mismatched brickwork and quickfit windows. The eponymous cycle was bolted under the eaves, along with a rash of hanging geranium pots that did nothing to convince the discerning toper. So far so good. The boozer stood far enough to the west to escape the worst excesses of the art mob, and far enough (just) to the east to discourage the shopping-centre rabble. It refrained from boasting of ferrety brews and its prices were steep enough to repel academics and other meths-drinkers.

Sileen dumped his trawl of copper on the bar. Sufficient, on the recount, for a cracked cigar and a pint of steroid-positive sample. An out-of-hours man with a choice of tables, he drank slowly; puffing away, fingers pinching the fracture, in something ominously close to content-ment. The bar was deserted – exclude the trappist pump-polisher in the ruffled peppermint blouse, and the couple subverting behind a fence of plastic greenery. Some steady hours of uninterrupted melancholy and Sileen would, so he asserted, conjure a fix on Hinton. Even now the threadbare flock was suspiring, its fused grey assuming the aspect of William Hope Hodgson's hyperenchanted ocean. An eternity of emptiness that rivalled his own. The caesura that predicts the rending of the veil.

Sip, swallow, stare. Agitate the oesophagus. Trickle icy liquid into a blast furnace of unassuaged nigredo. Whistle and wheeze. Sileen exhaled: a smokescreen to stifle demons. Say it, then forget it. 'Germy Hinton.' He indulged. He wrote, forefinger in a puddle of dropped ash and spillage, the letters of the desired name. H . . . I . . . N . . . T . . .

'Swindon mean anything to you, mate?'

Sileen ignored it. Such a voice was not possible, not permitted, it could not be. The rachet and pawl of East London markets – more Plaistow than the cosmopolitan sneer of Bethnal Green, deeper and dumber. Glottal virtuoso. The interrogative as a style, mini-cab garrulous. The arrogant stupidity of the man's stare, six and a half feet from the ground. Not the usual legbreaker, the fur-shouldered mesomorph. A merciless gargle of the backrivers, more swamp than estuary. Too many roll-ups on bunk beds. Rottweiler cough of abused throat. Intolerable.

'My brother, 'e wants to know if you've ever 'ad a poodle dahn Swindon way?'

It wasn't the potato sack. Not any more. He'd run out of chat. A bombhead had insinuated a stool at the bar; one of Pasolini's rough trade hoods. Paul Smith and white T-shirt. A long range ventriloquist, the man cupped his chin on the heel of his hand – and stared, unblinking, at the shamed Sileen. His mannerisms – scar tickling and the compulsive dusting of a Berkoffian No. 2 crop – were peculiarly offensive. The villain had all the dodgy trademarks of a resting actor. Some petty screwman, smalltime rudyard, called in as local colour. He'd bleed all over the leather of the getaway Jag, and be dumped after the first reel. The silent menace of his performance obliterated by gabbiness in the hotel bar. Vodka verbals. The geezer with the silver attaché case of bent Rolexes.

The lowlife wouldn't drop his gaze: a brothel-keeper's challenge. Swaying on the stool, he talked across his inert sibling – a flat-snout who should never have bothered to struggle up from his all-fours crouch. An underbiter whose horizons shifted from the throats of rivals to sniffing their extended fundaments.

'Won't go within ten mile of that shithole, will you, Anthony? Copped for eighteen months, lending his support to the Arsenal. Affray, they called it. Winchester, then Portsmouth. More of a bleeding holiday, weren't it, Tone?'

'Too right, bro. Time o' me life.' The big man drained his pint at a single pull and slid it across for a refill. All Sileen's nightmares were coming home to roost. ' 'Undred press-ups 'fore breakfast. Better than the fuckin' army. Fit? You could smash me in the guts with a sledge'ammer – wouldn't even fart, would I?'

The bombhead dropped nonchalantly from his perch and started towards Sileen, nursing a wash of port and brandy. 'Have another go, Tone. Get on the blower. See if you can raise Chris. I need him tonight. Nine sharp or he's dogmeat. Oh, and Anthony, manners – don't forget to enquire after Maureen.'

The donkey blew into the mouthpiece, tapped it against the wall, hammered coins into the slot. ' 'E don't answer, Nicky. Won't take no call. Must 'ave done a runner.'

'We're not on our own turf here. Give him respect, brother. You a poet?' Nicky jumpcut along the banquette until he was superglued, buttock-to-buttock, against Sileen. 'You don't mind my mentioning it. I could tell from the walk you had a connection with literature. Either that or some slag's put a couple of rounds through your kneecap. I know the signs, son. Done my turn across the water.'

Indignant bars of old man's vein stood proud from Nicky's covert wrist. Sileen played dumb – hypnotized by the snake tattoo in its thicket of blueblack hair. This monologue had nothing to do with him. His reverie was trashed, replaced by bad television. These characters, surplus stock, were pre-monopoly – from A.B.C's *Armchair Theatre*, where sets shook, and drying was interpreted as a menacing pause. Even the barman shrank from them, polishing his gin glasses to an embarrassing sheen.

'It was your plates took my eye.'

Sileen scuffled to hide the disgraced daps; one behind the other, the squelch of the river. Black mud oozing like ointment as he wriggled his toes. No point in disguising the fact. His rubbers had burst.

'You're all the same, you poets. Wystan favoured comfort over elegance. Famous for it. We knocked back a few shorts in our time. Did you know that? The Pennyfarthing was, I should say, one of his special drinkers. "A private sphere in public chaos." Right?'

This was not going to work. Sileen made a move to push back the table. These scallywags might come in handy when it was time to dispose of Hinton, but first the feathery Hodgsonian had to be netted.

Not so fast. The downward pressure of Nicholas Tarten's grip bit like acid into Sileen's good thigh. The poet's friend winked at the barman – who trotted over, smirking with malicious glee, and bearing an enamel tray of doubles.

'It's like your first contract killing, you never forget – the ineradicable charm of the spires. A meeting of minds. Ships in the night. Toe-to-toe on the cobbles with a Faber poet. Wystan Auden, across the road in Christ Church, early Sixties. A wide-open time. You had the lot: poetry, fashion, crime. I held the rent books for a couple of bibliothèques in St Anne's Court. Stuck an old Etonian in shades and hush puppies out front for the carriage trade. I'm in the book – the David Archer of the Psychedelic Generation, they called me. Phil Larkin, Bobby Conquest, Moisha Blueball, Sonny the Yank. No allergies to maidenheads there, know what I'm saying? A parnassus of spankers and chickenhawks. That was the mix, high and low, poets and perverts.'

'Ever run across any Hintons?' Sileen was too pissed to resist it. Playing the straight man, the feed.

'Hinton, Anthony? Ring any bells with you? Any previous?'

The sibling exchange gave Sileen his excuse. Arms folded, fundament clenched, he wiggled away from his tormentor.

'You're the scholar, Sweeney, what do you say? I've never been comfortable with born-again Auden. But I go down on my knees for the chances I had to get rat-assed with the old bender before he snuffed it. He's what I call a proper poet – rhyme, elipse, classical allusion. Master of his craft. Know what I'm saying? Beside which, in my opinion, he gave a very decent blowjob.'

Sileen made it to the bar, fumbling his pockets, pretending to mull over the vintage he was about to order. Anthony Tarten was propped in his corner, dutifully holding the dead telephone. Tears of pique sparkled in his babyblue eyes.

'My brother, it's not his night.' Nicky clamped an arm around Sileen's shoulder. They breathed menues of bad faith in one another's face. 'Fancy a turn in the ring, yourself? That's why we're checking out poxy Swindon. Pub show. Need a fresh face to put in with Roy Shaw. No bullshit, I've always got time for a gimp who hasn't lost his bottle. You got the look, son. A ringer for Boy Boon – take away the legs. Worth a monkey first time out, if you stay the distance. Think about it. Give me a number. Who did you say was your publisher?'

Wedged in the slit of the door, nose tilted to the evening air, Sileen would not turn. Tarten's demented recitation raged at his back. Jumping its grooves. Thuggish. Unlovely. False.

'*In Praise of Limestone*, that's the guv'nor. "Your kindest kiss, how permanent is death." Tell Chris – if he hasn't delivered by ten we'll feed his bollocks into a meat-grinder.'

Outside: ejected, reeling, Sileen went where the tin leg took him. He obeyed that which was least his own. He favoured fault lines, the zone where the light was thinnest. Disorientated by the alcohol's rapidly diminishing elation, he twisted and spun. No direction seduced him. A windlass of unenticing options.

The oily touch of a woman's sleeve checked him. A dream figure, unregistered, trailing the smell of life. Too late. The door of the Pennyfarthing was in mid-swing. There and here: distinct and independent kingdoms. Andi Kuschka, black leather holdall clutched to her bosom, had passed inside. Sileen was not included in her nightmare.

The woman was an obedient prisoner of romance, obedience was her solitary pleasure. She remained faithful to her narrative, when Sileen had allowed himself to be traduced and distracted. So far had the cripple fallen that he was willingly suckered in amongst the crowd pushing through the open glass doors of the Museum of Modern Art. Why not? Only the mindless mass could grant him the anonymity he craved.

FIVE

Her heels sound the polished woodblock floor: Helen, alone, circum-navigating the cloud chamber. Taking sound as affirmation. Confident. An expensive, well-cut blouse setting off the rest – the checked, mid-thigh skirt, the almost tarty heels. A dab of scent at the wrist. She directs the pattern of her movement through this retrieved industrial space, this roofed forest. White brick walls, low white ceiling. Iron-red pillars. An old brewery. She does not need to see green shoots twisting around girders, burnished copper vats, leather aprons, sweating bodies. She summons the heady languor of drying hops, the diuretic flush. A stately progress.

Helen assesses the reflection of her hair in the glass that protects one of the paintings. She walks, as she has always wanted to do, among the hierarchies of Luke Howard's clouds.

She witnesses a sweep of late sunlight over the marshes, the enormity of that emptiness, the distant city. She remains within the circuit of the echo of her heels on dead wood, not giving concentration to any of the sketches. Those rapid, excited seizures – pulse-takings – by which the amateur meteorologist attempted to codify the sky's moods. Clouds were to be analysed like broken minds. They never lie, but they do fabulate – crease, fold, brag, dissolve. Luke Howard's wispy water-colours illustrate tendencies as distinct as Freud's case histories. Dispersed fiction. Invocations of nostalgia. Helen loved them with all her soul. Not looking, not pausing; having them about her was enough. As they drifted across the white bricks. As windows opened on delicate shell-pinks, celestial blues, yellow, cream, silver, black rage. An articulate resolution of moisture. This was better than art, stranger than landscape. This was weather.

Balanced on the edge of a cluttered desk, legs crossed, in tailored slacks, Sofya Court swings her small foot. The day's business subsides into the temperature of the social: art gossip, names, cases. Who gets the cash. Who gives the clap. Who is dying. Who is dead. Sofya is good at this, but uninvolved. A long tight room dominated by its furniture, the prominent utility pipes a much-admired feature. Slatted blinds, no exterior view. One monitor to survey the street – where floating figures tug their ectoplasmic doubles. Another screen flicks between the empty galleries. Helen exists as an impersonation. Sofya admires the effortless lethargy of her performance.

We few, the friends of friends, cosily inside before the doors are opened to admit the throng. Cackhanded, undeft, the administrator (one of the sisterhood) breaks the cork, screwdrivers the remnant. The extent of their exertion: a choice between white and red.

They drink. Sofya sips, the administrator rinses, but Andi throws back glass after glass, splashing her hot face, shivering. She was high before she started, now the claret is an excuse to justify the state she has already attained. She was not free of the lethal coolness of the black holdall, the leather pressed against her bare thighs. She misses it and is liberated by its absence. The thing's done. She laughs with the others, bereaved, ready to sob, or scream out, smash her glass against the wall: feverish, her teeth chattering. She detaches herself and walks away into the upper gallery, the grander space where they are setting out chairs for the poetry reading.

There is always a poetry reading. She can hear them below, the babble and spit of culture chat – names names names, argument, envy. Expectancy soured in transit. It spirals upwards through the nightblue stairwell. Andi walks, her rubber soles squeaking against the polished tiles. She walks and stops. Stares, starts – moves closer to the monochrome prints, the photographs. They absorb her. They are her salvation. A remembered city. People of the banlieue who model anonymity. Occasions in life's careless expenditure. Fraudulent spontaneity. Surreal conjunctions. Coincidences of the light. A pair of newlyweds, squat and resigned, cross an acre of cobbles to the ugliest café in the world. Where will they discover the energy to step over the gutter? The bride's got up like a graveyard pigeon. The groom's an urban hunter, a strangler of things already dead. It's overcast, never-ending wartime. Artists crank their presses in the service of propaganda.

Andi doesn't care who took the photographs. It doesn't occur to her than anybody did. They exist. Summary lovers achieve transmigration by stopping to kiss in an unfocused carrousel of pedestrianism. Eyes shut, the girl bends her neck to receive his saliva. But it's the hands that touch Andi. Hers, so trusting – chapped, open-palmed; and his, pinched, thumb to first finger, describing the quantity of erectile tissue he wishes to violate. Or, perhaps, snuffing a cigarette. The hands are not implicated. They do not participate. Andi trembled for this maggot tenderness, asserted against the sullen grandeur of public buildings, headlamps, bumpers.

Stubs and coffee spoons of defeated eros. A prickle of damp overcoats, sunlight between showers. Solitaries dragging heavy packages, observed from above, as they march to the unheard beat of madness. A nude dancer, caught in the morning, buttoned to the chin, her painted nails squeezing the neck of an oversized milkbottle. City under occupation. A man with a pistol crouches at a window. Rooms commandeered to indicate a geography of terror.

Andi needs to hold each dark square until it becomes unbearable, until she knows every pore and pebble. Kill the flow of time. Retain the impossible present tense of the photograph. Become another. Give yourself up to a procession of unearned regrets. Guilty, yes, but of *unremembered* crimes.

What a magnificent mouth! The portrait of that young girl, Mademoiselle Anita, haunts her. They will exchange places. The ghost of the photographer, in the angle of the barroom mirror, is twinheaded: he stares down into his box at the reversed image. The dark V of his hair repeated in Mlle Anita's generous cleavage. Noticing him, Andi wants to know why he is staring at the back of his model's neck.

Anita is as alive as Andi. Their names are too close. Andi shares her blood, her subversive resignation: the shuttered eyelids, pearls, earring. Her autistic detachment. The girl won't look up. Andi wills her to submit to degradations worse than anything she, Andi, can invent. Andi wants to be beaten in alleyways, raped in coldwater Arab flats, dumped in couch grass at the canalside. Wants it for this other, this beauty. The café madonna, this child who is old enough, in real time, to be her mother. *There is no real time*. Andi has stopped it by the act of dropping her holdall, allowing it to be taken from her.

There's a story. A card 'explains' how Anita took off her jacket for the photographer – anticipating his request? She *chose* to direct her own appearance: bushy pelmet of get-out-of-bed hair, bare shoulders, black dress dissolving into the leather of a padded backrest. Fleshy arms, one above the other, on an unseen table. Lifeless hands.

The full-lipped, coarse/fine, hungry/replete, face will give up none of its secrets. Even to Sofya, as she leans forward – her reflection absorbing Andi's – to check if the eyes of Mlle Anita are open. And, *just*, they decide, they are. Sofya squeezes Andi's hand, brushes her cheek with her lips. On the surface of the glass they come together – and, marrying, make up the gravity and recklessness of the photographed girl.

A mannerless bluster of sound overwhelms the gallery. A chattering crowd frisks up the blue stairs, and floods the chamber, reducing the magical profanity of the images to background decoration. It's difficult to decide whether these gadarenes have been let out or allowed in. They occupy their chairs with an overweening confidence, asserting their inalienable right to participate as audience, to become children again – listening intently while some stranger reads aloud from a shiny book. Only when he begins can they relax, fidget, cross and uncross their legs, wonder when it will all be over.

SIX

Art politics is counter-punching – the measured response, the significant gesture. Survival is the only rule. In time the knotted philosophy of John Latham will be as translucent as a Hockney swimming-pool. Hang in there and anything is possible. Hermits, twenty-five years in the boglands, and bombsite anarchists: fashion grants them their moment. A decade of silence may be construed as a work in progress, and Tourette's syndrome as an essay in irony.

Dr T. C. P. Hinton had won the Newdigate Prize with his loosely-knit blank verse tropes on the construction, history, and mythological status of Oxford's Castle Mound. Alfred, Lord Tennyson, as a borough-surveyor. Henry Newbolt without the lyric dash. Those were the kinder critiques. But what did *they*, lemon-scented effetes, know of suffering? Hinton loved literature like a barking ulcer. He would go anywhere to snort it. Even here. Even this: the introduction of a combo of lesser figures, rivals, subterraneans backing timidly into the footlights. Traumatized trench vermin. A trio of future exiles, clapped-out headbangers who had made their reputations in days when poetry was still on the agenda – when grants were there for the taking, and primary schools clamoured for beards and tin whistles, language games and the pepper of revolution. Deleted, utterly: the flatulent comforts, the mesmeric decay of the Earl's Court poetry slum.

Sileen was pinioned in the belly of the whale, an outwash of ranting worshippers. He went with the tide, a new experience, and a cruel one. He was glad. Glad to take his hand from the tiller. Let them do their worst. They flattered his despair, these so public masochists. Better a paragraph in martyrologist Foxe's *Actes and Monuments*. Better disembowelled on the lawns of Balliol. He stayed resolutely on his feet, the swifter to escape. The mob bitched and nudged, worried thin buttocks against a doctrinal rigidity of plastic-cup chairs.

The theory of least resistance, formulated in the Pennyfarthing, was put to the test in the gallery. There he was, up on his hind legs, wobbling in the breeze of fans, the manifest Germy Hinton. Sileen's hurt embraced the shambling golfbag figure. Hinton. The name clanged like the Lutine bell: a charity line of disgraced surgeons, time cranks, cardboard-soled mystics. Germy – the last of them, an atavistic stooge. The green of his rayon turtleneck ('glacier' green the catalogue had called it) was a mistake – given the pallor of the man. He cried out for a transfusion of life-enhancing colours, oyster pinks, primary risks in crimson. His minder winced as he wrestled the verse Diaghilev out from under a sweltering blanket of topcoat.

Insanity. All the carpet-chewers in town are up for this gig, all the heads are giggling in the aether. It's a horribly unstable mix: parchment skulls from the Sixties riding herd on bandits who always turn out, carrier bags at the ready, in case they have snared the next Ian McEwan.

Sofya Court, Sileen noticed, was bottling it, backing rapidly towards the open door, escaping before the affront of the first belch. Poor child, born too late, performed poetry brought her out in hives. Hinton was undismayed at the loss of such a fragrant disciple: his eyes were shut. He was mumbling and grinning like an unassigned zombie. The audience ignored him. They were peevish, drumming their heels, unprepared for the standard forty minutes of introductory tedium.

The poets. Sileen had forgotten them. They'd been unhitched from their stretchers and were making noises. They lolled like imbeciles, feigning disinterest, popping pills, uncreasing scrota, leafing helplessly through slim booklets to find a poem they recognized. An instant of transcendent exposure and they could be wheeled back to the reserve collection of the Pitt Rivers Museum.

Now Hinton, in particular, caught the eye. Nude scalp gleaming like a roasted acorn. He twisted his arms and shoulders in unlooked for relief. The discipline of the straitjacket had kept him upright. He sighed, and made his pitch to an audience that had, intellectually speaking, decamped. They were *themselves* performers, frustrated, willing the torment to finish – so that the fun could begin. Question time. Why, why not, who, how, when, what, if – wrong!

Three poets, unadorned, is always a mistake. It's at least one too many – and, in most cases, three. The molar-grinding hell of knowing that surviving the first assault puts you on stream to face two more. Flesh cannot bear it. It's an endurance test, an exercise in public humiliation – humiliation of the public. The poets strain to drown each other out, to keep going so long their associates will have no chance. Bullocky, jealous-spirited, they're full of tricks and stunts, carefully rehearsed ad libs, false starts, stutters to damp the front row bibs, obscenities invented on the spur. They'll stoop to any gimmick – epileptic fits, coronary stumbles, copious vomiting. One minimalist never set foot on stage without throwing back a pint of seawater. Sileen was resigned. He'd seen it all before. Only Hinton mattered.

Who shall trill first? They squabble over precedence. Should they jump in while the crowd's still in good heart, give it the gun – or hang modestly back, barnstorm a finish, sit down to the ringing applause that always welcomes the final bow? The filling in the sandwich, that's the old bollocks, the spot nobody wants. Balsam and clinker.

Sileen wishes they'd read together in a fool's chorus and get it over. Sweatlets rolled their bearings down his neck. His black shirt blotted the lot. Claustrophobic, he churned and jutted his elbows in a Fashanu. Neighbours, suspecting the onset of grand mal, gave him room. A creamy curd lodged between tensed bands of lip. The clonic phase was imminent. He *wanted* Hinton – out on the street, in the snug, on his knee, anywhere but there. He felt that support-stocking neck within the circuit of his fingers. Heard the rattle and choke. Age was having its way with him, this uncalled for impatience. Half a century of bile skewered his heaving guts.

Doc Hinton, forgetting their names, and grievously overrepresenting their achievements, announced the performers – offering a running order they immediately reversed. The first poet is at his shoulder, slurping claret down the greengage slopes, before the Newdigate quisling can back into a neutral corner.

Has it begun? Is this a poem? Or is it the preamble, the excuses? He's quite tall, Sileen thought, for a poet. Drooping, sub-eloquent, weak-necked: a Stalinist noddy. A dead-voiced, language-abusing crooner. A gesticulator. A stopper. A starter. A self-eraser. A manic autodidact. A Charles Fortean assembler of inconsequential facts. A piddler of parentheses. An alkaseltzer ham. A white bebop. A parboiled rasta spat out from the ghetto into some tame rural retreat.

Take a grip. Sileen was running away with himself. He was becoming a poet. Time to make his excuses. He needed a dose, a pull at the bottle.

Eyes wired into Hinton's mushroom torpor, he wriggled towards the exit. Strict binocular vision: the bobbing schizo would never escape him, this custodian of shnide manuscripts. A sneak raid on the drinks cabinet and Sileen will be fit to pluck him.

REEBOK SIRENS CLIP THE GORGE / CHOPPER GRADIENTS IN A HAT. Screamed, then whispered. The poet's accusing digit pierces Sileen's scowl. He clams. Is forced to admire the motility of the ranter's wolverine ears: Vulcan Spock, script in hand. Sileen is transfixed beneath the lintel, thirsty, yet held by this torrent of urban invective. It works! A fragmentation device ticking in his shallow chest. It's true! City lobotomy, buildings alienated from the dream. A wizard, a speedfreak scissorhand cutting paranoid promos: snatches of street-talk, brand names, geology, news, technobabble, riot. *What* is the poet incubating in the bloody globe of his eye?

Scarlet filters. In a reverie, induced by this hypnotic soundtrack, Sileen migrates to the Sly Street room. Nightsky over Shadwell. Candles flickering behind muslin in the Kinder Street warren. Gulls tracking the river. The madeleine of Helen's perfume triggering his irresponsible responses. Isabel on the threshold, her black stockings. Cruelty of words: the poet dubbing their gentle pornography. The body's involuntary memory of pleasure, the curl in the cell. Things otherwise forgotten. Affection after hunger. Greed sated. A fond and comfortable separation. Looking out over roofscapes: a tile garden, a muddle of chimneys. How once, naked, he had put a leather belt around them both, standing behind her, at the window, witnessing the cloudrace.

Helen: coming up the stairs, away from the Luke Howard gallery, making her reluctant way to the office – sees the familiar bulk blocking the entrance, rushes at him. Sileen. Arms tight around his waist. No need to speak. Their private odours mingle. Call it what you will. Joy, habit. It's far removed from intelligence, calculation, the realpolitik of living. It's suck and swallow. Reciprocity hammered on the slab. Names spoken aloud to telegraph the pleasure centres. A wicked tango for the surveillance cameras.

She takes his arm, being more capable of movement, and leads him, blind, into the administrator's office. They don't have to watch. They can hear the second poet on the monitor: worse than the first. Repeating himself before he begins. A pethidine singsong, a cerebral insult. Too long in the weather, the old salt cements skulls split in forgotten wars, rescues colour from barneys in the forest. On autopilot, he doodles with a swinging watch. His faculties have gone up in green smoke. A wheezer, a fugitive seeking his justification in apocryphal texts, he calls for potato skins.

They kiss to the slow hawk of the bard's asthmatic choke. He patronizes those who will never fathom his scorn – townies gawping at an ursine freak in a roadie's satin baseball jacket. How does he shift the temperature then? An invocation of remote places: moors, seascapes, coal beaches. Recipes for honeyed anthracite. The mock-heroics of poverty. A druid of the welfare state, cast out, dumped like toxic waste. Tame anarchist, kippered by roll-ups: his voice scores their lovemaking. Dry juice. And is itself a form of love – generous, fractured, out of time.

Sofya Court, vivid on the pearl screen, moves and hesitates beneath their feet: she's not happy with clouds. Wisps, flocculate threads. The average specimen weighs 50,000 tons: a fact. 'Average'? What nonsense is this? Who held the scales? Luke Howard, sketching tendencies, reinvokes electrified instants of consciousness. Sofya wants to forget. She's dizzy, she sways. She shuts her eyes.

Helen's eyes in his. Sileen's dirt-crusted hand lifting the weight of hair from her nape. Pleasure. The flow of pleasure.

Andi Kuschka does not dare. To let her lids droop. To slide into the floe of sleep. The only one of them, the women, secure among the audience – passive, participating. Listless, heavy in her movements. Attending on every word, their shape does not touch her. They are without meaning. Formlessness *is* their meaning. The power of sound. Like a scorched wind. Her eyes stretched in terror: the curved reflection of the room, the ranks of chairs, the photographs on the walls.

Another poet, the last – solid as Satan. 'How far can / you raise the skirt / without taking it off?' A treacherously oracular question. Is he improvising or quoting? *Whose* skirt? Who does the raising? Andi can't remember skirts. The ambivalence of Heneage Street afternoons, sharing and being shared. Showing and doing. Provoking and suffering consequences of provocation. This voice: its catarrh-ripe insinuations, woodsmoke on wastelots, the struggle for precise articulation. The most dangerous of them. South London in a corset of vanity. A pomaded bison. His words draw blood. Independent of their author. The twilight confidences of riverside bars.

'A seer is what England needs.' Over Sileen's shoulder, on the monitor, Helen can watch the final poet: gravity of hock, chalkstriped, genial as one of Patrick Hamilton's psychopaths. Tieless – in an excess of collar and cuff. Sofya, Helen decided, would flinch at the presumption. The man was fleshy, old/young, brave: silvergrey hair flicked from the forehead, resprung to its bouffant glory. One of those who step from the shadows to model designer tat on the foreshore at Limehouse, in company with reformed hoods. A *Face* face. A made man. A lad on the make. He shivers the lectern, banging a fist to derange some self-censoring plug of inhibition. Language: it flows in a block. Swings like an anvil on a chain.

Alone, it's difficult. Sileen, on his monitor, admires the way Sofya acts the part – herself – a woman of discernment; circling the empty gallery, giving mind to this assembly of significant phenomena. The clouds are correct, unsexed. They are streaked with colour, tactful infusions of sunlight. Their shapes are generous, female. Or mean and thin and male. Nothing is fixed. Every captured curl is capable of transformation. This quietness is a fake. This attempt at turning the gallery into a Steiner shrine. The biography of light is more complex than Luke Howard would ever conceive. His clouds do not belong inside a frame. The frames catalogue (and stilt) a process of perpetual motion – drift, dissolution, rhetoric.

As the drawings spin, Sofya slows. She wishes she could masturbate involvement. She would love the sketches if only they remained what they are, decoration. Finite events to be discussed. Aerial snapshots recalling particular East London days. The brushwork is rapid, predatory. It nets moisture. Sharpens without achieving focus. The drawings are emotions. Clouds are the absence of eyes. Clouds damage the clarity of vision. She will not allow them into her head. This unease must find some physical manifestation or she will die. She'll empty her lungs to blow the curtains from the chart.

The big glass doors, secured as soon as the performance begun, are rattled. An angry face, urgent, ghetto-pale, unrequired – Mordecai Donar. He's squeezed like a curl of paint between transparent sheets. His open mouth howls in silence. He waves a plastic carrier-bag. Londis. Coat to the ankle on this sweltering night: her ape has found her. He trumpets for admittance.

There are only so many actions in the world, so many things they can inflict upon each other. They know it: no petty inhibitions, no questions of taste or inclination. Helen's checked skirt pinched a white line across her upper thighs, a temporary border. Isabel as much as Helen. Sileen, massively tumescent, needs to see. Needs to look on her black gash. The skirt raised as far as it will go. Isabel, resting on the edge of the desk, stretches out her legs, the sharp heels like crampons between the grooves in the wooden tiles. Sileen kneeling, as he should, painfully. The tortured joints, raw stump, blisters, abrasions, all the weary miles of his trek. Sweating, mumbling, gobbling at her. She laughs, pushes his head aside: the risk. An edge to their excitement. Pulling him up, towards her, locking strong legs around him. His awkward knuckles in her crease.

The sudden silence, applause from the monitor. A torrent of release, the scraping of chairs, rattlebabble of relieved voices: it drifts towards them. Sileen thrusts. Isabel's heels drum at his back. He nuzzles, she claws. All the fractured currents pull and toss. They cannot break away, break from the intoxication of the poets, egos critical with exposure, stepping across for a celebratory bottle.

Le Cheval tombé.

A white horse, blinkered, in harness, has gone down awkwardly in the street. A man in a trilby and shiny black raincoat tries to heave a blanket over the trembling flanks, token protection from the wet stones. A spill of gritty sugar-snow – the load? The animal is finished. Andi knows that spectators in caps and bicycle clips and overcoats will never coax the beast to its feet. Grey implacable buildings of wartime. The avaricious eye of a handbagged housewife weighing the future steaks.

The gallery empties. The hand of the administrator reaching out towards the office door. The poets gaze at their feet and wonder how soon they can escape – how many rounds will they get in before closing time? Andi is left with the photograph. The fallen horse. The aftermath. How it happens 'while someone else is eating or opening a window or just walking dully along'.

High angle video-scans populate the abandoned gallery with ghosts, a wash of displaced bodies, their warmth. Sileen knows the trauma of furniture and walls. Wiped narrative. He mops his cock on a tug of unbuttoned shirt. Helen smoothing the line of her skirt. On the monitor: alternative versions of the street. The smooth arc of the opening door. Then a woman flying. The administrator, a black bell, shapely in her velvet dress, arms outstretched. Glass shattering. Desk presented with crystalline shards. An exhibition that has gone wrong.

The twisted blades of the blinds in a roar of dark air. All of them on the floor: cups, bottles, documents, rulers, trays, pen-holders, shoes, coatstands. Hands over ears. Tears. Prolonged shock. The shudder and thump of the stillness after the roar. Bells, sirens.

Like the melting of hard ice, glass tinkles from the frames. Mordecai Donar's mug is printed into the door. He's featured, at last, among the posters of poetmen and art revolutionaries. Sofya bruised, knocked from her feet. Luke Howard's clouds are slashed, animated by reflected damage. Creased paper, thick splinters wedged in the watercolour. Smoke alarms. No-one knows what's happened. The poetry punters mob the street – the probable source of the drama. They scream: GAS/ FIRE/TERRORIST. HANG/MAIM/SHOOT. Or are brave, stern, facing they know not what. The poets, curiously, are calm as milkchurns. What else should we expect? This is what they've been chuntering on about all along. Some of the audience are less stoic. They blub and confess, won't be hushed. Some curse. Sofya sits now, rocking, hugging her knees, sniffing at the scorched cloth of her sleeve.

Spooky contrails scar the screen as ambulances rush down Pembroke Street. Sileen is fascinated. It's years since he sat through a film. The panning camera is unimpressed by action. It sweeps at random – a birdscarer's arm. Tops of heads are sliced like onions. The form of the crowd is clearly visible – how it clusters and darts, surges to escape; or flees, with equal fervour, into the epicentre of all it seeks to avoid. Video fascism: the machine talks the individual down, loves action – riots, death. The glamour of fire. This is better than cockfighting. Sileen could slump for hours. He gets himself comfortable, rescues a bottle. Now there is only Doc Hinton left to tag.

There he is, laureate of fools, whirling on the pavement, hopelessly clutching a rack of booklets to his breast. Time to descend. The wrench of duty: Sileen would prefer to wait in the office, swilling booze, watching his body-double wrestle the doctor to the ground. But the technology's not available yet. He swings out, bouncing his rigid heel down the unforgiving stairs.

Germy Hinton: in an armlock. Sileen shouts in his face, assumes that idiocy implies deafness. The moonhead understands nothing. Nothing can be arranged. There are claim forms for the poets to sign. The man's a total zoid. Sileen tries persuasion, reason, flattery, a subtle jerk at the shirt's tail. He fluffs Hinton like a pillow. He rattles his bones. No joy.

The minder, alerted, shuffles up – all threat in his appearance. And his odour. Stubble, dogskin jacket, xylophone of rusting facial rings. Sileen nuts him with a Swedish kiss, drops the greaser in the path of a charging mortuary truck. Save everybody time. Real blood to set-dress slack news. Arriving paparazzi trample the victim into the dirt as they stampede to snatch the first shot.

Tomorrow. Yes, of course. The sun will rise. The doc concurs. Scholarship will triumph. Hinton mutters a sketchy description of their meeting place – and is lost. The pack are storming the Pennyfarthing. It's gutted. A windowless ruin. Flames and evil twists of smoke. The drunks don't help. One of them is trying to balance on the bicycle which has fallen from the wall. Another has thrown himself under the wheels of an ambulance. They all want their confessions *immediately* transcribed. The Celts are saving everybody time by smashing their own heads against the paving stones. Sirens intensify the panic. Film crews are hosing playback imagery onto the banked screens in the shopping precinct. Analysis or incitement? Sleepingbag vagrants, and mall rats – stepping over them – pause to watch. Surveillance cameras watch them all, stamping them with the timecodes of retrospective fame. Circuits feed on circuits. Systems exist to justify their budgets. The only prevention of terrorism is terror itself.

Andi is drawn back. She retraces her afternoon walk, hunching forward to compensate for the loss of her burden. How did they know, all these journalists? Who told them? They were on the scene, hustling their close-ups and cutaway zooms, before the first wrapped bundle was hoisted onto a stretcher. Selective reality: the gloss of telephoto lenses. Andi misses the weight of the bag. She stares, expectantly, at the passing faces. Imar O'Hagan. She wants his blessing, the whip of his scorn.

Sofya is with Helen in the office, with the administrator who is vainly trying to use the phone. Sonya feeds on this rinse of soundless horror. She can cope with any amount of visuals. She knows exactly what her emotions should be when she looks at things on a screen. She knows about composition, balance, narrative drive. She talks about them with genuine conviction. Strong cuts are the morality of the desktop generation. Helen holds her hand. They are both shamed.

They can hear loudhailers appealing for calm, for witnesses. It's a wrap. The pages have been shot, a timelapse photoplay. All in the frame:

blue ribbons cordon off the tragic site. It has achieved significance. There's nothing left to finalize except the statistics.

Hinton looks down at his outstretched hands. They are sticky with some stranger's blood.

SEVEN

He withdrew one lingering breath from his ration of delight. Pilgrim Sileen struggled to bring the triumphalist script into focus. HONORI CAROLI REGIS. Struggled with rods and cones of sharp, clear light. The concept of honour. Magdalen Bridge: abrasive air. Birdsong. An intoxication of early flowers. The decorous fornication of midsummer Oxford. 'The linear strip / of the beautiful Jurassic lias.' Swung by the lodestone of his sex, he sidled to the gates of the Botanic Gardens.

Comfortable in his discomfort, he brushed sticky eyes with a mildewed sleeve. The morning was fresh, unused. Sileen inhaled its optimism and sneezed. This was dangerous, the elation of elsewhere. He did not belong. *That* was the buzz. Lightheaded, he paused to register a crusty triumphal arch. Twin niches occupied by handless royalty: sandstone ancestors – syphilitic, crumbling to powder. All stone aspires to the condition of dust. All things that live. Grit on the wind. A Jacobite salute, and Sileen attempted the turnstile.

The reassurance of footsteps on honest gravel, the crunch and drag. The very sounds evoked an England that was dead to him, privileged places from which he had been definitively expelled. The chesty whoop-whoo of wood-pigeons, the purring of doves. Sileen played the game, he stooped to read the visiting cards, the exotica of half-remembered names. *Rosa omissa, Rosa damascene, Clematis cirrhosa, Jasminum fruticans, Lycium barbarum.* Bees were at their tasks, work their joy. Should the bee stand as his emblem? That sturdy torso, the scent-drenched journeying in the service of an implacable queen. Anonymous, obscure – drunk on matutinal nostrums, settling nowhere.

A secret country. His soul's globe afloat, a bubble of ego, unpricked by leaf blades: it soared, paying homage to a diffusion of florets, ferns, liquorice herbs. All the microclimates of competing beds. The lifeforce returned to his wrecked body – the matted hair spikes, sarcoidal skin, blistered tongue. Filth shone. A great stone had been rolled aside. Sileen, premature cadaver, enjoyed the solitary freedom of the garden. He wandered at whim – rockeries, greenhouses, clouts of lavender: from grass to path, tracking the west-falling shadowline of a giant yew. He was relieved of himself, his pain remitted.

Was it a special day? Already the young gardeners, descendants of Bobart, were at their tasks – in ragged shorts and ponytails. They were busy with besoms, correcting the gravel. A disciplined clatter of motor-mowers coming from the far bank of the Cherwell drew Sileen out among the glasshouses. Another phantom Zion! Sileen was uneasy. These seductions were too blatant. Meadowland, fat green bolsters. The plashing of a plurality of fountains. Sacred cricket squares. Heavy rollers dragged over indecently smooth ground. Who could deserve these glimpses of paradise? They made Sileen's banishment hard to bear. Arcady rented like a cheap video. Melancholia possessed him. Cast out by his own hand. That other England a mocking dream: groundsmen, college servants, erectors of marquees, kitchen maids. His demons had found his flaw – a weakness for country pleasures.

Thus memory betrays us, recalling times that never were. Better tarmac the lot. Better the dogs of Whitechapel, the manners of the souk. Sileen, sweating, trifled with an imaginary buttonhole, a nosegay of cornflowers. His scalp prickled beneath a straw boater. You could see the white circumference where the sodden lining pinched like a castrating-ring.

Abort these riparian fantasies before they turn you out. Who *they*? Before they notice you – Sileen, humpback crow, molesting fritillaries. Before they hustle this alien from their water-meadows. Forbid all prospects of towers, domes, grazing cattle. Let Sileen cast the first stone; costive leveller, bent witness. Tip him back on the Queen's highway, traitor to his class.

Germy Hinton had commandeered a bench that overlooked the stream. And marked his territory with a flutter of papers. Sileen approached in silence, murder in his heart. There had been enough killing. One more could make no difference. Room on the ferry for another tenor. Act first, then publish your obsequies.

The slow track-in on the unsuspecting grouthead depressed the cripple. This creature was one of our own. The doctor had never been young. He had arrived, without noticing it, at that age when he was forever checking his fly-buttons. Not *quite* so decrepit that he did not care. That was ahead of him: behaving disgracefully without a qualm, waiting for death's tongue in his throat.

Hinton's head was in his hands. The tragic inevitability of the Cherwell, its scummy surface, passing uncelebrated before him: an ejection of vaseline. He soothed the fearful spectres of the night with ducks and willows, skimming insects, sapless trees. His was a reversed world. Any intrusion was obtuse.

Admiring that shellacked dome, the goldrim specs, the Trollope schnozz, Sileen was plunged into an elegiac mood. Could this university oblate, this clerk, be one of the true Hintons, terminal cough of the bloodline? Directly descended from James Hinton, surgeon, philosopher of pain, 'saviour of women', and from C.H., with his airfix time kit, his system of threadlike lines, 'multitudes of moving points in the plane'? Unlikely. But who knows? It was a singular day.

The doc, catching at the very last the stamp and sweep of Sileen on the gravel, leapt to his feet, rabbiting. He was fully primed, speeding like a tram, eyes on stalks. This geek took methedrine to slow down. He spittled Sileen's vest in a drench of rancid sputum. Everything was possible, ya – but not now, not here. Too late and always would be. Um. Mind elsewhere. In Latin vein. To-day. Encaenia – Oxford's Oscar show. Doctorates flying like clap remedies, hurricane rhetoric. Cash boasts. Newdigate. His speech from the pulpit. Chance to swish in ermine drag. Cameras, feasts. *Who*, Hodgson? Which one, pray? Ah, yes, the great White Hope, Hum. Ha. Les neiges d'antan.

All Sileen required was an address. If he could lay his hands on the goods, he could snuff Hinton like a pauper's candle. The town was awash with bombers, incendiarists, state-trained killers. Who would miss him? Who would even know?

'My theme,' Hinton declared, 'expressed in the blank verse with which Tennyson gained *his* chancellor's medal in 1829, takes the castle mound, or mount, and . . . '

Mercy. Sileen was surfeited with mounds, with every species of elevation, anathema on them all. Rhab Adnam had cured him of the urge to climb.

'The mound is the city born as man – beheaded, sacrificed. A covert presence, humming with implication. A cabalistic Adam with biology intact. I had only to unravel the labyrinthine paths, ascend with considered tread – fuse my energies with the energy of place. They expected me to muse among classical ruins, dabble in sunsets. Pah! I have decoded a vital entity. Officiated at the betrothal of seeker and source.'

'What were you on?' Sileen couldn't help himself.

'Good question. Something rather wicked, I'm afraid – an exponential tincture of bennies, glucose, laxative, chilled with a blast of Howard Marks' finest Afghan black. Lovely man, Howard. So grateful. You bring it all back.'

They spoke so well of him, his damaged subscribers. Worshipped the air the steel town Emperor of Dope had once exhaled, his bedmates and cellmates. Never a word of pique, even from those who played Judas in the witness-box. A Prince among Pranksters, a Celtic demigod. A psychedelic counter-revolutionary: Howard smoked out the shaky vermin, children of the establishment. Wasted them. Charm of the devil.

'Hodgson? The *Borderland* sequel? Of course. Not uninteresting. One of those fugitive reputations long abandoned to the mercies of obsessives, semi-literate tunnel visionaries, necrophiles who can't leave a dead bibliography alone. What did you make of Birchy's canard in *Weird Fantasy*, circa 1968? Sexual symbolism? Outlandish stuff. He should talk, a name like that. Moskowitz is dogged but unreliable. Everts, thorough. So many, mad as hatters, living by proxy. Sequel, you say?'

The gesticulating Hinton had jigged dangerously close to the riverbank. Sileen, reluctantly, hauled him back. What a temptation. Hold the germ under until the bubbles of frenzy ceased. Stay on the road. The mist was lifting from the meadows. It promised to be a blazing day.

'I *did* blunder on a cache of unrecorded *Carnacki* stories in a furniture shop down by the station, Park End Street. Undoubtedly genuine, but correctly suppressed. I torched them to preserve the integrity of Hodgson's standing. No better than the fabulations of a body-builder. Muscular agnosticism – like a Borges dictation transcribed by Arnold Schwarzenegger. No, no. The marvellous find was the *Borderland* manuscript and the storm photographs.'

'Don't miss the parade, doc. Leave them with me and go on your way.'

'The provenance. I must explain. Chad Hodgson, oldest of the brothers, became involved with a divorced woman, then exited from the script. He may have died in the First War, who knows? His child, a daughter, Una Hope Hodgson, married a certain Arthur Blair Machen – yes, only son of the Monmouthshire fantasist. Chad was, so I believe, entrusted with the manuscript. Never completed. But I read quite enough to ascertain its . . . '

'How much? What might it fetch from a demented collector?'

Hinton jumped back, flapping. '*Sell*? Out of the question. Too rich for my blood. As soon as I glimpsed the significance, I packed the whole lot off to Undark in Cambridge.'

Undark. One of the few words that may be expressed while the grip tightens around a windpipe. A confessional squeak. Unnn-darrrk! Croak of phlegm. All those miles walked for nothing. Simon Undark, famous for his goldfish tie. Famous for being unknown. Sileen squeezed. Hinton was the colour of raw liver and not so fresh. His tartan tongue lolled. He flashed a photo from an inside pocket and waved it like the emigrant's farewell.

Stalk lightning over a featureless sea. Veins on Hinton's protruding orb. Stupendous discharge splits the aqueous humour. Ecstatic hair. Sileen laughs. Something at last to grip. The card in his hand held up against the waft of midgy parkland. An electric demon in the fellows' garden. Would it stall Drage-Bell? Hardly. The score was Undark or total eclipse.

Coughing, spluttering, crowned in slime (where Sileen had dowsed his heat in riverweed), Hinton bounced back with a viral resilience. Gush of enthusiasm, the flipside of catatonia. 'Undark' was all that needed to be said. Undark was legend. And Germy his legman. A post-viva 2/1 to *the* starred double first, the best of his generation. At England's darkest hour, initiates muttered Undark's name like a password. In jungle clearings, fish brothels, hairy yurts in Mongol deserts, meeting unexpectedly, the Cantabs would articulate the masonic catchphrase: 'Undark!'

Hinton, being closest (or so he thought), put it best, quoting Menéndez y Pelayo. 'The alchemists, and other illuminati or gulls, began to take possession of his name and to invent apocryphal books.' They sub-titled his silence. Pirated pamphlets he had never published. Taped his table-talk and translated it into demotic Swedish. They went to law over the right to steal his private correspondence. They plagiarized pastiches and claimed them as their own. They took his tonsured squibs for reading lists. Taught themselves runic characters, mandarin calligraphy, twelve-note systems, Stock Exchange mumbo jumbo, meteorological data bases. They learnt nothing. Undark was blatant and opaque. Gnomic, lewd, swift. A multi-faceted gem. A beacon of darkness.

He was, according to Hinton, the most intelligent entity on the island. Our conscience. Sileen gagged, he hated the sod. Milton and soda water: the trash of invisible colleges, wise ones spooning marrow from dry bones.

'Undark,' Hinton persisted, 'lives for the coda, the sly footnote. He's delighted to begin where Hodgson lost his nerve – with the death of time, the immanent triumph of beast nature. All dogs are dust. Does he *identify* with the depressive visionary? Impertinent to speculate. The pit-creatures have surely come from hell to claim their Faust, to apply their branding-irons to his sanity. It's one of the great climaxes in the literature of the fantastic. "Stand still, you ever-moving spheres of heaven, / That time may cease." *Borderland* is overwritten, certainly – *pace* Lovecraft. But in this genre, you'll agree, excess is the norm. And Undark's question remains pertinent. "Can excess ever be excessive enough?" Is the realization of absolute horror a paradigm of stasis in the universe? What occurs if we insist upon trespassing beyond that final note?'

Trespassing was Sileen's game. Ingratiating himself was a newer trick. He patted Hinton on the cheek. Knuckled him till he rang. There was little to offer beyond companionship and the transitory compensations of the flesh. A best buddy, a willing chum. Perhaps the doc ran to wheels – motor, tandem, cart? After what the cripple had already endured, Cambridge was a puny step. He leered, faking interest, nodding his head in premature agreement.

'Undark sees Hodgson's achievement as prophetic – like that of Ludwig Meidner in Germany. Anticipations of apocalypse. He tapped the shockwaves flowing back from the psychic carnage of the Great War. Wrote, in advance of event, in fear and trembling – describing the instant of his extinction, blown to pieces at the Forward Observation Post in Ploegsteert. Lights out, he *became* light. The "universal water" that video cameras exploit. Hodgson's courage would admit, in his biography, no diversion from the trajectory of a written fate.'

'We must join him,' Sileen offered.

'Hodgson?' Hinton was anxious, but ready. He hugged his papers to cradle the blast.

'Undark. In Cambridge. He'll be expecting you to do the donkey work. We'll act as his soundingboards.'

'The Newdigate, the luncheon. My measurements, the mound. Not possible, not yet, not now. We'd never achieve sufficient enlightenment to pass through the door. We belong among the swine. Don't you follow? *One* step across the borderland threshold and the hybrid – pig/ visionary – becomes a god. Or tumbles to the deepest shelf of hell.'

Hinton was swooping, trapping scattered notes with the ball of his heel, scuffling gravel like birdseed on the floor of a cage.

'Wait. Forgive my vulgar curiosity . . . ' It was Sileen's last card: vanity. '. . . But do you have any connection with James Hinton the philosopher?'

'Ah. Umm. Yes.' Hinton goafed – a spontaneous nosebleed, a scarlet spatter down the grungy jersey. He rummaged for the relevant document. 'Rather exciting. Tennyson research. William Allingham, the Donegal customs officer, his diary. Monday, July 20, 1868. Allow me to quote: "Hot. Tennyson and Mrs T. on the steamer, I with them to Brockenhurst . . . We spoke of Swedenborg: T. says his Hell is more striking than his Heaven; praises Hinton's book on Man and Nature." Praises Hinton! Excellent. Must fly, Bullingdon Road. Robes. Encaenia. Sheldonian. Recitation. Alarming. To-night then. Bullingdon Arms?'

Sileen, the Hodgson storm photograph safely in his pocket, endured the parting, and did not trouble himself to watch Dr Hinton's scampering retreat. The morning was not quite spoiled. He was content to stroll. Indulge. The effluvium of sluggish water, the sight of new-mown hay.

EIGHT

The indiscriminate waters of Folly Bridge: Sileen's appetite had returned, only his inner eye starved. To be where he was, suffering the stones and locusts of unrequited bliss. The less deceived, the better enjoyed. Carnivorous whelp. Light could not dupe him. He forged his own delusions, and they were true – all those dire excisions of 'Morse's Oxford'. Phoney blood in the cracks of genuine granite sets. The tumour of sanctioned privilege. He bit. Waves of dispersed colour toyed with the flanks of moored craft. Salter Brothers boatyard. River rushing beneath a triple arch.

Sileen gnaws a hangnail of burnt bacon, splits the surface tension of a golden egg. It gushes mess. He mops. A rectangle of damp white bread. The blue plate is restored, a virgin disk. Reviving, he belches. Spits. Dying cells perish without fuss. He warms like a lizard, slowly. The cordite nightstuff fades, other people had been blown apart. The roaring, the sirens, the maddened crowd: he grew deaf. An empty coffee-cup to his ear, he listened to harps calling from a distant shore.

They were wrong, the terrorists, to pretend there was some cause worth more than description. They were addicted to death, a black pornography of secrets. Sileen did not judge, he feared. Feared what he knew of himself, champion of unreason. Killing is easy. Waiting hurts. He scraped back his chair and stood, trying to believe he meant whatever it was he could not express.

Sileen the *flâneur* was a novel concept. He strolled his dementia modestly, and at whim, not knowing where to turn. He ascended, easing himself, yard by yard, towards the clot of the town's centre, the crossing of roads. Was that too logical? Oxford, more than most, was laid out like a compass. He was untroubled by the 'tyranny of facade', the blatant coding of gargoyles and figurines. They flattered his mood.

He craved expulsion. The place was charmed. Sileen was a bullfrog, dodging wheels.

College entrances are barred to casual visitors, uniforms lurk in the shadows. Thank the Lord, it cuts down choices. Hissing buses evacuate their clysters of cameraheads – who cling together, waiting for instruction. Sileen offers them the elbow, tramples on tendons. He is boisterous and gay. A woman screams and frets her husband. Who rattles a sticky child. The distress is all in Sileen's wake. He climbs, immune, sniffing for the salty tang of intelligent women, and allowing himself to recall – it dates him faster than Criminal Records – the words of Edward Dorn. 'Variously do their cunts shine.' The lank American poet's cynical rhapsody in VI parts; at once, libidinous and irate. Daughters of tame dictators with shameless legs, riding out from Paddington, naked under their fur coats. No worse a fuck. No slower a train. Poetry is also a way of remembering.

Sun on stone. Watching the way his feet progress, coping with the slope, this marriage of opposites. They know something he has yet to learn. The whereabouts of Rhab Adnam and all Sileen's dubious connections. A day of innocent excess – processions, fancy duds, gluttony. To be outside is still to play a part.

It's not envy, let them enjoy it while they can. They are doomed, these gorgeous children, birdspit hanging from a hedge. Pink faces, barely inhabited. Billowing gowns, puffy white bows, starched cuffs. That's the women. Scuttling on skijump heels to claim their dole of glory. Stockings a bonus (for Sileen). Fingertip smokers, unused to the muck in their throats, drag nervously. Ratty, hungover males in borrowed blackout curtains. Give them their moment. Sileen is plague news. They run to pass him.

England's immortal youth – in clusters, or panting to catch up. Beauty is intelligence. Intelligent flesh. Sileen had never seen so many beautiful women and felt, physically, less affected. It hurt his brain. He slumped in the doorway of some Christian mission, buffeted by trippers honking to get at the *Alice in Wonderland* mugs. Tom Tower. Wrought-iron gates. Off-limits greenery. He is Caliban at the Lord Mayor's Show.

Struggling for breath, it hits him: an expediency of light. Oxford. He has come so far and achieved nothing. He knows nothing. He has learnt nothing. The light was there before him and will remain when he is dirt.

It breeds in oolitic stone, sand drifting down from the Cotswolds, effigies rotting in alcoves. The 'golden hour' is a statutory fixture. It lasts all day, this cinema of compulsory nostalgia. It models impossibly pale and laughing women. He watched how they ran. All shoulders and hair, patting their heads and letting their skirts ride. Virtuous legs defending virtue. White ties, black gowns. Coaxing the elder dead out onto their balconies: John Dee, Robert Fludd, Edmund Halley, Giordano Bruno. Visitors and disputants, their numbers called.

He is dying. His light stolen by windows. His exhausted blood circumscribes a hoop of medieval glass, granting colour to the sleeting murk. His skull is a poisoned egg, set out for crows, white among mossy walls. Light is dust, falling in columns. The tawny town is a shattered timer, a whirligig of abrasive powder. It is now and not now: attach himself to fresher lives, or become a pillar of salt, another misattributed portrait.

Head down, Sileen butted against gravity in a blind charge. He scattered mendicants and a quorum of the morbidly curious who had been drawn to the Pennyfarthing to validate the news. All true: blue ribbons, TV gangs interrogating bogus survivors; Plod at his honest best – doing nothing with authority, adding bulk to an underpopulated frame. Sileen didn't catch the papers. Except as winter underwear. Oxford, with its dearth of newsagents, suited him. A civic abhorrence of postage stamps, fag packets, gum, wank mags, empathized with the cripple's present mood. Read the firmament instead. Take instruction from birds perching on a chapel roof.

Follow crows. Fly with the piston legs of high-steppers. Young women celebrating the freedom of recently ruptured hymens. There has to be a second chance, even for Sileen, an opportunity to reinvent himself. Procure a sharper editor and a more convincing script. He was more than willing to bear passive witness to midsummer and all its Pimm's and circuses.

Too early for museums, too late for the river: he flattens his nose against the sealed door of MOMA. Peers into the vestibule for some trace of women and culture (in that order). The twin imponderables of his existence. Nothing. Mercifully. His face a chalk moon among posters, wimpish clouds and a city of rain. Some fat little tart inflicts Canadian Airforce exercises on flabby triceps to procure a more convincing cleavage. (Ever *seen* a Canadian airman?) PR and graphic design, plus explanations on a postcard: that's what gallery culture is. Least as best.

It was then that he caught the flow of scarlet across the paper mirror. The heady scent. Like blood droplets over the crushed ice of an eel-tank. Isabel. His weakness.

No fancy, she passed him, cometlike, brushing against his back. Without recognition, hurrying to some appointment. Something between a fast walk and a run – bare legs, tripping and awkward, mature *gamine* – down Pembroke Street. A metropolitan raid. The red suit – in honour of which cameras? Wrecking surveillance with the drama of her startling transit. Sileen's heart surged. Love in his hand. The sight undid him. He trembled, rushed breathless, to trace the passage of that crimson stain through the town's dull lint.

St Ebbes: a clog of slo-mo pedestrians, impoverished, addicted to acquisition. They slacken his pursuit. The drinking school around the memorial obelisk derive obscure comfort from that pee-stained stump. They wave their cans of Special Brew at the hustling cripple – and cheer. Kerry Gold voices, soft and mad, sweet with the purity of threat. Isabel is buffeted and spun. Lost in terminal crowds: the ones who cling to the station to be sure of getting out. Dole bandits, bum-pinchers, drunks, thieves.

He was tempted, time out of war, to join them, the blues boys. Serious pissheads, dosed with oblivion, always stake out memorial gardens. It makes sense. The centre of the town, all human life shuffles through. There are cool steps on which to cultivate your haemorrhoids and to exploit the anvil of war guilt, 'comrades who died'. Any trick to loosen the pockets. Timorous citizenry back off in superstitious dread, yield the patch, so that the fanciers of industrial-strength lager can sprawl and chortle, take the sun. Bonn Square is no worse than the rest. Sileen, thirsty as Morse, and less the hop-buff, is drawn by the hiss of liquid punctures. Lust is a dreadful thorn. He shocks himself and does not pause.

Isabel dissolves among a shuttle of buses, a dancer. Worse. A lunchtime diva between engagements. Clipclop. Too much paint for Brewer Street. Eyelashes like flytraps. Write her out.

Sileen's on heat. It's Helen he needs, not Isabel. Conversation, advice. Loot. He leans, groaning, against the perspex confessional of the Midland Bank's cash-machine, hoping some unclaimed largesse will tumble out. He'd feed his tongue into the slit if that would serve. Genuine de-vesters snort and poke. Helen's pin number is easy to remember. *Forty Lashes Less One* (40–01). If only he'd had the foresight to nick her card. HUNGRY & HOMELESS has been sprayed, like a Passover slogan, on the door – warding off the very conditions the institution is chartered to inspire.

Across Cornmarket Street at a canter, and into its diminutive, Market Street. Isabel is running again. The short skirt riding unwisely on her long thighs. Sileen was almost close enough to touch – until he was balked by a mob of gowns and waistcoats, outside the market pub, the Roebuck. The migrated name gave him pause. What were these flushed children so frantic to celebrate? The streets were lurid with exploded flour bags, carnival dye, shaving foam. The wilder lads looked like casualties at a field dressing-station: snowhaired, arms in slings, simpering for pocket cameras. Flashflash. They suckle empty magnums and dry puke into ornamental tubs. All is forgiven, the city *en fête*.

The publican, foot in door, tried to turn back the crowd. 'Go away. Too late. Position filled.' The winner paraded in his apron and rubber gloves. Disappointed supplicants hurled themselves at the narrowing gap. Those at the rear of the crocodile, back around Carfax, shoved hardest. They *had* to hear the worst from the Roebuck's mouth. Rejects. Failed washer-ups. They didn't even qualify as down-and-outs in Oxford, let alone Paris. Dirty pots would be attended by superior hands. Cold despair nibbled on their intoxication. It was their first pop at the real world and the real world had given them the finger.

In Whitechapel Isabel's microsuit, scarlet as a triple bypass, was a shriek against monochrome repressions. She was a brakelight skid, a cardiac stab for grounded tossers. On Catte Street, hurdling chains, skirting Radcliffe Camera in a delirium of jumpcuts, she bled, unnoticed, into a shuffle of tulip-coated initiates. The Encaenia procession: ego-inflatables, codgers with staffs and rods, pancake hats. Widmerpools and purse-snatchers in polished clogs. Corruption at a stately crawl. The worst of the Lord Jenkins lookalikes: Lord Jenkins himself. A chess queen on expenses. Some bibulous old fart in a tasselled mortarboard, having his gilt-trimmed skirts lifted by an unbroken page in knee-breeches, black stockings, buckled pumps. What a hoot! A two-by-two plod of crimson that makes the jealous Isabel seem discreet.

How they jabbered, these progress swellers, sashaying to glory. The plebs, herded behind crash-barriers, click and buzz. A première without stars. A martyrdom without martyrs. One manikin is up on his toes trading quips with an advanced case of risus sardonicus in an ex-stoat collar. In the gut of the pack, it's survival by handbag. Overtime for bootblacks. Boneless necks are strengthened in avoiding the scrape of scientific beards – those mean ones Brahms-loving dentists cultivate. No ethnics on view. It's uncanny. Like a hernia-in-the-throat Fifties newsreel, or an awayday to the Channel Islands.

'So this is what is meant by tradition,' they mutter. A freelance state funeral. To show the bastards who *really* owns this town (and half of England). Flaunt it, ladies. The Old Bill in their nippled coal scuttles are properly subservient, whitegloved like wine waiters, loitering with intent. Fists clenched. Regulation 'tashes in subdued converse with the bulldog pack – who confide only in handsets. An isthmus of daylight between their razor-creased flannels. One brass button secures the heraldic blazer, the truncheon of a blue college tie. Even the Rorschach manhole covers are stamped with hieroglyphs. Every slab a story. Windows of college servants, polishing their bawdy, hacking rough edges from cucumber sandwiches, wrestling with lobsters.

Sileen fumes. Is there no gap in this tide of privilege? Isabel has slipped him. An unpaid spectator, he's pestled by a genial constabulary. Lured among a banality of walnut-complexioned transatlantics. He hasn't the spit to gob the hornrims of Lord Toad, that latinate lisper.

It's endless: from the Sheldonian Theatre to the Schools Quadrangle, a stately convulsion of dignitaries with cold mutton jowls. Where do they find them all, crumblies who can stand up to an annual airing? They must have decanted the taprooms, sent snatch squads into rest homes, granted day release to the inmates of local asylums. Some impurity in the Folly Bridge black pudding: he was hallucinating. Surely no pressgang would risk the pestholes of Wapping to drag back S. L. Joblard? But there he *was*, the schnorrer, Sileen's Robinson, swaying with the best of them, in full gubernatorial fig, ketchup skirts and lambskin bib to catch the gravy. A porcupine magus. The unacknowledged Reichmann brother. A professor from hell. Had it come to this? The barbarians bagging the best costumes. Beggars in charge of the ladle.

At last, it's over. The sheep are in the fold. Sileen can only hope they are enduring a full-frontal rant from the addled and speeding doctor. He wants Hinton to go on so long they have to nail him to the pulpit. Yobs in the gallery jeer at this addition to the roll of honour: Matthew Arnold, Oscar Wilde, John Ruskin, John Addington Symonds, John Buchan, Laurence Binyon, Germy Hinton. Coppers and proctors rub hands in self-congratulatory fraternization. Bit of a bummer, lads. Not a waterbomb, nor a threatening gesture from Class War. No scalp-hair to hose from the floor of the van.

Sileen's back to pace – New College Lane, ducking under the horse-collar of a pastiched Bridge of Sighs; no time to spare a glance at Edmund Halley's grace and favour. He flinches from unseen faces in oblique, suicide windows. Brittle in highwalled lanes, nose to the double yellow, he yearns for Isabel, spear prints where her heels scraped the paint. A low-flying Concorde gives the punters a thrill, shakes the minarets of All Souls. Sileen is alone. Only the unqualified dead walk out in the midday sun.

His method, as always, is to erase the image of the thing he is hunting; break free from the bonds of sight, keep her at a distance. While she is visible, he will never get close. He pounds, sweat gumming hair-streaks to his scalp, blinding him with corrupted salt, as he brushes indifferently against the old city boundaries: Longwall, Holywell. He investigates any hint of coolness, vegetation, respite. He taps shadow-nests, ivy, drowned gardens. Pint pots on teak tables, his fantasy. The Turf Tavern then. (Is there a welcome clatter of hooves in that designation?)

The risk of a narrow, flagged passage: bad birth replays justified by the imposition of a large man, blocking the way. His head didn't fit; a scissors and paste job – runtish boat stapled onto meat-porter's shoulders. The dark glasses were an overreaction. You had to be somebody to try for that acreage of anonymity – Jack Spot, say, under a bowler, a newly declared bankrupt. The suit was worse, concertinaed at the ankles, short in the sleeve. The sort of affair a redneck suitor picks blind from a Sears catalogue. And regrets.

Averting his eyes, in unaccustomed modesty, Sileen recced the bar through a low window. Found what he dreaded, smiled. His scarlet plaything and her interminable, black silk legs dressing a pew. Teasing a glass of crushed ice: Isabel in company with a suspect razorhead. Tan linen threads, Milan inspired, Whitechapel cut – loose on the shoulder, tight in the crotch. White T-shirt and a ruff of throat hair. Who did you expect? The story was coming together like proper fiction. Sileen's drinking chum, the poetic armbreaker from the Pennyfarthing. Nicky Tarten.

The cripple steps to one side and the minder steps with him. They reel in affectionate futility, somewhat after the Politburo style – cloddish, vodka dangerous. Sileen, warming nicely, hooks his partner just below the second button and waits for him to fold. Pain freezes his wrist in an analgesic spray, screams aloud: the shock of punching your weight against a sack of Mormon bibles. The professional brute was delighted to have something to do, something that he understood. He lifted Sileen by the lapels and whacked him, wall to wall. Tickled by the vivacity with which his client bruised, he harped protuberant ribs – stood back to watch him slide towards the deck. And convenient range of the size fourteen boots.

The relief of mental agony given a physical form: Sileen, twisting, saw Isabel rise as he fell. A puff from the back of a gangland shocker flashed into his sabbatical consciousness. 'London's answer to Elmore Leonard.' Now he had only to recall what London's question had been.

Big CU: the silent working of Isabel's lips. Each crayoned groove. Like watching a butterfish through pebbled glass. Head thrown back, lustrous swat of hair, lashing the villain as she laughs. At her shoulder, a sudden cloud depresses the play of beams. Some weather portent? She disengages. Notices Sileen crash across the window and Anthony's bulk block out the sun with the formal routines of inflicted mayhem. The rhythmic prod of leather on bone.

Isabel: on her feet. Tarten the Gent rising with her. Following her out – to muzzle his excited sibling. Gentle Anthony and stand him down, a baked potato in each paw. Haul Sileen inside. A brandy and a handkerchief to smear the worst of the damage. In some ways it's an improvement. A bit of colour in his cheeks: purple, indigo, Danish blue. Nicholas Tarten grasps the victim's hand, drops it like the touch of death.

'We was having a natter about Albert Donoghue, 'ardest man in the East End of London, bar none. Ever run across 'im? Absolute evil Albert was. You ask Anthony. I had occasion once to send the pair of them out Loughton way – I was telling the lady – quiet word with a slag who was completely out of order. My life, Alby done the lot of 'em, the family, entire. God knows the mischief – if Tone 'adn't smacked 'im with a tyre-lever. Right monster. Topping the bill when we give Miss Izzy her intro – "The Wapping Wildcat". Prime location, Sheppey, week Friday.'

In the small sunken garden of the Turf Tavern, a man unused to gardens. Pint of clouded scrumpy in hand, the shade of a plane tree, a man who did not drink. Mordecai Donar. Donar scrubbed the slatted table, compulsively, with a balled wad of toilet tissue, then spread out the photographs of his mother and his sisters. He played a match flame against the slowly curling borders, scorching them. Under the table, wedged between his feet, was a Londis carrier-bag. In it, a revolver.

NINE

The town was defined, its energies cradled between discrete acts of folly and enterprise. It was the suspended hour when all things creep and crawl. Rhab Adnam, ignoring municipal prohibitions, went over the wall and onto the coarse grass of the Castle Mound. Nails hooked in turf, he favoured the direct route – tested the gradient. The tump fisted above him, spiked with thistles and half-wild bushes. He had rushed it, he reeled. The sky was black as Mary of Scotland's velvet.

Adnam slid, he rubbed at places where the skin was already broken. He willed darkness. A moral element to separate him from Oxford's dreamlike indolence. A sharp-edged pebble to squeeze in the fist. A pinch of grit to tease beneath his eyelid. Provocations to equal the risks he felt obliged to take. Small blasphemies were Adnam's bag. And it was working! The marram dune upgraded its status from a cough of stubborn clay to a site of potential sacrifice, a thatched skull – Tradescant! Rhab was catching the wave. It hurt and it felt good. Death might work out fine. Unhitch the rucksack and saw a blade of cat's tongue grass along the underside of a wrist. Detach. Observe. Withdraw. Notice, with no involvement, birdspit dripping from the scrawny sycamore.

The watcher's vantage clouded. He didn't know it but Rhab Adnam was making his own weather. William Hope Hodgson's *Eloi Eloi Lama Sabachtani* was his text. Dr Hinton had infected this ground with his musings. Bad poetry operates like a powerful insecticide, draining into tributaries, turning the urine orange. The culture geek had been on the nod, Hodgson's yellowback horror in his pocket, when the caretaker had palmed him a key to the Mound. How could he open the myth ducts (King Mempricius and his wolf pack, Empress Maud and the frozen river, Edmund Ironside) with the viral fear of Hodgson's prose nuzzling at his hip? What a tale, *Eloi Eloi*! What a dose! The chemist Baumoff resurrects (is that the word?) the famous Easter lightshow, the Jesus thing – psychic thunderheads of Golgotha, magnetic seepage, spongy black pith. Bruise-glamour from a sulky, post-coital cloudbase. Un-rain stacking the horizon like sheaves of condemned wheat. A dip of grey powder on the experimenter's tongue. A steel spike in the foot, 'between the second and third branches of the dorsal artery.' Pain becomes the *absence* of light, its withdrawal – the permission for light's contrary. Impersonations of light. Light borrowed from Limbo. Great suffering, maculate darkness; clouds of voices on an irreversible loop.

Which way had it swung for Adnam? Had his trivial torment admitted this premature De Mille eclipse? Or had the minatory sky induced him to audition for the Jeffrey Hunter, blue-eyes part? Whatever, it was all Hinton's fault. He'd got there first and botched the triangulation, salted the creamy green. He'd poisoned everything Adnam had journeyed to assert. Whitechapel, Oxford, Cambridge: a single, steady exhalation. The pleroma. God's theme park. The pilgrim's wedge. Adnam lay under the fallen sky attempting, futilely, to link the mammary terminals. To jumpstart the necessity of walking those extra miles.

The ranks of doctors gave themselves up to infusions of doom – as Germy Hinton pedalled the Sheldonian's pulpit, stanzas deep in verse that was not so much blank as lobotomized. Its nerve-ends had been clipped, nothing connected with anything else. Lurches of language that defied speech. Between the sixth and the ninth hour, they paid a sorry tribute for the feast that was to come.

Even the prisoners in the old gaol, who stood upon stools to look out on a vertical slice of the Mound, were freeer than Hinton's audience. They knew when the bell would ring. The poet conjured no images. In the noon dark, finger raised towards the skirted sun, he made his pact with Adnam.

The pages of an oilskin notebook fluttered. At the summit, Rhab illustrated Hinton's unheard text. Like a peasant with a ricebowl, the pad a couple of inches from his face, he scooped up the town's slack consciousness. Reported on things he could hardly see. Beside him was a pincushion doll, one of its legs broken off – a manikin secreted in the turf.

As Hinton climbed down, the doors of the theatre were thrown open on a blaze of light. Adnam watched the cloud-scarf break and decay. He took the reviving warmth on his upturned face.

These incidents, occurring simultaneously, at their own intensity, devour the available light; concentrate it, real or imaginary, light forged in earlier times – remote, prescient.

Summer is North Oxford's season – Summertown, Sunnymead – a writer's house, rented space, too much of it, too many distractions, brief tenure, can women live like this? Can this near-white room, this sunspill, exist without the cages and dungeons that newsreels sponsor? Sofya is troubled, guilt her portion. But happy too, happy to be troubled. She *has* to get back, fade into the warren, so that there is, once again, a territory from which to escape, a reason for exile. Madness makes her calm. She is so young, Andi thinks. So beautiful that she wants to touch.

A river (the Cherwell?) ripples across the white ceiling – a morning meditation, like dreaming on a streambed, beneath clear water. Trembling leaves frame the long window. It's excessive. Too like other rooms where Sofya could not bear to stay. She's dressed, ready – likes the feel of her clothes. She takes comfort from the shape and design of the cup from which she does not drink. It isn't hers. There are no appointments to-day, nobody has asked to interview them. They do not belong in this house. In this room, yes. The room accepts transients. It has to. Even the paperback books have been carefully left, they make assumptions. Literacy, women of the university, drinkers of decaffeinated coffee. Andi is naked on the bed, covered by a single sheet. She *smells* naked.

They are both waiting for something. A scratch at the door, a creak of the hinges. Sofya interprets this phenomena as the ghost of a cat. They have not discussed it but Andi knows. Knows when the cat is about to make her entrance. She leaves the window open so that the beast can take the sun.

The spectral cat rustles paper, it may not mew. It domesticates the eros of the borrowed room, the curiosity over other people's furniture and clothes. The (suppressed) desire to sniff and pry. Andi fluffs a pillow, Sofya passes her a wide cup with small red flowers on its brim. Mornings, late mornings, are difficult. It's like being in a hotel room with a stranger. There is no established sequence. The open window admits the city: bicycles, wives. Sofya admires the strength in Andi's body, the width of her shoulders. The meaty sweetness: one generation out of the byre. Cow breath. No English girl would travel without a wrap – risk Andi's modest display, sit, uncovered, balancing a cup on her knees. It's a decision she's taken. Why should they speak of it?

Andi drinks greedily. Tanned froth emphasizes her pale moustache, the generous lips, the indecently white teeth. There is something repellant about the way she slurps, so free of shame. She reaches from the bed towards a slipware bowl. Her richly furred armpits are deltas of sexual access, moist and unsplit. She chooses an apple. Her strong jaw mashes the green fruit. Sofya, in defence, lays her hand on the camera case.

She steals a glance at the bedside cabinet, anywhere, the blue pillow, headboard, as Andi throws back the sheet. A book. Christopher Marlowe. A grey paperback. *Complete Plays and Poems*. Everyman's Library. John Faustus, the conjurer, skirted and capped. Andi, biting the apple, revolving the shredded core, strides to the bathroom. A walk-on Helen. The curve of whose back Sofya may safely admire (and resent) – while the lifted camera hides her blushing face. The instrument limits itself to the play of light, the sharp angles of the stripped pine door.

Sofya puts down the camera to handle the book without opening it, the slippery smooth cover she cannot bring herself to read. Phrases insinuate. 'Filled with violence.' 'Relentless.' 'Sly and ornate.' She will not study the slit of light beneath the door, but cannot help overhearing – she wants it – Andi pissing into the bowl: the rush, pause, rush again. A horse, a mare. A running tap. The tap *does* run. Andi splashing water over her breasts. So Sofya imagines. She pictures it. Andi towelling. Andi's towel tucked around her waist. Brushing her teeth with firmly directed strokes, gargling. The mirror. Sofya feels the exchange of heat. Her blouse sticks to her, she picks at it. Her jeans are too rough, a brass button cutting into her belly. She wriggles, she shifts. Listens to Andi, whose head is twisted, hair in basin, drinking cold water from the tap.

Sofya changes position, drags the rocking chair, so that she can gaze into the skirts of the great English elm, localize her excitement. She's feverish. How *precisely* can she define the request to take a portrait? Did Andi's present behaviour imply such a request? Was it unselfconscious display? Or did Andi feel she should conform to the mores of higher bohemia? The ovate leaves were too heavy, asymmetrical – it troubled her. Unequal portions on either side of the midrib. She was uncomfortable with sharp serrated edges. They shivered fretfully in currents of warm air, protective spines choked with soot. The veins were scarlet, pulsing with unwanted life. She couldn't breathe.

Tilda Swinton, the actress. Derek Jarman's Queen Isabella in the film of Marlowe's *Edward II*. Remember shooting her on set? The first commission. Sofya felt she was shooting herself. Strung out, on edge. She knew Derek. Had to keep herself from telling Andi. It wasn't name dropping. Truth. It confirmed her reality. She was known by those she knew, the best of their time. Helen would have laughed. Helen/Isabel. Sofya fumbled the book. 'Be rul'd by me and we will rule.'

Behind her. Andi slips an arm, wet, around her shoulder. Sofya turns. Andi kisses her on the mouth. She responds. Her tongue discovering a shard of apple-peel between Andi's teeth. The swiftness of the kiss is its resonance. Andi increases the pressure, leans over, reads what Sofya is reading. 'It's got to be that bastard O'Hagan, right?' Sofya, childlike, follows the finger. 'Vile torpedo . . . That now, I hope, floats on the Irish seas.'

The photograph. Andi folds her towel on a radiator, faces Sofya. Enough of a justification? Nothing spoken. Andi tips back her head, one arm supporting the heavy breasts, the other protecting her sex. Not quite a smile, eyes shut. Negative tracery of leaves on her skin, shuttered sunlight. Water droplets dripping steadily from her wet hair down the back of her neck.

Photography is exclusion. Sofya's hand steadies as she raises the camera. She is in control, controlled by her subject. She absolves Andi, concentrating on what surrounds her – simplifying it, cropping out inessentials, fussy detail. She allows the dark mass of tied curtain, its rich velvety tones: diffused light coming from the side. She moves in. Andi, used to posing, does not pose. Used to teasing, does not tease. Used to being an object, is an object still.

She retains the advantage of her nakedness. Sofya waits. They both wait. Perhaps the moment will lose itself, become fraudulent, bad theatre – it doesn't. It happens. Sofya does not snatch or grasp, she cedes the instant of collaboration. There is only one: a clunk of conspiratorial solidarity.

They continue, long afterwards, holding their positions in the borrowed room, one dressed, one naked, until light sickens, and the coating of dust on the leaves mingles with the carbon created by Mordecai Donar's act in singeing a border around the photographs of his mother and his sisters. Donar: the habit of solitude. His ritual accuses them. They are childless, carrying a curse in the world. Andi's vigour is in that choice, not to bear a child, give suck, let an alien being feed from her. She could not watch it suffer her own fate – that it should, one day, die. Sofya had not yet made a choice. Now she *is* aware of it. She does not know. She does not want to know. Feels the ghost-cat brush against her leg.

Andi, pulling at her wrist, leads Sofya into the narrow bathroom. A full beaker stands on the rim of the bath. It is warm in Sofya's hands. Andi, coaxing, steers it towards her mouth. Sofya drinks. gagging, she swallows. Andi whispers, soothes: swears by the healing potency of her fresh urine.

TEN

Joblard, ducking out of the Encaenia column in a strategic withdrawal, laid hands on Germy Hinton. That way he would cop for all the complimentaries, the bottles handed up from the crowd. The doc boozed like an amateur, swallowed whatever was put in front of him; no notion of pacing himself. Ruddy-cheeked, he marched in the company of lost reputations, unfrocked rural deans, pillow-biters, deadmen. It didn't matter what happened to him now, his name was written in the register in letters of gold: T. C. P. Hinton, Ph.D., Newdigate Prizewinner. The boys could rejoin the procession at their leisure. They'd miss nothing. Time to tap a couple of barrels before the soup was halfway down the table.

A shnide of journos was manifestly in possession of Joblard's favoured corner: he reared over them, swaying. The sots ignored him. Even the ash trick enjoyed limited success. The victim stirred the crumbling grey knuckle into his cognac, pitched it back in a fit of bravado, and took the culture-shock as the excuse for a refill. The schnorrer was forced to endure their rabbit for a few moments more. He rehearsed a paroxysmal asthma attack. The Wapping mercenaries passed him a tranche of empties. They required the space to lay out (credited) colour-spreads of bomb damage.

Mega! The Pennyfarthing had come into its own, it had never looked better. Aesthetically, the dump was a show-stopper. Bleed it across the centrefold. Windowless windows, roofs made from bungy rubber. Shreds of flapping wallpaper caught as they waved. Boss imagery! Implosions of the unexpected. Chaos samples. Pavements trashed with non-specific debris: an instant ice age. With a smoking crater as its keynote.

Despite himself, Joblard was intrigued. He lectured in this stuff, iconography. Entropy porn. He specialized in found materials, street art, expenses-only war zone commissions. Arranged accidents preserved in perspex. Catalogues of the domestic given a sinister nudge. He wanted *in*. The heavyweight bricoleur prolapsed among the leather-ware, a smear of graphite to temper the post-prandial hysteria of the hacks.

'You lads saving for something special?' he asked – when they kept their hands in their pockets and failed to acknowledge his descent in the customary manner. 'Like a set of dentures?'

It took something unusual to pull the posh papers out of town: these blast colours, draped across five columns, were irresistible. The grey of the provinces hit by intrusive pinks, stonegreen twitched by mongrel yellows.

Joblard had to spill most of the first pint to get close to them. A vanload of doctored fertilizer – that's all it took to give Oxford a facelift. Urban renewal, community art: no problem. Excited, muttering, Joblard smeared his paws with ink. Silkscreen these atrocity blow-ups and we'll be in blacktie at the Tate, networking with Waldemar, winking in Nick Serota's spectacles as we fist the big one.

The leg is finished; hobbled by all this benevolence, honeystone bathed in pensioned sunlight. That's Sileen's decision. Creased with pain, wolf eyes staring back at him out of the window of a tie shop. Silver cups, wooden shields. Not so much the leg, the rest of him – it aspires to the condition of tin. He's finished with vergers and beadles, clever bitches, bonhomie and bow ties, leapers from bridges. The meeting with Hinton will be his last. It's Hodgson or the river. Out of it, definitely. Mongolia. Donegal. Territories where maps are no longer negotiable.

He crouches on Hinton's bench, a twist of the Cherwell, sniffing the linseed. Wickets set trim on the lawns of Magdalen College School, umpires levelling the bails. He takes out the Hodgson photograph, the storm-card, a sea that has died, extinct water. The lightning flash is all his own; fire-hair, Promethean anger. A bolt shot into this meadow. He curses the horizon with its simpering dentation of spikes and spires. Let green be grey. Slushfund silage. He wills trench fever, gangrene, rubber hoods. Corpses in hog masks to cut the wire. Negative roses. An apocalypse of brimstone on this city of summer. Make it fit for monsters. For Sileen the Betrayer.

Where *is* the rizzer? Where's Hinton? Did he say *night*? Some pub? Surely they couldn't be gorging still? (Two hours in and they'd hardly broken wind. Soup. Fish. And soup again. Cold, bluish, throwing itself off the spoon.) Sileen was forced to picture the affair. Striped waistcoats stuffing the doc with milkfed beef, cramming poached salmon under his vest, pouring sauces down a funnel into his throat, inflating him. Hinton would blush with illicit hormones. His scales would shine. There would be servants, queer probably, after the military fashion, bristleheads with a stiff gait, quilting him in eggwhite, fluffing his pastry. As an encore they might choose to dip his snout in liquid cheese – battery-acid Camembert, nosepicked Brie. They'd gag the geek with blistered cigars and a wadding of bitter chocolate. Then call him 'sir', sniggering into their white gloves – as they decant his watery vomit into their bowlers.

Fantasies of a starving man. What if they *kill* him? What if he O.D.'s on pride? Sileen tasted the panic on his breath: he must drag Hinton from the hall, asphyxiate the gibbering freak in the folds of his own scarlet satin, draw his guts like knotted twine through the bore of a rifle. The image was obscene. Sileen wondered if too much pedal celibacy had turned him nonce. He split the Botanic Eden at a canter. He was in danger of bottling the lot: Helen, Hinton, Drage-Bell, the rays. X-rays! To think of them was agony. He choked on sweet scents, compulsory drenches of bliss. He scattered gravel like a revving Harley: foreswore, for the last time, the soothing physic of persimmon, swamp cypress, maidenhair.

Through the Memorial Gardens at the gallop, damning memory. This botulism of pampered species and mourning cards. Sileen soaked himself, gratefully, in his own stench. A garlic priest, he plunged from the kerb, into the worst of it: the town.

You can dowse with pain. You have to. Mordecai Donar traces Sofya by measuring the migraine-hammer of his greed for her indifference. He wants her to gob in his face. He wants her spittle running down his cheek. (He hasn't shaved. Soft grey hairspikes will slow the warm spit's tumble.) He can follow her by the distance with which she withdraws from him, the speed with which she moves into the orbit of other worlds, truer affections.

His eyes. He could track her through space. Eyes of a predator, a night prowler. Glowing in scarlet. Inside her camera-womb. Under her arm like a bubo. At the bedside. Soul parasite. With her. He could swim, uninvited, into her sleep: a false memory of guilt. That she was alive. *For how much longer?* He counted the seconds like bad coins. He waited. He watched. His suffering authenticated. Unblinking, he witnessed all the horrors. Roundups, blacksmoke skies, caps and coats, pale faces in barred windows, haloes of evil light on station platforms. He would put the envelope into her hands. As they passed each other, here, this neutral town, in a crowd, on her way to the gallery, a restaurant – unsuspecting. Not stop, not touch, not speak. Nothing.

It has survived, it coheres: this urge to make treaty with ritual, to use life like an incantation, a charm against the unknown. Donar, mumbling incomprehensibly into his chest, bumps against Sileen, who is busy flattering his own demons. These two: standard inner city crazies thrown out of kilter by provincial elation. The cripple broods on a thorny question: how can you trust students who walk purposefully towards known destinations – wineshops, grass parties, reserved punts, suicide? Picking himself off the pavement, he takes a hit at the gargoyles, a coven of low-flying bishops. It is the day of *his* saint also. John the Baptist. An epiphanous conjunction. Wednesday, 24th June. Midsummer Day. Encaenia, feasting. Very well – but the spiritual side must not be forgotten. Magdalen commemorates the bloody caput, the head hacked from its support system. JB, unhinged gobbler of locusts. Warm-up man, famous beard.

Talk about elective affinities, even Sileen noticed it. The High Street was black with cripples. It was like the start of the London Marathon. Squadrons of lethal, self-propelling wheelchairs. And the other sort also: vegetal presences shouldered by goofy attendants. More lycra than you could shake out of Stoke Newington. No-motion slugs kitted like racing cyclists. Mexican headaches as a colour primer. Tea-cosy caps to retain the heat of deepfreeze consciousnesses. Things in hammocks. Unbottled accidents. The halt, incontinent, rabid, vacant: a counter Encaenia, a necessary rollcall of fetches and doubles, prodded and purposed by trailhardened old ladies. The capos of charity, Oxfam oberstleutnants.

It was livelier than the fancydress version on Catte Street. This was a parade Sileen could not resist: he was inducted, a card-carrying member, nudged into line by the caring boots of Class Warriors, sentimentalists with clout. Ruffians with brick-chipped edges – envious, hard-done-by, exhilarate. Olly and Strongbow chasers: they were humourless, raw as the wind. The jackals of the English summer, more faithful to the Season than any stockbroker. Henley, Ascot, the May Balls: they never missed. Lobbers of stones, chanters at the gate. Missionary outcasts in anthrax T-shirts and institutionalized anoraks, they were the true motor for this pilgrimage of discontinued bones.

The proctors had no option. It was custom: they had to let them through the gateway, into Magdalen, onto the gorgeous turf. The outdoor pulpit stood beside the Bell Tower at the south-east corner of the Chaplain's Quadrangle. Sileen was washed along with the others. It felt so strange to be tolerated, even welcomed. Sermons, he didn't need. He was gutted with sermons. But there might be some dole of broth or leper's dip if he stuck it out. He dripped resentment. His skin was a pablum for midges. His sweat the plipplip of calcium carbonate, a limestone nosebleed. At last, after all this time: satori. He is calm. He belongs among these stone witnesses, the carvings in alcoves: hippopotamus, dragon, werewolf, pelican. Like them, he was ready to feed on his own blood.

There are infinite justifications for paranoia, even without the chemicals, the lack of booze. (Seen the TV lately? Does your head in, the plots, the black propaganda. Can't tell fact from fiction.) It's bad enough to be babysitting the Encaenia rump. They stagger from the table like spongebrain cattle. The jacket-tapping minders, sponsored hitmen, are twitchy. They're paid to be twitchy. Twitchy is their shtick – but they shouldn't show it. They've been outside too long. Faces like hoofprints of stagnant water. They've been chatting to the civilians, woodentops, college ties. Fucking Rushdie, banged up in All Souls. That's the rumour. If they know, *everyone* knows. The towelheads know. All this glass, these alleyways. Oxford is the capital of windows. An assassin's wetdream.

The Pennyfarthing's already on the docket: black marks all round. Who's moving? Who's out there? Mad Micks, leatherjacket Moscow snowmen, Wops, Nig-Nogs pregnant with heroin condoms, Chinks with attitude. *We're* supposed to be the spooks. We're impassive, we don't register on video. Hairtrigger psychos. Try it, son, and you're dead meat.

Watch the way Lord Weevil follows his zeppelin cigar: he's doing his nut to keep one foot in front of the other. The Chancellor's top button, held by a thread, strains to keep his lunch out of sight. Tongue lolling like a flycatcher. The transcendent sloth of the Holy Hour, when all living things struggle for breath. What a bunch of tossers! Where's your Betjeman of old, your Spender? Where's Auden with his rubber lizard profile? It's the dead that flood our memory, the dead and the dying. We won't be fobbed off with Hinton.

He coughs. The blazers spun. Top-of-the-range hardware is fumbled inside black leather blousons. The doc's lucky not to be cullendered. In their private cinema – he *is*. Trained as they are to anticipate, to visualize consequences. Hinton's a leaking pillow, spilling rouge. The crowd is bored. Cocky French schoolkids trying to cop a feel without creasing their immaculate whites, without removing their dark glasses.

Something metal caught the light: it made a long white mark where it pressed against Germy Hinton's cheek. The wrong man, surely? But the dwarf, running alongside, was no fool. He balanced on his toes to squeeze the barrel of his gun tight under the doctor's left ear.

Sileen abseiled into Catte Street, cold with dread. He couldn't make out what was happening. His sightline was blocked by tallsided vans, pantechnicons, men fussing with mesh barriers. He heard it though. The shot. Felt it too, his heart stalling in its wrap of fat. Worse than some tabloid plagiarizing his darkest terrors in a block headline. Hinton was *protected*. Hinton was Sileen's prey. Across two hundred yards of guidebook ground the cripple could smell the shock of scorched air. Who *dared* to snuff his pet?

Medics found distortions of themselves in the doctor's hideously enlarged irises. The phantom blood on his paws, he knew now where it had come from. The pulpy thing that had once been the Chancellor's face. There were noises in the old man still. He lay spreadeagled on the paving stones in a gaudy splash of robes. His blood was yellow. He was screaming in the throat. Dazzling toecaps stamped, trying to scrape off the sticky slick – blood-varnish pumping from the open wound. Extreme High Angle: a twitching corpse in an increasingly complex maze of red footprints.

Fabulous shot. The bodyguards, the ones who haven't pinned Sileen to the wall, pour their retaliation into the former dwarf. The first dumdum scooped his life in a hungry twist. Repeated rounds give him another chance. He bounces, almost sits. Then rolls like tumbleweed. Explosive devices beneath his coat work like a charm. He fountains sauce.

They cut. And come to speed. Go again. Hinton doesn't understand. Nobody is really dead, not so as you'd notice. No obituaries, no floral tributes. It's television, a pseudo-event capable of infinite repetitions. Somebody has set it up. It doesn't count. See how the Chancellor brushes himself down, solicits approval. See how the girl cures him with a pad of Kleenex. It's a world of fragments. Restricted growth is the norm. Killing is something people pay to watch. The main man (you can tell that by the way they ignore him) is engrossed in a crossword. He never leaves his chair. He's like Sileen. He doesn't do action. Not any more. He's got a crook leg. The only difference is – he's paid.

Shock has made them all tame, collaborators in escapology. Even Hinton has to get out of town. He wants a better address from which to write a letter to *The Times* denouncing the affair. He decides that it's a high risk period, death-news provoking imitation, morphic resonance, copycat atrocities.

Singed and deaf, they creep away. They weren't in the market for embarrassment and boredom, the qualities that film sets copyright. They needed a better location. One that wasn't sponsored by Beamish's Stout.

ELEVEN

Straight on down Parks Road, why stop to think – more shots. Or the original is an echo they can't extinguish. Now they're fakes. Hinton ducks and shudders every time, bruises Sileen's arm. The usual ragged vacancies are blown against the railings of John's like the debris of a storm. They can't speak, these dismissed TV extras. Their tongues are too heavy for their mouths. They find a rug of grass, and crawl. Too exposed. They thirst for darkness, open doors. There's one ahead, an oblong of liquid coal in the side of some yellowbrick, Victorian Gothic stack.

Sileen cringes. It's his school come back to haunt him, the gymnasium, Ruskin's madness, muscular Christianity with a limp wrist, Irish labour patronized by prayer: a cliff of mock Venetian windows illuminating folly. They'd never be let in, not two of them.

But they *are* (like Jonathan Harker, hat in hand): Germy revives as Sileen wastes, grows sullen, stares. A boneyard, an ex cathedra abattoir. It's flooded with good grey light. A dream museum. Sileen is in X-ray heaven. Fleshless beasts in a dazzle of bone. Harp-ribbed horses with necks like melting candles, a yard of teeth. The evolutionary table scalped for parade. Vertebral sticks harmonizing with cast iron columns that branch into a sky of diamond glass. Porphyritic granite, carboniferous limestone: it's three-dimensional Darwinianism, the building conceived as a walk-through lecture. A forest where all the birds and foxes are dead. Their own flesh is so much excess baggage. Hinton's more than Sileen's, the cripple (where he didn't weep) was muscle. Contours of bone, the skull, worried his tight skin. He belonged there – in the saddle. He loved the coolness and the way this hall treated sound: deferentially. The silence of muted flutes and strings.

He's prepared to nest in the Iquanodon's breadbasket, but Germy

Hinton is the guide. The doc promises richer circles of hell, more suited to their state. The quest is shelved. Who needs it? What more could any reasonable man demand? A square plinth on which to perch; forget the illegitimates, the electrics and the straps, *this* is where Sileen belonged. He felt the marble rise in his veins.

They stumbled down some steps. Another door. Hinton's schnozz was a darkroom bulb. It was Sileen's turn to grab. The roof – was it tin? The weather came from the exhibits. There was nothing outside. An informed twilight in which all things decay. They tick like buried hearts. Like clocks attached to bombs. Like radiation. The public has no business here. This is a depository of secrets that have been betrayed; unmanned boats, empty skins with maps of blood, headdresses without heads, instruments that, being looked on, provoke surgery. Case after case, shelf after shelf, drawer after drawer. Exhibits breed. The more the visitor learns, the more he is undone. Bluebeard's trophy cabinet. Coins the dead give as bribes. Weapons that wound when their makers are dirt in the ground.

There were so many contradictory messages that Sileen reeled. He staggered from case to case. Or else he would not move. He gave precedence to his exsanguinated reflection. Waited, respectfully, on the power of things: bone, twine, feather, wax. Hinton had left him. The doc's orange boots squeaked across a rubber floor: unscrambled, blinking behind gold specs, his rabbit eyes, wildly, connecting everything to everything. His lips moved as he read the explanatory cards. Remember *all* the words or you will never leave this place.

Looking down from one of the high balconies, on Sileen's peeling scalp, you'd see him advance in jerks, straight lines, abrupt turns to the right. Like a pebble bouncing down a staircase. He floats through the dim chamber, hands over ears, struggling to keep out the incessant murmur of the tribes.

Overload. This storehouse makes the X-ray assaults feel like twenty minutes, goggles on, under a Finsen lamp. The shallow nicks on every twig preach rebellion. Whittle a clothes-peg and you rewrite your family tree, each cut an ancestor. Accidents are invitations. The silence: a Telegraph Exchange of competing voices.

Sileen thumps against the Haida totem pole, a memory spine of beaks and eyes. There are other attachments he doesn't see: Hinton on the first-floor balcony, and, above that, in the off-limits gallery, Rhab

Adnam. Unknown to each other, making their own circuits – particles flinching from the inevitable collision. An institutional clock ticks doom. But so do all the others, hidden in green baize drawers. All the dried insects, minerals, fossils. All the sandy skulls weighing out their dissolution. All the rusty blades that hack at time's sinew.

Adnam's task is almost complete. He has paced out the steps of the Oxford Mound. It leaves him a few feet short of the tin roof. The upper gallery is closed – to those who pay heed to signs. The Mound *will* fit inside this shed, envelope all its treasures, set them free. Adnam scatters imagined earth. He yells: an *Iron John* sweathouse man.

Hinton retreats to the balcony's edge, clings to the pole. Sileen sees them both: Adnam standing on the doctor's head. They're linked. *He* has linked them. They've each got a part of the story. Put them together and they can all escape.

Adnam's scream of affirmation spiked Hinton like a bad toxin, a dart in the neck. Uncut nails drew blood from his palms. Sileen couldn't prize the geek's fingers from the rail. Germy had the face of a jumper. Beneath him, the floor of the museum was a site of public burial: nameless stiffs incarcerated in horizontal phonebooths. Ex-directory gods. An orchestra of the dead. An outrigger hung in the air, ready to carry them out on the tide. Hinton tried to swim.

'Adnam!' Sileen bellowed the name, and waited – listening for muffled footfalls overhead. Hinton was painted wood. The hushed deck was otherwise deserted – apart from the odd couple, up to no good, by the cabinet of Mochica pots: pillage, drinking bowls snatched from shallow graves, dishonoured debts. How did they get in? There had been no visitors on the stairs and Hinton was alone when Sileen spotted him.

The pair were furtive, foreign; they talked too much. The pitchman was gaunt, half-collapsed, sucked in, teeth gone: somewhere between forty and the crematorium. A nose that had seen plenty of better days: grafted from a statue of the Duke of Wellington, it unbalanced the consumptive profile. Pipe-cleaner legs in suspiciously fresh jeans (pinched from the girlfriend). Collarlength hair in a damp fringe. It came off with the beret. They were a set. The leather jacket was secondhand skin.

The grifter yapped and gestured with a smoking paw, ground out his dogend on a PLEASE REFRAIN notice, bummed a straight from his pal, lit up with a blowtorch he carried on a string. Foreign was right, but English born. Foreign at home – disaffected, loud. Frog tobacco and habits picked up in the Algerian quarter. Cognac instead of blood. A bum on several continents, with residual airs and graces, manners that outlasted the inherited cash. A cashiered gent scraping by on a dose of the classics and the never-forgotten ability to deal a queen from the bottom of the pack.

He gave his patron the works, misquoted from an open book. 'The country was not worth the conquest. It is chiefly interesting to the antiquarian. There are marvellous aqueducts, and more particularly hauchas, or mounds, scattered at irregular intervals. When opened these hauchas prove to be burial-places; and beside the bones curious pottery is often found, chiefly water bottles, of which I secured a number of specimens. The chief enterprise of the place consists in despoiling the graves of the ancient Incas.'

The fat man scowled, his prejudices confirmed. Who wrote this book? Sileen could make out the title, *In Tropical Lands*, but not the author. The beret enjoyed playing messenger, delivering bad news without risk. His companion had the look of a spoiled polaroid. The tan had gone off the boil. Naturally sallow skin kept too long indoors, then boosted from a tube. The sagging dewlaps were yellow and spawned a nasty razor-rash. Dark glasses and a grubby trenchcoat didn't help: a Nazi abortionist on the run, pockets bulging with contraband. Our Gasman to the life. He might as well have printed the reward, in dollars, on his vest: DEAD OR ALIVE. Only Special Branch could miss him, the subtle prompts of paranoia refusing such a blatant target. They'd rather stripsearch Belfast housewives, batter labouring men who chanced on the wrong ferry, or construct intricate webs of conspiracy in which to plant evidence against themselves.

Unless he's busking for a hit, thought Sileen, this public jackal should abhor a guide who giggles and is at home everywhere, never short of a chum in the back of a taxi – with a detachable wedge. The beret was an Old Etonian tie for rent, a front for spivs, the gossip columnist's deepest throat.

The Gasman's finished. He belongs here, more than any of us. It's his broken crockery on the shelf. 'The head of a monkey, a crouching figure and a warrior before the spout, probably Mochica.' That's what the catalogue says. Sileen can't find a spout, it's missing – liberated, tossed aside. The Gasman reassembles the fragments with greedy eyes, he knows what they mean. The pot without a lid. The funerary offering that lacks its votive monster. How to proceed? This glass box contains his charter for all the machinery of terror. Ancient systems of sacrifice reactivated by a word. Inca: Coca: Mao. A condor on the bull's back brings the great beast to ground. You cannot stamp on a thing unseen.

The Gasman's ears, standing out like spigots, flush in sympathy. His anger is a form of madness: damaged kidneys, burdensome flesh. Throats can be cut with shards of baked clay. Sileen doesn't care for the way the Gasman's thumbs curve back. There's something overbred about the man, the arrogance of the grievously wronged. Revenge is a dish he's eaten cold. And wants to eat again.

Rhab Adnam reverses along the trail of Hinton's bloody footprints, reads them as the map of a journey still to be made. The mental travellers converge: the Three Stooges bereft of mania. They're ruined but unsurprised. The obvious solution depresses them: Exit All. Cambridge, capital of dolour. A city sponsored by Xanax.

He was the novelty, they nudged him: Hinton, the meat in the sandwich, the library beetle, checker of the facts, obligatory clown. He was their passport along the Cam, their *carte de visite*. The *in*. Adnam and Sileen seized an arm apiece and marched the protesting doctor out. They marched him as he moaned. 'My papers, my tapes.' The second leg of the Mound triangulation need not detain them long, they'd take it at the double. Another dune for Adnam, another chance for Sileen to pick a stranger's pocket. Addicted to pain, what did he have to fear from a seventy-mile yomp? Chiltern tracks, gravel-pits, snares: more pilgrims on that road than progress.

Their concentration faltered as they thought ahead, allowing a tropical storm to rush into the vacuum: rain, on the tin roof, bringing the exhibits back to life. Panels bounced and shook as they dodged between the drums and fetishes of beachcomber consciousness – deafened by the delirium of the fake monsoon. Together, all at once, they said it aloud. 'Undark!'

TWELVE

'Now the willows on the river are hazy like mist / and the end is hazy like the meaning.' Helen, an unopened booklet resting in her lap, has arranged herself at a particular spot, not previously known, where lightly-weathered steps descend into the water. Unmoving, she appreciates the cool of the morning, the filtered bleach of light. She is here, waiting and not waiting, studiously disengaged.

A squared wooden post, with the smack of tar, driven into reddish soil. A taut droop of wires (a netless tennis-net) straddles the river, the dark watercourt. Nearer her, a black rectangle (a mock lectern) is an empty frame in the uncropped grass: alongside the stone steps, two thin metal legs.

The slight weight of the card-covered book is, relatively, no weight at all. Face down (a dry stone wall, black intervals). So that, were she to prise the thing open, she would have to read from the back, come early on the poem with the river and the willows. ('Willow branches dip.') But the point, here, is *not* to read; to carry, appreciate the potential of just such an object. It does not insist, not yet. She picks it up, runs her hands over the monochrome cover, looks away. (Do not gay men have a code? Paperbacks positioned in visible pockets while they stroll across the graveyard?) To-day Helen's book is complemented by a fresh white skirt. The poems rest across the raised declivities of her bare legs. Crisp cotton folds. The dampness of the grass soaks her dusty feet: light gold sandals.

'Calm is all nature as a resting wheel.' Breath is thought. On the far bank, branches heavy with leaf decline towards the turbid surface of the rivulet; dull reflections throw back an alternate woodland, shivering in the sluggish drift. Helen hoists an ankle across her thigh, slips off the sandal, stretches out her foot, smooth and high-arched, places it, hesitant, in the water.

Is the ferry operational or discontinued (as it would be elsewhere)? There's a clumsy skiff on the far side – which could, theoretically, be propelled, voyagers working the rope, in against the steps. Not *her* choice. She's grateful for that. Let them come. Or stay back, forever, in the shadows. Her feet were white beneath the green water. Like mice inside cotton gloves. Her strong brown hand rested on the tensile instance of the book.

This section of the river, itself a tributary, is a kind of shaded tunnel, semi-private – not quite forbidden. Helen had come early, undecided about how long she might stay. She thought of swimming and wore a black bathing-suit under her skirt. But she had only the vaguest notion of where the official bathing place should be: not here. There was satisfaction in dabbling her legs, making small ripples. She sat on a spread towel. A few splashes, quickly absorbed, fell on the white skirt.

The stretching and separating of her toes. Her foot, swinging out, testing resistance, catches something mossy, brings it to the surface. Helen has to set the book aside, bend, scrape off the dripping weed. She lets her hand go with it, back into the river. She gives her attention to the languor of the trees, the lazy and remorseless pull of water. The crust of the stone steps shines like burnt sugar as the sun climbs towards its meridian.

Hands in the river, a skin cup in which to read the sky. Cloud watching. Indeterminate forms. She spills the water. Reaches inside her shirt, loosens the strap of her bathing-suit. A trickle of dampness down her breast. No visions. The thick black towel: all her relish is for what is true.

Crack or bay-leaved, Helen could not, at that distance, tell. Beneath the overhanging branches of the willow, on the opposite bank, stood two women, her friends, their faces obscured in patterned shadows. Their arms and shoulders were brightly lit. Andi Kuschka waved vigorously. Sofya, stepping forward, went first into the skiff.

Nobody called out, the space between them was awkward. Balancing themselves, the two women eased across the current, in fits, towards Helen. Sofya was clutching the large brown envelope to her chest, the scorched photographs of Donar's mother, his sisters. Helen, obviously, did not know what the envelope contained. She noticed it, a target, the sort of card drivers hold up in airports. Sofya could not decide what she should do with this most unwelcome gift – drop it, now, in the river, show it to the others, or return it, without comment, to Donar. The photographs complicated the reunion with Helen in a way she could not explain. Andi, for her part, was absorbed in the mechanics of shifting the craft, placement of hands on the rope, the steady draw: her strength carrying them both, safely, towards the steps.

Helen slid her feet, still wet, into the buckled sandals, and stood to greet her friends. She wrapped the booklet in her towel. 'Denial . . . always leads to political errors, of an / essentially Trotskyist order.'

THIRTEEN

The lads on their knees, in boiler suits and rubber gloves, the ones charged with picking through the rubble, toothcombing brickdust, pouching splinters and bone fragments, they had a name for the double act: the Cardinal and the Corpse. A talker and a graveside noddy. A rabbit specialist and a spook (the lads said *his* best snouts were cadavers). One of the team had the connections (the tickly handshake) and the other knew where *all* the saltiest secrets were buried. A very acceptable pairing. Of course, in the best music hall tradition, they loathed each other. The Martin and Lewis of Special Branch.

'Total fucking waste of time. But keep scratching, gents, till the newsreel boys piss off.'

Commander Cillick-Klaw – 'Monkey' to his mates. (Monkey's Paw, geddit?) The poor sod didn't have much going for him after the name: weak chin, worse teeth, boozer's beak, superfluous aspirates. Faceless, classless, a zero. If he hadn't existed it would have been quite unnecessary to invent him. His dress sense ended with his tie. The sober suiting was an attempt to talk down the sickening excesses of horizontal heraldry that winked at previous triumphs. Bogus. As was the moniker. 'Klaw' derived from a juvenile enthusiasm for the works of Sax Rohmer (Arthur Henry Sarsfield Ward), his conspiracies, his sinister yellow hordes, and, in particular, *The Dream Detective* of Wapping, Moris Klaw. ('When did Moris Klaw first appear in London? It is a question which I am asked sometimes and to which I reply: To the best of my knowledge, shortly before the commencement of the strange happenings at the Menzies Museum.') The question that troubled the Commander was: what occurred with that second 'r'?

Moris Klaw: patron saint of Grave Morries everywhere, the best of them. Mory knew how it should be done, this crime solving caper –

asleep, spark out. A snooze on a favourite pillow and the pictures rolled like a deodorant ball. A good lunch, a couple of bottles of fizz to promote the right mood. Feet up, wait to see what suspects the stilton can conjure. It's as good a method as any other.

(Cillick, if you're interested, came from way down on the credits of a solicitor's letter at the time of Monkey's first divorce.)

Careerwise, it had worked quite well. The name was the only thing anyone remembered. By the time the relief newsreader had got her mouth around that one, her oppo was cutting in with the next item: telephoto landscapes with flak jackets, skeletons in cots, suits – promoted beyond their station – muscling glass doors, long tables decked in flags and mineral water bottles. Locally, a few kiddies burnt alive in Forest Gate. Atlantic depressions on the move. 'Cillick-Klaw,' the punters muse, 'unusual that. Must know his stuff to have come through the ranks with that gobful.'

So much for the Cardinal's CV. But how should he *act*? He had a nose that could open oysters and nothing to stick it in. He dressed bombsites, shovelled gravitas over smoking roadsides, where bits of things still hung from hedges. He lifted ribbons, delicately, at the crater's edge, blinked into black depths, thinking of afterwards, the nosh. His brow was branded with innocence and his cheek was smooth as balsa. Blankness played back any tape his audience chose: righteous indignation, justly provoked anger, grieving concern. Monkey was a last rites bore, dancing over bodybags to make it official – in the tabloids. He converted an incident into an outrage. He had the manners of Pierrepoint and a batman to carry his kit. When Klaw progressed through the canteen the scoffing rozzers dived under the tables and waited for the bang.

The Commander was boredom personified, that was his charm. Mogadon man. Put him up and the newshounds yawned. He *invited* them to dig. One evening in Soho and he'd tell them precisely where to find the spade. And snigger as he palmed the envelope. Incompetence, sexual sadism as an addiction: who needs cover-ups? Give the hacks what they expect, fall guys with half a garbled tale, blabbermouths, their trousers around their ankles – small honours to the ones found out. Scandal diverts investigation. Expendable paedophiles, nothing *too* extreme. Time the release for the party conference, or one of the royals falling from a horse. The real business goes on as ever: understood!

'You weren't up at Oxford yourself?' Monkey Klaw, the Deptford teddyboy, threw Drage-Bell a bone.

'Actually, sir, no.' Bell's hyphen was genuine, but he'd never been 'up' anywhere. Informed (almost educated) by Popular Book Centres, radio serials on crystal sets, a sturdy pair of nightsight binoculars, Bell tossed between assumed servility and the unshakeable sense of his superiority to all lifeforms. Get shot of the Cardinal and he'd have the Penny-farthing tapes to himself, a clear run.

'Booked anywhere interesting for lunch, sir?'

'Bugger all. I'll snack at the Elizabeth and motor back to town.'

Drage-Bell (the Corpse) smirked. He was the trace-agent, the viral snoop. He'd be alone with the racks of video windows, surfing replays. Fastforward, freeze frame, enlarge, print: obedient controls. They were out there, flies stuck on tape, *his* villains, Whitechapel mound folk. They'd had the run of the sewers, he'd seen to that, keeping threat on the agenda, incubating controllable chaos. Good for insurance premiums, good for glaziers: a fear state. Deadbeats from Belfast cemetery estates helping to demolish unrented properties. Paddies, on the lump, to build them up again. Mug punters nudged into docklands, the swamp corridors. But not this. This was out of order. Oxford. City centre pub. Special interests affronted, not enough cameras in place. Here were corruptions even Drage-Bell could not corrupt. Terror was a permanent requirement (in small doses) to keep red eyes swivelling on vulture ledges. The only film worth watching is the film that *extends* time: everything there is, and then a little more. Cameramen, soundmen, editors: redundant. This is the age of audience-directed art, ultimate audiences – audiences of one.

Commander Klaw was away, skidding downhill to put an edge on his appetite. He felt suddenly old. He couldn't for the life of him understand why they hadn't made the usual cull of Shepherd's Bush Micks and hammered a couple of pages of script out of them. He never troubled himself with the broadsheets. He had a nice little graduette (in applied skirt-technology) to do that for him. The news hadn't reached him yet that such tried and tested methods were temporarily out of fashion. Impossible to nail the right bastard, so nail any of them. They're all guilty. They're not English. As his blood sugar slumped, he found himself considering the fiscal implications of early retirement, cashing in his honours for a brace of snoring directorships. This creature, Drage-

Bell, wouldn't have been trusted with the milk money in Kim Philby's day.

The rind of perverse intelligence that separated Drage-Bell from a sack of dirty laundry made him uneasy in the company of his peers. In any company. He simply did not belong. He didn't belong anywhere outside the Third Reich or Rackmaster Topcliffe's inner sanctum. Isolation was his strength. Inviolate: he could not lose. He shifted the wreckage of the bar with a prehensile toe. He reached out. One of the drudges, behind Bell's back, had unearthed, or so he thought, a survivor – a bottle with life in it. Bell waited while it was uncapped. Then poured the spirits over the glowing ashes. The lesson of John Bunyan's Interpreter recalled: Lay the dust and make it fit.

The tedium of evidence didn't concern Bell. He clocked the retrieved details with a yawn. Surrealism had never been his bag: the fossilized zip embedded in the flock wallpaper, the numbered thumbtip in its acetate slipcase – which was, in truth, a cigar butt dropped by Monkey Klaw. The aftertaste of drenched fire, ruin's foreplay: Drage-Bell liked it. Took it into his pores. Splashed himself with the carrion bouquet of death. Stirring a residue of gritty powders, he reformed a shattered wrist. He laid hands on leatherette fronds trapped beneath a twisted iron joist and released deferred smoke. A special odour he'd been missing for too long. Everything played back. Dust into tables, dirt into men. He eavesdropped on overlapping dialogue as it speeded into reverse. Something nagged, a footprint without a foot – Sileen! His golem, the sullen cripple, had been here, and was here still, supping ale on the company budget. He must be fetched and taught. Subverted, bent. Or freed from motion altogether. Returned to the river when the tide was at its flood.

The intelligencer didn't want to hang around. He called for a car to spin him back to barracks. It wasn't much further than Folly Bridge, but his need was bad. A physical ache. The pre-transformation Jekyll. Like a repetitive strain injury – muscles cramping, dull steady pain. The hurt came when he stopped. Returned to the editing suite, all was forgotten. Analgesic chemicals coursed in relief. Tape was live! Fishtanks of wriggling snakes. Grey Oxford streets: the same decisions, the same mistakes. Drage-Bell owned Sileen's memory and would wind him in, burn out the renegade cells, forbid escape.

He locked the office door and shot the blind. The spook poured himself a pint of barely-warmed black coffee and tightened his tie. With a series of ferocious clicks he pulled his finger joints like an imminent soloist. He hammered at the keys, a bone orchestra. Twin monitors flickered and released their patterns of interference. He could run aftermath before event. He was out there, invisible on the walls, flicking up the collars of their coats. Time could be sucked or shoved. It was feasible, elementary, to go back, re-edit – involve himself in things that hadn't happened yet. Debased tape was a self-fulfilling prophecy of acid rain. Thermal floaters with drifting heads. Bell cursed the museum administrators, art cranks too mean to keep their equipment up to speed. Those bastards would hold out until they could run this dreck as a video retrospective, an excuse for discordant thumps and bangs. Sub-Beckettian voice-overs with plural adjectives. A performance prompt. The image-stream broke up into primal soup, morse weather in the Atlantic deeps. Car headlights on St Aldates were matches struck in haunted rooms.

No rush, he's got all night. Drage-Bell runs the Pennyfarthing tape through, again and again, upping the damage in quantum leaps. It improved the closer it moved towards abstraction. He bungs a humbug into his cheek. MOMA's hormonal surveillance camera continues to get it wrong, tail some bitch, then cut before she waddles across the frame. Empty pavements like fogbound docks. Ghosts of lightbulbs shuffling in the rain. White holes in a negative storm. FREEZE, PRINT.

Looks like death, but it's still him: the slippery blackbird suit, yarmulka and stick. Todd Sileen on film. He's mugging some out-patient in the street. A basketcase defending itself with a stack of books. There's genuine feeling in Sileen's stranglehold. Give him the part. He's done it, snared Hinton. Now the intelligencer can net them both.

FOURTEEN

From the Tape Diaries of Dr T. C. P. Hinton
*(The present author acknowledges a degree of invention, made
necessary by the indifferent quality of the original recordings.)*

REEL I. O noble Hinton, wretched man, humbled in your pride, cast out
in the company of thieves and strangers. *They* sleep. I whisper these
words, not knowing if they will be my last. We sprawl in a ditch at the
field's edge. A fire of dung and thorn branches dries out our sodden
clothing. Nothing to eat all day: we dined, at sunset, on sour apples
(inducing severe gripes) and a tin of cocoa powder. Darkness, pitch
black, wet again.

They allowed me no time to prepare myself, to gather my effects.
Oxford, my bower, my refuge – libraries, gardens, record exchanges –
snatched away on the instant, prohibited memories. My dealer! They
say we are pursued. Bombs, assassinations – it's only the beginning.
Seeing the world through their eyes, I concur. I thought paranoia was a
privilege until I met this ghastly Sileen. Adnam's OK in small doses, a
little vague, doesn't read, always quoting, or misquoting, turning
himself into a book. Like one of the woodland refugees in *Fahrenheit
451* – a poor film, I thought, despite Julie Christie. 3 out of 10.

The Walkman and the pocket recorder (previously used for my lists),
that's all I got out with. They frogmarched me back to Bullingdon
Road. 'You can't possibly cross Cowley Road,' I told them, 'it's the
floodline that guards the city.' Joy riders, ram riders. Out of Blackbird
Leys, the estates. Transport's their inheritance. (I must re-read that
proletarian novel by Robert Westerby, *Wide Boys Never Work*. A strong
6 out of 10, if memory serves.) These backstreets are a Monza of
handbrake turns, burnt rubber. They bail out and torch the vehicles as
soon as they get bored. From Garsington, Oxford is a rim of fire.

We crossed Cowley at a run. 'No worries,' Sileen yelled, 'three's a safe number. One out of three always survives to tell the tale.'

I tried to rapidly collate my archive (it's floor to ceiling now), sort out the disks I'd have to put in store: the typescripts, artwork, autographed sleeves, the Moorcocks, Ballards, Philip Dicks, the *Avengers* tapes ('with best regards' from Honor Blackman in her leather shell), the *complete* run of *The Prisoner* (including the Thomas Disch paperback, 4 out of 10, the magazines and the strip cartoons). Sileen filled a bolster and lugged it over the road to my local. The shame! He flogged the lot for less than twenty quid. A collection that had taken a lifetime to assemble. A life dispersed. We'd need the cash, apparently, for our journey.

We'd be moving out as soon as he drained his Guinness. But which one? He's on his third and shows no sign of flagging. I've got nothing but what I stand up in, my best, my *Adam Adamant* suit, cuban heels, headset. Unnoticed, I slipped two cassettes into my pocket: the choir of St John's, Cambridge (leading us on to where we are going), performing Allegri's *Miserere Mei* and, it goes without saying, my treasure, my grail – the Nicholas Lane compendium. Straight 10/10! What a guitarist – improvises like a god, no ego, makes Clapton look very boring and provincial. A genius, what more can I say? I love the man. Savoy Brown, Mighty Baby – the Leonardo Da Vincis of their era. So many levels, so many shifting layers. I could spend eternity decoding them. They collapsed into bad debt, drug burns, affray in a yacht club. Murder witness, runaway, Sufi retreat. The comebacks with Aynsley Dunbar Retaliation, Fat Mattress, Lane's End. We all thought he was dead. Then rumours started reaching me, he was living in Paris and had lost all his teeth. The man could double for Villon, he's immortal, a work of art. I'd rather gargle with Sileen's spit than give up Nicholas Lane. Allegri for the roads, and Mighty Baby for the English landscape – weak horizons, amphetamine skies.

The suit's ruined, torn, crusted with filth. How far have we come, how many miles wandering helplessly, guided by unseen stars? We started along the dismantled railway in the direction of Wheatley, keeping together, avoiding roads, skulking from imaginary helicopters. Onto the nature trail through Shabbington Wood, by way of Polecat End and Drunkard's Corner. Surveillance cameras might have snatched us as we bundled over the M40, coats covering our heads. We waited hours before risking the A41 – which Adnam referred to as 'Akeman

Street'. God knows how he navigates without map or compass. Sileen hobbles faster than I can run, sticks at Adnam's shoulder. They shout at me, prod, poke, kick. I couldn't hear a thing. I was with Nicholas Lane in the *Jug of Love* – what a riff!

One of my heels broke off, I limped in synch with Sileen. I'd never walked so far. I used to hitch: Aldermaston, Beaulieu Jazz Festival, Horovitz and Brown, the Isle of Wight. But no more. I thought I'd found my spot in Oxford. I ache from head to foot. I wanted to lie down on the motorway and go to sleep, but couldn't shut out the bronzed imago of Simon Undark. His goldfish tie is a beacon of hope. They want him through me. Want the key to the Hodgson house.

The further we push out, the worse it gets. I'm beginning to think like they think. Like the dreadful Sileen. I'm copying the man, picking at my cheek, examining scurf from my nails.

Everything's changed, changed utterly. I've drunk for years in the Bullingdon Arms – friendly, lively, good crack. (I once caught Dominic Behan's turn. 2/10.) Photos of the great ones on the wall of the snug: Yeats, Joyce, Beckett, Wilde – and one or two published after my time. Such as Charlie Haughey. Now I saw what Sileen saw: the hardfaced girl hawking *An Phoblacht*, blokes I'd taken for ditch-diggers staring me out, graffiti in the Gents (IRA 3 SAS 2). Even the music, the fiddlers, the smoke – alien, wrong. Watching us with cold eyes. Guinness turning to liquid iron. The joke that puts its hand down your throat. Rebel songs. We dropped our glasses and ran.

'Enough to exist,' I thought. A sliced beam of light: the moon. Old onion eye. Smoke trapped in a toy syringe. Light, the message and the meaning. I rolled a fat one, the others safely asleep, and watched the hillock fade and form. Thin clouds racked at an unusual rate. Where do we come from? Where are we? Where are we going?

REEL II. Dawn is a messenger returned from the front, a black-bordered telegram. Now we can see the extent of the fix Sileen's left us in: a dank copse hiding in an undistinguished field. A plethora of wild appletrees suggests the failure of some farm, domestic virtues in retreat. A tump marked with a line of poles – a road? No sonnet takes shape in my troubled mind. I've written nothing for two days – since I met Sileen, verse's exterminator.

Adnam circulates a stale crust. Yesterday we lived off a single pint of milk. Sileen gulped most of it, then puked. My doing, I must confess. I lifted a bottle from a doorstep as we passed through Horspath. I wanted something civilized to carry out, some token of a better way of life. Unlike my companions, I'm not a natural thief. While they drank, tossing the bottle back and fore, I retreated – more than a mile – to leave my *Star Trek* wristwatch in exchange. They chortled. I dropped it into an empty with a prayer of thanks.

Twisting his crystal against a lowering sky, Adnam tunes us to the dragon line. Cambridge is easy. Cambridge is despair. A black hole. Flow in the direction that attracts you least, the absence of desire.

Three men ascending a hill, it's special – even a hill like this, slyly backing away from our advance. Three trees on the brow. Don't make too much of that, stick with the grass. Generally thick, coarse, worn down in riblike treads, bleached by cattle piss (no cattle to be seen). Not quite an earthwork, nor yet a natural form. We could be trespassing on the dome of a Secret State bunker. The slope – too late to run – is a gull's head: first, the beak, a gentle plod, then something sharper, something with a winking eye.

The summit. Looking back, between stunted box-trees: so much land, huge rolling distances, green, pale gold dispersing into blue. Something's buried here. I want to hide. The trees are tin. We're watched. All that wire. Perimeter fences stitched into hedges. A triangulation plinth and, behind it, telegraph poles that splutter and fuse against a Tarkovsky sky. (*Nostalgia*, 7½/10.) In the distance, but too close for healthy underpants, a fury of barking dogs.

Wherever you find blameless ground, tremble. It comes back to me. I *know*. I've been here before. Don't make me remember. Grendon Underwood, a sanctuary for the seriously disturbed. A pilot scheme for volunteers still capable of making their mark, and Rule 43s, dizzy with pills. Home for outcasts of a sociable bent. A halfway house, the Interpreter's mansion. The things they said I'd done. The fictions to which I willingly confessed. We lived without a mantle of clouds, circles within circles, no possibility of escape. And counted ourselves blessed.

I ducked behind a tree when they came, the blue raincoat and his wolves. Now we spotted, when it was too late, screened by a wood, the redbrick village. There has to be a place for wives, somewhere outside the range of the searchlights. The screw had clocked us – how could he fail, suspicion was his primary training. He approached fast, choking his beasts – trying not to appear *too* eager, knuckles white where they gripped the leash. Sileen elected to do the listening, I ran the tape. I didn't want to hear this guff in present time. Let the machine pick up what it would. I forced my finger down a groove of bark. I'd earwig the story in solitude – or solitary, as the case should be.

The moment the screw's mouth opened, I hit full volume, shut my eyes, scuppered reality with Nicholas Lane. The pirate track recorded while he busked. *Heroes and Prophets*. The keeper's pitch was double-tracked.

I listened to the playback while the others slept. The usual: weather courtesies, followed by unsubtle interrogation. Sileen tried to bum a smoke. They're used to that. Doesn't indulge, the screw. Bored. Ready to give his mutts their head. Sileen plays the local history card, strikes lucky – cops for the lot. Could we make out the church tower to the south-west? St Leonard. Fifteenth Century. Shakespeare, drunk, slept there, woke to transcribe *A Midsummer-Night's Dream*. My headset throbs like a graft of asses' ears.

Even Adnam comes to life. 'I was married there.' I think that's what he says. Could be 'marred.' Says no more. We are things translated out of sleep, returned to hateful fantasies. We settle where we fall.

The keeper, used to mutes, bores on, offering up the asylum's prize catch, one Dryfeld, a serial suicide. I'm almost sure it was Dryfeld. It might have been Renfield. Or Driff. English and untrustworthy, whatever. Stolen from a road sign. An ugly, low church sound, boastful in its modesty. The monster's crimes were huge: pyromania, libricide, anti-Semitism, pro-carrot, slander, libel, false accounting, failure to keep accounts at all, gender jumping, physical and verbal assaults, video exhibitionism, recidivist grammar, voice like a faulty cement-mixer, dress sense of Mr Toad, plays chess with vagrants (and cheats), writes for the *Express*, lives in Hackney, performs acts of charity with stealth worthy of the Krays. Bad news.

Dryfeld, they decided (the benevolence bureaucrats), was a useful resource, a fossil brought to life. A pre-Einstein throwback. The man belonged in the electromechanical culture of the nineteenth century. He belonged in Frankenstein's lab. They rigged him in a wire bib, a Hannibal Lector leftover. The stuff he gave off blew them away. His demented rhetoric was an unstable force-field, independent of the standard brain circuitry. His brain was, in point of fact, redundant. You could chop it up, mince it, feed it to the hounds: his rap was unabated. A form of wild excitement, sexual, salty – born in the skin.

The whitecoats got the message fast. They were the poets of a new (revived) science, a neat reversal of the Mary Shelley scenario. (They didn't read but collected videos. Loved Cronenberg.) You didn't pump electricity (via the Mother of Storms) into a collaged corpse, you *tapped* it. This made perfect sense to the Perrier sippers. Dryfeld was energy *in extremis*, self-stimulating, deranged: melancholia was his motor.

Then give the bastard something to be melancholy about: no books, no mirrors. Total success, the lads were writing it up now, Nobel prize-winning potential. Dynamite! The entire prison complex ran on Dryfeld's excess secretions – lights, waterpumps, internal phones, drills, surveillance cameras, sanitation. The faster they drained him, the faster he renewed his monologues. Guard dogs howled. Small birds fell dead from the trees. Just think of it, one bullhead madman fulfilling the energy requirements for a community of four hundred souls. Dryfeld, the one-man Chernobyl. What were the implications for our great cities with their population of floaters, rappers, freelance visionaries?

Downhill to a pub, the Swan, an Ushers' house. With the screw fronting us, we might get in. I hang back, the others are used to that, and notice how the dogs are waiting on the pipesmoker's slightest hint.

The bar's filled with off-duty warders (who never are); shirt-sleeves *too* precisely rolled, big glass boots, eyes not synchronized with their smiles. Conversation dies. They watch us to our corner (the most remote, greenflies exiting from the plastic foliage). Our escort drops off, interrogates the landlord, nods to his mates, but keeps apart. Dog-handlers are a special breed, unloved, even amongst their own. The others boast of obscure (in-house) events, of boats for sale.

Sileen helps himself to enough of my cash (the rest is securely pinned to my inside leg) to get in a half-hearted round. My guts are tied in fancy knots. Much pain in the bowels. 'Pulled as it were both ends together.' I dashed for the bog.

Red tiles and a glimpse of local fields, a pleasant space. I strained to no effect, watery squirts, not worth the discomfort of their passage. (Escape *now* before they lock us up. Window's too narrow. Lavatory paper would never bear a body's weight.) Wash, rinse, wash again. A bright machine. It dispenses thin packets, wrapped in cellophane. Not towels, not mints. Nothing to eat. Hard to unwrap. Condoms, I suppose. Prophylactic sheaths – some flavoured. I've read about such things.

Ordering an Indian tonic, pinch of quinine, to settle my cramps, I surreptitiously stuff one of the johnnies with complimentary peanuts from a bowl. I knot it, and, with the nonchalance of Roger Moore, begin to work it down my trouser leg. (The second rubber will store my grass. The last one, I'll hold in reserve – who knows what luck the open road will bring?)

Unfortunately, my erratic movements caught the pipeman's eye: his mouth agape, pipestem rattling like a woodpecker against his teeth. I grin and mime a rupture (praying that I do not induce the event). I point towards the street, fixing him with the kind of blokeish smile golfers exchange across a urinal stall, as they shake off the dripping residue of victory pints.

Meanwhile, Adnam was emptying the olives into his pocket. And Sileen was up. The cripple won't stand by and watch his investment take a solitary saunter. He's at my heels.

We're clear. Not a face in sight, not a car. But which way to turn – without joining Dryfeld in his cage? Adnam presses the green crystal to his brow. He leads us in single file. Curtains twitch at every window. The dogs, drooling venom, track us from the open door of the Swan.

REEL VII. I'm the one running this machine. The story's over when I say it is. I suppose that means it's all fiction, distorted for effect. I'm leaving lots out. I can't always remember. It gets muddled in my head with other times. I hide the tape inside my coat and whisper – censoring the worst insults, in case the boys are only feigning sleep. A strange day.

We're on licence, we all feel that. And being constantly observed alters our reality. Alters reality period. Even if these tapes are never called up in evidence. They have the authority to subpoena sound. No fart is secret. Sound stays in close-up, even where our figures are reduced to distant pinheads. The listeners heard me say, 'I expected Bedford, not this.' I gave away our destination.

Adnam admitted as much. He's our guide. He spoke of visiting Bunyan's sepulchre, back in the smoke, in Bunhill Fields. He inspected the effigy, the sleeping tinker, book in hand. The crust of white plaster representing the great preacher's skin had chipped and peeled: bird-lime, warts of orange hair. A deathmask rotting from the inside. A shell cracking before Adnam's eyes.

Now our guide's lost it, he's almost dumb. You think he's about to say something gnomic and witty: he never does. He's lost his past. The Bedford he holds in mind has yet to come into being. Could only exist on the lip of catastrophe – when flashback is prophecy. I share the man's blind reverence for the prison on the bridge, the bronze doors of the Meeting House, Stevington Hill, Hill Difficult, House Beautiful.

What a shock then to find a custom-built Slough blocking our path, congeries of suburbs, a necropolis of sunset tiles with no centre, a thought city, an allegorical theme park called Milton Keynes.

Are people allowed? Or is the landscape entirely reserved for panoramic cameras? The boastful cleanliness spooks you – if you're used to Oxford's medieval stains, the breath of centuries fouling the glass. M.K. is a zone without time. Nothing has accrued – no rot, no folk memories of civic discontent. The initials suggest armament, not habitation.

Nothing for it but to work our way across this red desert. (Richard Harris and Monica Vitti. 6½/10.) Day-for-night: feral creatures with dark-adapted eyes, testing unfamiliar textures with their fingertips. Sticky plants, coarse soil.

From the centre of a bridge, we're none the wiser. Ribbon after ribbon of polished silver road, cream-of-tomato maisonettes in formal clusters; no hope of anything beyond. We plough on: propellers on stalks, wind-machines. No cats or dogs. No travellers, please. (This must be where all the reps come home to kip.)

Lakes and mock-timber lodges, bits of farms with concrete cows, compulsory weirdness: the dim surrealism of ministry men. Street names are no help. Cul-de-sacs of cricketers: Sutcliffe, Hutton, Boycott, Milburn, Verity, Evans, Shackleton. A surfeit of openers with a polar glaze. Then sunset boulevards with no pavements and postmodernist lamps instead of wild palms. Chips of brilliant stone: a radium beach. Elder Gate, Albion Place, Avebury, Silbury – time to anticipate the season of sacrifice.

Striking towards what we hoped was more open ground (rumours of abbeys, museums of agricultural instruments), leaves us adrift, close to the railway and Stacey Hill Farm. Close to dead. Sileen achieved his lowest ebb, bloodflow clogged to silt, spine aping the curve of a ditch.

Adnam was troubled, and, for the first time, in doubt. Milton Keynes shouldn't be here, it's dragged us down. A test we'd failed.

The bushes shook. We were not alone. A vagrant, nesty chinned, with fretful borrowed hands, lurched towards us. 'Got a fag?'

'Who're you?' Sileen shot back, atypically curious. Seeing an avatar of his future self. Something to aim for – if his bad luck held.

'You can't go home again, chums, especially not on Saroyan's bike.'

A nutter with class, obviously. The face told its own story, a serial publication drunkenly assembled: the eyes all pain, cheeks bruised with cancelled date stamps. He fiddled in disbelief with a soft grey moustache. One of our own. More lines than British Telecom. Teeth in a glass, mislaid. Nicotine-tanned brows. A reflex grin that had lost its spring. Tears welling in the eyes.

'Nice coat,' Sileen punted. Calculating how long he'd have to wait before filching it from the corpse. Even by our standards the vagrant was done in. Not many we could say that about. This one assessed the colour of his phlegm, and copied it into a notebook, to report. I felt sorry for the old bugger but was determined *not* to hear his tale. Not in that throaty, smoky, Max Wall voice, with all the artlessly discarded *g*s. Too much like Music Hall: fine to be nostalgic about, difficult to endure. Especially when revived. I plugged a roll-up in his gob.

'Sorry,' he trilled, 'I can't meet your eyes. I *have* to stare at your crotch – that's me. And will never change.' A runaway granddad who had misplaced too many wives. Not hard to suss. Carpet-slippers and (good times known) camelhair over striped pyjamas. Off the lithium and sleepless for days. He'd made his way home across country. A writer of sorts with a telephone family.

'Forgive me, gents, I'm old. Have to squat to pee.' And without troubling to strip off his breeks. He's genuinely disturbed, sadder than us, seen more. Struggled back to somewhere that never was. Sileen, looking tactfully away, sheds his ambition to move up a sartorial notch. Let the vagrant go out in style, bury him in his camelhair. A Viking funeral in the ditch. As he makes water, he whistles. 'Love is the sweetest thing.'

'You don't know, do you? Don't have a clue who I am? Name on over a hundred book-jackets, not counting the paperbacks and pseudonyms, the short stories, radio, TV, films. I closed the Sexton Blake Library on my own. "You finished us off, sport," Bill used to say, every time he bummed a drink. The culture? I *was* the culture, poet of clubland – country clubs, snooker clubs, strip clubs: done 'em all. And done 'em twice – if I could think up a new title. Been at it fifty years. Laureate of those unromantic bits nobody notices, between the electronics factories and the defunct studios – St Albans, Welwyn Garden City, Harpenden, Hoddesdon, Luton, Royston, through to Cambridge. The Exit Corridor. And I washed up here, my biggest mistake.'

'Amen, brother.' Sileen snapped – with unrequired vigour. It was too late now. The vagrant was launched. Hypermanic. He had mania like the rest of us have fleas.

'Know what a hernia is?'

'Anagram. Rain, eh?' Sileen. Couldn't resist. Hands cupped to taste the storm. Pebbles danced, tickling our ankles. Lashed to the skin, comforted, we sat. Too weak to run.

'A – should that be "an"? – hernia . . .' The vagrant wouldn't be deflected from a good gag. '. . . Is the protrusion of an organ out of the body cavity. Story of my life. Buggered from the start. Dad died at the front. Mum's in a shoebox. House on the hill.'

The rain was coming down in rods. Our ditch a flood-channel. Were we saved, or would we drown?

'You've got a house?' It had to be asked. And Sileen did.

'My entire life's up there, gents, in bin-liners and cardboard boxes. I'll be a cult when I'm dead. I founded naturalism, you know. "The poetic interpretation of reality" the Third Programme called it. And reality didn't want to know. Had the last laugh and that's for sure.'

Adnam got his arm around the old chap's waist and pulled him up.

'My rupture, my feet, my shoes. Tramp tramp tramp. The length of those corridors, then back. Wouldn't give me time. Dragged out under a blanket. I'll never trust another doctor as long as I live. Tramp tramp tramp. We'll go on the town tonight, have a party, ring the girls. It's Edgar Allen Poe territory around here when you're alone with your tablets – diazepam, Priadel, phenothiazine. Rattle rattle rattle. Hear me dance the rhumba.'

A light was tracking us. A blue light in the rain. Visible above the ditch's bushy rim. I peeped. They wouldn't get out of the car on a night like this. But they kept stopping, headlights on full, sweeping the scrubland.

'What have you done?'

'Slept flat, facedown in wet grass. Travelling on foot. Robert Donat in *The Thirty-nine Steps*, that's me. Made a reverse-charge call. An old, dear mate. Won't let me down. He'll pick us up, run us home, omelette, bed.'

There was heartbreak in the way he stretched 'omelette' into three syllables. Prolonging the inevitable. We had to get away, or find ourselves adding a lurid splash of naturalism to the latest Sexton Blake.

The old man, arms outstretched, was trapped in the headlights. The fluffy wings of his hair a burning nimbus of gold. Rain hammered on his unprotected head. The car was talking him down as we crept along the ditch. We could hear the soothing condescension that comes before the stick. They hadn't decided yet if he would bite. He didn't lose a beat to his change of audience. Humming boyishly, he warbled to the death.

'It was the cocoa, Inspector. My teeth falling in the mug. Like a nudge from limbo. Time's up. I cried tears and waited for the windows to turn black. Watch out for the coat, boys, that's my Alfred Hitchcock option you're trampling on.'

Doors slammed. Wheels churned the soft verge. They were gone. But would they return? We wouldn't celebrate whatever it was that we had lost. He'd been taken in out of the storm. We still had our wilderness of this world to cross.

REEL X. Zion. The Shining City. Out of the woods we saw it. Like news of fire, far away. Flames frozen when the city is ash. Adnam woke up. Came to life, or closer than he'd come before. (I'm greatly helped by having to make these reports.) Sileen looked a fright. Breath like a sewage beach shovelled into a spin-dryer. Sherbet-yellow eyes, puffy and stuck with glue. He had to pull down his lower lid to see at all. Can't be bothered, he claims. Cambridge is a place he'd rather enter blind.

But it's not the city, is it? Those lights are moving. It's the M11, hellbent for Grantchester and places south. No night for flyers, this, fast low clouds, flatlands to tempt them down. And down they came. Trust Adnam to find us such a hideyhole. Rose of Sharon, firethorn, forsythia. Acres and acres of the airborne dead; Americans and volunteers buried beneath their flag. A permanent Military Cemetery: cartwheels of crosses, frosty and white.

I drank with the others from the lily pond, but I wouldn't sleep in the grounds – not on that reserved quilt. We were so tired and had come so far. Energy from a previously untapped source. I'd never have to walk again, I'd made my pilgrimage. ('That's the spire of Ely,' Adnam said. Pointing into the distance, where we did not care to look. We hung against the flagpole. The sun behind us tipped our shadows into a darkening pool.) The mind goes back, I notice, at the end of day, picking jewels from the dross.

It had to be the wood and not the dead. They would never be dead enough. Too regimented, buried upright in painted grass. The hush unnerves me, it's so loud. And that frieze! Portland stone giants up against the wall, armed to the teeth they do not have. Stern jaws, no smiles. Waiting to be shot. The wall is a directory of corpses: rank, squadron, place of origin. Comic-book albinos, not yet coloured in. *Sergeant Rock* without his cigar. His blood. The evening mist, creeping down from the trees, gives them speech balloons. ALL WHO SHALL HEREAFTER LIVE. The sentiment reversed in the lily pond. The text looks Russian from the other side. This linear, Mormon-scroll architecture doesn't belong on the outskirts of Cambridge – which is, I suppose, the point.

There's a ledge, for rest and meditation, on which Sileen sprawls. The phantom airman, like a flautist, fingers the holes in the barrel of his tailgun. There's nothing I can play. Allegri doesn't work. Tautologous. And Nicholas Lane needs movement and the road.

We are the wrong kind of dead. Underqualified. We like promiscuous sycamores, knocked-off marble doves, nettles, ivy, overgrown paths. Classical grids spook us. I puff out my cheeks to throw a fit. Shock the other two out of their dull respect, back where we came from, over the fence. Woodland and a keeper's cottage, the perfect place to doss. Leave the city beyond the trees as a leitmotif for shallow dreams.

Cambridge is the catcher and informer of sleep. So Adnam states, as he wriggles into the undergrowth. It was his home once, bits of it. They live in his pockets still, wearing them away. Nothing dies. Grandfathers, fathers, rivers, mounds. Cambridge and Venice, sisters under the pox. Adnam knew lawns, music rooms, studies heaped with books and hung with Alpine watercolours. Knew curtains, kitchens, exotic shrubs. The Round Church, Midsummer Common, the geomantic mysteries of King's. (Also markets, pubs, coffee-bars, as you'd expect.) His eyes blazed. The nostalgia of risk. To be the child he was, and old – old *then*, prone to fits. Overwhelming claps of light.

Only Sileen seems untouched, spark out. I don't understand what he wants. He's not like any scholar that I've known. It's personal with him, a ruck. He'll nut the dead who won't yield their secrets. He doesn't love Hodgson but he wants the manuscript so badly that he'll even suffer this walk, the watchers. Pure scholarship, disinterested, like nothing I've ever met. Scholarship like the three-day sweats. To hold those close-written pages in his hand!

I've purposely held back from my own Cambridge, Lachrimae Christi. But it has to be faced. Evil days – until Undark took me under his wing; gave me tasks, spoke obliquely to make all things clear. (Instantly, then lost, and *then* they stuck.) The clarity of language, language alone, capable of splitting dolerite. The language of light traversing a dusty desk. I'll never escape the awe, that first time, scratching at his double doors, opening the outer, terrified to broach the inner. Music I dare not interrupt. Unaccompanied voices in distress. Footfall of other students on the wooden stairs.

I was trapped inside my temporary cupboard like a mummified sardine. My head was ringing with inconsequential facts, answers for which I had not quite formulated the questions. Corpus Christi might have Kit Marlowe up on the walls, but Lachrimae Christi went out of its way to expunge all trace of Germy Hinton. Not a snap, not an initial carved in oak. I was abandoned forever between heavy doors. Doomed to spend my life in vestibules, picking at noticeboards, announcements of lectures that had passed. 'Mr Undark does not keep any fixed time for consultations.'

The hopes and fears of my sleepless night touched Sileen. He writhed and groaned. Did he accept the doctrine of the Invisible College? I gave him clear warning in the Botanic Gardens, back by the river. I tried to deflect his quest. There's a bloodline of the elect, so I've been told, seers and sceptics, a free community of the intellect spurning signs and passwords. Pace out the canonical dimensions, study the charts. Nothing is disguised. Or is this mad? Fever tracts, pamphlets snatched from car boot sales. Harken to that hum across the fen. The alchemy of conversation, no more. Poets accommodating scientists. Poets as mediators. A fiction. A gothic yarn.

I pass through the interstices of Sileen's sleep and enter Undark's room. He's smoothing out a map, the manuscript sheets of the *Borderland* sequel. It came first! Preceded its more famous relative. How can this be? Undark deals in specifics. He knows, a thing we never considered, that the Borderland is a reality, a site, a map reference. It can (and *must*) be visited. Otherwise the essentially debased nature of Hodgson's dictation (too loose, too vague) will unpick his startling thesis. The sequel was written *first* and in a simpler form. That's what threw me off the scent. I thought it was a fake, too pure. Hodgson's visionary instant required no framing device, morbid architecture, pits of uncleanliness, no terrestrial base. *The House on the Borderland* was a smokescreen, disguising the only detail that really mattered. There was, and is, a pivotal place. A gateway. A point of entry. Which Undark with his rulers and photographs is slowly locating.

Had Sileen somehow shared in the discovery? It was implied in the way he clenched and unclenched his fists. It was present in the tumours that were eating him alive. The crippled man, blundering, guided by disease – trading his life for knowledge. And Simon Undark, reticent, shuffling index cards behind a baffle of books.

Beams on the motorway, engine row. Am I responsible? Do I dare to accept the consequences, tomorrow, of bringing these two minds together?

FIFTEEN

Avoiding the town centre, that notorious clog of picture-postcards, they trusted Adnam's crystal-inspired meanderings. Worse. The mangy riverside was for cardholders, blokes with acrylic rucksacks, sauntering conversationalists. The cuckolded rear of King's College Chapel showed itself across a stubbled meadow. Vistas solicited through high locked gates. A drift of Stalinist hymns. They might have guessed. Adnam was shepherding them towards Castle Hill – by the scenic route, the cycle track. Hinton, nauseous, was on remembered ground: sweating, mouth wadded with cottonwool buds.

'What's your favourite Cambridge building?' A blatant attempt by Hinton to engage Rhab Adnam in a bout of insider-speak. Slow him down.

Sileen got there first. Exercising his venom.

'That monster, the ugly cloudscrape of crematorium brickwork.'

'The University Library? Like a tower out of *Vertigo*?'

'No. The factory thing you see as the train pulls out for London.'

Northampton Street. They passed, for now, on the School of Pythagoras and went directly for Lachrimae Christi. And Undark. Sileen, using Adnam as his mule, to keep him from the Mound. A trio barging in would be more impressive, justification for the manuscript's removal.

Open gates, opening inwards, gave them pause; a clatch of obelisks leading the eye back from the gravelled yard to a pinkish tower. NEC TAMEN CONSUMEBATUR. Ivy in two shades. Leaded windows. Hatchback cars. Everything except a door. They sniffed the atmosphere. India paper bibles and bad drains. You won't find this one in the book of views: strictly addenda (no illustration), visits by arrangement. An elbow-patch crammer for undermasters who want *Cantab* on the CV. A pleasingly perverse shot at cloistered life. Like St Trinian's or *A Chump at Oxford*. Sileen felt better already, the snob.

Jack Trevor Story had said, 'If you know Oxford – Ruskin College is the public-bar.' Lachrimae Christi was Ruskin without the self-improvement and the women. More like a drying-out cellar beneath a Hawksmoor church: table-tennis, plastic chairs, coloured photographs of chaps in turtleneck sweaters, waving from a rock.

There was no porter and no lodge, just passages, striplighting, walls blitzed with depressing leaflets: poetry readings, palm readings, choir practice, cutprice travel to places where the fighting hadn't stopped.

Morning was the only time to face the interior of Lachrimae Christi without a bottle of sleeping-pills: a play of sun-slats through irregular windows. The students were at their studies, or in bed doing something they'd regret. The long brown corridor, stinking of boiled cabbage and boiling gymshoes, led to a small square of untended grass. Dim passageways drifted back into the shadows. Stair-suggestions were prefaced by lists of names, rather elegantly painted on the wall. Or overpainted. Every name, other than Undark's, had been revised.

Nothing had been allowed to change, Hinton knew the turf. Undark rated a 'Mr'. Then came a 'Professor' Hinton swore was dead. The rest were untitled, lacking initials, pot-carriers in the status game.

They climbed, drew breath, and climbed again; not trusting their guide, they checked on every door. UNDARK. The name was there. A laboratory warning to be viewed under a red light. Sileen staggered over to the window, looked down. He needed a gash of the old world, the spiky rectangle, the paths. He wanted to fix this moment of triumph in his mind. *Before* they met the man, before Undark. The last fleeting granules of B.U. consciousness.

Hinton dragged a fingernail across the painted panels, Adnam offered a moody tap. The outer door did not flinch. Perhaps Undark was consulting; soothing a social sore, passing sherry, or a paperback. Hinton kicked, then gave it up. He slumped in the window-seat, deflating like a punctured mouth-to-mouth mannequin.

Time idled, spurted, stopped. Bells sounded 'eleven'. The hours flicked. Dawn/ daylight/ darkness/ dawn. Hinton covered his eyes. He was unpacing the Oxford walk, step after step. Adnam squatted, tailor-fashion, cleaning waxy dirt from between the boards; rolling it into pellets; tasting, then sticking them in star-clusters to the wall. Sileen was dead. He'd pulled the plug. His powers of invention had run out. Without Undark his narrative was finished; no conflict, no double-dealing, no resolution of the mystery. He was bored, too bored to breathe.

'It could be a sabbatical. Undark abroad.' The notion panicked Hinton, whose nerves were already shot. He paced from door to window, hopped from foot to foot, fingers pedalling frantically in his trouser-pockets. 'He could be resident in Peking or Prague. Advising on an opera by Ezra Pound. Or solving the impossible case of *The Silent Garden.*'

Down on his knees, Hinton prayed to the keyhole. Saw another hole beyond. Only Sileen heard the footsteps. Climbing the stairs. No flattening of the grass outside, no calculus of gravel disturbed. Closer, but not louder – matched with the arrival of the man.

Hinton, jerking upright, split an eye; fell backwards, dripping claret on the tragic suit.

'Ah yes.' The famously imminent smile. 'Our ambassadors from the Alien Nation. Ready to graze?'

Undark was just what Sileen had expected, a surprise. Not the anachronistic vulgarity of the greeting, but the physical appearance of the legendary dude. The goldfish tie, punningly shaped like a kipper (imported by Pyratt of Uppingham, on the way to his first bankruptcy), must be worth a bomb to nostalgia buffs. The last of its kind. Condition: distressed. More so the three-piece. Thames-green velvet crushed in a scrapyard. Flares! And Chelsea boots in badly shaved suede. (Chelsea Hotel, the Suicide Suite.)

Sileen could swallow all that, he'd dreamt about the man so often, sounding the depth of his own failure against Undark's articulate silence. The schmutter was a joke, irony pushed to its limits. (Current theory insists that 'the perils of irony are more severe than the risks of misconstruction.') Undark's 'look' had been acquired more by accident than design. Like the language. Mannered but precise.

'Let's split. There's a den around the corner that offers atrocious Thai food. The students can't afford it, the locals wouldn't dare. We'll be perfectly undisturbed.'

Time to study Undark as they walked.

The don explained to Hinton why he chose to avoid the skeletal centre of the town – Trinity Street, Sidney Street, Jesus Lane (drooping clavicles and a ravaged sternum). Gingivitic gums unable to support the pepsodent coral of the medieval colleges. Bookshops shot to hell. The trade gazumped by multinational charities. Straw sandals with every Patrick White. Sticking to the 'wrong' bank of the river closed down the options of rage, gave Undark space. He refused to hang out with academics who pimped for literary rags, reputation brokers, High Tory zippersniffers.

But *apart* from that? He'd come to love the dreary turf of Castle Hill, the boozers around Victoria Road, his allotment out beyond the Ninth Public Drain. (He was doing interesting things with carrots and eclipsing binary stars.) He was getting old and hadn't changed a whisker in thirty years. Fashion swings in predatory circles. It might be time to make his move, dig a little deeper into where he was.

Sileen read claims that Undark would never make. The scholar spoke only of ethical dilemmas, crucial choices: Chicken Leg Yellow Curry (at £4.10) or Nua Pad Prik and a top-up of Prawn Tom Tom.

They settled. Undark at the bar, where he could refill his porcelain pot with lukewarm black coffee from the hob. Keep up the caffeine level, stay sharp. Not eating, he chewed hard – like a bunkered football manager, busting to protest, blaspheme, applaud. 'The boy done great.' He was amused, pleasured by the world, what the day had brought. The travellers relapsed, reverted, slobbed out. Being there was achievement enough. Undark's peculiar gift was in not saying, or so it seemed – until he spoke.

'Jackasses! Frauds!'

Hinton jumped and burst his peanut sock, wriggled to shake the yellow crescents from his shoes. Rattled peanuts as he walked, spilled his soda. 'Who? Who? Where?'

'We're spoilt for choice. New World lavender boys who can't distinguish "thinking" from "thought". Do they seriously believe that electrochemical process arrives in convenient lumps – like basalt? Or, worse, revisionist weather consuls collectivising vision. Weather, they should know, is an infinite dance of observation in present time. Scour the skull, open the eyes. Imitate those eighteenth century parsons (who had nothing better to do). And now the clods have set Rushdie in the pulpit at King's to confirm their own . . . '

'Who's Rushdie?' Sileen was fascinated. He wanted to absorb the arc of venom, the tracery of argument that remade the world (beginning with this bar). Undark's web of facial patches was a starting point. The man was an anarmorphosic portrait of Ben Jonson brought to life – flat, until viewed from the appropriate angle (close to the deck). Only then would the bouquet of his manifold particular deformities spring into focus: the potman's flaming cheeks, the tangerine wart that kept company with a brawler's beak. Forget the fantasy Undark, the saturnine hawk – dissolved utterly. The Holmesian sneer, the Miltonic blacks and greys, the cocaine shiver: it's what we wanted. The don was the reverse. Fire, steam, bowls of bubbling mud. His eyes, all iris, burnt like precious scabs. They scorched you, drew your soul, then cut it loose. Disciples were a drag. Pecked ears pasted to a lantern skull.

He worried at his patches, slapping a fresh one at the centre of his brow, masking the Third Eye. 'Nicorette. Hideous sound. Wretched diminutive, castrating the stem-word. Affecting its host like an inward gangrene. Why can't they say what they mean? *Yellow Death* would sell like camel piss in a drought. The gum's worse but it exercises the jaw. Prolongs silence, confuses bones. I don't suppose any of you are carrying? No? Try the green curry then. It bites like monkey pox.'

It was marvellous how no-one spoke of Hodgson, the manuscript, the matters on which their sorry lives still hung. That wasn't the Cambridge way. Talk instead of crop rotation or the Platonic year, gossip from the courts, poets who had lost their nerve. When the small ovoid plates came, heaped with microwaved plasticene of a startling hue, Undark unleashed a showstopping courtesy routine: polite enquiries, discreet nudges, hints, bows. They bolted the glaucous swill and glugged on stout to wash it away. Undark did not indulge. He sipped his coffee and knuckled the irritating patches. Dullness grew an edge.

'I'm encouraged by the linguistic signifiers you hide behind, your names. Favourable, both. "Rhab Adnam" with that glorious Melvillean cadence, and its well-brewed East Anglian conclusion. Sounds as it means. Non-arbitrary sonar effects. Rolling thunder, bitten off. Admirable bounce.'

This was a facer. Sileen pulled himself together and faced it with a frown. The quack knew them. Yet nobody had bothered with the intros and the handshake thing.

'And "Todd Sileen", despite its crassly gothic overtones, is not without charm. Christened on Boot Hill, barbered in Fleet Street, trodden in silage, suicided by moonlight. Monoped – part pirate, part tree. Almost worthy of the trepanned Frog, L-F. Céline. Something Swedenborgian too, I'd hazard. Secretive, secure. "What you have whispered in private rooms shall be proclaimed upon the housetops." Release the glottal stopcock and you'll survive.'

'Fair cop, squire. Some unguarded reflex of the foot, I suppose, gave me away.' Sileen shot back, hating the notion of being so easily read. 'The mud on my boots being of a type unknown outside Wapping. You eliminated the impossible and interrogated the improbable. Seeds in my hair from a family of apple trees found only among the ruins of the first Swedish Church. My name, I assume, you recalled by having previously memorized all the minor public-school cricket photographs of the relevant era?'

'Not at all,' Undark remarked, waving a gold card to signal his readiness to accept the reckoning. 'Hinton belled me from Oxford. Names, descriptions, purpose of visit, history of participants – in so far as he could supply it. Let's split, guys. Discover a more stimulating backdrop against which to prolong our conversation.'

The publican, whose exotic menu had successfully deterred all other gourmets, wouldn't countenance Undark's card. (Lachrimae Christi: twenty-fifth in the league table of college equities. And falling.) Instead, he scratched the debt onto a slate that was already large enough to carry the calculations required to expound *The Large Scale Structure of Space-Time* (S. W. Hawking, G. F. R. Ellis, Cambridge, 1973).

How quaintly apposite, this mound. Sileen, at the rear, remarked on it to Adnam's back. Undark led them up a left-inclining track – phoney as the cardboard hump in *Torn Curtain*. But very effective, in its way. The happy conjunction of the physicist's blackboard and the hillock that oversees the dialogue of disclosure between Paul Newman and Julie Andrews. Revelations were in the air. Cinema had once been Sileen's guide; simplistic moral imperatives emphasized by a moody score. The falsest gestures were the ones to trust. A lump in the trousers or the throat. Call this molehill a castle, if you choose: its crest was as bald as a chemotherapy case.

Adnam and cinema were divorced. The visionary mumbled as he climbed. 'Let Allcock, house of Allcock rejoice with The King of the / Wavows a strange fowl. I pray for the whole University / of Cambridge especially Jesus College this blessed day.'

Whitechapel carried its mound away (the hospital would suffer no rival). Oxford's meagre dune anchored its meaning to a prison, then chained the gate (visitors should pay). Cambridge manages these things better, by pretending they don't exist. The mound is available, listed in the guides, but tucked from sight – just making the final fold of the 'Historic Centre' map. (Thanks to the mailbox and the pub: Sir Isaac Newton, red apple, gravity proofs superimposed.) Enclose it in offices, non-pedestrian grass, and it becomes a modest feature. Somewhere to stroll a lunchhour secretary. Though no-one does.

At the blunt summit, no quibbling over precedence, the four stood, leaning in, over the cardinal points of the stone-lipped brick plinth. Like mourners come to bury a wasp incinerated in an ashtray. Or masonic surgeons scouring bloody hands. The roofscapes (too much speculative orange tile) didn't carry that Oxonian jolt of received beauty (spires, domes, heat haze, choir of bronchial stalagmites) any clown with a camera can catch. Cambridge is leased sky, broccoli tree-masts blighting distance. The tower of St Giles, King's College (side on), the Gogmagog hills.

Hinton looked back, wanting to advise the innocent troop they'd been that morning to turn tail. He scanned the Library knob, lifting from the forest like a cairn of forbidden books. The clouds were heavy and late, expected elsewhere, to saturate farmlands and fill ditches. Undark had chosen well. They were ordinary, public, alert to intruders from any side.

'Ireland's our Mexico, a realm in which death lives. And we may learn.' Undark was granting them a consultation. At last. 'All the signifiers in the Hodgson manuscript, the supposed sequel, indicate a particular place. The generic vagueness of the later text – which now masquerades as the one and only – is intended to confuse. *House on the Borderland*. A childish conceit. Anagram of first letters: BOTH. *Both* texts compulsory, laid out side by side.'

Adnam's finger, fretting, traced an arrowhead in the dirt of the plinth's bowl. London – Oxford – Cambridge. Undark had earthed their quest. And offered something more: the unknown. He did not understand, this new destination was illegitimate. The wrong shape.

'By early August my way will be clear, duty done.' The lecturer was at his ease, resting on the stump, gazing out over the town, noticing small things, too local in their fascination to be worth mentioning. 'It's a plausible system for the disciplined mind. A window opens. Three weeks to call my own. Nothing rushed or marred in forcing. I've examined Hodgson's photographs, time and again. You'll see them for yourselves to-night. I believe I have located the one that matters. A large circuit on the map, the forty mile sweep around Ardrahan. The other textual indicators are conventional scene-setting: a river "without a name", an "inhospitable country . . . rising out of the soil in wave-shaped ridges." That's the better part of the West of Ireland, surely? Deracinated hippies. Frankfurt dykes peddling handturned wooden bowls. Neo-colonialism of the worst sort: De Valera's nightmare. I've made my arrangements through Thomas Cook.'

'Wasn't that a tad impetuous?' Sileen asked, alarmed by the notion of the Hodgson manuscript being carried out of the country. Risks were escalating with every twist of Undark's outrageous strategy. (Were they, even now, being bugged from the blind windows of the council offices?) And, with tides of inky coffee ringing all his bells, nicotine winching up his lids, *how* would Mr Undark ever fall asleep?

'The green folder remains untouched upon my desk,' Undark replied, divining the sub-text of Sileen's panic. 'We are constrained to work backwards from a given point that Hodgson is at pains to define: the ur-instant when all things are possible. Strictly speaking, is the door half-open or half-shut? The mental journey having been made, allow the travel agent to claim his tithe.'

'You're a fatalist, then?'

'Fatal to confess or to deny. Irrelevant. The only direction worth assessing is "on". Even when – especially when – "on" involves retreat.'

The weighty compass of their inwardly inclined heads, drooping over a tray of dirt, broke apart. Their colloquy had done something bad to the light (even Hinton, inferring no blame, noticed). The flaring, hungry white of random negatives they hadn't been programmed to read.

Rhab Adnam, uneasy, eyes on their eyes, backed away. Proving Undark's thesis by refusing to hear its conclusion. Argument inked their outlines against a fugitive sky. Sileen and Undark: horn to horn. Hinton: slack – his purpose as linkman expired. Adnam dowsed for a shallow trench. He would wait for darkness, dig in among the trees on the mound's flank. A meditation on loss. Remaining here confused the issue. He should bury himself alive and wait.

Undark, who had the slenderest investment, played host: anticipating their needs, he'd led the ascent. Now his chat was cleverly contrived to draw Hinton in, without antagonizing Sileen, by sustaining the illusory politesse of common ground. As if guru and disciple had once shared a single mind. Without breaking sweat, he improvised.

'Hodgson's great gift, of course, was to exploit the sense of premature bereavement that obtained *before* the Great War; the final Edwardian summer – long shadows across the lawn, from larch and walnut and yew. Crisp linen. Sepia transfusions from a silver spout. Postmortem tea-parties. Invaders in the shrubbery. Spirit photographs of the coming dead.'

Doors slammed, cars revved below; a tidal exit to empty the town. Strollers on Castle Street (few) might notice how the contours of the mound were more sharply exposed, the ridges and paths. The silhouetted figures had taken root. One moved: Undark. He craved a hit of coffee, a more virulent nicorette patch.

'Fame is oblivion postponed. Hodgson knew that as well as Goethe. "Es kann die Spur von meiner Erdetagen nicht in Äonen untergehen!" The price of achievement is death – but death is also the reward. Hodgson made an energy withdrawal that could only be mortgaged by the supreme sacrifice. Witness, if you will, his ferocious attempts to enlist, an over-age volunteer. His recovery when trampled by a horse in training. His insistence on getting to the front, at all costs, to keep his bleak appointment at the storm's edge. Unless he could be blown into dust, he would never achieve the immortality that was rightfully his. The fiction he had laboured to contrive would be fated to remain just that and nothing more.'

Sileen blanked out the townscape to follow Undark. Hinton too. Rhab Adnam, he could hear, crashing blindly through the branches, gathering twigs to shape his hide. Conscious of the act, Sileen tried to move his foot. The signal went astray. He urged the mechanized boot to kick from behind. No use. A hand to lift. A wrist to bend. He no longer knew how it was done. Voices were clear but remote: Hinton's excited pedantry, Undark's consumptive cough. The twilight wildtrack: bicycles released from their chains, the clearing of market stalls, damp oarsmen dragging out their sculls, charity shops shooting the bolts.

There was a reason why he couldn't move. It had nothing to do with morbid anatomy. Leave that stuff to Olly Sacks. This was much simpler. A crack had opened in the earth's crust, a split in the world. An intrusion of all that Sileen had previously suppressed. X-ray visions liberated from the timid rationality of the machine. His furies had come to visit and to fetch him back. He saw what had always been there, psychotic nature on the march.

A ruptured blood vessel? General paralysis, diplegia, hemiplegia? Loss of nerve? Dry fire spat through the grass. The triangulation made literal – like a preacher's boast. The nifty logo of apocalypse; high-speed British Gas. Twin mounds as hemispheres of a reviving brain. Unable to speak, the cripple froze. He summoned the cynicism of belief, and fell. Believing, in that instant, he was lost.

SIXTEEN

For Sofya Court, the world was eyes. She drank Cobra lager with gay boys in cool, quiet bars. (*They* chattered and died, thin-chested youths with lovely shirts.) She was too bright at windows, then spooked at lunch-counters – facing outwards, half-watching the street. Extended phone-calls at safe times, office noises when she came to discuss commissions she could never bring herself to accept. Bad mornings, waiting for the day to start. A karmic makeover by the act of cropping her hair. Men met, travelling in the opposite direction, midway across a busy road. Smelling fine. Dressing with care. Posters she couldn't read. (Moustaches, red lettering, exclamation marks. Leather jackets. Guns.) The camera was a penance, a lad's thing in its heretical holster. No footsteps. Nothing to see. Who was following *her*?

Eyes everywhere. Her cats on the bed, unblinking, cold. She suffers their indifferent, watchful gaze. (Time to move, try another place.) Stoppers in bottles. Pub signs. Curtains of beads. The portholes of the Monster Doss House. Coins in her hand. Dead eyes. Eyes that refused to see. How much longer could she live like this? A black sheet draped over the looking-glass to conceal her nakedness.

She was tormented by the photographs that Mordecai Donar had forced upon her. She took them out from their envelope; a glance of confirmation and she put them away. They were genuine, lies of the worst sort. They stank of nicotine. Donar had killed his sisters to get Sofya into bed. He'd informed on his mother, fifty years ago, to sniff her pelt. He'd witnessed the procession, arms in air, cardboard suitcases. The gold spectacles that would outlive their owners and continue to glint, whenever light was allowed into the warehouse. She damned him for her own bad faith. Burnt paper marked her cloth. She tried to sweep up the ash, making it worse. She wanted to smoke, to drink until she couldn't stand, to talk, seriously, all night long, with older men. The packet was foul. Donar should have been honest and sent his soiled underpants.

The sun caught a window across the square. She feared to swallow her orange juice, in case an eye was hidden in the glass's heavy base. Donar's eye. That pleading hungry look. She trembled when she heard the rattle of the flap, letters threatening onto her mat. His gifts kept her locked indoors. Musty chocolates with the frost of age (stolen out of his mother's bed?). Pink cloth roses. (She saw him stitching them from retrieved petticoats.) His packages were so intricately wrapped. She sobbed as she slashed the string, the bubble-pack secured with elastoplast. She dreaded fingers cut from children, silver-varnished nails torn from crash victims, waving out of wrecks.

The roll of film was winding onto its spool as swiftly as a cylinder in a mechanical piano. The spine of her life, the last. Posers caught with superglued lids – or performing at Sofya's request. The act itself, she decided, would constitute a contract.

A regal landlady, in spotted blouse and pearls, crossing her legs on a high stool (accordianist framed out, except for huge hands interfering with the keys). Her eyes are clamped shut, mouth wide: keyboard of equine teeth. There's the blushing amateur, tickled by a mike, colluding in her own exposure. Two fancy lads against a wall. They took so long striking an attitude, arms around each other's necks, then not, that Sofya had time to go home to water her plants. Jackets on/off, sleeves rolled. She snapped. A razorhead, swastika lids, pumping iron with his tongue. Friends on a bed. The not-quite-famous in hospitality suites. Shocked civilians on stretchers. Drunks with bleeding heads. Stripshow patrons waiting to be let in. A publisher, being shown the waterfront, winding herself into a headscarf. A pilgrim with severe cheekbones sleeping on a satchel-pillow under a tree. Faces in the morgue who have finally come to terms with an inadequate narrative.

Thanks to Sofya, all doomed, fated; cursed by the theft of light.

There was a spectacular shot of Imar O'Hagan, smashed, masturbating on a railway bridge. High, rivetted sides, slogans, and, weirdly, from a signal-box, a giant's hand aiming a pistol (Makarov, 9mm., self-loading); a Czech artwork they'd forgotten to take down. O'Hagan's eyes, she assumed, were white, rolling back into the top of his head: a hypnotized clerk believing himself to be black. (O'Hagan swore mightily as he came. They walked on and had a few in the Carpenter's Arms – before he fell asleep at the table.)

But Mordecai Donar was the flaw she couldn't shake. His persistence was equal to her own. The treachery in his eyes: it's the camera he's looking at, not the photographer. Questioning her competence. He's in charge. He's laid himself bare. She's above him, on her feet. He leans on his elbow, sneers in her face. There's nothing she can do, not now, he's with her to the finish.

Sofya purchased a knife, a fish-shaped switchblade, decorative, nasty – with an evil, serrated edge. She carries it in her pocket. Doesn't go in for handbags. One of the boys. She tests the weapon when she checks her hair. In the Ladies, she can hear the tape upstairs. Not a mistake, the warrior crop looks good. But the shirt's chancy, shows too much. A cruising single with no make-up and translucent skin. Click. The blade, flashing out, skins her fingers. How does she force it back? Is there a safety-catch? Hurry, girl. She wants to be first at the meeting place, a pub she doesn't use. Narrow Street. Far enough to make him walk, throw Donar off-balance.

Waterlight streaming over weathered wood. In the window seat: a haze of particles skidding, wavelet to wavelet. Launched on the river's lovely indifference. When he arrives she'll force him to take the photographs back. She'll scratch out the mamzer's eyes on the negative. Violence will compensate. She'll recover the project's necessary edge. The images she still has to execute will redeem her one mistake.

She looks at her wristwatch. Donar is late. Cunning. He's granting her time to plan her strategy. Lose her nerve. He won't come. Not yet.

SEVENTEEN

The meal in college was dreadful: more high-stool than high table. Nursery grub in gigantic portions, warmed just enough to dent the permafrost. Premasticated green sludge, and potatoes gathered from a limestone shelf, fixed in bituminous gravy. Knives and forks were held in reserve. Coloured plastic straws and ice-picks were the favoured tools. Old babies, with bibs and angry rectal faces, were mopped and sponged by attendant sizars. Claret wrung from rabbit fur. The noise was an equatorial sunset, payday in a mining camp: riot on the lower benches, spiteful eructation among the nobs. A mumble of dog latin concluded it.

It took a case of the college's best red (pod-popping fusillades of cork), and a whisky so smooth they were incapable of appreciating it (inbreaths of rolling delight), to lift the gustatory gloom, the griping and slooshing of abused digestions. Hinton felt better than he had for weeks. His kind of scoff. Alimentary distress gave his previously non-specific worries something to get on with. Death fizzed like alkaseltzer in his guts. He drank to provoke sweat. And mused on Adnam starving on his hill. The softer path to gnostic bliss.

Undark hadn't done much with the room, granted books permission to breed, curtained the window, tolerated a splintered cello – on which he hung his coat. He fiddled with an antique projector (coughing steam) and sent Hinton through to the bedroom to filch a sheet. Sileen luxuriated behind a gentleman's cigar: fantasies of collegiate life. The Sherlockian respite from the chase, the consulting of Bradshaw, the planning of trips: newspapers, gazetteers. Licensed bohemianism. Silver service. Breakfast on a tray.

'Sound *is* sense,' their host insisted, as the crumpled sheet was stretched and pinned. 'Kraighten – attend to that name. Hodgson's fictitious "hamlet". The shapes those nine letters make when they combine. *Nightrake, Kaneright, Raithnegk*. The tonal mood they suggest: greyness, kraken, fright. Now sample the map at random, anywhere in the forty mile circuit around Ardrahan. Chant like banshees. Slip inhibition. Sing out, lads. Kilshanny, Kilbrickan, Keeraunnagark.'

He kept their glasses primed, scarcely indulging himself; wetting his lips in a gesture of encouragement. The cyclopean engine, its chimney ablaze, scorched the first of William Hope Hodgson's glass slides onto the screen. A circle of intemperate light that left them blind. They were not yet drunk enough to stall the rational mind. Undark played with the focus. Rocks turned to meat. Moss to maggots.

'Hodgson, at first, worked close in, producing hard evidence of the appalling conditions at sea. Foul rations. Steaks that ran from the plate.'

Spectral images shuttled to a cranking sound. Some Sileen noticed, more often, his eyes were shut. Darkness and its faultline. Tracings of landscapes that never were. The plate camera's allusive prose. He drank in furious spurts, snatched sleep, woke among blue (imagined) polar floes. Hinton stayed alert, firing questions that were provocatively out of synch, disposing of astonishing quantities of gin. (Nursing his green bottle like a spinster's friend.)

Shakesperean seas. Forked lightning. Bar code rain. All the infamous weather spats. Hodgson and his tripod were always up on deck (when he wasn't weaving rope doilies, hefting barbells, or punching sacks). Undark worked in silence now. The photographs said too much.

The trumpet beam of white light was artlessly fouled by Sileen's smoke. Hinton observed: a pompous cobrahead of twisting blues. Sileen's face like something rescued from a grate. A concentration that would split stones. And there were plenty of those. The wretched state of the screen (buttered, marked by nocturnal and diurnal emissions) cast oceans into devastated fields. Convulsive vomitings. Earth showers that would never complete their dying fall.

The ethically challenged guest sprawled on the upholstered bench, easing his stump, bottle backgripped like table-tennis bat, brooding: how to fill Undark's glass. The scholar, stoking his light-machine, always managed to shift his tumbler that inch too far. Sileen's last hope: keep the slideshow running through the night, drink the gaffer into a coma, snatch the manuscript, run. An unconvincing scenario. (These fleet images, prompts for a silent lecture, were a privilege: beyond X-rays, or surveillance valentines. Must *never* end. They formed a border around the borderland.)

Plastered Undark was a bad pun. Legless Sileen. Alcohol was a social fragrance, killing the arid selfishness of nicotine. (The man with the kipper tie knew that Sileen knew the game was up. And knew that Sileen knew that he knew that Sileen knew. But all would play it out. What else?)

They lost themselves in what they saw, adding pigment to the graded fog. What intrigued Sileen (who had no contract to become involved) was the relation between body-building and seascape portraiture. First: hides of muscled wave. Next: a slice of Hodgson in an oval window, stretching a sleeveless vest, biceps deformed by use. The background took the breath away: a raging, rhino sky trapped in a pool, Scottish curses unfulfilled. (Accidents lovingly pressed between sheets of glass.) Behind the poser's back, a hint of wings. Inscribed name blotted out in cloud. The shuttle sticks, the window takes flame. Our indoor athlete, in his heated spoon, melts to demerara. Bubbles, spits. Is martyred where he stands.

KNOCK KNOCK.

Sileen attempted to read Undark's vices in the stains on the sheet. Couldn't be done. Like imagining Drage-Bell's habits as anything but solitary. Like finding the intelligencer dining *à deux*. (How many children had Simon Undark?) The puff of unspoken things lifted the air masses, exquisitely delineated heaps of meaningless moisture. The weather was loose, seeping from the screen. Surfing wave fronts of Irish light: Huygens principle. Hinton failed to find his feet. (An urgent act of personal hygiene. He needed to withdraw.)

'I'm encouraged to wonder.' Undark's voice. Behind them. 'If there is any exculpation to be discovered in our climate for the infliction of terror. A rancour in the pressure of spite. Telephones, tuned to the random violence of the streets, become instruments of harm. They wire the tongue to shriek. We are altogether hemmed in by devices that prevent the dispersal of threat. Gloatingly, they play it back – suborning us to hoard our petty hurts. Unprepared, we're urged to speak. Terror, in this infinitely reductive world, is offered as the poetry of the inarticulate.'

Too rich for Sileen. KNOCK. He thought better of the man than that. Too pissed to risk a refutation. (Dr Johnson's kick at Bishop

Berkeley's stone.) And too fearful. Undark and the room (books, town, mount) were a single entity. It would be like nutting smoke. Bruise Undark and the walls would shake.

Germy Hinton, in real time, had to micturate, or wet his pants. He stumbled blind, fondling objects creped in gloom; cracking his finger joints to dull his bladder's swollen ache. Drank from the bottle, soothing by making worse. Rolled relief lettering across his damp brow, printing GORDON'S widdershins. The screen was blank, his blundering had eclipsed the beam. Monster Hinton *was* the show. The cold fronts had, wisely, decamped.

'How can we take sides when terror's an ellipse?' Undark again, racking an argument they did not want to hear. 'Does it matter if the cause we champion is unjust? Myths once invoked – Cú Chulainn or compensatory High Andes dreams – cannot be withdrawn. They feed on blood when all the blood is drained. Innate stupidity. History as a hot flush.'

The sound of those words set Hinton's belly churning, woke Sileen. Peristalsis like a spiked saxophone. A riptide of cisterns as liquifying suet climaxed through their tubes. KNOCK KNOCK KNOCK. Undark groped for another slide to mitigate the shame. A triangular field set into the side of a steep hill. Sileen speared with shock. His memory's been raided. It's part of the faulty circuitry. (Adnam, in his ditch, saw brooches and clips of stars, ornamented animal forms: cloisonné. Celestial pub signs painted on angel glass.) The next slide would surely make everything clear.

Hinton, in remission, found the door. His prayers were answered. There *is* a god. Wherever she might be. One hand to turn the knob, the other to unzip. Clamp thighs: still in the dark. Another door to spring. He'll spray from the window, if he can get that far. Dangling and fumbling, gibbering too. Gin cleansed the palate like a phenol spray; he spoke in tongues. Flung himself outward into Drage-Bell's arms.

See it through Hinton's eyes (the reverse angle would make Max Miller blush): a smirking interrogation of porters, uniforms, keys. Lodgemen first, resentful and out of hours: counting their buttons (supernumerary nipples). Then local filth, trespassing on forbidden ground, incubating nervous helmets under steaming oxters. Two or three who exploded the concept of 'plainclothes'. Stubbled ennui in elasticated binliners: Goochy's jetset cricket squad in weary transit. And, finally, the one who had the doc by the throat. The skeleton with hair. The boss.

Hinton howling. 'I am not a number. I'm a free man.'

The classic dawn raid – without the sledgehammers and the obscenities. College property was protected by sanctuary taboos too heavy for Plod to violate. (Ditto, tenured scholars. Still open season on fly-by-night dossers.) Drage-Bell, on foreign turf, marched directly into the beam of the projector, casting treacle over the field of stones. The low lighting flattered his capacity for the sinister. Baseball cap, checkerboard charity jacket, the lipodredged cheeks of a toothless vampire: Harry Dean Stanton on walkabout. Harry Dean with an attitude.

'Good mornin', sir. Very sorry to disturb. But we have reason to believe . . .' One of the turnip-tops had been delegated to go through the motions. Obsequious thuggery. Sileen had his elbow resting on the green folder, the Hodgson manuscript. It was all his fault. He had got too close. Done what he was supposed to do.

Introductions by the constabulary are usually terse: 'Name? Address? You're nicked, my old beauty.' Drage-Bell was the exception. He was delighted to make Sileen known to allcomers. He treated the amputee like a recovered pet.

'Mr Todd Sileen, formerly of Wapping, a registered snout. A recidivist, a runaway. A sneak thief. Even now, sir, as you'll observe, he has his sticky fingers on your property.'

The intelligencer shot out a claw. The green folder was swiftly deposited in a non-regulation reticule, a Tesco's carrier-bag. ('Pile 'em high and sell 'em cheap.') It would precede the pedestrian troop to London. The triangulation was complete. Drage-Bell's goons were boxing the slides, wading through bookshelves (one book looks so much like another). Bell himself was autographing the pink chitty. Information is power. Absolute information is nuked paranoia. Nothing is too trivial: black bags of correspondence (that couldn't be a West Cork postmark?), unpaid bills, Arts Cinema ticket stub, annotated dissertations, 'Average Smoke Concentration' charts, wind speed tables, accounts of the famous Lea Valley temperature traverse (allowing for warming of elements by car engine), photocopied extracts from the diaries of the poet James Thomson ('5pm. The sun, large, defined, tremulous, like a beryl or crystal globe full of amber light, stood on a long ridge of ashen cloud').

Sileen was cautioned and asked not to leave town (implying, quite urgently, the reverse). Hinton, the prospective flasher, was offered some assistance in his difficulties with the stairs. His jowls erupted, spontaneously, in a thatch of blood-crusted splinters. The intruders, running out of ideas, withdrew; stamping meaningfully over the dewy grass of the quadrangle, badmouthing their booty.

Sileen watched them from his high window. What now? (If he didn't jump.) The intelligencer had used him to track the Hodgson manuscript across the south of England. Used him without payment. There would be no more 'little drinks' for Todd, there was nobody left to shop. The monoped was finished. The comic interlude in a rock 'n' roll melodrama.

Simon Undark, tipping back a metaphorical stetson, stepped forward into the beam. One slide left. More Ben Johnson the roughrider, now, than the fruity playwright, he galloped into those wild and rocky hills.

Outside: the first streaks of sunlight infiltrated Rhab Adnam's sandy ditch. The shivering visionary, lying on a sharp stone, felt his assemblage point make an abrupt shift. Tree roots laced him in a tight vegetal corset.

Sileen was not a part of it. He bled for his old chum. He needed Adnam like an incipient migraine, a means of reasserting his dispersed identity.

EIGHTEEN

On the flat roof of the White's Row multistory car park Andi Kuschka digressed on eyeballs for the benefit of her respectful group. She knew these streets too well to have much time for such an exhausted fable. William Stewart's theory. Didn't he claim (Toronto, 1939) that a *woman* was the Ripper?

The twin clock faces of Christ Church were mad eyes, unevenly set. Different hours in south and west. The Germans were intrigued by (and dismissive of) her shaky optics. The Americans were credulous, eager to interrogate. The Japanese loved this fairy tale of the camera: a pleasing anecdote of formal cruelty. (Like John Evelyn's yarn of the young lad with scriptural texts engraved on his lenses. To be read from which side?) They knew it all, but wanted to be told. The experiment had been Tokyo published in one of many Ripper homages – tinted studies of Victorian Whitechapel. Top hats, carriages, spread legs. Pictograph explanations shaped into ornamental borders. *The Double Event* or *A Lost Woman*. Their end was our beginning. Sir William Gull's portrait on page 241. The solution announced as soon as we open the book.

The white raincoats moved closer, encouraging her. It was the finish of their tour, the finale. Andi, vertiginous, rested her hand on the rail. Clear sky. Trees in the churchyard. The church perspective as clean as the architect's original drawing. A corner pub, the Ten Bells. She thirsted. Stifle repulsion, get it done. Drinks, photographs. Bloody Marys waiting on a tray.

Shutters were hammering. She steadied herself. The Japanese never pressed, stood off. Big CU: her eyes. A ring of them like a ship's chain. She must not blink. To close her lids, even for an instant, would be to lose her place in time. To erase the magical, life-affirming script. She held out a hand in front of her face. No, no. It was wrong. The story was apocryphal. A rumour that had outlived its usefulness, a rumour that had found its moment. The Black Museum was justifiably sniffy about the whole thing (which only convinced the conspiracy nuts that they were on the right track). A photograph *did* exist. Taken here, beneath their modest feet, on the concrete ramp of this building: a mapping of Mary Kelly's eyeball.

The rented groundfloor room, with its cooling meat décor, became a studio. A site of ritual and curious intimacies – attended by those ancient bedfellows, etiquette and obscenity. It was their forlorn hope that the frozen hemisphere (stretched with tape) would retain, printed by trauma, a retinal portrait of the assassin. An aqueous miniature. (Should they arrest the culprit or hang him in the National Gallery?) Death, these speculators imagined, as a spontaneous ingestion of light, converting the woman into an instrument of memory, a camera. Their investigation: the ultimate injury.

As she spoke, standing back from herself, looking down on the tight group from the tower of the church, Andi believed everything she was saying. She listened (by simultaneous translation) to the lying words that flowed from her mouth. Men in dark coats peering expectantly into the face of the dead woman. Extreme suffering had made her oracular. Death was no bridle. They had only to probe the wounds to extract the name of the killer. Microscope the tender pupils to recover a map of his motives.

Andi's performance – and it was a performance – hushed their excitement. There were strange requests (she busked for them, they were implied in the risks she took). Gratuities were forced into her hand, folded banknotes. She always refused the private theatricals they whisperingly insinuated. Once, it's true, needing a tuition fee for her painting class, she *had* come across. There were two of them, safety in numbers, and the hotel was in Bloomsbury.

Like state hospitality in the old East Germany. A courtyard of windows. Regimented quantities of greenery. Busy foyer of tourists and prostitutes and salesmen. Air terminal bars. Drunken Russians. Ballrooms given over to the sale of cheap leather jackets and used books. Long corridors patrolled by cameras. A good place for out-of-towners to kill themselves.

The young man greeted her at the door with a bow. Attempted a gesture of introduction which the older man brushed aside. He signalled for the curtains to be drawn. Did not rise from the twin bed on which he was sitting. He had the authority of a father, or an employer. The walls were thin. Andi could hear excited conversations, TV, airbrakes in the yard, doors creaking and slamming. This was a building made from sound: solitaries on harsh mattresses would be listening to FX they could not avoid, to the young man's over-emphatic pleasantries.

Andi wanted to tell an Irish joke. She was not invited to sit down, she walked. The older man, watching, said nothing. The young one hovered at her heels, shadowing her circuits. Turned to his mentor for instruction. Tea. 'Ahhh!' He hissed, nodded like something rabbit-punched. It amused Andi, the boy's difficulties with the tea bags, the button on the electric kettle.

The oldie sipped with style. Andi was offered, and accepted, a whisky. With a splash from the tap. She was told what she should do. The father sat, stiff and silent, staring into her face. The young man, behind her, talked.

She must undress. She did. It was what she expected. The domesticity was less predictable. The way the old man sucked his cooling tea. Or the boy filled a hotwater bottle and wrapped it in a towel. They waited.

There was no anger, none of the aggression she felt during the modelling sessions with the St Anne's Court sleazos. None of the flirtatious gamesmanship she indulged in with the camera club buffs. There was such venal detachment in this old man, in the saucer held in front of his mouth – as if he had taken out his teeth and couldn't remember how to replace them. He had seen everything, at least twice. Corruption had exhausted him. His life was a retrospective to be endured. The efficiency of the son, allowed no feelings of his own, was a badge of subservience. Andi was stronger than either of them, than both together. She wanted to fuck the boy until he howled for mercy, to see tears start in the father's eyes.

A book. A Japanese book taken from a slipcase. The old man nods. Rapid shuffle of pages – to demonstrate the lack of harm? Columns of excited script. Buildings she recognized. The brewery coldstore. A car parked in an undistinguished square. The Roebuck. Dull, flat transcriptions: the suppression of light and atmosphere.

A Lost Woman. His long, beautifully manicured finger holds the page. A steel engraving. Left hand on hip. Jaunty hat with a nonsense of ribbons. Anklelength, double-breasted coat secured by a single button.

The father signals. The son opens the suitcase. He has the coat. Nudges a hatbox.

There is no difficulty in recreating the pose: it belonged to Andi first. She sees what the Lost Woman saw, when she paused, turned. An anonymous hotel room, two men. Andi has the same sturdiness, the quizzical tilt of the head. Her wrist bends to take up the required gesture, hieratic, mocking. The hat's awkward. Comic or pornographic? A performance tool. The double-breasted coat is hardworn, but thin. She fumbled for the button, allowed the skirts to spread. She was more naked than before.

A clockwork bird in the room. The hum of the camcorder was an intrusion only she could hear. The young man had gone to the trouble of setting up a tripod. Andi was arranged at the door of the en suite bathroom, right hand (in shadow) on the knob – about to enter, looking back at whoever dared to follow her in.

The eyes. That's all they want. No need to zoom (his hand is trembling too much). Monster CU, then let it run. She listens to the muted traffic, bathwater running in another room. The click of the saucer as the old man sets it down on the bedside table.

Evening coarsened behind the church's spire. Remembering the business with the camcorder brought back the hurt. The horror of her optician and his carrion breath. There is a fetishistic device for measuring the pressure of liquid inside the eyeball – a sudden puff of cold air. The subject is helpless, trapped by the faint red light she is forced to watch: a light she intensifies by squeezing her forehead against a pliant restraint. Unprotected pupils wait expectantly for the shock: the needle, the scratch across the lens. A thin beam of sunlight. Darkened windows drawing her deeper into the building's depths. The horrid aperture of the porch.

Victorian light had sickened and died. They should have photographed the men instead: starched worthies, butchers, anarchists, loungers. Men on their way to the races. Men cutting cloth. Strollers anticipating breakfast. Clamp them. Shoot the fear in their eyes, the hunger that never gets out. We are not trawling for malign homunculi, Hilliard limnings. Eyes are not medallions. The eyes of the killer are blank as porcelain. Nominate the dullest grape. Publish eyes as pamphlets. Let there be ocular directories, corneal encyclopedias. Study them until they start to blink. Use exhaustion as a guide. The one with least life: that's your man.

Andi tasted panic. Like a waxed knot. The street twisted below, cars slid on the ramp. The church: a ladder on its side. Fournier Street: black sprockets in a torn film. She couldn't finish her story. The tourists touched her arm. She recovered, smiled, dispersed the group by pointing to the pub. Voices faded down stone steps: ammonia assault, gusts of tired city air.

Gripping the rail, breathing slowly, she watched them cross the road. *Sofya!* Andi had to run, get back. The flat. In this heat, race. Squealing tyres. Horns. Men hooting invitations out of cars. Suck me. Swallow me. Drink my seed. Bumped, thrown off balance by the drift towards the underground station. Groups of men talking on pavements, in doorways, leaning against polished motors. Show us your tits. Drop your jeans. Piss on my face. They reach out. Skin-traders, kitchen workers. Honks, whistles. She's crying.

Stalls of tat on Whitechapel Road. A drinking school on the corner saluting her with their upraised cans. (One of them, probably dead, has been dragged into the alley beside Wood's Buildings.) She has to rescue the flat, make that space inviolate. Perhaps Sofya will be waiting for her, returned from her adventure with a tale to tell. Perhaps she didn't go. (Won't wash: Andi sees the empty bench in the riverside pub, the locked door of Mordecai Donar's Wellclose Square retreat.)

Andi *must* press her lips against the feet of the bronze angels on their plinth opposite the hospital, touch them before she crosses. Keep Sofya safe. The angels have been removed! The memorial plaque chopped from the stone.

One of Sofya's mad old ladies is wrestling with the street door, buckled by the weight of an almost empty shopping trolley, a dog on a string. Andi wants to scream. But is calm now; listens, nods, holds the yelping, furry thing. Follows the old biddy inside: a stream of forty-year-old grievances. Then the stairs. Uncollected letters, brown envelopes, picture postcards. Sofya will be waiting.

The bell sounds a long way off. A soft footfall, that's what Andi heard. Pressing: again and again. The old woman shouted up. 'Is out, she. Gone, my darlin'. Never said.'

Andi wriggled the key. Never used before, this emergency spare. She shoved too hard, threatened to break it off. The lock yields. She steps inside. Stay calm. Be here. Assert a presence. The flat is empty: sitting-room, bedroom, kitchen. The plaintive moaning of an old-fashioned fridge.

Sofya's absence made the flat too small. Andi was an intruder. Too clumsy for these low ceilings. Too intemperate. When Sofya let her in, the rooms were neutral, extensions of the woman who occupied them. The girls brushed cheeks. Andi would notice Sofya's hair, the earrings, her shoes. Now objects challenged the stranger's gaze. Books flinched from her touch. Flowers wilted. She had to follow Sofya's pattern in order to retain her, bring her back. She had to *become* Sofya. Share that risk. It should be Andi waiting in the pub. Andi nursing the last half-inch of beer. Andi is already damned. Sofya might survive.

Coffee, that's first. Spilling grains in her haste, they melt and stick to the damp cloth. Bubbling percolation, boiling rust. Draw out the ritual to stretch time. Moist windows, nothing to see. Quiet darkness cancelling fear. The kitchen shrinks to a black box.

At the table: Andi nurses a mug from which she cannot drink. Lips scorched at the first taste. Sofya's bite. A rattling window. Andi starts. How long has she been here? Catface. Imperious tapping of a grey paw. The traitor rubs against the alien leg, and mews. Avoid the mirror and she *is* Sofya. Slashing her thumb to the ball on a can of whale pulp, scooping red mush into a bowl. The stinking cat won't eat. Arches its back and whines (a vile sound – the hunger of a fledgling thrush). Purrs, twists. Sniffs a second time, refuses. Won't be coaxed. Spurns Andi's food. Blood drips from her gashed hand into the coarse shag. Splashes on her white jeans.

The phone. That's what's wrong. It doesn't ring. It should be ringing all the time. Sofya's a busy girl – galleries, picture editors, friends. Cut herself off and she doesn't exist. She's buried in this hole, a hostage to fate. This is the time of day for Sofya to work the wires. (Mornings are her own.) Andi wants to pick up the period piece, this Edgar Wallace prop, and talk – to anybody. Imar O'Hagan, Sofya's mother, the faceless rapist who's watching from across the square. She fondles the short black arm, obsessively: tastes it with her blistered tongue. It shrills. She backs against the wall.

The horrible answering machine has come to life, it clicks and whirrs. Silence. Drowning cheeps. Then Sofya's voice! Sofya talks to Sofya. Andi hugs herself. The real Sofya is in the room, a recording sponsored by an effervescent tone. The other Sofya, the one in the pub, is romance – a character Andi has invented to salve her guilt. Someone to punish for being loved. (What if the pub was targeted? What if Sofya's camera case contained a bomb?) Write *that* Sofya out.

The real Sofya's voice is troubled, tense – she doesn't want to be bothered. She does what Andi does, listens while strangers talk to her absent self. She repeats. 'I'm sorry but there is nobody to take your call.' Reads it like a boring script, fast and flat. She's preoccupied, has other things to do.

All Sofya's neurotic rituals must be observed or she will be carved like mutton. The hairbrush touched against the open drawer. The position of the jars of facecream switched three times. What could this Sofya impersonator want? Go away. Leave her alone. The false Sofya, speaking too loud above the din of last orders, wants to know if Donar has left a message.

How could he? There is no Donar, no such man. Andi made him up. It's Andi, in Sofya's gear, waiting in the bar, asking if she can use the phone. Sofya's exasperated with having to repeat her tedious message. You can tell. 'Nobody to take your call.' Why doesn't this other girl ring off?

It's important to stick to Sofya's routine, allow the layout of the rooms to dictate her movements. Think of nothing else. Andi remembers, remembers what she has noticed, sitting as a guest – talking, laughing. Is *this* how Sofya behaves when she's alone? Andi, suppressing knowledge of anything beyond these walls, anything that happened before or is still to come, taps directly into Sofya's unconsidered actions. Strolls, smooths curtains, adjusts the line of books. She sits tailor-fashion on the sofa, strokes the cat.

She keeps time to the irregular drumming of Sofya's heart. She reasserts the particular rhythms of her friend's breath: the fret of demons Sofya has to quell – so many paces, a pause, the sounding of a loose board. It *works*. It must be true. This spell. Invoking Sofya, losing herself.

Andi grips the propeller-head of the brass tap. Spasming water, steam. Sofya's pink bath foam. Back through to the sitting-room: TV on, sound down, low but distinct. There should be a glass of chilled white wine. She doesn't want to listen, but from the bath, she can't help it, she does. Check water level. Top up her drink. *News at Ten*. The usual montage: columns of exhausted marchers spitting at/for the camera, ordinary buildings – doomed if shown. The tide of imagery, un-explained, tells it all: how conferences beget disasters and peace formulae assure us of war. Processions of planes held on runways, carpets, umbrella carriers, men who photograph other men opening doors. The salute triggers the explosion. Camera shake ordains a thunder of mortars. Flak jackets spit tracers. An opentop limo cruising through a complacent city should guard against Super-8 cameras, before considering the potential angles of fire. If an event isn't covered, it doesn't happen.

Andi adjusts the volume, turns off the tap. The misted mirror, a woman's face. Not her own. Not Sofya. She undresses, tests the water, kicks her clothes into the corner: sound persists through the open door, jaunty summaries, weather. She rinses out her pants in the basin, hooks them over a towel rail. Ties her hair in a chiffon scarf. Lowers herself gently into the water, as hot as she can bear. Lies back, wine glass within reach, scarcely attending to the human interest fillers: a man's face rebuilt, after it had been torn off by a pit bull. Ears, forehead, nose. Brought to the hospital in a plastic bag.

Now, with a towel around her waist, she investigates Sofya's medicine cabinet. Skin cleansers. Dental sticks. Adult Expectorant. Nurofen. Coconut milk balm. She thinks about painting her nails. A white dressing gown with a hood: tight, splitting as she flexes stiff shoulders.

She plays back the video that Sofya set. Isabel's weather mime. Hears the bath draining with hungry swallows. Swooshing away the foam, the dark hairs. Isabel directs the clouds. She doesn't gabble like the motormouth men (who feel obliged to busk the history of the world in 10½ seconds). Elegant but stern. Isobars are chided. Cold fronts tidied away. She swirls her hair, plenty of it, with such style that her audience identify the effect, correctly, as a shampoo climax. The country admires her maquillage. The spontaneity of that final smile. She demonstrates weather they are obliged to buy. Adverts follow in a seamless wipe.

It's almost that time of night when the programmes lose their nerve and opt for self-cannibalization. Old movies like wrongly assembled dreams. Sofya pours bourbon into a shot glass, too large to hold. She sets it on the floor. Local news is always weird: cash points ripped from Building Societies by earthmovers, Indian takeaways operating out of the City Airport, a hitman in a parkside pub. No Sofya. No Mordecai Donar. No photofit. They haven't heard. They haven't mutilated the 'twenty something East London woman' by showing her unblemished face.

A taller drink, more ice. Andi never touches spirits. (Hotels don't count.) She'll happily nurse a single spritzer through a two hour session. Back to the fridge. An apple. Bung in a CD, top of the heap. Another video – with the sound off. An anthology of Isabel in different suits. Weather prophecy: undercranked. Red skids fill the screen with knitted warning lights. Izzy's face shines with health, but the forecast's bad. Shoulders of an athlete, a bedroom athlete. That's what we're supposed to think. Nothing underneath – except the mike. Clouds wheeze, suns wink, cherubs ejaculate. Bikinis and raincoats. The hottest on the map: St Helier in the Channel Islands (where gold bars melt).

Andi sways. The booze doesn't work. The tape switches itself off, rewinds. The CD goes on and on and on: ethno-discriminate, Jazz Café. With the window open, the room grows cold. Sofya's dressing-gown doesn't fit. She's not Sofya and never could be. She sits, shaking, at the kitchen table. Expecting the worst. Her bottle's dead. (She wants to want O'Hagan, bursting through the door, belt in hand, to thrash them both.)

The bedroom, a more private space, has absorbed the quantum of chaos that rightly belongs to the other rooms. Duvet thrown back, pillows tossed aside. Andi, in her isolation, tests the sheets, presses her face into the mattress. Drapes Sofya's nightdress around her neck. Moans. Like something on the fjord's edge. Fingers into lidless pots. Golden hair strands picked from brushes with her teeth. Pink tissue-balls uncurled.

Andi slumps. From the bed: a chair mounded in castoff clothes. A reverse striptease. Sofya's week read backwards: baggy white raincoat, leggings, blouse, black bra with powder traces, half-slip. Tumbled, shed. Things Andi would never have imagined – so how could she trust her own feeble impersonation of Sofya-at-home? Each garment had its history, represented a specific occasion. Times that Andi can now replay.

Holding the dressing-gown tightly across her chest, she runs back into the studio and rings the police.

NINETEEN

Who would bother to follow them now? They felt the absence of Drage-Bell's dogs like a skewer unskewed. They were cloddish, dull. Their quest had been stripped of its subversive glamour. Futility, silence. They were off the list. The lack of eavesdroppers bleached all purpose from their walk. Nobody watching means no-one to watch.

They stalked, zombies, through the early, tessellated streets – in a stereophonic hiss of bicycle wheels. Lucifer, the gorgeous angel, was abroad. Fresh light picked gilded scabs from historic porticos. Such arrogance in the modesty of rosy bricks! Undark, risking the town centre, treated them to a farewell breakfast in his favourite grease caff (proximate to the market's lowkey buzz).

There was nothing for it: limp back to the old hutch, Whitechapel, the river. *Which* river? The river had betrayed them, gifted them with reflected arcadian follies. The river was a lie. London was cellars, noise, dirt, corruption – life! London was what Sileen needed. His travels, if nothing else, had proved that. Daemons were everywhere. Movement fretted them, shook them up.

Look at Sileen's hands. Blotched, blistered, can't hold his cup. They belong in a burns unit. A rejected graft. The Guinea Pig Club. He's got the shakes. Look at the tits on that calendar. The dairy potential going to waste. He wants to feed and suck. Look at the date. One of those numbers is his death.

Hinton was white as water (post-leper dip). He had glimpsed the future and she ran away. Banishment hurt. If Undark cut him loose he had nowhere to go. Oxford, he accepted, was in purdah. A clap of sunlight unilaterally withdrawn. A privilege suspended – to increase, by the same amount, the privileges of those who remain. Oxford exists in retrospect. Better to talk about than endure. Brian Howard,

Evelyn Waugh. Where could he turn?

The House had disappeared bodily, and a stupendous pit now yawned in the place where it had stood . . . Sometimes, in my dreams, I see that enormous pit . . . And the noise of the water rises upwards, and blends – in my sleep – with other and lower noises; while, over all, hangs the eternal shroud of spray.

Hinton slept where he sat, his eggs untouched. He toyed with his cassettes, leaning them against each other to form an arch. Simon Undark, not watching, watched: he journeyed through that plastic gate and saw the rack, the pinion, and the screw.

The triangulation was a sugar dendrite that Adnam moulded with a knife. His nails drummed on the upturned bowl. 'Yes. Like like like.' The weathered visionary had been retrieved, delirious, from his open grave – babbling of darkness consumed and light that surged like a flamethrower's cough. The night was a revolving cylinder: cold, bright, then black as the pit of hell. Shooting stars, field mice, contracted buildings groaning in the chill. Adnam had nurtured gloom – in order to provoke its contrary, a pinprick beam to fire his pineal bud. The crystal of consciousness splitting into a blizzard of fixed stars. 'Knowing,' he said, 'the answer is YES.'

The luminescence of Robert Grosseteste's prose, *De Luce*, never read, touched Adnam, profoundly (at the very moment when Simon Undark slid the slender volume beneath his projector to raise its beam). The visionary, in his slit on the mound's side, saw Hodgson's monochrome seascapes invade the clouds.

Then came the shocks, the shudders, and the grief: a child again, lost, an ancient man pissing himself in proof of weakness, waiting to be born. Came rage, the knowledge of what was still to be done.

Adnam survived, his spirit sang. He greeted the others, when they came for him, as wavering flames: colours not shapes. Interwoven, beam to beam, soul to soul. They descended like a courteous whirlwind on the town.

Across the breakfast table, Rhab's madness rang like truth – freezing Sileen's vertical fork. He could have snuffed the bearded scrote for spoiling a buckshee feed. Adnam was one too many. Four men breaking bread was bad news. Adnam's Lazarus act condemned them to the road. Hinton knew it first: scraping their leavings into a bag. Civilized Undark spiked their final coffees from a silver flask.

The curse with this New Age we're-all-one spiel, as Sileen recognized, lay in having to see with Adnam's eyes: noticing that Undark, who never touched food, glowed with the inflorescence of the *perfecti*. A man apart. Dangerously pure. White highlights where the nicorette patches had been peeled. Put it down to dodgy phosphors in the tube, but Undark shone like an irradiated herring, the X-ray of a suicide. Sileen was fearful. If the scholar spoke, as he was bound to do, they'd have no option but to act on his refusal to advise. No more quests, no more kills. The Hodgson manuscript was lost. Better the certainty of extinction than the cruelty of rekindled hope.

'Under the turbulence vector, the pleasure in last night's furious farce,' Undark opened, 'lay in the confirmation of a hunch I've toyed with for some time – we're opening the oven to late-Elizabethan or early-Jacobean methods and manners. That thing Drage-Bell belongs in *Volpone*, "feigning lame" till he be "sick and lame indeed". Language as assault. "Sudden privy injuries." Espions, blasphemers waxing lyrical on the rack. Madrigals of love and submission, blushing with syphilitic sores. Bright diamonds polished from sedimentary gleet. Homages that poison as they praise. Thefts, anticipations, mobhanded composition. Blank verse clattering like the threat of blades. Glorious conceit! A fold-over, guys, *not* a palimpsest. Arright! What's your view, Hinton?'

Not good. Head in a sack. Counting sausages, checking for leaks. Elizabethans were retro funk. Literature began with *Maude* and ended with Bob Dylan's chopper disappearing over the Needles.

'I can forgive anything that makes Cambridge tolerable,' Undark continued. 'But to have the dismal impedimenta of research dematerialized at a swoop was an unlooked for benefaction. Virgin pleasures are renewed. The dull'd ear pricks. Language, reviving, revives all the senses: taste, sound, scent, sight. We can be proud of our culture again – where else would a salaried servant of the state confiscate an indifferent literary manuscript, not to assess the weight of subversion, but to display it in a private library?'

Germy Hinton couldn't hack it. Fuck Cambridge. Pressure leaks from Gaggia coffee machines, and unbroken voices braying in complaint, brought back the original pain of his student days. Interrogations, hooded chambers, sleep deprivation: he wanted out. Electrode prosody is conditioned reflex. The ventriloquism of torturers. Bound transcripts of whatever the man with the cigarette dictates.

Undark's genius for improvisation was a lure to pull them from his best shot: Ireland. Now that the manuscript had been removed, the site of the mystery had come into sharper focus. An arrangement of rocks, the side of a hill. What could they prove? Why, nothing – hence the charm. To be free, at last, to talk of other matters, with the borderland, in balance, as a moral counterweight.

Such niceties were of no use to Sileen. His game was collaboration by stealth, creative deceit. Visions purchased with corrupted coin. He fancied Hodgson's interplanetary maunderings in his hands. There was no flesh to spare. Another X-ray binge and his bones would be Emmental. *Reading* the manuscript was the easier path. What happens when the seeker procures his much desired end? Sileen would know. (Failing that, he'd photocopy the papers and flog them, in a fancy binder, numbered and signed, to every collector on the coast.)

London. Say it. Hospital, market, pub – woman. Drage-Bell owed him. So why not draw the spider from his hole with false intelligence, spurious confessions? Trade Hinton in, the slag, fit him up as a Howard Marks connection. A bagman for the Highland run. Collar Adnam as a Swedenborgian freedom fighter. Who else? The pair in the Pitt Rivers. Slash a whore. Castrate a queer. Plant rumours of coming Holy War in the *Gazette*. Blow the whistle on Muscat's bareknuckle show. Perfect! Maroon the filth among the storage tanks of Canvey, then kick down Drage-Bell's door. Do it fast, before the cankers eat you up.

Sileen knew that he was too far gone to drag himself along the towpath. He was no peachy ambidexter hobbling from Calais to Rheims to sign on at the seminary. He needed class wheels, man. And soon. Like now.

They left Undark to settle the reckoning. Or talk his way out. A landslip of denim disciples, mannerless, were disputing the deserted chairs – primed to bore the Carnaby Street don with niggles concerning paraphrase, copulae, prepersonal forms. Parataxis: everyone in the wider world thought that one had been talked to death by Olson in Vancouver. The guru flashed us an owl's wink, then, effortlessly, began to work his shtick.

Outside: the lowlife trio passed the word. 'Undark is in town.' Then snatched the abandoned bikes.

'Hurry, kids, we'll hold your transport while you grab a place.' Sileen. 'The gaffer's doing his annual number on *The Epistemology of Loss*.' He shoved an outsize, midwife's mount, complete with wicker basket, at

Hinton. Once in the saddle there'd be no getting down without the help of a library ladder or a pageboy's back. Inhibitions would be doused in fear. Any direction would serve. Peddle or fall. Adnam accepted a radically stylish affair from a Brazilian girl (with dimplomatic English and *Party Girl* legs). She thought he was the restaurant valet and tipped him a freshly-ironed note.

Sileen was left to tease a boneshaker from the arthritic grip of an elderly female pedant, inconvenienced by a trailing gown and a cargo of primary sources. He guttered the dame with an overemphatic nod. The hoodlum windows of a pizza joint, garnished beyond their station, replayed his crime.

The dud leg was a local difficulty, horizontal as Boadicea's scythe, slashing a track through the hapless pedestrian flock. The good foot had to do the work, pump like a bilge rat in a sinking ship. They slipstreamed when they could, took the rough with the smooth, flicked midges from their eyes. One-way streets were a sophistication they ignored: St Mary's Passage, Senate House Hill, Trinity Lane, and over the water. They flew. London was the gravel in their hearts.

Only Dr Hinton, disbelieving, glanced back. Could it be so easy? Cycle tracks through grass tall enough to entertain one of Francis Bacon's baboons, the Backs vanishing like icebergs, the river – intimate as a catheter. Call it what you will – Cam, Granta, Rhee – as long as it points in the right direction. Out.

Inactive playing-fields and drains to leech the flood. Cambridge expelled them with a yawn. From a distance, under glowering skies, backs bent, buttocks raised aloft, their humiliation was complete. Give them megaphones and college scarves, these boys belong.

TWENTY

Ian Askead (piker, coiner, professional witness) is discovered within the Grave Maurice, disputing with doctors. The question on the table: 'Where, pray, did Dr Dee acquire his doctorate? Cambridge? Louvain? Prague?'

The company, swayed by the campy erudition of a medical groupie, familiarly known as the Duchess ('tash like a Lucozade afterburn, wrestler's neck ruffed in fatty wavelets), settled for the school of life. (The Duchess got his laughs first time: after three bottles of white he was on a loop. Name, sex, date: all wiped.) Was Dee truly of *our* company? That was the sticking point. A bone-setter or a pass degree geographer? Askead couldn't have cared less but disputes were good news. Heat, the vapours, fisticuffs – plenty of booze to quench the rout, and nobody sober to count the change.

Life was hard, Askead conceded, with Sileen out of town. The newest quacks refused to live down to their reputation: morose, tobacco-hating management freaks, slopped out in trainers and rugby shirts. Where were those little earners on the side? Abortions had become a literary device, rare as well turned villanelles. Dustbinned, he supposed, with the last proletarian novel. The British Marriage was in vogue – licensed celibacy. (Doctors cultivated mortgage relief instead.) Sales of surgical spirit were way down: even winos had to graft, up early to audition for a documentary spot. The rare guest appearance in court had lost its kudos (and its budget): the Micks he'd fingered had been let out. And so many of the S/M fraternity had self-culled that the leather straps and thrones were abandoned under dustsheets in a damp basement. Back to basics. Sorry times.

The Maurice was a great bar for those not quite brave enough to leave the street behind: an open door, private islands of woozy light, a line of mirrors to double the gloom. Askead, incognito, worked the tables. Newcomers, assuming he was on the firm, watched while he swept their barely-touched glasses away. Clean-shaved, the Scot remained a bearded man. Radon shadows (like John Major's phantom moustache) discoloured his mandible.

Askead ferried trays, miraculously converting ordered beer to spirits (swilling, in transit, his commission). His dainty feet were swift, dancing pumps to dodge the slops. He gave the kiss-of-life to cigar butts pronounced as clinically dead. His prim mouth too ulcerated to endure amateur infections. (The necessary frisson of excitement, keeping him hard, he engendered by wearing secret black-lace panties, lifted from a traumatized accident statistic, while she waited to be swabbed. Blood was a bonus. The lady, thinking ahead, had dressed with care for the eventuality she now endured.)

Religio Medici. The philosophically-inclined sawbones pitched into Askead's cleverly trailed Swedenborgian flyers: the circuits of hell beneath their feet. The *plenum* through which they moved. Fields of force turning to water. Dry water. Water as a residue of ancient light. Vibrations of ineradicable crimes. Intoxicated by their own metaphors, drink sobered ambition. They yawned and scratched. Swedenborg was a bore. Askead was forced to pepper the complacent moons on their churns of stout, spit in the brandy. Provoke. (They were too far gone to require the personal services of his stable of Celtic Watchers.)

Cut out the extemporizing d.t.'s: specifics.

This floor (where Askead, lurking behind a deco lamp, misheard the yarn) is where unreliable joists totalled the Swedish visionary's celestial survey.

'Gobshite!' They chortled – as a man. Thus satisfying the trickster's design. He semaphored another round. The conceit was too obvious. Hell, being visible, needs no mezzanine. Whitechapel was a rootless pestilence, a state of self-renewing bile. Terror beyond terror. Terror like a cataleptic calm. Brain/lung synchronicity, ductless glands: OK. But Swedenborg's theology was for the birds. Creatures under surgery had, it's true, called out his christian name. A reflex plea – like those who, buried for eight days in a box, see wise women with a finger to their lips. Reports of skulls wigged in maggots were the downside of the same cortical upset. Their presence in the hospital kept under wraps (unlike the sordid photographer, John Deakin, whose lung had been removed in the Marie Celeste). Unfortunate as dry rot, no more meaningful. A heresy too expensive to root out. Stress breeds such things. The hours we work.

Askead applauded the rebuttal. And ignited the venereologist's Havana – moistening the glans so copiously that the donor waved it away. A hand on the technician's shoulder spun him around. He didn't welcome creepers who insinuated from behind. He felt inside his labcoat for a blade.

The Watchman, rubberized torch in hand, wanted advice. No worse than that. A woman known to Askead (weren't they all?) had vanished. A snapper, Sofya Court, was awol in the streets. Her tribade, failing to count her in, had raised the alarm. Mum (well-connected in Cambridge) was going spare. It was Askead's civic duty to guide a posse to the suspect's den. Some yid with form, a school-gate snoop. Askead could sell the story to the tabloids. They'd case the victim's gaff on the way home and sort the juiciest pix.

'Pubs,' said the Watchman – who had all the makings of a Coach and Horses bore, 'have always been the annexes of death.' No need to spell it out. Even sewermen feel obliged to mythologize their craft. Askead understood and was more interested than he'd care to confess. The car that pulls up too pointedly outside. Murderer and murderee deciding whose turn it is to play. Nothing special on the jukebox when the needle sticks. Selective amnesia of witnesses who, ever after, remember lyrics they never knew. Drinks untouched on the bar. A shift in the light. The flash of recognition that justifies a lifetime's fear.

The Duchess, splaylegged in the Gents, forgot why he was there. The tap was running and the floor was wet. He pressed his swollen ear to the ground and listened for the empty trains. He knew himself. He wept.

And, all the while, time digressed – uncurled in spurts, eddied, raced. Andi Kuschka waited beside the fence of the wreckers' yard. The wolf that guarded the place licked her hand. The sky was clear, bits of stars threw back the city's lights. While the men talked, Sofya was intact. Nothing should break this spell. The factory-alarm, a mile away, must never stop.

Andi was running to stay at Askead's heels. The Watchman and his gang of turncoats (available for hire: lynchings, blags, bar mitzvahs, freelance circumcisions) stormed past the hospital and over Commercial Road. A peevish football mob hellbent on aggro. Only Askead knew where Mordecai Donar hung his kapel. (No address book required. He'd followed them all, man and boy, trading present misinformation against future favours.)

Not Cannon Street Road. Not Cable Street. Andi's loving involvement allowed her to jump ahead, eradicate dead ground. Her journey wasn't strictly necessary. She *knew* where Sofya was. Samuel Jacob Hayyim Falk, 'kabbalist and adventurer', man expelled, arrived in England in 1742 (as Swedenborg's spiritual sight was cleansed). Falk went to earth, establishing a private synagogue in Wellclose Square. Anyone responsive to the flow of the city's true energies would do the same. Nothing dies. We have no choice.

Andi's London researches had given her too many facts. Houses matter when their stories have been lost. She'd walked too far, explaining things that ached for silence. Corbels, keystones, shutters have their natural modesty. It was *her* fault, this drama. She'd linked Rabbi Falk and Mordecai Donar in a treaty neither man deserved. A psychic bawd, she'd forced them to share a bed. Falk had turned back fire by placing magical inscriptions around the same doorpost that his tenant now defamed. Donar was too greedy a temperament for alchemy. He botched the purity of repetition with haste. A fever to possess Sofya's soul. Coaxing her towards blasphemy with his open eyes.

She didn't have to believe. Perhaps Askead would carry on towards the river, not branch, not dodge among the shrouded mounds of Swedenborg Gardens. Chilled with expectation, hurrying to confirm the worst, she overheard the Watchman's self-priming recitative. 'Get what they deserve, these slags. See how they dress? More off than on. Drinking alone? Asking for it, I say. Definitely on the game.'

It was obvious what they would find, why drag it out? Eyes were opening like tulips in Sofya's film. Lids burnt away. Only Donar was left without sight. His tilted smile, looking up from the table, no smile at all: mouth caught, mid-sentence, protesting. Woodgrain on the wallpaper brought to life.

Under the railway bridge; hard right into Cable Street, then left. Askead has it sussed. Cheap smoke sharpens the synapses, the reek of blood. Stories to be sold. Snuff images to direct – so vivid, they made it hard to walk. He edges closer to Andi, rubs her like a lamp. Fishes for background details, phone numbers, associates. Intrusions that could be constructed as sympathy. He takes her cold hand (large) in his (childlike) own. Has to work her while she's still in shock. Mainline the brandy and a steady drip of soothing words. Keep talking till she's pliant, find out if Sofya was banging the Jewboy.

He panders for news (super-sensitive to the fluxions in Andi's wrist). She's out of it, back in the flat, welcoming Sofya's return – and also here, anaphylactic, struggling for breath. This junk scenario is doing terrible things to Askead's lace-trimmed pants. He can't help wondering – he doesn't try – if the Amazon will, in the aftermath, come across; give him one. Handjob or something subtler that'll scratch her knees.

Who called Wellclose a square? Some mason on the piss? ('The square at night –all wind scudding and black cobbles.' Lee Harwood.) There's nothing left but a skip of bricks, gutter projections, floating stairs. Grace's Alley is a vestigial tail the vandals haven't noticed yet.

The door's fiery grid threw Askead back. The faded pink of spiral shells. Capstone like an Egyptian crown. Frieze panels, in relief, profound with fruit. Pineapples, grapes. All upsidedown. No way was he going to be first across the threshold. The psycho was probably tooled up, in the dark, cradling the stiff. Undecided. Blast his way out or top himself? Let the other cunts, the gong chasers, go over the top. He'll hammer out the headlines. DYKE AND KIKE IN SUICIDE PACT. CAMERA GIRL'S DOCKLANDS HORROR. He'd pocket the Leica while they chalked the victims' outlines on the boards.

Trouble was, nobody was quite sure how to go about it, the assault. The only light in the building a glide of ignis fatuus, window to window: the phosphorescence of a decomposing human battery. Askead, in gothic vein, imagined candles of woman-fat, wicks dipped in sweaty tallow. Perhaps Donar had decamped, booby-trapping his attic? The structure was condemned, entrances boarded over, primed with warning notices. The whole pile kept upright on an armature of medieval timber.

Leave well alone. Walk away. And Sofya will come through. Andi Kuschka, leaning on Askead's arm, gave herself to the unassuaged house. Silently promising that the lab technician should be serviced – if Sofya was unharmed.

Askead ground out his cigarette. The Watchman asserted his small authority by kicking the street door from its hinges and waving the first man in line forward into the darkness. The paroled drunks preferred to wait and see. Some tied their laces, others slid into the bushes. The keenest (those for whom stupidity was pride) advanced, paused, shook themselves. Mayflies dashed against a sheet of glass, they had encountered an invisible barrier. They were confounded. The orders they survived by obeying made no sense. Night froze around them in a cryogenic spray. Martial tattoos rose proud on pointless biceps. The biggest of the bunch posed, sledgehammer raised aloft, like J. Arthur Rank's oiled bombardier. Waiting for a word that would never come.

Andi *had* to move. She pushed the rabble aside and bounded up the stairs. Finding no rail to guide her hand, the ascent was dreamlike: instantaneous, drawn out. The decision, once made, carried her immediately to the landing outside Donar's flat. She heard an echo in the creaking beams and realized who was screaming Sofya's name.

Hysteria was a pose. Now she was calm. The mercenaries, fearing to forfeit their share, gathered around her in the murk. The Watchman's timepiece ticking like a bomb. They were hanging above a crater and about to fall.

Together, as one, they charged. Plywood panels splintered to dust. They were inside. It didn't help. Inside was darkness of a darker kind, the absolutes of space folded to fit a lady's case. Darkness as the richest cru of light. Their eyes were useless, leaking fear. The attic was a cave. And, seeing nothing, it forced them to invent. Infra-red monsters. Flying serpents. Creeping bats. Nightmare menageries that peck when you take a standing count, shaking a sandbagged head. Why had they come? Who did they think they were? They dropped to the floor, knees clutched to chins, and moaned.

Andi tracked them. An awful noise, excessively feline: a cat's vocal chords grafted into a child's throat. Darkness, suppressing information, informed too well. A woman suspended, head downwards, from the wall. Sofya: stripped. She levitated as a melancholy hieroglyph. Impossible to eradicate.

Reaching out, Andi felt crumbs of plaster in her nails. The flickering icon announced an absence, nothing more. The student of the streets didn't need to hear the rest. She understood. Sofya had courageously delivered herself up to the labyrinthine beast.

There was a gap, a pinhole, in the heavy drapes that kept the kitchen separate, some brightness beyond. The room itself was the camera. Sofya's solution was rigorous, but pure. The wall had been treated with light-sensitive paint. She stood in the kitchen, unmoving, bombarded by escaping photons. Her image was then reversed, reformed. The portrait wasn't sharp, only Andi would have qualified to put a face to the crude sketch. It was fixed like a mural of Death, made in earth colours on the whitewashed screen of a primitive chapel.

How long had it taken Sofya to refine this narrative? How long had she stood in front of Donar? Was she there still, behind the curtain? Was *he*?

Mordecai Donar was the source of light. Andi drew back the curtain and stepped through. Her action restored the Watchman's trash to life. Mobhanded, they captured an undefended set. Everything strictly by the book: they stomped, smashed, tore. They elbowed, punched, butted, leapt. Shouted in unison and dragged out all the drawers. Cutlery spun in lavish arcs, bottles burst. Books reverted to ungathered leaves. Poofy chairs, they gutted like fish. A satisfactory but inconsequential rout.

The Watchman, taken aback, gave them their head. Andi waited until they flagged, the drift of feathers settled like a turkey pluck. She was not unused to panting men in dingy rooms. Their brutish heat was staunched. Sofya, her original error repaired, had gone.

A votive candle on a plate. The dreadful whimpering was Donar, revamping his kitchen table pose. Face hidden in hands. Andi couldn't bring herself to look. He twisted, seeking her out, this female scent. Tired boards creaked beneath Andi's weight. She has to know. Reluctantly, she touches him, whispering Sofya's name.

He grips her wrist. His sight has been absorbed into the candle's dipping flame. His cheeks are crusted with tributaries of blood. He can't let go, he's blind. Some fury, in the night, has come to tear out his eyeballs with its fingernails.

TWENTY-ONE

Mornings forgive and the slate is wiped. Wake in a ditch, or lift up your eyes – all one. You can rely on it: the blue hood, the sky. This exhalation of the city's breath, the snore that lifts the sheet. Mutability that doesn't hurt. No compulsion to get involved.

A ribcage sprung over unconsidered lands: puffball speed, white breath, then, the slower, higher mass – rivers in abeyance, potential angst, stair rods, thunder anvils, cats and dogs. No call for Helen's cloud-scrying cup. She's not alone and not herself. Luke Howard has yielded his role as spirit guide. Replaced by Robert E. (begetter of *Conan the Barbarian*). An augmented posing pouch, dumb with steroidal rage, is godfathering this pre-breakfast jaunt.

The East London sky knows, understands her betrayal. She's acting a part, vixen, glamour puss with claws. Muscat's latest protégée. Sliema Felix: the Tartens' frontman, the lifer with the Egyptian skin and classic Sixties' suiting (mean lapels, single button like a bullet-hole, mothballs). Hair *just* so (the barber's friend), curling to protect the naked neck. Nothing-for-the-weekend spoils the tubular line. Shoes with gloss to embarrass a guardsman and enough lift in the heels to bring him up to a respectable Cockney height (the armpits of a toff). Height, for Felix, was a moral matter: Clint Eastwood, his Socrates. The twin-peaked handkerchief in his breast-pocket (breasts worn high this year) looked like a concealed weapon, a throwing star.

That was Felix, dressed for the street. Nothing flash. A polite warning. A broadcast threat. Unbending, with baleful glare (cold as the clear mirror that confirms the loss of breath). Holding court in the Roebuck. Taking bets. Talking childhood and the good old days. Revisionist crap. Airbrushing his legend, puffing his place in the pecking order.

Helen smiled on Muscat's human side: the urban sentimentalist, memory slave. They made a striking couple in the great outdoors, stalking the Marshes – for which Felix had a genuine, physical love. Eyes welling with teardrops, he reminisced with heartfelt (and very marketable) sincerity. Cameras worshipped the depth of emptiness in that stone-lion face.

'Them 'orses, give me the 'appiest days of my life, they did. Stables on Lea Bridge Road, under the railway arches, by the canal. Down the Elephant, the knacker's yard. Clipclop of 'ooves on the towpath. See them ramps? That's for to get 'em out when they slip in the water. Under bridges where we 'unted rats. Ears ringing from the Old Bill's back'ander. Made a man of you, straight.'

Canal ticked off, Felix reversed, spun the Cortina's wheels; a showy twist that sent a ripple down his sleeve. Gymnasium pallor contradicted on a sunbed: a mistake that only lacquered his flaws, faulted the flesh with all the threadlike cracks of a badly restored Venetian doge. Excessively showered, rubbed down, he ponged like a high gloss man's magazine. Like the newsagent's shelf, when freshly sprayed copies of *Esquire* and *GQ* have just come in.

Helen crossed her legs. Muscat's response was disappointing, a growl, a single pump of his balled fist. The old villain's vanity had been compromised by the goldrim specs he needed for driving (tinted or not). He was still wired to prison reflexes, the olfactory triggers of Maidstone: overnight piss pots, two-week unwashed denim, hair oil, testosterone. Women were topheavy pullouts, gifted with puncture holes on either side of the navel. Nocturnally, they leaked confusion, blending into muscle boys.

'Handy little runabout,' Helen offered. As a gambit. Felix rolled coathanger shoulders, the tense knots of a life on licence. Stunts natural instincts. Can't hand out a slap by way of a conversational loosener. He wanted Nicky Tarten's skilled hands massaging the neck, the old sweat's relief, before going up the steps for sentencing. Reduced to this: a fucking Cortina! A jamjar nicked off of a spotty scrote doing his first stretch down St Vincent's in Kent. Christ knows where *he* pulled it. (The old cons are still favourite: punt a toshed-up banger from the pitch at the end of Brownlow Road. Keep a set of keys. Give it two/three weeks, then repossess. Spray job, new plates – you've done your bit for the ecology.)

Fumble for a Winston. 'I'm living on my sodding nerves,' he thought. The filth could have him any time they fancied a suss at his documents.

He slumped on the leopardskin, letting the motor find its own way down Homerton Road towards the Marshes. A dazzle of worry beads, dangling from the rearview mirror, flicked his cheek as he took a sharp left into the clinkered car park. The lemon and lavender respray bubbled in the harsh sunlight. He parked, for safety, down the far end; away from the laptop picnickers and insurance burnouts.

They sat, strangers, shoulder to shoulder, gazing on a prairie of industrial grass. Felix Muscat and the bird with big hair, the one who wanted to be a scrapper. Helen. Funny name that for a female contemplating a showbiz career. What's wrong with Tanya, Suki, Debra, a handle with a bit of class? 'Helen' was the missionary position and think yourself lucky to get it. Felix didn't like the way she raised her eyebrows – and they could do with a pluck – when she clocked the Black Madonna and the hoop of cat fur stapled around the steering-wheel. He didn't care for that overgenerous mouth. He knew the type, impossible to satisfy. Miss Prim (a.k.a. Mlle Hot Pants). Wide-set peepers, all innocence, while brilliant black pinholes reduce you to your component parts: mounds of ash, fat, fear. What did the bird expect for her first training run, Eddie Fuchs and a stretch limo?

Painfully decanted, sniffing at the rush of non-pestilent air, Muscat shook himself, sparred, coughed green, wiped his sweating hands on the towel that was carelessly draped about his throat. He didn't like it: too much sky.

'Love the jacket, Felix.' Helen ran her nails down the satinette finish. A two-tone bomber affair from the Greek shop in the Roman Road. Muscat, blushing, didn't know where to look. He pouched his mean specs and solved the problem: the Marshes became, at once, a sylvan swirl, a detail-free zone. He tapped another Winston and bunnied for time.

'Know where the craze for chalkstripe come from, darlin'? Churchill. Winston Churchill. God's truth. You seen that picture with the tommy, bowler, cigar? Siege of Sidney Street, as it 'appens. Very well-known affair in the East End. Patriots to the last man, all the lads went in for stripes. I won't touch no other fag. Winstons. 'e 'ad them made special.'

The recidivist's grip on legend was as shaky as his moral sense. History, the scoundrel's friend. Helen was growing fonder of him all the time. She took his arm, in memory of the barre, and compassed a prodigy of leg onto the metal fence. Long on tradition, short on imagination, these gladiators. She loved the genial brutes, wanted to ruffle Muscat's iron hair. It was Nicky Tarten's idea to land him with the job. Tarten was a humourist whose puns left scars. Felix must teach Helen how to box – or end in one himself, alive, and kicking at the lid. She had to be a recognized contender before she could lose. And Muscat had always been the loser's pal. Known for it on the manor, winking at his mates while he took the full count.

Along the path and over a bridge: the bounce comes from Helen's new airheel trainers, her crisp grey jogging suit. The drag's in the sand-filled gauntlets Felix has attached to her wrists. Fetishism with a purpose: adding menace to her jabs.

'Knees knees knees. Keep pumping, gel.' Muscat gasps, a good ten yards off the pace. The thin bridge shudders as he grabs the rail. A poison garden where evil plants feed on illegitimate chemical spill. Blooming decay: infertile hybrids, giant hogweed, Russian comfrey run amok. Squats of willow herb. A bilious rivulet humming with sewage lilies and demented flies.

Helen moves off first. It feels perverse to be trespassing on Luke Howard's cloud reservation with another man. Muscat doesn't belong outside. Previously, he's only ventured among the pylon-bordered stadia to dump a sack, run a dog, sledge a motor into the Lea's forgiving slime.

Felix can't sweat. Up on his toes, all the old nonsense, theme from *Rocky* ringing in his ears; feint, duck, weave. Truth to tell, he's overawed, gutted by landscape: it happens to the best. Agoraphobic from decades of close confinement, he'd give a week's wages for the comfort of the cell. What can you *do* with miles of nothing? Figures in the distance could be friend or foe. Artisan golfers or hitmen from across the water. Snipers in every bush. No effort of will pierces the cloud of melancholy. Give in to depressive fugues and the sky will fall.

He shoots his cuffs and calls a halt. Doesn't know how to talk to gash. He treats Helen like an inflatable princess, a mink quim. He speaks slowly, translating initiate's terminology into dingdong fact. He pats her flanks, comforts her like a nervous whippet. He *has* to touch or crack wide open, beat the ground.

'First off you gotta learn to move. Bob, jab, left left, run. Guard up.

Chin chin. *Now* stand. Cut off the corners, gel. Dominate the ring.' He has to gabble. Repeat instructions he signally failed to understand. A pain mantra before the lights went out. How can you think with a Scouser's thumb in your eye? Stay on your feet long enough to take a dive – when a mad Jock is scrambling your brains? Felix surrendered to the vacant majesty of a wilderness where his only purpose was to carry a spade. That's what's wrong: it should be night, a scatter of windows blinking in the tower blocks, a dog howling over Clapton way, and some defaulter begging to be put down.

The problem with these Marshes is they're not like fields (hay, cows, oilseed rape). They're empty, a city that's gone missing – white outlines limed on shifty grass. Felix wishes he'd brought a bike. He can't keep up. And the law would pull him if he took the motor onto the pitches. He never considered running, not in this Versailles-casual clobber. Blouson with an upturned suede collar. Vertical pockets slit to hide the meatporter's mitts. Surgical creases in the tan slacks. Jog and he'll drip. Trot and he'll split the seams. Static, chin aloft, he's a significant presence.

So what they decide is that Felix will stand firm, a fixed point, while Helen does a couple of laps – over towards the river, and back in the shade of an avenue of Lombardy poplars. Felix set fire to his mouth and blew out smoke. He'd have nothing left to sacrifice when his lungs were lace.

Watching's hard. Ask any pensioned pro. Leaves you dizzy, following her round. What should he shout? 'Pick 'em up, gel. Don't mince like a poof.' Muscat's redundant, a nail to keep her in orbit – or she'd never return.

She settles into a smooth ellipse: each circuit weakens her trainer, peels another layer. He's fated if he doesn't shut his eyes. His knees are buckling. He's alone, this sharp-beaked Maltese falcon. (The bird who cannot hear the falconer.)

A becoming flush to her cheeks. If only Felix could see it. Youth, health. Moist and sweet, darkening rings on the sweatshirt's bib. 'A little goer,' he'd report, 'puts her back into it, tasty mare.' She shocks him with an aerobic kick. Confusing messages. Tights stretching as she presses her palms to the deck. He shrivels, as she forces him to focus on the rectal crease.

Who said violence was a profession? It's a calling or a refuge for inadequates. (Much like the C of E.) Felix couldn't fight a bird (except in the way of business, which didn't count – the recipient would know the rules and *never* hit back). This whole shebang is down to Nicky Tarten. Crust! 'The bugger's pissing 'isself. He knew how it would go.'

Helen entered into the spirit of the impersonation – the Wapping Wildcat – but she didn't know how to punch, the mechanics of the thing. Felix holds out an open palm for her to pat. 'Nah, nah, darlin'. You're all arm. Roll. From the ground up, throw your weight.' *This* he can demonstrate. Balls a fist. 'See what I mean?' The afterhours two-step, downstairs in the Gents, with a mucker barehugging the target's arms: short jabs, swift combinations. 'Nothing fancy dan. You ain't got room to be clever.' A scrapyard salute, flat of the hand across the windpipe. The unexpected nod that deltas a Roman nose.

No backswing, that was Muscat's special gift. That's what put him in the reference books. One-shot Felix, sledgehammer in each paw. Watch how it's done. Watch and learn. Comes out of nowhere. The first hit has to count. You only get one retaliatory strike – even when your client's in catatonic shock. Then it's the Colonel's turn to flash his blade. Who pays, carves.

'Basically,' Muscat warned, 'the jobbing heavy's responsible for the anaesthetic. And it's a kindness not to take too long.' Worked up, and working well, he treated Helen to a reprise of the Look. Once it would have put skin on semolina; without specs, he couldn't make out if she paid him the respect he deserved.

Smack. She swats his ear, follows up with a dig in the breadbasket. Dead liberty. He wants to demolish the bitch, rip out her arms and fuck the sockets. The Marquess of Queensbury would have a fit. She jerks a knee into his wedding tackle, bringing tears to the sad old eyes. Ingratitude! He'll let her have a special in the mush. But she's tricky, fast on her feet; moves like a featherweight, dropkicks like a kung fu vixen. Stamps on his dodgy ankle before he can trip her up.

He tries to con Helen with his voice, the fatherly base that charmed his paperback ghost – sincerity like chopped onions and a shuttle-service of gin. *She* did him proud (moonlighting from the Woman's Page of the *Guardian*): typed the book that bears Muscat's name. The auto-hagiography that took him onto all the talk shows. Once.

Helen, going over the top, closes his good eye with a whiplash left. Getting the hang of it, definitely. Nicky's investment is safe as the Albert

Memorial. Decked, Muscat got serious. His jacket (which set him back two and a half, off the peg) was grass-scorched, and his dignity adrift. Using his favourite chokehold, he attempted to force a face-saving submission. Meekly, she nods; then tumbles backwards to scissor-lock his pharynx. Outraged, he filters down: olive to indigo to black. Musky gusts he's never met in fifteen years of married life. He gave her best. And beat the turf instead.

They shake as equals. She helps him up, brushes off the worst of the damage, kisses his cheek. The martial arts (pupil/teacher) bullshit is intact. A fair workout, he admits. 'You got aggression, now learn yourself glove craft. How to make an ordinary shot look good. Sneak a rabbit punch on the ref's blindside. Open an eyebrow with a trailing lace.' Tomorrow will be time enough. Felix goes easy on the girl, first day out, lets her walk back to the motor.

Juggling the furry wheel, his confidence floods back. He idles at the lights, anecdotes on autopilot, arm slipped conspiratorially around Helen's shoulder. The car could drive itself: Morning Lane, Mare Street, Cambridge Heath Road. Quick glance in the rearview to check his barnet. Taps out a Winston and waits for her to match him. Narrowing of the eyes. He's ready for his saraband, Mr Bailey.

TWENTY-TWO

Further Extracts
From the Journals of Rhab Adnam

DAY TWENTY-FIVE. To the spies across the water, the bailiffs of Holyfield Marsh, we must present a curious sight. 'What's wrong with these men?' they ask. 'What's their hurry?' We'll never be allowed back into London. As soon as darkness falls the agents will be on the blower.

On our bicycles, under the highway of pylons, we shimmer like phantoms in an electromagnetic field. We are, as the reviewers say, extraordinary. We challenge belief.

You have to admire the sadistic refinement that has gone into laying out the towpath: narrow metal gates (above cattlegrids) forcing cyclists to dismount, slippery cobbles under dark bridges, obstacles to play havoc with our internals. Hay fever also – for Doc Hinton. Hay fever as a consequence of metal fatigue. Plants cunningly selected to trigger allergies. Pods detonating at the slightest tremor of traffic. Sticky sedges capable of creating their own wind. Secretions flicked from tyres, and bred to defy all known anti-histamines.

Sileen succumbs, bleeds tears. His sickness is in VistaVision. His mood swings are complemented by the geology of the landscape through which we peddle: bits of Lincolnshire and Yorkshire (ice-delivered) litter the ground, flints to provoke punctures.

O Cheshunt, borderland jewel, where eocene yields to chalk, forgive our haste. I refused to be alarmed by the caravans plodding north up the Lea Valley, a diaspora of Hackney cabmen and other endemically aggrieved citizens. The wobbly crocodile through which we weave is a protest march of premature millennialists, each man attempting to outrun his identikit portrait. Felons with shaved heads and abbreviated ears. Branded thieves, runaways, recusants.

We come across our first encampment of travellers: savage dogs, wrecked cars, pyramids of spare parts. A coffee-stall where fat men (lacking shirts) can groom their luxuriant armpits, de-fluff their navels. And blame it on the blacks. ('I told that Paki down the yard to fuck off.')

Beneath the road bridge, the A121, we dismount again. Refugees block the path ahead: a Swarfega river and late skies so confused they defy interpretation.

Sileen has been written out. That much is clear. Even if we go in by night, it will not be our city. In our absence we have been replaced by more spirited subversives. Sileen will be a blindman in his own warren, obscure as a novel by W. Pett Ridge. Affectionately remembered by a diminishing cult of fanatics.

Waltham Abbey is reputed to offer shelter to distressed pilgrims. So let us make the detour: the gravestone of King Harold, another eye-pierced martyr, another marathon limper. Another man famous for failing.

I took Sileen's arm and led him gently away from the bicycle track, east, in quest of sanctuary. A twig, trapped in his wheel, clucked like an imprisoned bird.

EVENING. Dusk flatters the Caen-stone tower, flatters us. Forgetful, we think it might all turn out for the best. The door to the church is open, the dim interior draws us on: an ancient vessel eviscerated of implication. I must pause here to sketch William Burges' Zodiac ceiling, a diamond sutra pathway on which no human foot shall stand. Figures represent Past and Present. The Past is an old man with an open book. The Future is a young woman whose volume is closed and sealed. The dying light interferes with an immense stained glass barrier: a rose propeller.

We trade with silence, a baffle of pier arches. The roof grander than the floor. A winged lion sleeps with open eyes above the west door. A symbol of Resurrection. Breathing life into the dead cubs.

Breathe on us. My own efforts would scarcely lift a wafer of ricepaper from my face. Hinton, in travail, groans. The racket! Sileen's bronchial psalming.

The snores of the fourth man, the shrouded stranger sprawling his length on a pew.

'Sanctuary,' I whisper.

'Sanctuary?' he replies. 'That's rich – coming from a trio lucky to be called extinct. I took you for superstars on the bum. Seen nothing half as rough since the opening of Planet Hollywood. Wait till I tell the others: the dead have returned to us, looking like Brighton Lanes on a bad Saturday.'

We followed our host into the grounds where the Norman Abbey had once stood. The high altar, beneath which King Harold's bones (gathered up by Edith Swan-Neck from the battlefield) repose, is a wonky milestone. Gifot (for so our sponsor is called) lets the shrine pass without a word. Black robes, sandals. He calls his order the 'Light of Cain' (an obvious theft from Cluniac).

I've read my M. R. James and know the tale: how a blacksmith, obedient to visions, digs under a marble slab on St Michael's Hill, Montacute. Cart, bell, book: cross-country, drawn by 12 red oxen, 12 white cows. Waltham. Holy Cross. A fable invented to give form to the portage of power. England is nothing else. Migration, remembered light. First in dreams. Then plodded out.

Orchards and gardens, good. But Gifot hustles on. Hinton is tranquillized by having someone to obey. Sileen is out of it and sulking for the slums. He sees the herb beds as outcrops of his sickness, cures that promote disease. At the fishpond I had to drag him from the reeds. He lusted to strangle his reflection in the green muck.

East-running shadows from stunted apple trees were the ghosts of forgotten hogs. Phantom smells of pork charring in a pit gave us encouragement. Hinton dribbled, said his prayers.

A foot-tunnel under the motorway. Everything transitional, nothing you can hold. The walk progresses in a series of nightmare dissolves. We pause by a five-barred gate (like discordant notes on a sheet of music) for our spirit doubles to catch up. Gifot bombs a spliff. A well-tramped path runs away into Cornmill Meadows. Lammas land. The privileges of the celibate brothers survive – only the cattle have been butchered. The black robed ones want something more from us than our bikes.

I'm captivated by the silver circle on Gifot's back: a cult of nothingness. Gravity stretches as we struggle to walk the line of Zero Longitude – prisoners in a temporal park. Bits of what happened before come back. Bits we forget. There's a special quality to the meadows at this hour; a formal wilderness restored.

Meditating these things, we plod the old straight track. The abbey is lost as we creep closer to a plume of smoke.

A conference of friars burning a headless animal in a pit. Cider swillers in hooded dressing gowns. Out-patients on the lam. Orgy extras too ripe for Ken Russell. Market gardeners given their cards for cultivating illegitimate crops. Alignment freaks who got it wrong. Nursing mothers chasing deficits. Freelance mongrels. It's hard to believe we're 15 miles (a one day progress to Henry VIII) from Canary Wharf.

Sileen, enquiring after the *necessarium*, is gestured to a tributary stream. His bowels are twitchy, in affectionate remembrance of Dorchester, their most recent outing. He squats, straddles the flumelet: a sympathetic accompaniment of water gurgling over burnished stones. The illusion of a better life. Sticking in one place, cultivating our own patch, giving praise. Gasping, Sileen dams the creek with foul spill. As filtered sunlight shines his scabs.

We each own a clearing in childhood that feels like this (nomadic ancestry recalled). A time of day when, sniffling, we think of home. The rays lengthen and we sing. We draw closer to the roasting carcass and the pit. The monks are clots of encroaching darkness, as they gather to occupy the fallen logs. Gifot's particular friend, barechested in a leather coat, ladles sump oil on the spittling meat.

NIGHT. When we'd eaten (half-raw, half-burnt), Hinton talked. We were all high: cider-pulp cut with blue, grass, olly, the jug of stars. The doc spoke in heroic couplets and the company was mute. Faster, wilder – fearful that when he stopped they'd chain him up or fling him to the dogs.

Sileen kept his own counsel, spoke only to me, his conscience. I couldn't follow what he said: how he decided, scalding his lips on hairy pork, to convince himself it was mutton stew. A wooden bowl, barley grains, pumice bread. Watery milk jetting from the den mother's tattooed breast. The gnostic gospels droned to stimulate digestion.

Who can tell where the truth lies? Sileen's vision of monastic life – refectory, brewhouse, cloister, misericord (how he loved that word!), or Hinton's nostalgia for the fallen angels of Rock 'n' Roll? I shared this sense of a parallel world, unrisked alternatives. Einstein's mental proofs: a building, explored in thought, is truer than its photograph.

If I were writing a true journal, I would have to list the buckled portakabins, the botched tepees; a community of losers too timid to split. They *had* their strengths, granted – tricky to name. Brotherhood, teaching and sharing, the rejection of an increasingly self-deluded society. Dirt on the hands. Zero as the primary option. But why should they live in the lap of everything they professed to despise? Why should they strip motors, deal drugs, thieve?

The inner circle, black cowls, were a different breed: celibate or favouring their own sex. Manichees. Fire freaks. They hung around the smouldering pit when others stalked away to kip. They regarded this glowing concavity as an extracted eye, a substitute sun. The flames modelled starveling faces, beards, blains.

They take a lively interest in Sileen. It's not surprising. He could have been one of them if he'd kept the faith, stuck with predestination. His sores outrank the foulest they can flaunt. He is so ripely present, he stinks. Rot chokes his breath. Infected blood. Gifot's campsite is a survey of his soul. The monks know him, receive him, covet him: he's a long-expected visitant.

'For in the day of David Man as yet had a glorious horn / upon his forehead.' Sileen is horned. Gifot is a rhino bent by cuckoldry. The black sodomites watch Sileen, while seeming to meditate upon the action of the flames. They chant: a doleful interference, mouths filled with bad Peruvian sand.

Two were beardless, young, or, by my guess, self-castrated ecstatics. These novices, lifting their skirts, dropped into the pit. They ran the hot coals; head back, eyes wide. Plenty followed their example; some buck naked, arms thrown out, balancing on an invisible ledge. The humming never stopped.

I was unbuttoning my shirt, judging the temperature, when I noticed Sileen. Distracted, I'd been careless of my nearest concern. THE SOLE BUSINESS OF THE ARTIST IS TO LIVE AN ARTIST'S LIFE. The cripple was in spate, performing with the best. Mouth agape, massaging his chest in the attempt to swallow air; blackberry lips, dagger tongue.

The cheeks of a drowning man in a helmet of glass. Eyes like tennis balls. One hand held out to block the heat. He had disowned it, this fin. It wouldn't mask Gifot's sharp-boned face. He tried to wriggle to the edge, to dip the troublesome fist, singe pain among the hot ashes.

'The hogs!' he cried. 'Hodgson's pit!' The curtains of probability twitched. He saw the monks' hoods as fur. Pigs with human hands. The cloying stench of the roast. The sweet fat oozing from our lips. Pain had tripped him directly into the old X-ray fantasies. His shriek woke Hinton. Which made things worse. Hinton *was* the Recluse, the tenant of a cursed house (his body). Hinton, in drink, was reeling where he stood.

Then it became, as I must transcribe these events, provocative. I've always regarded myself, pen in hand, as the author of my destiny. Where would *The House on the Borderland* be without the mediation of the manuscript, the tattered journal? *Quaint but legible hand-writing, and writ very close . . . the queer, faint, pit-water smell of it.* Writing, the physical act of it, dissolves ego. Lets the elder voices through. Everything I write, even the act of ventriloquism, is autobiography.

No more. Not here. We've dabbled too much in fiction. The events, rapidly unfolding, are fiction's revenge. An ashpit overlaid with swine demons, revengers, cultists. Hinton gibbered; he spoke in tongues, all Hodgson's rhapsodies as a single stream.

The red spheres bearing down helpless to move deep red mist the flame-edge mass of the Dead Central Sun.

Keeping must keep my journal sure to be lost the lip of the pit recalling Hodgson's conceit the Recluse's journal a trap for the unwary lost to be found on the lip of another greater pit another country torrents welling out of rocks cascades *myself* inspiring imagine it another journal another recluse discovering *this* pit another life strange cubes of doleritic stone overturned obelisks marking the dread path the philosophy of *zero*.

I *must* try to be clear, not inveigled too deeply into the mental universes of Hinton or Sileen or Gifot (who must receive their dues). I can share (while I write about him) the psycho-chemical impulses that generate Sileen's original energy field. Within a sphere, a scarlet globe, I am bumping over jagged rocks. A coast path. A beach at the dawn of consciousness. Another ruin, tumbled walls. A field of horses. Catching the currents in the excited air. Hedges dripping gore. A white stalk-tower with puddled concrete steps.

The monks have Sileen pinioned like a star, like a flesh compass. He's saved. One of the women from the portakabin brings him a bottle, forces him to drink. I chant from Kit Smart's *Fragment C*.

'For H is a spirit and therefore he is God . . . I is person and therefore he is God . . . For S is soul and therefore he is God . . . For every thing infinitely perfect in Three.'

I watch Sileen watching Hinton. We are in it together, sink or swim. Gifot, a candled skull, wields the bowie knife. Will he tear out Sileen's exhausted heart? Reveal it as a crow, set it free? He takes the victim's sacrificial hand. Three fingers at a stroke. The little one pruned with an upward twist. Now spirit is splashed. Now heat the blade and cauterize the bleeding meat. Gifot has made his mark, defined the border at which the infection must be repelled. He rescues Sileen. Butchers his sickness with swift sure strokes.

The cure hurts. Sileen moans.

DAY TWENTY-SIX. No end to this night. The monks have retired to keep the canonical hours: prime, tierce, whatever. Sileen the Heretic is left, a stump of old knowledge, lying on the damp ground. The residue of his fingers – warts on a paddle. He'll live. Agony has brought life back to his eyes. The lost offcuts have effected a spectacular realignment in his psychic map. Less protein to drag about, effortless weight loss so good for his self-esteem. By amputation, he is made whole. Returned to the story. Our passage into the city is secure. The line of zero that runs directly into Drage-Bell's protected room. Where Hodgson's manuscript remains, unread, upon a scrubbed table.

Sileen sat up. Hinton was wrapping strips torn from his shirt around the mutilated hand. The woman, supporting Sileen, unpinned her jacket. Body heat: the odours of the slaughterhouse deflected in a patchouli drench. A long brown teat thrust into the cripple's mouth.

He sucks, milks her. A sugary draw of comfort. Her cunning fingers soothing, nursemaiding his cock. He is confused, renewed. He gnaws, guzzles, breaks off – buries his full face beneath the abundant ripeness of her bosoms.

DAY TWENTY-NINE. Asbestos wool – or the smoke from distant, burning synagogues. The sky is a pond of unmoving smoke photographs. We lie on our backs at the epicentre of a gigantic field and let the weather happen. The clouds (thick, white, masculine) migrate. (But only when we shut our eyes.)

Sileen wears the missing digits in his breast-pocket: a row of trainspotters' pens. Anything is possible now that his sense of the ridiculous is recharged. We're marooned on Hackney Marshes, the Cockney Fen, the 'Empty Quarter'. Like Speke and Burton, we're not quite ready to pay off the bearers and complete our triangulation. The city flaunts itself on the southern horizon; but it's not the *real* city, it's the docklands surrogate, the set. A grinning mouth that has just devoured its ancestors.

Is this the London that we left? Are we the same characters, or do we simply occupy the same clothes? The thing is not to be hurried. The end's in sight – which is where we'd like it to remain. Stay put. It's bliss to be shot of the bikes. A small price to pay for cosmetic surgery and *demi-pension*. We've traded our future incidents in. Progressive medicine. Casualty wards could learn a dodge or two from us. Reassert the honourable bond between hospice and market, the barter system: wheels for fingers, fish for a blood transfusion, a sheep for a set of lungs.

The heat was on the deck, tower blocks tinkled like mirages. Nobody wanted to be the one to get up, initiate the march across the grassland, our parting. It was a moment of obligatory quietness. Hinton was wired to his tape, while Sileen stared at the sky. Hanks of refuse, bits of stuff dropped from prams, spun in tight vortices. Grass spines quivered in expectation. A drop in the barometer. Rain: observed as a backdrop, then felt. Advancing fast.

We were so hungry for negative ions, the cleansing sweep of a storm. We had caused what we now saw: our excesses demanded a geo-physical response.

Sound followed sight, a geiger of excitement rushing through the broad leaves. We raced for shelter. Behind us, incontinent skies chucked it down, erasing the lime-marked squares, the outlined football pitches that looked like the foundations plans of an unbuilt city. Needling columns of rain were visible against the folded trees. We froze in our tracks, fearful of losing a single frame of this Caspar David Friedrich lightshow.

I had to sketch fast to catch the atmospheric effects: fleet silvers, critical mauves, hypochondriac thistleheads. Sileen and Hinton slithered and stumbled, arm in arm, through undergrowth, till they chanced on a bicycle shed with a corrugated roof.

Drumbeats overhead. The ideal shelter from which to spy upon the scene. The hut is enclosed at the rear but open to the fields. A urinal without the stalls: a deficiency that had in no way inhibited previous visitors, who left acid ferns bleached into the pinkish wash of the plaster. We are enclosed, yes, but not imprisoned. It's a bathyscaphe looking out on deeps of chlorophyll. Green on our faces, green everywhere. Parrot green, the green of gold, green shadows to complement black. The green of Elizabethan teeth, mildewed camiknickers. Cash.

Do the others share this with me?

Sileen – I don't know. Can't read his mood. I think he'll split soon, break away. He doesn't need us any more. Doc Hinton, on the other hand, is delighted to have found a text to work on. The habit of literacy is a bad one to kick. Words sprayed on the wall give him an excuse to turn his back on the undersignified prairie, to go for the spurted urgencies that decorate the breeze blocks. Such messages have no author. Telegrams from a doomed stockade. They were there before the shelter was built.

I LIKE TO SUCK / BOYS ANY DAY HERE / 2pm or 7pm / PAY £10 / JEN.

Jen sounds more reliable than a doctor's surgery: two sessions per day and a modest fee. More services than the Jehovah's Witnesses.

Hinton, it's clear, is indecently aroused by the lingering scent of kiddy pee, tom cat musk on wet leaves, bicycle saddles. He thrills to the supplication of icecream vans prowling riverside estates, cranking out doubly-plagiarized Lloyd Webber riffs.

I understood it then, Swedenborg's credo: all motion must obey the spiral, the spiral is the most perfect figure. The Mounds we have visited, that's all they are, spirals, time turds. I embraced Hinton. Fell to my knees and worshipped Sileen. Their contrary energies had gifted me with this insight (as Swedenborg penetrated the mysteries of magnetism). In fulfilling the Whitechapel spiral we had achieved our PARANOID MILLENNIAL VISIONARY destiny. We had made ourselves redundant.

Two girls, ages difficult to assess, stood dripping on the shelter's step. Hinton wheeled, gawping like a dab. They were beneath the age of consent, he was sure of it. Said as much. One wore a denim jacket, soaked, with the collar turned up. The other was in a chunky baseball blouse, borrowed or stolen. Miles too big. Jeans, *not* jeans. Leggings. Those tight black things kids wear.

The mixture as before: the talker and the mute. Solid, scowling, broad in beam tugging at her mate. Who is tarty, chewing gum. A botched lipstick attempt and a scent that kills all known germs.

The girls giggled, whispered, nudged. They clung to the pillar, playing at indecision. Denim jacket waited in the rain, plucking at the midinette's sleeve. Sileen dismissed them, dismissed it all. His spiral has been stretched into a long straight line. He lurches out of the shelter, storm or no storm, heads south, easy to follow by the flattened drag of grass.

I'd love to go with him all the way to zero (discover what Swedenborg debated with Flamsteed on Greenwich Hill), but I won't abandon Hinton.

The sturdier delinquent has taken fright and is trying to pull her pal away. The situation's too volatile, Hinton on his tod. Break it off now, before they start to chat. ('He's *weird*, the old bloke. Got things in his hair. Wears his vest outside his shirt.')

'Got the time, mister?'

'Time?' Hinton, discomforted, doesn't know what the word means. If I intervene, I'll lose Toddy. Keep him in sight and our alignment is preserved. Secondary rain leaking from trees. Drip drip drip on the shed's roof. Passion damped down. The stoic calm of a roadside casualty with a broken back.

The headiness of moist fresh earth, ammonia washing from the bricks. The woolly jackets are drying out. Hot spearmint breath in Hinton's face. The girl tilts her head to read what Hinton's reading: the safety of a text.

PAY £10.

'Come on, Jen, 'e's a nutter. Your mum'll fucking kill you.'

Hinton feels the need to explain himself, why he's here. He flaps his hands like a man scaring crows.

'Swedenborg, girls, found himself able to talk to people who were dead. Can you imagine? Angels upstairs. Like lodgers. Characters in *Neighbours* or guys from comic books.'

'Mister, got a match?' She was patting his pockets. Could it be seven already? The Captain Marvel watch: I see him sneak a look as he lights her up. The one in the big jacket. The one who cups her hands. Her fingers are lolly sticks, nails bitten and fire-engine red.

Jen holds out the ciggy for her mate, trying to call her in. The fat one snatches but stays out of range, scoping the lights in the tower blocks.

'Lend us a couple of quid.' Jen again. The dialogue doesn't improve. 'We gotta get a bus.'

'Honest, mister.' The fat one. ' 'er mum'll do 'er fucking nut if she ain't indoors 'fore dark.'

'Go on, two quid. You got it to spare.' Jen auditing Hinton's pockets with expert hands. She snatches the cigarette from his mouth and puts it in her own. Small, hurried drags. Lips in a pout.

She'd fingered the stash pinned to his inner leg. Hinton flinched. She tried to tease it out. He stands exposed. Dope freak suborning the innocent. She lets it dangle, his winkie, to her friend's alarm. Yuk! Pearl grey, short and thick. Lolling like a dead pigeon's head.

Hinton felt obliged to roll a joint, pedantically demonstrating what had been familiar to them for years. Boys any day here. She's counting his coins.

But of course: it's the *other* one. The money's on the floor, Jen feeling for it. The plot twist before the curtain falls. Jen's the mouthpiece, the promoter, the bait. Denim jacket does the business. *What* business? She waddles resolutely towards Hinton: grim as granite. It's too dark now to describe it further. Too dark to write.

'Wait,' I shout, setting off to search for Sileen. Hacking through the scrub until my heart pounds. The magnitude of the marshes. Terrible groans from the shed. Hinton's humiliation. Everything will change the moment Sileen takes that final step, back to where we began. As ever. Speke and Burton. Whoever reports first, dies by his own hand.

TWENTY-THREE

Lacking Sileen, Helen enjoyed no covenant with the skies. No weather orgasms. Benign and alert, she strolled – lips moving, mouthing silent arguments. She was incomplete. The letter brought it home. She wanted Sileen's wanting, his presence. The quietness he displaced. The engendered turbulence. He gave her a reason to leave the house.

The letter was from Sammy Taylor. Can you forget the broken typeface of your first lover, the one who performed the mystical act, plucked the cherry? Quite easily. A blush of shame, holding the dun rectangle in her hand – deshabille. She found a wrap in which to hide herself, before returning to pick the horror from the mat. Sender's name on flap. Addressed to 'Butcher Sileen'. She had to carry it into the open air. She would not contaminate the flat, the room in which she slept.

A good excuse for an early walk. Pleasure insisted upon its mandate. Isabel was dominant. Isabel no longer cabbed into the office, Isabel exercised. She jogged. She sculled on a machine that was innocent of water, locked to the floor, while she hurtled, sickeningly, backwards and forwards. She skipped, chased shadows, hefted weights. Punched Felix Muscat's padded hand. She rode in leathery cars to Canning Town. She slept through afternoons. Obligingly, she listened to the crack in private clubs. Stuck faithfully to her regime, smiled behind a squadron of blue water bottles with the other girls.

She was performing, exorcising the time that Sileen had shared. It worked too well. Her man was reduced to a stinky notebook, small, thick. Fusty to touch. Unopened – as yet. All he'd left behind.

Helen stretched her legs, using once familiar ground to recapture the potentialities of a previous self. The Outfall. *Nostromo* like a breviary in her hand. Taylor's letter tucked from sight in the deep pocket of her long black coat. If she *did* read it – would Sileen be lost forever? Would she take on his guilt? Become Taylor's target in his place? She knew the letter was a curse. She halted on the bridge.

Remembered, not what she had felt those other times, but the appearance of the water, Channelsea, the oily smoothness (like developing fluid in which herringbone clouds could find their form), snouty grass islets, gasometers, pylons, the teardrop ironwork of the bridge itself. But the water was not there, the cloudrace she had anticipated – lush green mud. Fizzing puddles left by the tide. A greasy cloacal carpet. Unobtrusive stench. The treacherous possibility of taboo breaking, trespass, walking over. What could be more appropriate, take out the letter and let it float down onto the mud? She recalled Taylor's voice, she *heard* it, drawling, ranting, the furious intensity of the worst, the hysterical pitch of disbelief that the world could treat *him* so. 'Oh come onnnnnn.' With anguished *r* in the middle of it. McEnroe. That's it. Spoilt, fucked-over rich kid trying to tough it out.

Well-being shone in Helen's skin, the brilliance of her eyes, the lustrous close-cropped hair. She'd never been so fit, or felt so lost. It was easy when she sauntered and the landscape moved – but when she *stopped*? There were decisions to be made. She knew herself in ways that invoked Sileen, always Sileen, his consciousness closing from behind. The power of her image made her untouchable. She could afford to walk without purpose, clasping a book she wouldn't read, collar turned up on the mildest day. A girl played by a boy, one of those implausible Shakespearean reversals. Changes that recur spontaneously: girl as boy as girl, whatever turns you on.

She mimed a contemplative style exactly suited to the mood of worldly withdrawal Sileen's absence had induced. Couple that with the spiritual exercises of the gym – the sweat, the burn – and a total makeover was achieved. She could enjoy the purple nights in drinkers at Muscat's side, his tart. Long rides back, chasing the dawn, cold sober, indulging his sozzled rap. The bragging, then the weepy spaniel eyes. He kept the engine running. The perfect gent, he'd drop her off, never permit her to clock his council flat, that probationer's shoebox across the water. If she touched his knee, he'd jump. But she was tiring of the game.

This Outfall walk, man-made prominence, was her secret place: river and cloud. Illusion. Luke Howard. She could fancy herself, she did it so well. The breeches parts and the little black numbers that made men gasp. Trainers or six-inch heels, the same. Coronary lips, lips on their own. A fetish. Licked. The most respectable punters lost blood. They thought of painted pussy, worn aslant. They flushed. Her moue of contemplation. Playfully cusped to show her teeth: laugh or bite. She wavered between engagement and boredom, a territory once occupied in her life by cinema. Something less than an affair, a voluntary dreaming. Once she would have mortgaged time in the Everyman, railway terminal Classics. Seasons of cold Swedish light, blonde heads obedient to her whim. Paris on the jump, overexposed. All those shots into windscreens, trains of fitful leaves. Cocktail dresses subsiding into sandtraps. A procession of elegant skills. She was directed and she was free. She chose to make no choice, allowing others to supply the theatre she craved. Rain on the streets. Coffee in bars she would never visit again. A culture of afternoons. Old indulgences fondly brought to mind. Now mornings rule. We work. Cinema has crept back into the tentshow from which it emerged. Dreams on the spike.

Helen casts herself in an interminable Antonioni travelling shot, black and white, Gianni di Venanzo. A fake. Ambiguous gender – submerged in her Milanese coat. Slumming it, destitute. Posed against a doleful backdrop of industrial retreat. Nothing for it but to play her part: open the letter.

SAMUEL COLERIDGE TAYLOR (PHILOSOPHE)

MORTZESTUS, Bantry, W. Cork, Republic of Ireland
August 3, 199–

Gertrude –

uncool. think youll get away with dispatching paramilitarys to take me out? ive been on the street too long, best buddy. i KNOW why none of the cocktail party crowd will accept my calls. the famous anglosaxon sphinxter, right?

shit, i pick up enemys the way a magnet picks up iron filings. big city queens piss acid when a man pays for his own work to be published. EZRA POUND DID IT so fuck you, jack. im hip. itll need more than a silver bullet to put ME to sleep.

'when danger threatens, every man becomes a soldier, when wars end, men return to the plough.' ya!

bank holiday monday, sun stroboscoping thru misted cold windows, thin red cow all ribs plodding up lane, worried by old johnnie's switch his greasy checked cap down over eyes. the dense green of almost metaled grass. no sentient being on this earth can prevent me taking my evening walk – solid luminescence of light reflected off sea, outhaul moaning like dead, vapid sky above. i herd barrel break & dove for the ditch before the raw terrible blast tore my washingline to shreds, hanging up there like a klansmans knecktie party.

ive quit on the tractor & the car, could be wired. sold rowboat to a chick from Frankfurt. let her get blown away like mountybatten, nazi bitch. i thrive on hate, man, it swells my dick. i can go all night.

meditate carefully on what i say. i know youre coming & ill be waiting where you least expect it. could be the ruset gorse, the burnt sienna of the rocks, the crinkled field edge, the inkblot stains of kelp & bladderwrack. dead, ill KILL. i was born for WAR. i dedicate my life, whats left, to youre destruction.

> *respectfully,*
> *SAM*

Helen had forgotten how clinically weird Taylor could be. The generosity of Saddam Hussein. Innocent and depraved. He wasn't improving. Isolation, wretched diet, emotional instability, chemical excesses, chemical deprivation, they'd screwed his head. Justified paranoia, the worst kind. Those 'vapid' skies and 'ruset gorse'. A sick man. Ego hammered out like a silver thread (he had her doing it now). Indestructible. After all that craziness, those snakepit threats, he actually encloses a photograph. An intended author portrait for some never-to-be-completed masterwork. The maniac is squatting on his heels, out at the cliff's edge, convict-stripe rollneck, whaler's stockingcap. Drawing deep (it sucks in the cheeks) on a long-ash roach, fingers clenched in a defiant V; Mark Twain's Yankee abroad. Eyes hooded, not quite closed, against a pale sun – the curl of smoke. Taylor was an original. All heart and wind. Who else could combine a pre-emptive obituary and a Valentine card? Was Sileen supposed to have the picture framed? To study it, learn to love the instrument of his annihilation?

Pull back. Crane up and out. Read this set-up from a respectful distance. Helen as the mysterious woman in black, sick soul of Europe in couture drag. Most of the directors were faggots, pill-poppers, closet psychopaths. Licensed voyeurs. She is ready to play. Notice how she leans so meaningfully on the decorative bridge, offering her best side to the effluent creek, the fires on the lammas land. She arranges the line of her coat, the outstretched leg. Thinks of nothing (which *is* hard): the chilly handrail, she thinks of that. An achieved absence, a mask in which any passion may be found.

Helen had reduced landscape to the status of a still life. Its agitated elements were charms to dress her pose. Absolute control. Clouds sprayed on glass. Mud as brilliant as her boots. She attends – all drilling has ceased, no horns, no planes, train-hiss only when required as a stand-in for the sexual act. She listens, she can't ignore it, the torrential, tumultuous urgency of some allnight binger voiding his liquid load, steaming the pebbledash from the pentagonal walls of an abandoned observation post. Horse piss. Steam clouds rising above the white nettles.

Concrete walls gentrified by scarlet splashes of Virginia creeper. Did he sleep in that thing, the machine-gun nest, this man? It had to be a man; no woman could micturate with such careless self-satisfaction, no animal would untank such a drench in one place. She couldn't help herself, she walked across the path, watched, waited for the culprit to emerge.

Straight from central casting, but not often called. Almost tall, long-wristed, scrawny tough. Lank hair improving the handsome ruin of his face. The aggrieved, shocked-by-daylight look of the remand prisoner; blaspheming and bullshitting in a single breath. He shook himself, shook off the drops, waited for the blanket to cover his head. The buttons of his paint-stained dungarees were still too complex a task. He coughed, racked, honked up some slime – which he spat onto the wall. It stuck, grew a tail, slid down between the crushed stones and shells. This bunker was his den, his *foco*. Dear God, the tattoo! The legendary Imar O'Hagan.

The painter waved. A boisterous greeting, laughter. Instant chums, that was his assumption. She was a woman, wasn't she? Helen had come a long way, redefining herself by the men she knew – but *this*? Taylor, Sileen, the Tartens, Muscat, O'Hagan? Russian roulette with a bullet in every chamber. The odds weren't good. He reeled towards her – too late to run – manhandling a suspect mountain-bike. He'd had the idea, a patron put it in his head, of cycling the entire Outfall track, down to the river: boneyards, follies, nature reserves, a dry ski slope with an amazing view. Thought it might clear his head, give him a few ideas. Worked best, he said, at night.

Sod it, there were more effective methods close at hand. Hair of the dog. Nice little boozer alongside the Hertford Union Canal. 'Know it? St Mark's Gate, Vicky Park. How about a wet one and a bite?'

Revoking Helen's superstitions, they walked north: side by side, talking as they went.

'Amaze me then,' she said.

TWENTY-FOUR

Cold eyes. Strong hand guiding the bicycle. O'Hagan was a riot. So full of himself that Helen was obliged to fall in with his mood, excuse the throwaway baroque of the hamlets wasting below them, colours never seen outside the painter's more deranged canvases. Why speculate? She relished the way he saw London as his personal fiefdom.

The narrative style of the story he was telling – oblique, never connected clauses terminating in fits of the giggles – held her attention, held something back. The absence of shame. O'Hagan's emotional life (the physical expression of it) was complicated. An everyday involvement with a married woman, one of several in play, had put him in bad odour with one of the more primitive South London families. The painter was genuinely shocked at such anachronistic posturing: the threat (promise) to have him blown away.

'The Nineties! A woman as some cunt's private property.' He laughed. Hooted. His teeth fascinated Helen. They were so experienced: lupine, nicotine ivory, interleaved with green shoots that he treated as dessert, by constantly probing with his tongue, currying with a fingernail. His teeth, she decided, *were* the man. Incapable of lying. The rosebud mouth was pure deceit. Lank delinquent hair having to be ostentatiously flicked back. Shoulders, strong neck. An amusing portrait – rapidly knocked out to please the ladies. The accent was flattened Brummie. Apart from the name he signed on commissioned oils, the pale irises were the only Celtic bona fide he possessed. The name was an unexplained inheritance, a job description.

Imar chained his bike to the park railings, watching with interest how rapidly a pair of primary school Hackney Wick-Caribbeans ripped the wheels from the choicer motors without the assistance of a jack. Helen waited by the pub door. 'Historic buildings of Bow.' Can you believe

this shit? A MEMORIAL TO / THOMAS BRIGGS ESQ. OF CLAPTON / . . .
VICIOUSLY ASSAULTED NEAR HERE / ON A NORTH LONDON
RAILWAY TRAIN / CARRIED NEAR TO DEATH INTO THIS / PUBLIC
HOUSE HE DIED AT HOME / LATER THE SAME DAY / HE WAS THE
FIRST PERSON TO BE / MURDERED ON A RAILWAY TRAIN. Heritage
piracy at its worst. Inventing fictions to map districts where only fiction
fits.

Imar helped her, sniggering, inside.

They were comfortable. They had nothing very significant to say. It
didn't matter: an interlude. Black coffee and cognac, Imar's healthfood
breakfast. Indoors, and pushed for time, he'd let the coffee go. Bacon
sarnies, thick as two-by-fours, dripping with melted butter and with
juice: the hog's revenge. Coffee was needed to fire the start. Conversation on hold as Imar gummed the soft wet bread. Brown sauce trickled
like a haemorrhage from his lips. Helen leant on a hand and stared,
fascinated, as he munched. Finishing up, the painter shoved the plate
aside, reached into his canvas rucksack to find his snout-tin. Might
Helen care to fetch the bottle over? Pity to let the coffee go flat.

Halfway to the bar, she heard the thump as O'Hagan set the bag
down beneath his chair. She turned. He winked and stretched his legs to
obscure her view. Or did he simply stretch?

The publican, talking with two other early starters, wanted cash on
the nail from anyone desperate enough to take their rotgut wholesale.
Helen counted her change, not caring overmuch, but certain he'd
impose an unofficial service charge. The way, smoking, he looked her
over, using smoke as a screen, narrowing his eyes. It brought back
Sammy Taylor. Taylor to the life: lyrical/pedantic barchat – when he
tried to ape the fishermen's soft accents. Empathy as practised by the
CIA.

The click of pool balls at the far end of the room. A cardboard
Guinness harp on a dusty shelf. Costain voices talking fights. That was
what she'd seen in him, in Taylor: he wasn't Irish. She didn't have to
listen to the drone of single street towns, where collecting a Librium
prescription was the nearest thing to a night out. Taylor had money to
spend: restaurants, theatres, sports cars – like the ones Oliver Reed
piloted through Michael Winner flicks. (They saw those too, out in
Rathmines, wrestling in the stalls.) He was about, he convinced her, to
do great things. Talk as a form of energy. Gesturing hands. Chain on

wrist. How did it slide away? A patch of rock on the Atlantic's edge, a tribe of pigs. Stone crazy in the endless rain.

Helen found herself reciting the whole tale to this stranger, to O'Hagan. Who smoked his tight little roll-ups, splashing brandy into her chipped cup, laughing. He didn't interfere, he let it happen. Her increasingly hysterical account of Taylor's virtues: the rented house at the end of the long drive, space in which to withdraw from the city; sound system, records, feuding, midnight monologues; the phone calls, the restless combing through shelves to locate the only book in the world that could solve it; the swimming parties in the mill stream, showband saxophones through the open door, fancy dress, ruffs, wigs, bustles, not noticing, not caring about the rain; a strange mix of period posers in pancake make-up, drunks fighting over adjectives, lowlifes boosting Beckett first editions, fresh-faced Ulster beauties in riding macs, notoriously well-connected Anglo-Irish tarts in shabby black underwear, all those white bodies thrashing in the race of cold water; the man himself, the instigator, paymaster, alone in the kitchen, feeding his dog. She saw him from outside, came back, dripping, tartan rug around her shoulders, sought him out, kissed him. He was the child, the hurt boy, happiest at cook's side, happiest close to the food, the long table, the hound in its basket.

How had she ever swallowed it, Taylor's pitch? She can't keep a straight face now as she, head to head, yarns O'Hagan. Snow job and accusation. Taylor's way of hitting bad prose with pepsins of nostalgia to break down sales resistance. The painter was the perfect antidote. His indifference to anything beyond immediate self-gratification was an inspiration. He would stay as long as the drink held out. The promise of a future bundle (the future compassing half an hour). There was no future that Helen knew. Her weakness for these overdue Romantics survived. O'Hagan would plant his paintings in sealed containers deep within the earth. He would drop his bronzes over the fishing-boat's stern. Versions of himself to solicit the processes of decay.

'Sure, that's right. Yeah.' Apropos of nothing. O'Hagan came in fast, after a tactfully prolonged silence, during which they had abandoned themselves to the trivial but insistent FX of the city: jetmoan, playground, beer pump, Swatch circuit, coin tap, chaos siren. 'I'm not a nihilist. It's the job of the artist to record his own time. Self-portraiture is the only honest form.'

He cackled and they shared the joke. They were intimate in ways that didn't matter. And never would. O'Hagan even offered to freshen Helen's coffee, told her to stay where she was, he'd get them in.

A nod to the barman. Strange boy! He dragged his rucksack with him, kept it at his side, touched it secretly with his boot.

What could the painter find to say to a man with so much body fur he didn't need a shirt? A publican who drank neat lemonade by the quart? Were they shaping for a fight?

O'Hagan vultured his head, edged closer, shielding himself from the ditch-diggers, who were grimly working their way through the reserves of black stuff.

'Hey, Sean,' called one of the Micks, 'is it right you're one of them ex-alcoholics?'

The guv'nor took his inquisitor's glass, twisted it to speed the flow from the pump, scraped viciously at the yellow head. He had no taste for trading witticisms.

O'Hagan, seizing the moment, passed up his weighty rucksack. It vanished behind the bar. Weirder and weirder, Helen thought.

'Cheek of your man,' the lemonade drinker muttered to O'Hagan, their transaction completed, 'calling *me* an ex.'

Imar resumed his place at Helen's side. She asked after Sofya Court, the missing photographer, her friend. He'd heard nothing, but promised to keep his eyes open. And that, Helen felt, took care of it.

The possibilities of their alliance.

When the painter, demanding calories to counterbalance the vigour of the spirits, rolled over to the bar to solicit a churn of stout, Helen pushed back the table, and headed for the door. She looked, for the last time, into her cup, swirled the mix, drank to the dregs. Away. No backward glance. She carried the telegram of warmth with her through the stone-flagged garden, taking exaggerated care not to bump into the teak benches. Then, wrists out like indicators, down the tricky slope to the canal.

TWENTY-FIVE

We are the calyx of our dreams. But are they our own? In dread, we fall victim to random nightmares. Outfalls of melancholy. We fear to close our eyes.

Sileen couldn't make the words work. A glossolalic outpouring in which the components achieved some kind of sense, but the sentences, taken as units, fell apart. Blood sang in his ears.

Reluctant to give up a bad habit, he stuck with the canal – furious for the colour blue. Ha! Tide slurry reflecting carpet skies, road bridges to darken the plot, a spongy field of algal stars. Tempting to walk on water: birds did, pecking at polystyrene trays. Sileen noticed, with repulsion, the silver skull of a lightbulb submerged in the primal soup. Scum islands like computer-enhanced weather maps. At a better season, unharried by the deadlines of fate, he might have wasted breath on the magical passage beneath the Eastway flyover: watery refractions pebbling the overhead piers, the double nature of the whole conceit.

He slumped, rested. Rest was a mistake. Rest brought Helen back. (She'd been there all along, but now, closing on the town, she hurt. He tasted her on his skin.) He wanted to steal her sleep. Go where she went. He walked on.

'He absorbed himself in his melancholy. The vague consciousness of a misdirected life given up to impulses whose memory left a bitter taste . . . He felt no remorse . . . Sleeplessness had robbed his will of all energy . . . He beheld the universe as a succession of incomprehensible images.'

Since Tottenham Marsh there had been, he hated to admit it, a guiding spirit, a heron. A bird of dusk, loping ahead, gliding awkwardly, out of scale, a pterodactyl-kite with legs of string. Clattering to rest on the path before Sileen could find a suitable rock.

The scrawny augur perched on the roof of the Courage coldstore, where the Hertford Union Canal divorces from the Lea. Sileen grasped the hint.

He had come through, asleep/awake, living/dying, the river was done with. The canal: a venepuncture. Sileen was a fatal toxin aimed at the heart. He knew this place. Memory plagued him, avenues of moulting plane trees, rose beds, a clearing in his earlier life. The glint of a lake. Some estate or public park, the other side of the railings. He was back. His curses were reserved for the towpath mob: a sodality of crash-helmet lycralists, maggot-box fisherfolk with their telescopic poles, idiot radios, bivouacs of iron rations.

Nature was out of scale, clover tickled the cleft in his chin. A gate. Sileen, on all fours, crawled in: the instinct to find shelter for the night, some pit or den, was strong. A tragic Darwinian progress, a stumble on the evolutionary ladder. Out of the water and into the grasslands. He was so close to his base gradient, the foreknowledge of where he belonged. He was not in his right mind.

Fear made Sileen chaste. Let him have surgeons. He is cut to the brain. A few moments rest will restore his bile. Cheek to the ground. Head among the cool sensors of evening grass. It stinks. A spiral stool, fulginious and wormy, lies in his way. Magnificent!

Forced to pinch the nostrils and retract the neck, he saw the statue on the redbrick plinth, a sharp-eared hound. Toothless, a howling pest. One of a pair. Bookends. The dogs of Alcibiades, guardians of the park's entrance. He loved it. A real turd from a plaster beast. London on a plate.

Too fantastic. He must have sparked out, yielded to a microsecond of uncensored sleep. Imagined rain, the steady pelt of a tropical storm. The iguana canal bursting its banks. His black suit sticking like a skin.

He woke, bolted to darkness, scufflings in the undergrowth. Disorientated, he spun. Balls of cotton in his throat.

A rough tongue licked his brow. Too weak for flight. A flesh dog with a flat black face raised its leg to drench him. Circled, sniffed. Unworthy prey, a bite would be wasted on Sileen. It snarled regret. Breath like Lazarus. The seductive odour of decay, which had enticed the cur, was a false lure: death in life – gamey, rank, unbutchered. The disappointed predator backed off, whimpering, to savour the rump of a more agreeable companion, a starveling bitch so dainty she came from another species entirely, a depilated squirrel, a Camayed rat.

The thwack of this conjunction promised disaster, a gridlock requiring veterinary intervention. A woman of the dog-owning tendency, carrying a torch, stuttered towards the fallen Sileen. 'Keep your fucking dog off of my bitch, filth. I'll fetch up my old man. He'll kill you. Rip out your lights.'

They dressed for their nocturnal rambles, these women of a certain age, as for a trot up west. Teetering heels, Theda Bara eyes, sooty curtains of lash, thin red lips drawn back in a snarl over steelcomb teeth. Retired toms.

Sileen was thrashed with a metal dog chain. Thrashed like a grateful parliamentarian. Thrashed till he bled. He curled in a ball, blanked the torrent of unsolicited abuse, accepted the misguided tribute: that he could be one of them, a dog's sponsor. Sensitized by the blows, his perceptions were preternaturally acute. It couldn't last. Winding, coiling motions in the grass. The fitful pattern of earth energies revealed.

The crossbreed's true owner, bored with hanging his pet from a tree to strengthen its jaw for combat, was resting on a bench, syphoning warm lager from a punctured tin. A sandpaper head with a saltpetre temperament, he was happy to watch Sileen take what was coming to him, but less enthusiastic about his pampered warrior straying into the firing-line.

'Oi, cunt!' Well out of order. The old bat had turned her scourge against the quivering stud, who was hopscotching on her darling's back, pumping and gasping, tongue trailing in the leaves. The savage strokes of the chain were foreplay of an unexpected kind. The pug shuddered his genetic load.

The skinhead caught the dominatrix a fearful slap. She gobbed his face and hurdled a spike into his thigh. Their argument made up in intensity what it lacked in lexicological variety. They spat privates back and forth – while Sileen crawled, forgotten, into a laurel bush; set-dressing funded by sentimental revisionists with a bad conscience. He weakened, he wanted rest.

It faded. It wasn't there: the screams, blows, barks, snarls of rending flesh. All over with nothing gained. Perhaps anger irritates the soil, carries sap to dull roots. Sileen's brain was in bother: short-circuits, forward flashes, cutouts. The night was used up too fast. Confederate sunlight invaded the speckled greenery like a jolt of speed.

Inch by inch, he poked his bald head out from its hideyhole. The river was back. His sight, never good in the mornings, deserved a second chance. He paddled towards the distant barges, the landing-stage, ready to dip his face.

Like looking at landscape through a letter-box, a bumpy spread of waterways, orchards, country lanes. The rural idyll we dream about, the purgatory through which the questing trio had ploughed. Ware. Broxbourne. Waltham Cross. Drage-Bell and his agents would not beat Sileen so easily. Even if he was doped each night, returned to the precise spot from which the previous day's journey had begun. He would push on. Beaten, he would creep. Limbless, he would writhe like a serpent. Nothing could prevent him breaking into the secret Hodgson chamber.

The river was on him – but the river was brick. A community mural, a soft-focus account of what the Lea Valley *should* be. Like spraying the Black Forest over the Berlin Wall. A peeling mosaic of fawns and washed-out greens. The blue that Sileen had hungered for. Red dust under everything. The emulsion river blocked the genuine suicide ditch from sight.

Sileen could lose himself among these dappled meadows and inhale the canal's fecal drench at the same time. The painted wall was a prompt for timid travellers. Turn back, imagine the rest. The cripple traced the blistered road with his mutilated hand – a white wish dipping between hedgerows to a half-remembered hill.

The wall ended and Sileen was lost. A yard where park labourers kept their cars. Beyond, in the world outside, a pub. More fantastic than all the rest: Top O' The Morning. Believe it or believe it not.

Unfunded, derelict, decayed, Sileen marched boldly through the open door, spurning all published prohibitions against travelling men. He blustered to the bar. Get one in and toss it back before there's talk of recompense.

His luck was in. He spotted a musty bottle of Russian stout, called for blackthorn cider to complete the measure. While the hirsute fumbler behind the bar worked his alchemy, the cripple checked for escape routes, back passages. It was bound to end in tears, he was sure of that. The day had started out so well.

An acquaintance, with an enviable reputation as a pussy pirate, Imar O'Hagan, was drinking with two other men: in querulous debate, a couple of shorts shy of violent resolution. Feeling the intruder's eyes burning into their necks, they turned, as one, to face him. O'Hagan, with difficulty, lurched to his feet; led Sileen outside. A garden with tables and slatted benches. The painter promised drink, food, shelter. Sat him down. Left him there. Alone.

The beer garden tilted to the canal path. Sileen had to hold the furniture down. This O'Hagan must be part of it, part of Drage-Bell's protective web. The drink would be spiked. Sileen would wake up, if wake up he did, on the Marshes, or in another bush.

So be it. The air was balmy, almost good enough to breathe. He could absorb the raised voices of the labouring men, the lapping of water, the rustle of leaves. Fetch me poison and I'll drink it down. The wood of the table is warm to touch. No human agency can stop me now.

TWENTY-SIX

Drage-Bell offered the blind man one of the best views in London. Solicitous, oversteering by touch, he helped him from the lift. Nauseous, skating on flat feet across carpeted halls that refused his sonar, the blind man, the follower, went first.

The pressure hiss of automatic doors. Snatches of conversation he could not unscramble. Fresh coffee traces. Women's coats and scarves. The open-plan office: Donar knew it. A dearth of information, nothing coming back. Breeze in his face (a fan). Had he been brought out onto the roof? Would they invite him to jump?

'Look down, professor. You'll never get a better chance. It's what they call a Free Enterprise Zone. The enterprise is free, the rest you pay for – with your life.'

Mordecai Donar couldn't locate the voice: it might be a recording, or a team of actors. Was it behind him or twenty yards ahead? The spook had introduced himself as 'an intelligent servant'. Which sounded like a threat. Sensory deprivation. All the air had been sucked out. It was like walking, inside a transparent tube, across the London skyline. Nothing in this terrible space played back. Drage-Bell's prodigious desk had the displacement of cardboard. His deckchair, set to oversee the river, was a clash of stripes, so loud that even the blind man was not immune from shock.

Donar stood in silence. Waiting.

The glittering honk of the East. East India Dock Road. Hong Kong without the buzz, the yelping canine takeaways. Millwall basking in promised light – IOUs of bottled summertime, rainbows of capital. Downriver, the future was a silver road: oxbow curves, unexploited land. Sunsets free of copyright. A bullish purple horizon to trump any previous definition of greed. Olympian squalor. Yorkist pragmatism.

The Rose of Blood reflected in a thousand-thousand panes. Isle of Dogs. 12.5 million square feet of office and retail space.

This was not the infamous Magnum Tower, some lesser husk – customized, unlet. The black torture palaces were all upstream, swanking in Late Night videos, denounced by amphetamine pundits in playdough spectacles. Drage-Bell's mob were squatters of the Queen, obediently making use of a shnide investment, a portfolio that had gone belly-up. There had been miscalculations, it's true. A blizzard of photographs: the kind that kill unsuspecting lifeforms. Now even the Kowloons had shipped out. The fixers and fraudsters swiftly relocated to charity scams in the Balkans, or grace and favour spots with the Church Commissioners. A few cowed civil servants had been press-ganged to work their ticket. And a coven of Fleet Street hacks co-opted to talk up the values that made Britain great – while dazzling potential advertisers with riparian production values. Budget you could taste. The rest of it, the promontories of fear, were hidden fiefdoms of record. Memory vaults, detention centres. Tunnels in the air. In which Drage-Bell and his clones could conduct their off-the-record affairs.

'Pure poetry. "The steel is starting to rise." Don't you agree? There's a Wordsworthian directness in that phrase. Found it in the Olympia and York prospectus. Says it all. Metallurgic sap.'

Drage-Bell, thin as rope, had declined into his deckchair. Long legs. Atrocious taste in socks (white towelette with blue anchor motif). Filthy plimsolls, laces drooping. Arms over the side, as if he wanted to trail his fingers in the water.

'Can you appreciate the elegance of the solution, prof?' The intelligencer was talking to himself, one of those megalomaniac monologues no conspiracy theorist can do without. 'Here we sit, two and a half miles from the City. No more than the distance from Bank to Bond Street. And the City is a graveyard with SAS roadblocks and the notorious ring of irony. How did we manage it? Simple. We fake a bomb attempt on Canary Wharf – but conveniently "discover" the abandoned van in time for the ten o'clock news. Then, when the clerks are good and jumpy, we blast hell out of London Wall. Scream foul. Scream louder than the rest. Demand increased security to safeguard the City's position as a financial centre. The grey men do the rest. A couple of lunches and a red line chat.'

He was hugging himself in perverse delight. 'Upgraded budget for the Secret State. Docklands revived. The City rubbed from the map.'

Donar, groping for a door, came close to mincing his outstretched hands in the giant fan. Better to stay put, hear the madman out.

' "Where do *I* fit in?" you ask.' Drage-Bell, out of sympathy, had closed his eyes. 'Blame it on the reprehensible fiction that formed my literary taste, but I divide blindmen into two quite distinct categories. One: the seer, the armchair sage with a weakness for numismatics, the Max Carrados type. Feeding on darkness, converting his disability into a source of occult light. And two: the other sort, Blind Pew revengers hissing spite, tapping white sticks like the Armageddon countdown. Messengers of evil. That's you, prof – wearing your hurt like a leper's bell.'

The breeze from the revolving fan soothed Donar's scorched face. He'd been burnt, without noticing it, under pewter skies. Turned out. A schnorrer, a beggar in the streets. He had no voice of his own, it was impounded with his previous life. He was a witness now. Things happened around him. He was ticketed for relief. He picked at a loose thread and waited.

There were mornings, this was one of them, when even Drage-Bell was charmed by what he saw from his window: the bent spine of the river, the S, the biggest lie of all. London was a zone of control. His Hodgson collection was safe. It would never be penetrated. The act of penetration was death. Devices, covert and mundane, ringed the secret chamber. The intelligencer, in visualizing them, brought the fiery bands to life. Kinder Street shook like a Range Rover in a layby.

' "Scour out their eyes, when next they come. A fit reward for spies." Did you know, professor, that when they opened the files after the Velvet Revolution in Prague, they discovered that there were more paid informers than ordinary comrades? Any intelligence experience, Mr Donar? In your own country? Could narking be your métier? To be blunt, you've not got much going for you. Holes in the head, confiscated eyes. Therefore the victim must be a spy. Take a peep across at the other side. Kit Marlowe in Deptford. A pro hit, straight into the brain. Textbook stuff.'

Trained eyes noted the byplay of their body language, the unequal struggle for dominance. Boredom addicts logged Drage-Bell's recitative, Donar's culpable silence. Shellsuits, behind two-way mirrors, nursed screwtop beakers of black coffee and activated memory machines. C11 (the elite squad of 8), SO11, E4A: they were all in it, all

the bad numbers. Weaselmen, capable of living for three days in an 18"
space beneath the floorboards, periscoped Donar's hand movements,
the clenched fist behind his back, the mute insolence. Wetsuit spiders
submerged in tanks of drinking water. S/M contortionists, who'd been
turned, fish-eyed from overhead light fittings. The intelligencer's office
was webbed in lenses. The entire building was a nest of restricted
breathers, a blueprint of counter-terror terrorists.

The state of zero. Dysfunctional image smoke. Real time asserted
itself in car pounds where the drama of nothing was unbearable.
Cameras abstracted the exterior world in coded segments. Film was
truth, an invitation to future criminals. High angle pavements solicited
bombers. Nothing was shot that would not, eventually, justify its
budget.

'Rosebud.'

Mordecai Donar couldn't understand why he said it. Why he had said
anything. But it was a start, echoing single words, reading the lips of his
interrogator. 'Rosebud.' He carried the sound of it back out into the
streets, the doorways, the lost afternoons wandering between Wellclose
Square and the river. Where had it been? That night in the forest,
paddling downstream, drifting on the tide, snowflakes on the dark
surface – a quilted hush. Let it go. A storm in a glass globe. Tower
Bridge. An opening hand. A city under threat.

'Roebuck!'

Drage-Bell was out of the chair and screaming in his face. Mordecai
had missed the link, the explanation. Roebuck was not an animal, it was
a map reference. It was in the brochure – number 13. Drage-Bell read
the entry out. 'A popular venue for large political and Trade Union
meetings. Early on 31 August 1888, the body of Mary Ann Nichols,
Jack the Ripper's first victim, was found on Bucks Row. The Roebuck
will take you back a generation to the "boozers" of another era. For a
great night out or an afternoon treat, Cockney Capers will arrange a
guided visit for you, with transport.'

Era, Donar thought, funny word. The shamus was offering him a job!
Not so much an offer, really, as a chance to stay alive. The blindman
would be fixed to the board, allotted his corner. East London was a
pattern of marked squares, black and white. Like strolling through
Hatton Garden, you understand, between clumps of Rastas and the
ginger-bearded frummers from Stamford Hill. Donar, the rook, would

wash pots, slide obliquely through a public-house, God forgive, report what he saw. Call him a cellarman, a willing ear.

The shame! He was not bred to be a labouring man, to skulk like a dybbuk in low dens. He was a scholar, a student of the cabala, custodian of maidenheads. He was Mordecai Donar. He had been visited by angels.

'You will be my eyes,' Drage-Bell said. 'And I will be your protection. I will find the woman who did this thing and deliver her up to you. You have my word.'

What woman? He had said nothing about a woman. What thing? A thing was an instrument. A thing had no life. A thing could not hurt. Nothing had *ever* happened before this room.

Since becoming blind, Donar had tolerated no eidetic spasms, no imagery. He hoarded reservoirs of cold, sour light. Now he was undone by the policeman's request. He knew, on that instant, the geography of the room. The desk's edge, the photographs. No women left. A contracting border of fire. No mother. Ash instead of breath. No sisters. The grey cobbles of an empty street.

The cage again. His stomach fell away. Bells for each floor. The intelligencer talked him down. 'Cultivate perpetual night. Navigate by revenge. Trust your worst instincts. Tap her. Invade her sleep. Hear everything, evaluate nothing. Aspire to the condition of blank tape. Lick, swallow, retain.'

Alone, returned to the company of silent watchers, the spook opened a desk-drawer and took out a slithery bundle of X-ray plates. They were dated and in strict chronological order. Model's name: Todd Sileen. The plates, when they were held up to the light, blustered like thunder on the radio. The ghost tributaries of Sileen's ribs blue-filtered the spread of docklands. Hazed lungs promised storms.

Drage-Bell taped the sheets, in groups of three, across the window. Resumed his deckchair. Mused on what he saw. Cigar smoke melding into streets of cloud. The journey Sileen had not yet embarked upon. X-rays were the spymaster's codices, an unbound folio. Ian Askead had faithfully delivered every page.

Was there a faint migration in the sky behind? Sileen back in the city? Somewhere out on the fringes, wet feet, busking for tea and sympathy? The cripple's futile progress had been traced on the celluloid skin before he hazarded his first step.

BOOK THREE

DRAGE-BELL'S LIBRARY

Success: he talked spook to the spook.

James Ellroy, *White Jazz*

ONE

Was it the same man? *I don't want this*. He limped over the flattened cobbles, hauling his rancid gymshoes, painfully, across their irregular contours. Unconvinced ghosts backed off. *I can still change my mind*. No, sorry, you can't. It's far too late. Written. Sileen had come full circle. The mound *was* back. Peeping over the tenements, a conical oilskin alp. Rhab Adnam's visionary quest was achieved, leaving Sileen a mere cricket pitch short of his starting point. Once again he dragged his tin leg – like a sacrifice – towards the delicate roebuck in its icy panel, the orange light of public celebration in a private place. Imar O'Hagan, who was pushing a bicycle, supported him.

I will pay the price.

An acid moon bobbled over the cataracted warehouse, Durward Street was rubble. Had it ever existed, the catacombs, the openair chapel? Sileen didn't trust his memory. He was a victim of implants, reveries blowing like tumbleweed, X-ray hallucinations, things he had read, things that had happened before and would always happen, films reinvented as much as recalled. In a rare episode of self-consciousness, he tracked a limping figure to the door of a pub. A cinema of mood, photographs that refused animation: proletarian, romantic. A long-haired woman in a postcard, arms thrown back, a carving, part of a cemetery wall, stone blocks, the eyes of men, judges, black mouths. Sileen as saviour. Sileen advancing towards some final gesture, a farewell. A flick of the fingers. A tender obscenity.

The old set, London, *had* changed. Or his perception of it had been fatally worked over by the walk. A lock-up garage stopped Sileen's breath, the subtlety of colour bands, the excited arrangement of forms. Art that had dodged the galleries. Undescribed (until now) and therefore pure. Let the experience be the art. (He was half-starved and crazy for a drink.) The city pulsed. Routine epiphanies. Crushed milk-bottles as a crystal field. Moss as the complement to blood. Detail on detail: transformations, metaphors that bit. He was tempted to ask O'Hagan for a notebook and pen.

They fought their way to the bar as the muezzin sent out the call for 'last orders'. A crush of brutal thirsts. The gaffer had his hands full servicing the regular dead. They were all present (and then a few more): the lads from the breakers' yard, the Maltese pimps – mourning their squandered status, Scotch Dave the Bookseller – pampering his shingles with a whisky drench, the savage and generous Sligo mob, tinkers and poets, kissing and cursing. Sliema Felix Muscat with Ian Askead in attendance to torch his Winstons.

Sileen experienced nostalgia like a hot flush, an in-your-face frisson of sentiment. Safely reunited with the lowlife, villains, snouts: he was ready to blub. Home. Hiraeth. He should be so lucky. O'Hagan propped him on a hard bench, alongside a sozzled gammer with a troublesome slip. Between gargles of stout, she plucked convulsively, pulling yards of black rayon from beneath a mulberry coat.

The painter, as ever, worked some arbitrage at the counter. He had confidences to exchange with the ancient revolutionary (who had Swedenborgian whispers of his own), and who chose, consequently, to feign deafness, forcing O'Hagan to yell. There was another package to collect. Roadblock riflemen only pothered cars, culture couples trying to find their way out of the Barbican; pedestrians were free as birds to shift their contraband from zone to zone. They might show up as a potential flaw on distressed videotape – but, by the time the image was enhanced to produce a human likeness, it would be too late.

When thirst gets as bad as this, you think of sucking copper coins, ringing sweat from old socks, running your tongue down bus windows to catch the fog. Something had to be done before Sileen reverted to a cone of sawdust. Sensitized to every shift in the flow of traffic around the pumps, he spotted a gap. At the short end of the L, there was a lull in the riot of upraised mugs, a fissure in which any punter with sufficient vim could squeeze – side on. No sooner clocked than acted upon. Sileen was in.

In? Hardly. He couldn't move. The reason for the hiatus was clear. The deck of the bar was awash with a tide of spill. (Desperate vagrants, tongues like rulers, squatted beneath the rim to catch the drips.)

Attempting to pull a pint, the relief barman returned a damp-bottomed ashtray. The rest went down his trouser fronts. No joke. The man was in terror. His hands shook. His eyelids were stretched back and his sockets bare. He was blind as Homer. Old Gloucester with the cork arms and eggwhite down his cheeks.

Too much, even for Sileen. The world's gone mad. A drive-in movie for people who can't afford cars. You'd need a wetsuit to risk a short. Who's buying?

The robotic dispenser's sole client was a geek in a French beret, bent (in the old sense), gone in the legs. Sileen had seen him before – and knew him as a harbinger of grief. There was breeding in that nose a Derby winner would be proud to own. The rest of the profile was spareparts surgery from a knacker's yard. Polish cheekbones from which the chin had taken a suicide dive. Intelligence still present, burning like the last cinders of a barbecue.

The beret spoke without turning, drooped a hand. 'Royboy to you, old chum. What's your poison? No problem catching the garçon's eye. Eh? Eh what?'

Sileen on his guard. Better watch out. Nothing shafts you faster than charm. Royboys came with the fittings in Soho drinkers (somehow vanishing from the Farson snaps) – but *here*? The cashiered chancer was way off piste, a serial killer in a *Carry On*. Sileen almost refused the pint. He didn't accept favours from strange men with their feet on petrolcans.

Royboy reminded him of a missing file, something that had gone right off. A slice of wedding cake buried under the floorboards. He was DOA, a floater. Half a face. Sileen was frightened by seeing Royboy's other side. Royboy in Oxford, the museum, a pale reflection on a kiosk of Peruvian grave goods.

Where was his mate? Royboy was only permitted as a parasite. He was not to be countenanced without an obvious host. He was the spieler in a double act, the privately dominant stooge.

Sileen's liver felt the tickle of fear. Royboy, smiling, had unsheathed his claws. Felix Muscat, down the other end, missing nothing, shook his ashy lion's head. All the old values, he thought, are shit in the mouth. Rubbish like that, no respect for themselves, wouldn't line a bin with that jacket, stupid fucking pancake on his head – and no tie! No silk to hide the scraggy chicken-neck. Standards have gone to piss. The mother country's stuck her bonce right down the khazi, and there's no way back. What's happened to class? None of the riffraff peddling pills out of Marbella could hold a candle to my brother Georgie, may he rest in peace. What was it he used to say? 'Felix, my son, I ain't got no prejudices about coloured people, as such. I'm just choosy who I socialize with.'

We were the last of our kind, he decided. Knew how to present ourselves to advantage, fit in anywhere. I read a book in the nick one time – biography, teach you a lot, as it happens. Some Yank pillow-for-hire, rabbiting about the Mafia boss, Sam Giancana, at the Cal-Neva Lodge. 'He had beautiful shirts.' Says it all that. No-one will mess with the right shirt.

('Sam Giancana? Rings a bell. Didn't I meet the geezer on the Dallas trip – with Ron?')

As he brooded, Muscat tightened his grip on Askead's wrist. The blood drained from the fink's face. Posset white – beneath the growth, the matchbox stubble. Askead slipped free, liberating a pack of Winstons, crinkly in cellophane. He ached for Sileen, the cash the crip represented, the intelligence he would import. He must tap him before he drank his memories away.

On his feet, he touched the stanley knife for luck and bundled into the crowd. He had cultivated a New Look that bought him space: pearl droplet in the ear, red shockwig (household gloss), black corset, silk stockings, gumboots rolled down, pirate-style, a crow appliquéd to his nicotine labcoat.

'We've missed you down the hospital, old morrie. Empty beds, no action.' The Glaswegian insinuated in Sileen's ear. His head was full of it, quotes, playback, recycled angst. 'Any dosh left, Baron?' Everything had happened before.

The overhead TV was clipping the interior of another pub, blood on the floor in black and white. Real sirens in the street outside. It's the best way to make a splash in the broadsheets: sponsor a hit on the premises. They'll bike round one of the Big Macs to do a serious 'been there/done that' slab. Cal McCrystal, John McVicar. Just bell the Twins on a bad night, when the Colonel's got the hump. Tip the wink in the Walworth Road. The villains will gift you a blue plaque. You'll be on the heritage trail with the Beggar and the Royal in Vicky Park.

Who was this man? Sileen wanted to know. Smelt familiar. Jackal with a bunch of keys. *Show me the path*. His tin leg underwent an involuntary spasm. He started for the door.

The painter, O'Hagan, on a bench with the old girls, was hooting like a Bedlamite. Rapid-fire non sequiturs and ribald anecdotes lacking punchlines. A naked shoulder pressed against the sporting granny, while his free hand groomed moist ginger tufts in an exposed armpit. But, even as he plunged towards blackout in the lap of her coat, his boot never surrendered its guardianship of the bulging knapsack.

Tasting the night air, bone flakes and meltdown rubber in a smoke solution, Sileen revived. *Any price*. The cobbles glistened. Askead gave him support. This is what should be happening. This is how it begins. O'Hagan's laughter and Royboy's taunts were sidebars to the quest. He drank the noxious eddies that hustle between blind buffers of stone, a castaway on leave.

Would Askead reveal, on a promise of future reward, the whereabouts of Drage-Bell's secret bunker, his Hodgson room? Askead revealed nothing but flattened canines, a gobful of ruin. 'Cash money, pal, or zilch.'

Could he be threatened, hurt? Sileen's surviving hand locked like an arcade grab between the Scotsman's legs. He whistled as his purse was pinched, squeaked submission, pleading for an agent's cut. 'Say, thirty per cent?' (More a castration than a vasectomy.) In his favour, he offered a better deal than most agents: he was available on a twenty-four hour basis, and he didn't do lunch. (Neither did he charge a premium for sending copies of Sileen's book on useless quests to farflung Siberian outposts of the trade.)

Shouldn't Sileen reconsider before he signs in blood? Drage-Bell's room is guarded by rumour: surveillance, false walls, pit bulls, bugaboos, skulls on sticks. Pinpricks! Snatch the manuscript and the intelligencer is amputated from his energy source. What's left to risk?

The bridge over the railway, urine alley, the hole in the buildings. Black windows blazing with light. The warehouse on fire. Bundles of evidence going up in flames. Affidavits coughing smoke. Sileen sweated in the halloween heat. They must escape before the alarms begin to shriek. A tremendous backdrop – but not, strictly speaking, their fault.

Royboy watched from the doorway of the Roebuck, lounging like a stripshow tout. The ash on his cigarette had achieved its optimum growth. He shouted something to the blind barman. Mordecai Donar bolted. Smashed his way along a congested shelf, toppling bottles, clearing glasses. He found the phone, and croaked into the mouthpiece, frightened by the sound of his own voice. A reprise of the evening's events, accompanied by vivid hand gestures, suitable for the cerebrally shortchanged.

Sliema Felix witnessed the cameo. So did the publican and his ruptured son. Royboy, semi-tumescent, stuck with the conflagration.

TWO

Ian Askead's cover was the coverall, the ubiquitous nicotine labcoat. It took him anywhere, blessed him with instant anonymity. A jobsworth on the prowl: pet handler, relief caretaker, stacker of mortuary trays, shoveller of dogshit (by appointment to the Hawksmoor churches). He'd done the lot and was still drawing the wages. The labcoat was his visa. It conferred a freelance, quasi-official status – somewhere between a traffic warden and a beagle in a cage. Before the recent trope of the earring and the ketchup beehive, he was as invisible as the inscriptions on parish boundary stones. Short arms swallowed in deep pockets, a clip of pens, he darted through the hospital shallows, privatizing unconsidered broom-cupboards.

Too cruel. The Whitechapel Mound was revealed, on closer inspection, as a slithering heap of rubbish sacks, a protest by refuse operatives. Untethered landfill attracting the attention of the usual scavengers with shopping bags. Sileen was still protesting when Askead bundled him up the steps and into the hospital. Could Drage-Bell's safe house be located within this Vatican, secreted among the silent wards? That, surely, was too coarse a fiction: to contrive a cell of static time in the one place where every window was a codex of lies? Askead was dancing him into a trap, working him over with the smells and sensations of his former addiction.

'Melanie Klein,' muttered Askead over his shoulder.

Sileen couldn't take any more names. His index was oversubscribed. There was no-one left to bribe and the float was dispersed. Funds were at zero. Was this person a medic or a password?

The entrance hall was deserted, suspicious in itself. No idlers, no crazies begging to be let in, no hawkers flogging ex-Soviet optical lasers, no whores, no punctured gangsters leaking on the lino. Where were the courtesies of the Golden Age? Askead, nervous inside his nicotine envelope, mimed caution, pulled Sileen into a curtained examination cubicle.

'Melanie Klein. She asserts that the individual, under stress, moves either towards integration or disintegration – thereby conditioning his or her perception of the world. It fascinates me, sitting alone at night, to chew over that conundrum. Bit of an imponderable. Which way do you hang, Baron? Integration or disintegration?'

Sileen did not hesitate. He got his fingers around Askead's throat and squeezed until the weasel's eyes were rhubarb stalks. 'Drage-Bell!'

Uncalled for. Hurtful. The injured man, sniffing, groped for a match. He couldn't understand Sileen's frenzy, this charge on oblivion. He integrated with a few fast drags. What did Melanie Klein say about suspicion of the breast, the infant's paranoid-schizoid bind? Hating to love the milky spurt. I can dig that. Sileen was a mannerless brute, unworthy of serious philosophical dialogue. Give him what he wanted – but not quite yet. There were drawers to open, flat tins to tap, papers to be shuffled, pill bottles, loops of wire. Whenever Sileen tried to speak, Askead wagged an admonitory digit. He was enjoying himself. 'You should make the time to read, man. Debate with yourself. Tease out your anima, the female side.'

Ripping back the curtains with a *Psycho* flourish, Askead was away. 'Can't speak, not here. Too many eyes in hock. Too many ears buried in the wall.'

Again they were squelching on rubber ramps, clamped in antique lifts, wheeling down stairwells, passing like bad light through cloche corridors that linked blind buildings, doubling back, bypassing previous selves.

The torchbeam slid along tiles so blank that any shape could be projected onto them. These depths were worse than the cupboards of decaying specimens, the shrouded machines: they were cold, faintly humming. Askead, in his costume jewellery, stocking slither, corrosive perfume, was an usherette after the heart of J. Edgar Hoover. He was ready for his final trick.

'We're there.'

Sileen knew he was lying. There should be a stillness in the air, a field of beneficent influence, around the Hodgson manuscript. *The pale and gentle light that lit the Sea of Sleep*. Rooms withdrew. Tables floated. This was not it. This was an outer court, squatted by knaves and criminals.

The oily, overpowering smell of paraffin. Shadows rearing. Askead swung the lamp. A canvas curtain. The pain returned with the imagery. Slow-burning flesh – cooked from the inside. An unkind jest. Sileen had been brought back to the borderland theatre, the technician's wash-room. X-ray plates hung around him like abandoned armour. Nail-clipped celluloid. Prints stolen from the history of his body. Intrusions. His name, the date, on every one: Todd Sileen, Ted S. Ileen, T. Silone. TS Ill-One, Todd's Alone. An autobiography of flaw. Landscapes in negative. Memories that should have been destroyed. He was un-manned.

It could take Askead, when he put his mind to it, a very long time to roll a simple spliff.

'Like it? The way those weather fronts run, east/west, across your lungs? The inevitability. The way you can cheat fate by monkeying with the arrangement of the plates.'

The bruised squares were dull as views of St Paul's shot by incompetent tourists. X-rays were for the literal minded. The past prophetic. Sentiment. Like taking home a necklace of gallstones. Sileen was only interested in displacement effects, using the extraordinary persistence of the waves as a method of escape.

Sileen walked over to the basin and splashed water on his face. Every time he tried to speak, to question Askead, the Scotsman touched a finger to his nose, and took another shuddering drag. The phlegmy insuck blended with all the other sounds of the ancient building – the hiss of gas, water pipes thumping and juddering, rats gnawing through Edwardian wiring. The hospital itself was sick, its crumbling plaster infected by the diseases it had overseen. Wards were obedient to their titles. They incubated fevers and distilled despair. The empty Cambridge Ward was a begetter of argument and the Blizard Ward a convener of cerebral storms.

Sileen, staying put, would be usurped by X-ray plates. He would fade with the night, melt like a candle. The Glaswegian had only to wait. To wait and smoke. Sileen must beat the truth from Askead or give the building best, accept the verdict of the rays.

The weasel sensed it, the point at which Sileen would act. It wasn't difficult. Sileen had kicked the table over and was reaching again for the still tender throat. Askead, nimble in his wellies, nipped behind the screen of prints, setting them creaking and complaining, suits for ghosts. He turned on all the taps, full pressure, such as it was. A pounding, spattering of water: the Gents at the finish of *Hamlet* performed without intermission in the Cottesloe.

'Don't speak till I drown the bugs.' Askead found something loud on the radio, a bedtime book, quirky but tame.

Sileen couldn't wait. He wrenched the cap from the paraffin lamp and splashed the hem of Askead's labcoat, his rather shapely legs.

'Precise location – or you'll fry.'

'Chill out, man. I'm hustling here to save your skin. Don't forget the wedge we've got riding on your chick. The cat scrap. Tarten's bareknuckle show. I'm in for a heavy slice. I'd never let an investment blow.'

'Fuck that. Give me Drage-Bell and we're made. Write your own ticket.'

'No chance. Can't be done, boss. I'll sneak you to the door – that's it. The spook's carrying too much heat. His first defence is anonymity, right? I've seen it, man, and I don't believe it's there. You've clocked those nuclear/brain-bend gaffs that don't show up on the ordinance survey? High profile compared to this. Take a photo of Drage-Bell's pad and what you'll get is fields and orchards. Weird!'

'I don't want to record the shit, just get inside.'

'Take my word, even the schvartzers won't touch it. Crackheads would rather deal from the Stoke Newington holding tank. The building looks abandoned. Bell lets squatters have a couple of floors. Anarchist slogans. Tagger's calligraphy. GASMAN LIVES. All that yak. Any street zombie can get in, no sweat. But none of them do. They know better. Forget it, baron. Sleep it off. I'd climb into that fridge of stiffs before I'd chance Bell's library.'

Enough PR. Sileen wasn't optioning for *New Worlds*, reviving H. P. Lovecraft as a Neo-Gothic scam, he had to keep moving; stay still and the tin in his leg would spread, clot his veins, sheet his eyes. Movement was truth. He was hauling the tiny Scot like a poddle in iron clogs. He *knew* the way. Askead was excess baggage. He led from behind.

They processed through an overlooked garden – cringing nightstock, sour geraniums – and out, by a hidden door, into the street. Poisoned earth would not be so dead. The soil, Sileen decided, had evolved from pellets of stale bread dipped in ink.

They drifted towards the river: Askead stuttering ahead, then ducking into doorways, choosing the most obscure and ill-lit tributaries, the meanest slits between undemolished ruins, cul-de-sacs without names that somehow, at the very last moment, offered a release. Wheezing, the shifty guide gave up, pulled back against a slimy wall, and pointed up – a reflex action, nominating any husk, in order to discharge his duty and retreat.

Sileen was home. Prodigal now, as he could afford to be, with his emotions, he watched the only illuminated window in Sly Street; brushed his eyes with his fist, blinked for focus. Figures drifted behind gauze. Helen! The contrived peepshow of TV drama: the way lurkers in dark alleys always confirm their paranoia. Lovers who can only perform with the photofloods on – and so close to the window-ledge they're in danger of falling out.

Helen was dancing. Or so he thought. He was swamped with tenderness, the randy sod. Nothing else mattered. Sileen was incomplete. Love's sorry curvature. Dry throat, pumping head. He nearly lost his lunch. Who was the other one, her partner – the man?

Askead whispered. London froze. *Not* Sly Street. Further down, Sileen could make out the pepper-pots of St George, a bit of the Crown & Dolphin. *Where?* A confluence of shadow nets, a heap of nothing held together by inertia and scaffolding. The hole from which all rumours oozed. Swedenborg's pit. Askead shouted the name as he ran away. Kinder Street.

THREE

When he succeeded in bringing the block of Kinder Street into focus, everything else evaporated. It was an either/or situation. The kind Sileen thrived on. No aphrodisiac like the char of burning lifeboats. Unconcerned with the risk of being observed, he made an open and leisurely examination of Drage-Bell's rumoured stockade. (Askead might be lying. He might have pointed to any fire-damaged shell and done a runner.)

No signs of life, no indications of squatters within. The usual slogans and cheerfully misspelt obscenities had been replaced by flowered wallpaper and plaster ducks. *On the outside*. Ledges, chimney-breasts, shelves standing proud – most curious. Sileen thought at first he was surveying the borderline where the demolition men had given up for the day, leaving half a room exposed to the air; floating baths, grates instead of windows, bunches of loose wire, like limbs stripped of flesh. Not so, it was stranger than that. The building had been turned insideout. Whatever had been trapped inside was expelled into the night. Whatever currents surrounded and protected Kinder Street had been drawn up and imprisoned within this brick lung. The process might be in flux. Sileen, watching too closely, would be utterly absorbed.

Wet rot: the soft, creeping, woodpulp breath of masticated skirting-board, peeling albums of paper, blisters of glue, sawdust porridge, size. The tubes of the house sliced. Sileen studied the futurist diagonals of former staircases. He had come to the end of it, the quest. Drage-Bell's redoubt had been emptied of everything except the manuscript. All other qualities had been loosed, drained away into the indifferent neighbourhood. A dispute on the steps of the minicab office. A barely perceptible flaw corrupting the green plastic wrapper that protects the latest temporary glass tower. The guard dog, roaming the long grass beyond the Swedish Church, who cuts his mouth on a broken bottle. The film producer who cannot sell her flat. The photographic model, newly arrived in the labyrinth, who develops a mutant strain of serum hepatitis. Kinder Street was a memorial block. A sepulchre constructed to contain a single item. It was so dense, there was nothing left to penetrate.

The manuscript which, until this moment, had been an impossible abstraction (that was its charm), was overwhelmingly present. Everything and always. Sileen knew it, knew that he was part of the story. He no longer belonged on the streets. The pain had left him. His skin was moist and new. A wraith, he drifted under the eaves, and was lost.

Helen, preoccupied, resting, looked out from her window – enjoying the night, the stars, the exhalations of the miraculous orchard. Sileen passed through her mind. A thing with horns. A beast separated from the herd.

Breeze blocks had been neatly stacked and cemented together to fill the window apertures (Sileen rather took to the style). And planks nailed, in Xs, across the frames of the doors. Irrelevant. House and pit. If only Sileen could solve the riddle of their relationship. Were they aspects of the same energy, reversing, evolving, exchanging identity?

Impulses were actions. He was pressing against the east flank, a rubbish-heaped passage that hadn't been there before; wriggling between Drage-Bell's defended stockade and a high brick wall. How could he gain access to a building whose entrances were concealed on the inside. A trick that repulsed any advance. The closer he came, the stronger the urge to run away. The book alone held him, his place in the text. He had been written into its pages, he was integral to the development of the plot.

There had to be a way for the squatters to come and go. (*Were* there any? Guerillas, Sendero, bullion thieves, Angry Brigades – slightly peeved eco-bandits?) Sileen was vulnerable, confused. He couldn't handle confusion. He was used to being wrong, acting from the lowest motives – but acting, always. He drove forward. There was a goal. This sighting of Helen had stirred ordinary human desire: the need for succour, confession, revenge. He began to explain himself. To himself. Fatal! He couldn't move. Sweated where he stood.

Suddenly, all the newspaper legends of Gray Hood, the *Hackney Gazette* bore, came rushing back as a torrent of renegade images. Prisoners in cages. Beatings. Animals flung from balconies. Black-window limousines. Floods that vanished without trace. The Kinder Street dwellings filled with seawater. A necklace of burning warehouses to mark out the divisions of the city. Calcified evidence. Spiked scandals that wouldn't connect, or that connected all too easily.

He was alive, overwhelmed by the presence of things, others – or did he mean the opposite of this? Integration: rags, split rubbish sacks, wet food crawling with maggots, broken-necked pigeons, hubcaps. A cumulative portrait. He was the only reader, the author of his own equivocation.

A leap of imagination *was* possible. The sky: a velvet ribbon between the boundary wall and the toppling tenement. Sileen, in losing his name, had given way to the ecstasy of selective amnesia. He could step beyond the extinction of Hodgson's visionary, the moment when the morbid traveller cracked – and allowed the apes of unreason onto the stairs.

Soggy newspulp wrapped itself around his tired feet: all the torn lavatory fragments and masturbatory spills were edited, smoothed, joined. This supplicant, who was no longer Sileen, learnt all the stories of the city, each small disgraced act, each terse para. Memory feasts coagulated from the stink of rotten vegetables. He dribbled over descriptions of forgotten meals. Winos' spit-bottles were recorked and granted a vintage. Pawless cats sprang from their drowning sacks to claw his cheek. Even the black suit, which had been an envelope of grease, was steamed, laundered by expectation.

Sileen was dressed in crisp execution tailoring. The kind that is worn just once. He was empowered by risk. (He used that verb, for the first time, without blushing.) The cripple was writing his progress as he endured it. He was improvising, going with the flow. His bowels jingled like a pocketful of loose change. He heaved himself onto the only sill he could reach. A window that was not bricked over. The tradesman's entrance.

It was the missing fingers that gripped, the amputated leg that drove him from the ground. He rolled. Between worlds. Having forfeited terrestrial wisdom and not yet entered Drage-Bell's cave. Let the head droop, follow it down. Inside. The darkness exceeded expectation, it was absolute.

Seeing nothing, feeling no pain, he lay where he was. He panted, listened to the rasp of breath. Not dead yet. He waited – waited for what? Losing his identity, he had lost his purpose. The quest was nothing beside this darkness. Fathoms of unprocessed light. Un-light. Post-narrative, sub-genre – inhuman. Sileen was not informed, he was consumed. Now what should he *do*?

The space he occupied filled with amniotic water. He didn't have to breathe. He was learning to forget. Names, districts, lovers. Hodgson's visionary in his impotent Galway tower, erasing the bright particulars of everyday life, irritations of mere fact: he floated out, guided by willed lesions, aphasic episodes, in his grid of information. He swam in sentiment. Dead cosmologies.

A dim far mystery of red.

Helen's intrusive perfume moving through the imageless darkness, bringing him back to himself, conditioned reflex, the need to touch. Helen here! He crawled in search of the perception of that scent, the red dress. Helen becoming Isabel. She leads him, the figure he glimpsed in the Sly Street window; he gives her his trust. The fond betrayer. Without Helen his frenzy was meaningless.

The musky trace brought him safely past mantraps, weighted boards, daggers of glass, unhinged doors panelled with nails. Brought him to steps he couldn't see, over floors as soft as feathers. The redness was the quality he clung to: a slash across the eyeball, too sudden for trauma.

It fades. He's not hungry enough. His lust is slack. He can't hold her. Helpless, he turns, twists, sniffs at the cobweb damp. Boxes of meat-earth broken beneath his foot. He gags. Helen can carry him no further. He stretches out a hand. Winces from some undefined sharpness: spikes, range wire? Not daring to move.

He fumbled for a vesta. A box had survived his travels, palmed in a pub. He counted five sticks, rolling sharp-cut sides between finger and thumb, licking the bulbs – working up the nerve to attempt a strike. He knew his own habits too well, collector of dead matches. Five was an awkward number. Snap one and you'd have a nuclear family.

He knuckled the sandpaper strip, then scraped. Nothing. The match was damp or burnt out. Again. Nothing. He worked the splinter till it cracked. Again. No. Again? As before.

Bored, pursuing the matter as a disinterested investigation, a juggling of odds, Sileen continued. The last match flared, blinded him, troubled the coherent mantle of darkness. The flame stretched, bent away. A window must have been left open. There was a second exit from the house.

The pale wood gave up its moisture, sweated, withered into charcoal. He remembered, when fire pinched his fingers, to check what lay ahead. Barbed wire, rolls of it, fixed across a black doorway. It would have trapped him – if he had taken another step forward. If he had followed the direction of the scent. He would have been pegged, helpless, a trophy in no-man's-land, caught in the arc of ordnance, night's day, exposed by flares, waiting for the dawn snipers.

Down on his belly, shuffling the shoulders, wriggling like a worm, he might work himself under the obstruction. It had been imperfectly set, a gap left, generous enough to admit an anorexic shadow. Thorns of wire groove the dirt of Sileen's neck. Cloth tears. He's through.

An arm sent out like an antenna. A hand to report on the nature of the ground. Nails to receive splinters. Eyes in his fingers. He hears things that haven't happened yet. Not quite. He sweeps dirt, advancing by peristalsis onto a clean page.

His fist closes on nothing. No floor. The loud stench, no need to see it, of Hodgson's pit. A roaring of lost rivers, subterranean storms. We hear them first, and then we drown. (The sound effects for the closing scenes of *The Third Man*, the pursuit of Harry Lime, were recorded in the sewers of the Fleet. Euro terror. Vienna *is* London.) Victorian fogs, sluiced from the streets, bubble and ferment. The almond smell of hydrogen cyanide from the electroplating works. Carbon dioxide from hospitals and icecream factories. Miscarriages, abortions. Medieval cesspits. Purifying sand. It rushed at Sileen. Overinformed, he hung on the pit's lip and retched.

Sileen elbowed rubble and waited for the sound, a distant splash, a clink. Silence hurt. No matches left. He strained to interpret any oracle from the deeps. Solid darkness. He could not penetrate the reek.

I might have been looking down into a bottomless, sideless well. Then, even as I stared, full of perplexity, I seemed to hear, far down, as though from untold depths, a faint whisper of sound. I bent my head, quickly, more into the opening, and listened, intently. It may have been fancy; but I could have sworn to hearing a soft titter, that grew into a hideous chuckling, faint and distant.

Drage-Bell's secret was protected by echo chambers of loose fiction, generic set pieces to cover every eventuality. Sileen's intrusion had provoked this gravitational force-field. Balance was shot to hell. *The House on the Borderland* had, until now, been held together by its exhilarating surges from celestial vision to swine pit; universes flowering and dying, contagion in the cellar. Kinder Street had no history of revelation to palliate the dementia. It hoarded what it had. Paragraphs mixed and mingled, uncensored in the air. Sileen's every movement was preceded by terrors *already* refined and concentrated in language by one of the speculative masters. Published. He had to forget all that he knew. If he anticipated, constructed a logical progression through the labyrinth, he would be doomed to mere obedience. If he allowed himself to act on his faulty recall of Hodgson's rhapsodic prose, he would suffer the precise fate of the recluse in his tower. He *dare* not think. He must behave as Helen would behave, instinctively, and with grace. Suppress reason, make contact with a swifter intelligence.

With a calmer mind, I became again curious to know into what that trap opened; but could not,. then summon sufficient courage, to make a further investigation.

Sileen shaped words, scratched them in slate air. After his adventures in the cellar Hodgson's recluse would withdraw into winter sunlight. He would wander carelessly through uncultivated gardens. He had no interest in the taxonomy of plant life, no relish for scent and colour: the wilderness was a morbid margin for his tale. Something to look away from. The man was adamantine, unyielding – alien. Sileen thought of him with contempt. His own skull had softened to a cheeselike consistency. He was unboned, ready to pass through the next stage of his initiation.

He risks standing. Edges forward, testing the ground with his good foot. The floor is spongy but secure. Either he is circumnavigating the pit, or he lacks the capacity to sustain such a tediously gothic concept. It's like skating across a slackly pinned leaf of India paper. Like dancing on rubber. He knows it's going to give, to plunge him into a bottomless shaft. It wavers, holds. Sileen's weight causes the page to bow. He daren't move. He's lost his place. *Senses dazed, through the space of an eternal moment.* Gigantic words are projected on the floor, the walls. Any sudden shift and disbelief will falter. An abandoned draft crumpled in the wastebasket.

Hush! I hear something.

This was Askead's *Book at Bedtime* gone mad. Actorly baritones lending unwarranted emphasis to Hodgson's riffs. (Trollopean placemen. Iraqi ambassadors on the run, pulpit-posh. Voices of the condemned.) Sileen couldn't stop his ears, block out what he himself composed. The feeblest advance might turn a page. And when it ended, when the hogs broke in? Would Hodgson's unpublished sequel reveal itself? Would Sileen's fatal wounds be dressed by sentences he might never read?

Steps on the stairs; strange paddling steps, that come up and nearer . . .

Paddling. What a terrible word! The suggestion that the stairs are wet, that webbed feet bring their own liquids from the depths. Not just the neutral script: sound effects. Sileen, as he shuffles, is accompanied, cursed, by memory – what he remembers stays at his side. Footfalls in a drowned basement. A rising river tide. He's seen too much. He obeys, climbs the spiral that he cannot see. Too many years of grazing on quota quickies, budgets that barely ran to secondhand sets, dwarfs in monkey pelts, taxi girls with mousetrap grins: he knew that *any* ascent was a big mistake. (Van Heflin in Losey's *The Prowler* scrabbling up a – mound!) Victims develop a congenital stair fetish. Child stars make their comeback to find something nasty in the attic. Peculiarly dim snoops abseil towards the camera in an old dark house. Punks on the run. It always boils down to: jump from the roof or catch a bullet in your teeth.

Fear, that formulaic hack, stocked Kinder Street with out-of-copyright ghouls, swinefolk, hitmen, Emanuel Swedenborg's mantic skull. Amino acid steps conveyanced parallel versions of this raid. The plunge into nightmare. Rungs of ladders twisted into pairs: adenine, thymine, guanine, cytosine. Hodgson and Todd Sileen. Word for word. *Fumbling at the doorhandle.*

It opened at a touch. A thought. Opened before him as he approached. *Somethi . . . Unfinished. A faint line of ink.* The options had run out. A serrated leaf of light. There must be some mistake. Was he back in the hospital? Had the wind blown the pages over?

Glass and mahogany cabinets, a time-defying immanence of wood. Sileen thirsted to sniff the varnish, lick the glue. He'd been granted a second life, a final séance in the X-ray chamber. The walls were self-reflecting, packed with grey and hooded books. Sileen peered closely, trying to make out the titles. There were no titles. The books were jacketed in soft lead to protect them from the siren songs of radon daughters. The cabinets were locked.

Drage-Bell's library was an installation that would win no prizes for originality. Windowless, stark. The cabinets overlooked a high solarized bed – which still retained volatile heat impressions of previous occupation: scarlet and green contour lines. Only here was the intelligencer safe. Unobserved, he could endure protracted transfusions.

Surveillance cameras could not operate within the electromagnetic maze. Drage-Bell would lie back, feeding greedily from his captive texts: books, uncorrected proofs, manuscripts. The spider of the Finsen Light Machine hung over the black couch, its telescopic arms emitting silent, soothing pulses. Etching sentences into the spook's carotid artery.

Light was withdrawn from the shelved books and played over the cadaverous form of the hibernating bibliophile. Drage-Bell drained the paper husks of their vital moisture. To bask on this bed was to pass into negative, renounce form and structure, erase all boundaries.

Rest. Sleep. Sileen's presence was evidence, his breath a signed confession. He circled the upraised plank, reading it as an altar, then a chopping board. Perhaps there had never been a manuscript, only the dream, the perfect uncommitted prototype. What if he laid himself down on the shining slab?

The door is opening slowly. Something marvellous. A soft white light began to glow in the room. The flames of candles shone through it, palely. I looked from side to side, and found that I could still see each piece of furniture; but in a strangely unreal way, more as though the ghost of each table and chair had taken the place of a solid article.

The text was folding back on itself. There was no knowing which – if any – of the lead books secreted the *Borderland* manuscript. Sileen brushed the mahogany with his hand. The cabinet moved. Glass, revolving, distorted the cripple's face. The cabinets slid noiselessly around him. There was no longer any gap between them. No ceiling, no floor. Glass everywhere. A globe.

As the house had been reversed, so now was the room: like William Yeats' egg. Sileen, the outsider, trapped within. Too close an attendance on the rhythms of the text had blinded him to events elsewhere, the broader picture: failure to deconstruct. Antecedents, disciples, alternate realities. He had followed Hodgson to the exclusion of Poe, Borges, Wells. Lead spines melted to scarlet blades. Time paradoxes, derivations, spectral twins. Machen, Catling, Shiel. Biographies lasered into glass. Stoker, Stevenson. The room of flesh. Memory gills. He was inside a cell that could no longer be entered, which did not exist – and would never be found from the street below. The building was demolished. Kinder Street struck from the guidebooks. A conversation killer in forgotten bars. A misquotation in the hazy mythos of East London. Waves of corrugated silver, scaffolding screened by translucent sheets that distort and intensify the passage of clouds. Sycamores bursting from the roof.

Sileen staggered, fell. He pressed against the now vertical couch, clung to it for life. Solarized disturbance. The chill of rubber. He tumbled and spun as the room settled. Sweated from its magnetic core.

Nothing beneath him, black sky. His pillow was hard. He thumped it, shook it, beat its shape. (Thought of the notebook he had lost.) Not feathers, nor foam: the pillow was bundled paper, tied with string. Tarred knots marked his cheek. He sat up. The glass walls retreated. His couch, beneath the steady drip of Finsen Light, was isolated. If the room had edges he couldn't see them. Warehouse space, a clicking from contracting (or expanding) panes. Like the depth echo of whales.

The manuscript!

The creosoted twine was difficult to slip, the brittle yellow paper torn. A covering letter, an introduction with the author's address: 'Glaneifion', Borth, Cardiganshire. Date: November 1907. Was Hodgson's sequel written *before* the *Borderland*, perhaps even before he moved to Wales? Or was it composed concurrently, in a single sitting? At the conclusion of the earlier book?

Sileen shuffled the pages: he was terrified to read, to conclude his ramshackle quest. He could not step into the marvellous light of intelligence that invaded the recluse's chamber through this partially opened door. The soft gold of unlearned poetry. Candles without heat – causing solid objects to give place to kinder accounts of themselves. A light in which visionary and vision are one.

That is what Sileen *wanted* to believe. Whatever was most foreign to his spirit. Whatever, most effectively, betrayed his darker self. The abdication of motive and will. Silent obedience. The witness who is forbidden to report.

He lifted the first page of the manuscript into the beam of a Finsen telescope. Veins in the paper, clots, creamy obstructions, interwoven pith. He was unable to separate subcutaneous fat from polished surface. He could see no words. Black letters were printed into the curved lens of his eye. They *could* be read – but not by him, not by Sileen. By some impartial observer, a joker with a cosmic budget.

He was weak. He couldn't keep the pages up. He sank, head on pillow. On the unbound manuscript. An obstacle between the closely-written pages and the persistence of light.

FOUR

'Fucking miracle, Tone, what they done to that church.'

'Nicky?'

'Better than new it is.'

'I'm tellin' you, bro, this *is* the place. We was bunkin' off school with the Moody Boys and Tommy South. Don't fuck me about. Poxy shed round the back of the swimming-pool, what they chucked us out of?'

'Money well spent, son. Look and learn. Urban fucking renewal.'

Insulated behind a blue-tint screen, high on the engine's cash-burning purr, they argued the toss down the length of the Highway. Fraternal banter, that bilious eructation of unattributed opinion, evolved into argument. Obedient to their roots, conversation was seen as the necessary foreplay to violence. Keep it in the family. Like Oedipus.

The white church jackknifed as Nicholas Tarten made the difficult right-hander into Cannon Street Road. Anthony was still kvetching. He wouldn't let it go. His displeasure was specific. Nicholas clucked, shook his head, lifted manicured mitts from the wheel in a gesture of resignation.

'We're talking power steering, Anthony, and you ain't even got no provisional, son.'

'I'm down as the fucking driver, Nick. I heard you tell the bint with the hair.' He might be outranked, cerebrally, by his sibling, but he knew how to needle. He had enough of his old mum in him to support a wicked tongue.

'Call me Nick one more time and you can walk, you fat cunt.'

'Leave it out. You show yourself up, Nicky. You do. Ponce in without a minder – and who's the cunt then?'

It was agreed. Anthony would be allowed to *park* the Merc – under supervision. Nicholas Tarten swung the gunmetal investment in through the gates of St George-in-the-East. He pulled up, engine running, while he checked his presentation in the rearview mirror; sliding Belmondo glasses onto the bump of his nose, palming the razored scalp for a fast buzz. He flicked up the collar of his camelhair. Magic! Went a treat, he thought, with the freshly ironed white T-shirt. A calculated blend of boardroom and gym. The spirit of the times made manifest. That's what fashion is all about.

'Know what, Tone? I could have pissed the Jagger part in *Performance*. What's he got, little tart? You could do Foxy. Why not, son? We knew all them faces from the old days – Johnny Shannon, David Litvinoff. I could have been the next John Bindon. Walked it, brother.'

Anthony shlepped around to open the driver's door, still muttering darkly. Nicky had persuaded him, or most of him, into a suit. More off-the-wall than off-the-peg. He hadn't heard that the double-breasted cut was reserved for wallies from the sticks who used hair-gel to keep their ears back. The jacket gripped his shoulders like clingfilm, while the compensatory excesses of the trousers concertinaed over lacquered hooves. Anthony was not himself in stripes. The shirt had been wrenched open at the throat, and the tie, coarsely knotted, was stapled – like a rasher of bacon – to his dewlaps.

Cheap material split in a gash as the chunky minder craned himself in behind the wheel. He revved, ground at reverse, backed a few feet, shot forward in a spastic lurch, came to rest against a family-sized sepulchre. Honour was satisfied.

Novice pedestrians, they moved awkwardly north – pausing to exchange non sequiturs, unwrap wafers of gum, pass remarks on dogs and the buttocks of women. The Pakis were another thing. The birds in bags. Nothing but eyes. Surgical masks. You need a drink to look at them. Turning the city into a hospital ward. If you've got it, show it. That's the Cockney way. Call a spade a coon. Unless he's mobhanded. No disrespect. Anthony was shocked to the core, the way the area had gone down. A geezer in polka-dot Bermuda shorts looned past, jabbering into his mobile. 'Would you care for fifteen ounces of heroin at all?' These yuppies were a pox on the streets.

Where *was* Nicky? Anthony sussed the doorways. His brother had vanished. Maybe he was taking a piss behind some motor? On his own, Anthony was a few cards short of a full deck: he fretted. Was reduced to earwigging his own unbroken monologue. 'What's 'e mean, provisional, 'e ain't got no licence 'isself. Only the one 'e's out on. And the Merc's bent, lippy cunt.'

He had reached the corner, the junction with Cable Street: a tricky one, this quadrivium, the choice of cardinal directions. Anthony swayed, undecided, on the kerb. He looked left towards the promise of the city, and right – towards nothing in particular. He was reluctant to go on, determined not to remain. Unprimed, he waited for orders. Sophisticates would define his behaviour as as 'anxiety attack'. He hyperventilated and hugged the Crown & Dolphin. Truly alone. An existential nettle that takes some grasping, even by the best of us. There was no comfort to be had in the opaque windows of the public-house, no salvation in the fancy tower that monitored Swedenborg Gardens.

Lacking a mandate to advance, Anthony turned back. Pavements, already travelled, were stranger in retreat. Starboard out, port home. Quite wrong. Nicholas Tarten stood where he started, legs apart, eyes behind mirrors. Anthony, finding no reassurance in the face, zoomed to his brother's fingers. The focus of his rage. They were rolling a tighter and tighter ball of silver paper. 'Alright then?' Anthony remembered the gum. It wasn't long ago. Their separation had been a blip on the screen, a temporary assertion of individual identity, not a divorce.

'*And*?' Nicky was smoking. Not good.

Anthony gloomed at his brother. 'And?' What did that mean? Swift-footed Bengalis brushed, like shaken blossom, against them. Nicholas Tarten was rooted. A twist of blue smoke hung in the still air, an arabesque with which the occasional smoker had colluded.

'And – where fucking are they then?'

'*What*? Where are what, Nick?'

'The bags, cunt. The poxy bags.'

'Don't call me cunt, cunt.'

'Cunt's flattering you, cunt. You got more mouth than Muscat's best brass.'

'You what?'

'Fetch the bags out, Anthony. Anthony? OK, son? The cases.'

'Right then. You should 'ave fucking said, Nick.'

'Anthony.'

'What?'

'Give your brother a kiss.'

They patted, slobbered, feinted, jabbed. Manners, that's all it took.

He wanted to watch his fucking lip, Nicky did. One day some cunt who couldn't appreciate his sense of humour would shove a shooter right down his craw. He loved his brother. Loved him to death. Grow up sharing a bed, you're bonded. Mums, brothers, motors, dogs: the Eastenders' code.

Blocking potential peepers with his bulk, Anthony sprang the boot of the Merc and hauled out two brand-new sportsbags. You could snort the straw in the canvas, the bull in the tough straps: no poofy plastic held together with sticky spikes (like strips of old hairbrush). Nicky was a traditionalist where accoutrements were concerned. The bags felt good to carry, their weight was nothing. Anthony was a man defined by his luggage. He could walk in anywhere.

Nicky's arm around Anthony's shoulder. Blaspheming, spoiling for it. Hip to hip. Stopping, setting down the bags, squaring up. Slapping palms, giving tongue. The brothers forged their eccentric progress towards the Sly Street call.

FIVE

Anthony knelt to unbuckle the straps. 'Unzip for the ladies, Tone.' The remark was in poor taste, but Nicky could never resist a demi-entendre. Playing patron aroused him. The ladies, sitting rather stiffly on the new chaise-longue, held their breath. Helen couldn't get used to this furniture: the kind of stuff that would be far happier on a pavement in Bethnal Green. Flash repro – as touted towards the rear of the colour supplements, alongside designer rubberwear, *drif's guide*, fishermen's smocks. The brilliant red leather faded by sunlight. It still amused her to play Nicky Tarten's game: to watch the guileless web of corruption unravel.

Helen was going up in the world. Or so Tarten thought. The chaise-longue was his gift. He had an interest in a local sawdust and horsehair establishment, and a fondness for the environs of Columbia Market, out of season – baking bread, cobbled laneways, pot shops that were never open. Nicky had his sentimental side. Life wasn't all gash and gravestones. Helen/Isabel, his protégée, she needed, in the nicest possible way, a bit of a kick up the jacksie. The ambience of her flat was a downer. Bare boards, khazi behind a curtain, mattress on the floor. She might call it bohemian, he reckoned it shamed her. Living like an immigrant. He decided to put a few bob into brightening things up, exorcising that slag Sileen – the one who had slung his hook, turned tramp, taken to the road.

'You want to be a headliner, darlin', start indoors. Live like a celebrity and you're halfway there.' Nicky had built the set from scratch. Like an artist, a writer. James Herbert, Shaun Hutson. He used his imagination, mixed and matched: World of Leather pastiches in knobbly claret – but polished. New antiques. Brass (both senses) bed, Italian blinds, glass table (like a window on its side) – heaped with chunky mags, catalogues, paint news. A showflat for a showgirl. Mail-order loft living. The Big Apple pressed till the pips squeaked. Dockland detritus liberated when the Aztec anthills went belly up.

Helen enjoyed Nicholas Tarten. He was her Mills & Boon, a harmless addiction, something to binge on – infrequently. He stayed so resolutely in character that he began to frighten her. There *must* be more. Fear was the buzz. He was predictable but not secure. She'd never face him alone. Andi had responded to her request and moved in; spending her days roaming the streets, making enquiries, searching for Sofya Court. She carried Sofya's camera, no film. There were rumours, people who wanted to talk, but no definite sightings. They all remembered the Leica, not the girl. Always some disaster after she'd gone: a crash, a fire, a handbag snatched.

Nicky stood beside the ultra low coffee-table. Stooping to lay out the items Anthony passed him from the open bags. Still in his coat, he handled the merchandise like a market trader, fondling it, pinching the cellophane, whistling at labels. All top dollar stuff. He talked up colour, texture, style. Then shot the cork from a bottle of fizz. Foam gushed and rapidly overspilled the flutes.

The women dutifully sipped, suppressing laughter. They'd never been to a lingerie party before. All it needed now was for Anthony to step forward to model the range. Laurel and Hardy repping Ann Summers. They kept their eyes modestly in their laps. One false move, one nudge, and they'd have to stuff pillows in their mouths, roll on the floor, shred the Peruvian rug.

The lace-up boxing boots had distinct possibilities. Helen immediately tried them on, lifting her long skirt, lying back, kicking her legs. Nicky agreed, very effective.

'Don't take my word, girl, 'ave a gander in the glass. Knock out. Anthony, what snappers do we know, you'd trust not to bottle it? Bailey? You're right, my son, passé. Too flash. Lord Lichfield? One who does the calendars and the portrait of Ronnie's second bride? Pricey. *White Women*, that's what I'm thinking of. The kraut with clout, Newton. Something you'd fancy, but can't afford. A collector's piece from the off, this poster.'

The shorts, loose at the sides, tight on the crotch, were acrylic tulip heads, a slither of counterfeit silk. The kind Page Three girls model when they promenade, bums out, arms aloft, tuft-free, holding up a numbered card between rounds. No, thanks! Helen vetoed them on sight. Nicky, setting down his drink, was sleighted. Took her point. He'd see what else he could lay his hands on.

The wrap was a beaut. Anklelength, hooded, a yellow tiger with rhinestone eyes stood in for the Wapping Wildcat. One of Nigel Benn's rejects, Helen guessed. Too reticent for the Dark Destroyer.

Up on her toes, she threw deadly combinations at slender shadows cast by floorlevel mushroom lamps. Sh-nuff, sh-nuff. She managed the sound all pugs make – like snorting pepper backwards. Sneeze foreplay. The new boots squeaked and teased.

'How about vests? Deco eyes and claws on a black background? Or just the name, sans serif? What do you think, Anthony?' She wheeled, to bring him in: one-two, one-two-three-four to the midriff.

Tone coloured. Nicky wadded gum into his cheek and bunsened a fresh cigarette. Both men were suddenly devoted to the pattern in the rug. Studied nonchalance, elbowplay.

'Nah, see, point is, darlin' . . .' Nicky planed the dark glasses up and down the bump in his nose. 'This is proper pro fighting, innit . . . Isn't it? Vests is ama-chers.' He could do the voices for hours when he needed to play dumb. Not for nothing was Muscat on the payroll. The Maltese pimp was the perfect model for a linguistically-challenged rube.

Helen's nails flicked at the rim of her empty flute, waiting to hear it all. Nicky, bringing a refill, planted himself beside her on the couch – a fatherly hand to gentle her knee.

'You've seen the pros on tele, barechest. Like Chippendales. Victor Mature. Play fair, girl, you can't go up against the expectations of your clientele. There's ample gear for the pair of you. Take your time, anything you fancy. No charge.'

Tarten shook out the last reluctant drops. Should he send Tone to the off-licence, make an evening of it? The brothers were at it again, on the couch – swearing, threatening mutilation, having a great time.

What was the closing score between Erskine and Cooper? Amateur and pro. 'Jolting Joe' and 'Our 'Enry', the Lloyd's name. Nicky, it turned out, was an Erskine man, a ringcraft buff. Lose a few pounds and he'd have walked the cruiserweights. World class. The night with Willie Pastrano? Masterly. We had a few laughs, over the years, down in Tiger Bay. Benny Jacobs, one of the best. Cooper? Nice sharp hook, but a bleeder. The Bishop handled him like a diamond in a lump of coal. Jim

Wicks, what a pedigree that man had! 1936, Wandsworth Greyhounds, he was there when Massimino Columbo got carved.

The girls had slipped, unnoticed, behind the beaded curtain, into the bedroom. *Girls?* Why not shaft Tarten at his own game? Let the lumpen brothers hear what they wanted to. Let them picture it. Squeals of fake/real pleasure as Helen rescued some novel vanity from the sportsbag.

Nicky was at the window. The booze was gone. He smoked in expectant melancholy. Separating the slats with his fingers, he looked down on the rain-slicked Sly Street. No action. Anthony, panting, glad to be of service, shifted furniture, made room for the show.

Sputum in a dry swallow. Nicky was usually immune, blessed with the smoker's desensitized mouth. Beef tasted like cod. Cod tasted like codpiece. Footsteps on his grave. Telegraphed intimations of mortality. It came together in an instant: the sampling of essence, nose sand, and the sight of his brother, arms hanging like an idiot, making faces at himself in the mirror. It had never occurred to Nicky before, as it occurred, cogently now, that his brutal sibling should, in his physical pomp, be intact, untested – a virgin. And might this assumed celibacy not be an affective factor in Tone's lacklustre presentation amongst his peers in betting-shop and boozer? Would it be feasible, even at this late juncture, to ignite that slumbering consciousness by a quick dip at the furry oyster? What, in point of fact, was the nature and extent of the inner life of this creature who had, thus far, been defined exclusively by physical acts? Does he dream? (Is the comedy taking place in this gaff a function of that dreaming?) Is he bent? Has his longterm institutionalized lifestyle gifted him with a taste for shirtlifting? Must Nicholas Tarten, the biblical keeper, take responsibility for Anthony Tarten's moral welfare? Is he responsible for his brother's distress? Does Tone, without Nicky's 'writing' of him, have *any* independent existence?

A bit of a facer, this. Postponed by the sound of beads parting. A jazzy shimmer: shattered cocktail-glasses reforming. Smarties dropped into the neck of a milkbottle. Teasing feet were peeping through. The curtain was the costume. Red boots. A musical interlude to lift the gloom. A snatch from *Gentlemen Prefer Blondes*. Helen had activated something brassy and dangerous. Various blues and greens upstaged each other as more and more leg appeared. Tone chose to keep the action within the frame of the mirror – which made it more like art.

Nicky toughed it out. A shrug inside the camelhair, fists clenched: nothing given away.

How to phrase his offer with delicacy: that the big one, Handi Andi, should take this boy into the bedroom and give him a seeing to? Nicky's palms sweated and cracked. How much should he lay out? A pony? Fifty notes? Not too heavy, but enough to show good faith. She wasn't a slag, this salt. Educated. But she could certainly use a few bob for tights, cosmetics, the full body wax.

The girls had stymied him with this turnout, it would be gauche to interrupt. Anthony was like Gibraltar – immovable (with monkeys on his back). For him, the scrubbers were figures in a frieze. Nicky was the audience: attentive, distracted. Spiked by social niceties.

A buzzer shrilled on his wrist. He should have been out of here hours since. The girls took it for a sign and touched gloves. Circled, sparred. 'Throws plenty of leather, Helen,' Nicky admitted, 'give Felix his due. But the other salt's got the punch. Moves well inside.'

The red boots screeched and slithered on the boards. Sh-nuff, sh-nuff. One-two, one-two-three-four. Faked leads, swift combinations. Their naked bodies rosy where the blows fell. They shone, warming to their work, as Nicky, hidden behind dark glasses, regressed to stone.

SIX

The dizzy, hazy feeling passed, and I saw, clearly. The ocean. The outhaul. Rolling and turning. Within it, a cell of light, breaking from a breaking wave – rushing, somersaulting, disorientated, breathless. Left behind, exposed. A stereophonic persistence of surf. Sunlight absorbed. Salt crystals. Warmed. Shrunken. Dried.

Into the beam. Radiant ropes. Extinguished. He dies. *Senses dazed.* Sunlight and shore. Warm milk trickling into an earth trench. The fountain! Sweet watery milk of the nun's bosom. Chest torn open, pelican pecking at flesh, gorging on blood. Old man with fish beard. Rain.

The broad meniscus of the bay. Cyles and generations of waves. Wind-ruffled surfaces. The sky: uniform, complementary greys. Fresh rain cutting his face.

The heap of pages beneath his head, the pillow of burnt words. Uncollated? Unread! No human had looked on the manuscript since the time of its composition. His head is shaved, his eyes masked. Body strapped. He cannot turn or twist. *A murmurous noise of Swine-laughter. Silence . . . clogged with horror.* Drage-Bell. The intelligencer. That voice.

The Finsen Light Machine overhead, its ultraviolet whispers. Soothing and healing the flushed and insulted skin. Inch by sorry inch, assuaging cancerous growths, the warts and chanterelles of a spiteful fecundity. Repairing him, scouring his spoiled crust. Tender Sileen, flayed by innocent beams. The machine is an udder, dispensing hot texts onto his new red body. Anonymous hands have washed away the dirt of the road. He is prepared: patient or sacrifice.

The voice again, it had never ceased: councillor, conduit. Drage-Bell. How he hated (depended upon) that name. Something encountered in a previous life. Droning, uninflected, a throat lacking all lubrication.

Dust. A self-denying sperm-drinker. Bricks have more animation. Not many know: they use them, Cockneys, to castrate dogs. Sileen couldn't take in what the copper was saying. The instructions were overlaid by moaning from the other side of the wall: o-oh-ohhh!-o. Dulcet apologies of sexual congress, the fluting rush of the woman, the appeasing growl of the male. What has *this* to do with the case?

Conditions, clauses, contracts. The impotent spook is giving him the score. Sileen's a prisoner, an experiment. He's read about such things (dot matrix composition). But *why*? There's no news left in him, nothing the man could want. Todd Sileen? Ask any of the faces, he's an open book.

The humming stops, the machine withdraws. *A white haze of light*. Rain falling on Sileen's exposed face. Cold hands remove the blackened goggles: war! His enemy is in the room. Sileen can smell him: aniseed and mouse droppings, immutable socks. A hole in the roof. Rain streams vertically out of the night.

The voice. Drage-Bell.

'Say hello to the "Starrs Mall", kaffir, our theatre of secrets. You've earned it, old son, you really have. A commendation in the Book of the Dead – for pig iron stupidity. Good sport, my efforts to discourage the mob: cheesy rumours, Swedenborg's skull, flash floods, Shining Path. Penny Arcade mumbo jumbo. All for your benefit.'

'Bad,' Sileen thought, 'the worst yet. Renouncing fiction, I've landed myself with a plot so preposterous it would make Dame Agatha blush, a Masters-of-the-Universe pitch too crass to be tacked onto a posthumous Ian Fleming flick.' The gimp cursed the failure of his imagination. Couldn't he, a card-carrying masochist, conjure up a more convincing torment? He was drowning, yellow on the table, in a house of expired narratives.

Try poetry as an antidote, a purge. What have we got for asylums, light you can't trust? Scrape the memory. 'There is something in this madhouse that I symbolize – / This city – nightmare – black –.' No use, much too close to home.

Drage-Bell's auditory hallucination bored on, the transcript of Sileen's agony. He became the editor of his own grief. Returning consciousness, tuned by the building's Osirian alignment, required a spokesman – an update for the storyline. What was he facing now? Rebirth among Orion's Seven Stars? His jaw, broken open, postmortem, by a hook of meteorite? Bell's limited tonal range inspired flights of interstellar fancy. Bell was what must be left behind. But Bell was unstoppable. When the ringing ceased, Sileen would be dead.

The rain, he decided, was time. No going back or forward, or even staying put. Boundaries lost. Pellets of wasted light fall from somewhere infinitely far away and are converted into sound. Drage-Bell. The drone. Sileen twisted in his restraints. He was wired. They were feeding him gash cinema, degraded tapes. Forcing him to open his eyes on the field of stars. They were tapping him, leeching confessions, monstrous essays he thought he had destroyed.

This was why they had pampered him with such subtle torments. This was the essence of their care. Drage-Bell wanted to scan the Hodgson sequel through Sileen. It wasn't enough to collect and entomb the books. Not enough to gather dust jackets and art work. Not enough to possess proofs, typescripts, manuscripts, notebooks, photo albums, lockets of pubic hair. *He wanted the man's brain at his service*: a larceny of engrams, neural traces to capture the persistence of memory. Drage-Bell would feast on Sileen's skull: a silver-spoon cannibal. Hope Hodgson could then be forgiven the solecism of death. He was disposable. Sileen was now the conduit. His suffering mitigated the over-excited prose, translating it into sidereal symbols. He would dream the unwritten sequel, smear blank nicotine pages with language coordinates.

The cripple was flawed: a natural medium, a pain addict. He was the perfect future plagiarist, thieving fictions that could never be completed, cruising slush piles like a resurrectionist. Nature, jesting, had made him an artist – fit only to soak up experience, with no mandate to explain or defend. The intelligencer had simply to hotwire Sileen's fantasies, transcribe the paranoid fugues, shadow him into fractal landscapes of anxiety.

The wretched man had been monitored from the beginning – and told of it, openly, so that he might grow used to the condition. He'd been tracked through all his absurd travels, fed clues, starved, beaten, humiliated, brought to a state of complete physical exhaustion. Nothing was left but the dreams, the images: beach, triangular field, watchtower. How had Hodgson managed to refine his vision to such basic elements? How had he freed himself from them?

Sileen still did not understand. They *wanted* his weakness, his stupidity, the absence of any moral inhibitions. He must put aside resistance, give himself up to the experiment. It was his best hope, the only hope there was. To let go, disembodied mind, an aspect of the climate. Out of that darkness he would dictate William Hope Hodgson's suppressed masterpiece.

The Starrs Mall. Sileen: an insignificant extra. This cunningly contrived and painstakingly aligned theatre was a special kind of cutting-room. They were cutting his flesh, burning off the skin – slowly, painfully, sentence by sentence, allowing time for reason to make its escape, move outwards and upwards, into the night, among ice stars that had no purpose beyond reflecting and distorting events on earth. When the rain stopped and the clouds cleared – he could surely achieve that by his own volition – beams of intelligence would trace their symbols on his purged skin.

A fretful soliloquy. The cause of his agitation. Silence.

SEVEN

Something brought Imar O'Hagan to the window. Usually, painting, absorbed in the familiar reflex gestures of self-portraiture, he was oblivious to noise, conversation, natural phenomena. He had wielded his pallet knife through proximate miscarriages, bathtub abortions, meths' drinkers laboured expositions of Blake's Los entering London (the 'immense artificial mound or hill' in Old Ford), serial buggery, feast, famine, all the average egoic excesses of invading architects, social visionaries, starvation-budget TV crews, the unceasing kisses and collisions of midnight throngs on the pavement outside.

This was different. An absence, something missing. He stuck his head, paintbrush in mouth, out of the window. Shocked hair: an aureole of linseed eels. His vest hung loose above baggy (and punning) dungarees.

It could hardly be called a silence – a pre-storm lull, voices dropping before the boots fly in. Threat as a condition of light. Irritations which, being removed, seem necessary to the locale's amour-propre. The migraine thud of helicopters overhead. Watchers, pursuivants. They weren't there. The lack of smell from fire-damaged stock, drenched by high-pressure hoses. Even with soggy bread jammed in your ears you could always register the street brawls, the slap and tickle of robust domestic altercations, hissing steam-presses, revving vans.

Imar was a fatalist, not a cultural historian. 'Fuck 'em' was his code. Leave well alone. He rolled a scrawny cigarette and went back to slashing at the canvas. Pile up the paint, draw the living skeleton out. He was working from the wrong side – building up, scraping away, smearing. The canvas was a barrier, a resistant veil. He had got the blistering of the lips, the wet pink of the eye – what did that achieve? Nothing. Worthless – until the portrait spoke back, cursed him in his own language.

Sweat dripped. He panted, let the knife fall and went at the bleeding likeness with his fists. Boredom and ecstasy were a feather apart. Exhausted, he paused – peering intently into the glass which was propped alongside the upturned trestle to which he had pinned the canvas. Time was with him. He had knocked out a couple of small Bacons and an undernourished Auerbach, the tubes of paint were rolled and flattened at his feet in a snail-world suicide pact. The walls were smeared with years of false starts and wristy flicks of overload. (He thought he might pass them off as kosher Lucian Freud.)

The noise thing would not have concerned him if he hadn't been listening, keeping half an ear open, for a hammering at the streetdoor. He'd invited Helen round, to discuss a portrait in her boxing gear. Tarten's notion. He wanted a picture worthy of its frame to hang on the walls of his office – when he had one. When he was promoting at York Hall and the Docklands' Arena. When he'd made it and the *Insight* team were publishing mass-market paperbacks about the complexities of his off-shore empire (golf clubs in boot, bullion under bed). When he was a two minder villain with an outrageous mohair habit.

The street was dead. It felt wrong – as if it had been sealed for a shoot. The usual bricks, the bench outside the pub: no people, no companionable buzz of conspiracy, no undertow. Freakish. Heneage Street had been stripped of its wildtrack: road drills, planes, ambulances, wind, weather. Cillick-Klaw, a film-on-TV buff, sensed it himself – his impersonation of the last-man-alive-in-city-under-threat (fawn raincoat to ankles, tattered briefcase, snivelling/sinister Dickie Attenborough eyes). More paint, deeper shadows required. A neurotic motif on the soundtrack, reprising the main theme. An expressionist sequence featuring tilted doorways, undercranked clouds, the black eagle on the brewery pediment, church spire beyond a chaotic assembly of roofs, cat arching against trouser leg, Klaw's reflection in horsetrough filled with rainwater.

He posed, a snatched glance over the shoulder: he'd got it. *Seven Days To Noon*. Barry Jones. The power to blow up London. Big CU: key in lock.

In the dim hallway Klaw thumbed his lighter. Terrified the air would burn around him like curtains of gauze. The gas of ages whistling from sacks of old books. Lumps of things that had been called art. And were now things again. Silver-skinned catering cans. Bottles of hair.

Unsorted evidence. A horribly faded photograph of faces in the crowd, graveyard sepia, staring at the sky: some unrevealed horror, an endless fly-past.

Klaw's instinct – stop, search, evaluate – countered by footsteps overhead. He wanted to break in on O'Hagan unannounced: soft-footed, enigmatic. Catch the bastard at it, pants down. Manifest himself (*The Dream Detective*) when least expected, a cutting remark scripted and rehearsed.

'Bugger off out of my light, for fuck's sake.' O'Hagan, dripping carmine, is justifiably aggrieved. It's no longer *his* light. He loses himself, loses the moment. Klaw, like a sinister portrait, has been pasted in his place. O'Hagan, on the canvas, is only partly there: an interrupted transplant, a half-invented man. He's forced, he doesn't drop the brush, to incorporate the spook into the evolving mess – rip off his sunken cheeks, his hooter, the hair. While Klaw, for his part, preferred to catch the eye in the mirror, and leave the real O'Hagan well alone. Bound by shameful secrets, they collaborated to bring each other down.

'Do you happen to know the origin of your street name?' Klaw offered, falling back on bogus pedantry. 'Heneage. One of those vanished London sounds, compound of silage and hay, recalling an arcadian past, orchards, hens, a white and dusty road. Evocation of better times, come round again. Thomas Heneage, knight, Walsingham's paymaster. The George Smiley of his day. Unacknow-ledged magus of Elizabethan counter-terror. I've always modelled myself on him. No headline-grabber, no grandstanding fraud, he pulled the strings, guarded the realm while lesser men slept. A face at court, a keeper of accounts, runner of agents. Heneage was death's purser. He scored out Christopher Marlowe's name in the ledger, jingled coins to satisfy furious men, men without conscience – men like you. Lice. Maggots. Grubs. Celts, cod Papists, versifiers. Playmakers pandering to the mob. Follow my argument? The street itself is tainted. You've got no choice. A name, properly lodged, burns through time, revealing everything to those who've learnt to read.'

O'Hagan moved in front of Klaw, blocking him out, reclaiming the glass. The new perspective revealed a new man. Angel magick on the cheap. He stretched to repair the damage.

'As your landlord and sponsor, I demand no kickbacks,' Klaw lied, testing the tackiness of the loucher Bacon by scratching the snotty green with his nail. 'But I must consider my actuarial responsibilities – book-keepers wanting chitties for every coffee consumed. You wouldn't believe the bumf it costs me, son, letting you run. Funding is under the cosh. They're threatening VAT on snouts. I need a major spectacle and I need it soon. The boys in Five are jaded. Pubs and shopping-malls won't get it up. You've got to grab them with a primetime blitz. Battersea Dogs' Home springs to mind – but the outcry might cost us our majority. A moderately offensive strike is what we're targeting – kiddies' playground up north, or the London Hospital. Don't go mad, not the whole edifice, just one wing; Out-patients, Isolation, whatever takes your fancy. Grand Hotel, Brighton, on the Richter scale – collapsing floors, oodles of photogenic smoke, wraiths in bandages wandering confused. Nothing too baroque. Honest indignation. "Bring back the rope." Provoke the couch-potatoes to channel hop, not burst into the streets. Wave down a cab with your AK47, send in a mule, one of your women, corseted in plastic. But move before the bedroom capers bring us down.'

A discreet rattle at the streetdoor. Or had it been in Klaw's throat? They changed position. O'Hagan to the window. Klaw addressing the portrait. Confusion.

Helen outside, looking up, sees O'Hagan. Under the normal rules of engagement he would have to let her in. Klaw panics. O'Hagan doesn't move. Scratches himself. Warms a hand in the crook of his arm. Pumps that arm to make a leathery, sucking sound. Klaw is a gyroscope of unease. He *can't* be seen. Not here, not in East London. He's one of the Invisibles, a hologramatic insert at times of national tragedy, frowning at craters when the smoke has cleared. Insiders might catch a glimpse in clubland as he steps out of a black Daimler. Spot him through binoculars at Bisley. The Burghley Horse Trials in an unsuitable hat (like Douglas Fairbanks Jnr with a Tyrolean feather!). Two ladies, talking, might nudge each other. Klaw's bodyheat never violates the emulsion. He's never taped. His minders sweep strip-joints and peep arcades before he ducks downstairs to conduct one of his social surveys.

Heneage Street! Members of White's were not supposed to know where that was. Tower Hamlets meant a box at the Barbican. Bloomsbury was where the glaciers began. 'For God's sake, Paddy, get me out!'

O'Hagan, swallow-diving, brought him down; winded him as he tried to flee.

'You can't go up there.'

'Whyever not? I own the sordid hovel. I'll go where I want.'

'A woman. She's taking a nap.'

'You've killed her, you bitch. Done her in.'

Cillick-Klaw previewed the headlines, blood on his hands. His 'K' was bollocksed. This fellow, O'Hagan, was an animal. Where did he find them all, the compliant drabs? What was his secret? The old art scam – or a mule's dick? They should have had him doctored years ago. No woman was safe. (That's what they loved: the interest he took.) Wives and daughters to the hill-station. These tinkers from the bogs (O'Hagan was a West Midlander, born and bred) are all the same, gas and gonad. He was well overdue. Take him out. Whack him along with the hospital. Pin the whole caper on the bastard. Clear the backlog: Baltic Exchange, London Wall, Colchester, Oxford.

'This can't be happening to me.' O'Hagan was shoving him into a metal cupboard, folding him like serge into a tall narrow space, one of those locker room affairs: plunder from the Monster Doss House. A vanishing trick for grey men. Key turned. Click of the lock.

Keeper of the Queen's peace, he crouched in the dark, elbows rubbing against cold tin, grateful to discover three points of light – which could be adapted, if he stayed on his knees, as peepholes. He heard it, then saw it: the woman's legs, sheathed, sheer black – a mechanistic, Allen Jones segment of calf; under tension, curving, narrowing towards the ankle, the artfully elevated heels. He panted. Textures in the gossamer, darker zones emphasizing the tendons. Denier: that was the word. *He* wouldn't deny any of it. The model paraded with such exquisite flexibility, control. Which weather girls aren't trained to do, no call for it. Unless they're promoting an acceptable product, opening a video store. Klaw wanted her to walk up and down his back, ease his cramps. He wanted to lick her undersoles. The metal box stank of burnt paper.

He was forced to watch while O'Hagan picked fluff from his navel with the sharp end of his paintbrush. The oaf was grinning like a baboon at feeding-time. When Helen, tactfully, strolled to the window, he took down the portrait and turned it to the wall.

EIGHT

Sileen talked with the dead. Black verticals dominate the horizon: a crucifix forest waiting on a future pope. Poisoned mud, slaughtered armies, mess cans, white hoods shrunken by gas, tobacco teeth, rusted weapons – impossible to date.

'Join us.'

From a flooded, icy trench, he watches for Hodgson. Not a trace. You can't kill a scattered corpse a second time. The graveyard earth relents. They keep coming over the top, the skeletons in helmets. All the hunts gathering in the clouds.

Sileen tried to focus on the Inquisitor's face. Silver beard. Chin like a rubber sock. Beheaded by an overstarched ruff. Eyes not frightened to condemn. Cruelty as a creed. He tests the cripple's pulse, nods to his scribe. Swedenborg's trepanned skull: a candleholder.

'In the spiritual world natural memory objects cannot be reproduced, but lie concealed . . . Whatever you have said in the dark shall be heard in the light.'

Intrusive lenses burn the vein channels of Sileen's naked body, ever closer to the broken fork. Healing and killing. Returning him to mammal existence. Neutrality is not acceptable as a plea. (The machine's operative is elsewhere.) There must be a great cause. 'If you see a cripple walk, you can be sure he wants to get away.' (The Inquisitor is not without a sense of humour.)

Remorselessly, the attendant scribe, bent over his desk, fills the page. With what? Keeps pace with the shuttling beam of light. On his head: a mortarboard, with the board hacked off. Doctor Syntax in a touring company melodrama. He dips his quill, splashes ink, annotates the intervals of Sileen's torment. Rondeaux of collaboration. The prisoner's screams, the Inquisitor's lyrical prompts. The Racksman (a dialect part) holds to strict metre: plucks bones from their sockets, manicures with garden shears. Cracks the stiffened bodycase into a hoop, scores Sileen's alphabet of shrieks.

The clerk or scribe, a pseudo-author, sits apart: deferential, attentive. His floorlength robe tightens across avian shoulders as he twists his spine. An artist of sorts, he transcribes gradations of noise with a crow's feather. Infers meaning in the victim's self-absorbed gurgling, the puddles of mucous and broken teeth. A ritual, a performance recorded as it is improvised. He's seen it all before; each time is, miraculously, unique.

Quite useless, all the fuss. Sileen's body is dumb. He can be unpicked to the last functioning cell, sacrificed upon the Starrs Mall, immersed in fathoms of psychosexual flood. He will not serve as a medium, transport Drage-Bell over into the landscape where William Hope Hodgson's spark of consciousness survives. Can't be done. A conflict of interests. The miserable wretch has given too much of himself away. The book he published, the woman he screwed. As a necrophile, he's a total flop. Suppress it how he will, he's a writer – nothing else. A memory thief. Exploiter of coincidence. Hodgson cannot be disentangled from his bibliography.

Very well. The Inquisitor orders Sileen's immediate removal to the London Hospital. Plenty of room among the prison wards and tunnels to lose one more. Confine him. Set him down where he belongs – among the sick, the criminal, the deformed.

The disappointed racksman clips the Hygieia token around his neck. A dubious favour: this badge of admission – with its dim goddess offering a hand to all in need. Her outline doubles for the missing mount. Behind her they're carrying out a corpse.

The cripple must shape fresher fictions, more seductive lies. Pale as something rescued from the waters, he might still be profitably bled.

NINE

'The body is always something that is true.' Klaw read that. In a book. A fat black book. Not for yonks. Near the top of the lefthand page. How true? *Whose* body? Whose title is *Whose Body?* Unwin. Un-win. He's going mad. Claustrophobia. Lack of air. A scurf of brain cells on his lips. They must hear him gasping for breath, Must hear his self-interrogation: the way he forces his defunct retrieval system to trawl back through dictionaries of forgotten names to fix quotations, date first printings, dead writers, midnight movies. *Stakeout on Dope Street. River of No Return. Chinese Boxes.* Who? When? Fighting the panicked rush of senility. They say you have to imagine a journey, a walk, associate objects with places. Too surreal. Memory goes first. Blank. Stripped of dignity: on his knees in a vertical tin coffin.

Dorothy Sayers. Dorothy *L.* Sayers. L. Ron Hubbard. Ronnie Reagan. Dutch. 'Where's the rest of me?' Jack Regan. *Sweeney!* Sweeney Todd. Tod Slaughter in *The Demon Barber of Fleet Street.* 1936. He makes confession, sucks greedily at the stifling air. Partakes, shares their communion: the room. A single eye, swollen, pressed against the nailhole. He doesn't dare to breathe. Stink of used clothes, women's clothes, coats, skirts. Hung here while . . . While they . . . O'Hagan's boots, vests like bluefin tuna nets. Something soft, leathery. A jacket? Dear God, the holdall! Sweating *plastique*, detonators. He's cradling it, Armageddon.

The box is an oven. Become what you see. An acute sciatic spasm convulses Klaw, limits his POV. Transference to Helen's leg and foot, encircled in an iris shot. Her longitudinal arch, the lubricated spring of her step. She pivots and turns. The fluidity of her flexors. He tilts to secure a better scan, presses down on the creaking holdall.

Helen leans forward (away from Klaw), watching O'Hagan as he takes her bag. The tight skirt rides, seams on the stockings lengthen alarmingly, alarmingly fast, a throat-choking slither of (token) resistance. Such stockings, Klaw submits, cry rape – when it's safely over. When the damage has been done. He trembles in such provocation that the cupboard shakes. O'Hagan stalks towards him, bag in hand, fumbles at the door, patting his pockets for the missing key. The comic! Fine, that's it – the clincher. The Irishman is dogmeat.

They vanish from his sightline. Klaw's alone. He can only imagine it. Which is *much* worse. So undignified: a sort of scriptwriter, second-guessed by fate. Guilty, of course. Like all those scum. Stern feminists will roast him on hot coals (or so he hopes). He imagines what he wants to imagine, and calls it art: savagery, whippings, cries of pain. The woman sobbing for pleasure. O'Hagan, that shameless monster, penetrating every orifice.

What *is* this? Some new perversion? They stroll around the room, the pair of them, as if nothing had happened. Klaw hears – but can't see. Helen blocks his view. Then it's O'Hagan's turn: his back, the hair on his shoulders. The laughter of reefer madness. (Louis Gasnier. 1936?) The maniac should be certified. She's talking to him about . . . the weather, art politics, food. He spreads himself like an hidalgo on the leopardskin settee, rambles, eyes ablaze (you'd think he meant it), whacko stuff on storms. He wants the city scoured of its trash. All the towers blown away. An ice age. Hebridean winds hurtling south in Jacobite fury. Standard millennial waffle pitched with style. Rhetoric heats him to a becoming flush. He's canny/cracked, his rap responds to the temperature of her reactions, doesn't wait to bore. Keep it crazy, but keep it light.

The painter ducks from Klaw's frame, returns with coffee in a jug. Helen doesn't sit, sips at the window, protecting her space. She's in control. He's not going to paint her, not to-day. The light dies on them as they chat.

It's all so civilized, Klaw screams for a shock cut. An ape in a trenchcoat to burst through the door with a smoking gun in his hand. He's crippled. Seedy visuals no longer wean him from his pain, the rapid degeneration of an intervertebral disc. This ludicrous posture O'Hagan has forced on him. Alec Guinness in his sweatbox. *River Kwai*. Klaw wants revenge. Wants O'Hagan to thrash her until she bleeds.

Now Helen takes her turn on the sofa, long legs demurely tucked from sight. All very Nineties, most agreeable. Take your time, old son. Cold beer to chase the coffee's speed. She drinks from the bottle, mockingly. Lips pursed to the absent hunk of lime. Why doesn't she get down to it, unbutton him, lick salt? What's *wrong* with the bint?

A terrible thought came to the voyeur at his camera obscura pinhole: would any of this be happening if I wasn't playing the captive audience? O'Hagan knows I'm here (doesn't care) – his lowkey approach is a performance, nothing more. Stay calm. He'll turn it on when he's ready.

Then doubt clawed back. Why should that bastard give a damn? He'd do it cheerfully in the street. He lives for the instant or not at all. He's forgotten me. I'm part of the furniture. Sexual congress has done in his brain. I'm dead.

Nothing to eat. O'Hagan has no cash to take her out. He pees in the sink. Klaw hears him. From the sofa Helen can see it all. Klaw watches her watching, the studied indifference. She gets up, obviously disgusted, walks away. There's nothing in his tiny oval window but the sofa – and that awful gushing, on and on and on. Her heels irritating the boards. The markings on the leopardskin print swim like bile ducts in a degenerate liver.

He was mistaken, an understandable misinterpretation from limited data. Only the tap. O'Hagan washing out her dirty cup. Gulping down a pint of water, towelling his shoulders, his drenched hair. Helen follows him into the kitchen. Klaw can't see a thing. He has to work from the soundtrack. They're kissing (the unblocking of the sink). She's sitting on his face. The tap's still running. They'll flood the floor, bring the ceiling down. She's washing. He's helping her to wash (the cup). Rinsing her mug. Soaping together. A mutual shower before they . . .

The cupboard opens. A slit of light. Klaw, caught off-balance, tips forward, arms outstretched. O'Hagan snatches the holdall, shoves the spymaster back, boot against chest. A very smooth switch. Forces the twin bag, the woman's, into Klaw's arms. Too late to protest, the lock's already sprung. He's clinging to his sanity, a pouch of female kit. Helen's torso in his arms. The swine's going to blow her to hell. Quite right! Sound strategic planning. Just what the manuals recommend.

She's going. Or has she already gone? Klaw knuckles his eyes. O'Hagan has his paintbrush in his hand. No gentleman, he declines to see her out. Footfall on the stairs. Can't wait. Stripped to the buff, unlaced boots, he stabs at the canvas, ladles pigment over the deceitful face. Buries his treachery. Breaks off. Rattles at the window. Calls her name.

She returns. Those legs again, stockings, heels. Klaw's furtive peepshow has come full circle. (*Diary of a Chambermaid*, Bunuel version.) A talus to be worshipped. Chiropodal bliss. Lovingly cured hide. Stitches delicate as an episiorrhaphy. Will she oblige? One small favour on her way home to Sly Street? Could she drop off a misdirected letter, intended for Ian Askead, at the desk of the London Hospital? Certainly, why not?

Obligated, the nude painter accompanied Helen to the stairhead, valeting her bag. The unequal exchange is made. He grips the holdall until the letter is safely tucked into her pocket. Then it's her turn to ask for something. Does he fancy a runout down the A2? Kent, a sniff at the Medway? The boxing gig. Helen and her friend, they're trying to find a face with wheels – to help them locate an inexpensive property in which to taper off her training.

No problem. O'Hagan knows people. Fishermen who fancy the occasional bit of coarse. Give their ears a rest from the usual sticks of dynamite and a net. An awayday, what could be more charming? Picnic basket, tartan rug, silver whisky flask. Oast-houses, the bouquet of drying hops. Guidebook to National Trust properties. They might take in a walled garden or a ruined tower.

Klaw couldn't bear to wait for the thud of the streetdoor before he began to knock, rattle and shout. O'Hagan can live with that. He's wasted enough time on politics. He models an ear with his knife, then lops it off – one's more than enough. He has to junk the symmetry of the composition. Work purple into the grooves, oxbow a flaky pink. He's smoking again, letting ash drop onto his palette, adding texture to the pigment.

A woman, coming out of the shallows of sleep, screams. Calls O'Hagan by name. Upstairs. Earths a nightmare. The painter thumps in a tape cassette: full volume. Heavy metal, clash of demons. Rescues a bottle from a drawer. He's primed, attention on the job in hand. He can go all night when he's in this mood. The portrait *has* to be finished before he sets the house on fire.

TEN

Not so bad. A ward like any other: bars on the windows, pillows on the wall. Cleaner than the areas of the hospital Sileen had previously visited. There were even sheets. The room had the remote interest of a postcard thrust into his hand at a party. It was an anthology of negatives: no surveillance, no conspicuous mirrors, no books, no flowers, no fruit. Bugged, certainly, but that was nothing new. Sileen had renounced his claims on posterity. He wouldn't be invoking copyright. This brief coda to his life was off-the-record.

Obvious indications of budget made Sileen uneasy. Budget had always to be justified. Somebody would be paying the price for such indulgent board and lodge. For the moment that didn't matter. There was a jug on the shelf beside Sileen's bed. No longer in restraint, he drank. Thirstily. Doped? Without question. Tranquillizers couldn't keep pace with him. His blood was the breath of fire.

'Welcome to the Topcliffe, old man.'

Was the ward wired? Sileen's eyes were shot. Basins flamed with nimbic doubles, better selves. Mescaline déjà vu: the X-ray burnout's equivalent of the BBC. All life comes round twice, diminished, drained of pep. Sheets were scarlet, emerald the walls. Radon shadows made scorpions of the beds. Faustus/Sileen.

Who spoke?

'A stroke of luck, Toddy. A right result. Someone up there's watching out for you. Politicals generally find themselves in the hole: Limbo, Little Ease, the Pit. Jankers for the duration. I caught your alias on the end of the bunk. Mine's Royboy. He's MacLin.'

Sileen, head throbbing, panned to locate the perpetrator, the glasshouse lawyer. Were there really two of them? The stripes on their pyjamas strobed and divided as they padded in. One: scrawny as a vulture. The other: long and lank. Woodworm on prescription. Bailiffs of despair. Carrion to snuffle up a potage of lights when the ruck was safely done.

Royboy, settling himself on the bed, offered Sileen his tin. 'Snout. Try a roll-up, decent herb. MacLin doesn't, straight as a Roman mile. G.M.F.U. Shouldn't be here at all. Underqualified. Boozehound on the cure. Miserable streak of piss. No good for anything apart from running the odd bet. We're inseparable. Right, Mac? Best of pals.'

This Royboy, he's horribly familiar. Normally Sileen didn't care. Faces were interchangeable. No more significant than hats. But Royboy led him back to the place where it started to go wrong: Oxford. When the trio had struck out, attempted to defy their destiny. Sacrificed pawns.

Topcliffe. Wonderful how they hang on, the old names. Richard Topcliffe, rackmaster, waster of Catholics, Burghley's man; decently born, a Fenlander, backwoods MP. What's so different now? Granted a privatized torture chamber, he worked from home. His boast: licensed to fondle the Queen's alabaster breasts. All woman. From the waist up. Paperwork? Handwriting and spelling? Quite equal to today's GCSE standards: execrable. One of those who, in righteous indignation, exceed their instructions. Bless his nativity.

While Royboy blathered, MacLin stared. Sileen was uncomfortable with the stooge, his size, his freakish ability never to blink. MacLin seethed with spite, unspent anger. The world had played him a cruel trick by keeping him alive. There was a chameleonlike quality to his malignancy. He became what Sileen feared him to be: agent provocateur, an informer turned so many times his spine was smooth as soap. His silence gave form to Royboy's sardonic parables.

As the days drifted, Sileen grew used to his companions and the long room in which they were all held. He must have taken food from time to time – he couldn't remember it. He remembered the smoke whenever Royboy opened his mouth. He remembered it before it happened. Unfocused eyes. Eyes borrowed from an abused child. The prim jawline and the perfectly horizontal smile of the confidence man. (Confidence misplaced. Teeth: a mush of broken cement and Irish coins.)

They were playing Sileen like a disadvantaged trout. Weeks, months – or was it still the first afternoon? The timbre of Royboy's pitch was hypnotic. Always the same cast of spivs, the same quixotic, outdated slang: morries, wads of readies in a cab, a double dingaling in a dirty glass, chums from school who turned out bent. A nightmare Soho drinks party – without the booze. Sileen stayed in neutral as they worked in shifts, to threaten or to charm. Readers who had invested too much time to abandon a tedious book.

Closing his eyes against their remorseless interrogation, he almost convinced himself that he'd managed it: sleep. Forgetfulness. No more. Once, he was sure, Royboy went away – leaving the silent MacLin. The maniac at the end of the bed, hands twitching, waiting on the nod.

Bruised, puffy, living up to the promise of his teeth, Royboy limped back. (He'd limped before. Born limping. A badge of caste.) It must have been a memorable 'do', or the latrine ensign had been worked over with broomhandles and socks filled with jaffas. 'Tell the purser to get the stairs seen to, Mac, before some poor bugger breaks his neck.'

The stooge helped him back to bed, fluffed his pillows, lit a cigarette. Royboy couldn't raise a yawn. He sat stiffly, on parade, letting the ash glow and bloom, fall into the neck of his pyjamas. The eyes stayed open, but he'd marched into darkness.

'You. You next.' MacLin bent over to whisper in Sileen's ear. 'They'll be nicely warmed up now. Can you hear the bath running? There's nothing you can say to make them stop. They know it all. You haven't got Royboy's class. You're scum.'

A notable hush. No screams, no drills. No tea-trolleys rattling in another corridor. The gaps in Sileen's blueprint spread: memory lace. The ward grew blacker by the hour. Royboy like a patch of burning phosphorus. A candle under MacLin's skull. Eyes that could never be extinguished. Eyes that followed Sileen everywhere.

The room was a corridor. Sileen *had* to move. They had taken his leg away, forcing him to hop, bed to bed – never getting any nearer to the door. Hand stretching out for the nearest hoop of metal. Foot skidding on the linoleum. About to fall. Falling. Steadying himself. On and on. MacLin and Royboy left behind. Faster and faster. A heron on a hotplate – pouring with sweat. Throws off his jacket. High window. Must haul himself up. See where he is. Has to look out. Be sure he's awake. The journey down the ward is as pointless as a dream. But the bricks taste real. Coated in greenish-white emulsion that never quite sets. Coagulates. Too much lead.

A strip of newspaper had been pasted over a diagonal crack in the glass: puffs, breathes. The image fascinates Sileen. He strains to see it better, rocks his head. A fat man from a silent comedy kept in a cage. Longjohns, jailbird stripes. RED SUN OF TERROR SETS. The Gasman's beard and dark glasses. His weakened eyes. Folds of stiff canvas around the cage's base. They evidently hood him at night. (Perhaps all the time.) The prison yard is marked out like a five-a-side football pitch. Andean Indians in suits, hands clasped, block the goal. More suits, dark, against a whitewashed wall. Marksmen with automatic rifles on the roof. Damage contained: the wild beast in his pen.

It *could* be faked, a report from far away. A production still from the film of the book. (Prison confessions don't count. Ghosted memoirs are for ghosts.) This is an obvious set-up to boost international confidence in a disgraced regime. A ringer hired when the Gasman, posing as a whisky priest, slipped the net.

Sileen bites the paper down. Palms on the sill, strength of rage, pulls himself up. Hot eye against the missing sliver of glass in the opaque window. The corner of a private kingdom. A yard. White walls. Snipers. Flak jackets with binoculars. Well-built men in dark glasses standing purposefully around. A low cage. A numbered prisoner in a striped vest. The Gasman! Royboy's patron to the life. Betrayed. An unoriginal copy of the newspaper photograph Sileen has crushed into a ball and swallowed.

ELEVEN

He thought he could smell burning, but he couldn't be sure. The tin locker was salvage stock, impregnated by arson attempts, cigarette stubs, clothes saturated with smoke from the Thamesside ghats. Klaw told himself he was being paranoid – but that's what paid his pension. Chill out, gather and evaluate available information.

O'Hagan was long gone. Klaw heard the door slam. The painter was unreliable, a psychopath. Of course he was. What other reason could there be for tolerating his insolence? The man drinks to excess, he's promiscuous, violent: a model CV. But he's Irish, that's the rub. Even the snakes have slung their hook.

It has to be admitted, after all these years of benevolent condescension, we know sod all about the bastards. Ireland, it's like another country. Provos, Officials, Fenian swine, INLA, Irish Revolutionary Workers' Party, Irish Socialist Republican Party: more parties than Sandringham Road on a muggy Saturday night. More wakes. They know nothing, nothing about what they want. The killing addiction. My streetwise counter-terror shtick, all bluff. Picked most of the blarney out of cheap thrillers. ('It's all in bed the lazy divvils is, sor.')

LET ME OUT.

A Dublin comedian in exile might make something of this. Interior monologue in a lightless vault. But Klaw's a down-market action man. (Celtic twilight – school of Mickey Spillane). He kicks, drives his heels against the door. The metal sings. LETMEOUTLETMEOUTLET-MEOUT. The ashtray stink is getting worse. Petrol on wet rags. He chokes from smoke he can't see.

The spook leans back, draws up his knees, hits the door with the venom of a hobnailed drop from a fifteen foot wall. It gives, bursts. He's out. He's been tied up so long his minders will be twitchy, asking permission to send in the dogs. Sure enough – the window – a chopper circling overhead: hammering attics with furious noise, lifting slates, swirling rubbish drifts. Reasserting normality. The status quo: a visible fear to keep us sane.

The shambles of O'Hagan's room is such that no man can be held responsible. It would take a squad of bacteriologists, dust technicians, midden archaeologists, to make any sense of the impacted layers of filth. The room was a shorthand history of postwar art – always inherited by each generation's least deserving participant. Exploited, abandoned: the washed-out surrealism of sunset churches as a ballet backdrop, action painting by art school lumberjacks, hairy performance tableaux, tactfully distressed sex in hoods and gloves. Worth preserving in the Chamber of Horrors, but lacking in basic amenities (viz., a phone). The Irishman was an egotist who refused to interrupt his carnivorous tutorials, his binges of narcissism. Integrity was the right to prolong his gynaecological explorations: bruise ripeness, salty-sweet decay. The crusty rim on the tequila glass. Undressed wounds, the gradients of the oyster garden – meat flaps that are still attached. He grafted flesh tones onto his own face. Cannibalized portraits. Satisfied women, drowsy as wasps. All voices O'Hagan, his cock.

All too clear to Cillick-Klaw: the loping Mick closing on the bomb-carrying female, shadowing her progress through a warren of streets – Heneage, Spelman, Chicksand, Old Montague. Released, exhilarant, she sways, swings. He watches her rear. She bends to set the burden down. Kids coming home from school in clean white shirts. Bollards given a lick of paint. She seems to notice things, but is on auto pilot, thinking ahead. Shooting alternative endings, mixing the cast. Wasn't there something she was supposed to do, a message, an errand?

She speeds up – Whitechapel Road – in response to the wider pavements; catches sight of herself in a showroom window. O'Hagan, on the far side, tracking through the park, enjoys her enjoying herself. He stumbles over the envelope of ground on which a church once stood. Is that a detonator in his pocket, or is he justifiably pleased with the way his plan is working out? Together, pursuer and pursued, they make a handsome item. You'd say they were the only ones in the crowd who knew what they are doing. A crowd? Inconsequential drifters waiting for darkness, waiting to be let in.

Flirtatious, doomed to remain unconsummated, this relationship.

O'Hagan, without conscience, stalks his target. No retrospectives. No morning-after fuss. Admires her without reservation, as he is supposed to do, as she intends – high-stepping Mensa showgirl, at pace. Last second swerves rescue her from a chain of collisions. Sauntering, she motors through slow-witted pedestrians who aren't given time to appreciate her singularity, the clods. A colour-coded warning: redness. The grace with which she swings the bag onto her shoulder, waits for a break in the traffic.

Excited, unobserved in his borrowed room, Klaw toyed with the fastenings of Helen's leather bag. A forensic curiosity: ran his hand over the cool black flanks, picturing the orgasmic conclusion in the hospital. She led him on. And the earth moved. He could feel it. The floorboards warm beneath his knees.

His fingers, true to their conditioning, trembled. Had the switch, in fact, been made? *Was* this Helen's bag? The zipper stuck. He wrenched at it. Aroused, plunged his hand into the unknown – the safety of silk. Lusciously scarlet shorts, laced boots, shiny boxing gloves (like the heads of boiled babies). He lays all the stuff around him on the floor, to examine it at leisure. Kit inspection. Not a handkerchief out of place. Buckles polished, bootlaces ironed. Olfactory flashback: a special lieutenant, fresh out of Sandhurst, risking eau-de-Cologne.

Andi Kuschka, barefoot, comes on him from behind. On the intruder. A pair of O'Hagan's soiled dungarees held up with a workman's thick belt. Naked otherwise. Woken by the assault on the metal cabinet. His scrawny neck. In the crook of her arm. She chokes the life out of him. Unable to breathe, blacking out, he responds to the investment made in him, the demented shriek of red beret instructors. 'Kill!' He stamps on her instep, pistons an elbow at the bridge of her nose.

Blood gushes down Andi's face. Nasty little pervert rummaging through Helen's things. An autopsy sniffer, proxy rapist. She jerks him around and – pivoting – lands a short left, just above the eye, a bolt from the stungun. Instant shutdown. Doves and bells. He drops like mutton. She's over him, legs spread, thrashing him with her belt. Klaw doesn't feel a thing, he's not accepting any calls. Pain is a crinkle of distant surf. The White Strand: sun spokes breaking out from a dour Atlantic sky.

If the peeper has the run of Helen's bag, where is she? What has he done with her? What is *she* carrying? Another Oxford? Another of O'Hagan's favours?

Andi flails. Strikes with surgical precision. Klaw won't speak. What is there to say? What's left when all your fantasies are gratified? What sliver of meaning adheres to the rest of your life? (Purple stormclouds over the limestone pavements of the Burren.)

He tries to roll over, to better survey the pallor of his Sapphic tutor. The situation was grotesque. That was its charm. Klaw was outside himself, lolling on leopardskin, applauding the theatre. This is how the French love to describe the English upper classes: active in translation. Pornography by Guillaume Apollinaire. Predictable violations. Art criticism as an obscene fable.

Andi's upraised arm. Her ungroomed tuft. The heavy, womanly breasts swinging as she swings; as the arm goes back, and the bib of the blue dungarees flops. She gets into it; grunting, she swats.

O please let it last forever. Klaw has floated out beyond the window's grime – cut his communication with the bombers – and is looking in. The room is all there is. Andi's ardour would cost him a month's salary in Streatham. The girl's demented, screaming as the buckle chews flesh. Why do the discipline professionals always have to talk? Why does there have to be a cup of sweet tea and a bourbon biscuit afterwards to bring the rhapsody to ground, surburban banality – like a visit to the chiropodist. Military chaps in pinnies. Masons in the wrong lodge. The whistle of the leather's edge becomes a kettle on the hob. Tears of frustration, not of pain.

Why does the woman have to speak? She's magnificent – Silvana Mangano in *Bitter Rice*. The blows have lost none of their original furious strength. If anything, frustration has increased her snap. The zip Klaw fondled once is now a livid streak opening his back: spine-teeth.

'Where's Helen, creep?'

She holds his face between her hands, holds him by the ears. The belt droops, useless, spent. Tell her, tell her anything.

'Too late, Miss. Don't stop. Stay with me and listen for the bang. Long gone. The Irishman conned her into hitting the hospital. He's your man.'

Crawls after her. Andi: pulling on a pair of O'Hagan's boots. Leaving him. 'Sweetling!' The door opens, smoke rushes in. A transformation scene. A staged diversion out of which devils appear.

Feel them, taste the smart.

'Come back, love. Save yourself. Save me.'

He can see nothing through watery eyes. It's not a proper fire. Not yet. Turns the tap on himself, head in sink, tips the jug over his head. To dare descent. Walk calmly through the furnace and back to the car. Get on the blower, call out the cavalry. 'Abort, abort.'

The lumber of the stairs ablaze, book bundles, jugs of hair. The streetdoor: a show of blistered paint. So far so good. Head cradled, hair wet. Glass crackling like frost wakes him to the truth of things. Flamelets leap on his thighs: fire dogs. Now he knows, now he can see, quite clearly, what it is that the mob in the framed photograph fear. Cillick-Klaw, burning like a torch, is the long-awaited one.

TWELVE

Doctored, Sileen slept. And in that sleep explored the house of memory: each ward, cell, theatre, cupboard, file. Starrs Mall, Medical Museum – retrieved episodes from his fabulous past. Windows had to be counted, tiles numbered, pillars touched. An endless tracking shot with no dissolves. Cornices, lintels, pipes. Corridors like conceptual art: shaded bulbs dripping wax down lengths of black wire. Sounds that become names: Askead, Adnam, Hinton, Helen. Schoolmasters, priests, dead parents, animals. Racks of meat. Beef orchestras. Scrubbed tables with a spread of gleaming blades. Sammy Taylor the West Cork revenger. Taylor hunting him with a bowie knife through the arteries of the dream hospital. Taylor composing his version of the borderland on a VDU. Fixing landscape, flooding roads. Taylor and Helen on the cliffs.

The black-robed confessor brought his own lighting effects to Sileen's bedside. He leaked Thames mist. The broad dome of his skull was nibbled by the radiance of internal fires. His sullen jaw was occulted with menace. Royboy and MacLin, nuisances, parasites on evil, had been banished, or had slipped away into the shadows. They were too fussy, too human, for this new development. The golden crucifix in MacLin's ear was a redundant irony.

Maliverney Catlyn, prison spider, stood over Sileen's pallet like a frozen waterfall. The fear-displacement from this man's bulk was awesome. Any word, however dreadful, would have been a relief. Drage-Bell's pet interrogator (double agent, trickster, magistrate) encouraged speech, the invention of petty histories, the recitation of names. He was a marvellous blank, a pond on the move, a sepulchral book. A shape on which the guilty (the accused) could project the face they needed most: sympathetic idiocy, the wisdom of the ancient dead.

Catlyn: look it up. Transpontine. The name's a South London

inheritance. Ducking and diving beneath the arches. Picking pockets in the precincts of Southwark Cathedral. Insinuating into the households of the nobility.

'Tell me.'

Sileen yearned to confess. Confess to what? There was nothing left, the marshlands had been leeched, the rivers sweated out. He clung to where he was, rooms that were lives. Rooms the interrogator threatened to rip out at a breath. Sileen was a character in Sammy Taylor's abandoned script, his actions dependent on that madman's whim. He'd been 'given up' to save the starving of Africa. Taken down from the walls of Taylor's cottage with all the other daubs.

Catlyn smoked a cigar, revolving it like a rusty bolt. A greasy soutane disguised his mass. His was the slowest presence Sileen had ever met. Objects stuck to him and knew their place. Feathers, needles, shavings of reindeer skin. His face keeps shifting. Sileen wanted to start at the beginning, the Roebuck, and tell him all of it. But he already knew! Watch how the silver whiskers retract to leave the cheek smooth as a girl's. Or: elephant ears filter whispers from another town. A compost medium: his head's a cup of mercury, his tongue is grey. Hands of a working-man and the eyes of a woman who died in childbirth. Maliverney Catlyn was Drage-Bell's final card. After him there was only the cage in the courtyard, the river. Catlyn could draw demons at a touch.

Neck to floor: black. The interrogator's caput lodged like a cannon ball on a hooded tripod. Sileen felt, as canny victims often do, a surge of tenderness for the hand that held the whip. He *wanted* to be purged. The congruence of star and scar. Focus of attention: scribes at the ready to immortalize his most casual aside. (He felt like Barbara Cartland feeding chocs to the pooch.) Groans are scored. And curses, prayers. Nothing to say. The modernist impasse. He functions neither as author of his destiny nor as the villain to inspire Sammy Taylor's litanies of hate.

If only Catlyn would press the biscuit to his lips, offer the dish of blood, he might find his way back into the low hills, the field of stones. Rocks, fence, tower. The news that Drage-Bell demands from the far side, the leap into unstable light. Starting from ignorance, Sileen must arrive at the words with which William Hope Hodgson began.

Many are the hours in which I have pondered upon the story that is set forth in the following pages . . .

Catlyn watched him closely for a drop in temperature. 'Did you know,' he said, expelling an Olympic cluster of smoke rings, 'that my Lord Burghley frequently boasted of his gift for seeing devils swim beneath the skin like shoals of fish?'

The cigar's orthopedic eye glowed at Sileen's neck. He felt the vigour of its heat. Blood pumped in his throat like cancelled speech. He couldn't scream. Anchovies were massing in his wrist. Silver and blue. Sharp wings of spotted dragonets. Catlyn's suggestion hit like morphine, spread through his veins in a rush of shame. Scorch marks. Rapture where the flesh burnt. He was branded with bliss.

The benign interrogator would open Sileen's dangling arm with a swift sharp knife and bleed his devils into a porcelain bowl.

'Confession's overrated as a sacrament, John. Play dumb. A classy evisceration will get you into the history books.' Catlyn, marble-mouthed, yarned as he worked. Talked to himself, sucked on a Fisherman's Friend. 'Martyrdom's the game, old son. Basted on a gridiron, drowned in milk, funnelled with castor oil till your guts run out. It's a seller's market out there. Take my word. Self-incrimination's the vogue. Nutters in every mall putting up their hands for uncommitted naughtiness that'll get them two minutes on *Crimewatch*.'

The skill of a conjurer who blarneys to deceive: the pass in the air, the sleight of hand. Catlyn offers Sileen the blue bowl. Goldfish swirling in a question mark. The switch has been made. Demons exchanged for cheap fairground trash. Smoke blown in the mark's face. A nudge from the shill. Flutter of linen to cover the crime. 'Look again, sir.' The fish have vanished. The bowl sits on Catlyn's head like an Hasidic kapel.

Sileen had been turned, no question. Buried within the hospital's labyrinth, he would, like Royboy, use his derangement for the general good. That's what the contract stated: be what you are, then die. A deed of gift in his own blood. Catlyn the scryer would interpret Sileen's wintry voyage, his yomp across the borderland.

Now there were two of them. They would have to trade identities, try another trick.

THIRTEEN

Helen/Isabel on the steps of London Hospital. Striding out. Legs, stockings, heels. Rapid tracking (L/R). It could be another: a stand-in, a body double. A feller even. Who could do the walk. Walks well (on the cusp of breaking into a run). Two steps at a time. Gallop of trained athlete.

Red suit. She mustn't die. Not yet. She *is* the picture. Beauty hurts. She'll pull the punters. Strong woman taking responsibility for her own destiny: appeal to the hyper chicks in the Big Apple. High angle (apex of pediment) down onto steps. Wheelbarrow bumping towards street. A body or a cripple. Doctors in white coats.

Tight on Helen. Camera inside entrance hall (anticipating disaster). Tracking back: behind grimy columns. A crimson scratch against blue-grey of stone.

Reverse angle. Long shot (from upper floor of Grave Maurice). Helen: crushed by intimidating mass of building.

BCU: her lips. Helen's lips. (Doubled?)

BCU: O'Hagan. Expressionless. The pursuer.

Helen. Towards the lobby. Walks out of shot, revealing O'Hagan. Keeping his distance.

The doorway of the Grave Maurice. Empty angel plinth. Puddles and shadows in alleyway. Pedestrian crossing. Railings. Face in crowd. O'Hagan battling against stream of out-patients exiting hospital. Clouds in windows. Blackout. Music.

Crane down. Andi Kuschka running towards camera. Chicksand Street. No sound. Kill sound. She slips, falls, picks herself up. (Keep it cold. No empathy.) Wet pavings. Rubbish bins overturned. Tight on Andi: the black arch. Walls pressing. The alleyway.

Reverse angle: behind Andi into overexposed road. Wildtrack: harsh, exaggerated. Heavy traffic. Whitechapel Road. Evening sunlight in windows of hospital. She can't cross the stream. Panic.

Blackout. Music.

Out from noise and light of Roebuck: Ian Askead. Weaving, drunk as a skunk. Hands deep in pockets of sepia labcoat. Scratching, playing with himself. Follow Askead. At a discreet distance: upwind.

BCU: the wrecked face. Cigarette. Face that knows itself, depths of self-disgust it is happy to tolerate.

High angle: from roof of torched warehouse. 90 degree pan as Askead swings south, over railway bridge, into passageway. He spots Andi, waiting on kerb. Tries to run. 'Bugger this.' Tails of labcoat flying back.

Floorlevel shot of reception desk (hospital): Belgian in its weirdness. Highly polished floor. A frozen moment.

From behind glass doors (reflections, distortions): tracking back. Helen enters hospital lobby. Let light values freak. Overexposure is good for the soul. Black bag on shoulder. Hair flicked from eyes. She could be the next Sharon Stone: a one-picture wonder. Camera waits on her. Which way to turn? She hesitates (looks good). Make the best of it.

Blackout. Silence.

The clunk of an electronic digital clock. Dull as a boffin tapping plastic teeth. (Corny, I know. But you can't underestimate your public on a TV budget.) Then segue to consciousness of hospital: surveillance footage, dated and time-coded. Meaningless white numbers. Grey reverie: dream stock. Posthumous present tense. Floating figures limed with fur of waterlight. Disquieting POV: halfway up wall.

Digital clock on desk. Over shoulder of woman in charge. Colour. Fate counters stuttering. Helen's scarlet nails. Setting down the holdall.

The woman doesn't hear what she says (positive discrimination in favour of eccentric deaf?). Helen's annoyance, tapping bag with shiny shoe. Woman preoccupied: fends off enraged pensioner, misdirects pregnant woman. Helen split in reflective glass.

Surveillance version: swirl of hospital fauna. Like station booking hall.

Shuttle of digital clock. Holdall. Helen's nails tapping on desk.

High angle (repeat of pediment shot): down on steps. Askead closing on Andi Kuschka.

Tracking behind stone columns: O'Hagan. His shoulder. The tattoo.

Surveillance camera: Sliema Felix Muscat approaching desk, his arm in a sling.

Helen's silhouette. At the desk. A telephone. The deaf woman stirring her tea. Let this moment live. (The cast assembled, catastrophe is certain. The bigger the budget the greater the carnage.) Let Helen become a postcard of Isabelle Adjani, Nastassia Kinski. She's nothing like them.

The freelance loonies are pouring back. Hordes of them, extras running amok. The ones who belong here, have always belonged here: the endemically aggrieved, Asps, casualties holding their wounds together, mumblers with the wrong paperwork. They swallow Helen. They rage at the desk-keeper. She's seen it all before. Gives a refined (counter-clockwise) spin to the oily orange surface of her tea. It slops. Another ringing telephone. A whitefaced Irishman. Looking at his boots.

'My name's Patrick Golden – I've been stung by a bee.'

Muscat didn't have a prayer. He wasn't going to risk creasing his oatmeal strides in this mob. Poor Felix. Somebody had been telling tales. A raft of gangland documentaries: tearful faces playing the old soldier, haemorrhaging regret, fingering Greeks in vans. In the latest ghosted pronouncement from Broadmoor, jealous of the coverage he was getting, the increasingly paranoid Colonel denounced Muscat as 'a lackey and a grass'. 'He ponces off our name.' Felix had to act fast. He cut out the middleman and broke his own arm. Made a good job of it, as it happens. Traditional method: door slammed three times. Now he needed a kosher certificate.

Click of digital clock. Blackout. Music.

O'Hagan manhandles Andi – who he knows so well (and not at all) – backwards down the steps, zigzagging across road towards the Maurice. Drags her into alleyway. Ian Askead, playing the drunk with considerable chutzpah, tracks them both.

Andi was so close. She tried to shout Helen's name. Then bit O'Hagan's dirty hand. She loved him too. The painter required a solid bulwark of brick and a good view, over the woman's shoulder, to where the action was. He wants to have her against the wall. (Askead is no less keen.) And, since she is wearing his clothes, he wants, in some senses, to have himself. Have her have him. They wrestle – as couples do. In ways respectable pedestrians can ignore. She kisses him and swallows his warty tongue. She slumps.

BCU: O'Hagan's paint-smeared hands. About to touch the wires.

Flash! Information burnout blinds them when they least expect it. The septic woman shuts her eyes. A patient on the drip, in the terminal ward, screened, fed with sleep. Flash! Weather freaks huddling in the shadows of their quilted dusk. Flash! The newborn in their perspex trays. A smoking circle of Tommies invalided from the wars. Tartan carpet-slippers ordered one at a time. They cluster around a coalfired stove, unable to sweat. A child has swallowed a tin bicycle. Flash! Prisoners spotlighted for the files. Eyes closed, all of them. Only the dead stare back.

Sofya Court, spectacles, dyed hair, is on patrol – working her ticket among the ranks of empty beds. The Lady with the Leica around her neck (where you'd expect a sales rep's laminated card). She's cropped and fit, hidden under a labcoat borrowed from Askead. He alone knows, knows everything, knows where she is. The time to sell her out has never quite arrived. He does feel something for the girl, a respect for courage that knows its place, that risks so much – knows when to hide. He likes her smell. Her putdowns. The way he thinks she'd taste. He likes her enough to wait for a worthwhile offer from the filth. He doesn't bother to ask around.

Sofya is a ward photographer – like the ones on Brighton Pier, but less well paid. (They don't have to bung Askead.) She takes what she's told to take, responds to requests, prints up souvenir postcards. A swimsuit under the labcoat, cheap gilt cross at her throat. Treat your clothes as props: create a new identity from that. A game for solitaries, people who eat alone in the canteen – by choice.

She's anonymous, it's true. Literally, without name. The hospital has no record of her employment, so she can't be rationalized. She hoards the negatives: shoeboxes of unprinted patients. Albums of fog faces. Dark sockets leaking kaolin light. Marram grass hair. Carry them home in a Gateway bag – the souls from limbo, her family. Unfixed: oval portraits they stick on graves.

Home? Ha! An attic room in Charlton, near the park. Corner house. Cemetery Lane, SE7. Joe Orton. Early Shena Mackay. A complicated journey taking her where she doesn't want to be: District Line to West Ham, overground to North Woolwich, foot-tunnel beneath the Thames. Third World precincts, boarded-up dockers' pubs – she put herself on the edge. Where there were choices, she picked the one with least appeal. Challenged fate. Footsteps echoing close behind, under the river where her breath came fast: the stretch in the middle that the surveillance cameras can't cover.

Unmolested. Unpunished. She didn't show up on the screen.

The first morning, when she had run away, after the thing with Mordecai Donar, she would not look at the light on the river. Offered the tunnel or the ferry, she went underground. Claustrophobia pinched her lungs. Travelling east, and making a bad decision at every junction, should lead her to the worst of London, a hell that was all her own. She failed.

Noticing a sign for the Thames Barrier, she turned the other way; sharply uphill, a gap in the houses – found herself where she needed to be. The deserted tennis courts, amphitheatre, severely angled steps cut into a gentle gradient. She recognized the set at once. Antonioni's *Blow-Up*.

An old Chinaman in a white coat was sitting on a bench, holding a newspaper he didn't read: the only visible human. She climbed, stiffly, into that which was misremembered, falsely anticipated, unknown: distortions of selective reality. He'd got it right the first time, the Italian. An atmosphere of conspiracy, concealment: the screen of trees. A celluloid rustle through the Lombardy poplars. Latent threat. Sharp leaves that gossip and agitate.

The Huysmans-weary decadence of Antonioni's choice: to nominate this site, a terraced enclosure of singular resonance. (She'd read about the director's unease, the facial tic, his wanderings, with scriptwriter Tonino Guerra, in and out of South London dancehalls and knocking-shops.) How could he perpetrate the disastrous vulgarity of the jeeploads of student extras, hooting as they gatecrashed the apocalypse? That mimed tennis match! For which he should, like Giordano Bruno, have been burnt alive.

She squatted down to examine a broken fence-post. Still here: traces of the dark green paint that once disguised the pallor of the natural wood, a rich lime mould creeping over it, covering the urgency of the set-dresser's brush. Sofya saw herself as an investigator on the perimeter of a great mystery. But it was all over, it happened long ago. Hanging Wood. Only the climate of menace has survived, seduced her, drawing her to the summit, the boat-shaped plateau: to confront the silver-haired man in the expensive overcoat, her father/killer/victim.

Curtained by woods, the turf mall spoke of absence. She stood still on the heaving ground, and listened. She waited to become. Frustrated, but not unpleasantly so, she turned her head. Perspectives shifted, her truancy was secure. She staggered, put out a hand towards the fence. Hawthorn wounded by bright globes of holy blood. She ran. Slithered on the damp steps, down to the blunted bow of the grass arena. She had to pee.

A few parked cars, but no keepers. The Women's shack was padlocked, she took the Gents. Nowhere to wash, no door on the cubicle, flooded floor. Lacking paper, they write on the walls. COCK FOR HIRE MAKE DATE / IF INTERRUPTED LEAVE MESSAGE.

Missage is all she had left. More than she could handle, forgiveness. A penance to endure. Around her: steep woodland terraces. The light belonged in another tale. Impossible to photograph. Receive me. Heal me.

Escaping, getting away, on the far side of Thorntree Road, in Maryon-Wilson Park, she stopped to dangle her wrists in a cool clear stream. Letting the steady flow of water wash away the dirt, the filth of eyes.

The white rectangle. Imar O'Hagan's misdirected letter. Helen's scarlet nails and the desk woman's whiter, fatter hands: rings, liver spots. 'Ashmole? Who? Who did you say? Askard? Definitely, no. Not here. Sorry. Next.'

Favour glass. Favour reflections, polished surfaces, revolving doors. Signal what's to come. The *Evening Standard*'s black placard beside the confectionary stall. RAGE. Full text blocked by Ian Askead's dicky shoulder. He's chatting up the chocolate girl, filching peppermints. (OUT)RAGE? (COU)RAGE? Rabies for Frogs? A feelgood transplant puff, or bangbang in Derry?

The little Glaswegian snatches the letter, arm around Helen's waist, walks her away. A cheerful obscenity tossed at the desk. Surveillance footage as they shove against the mob, head for the street. The mounted camera, not in on the secret, lets them go. Suspense should be maintained by cunning inserts (a repeat of the low angle desk shot), and doctored sound.

Askead was not conventionally brave. But there were many things worse than death. Thirst, for example. Tights that laddered first time on.

Dogs who wouldn't run. He was protecting his investment. The bareknuckle show. His status as Muscat's bucketman and clown. The cash that was riding on Helen's fall.

Galleries of glass redefined, on the instant, as sugary flints. Blizzards that stung. A fireball. The gonging, the fearful shuffle of bone, comes later: an avalanche inside a diving-bell. The floor is unilaterally withdrawn. It's not an option. Trampoline levitation. Askead cedes his hair. His eyebrows are a dab of ash. He's lying on top of Helen, shielding her, as the roof comes down, and Boulton Mainwaring's building composes itself in a more democratic form – greater account-ability, books open to a whirlwind inspection.

The black pint jumped in O'Hagan's paw. A grin formed in the creamy curd. Bottles rattled on the Roebuck's shelves. Windows fell out (a forest of fractures around the heraldic beast). The TV, unprovoked, channel-hopped. The blind barman was certain it was something he had done.

An orange helicopter, on its launch pad, became an elevator: going down. Buckled blades smashing medicine cabinets, provoking bells. Beds in the air storm the Mosque. Andi screaming as she watches slo-mo falls of masonry, Portland blocks turning to dustwater. Girders like twisted roots. Cars on their backs, wheels spinning. The wounded on walkabout. A pristine snowfield of powdered glass. Manic ambu-lancemen giving the kiss of life to shopwindow dummies. A dawn chorus of sirens and alarms. Pleistocene flashback: a smoking crater where the entrance hall had been.

It had been waiting all along, Swedenborg's terminal. The careless subtraction of the Mound.

Sileen was dressed for travel: leg, cap, blackout suit. Maliverney Catlyn had him fine-tuned: twisting in the straw, near dead. Catlyn, at the window, legs spread, keeping his cigar wet, followed every move. Grease reflections. He waited to track Sileen's dream migration, his escape. Scry that face: borehole, tunnel, fault.

This was not for Drage-Bell, not any more. Catlyn wanted to complete a subterranean map, then put Sileen down. Strangle him with his bare hands. Assimilate the lost rivers. Choke him like a dog.

The chemistry was right. The feral dreamer and the one who knew what dreams meant. Who followed Sileen underground, shadowed his attempts at flight. The desperate connection to sluices and rivulets that had been bricked in. Walbrook. Black Ditch. Bazalgette's Middle Level sewer. Obscurities. Visionary hoops of brick. Rainwater flooding the dross.

Skinned to cork, Sileen drifted out, drawn on the tide. He paddled through broken mazes, deeper and further, troughs of addictive hibernation. Somnambulist voyages: in sympathy with flow and spill, streamheads, springs, the wash from stormdrains. Out of the hospital and away. Crypt of St Philip's ... Kinder Street ... roots from Swedenborg's orchard poking through damaged brickwork ... cellars of the Old Rose ... Wapping Steps. Catlyn, memorizing the procession of clouds, anticipated every step.

An iron portcullis, the river beyond. Ferret Sileen had achieved the tunnel's end. Crescents of dazzling morning light. Scintillae: a golden field he couldn't reach.

If he could solve the final riddle, he would be free. Gills in his neck, fins on his back. His deformity reclassified. Fin de siècle? Fin de tout. Finished. Gone. Not Sileen, he falls.

In the yellow mud, catching the reflected riverlight, a silver ball. He took it for the moon brought down, a dish of liquid lead. Intrigued, he stoops. The weight's immense. It weighs as much as the world. A silver-red ball of metal (coins, screws, bits of forks) fused by the surge of tides. Perhaps it's the spherical book that will explain everything Sileen needs to know. It's cold as frost. He's fearful for the skin of his hands, the wafery gloves of flesh. Materialists would call the find 'treasure trove'. Tosh-fakers and sewer rats know the ball is worth all their lost lives, the children dashed against the tunnel's roof.

Sileen will never carry it away: his mortgaged lunar future, his soul. So drop it back into the stink, the meaty slop. A wad of copper, a blood head.

Jakob Boehme's 'Globe or Eye of Fire'! Fit it to the right symbol on the rivergate and the iron doors *will* open. He has seen the decoration before, the spokes and wheels – on Twickenham Bridge. The phallic skeleton of the rising sun moulded into the piers. He wished he had the time for a closer look. The labour might yet be accomplished. He's losing his grip, the mud is churning behind him in the dark. A grunting and honking, deeper in the tunnel. Other dead ones, animal familiars, come to fetch him back. The terrible noise would, he knew, stop if he abdicated his silver ball.

Meazled hogs. Descendants of the herd trapped in the Fleet at Hampstead, brutes too stubborn to turn (too fat). Half-butchered things tipped from the cleaning sheds into the ditch. Eaters of excrement. Pink-eye inbreeds, matted, blind, festering with wounds. Sileen's own, his tribe. They bristle against his bare leg.

Swinish noises . . . a semblance in it to human speech – glutinous and sticky, as though each articulation were made with difficulty . . .

The strength in Catlyn's diceratherian neck. A cloud across the moon. A spasm of pain in his lower back. He pinches the cigar. It's bearable if he does not breathe. Concentration falters. He can lift the fleshy hood from the bone, convert a doubting frown into a clubman's smile. Sileen is alone out there. Crushing his knuckles against the symbols on the gates.

The dreamer, suit in rags, came through. He fell with the house, the landslide of floors. The ball of conglomerate scrap was fixed to his ankle as he somersaulted through the scalding air. Catlyn, his tutor, was luckier – he was killed outright, chest crushed like rotten lumber, head wrong (the mighty hands shot out to protect the gonads instead). The spasm in the neck had been a true prophecy. Some satisfaction in that. The river map went with him. His wolvering howl fitted Sileen with gravity-enhancing boots. He tumbled like a water-tracer, a bullet so old it could no longer be fired. It had to be shaken from the chamber.

All the cells of the building that stood in for Sileen's memory, his prisoner's filing system, were deleted at a stroke. The hospital destroyed, he could start afresh – his priceless stupidity renewed.

It's as quiet as Christmas in the city. Frosty Sileen reaching for his scarlet queen, helping her to stand. Askead, Helen's page, had vanished. (Dwarfs. 'Don't try to pick them up. They don't like it.' Jack Trevor Story.) The deaf embrace. Andi hurdling up the steps. The lens of Sofya's camera is cracked, riddled with fine lines. She's laughing. A striped swimming costume, red and white. She wades towards them. Arms open, each for the other. A crab with a broken shell. Boredom is better than a protective hood: the girls, by having no vested interest in the building, have all survived.

A blast to wake the dead. Elbow on the horn: Askead in a liberated ambulance, siren full tilt, blue lights revolving like a showband dancehall. Cheering crowds. The Fall of Paris. Nylon favours. Spearmint in bed.

Individual identities are in the clouds, provisional. Felix Muscat, bandaged, is mistaken for a hero – offered the first soundbite. ('I can look at myself in the mirror without shame. We only went after our own kind. I know what it is to cry.') All the survivors tumble down the broad stairs – like the finish of a pantomime. Leaving the crater to those who need it most.

Askead honks in triumph as they climb aboard. His voice sounds weird, he's been taking hits from the wrong mask. A Gallowgate Mickey Mouse dubbed into helium: he raps too fast for them to understand. One of those backward talking David Lynch aliens who hide in the badlands and have faces that don't fit. He sweeps aside the stuff he thieved from the medical stores (sweetie jugs of poppers, syringes, cotton wool, flavoured suppositories) to let Sofya slide in beside him. The others, grateful, choose the back – crash out on the bed as the ambulance spastics into the traffic.

Away, away at last, jumping the lights: Cannon Street Road, hard left, the Highway, Commercial Road, East India. A litany. Names that invoke better times, lost faces. Into the Blackwall Tunnel, river upstairs.

Their chauffeur kept his foot to the floor, when he could reach it – shunting pedestrians, carnage apostles (who had to see before they'd believe). The rescue armada – one short – had to revise their ETA, circling around the block to arrive back at the hospital where they were based. Details on the radio were all wrong. They had Guy's on fire, hundreds drowned.

One-handed, showing off, Askead rolled a kingsize bomber. Gave Sofya some chat. 'Any idea how you get this bugger out of first gear, hen?'

FOURTEEN

Allhallows-on-Sea is a ghost, a resort that never was, a blemish. Bullied by marshland, it squatted the shingle of the North Kent shore, gawping enviously across the mouth of the Thames Estuary at the twinkle of Southend: the shortfall of a pier which could, with a little more front, have turned itself into a bridge, a way out.

Cutting the engine, Askead cruised silently down the long slope. Bungalows, dead-ends, resentful cul-de-sacs. A delicate marine light (wasted, wasted) in which each roadside weed was outlined in charcoal. The acid clarity of telegraph poles closing on an undesired horizon.

The expelled urban chancers bunged their ambulance into the car park of a monstrous pebbledash barn; a windswept lick of gravel, where the vehicle was immediately at home. It sagged comfortably on its wheels, welcoming the advance of salty grass, blue rust eating the bodywork. You'd swear it had always been there among the other wrecks, feral caravans with drawn curtains.

The pub. An off-limits anachronism proud of its non-history, its forgetfulness. A frontier boozer cleared for action – jukebox, stage, plywood furniture. The only customers are inbreeds with mercury eyes, their credit exhausted, and a few conscripts who went over the wall in '42, and who cling nostalgically to some part of their uniform, battledress or cap, boots that still don't fit. The guv'nor is obviously fucking his daughter, the only barmaid he can get. A blonde shellsuit with tentacles, she's been granted the run of the deepfreeze: choc-ice in one hand, pork pie in the other. The fat man's flies are held with a safety-pin. It's almost legal. He's not sure she's his anyway. Who *is* these days? The missus ran off with an armed robber from Forest Gate, down for the fishing.

Askead is accepted at once. One of our own. Diamond geezer. Only the dog considers him an exotic, worries his coat-tails while he enquires about Rachetts Farm. The interrogative mode demands compensatory gestures, rounds bought – doubles, trebles, a choir of chasers, steak 'n' kidney pud in its molten wraps, fresh from the microwave. Belly sufficiently tickled, the guv'nor recalls the place. They must have passed it on the way in, set well back, up the hill. Return to Allhallows and hang a right. Quiet enough – a couple of the Haward mob weekended there after the affray in Mr Smith's at Catford. Blood came out of the curtains a treat. Worth a pony a week of anybody's cash, overlooks the mudflats, the open sea. Won't be disturbed. Even the postman gives it a miss. Publican would be happy to provide an accommodation address, hold any royalty cheques. The girl will see to the milk.

A lurid twilight eavesdropped on the negotiations. The other freaks had, wisely, stayed outside. They sat, without talking, on a low wall. The steel in the sky clamped hard on the flatlands, the curve of stone-powder track, the peppery redness of the soil. Damp cattle kept their heads down and scrunched the coarse grass with greedy hoovering sounds. The power station on the far side of the creek howled, pouring out paprika smoke you could taste five miles off. Detached from the city, the voyagers had no life, no points of reference, nothing to hate. London Stone was a mockery, a name on the map, a minor geological feature marking the entrance to the rivulet. They ached for *visible* hurt: British Party foot soldiers, pit bulls, cars. Their metropolitan neuroses, not yet slaked, withered from lack of honest irritants. They allowed themselves to drift, in sympathy with the evening fret. They hung above reed beds. Only the light meant anything, its shifts and dramas – the quietly raging sky, the slap of water, the moody wails of estuarine birds, tourists like themselves. What were they all waiting for?

Now the characters are gathered in, Sileen thought, whose consciousness will underwrite the plot? The grammar of events, he understood, was set by the active participants – syntax, pacing, vocabulary. Travelling to Oxford he'd been happy to reserve his energies, let things evolve in Rhab Adnam's frantic crystal (kaleidoscope clouds, wanton hermeticism, telegrammatic prose). Cambridge was loosely cut from Hinton's cloth. Entropy as civic discourse, post-revolutionary modernism talking to itself. The retrospective as the hottest news. About the women, he was lost. He'd never understand them; moon stuff, jealous tiffs. They live in their biology or they wither to greasy string. Their prose is a provocation reverie. They demand a response. But not from me, not here. Does brooding on it grant us title to this dismal landscape? Our final retreat?

Rachetts Farm: a hideout from central casting – Joseph Losey, *The Criminal*. Even *Robbery* by Peter Yates. One of those Stanley Baker pictures that hint at insider knowledge, the *film à clef*. Never missed a gangland funeral, Stan. Paid his respects. Photographed in brown trilby, unbuttoned camelhair, chelsea boots, posing with the lads of Soho Rangers, F.C.: Albert Dimes, Geo. Wisbey, 'Mad' Frankie Fraser, Eddie Richardson. Break a leg.

The caravan's moved on, no cameras have been near the farm in decades. Roof's gone (red pantiles), unsupported chimney stacks, asymmetrical windows, grey cladding over brick, a porch of sorts, plantation verandah. What a waste! Sadly, the action's all in town. Rain on the motorways. Canary Wharf from the elevated railway. Forensic scientists busking one-liners as they ram home a rectal thermometer. There's room for an industrial-strength Barbara Vine crew to spread itself in this dump. The runaways can avoid each other, while they wait on the advent of the counter-terror goons. Askead's behaving so well, he must have grassed.

Sileen sat outside, lizarding the weak sunlight, adjusting to distance – the hurt eyeskin – ceding mental space to the dip of pre-urban land. He was uncomfortable with his present contentment. It should have had his teeth on edge, this absence of streets, damp paddocks creeping to an undramatic sea. He siphoned himself into the width of field and sky. He was glad.

Inland: a spindly water-tower on the horizon, the minor asperations of scrub woods – nothing else. The rest was sky: swift, boisterous, prophetic. Rockwater weather systems from the west, swollen with venom, slate. Hatred as a passing show. Black calligraphy on sheets of silk.

The whereabouts of the Whitechapel renegades *must* be known by now. Why were they still at large? Why was there nothing about the bombing in the prints, no tabloid spleen, no broadsheet analysis? Had they died back there? The Isle of Grain was an acceptable limbo – its refinery tanks, fields of stubble, corn wheels (like remnants of gigantic vegetable tractors), ditches, puddles, creeks, fences, pylons, pleasure boats beached on mud, secret villages. The usual pattern of misguided settlement and post-industrial surrealism. A hedgeless battle zone of binoculars, timid glimpses in the rearview mirror. Apparent movement in the windows of deserted outhouses. Concrete pillboxes on the shingle, game birds rearing out of ditches.

Flesh healed: salt breezes, woodsmoke. Hurt came back to Sileen, anger. His friends. Lying out there on the porch, a non-participant, shotgun across lap (apeing Sammy Taylor at his J. P. Donleavy, Donegal tweeds, worst), he thought of Rachetts Farm as a training ground, a transfusion of virtue, before they went up the line.

Taylor was much in his autumnal thoughts, the promise of revenge. 'I dedicate my life to your destruction.' Isn't that the warning Helen had read out? From the obsidian mirror of the ex-Irish clouds, the crazy Yank returned, possessing him. Was he supposed to be Karl Malden or Marlon Brando in *One-Eyed Jacks*? The guilty watcher on the stoop or the gunman/narcissist crossing deserts for the whip. 'I am another.' The cripple watered his hair, what was left of it, trapped the lank tails with a rubber band. 'Give up art.' He brooded on imagined sleights. Blasted potato sacks, jerked tin cans from fence posts. He knew the form. Paranoia was his candle in the night. He rhapsodied dawn and dusk in the most extravagant terms. Adjectives bred like the purple pox. His lovemaking was baroque.

Helen brushed his cheek affectionately, then bounced from the porch. He followed her, without moving in his chair, seeing her with Taylor's spiteful eyes: the wildness, the quest for something to obey. She ran easily, stride for stride with Andi, down towards the sea.

The women grew stronger by the day. The training went well, there were no distractions. No Muscat to slow them down. (Sliema Felix was closeted with his lady ghost, cobbling together a sequel to *Hardman! the Untold Story of a Hackney Gang Boss* – which Andi had mischievously christened *Handjob! the Confessions of a Motor Masseur*.) Every fresh morning the same circuit – past the gravel pits, and out along the marshes to St Mary's Bay, staying inshore of sea events. Splashing over wet shingle, their ankles make the necessary adjustment – springy turf, jumping across streams, racing the tide. The pillbox already washed over to its roof. Panting, hands on knees, they rest. Turn for home. They could see the farmhouse perched like a Monopoly block on the lip of the hill. They sprinted through the caravans, the Blue Green Algae warnings

– followed the coast path all the way to the pub. Picked up milk and groceries, walked back.

It was unreal, but it was the only shot they had. Blood Money. The cash in their pockets was gone. They lived on Askead's credit – like feasting on wafers of ambrosia. Taking dung for honey. The dwarf was blown. He'd proved a grievous disappointment to the barmaid, his repeated inability to do it standing up. (It would take a forklift to hoist that rump.) The gang needed Tarten's prize money. Before they were taken for natives. Grew skin between their fingers and developed tails.

In the evening, sitting outside, smoking, watching the sun expire, they took it in turns to script alternate endings. A triumph in the ring. A wager on herself. (Sileen didn't mention that everything he'd once had was riding on defeat: 'It's not your night, kid. Take a dive.') Knock Tarten over, then away. Sharpish. A fresh start, West Cork. Russian cruiseboat out of Tilbury. Drug runners on the Medway. Immigrant importers on the Swale. Awaydays to Holland. Danish bacon porn. All the bus pass villains were at it, Europeans to a man. Investing in rock crystal. Excellent returns. Flights to the Isle of Man. Suitcases of paper to Jersey. Gold bars in the duty free. Tot up the VAT.

Collective laughter of the herb. Animal movements everywhere across the drowned lands. Predators and prey. The sun goes down like a rusty tanker in the deepwater channel between Blythe Sands and Mucking Flats. Connections have to be made. Percentages agreed.

Askead was working at it fulltime. Shuttling in to Maidstone, early morning meets in the market, frosty, fern breath, back-of-the-lorry, cigarette tutorials at the tailflap with demi-gypos, ringmen. Bundling on, in a lather; carton of moody videos. Down the coast, Margate. Grease caff in Sheerness, blather with sailors. Frequently, from out of the way kiosks, he belled Nicky Tarten – kept the paymaster in the picture.

Nicky, for his part, affairs boring to a climax, death or glory, supplied Askead with class wheels, a driver – a minicab bombhead, a culture bandit, the least focused speedfreak on the North Kent littoral. A gabbler, Tarten's bad lieutenant: he let rip as he jolted the dwarf over the backroads, making drops, clearing premature antiques from country houses, shredding documents. Too much, even for the Glaswegian, this gulag motormouth. Banged up, seven to ten hours a day, in a sweatbox, windows stuck, ashtrays emptying over his best tights with every handbrake u-turn. Bungalow estates by the Salt Marsh Marina, trailer parks, padlocked sheds. Askead wasn't trained as a passenger. He held no qualifications in landscape.

The driver, Danny Egypt (né Seabrook, his Wapping a.k.a), was a curiosity in the sticks – a curiosity anywhere. Better here, Askead concluded, where he can do less damage. His old man, apparently, got his start as Tarten's indoors barber. Danny was favoured. He could initiate a rumour in the mortuary. Manufacture a thesis from an advert on the floor of his dad's shop. Golden showers. They tickled him. 'Nearly pissed myself.' Golden showers and George Eliot inadvertently linked in some O.T.T. copywriting for Waterstone's Bookshop.

The nutter had a take on everything. The Isle of Grain couldn't contain him. He could have presented *The Late Show* between deliveries. He'd stare into Askead's face as he drove, hands off the wheel, gesturing like a paraplegic. His opinions ran to twenty minutes without drawing breath, chains of amphetamine eloquence. His auto-critical faculties were needlesharp: he sniggered at his own wit, sentences before he delivered it. But cash? 'Forget it, man.' Not a jingle, potless. Tarten's tentshow was his last punt. The last of many. He'd pawned his coat, one of Nicky's castoffs, for a tank of petrol. Now he quivered on the forecourt in dishrag denim, black polo-neck (hostage to moths), laceless lace-ups: a welfare state existentialist. Laughing like a waste-disposal unit.

The dream team! They returned to base by moonlight, weaving across the horn of marshland, the cyclops beam of their single headlight silvering the storage tanks. The flint-eyed Askead, alert, unblinking, no angles left to calculate – and his bubble-blowing chauffeur, nodding out, shuddering from ditch to ditch, the Mandrax manciple. Egypt's monologue, independent of its host, fibrillated the windscreen.

'First sight through the french windows Nicky says Danny cut that fucking thing down before Lola gets the hots for it. Geezer topped himself big place over Sittingbourne way Faversham I think it was we had the clearance schlepping the effects for the new mob's decorator Regency tat. French slag marrying a rock ponce Nicky in the middle drinks from both ends. Leave it out mate he's only walking up to the stiff with his polaroid. What you after I said a Pan paperback jacket circa 1968 melon-breasted manacled mulatto miscegenation *Mandingo* style William Faulkner I said go for it my son. Not clever got to be some heavy comeback. Cicatrix! Worth a shot on its own. More stitches than the Bayeux tapestry. Webbed up with Chelsea poofs cardsharps bent filth. Don't make me laugh. Nicky's one of nature's. Always on the go. Language school Broadstairs portakabin. Barebreast boxing birds. Posters in every boozer on the coast. Don't fancy yours. Got the cadaver down bunged in a flyover end of story. A few quid to the Micks. One of them jams a 50p coin in his eye-socket couldn't believe it myself.'

Believe it? Askead didn't even *hear* it. Danny's compulsive rap slowed the dwarf to M25 pace. A persistent vegetative state – in which it took him ten minutes to part his lips and groan. His fingers, spilling tobacco from the paper tube, were gauntlets inside a plutonium jukebox. Smoke was too weary to invent itself. It sulked like a bad smell, a nameless marsh gas. The car stank like hedgehog cooking in the radiator. Askead turned over the rubber mats. He checked out Egypt's shoes. He had to discover the precise location of the pong. Otherwise the curse would stick, he'd never get away. Egypt would cruise him through the gates of hell.

Sofya was the only one moving about the house. Nocturnal. Excused dawn jogs. She set up a darkroom with equipment Egypt had been ordered to fetch. (He brought gear for Helen and Andi, knocked off Canning Town sportswear.) Tarten expected Sofya to provide posters, intimate training camp pin-ups, to whet the punters' appetites in clubs. He was out of luck. Sofya would never touch a camera again.

She worked all night, and was working still when the other women set off on their run. She stayed inside while they skipped and sparred, lifted turnip sacks, cut wood. Madness. Sileen, from his lounger on the stoop, watched it all.

Taps running, red light: it was cool in the old scullery. Sofya handled the strips of film – revolving, washing, pegging out. Most, she destroyed. A single roll, thirty-six frames, was preserved. Helen's face in the hospital lobby was the last of them. The shock: cracks in the lens transferred to that flawless face, distancing the subject, validating the portrait with spurious age. Sofya blew it up (a conscious pun) – the closer to life, the more unreal. Like cutting around a cake, she trimmed the background. Helen's terror, eyes closed, became a mask in fact.

One for Helen, another for Andi – so that they could shadowbox without the interference of the mirror. Hairline fractures, the afterblast.

Behind the farmhouse, in the yard, they sparred by touch, by sound. Hooded like penitents. Standing still, aiming by instinct, the hollowness of gloves tapping a target card. Sweatgrey tracksuits, baggy and worn, scuffed boots. In the dirt. A flick, a feint. Until both stopped, scarcely breathing, waited. Late afternoon: night-spilling trees, a pale sun extinguished in the sodden paddocks.

Sileen, just then, was lost. Inattentive, but aware of the actions of others, unconcerned: he listened to the night. There was no strength in him to shift his weight in the chair. He saw a slippage of earth and water, vanishing landfall. For the first time in all these months the X-rays didn't matter. Radon daughters, Drage-Bell, Hodgson, limestone fields: terminated. Pursuit had kept him alive. Now it was meaningless. He was adrift.

Innumerable rays, of a subtle, violet hue, pierced the strange semi-darkness, in all directions. They radiated from the fiery rim of the Green Sun.

Sileen's hearing, in defence, grew preternaturally sharp, rebounding, batlike, from the water-tower – a single car on the road, out of Rochester, St Mary Hoo, the long hill. It will turn at the gate, jolting up the track. Cancel it. Withdraw that sentence. The chart of Sileen's protofiction is laid over this small patch of ground – borderland, triangulation, women, gangsters. Correlatives. Keep the Isle of Grain intact and the mysteries will solve themselves. He wanted that intrusive car to explode, a fireball. He wanted the sight of it, far away, from a hiding place among the marshes.

He'd lost the novelist's power to destroy. Powerless, he was freed from all his obligations – pain. Stay here. Enjoy what is. The car. The car forbade it. The car was fate. A Mercedes gliding beneath skeletal pylons, dim bald fields. A torpedo in an X-ray world. Fat wheels splashing orange puddles over soft verges. Danny Egypt, chewing dry lips, running the Tarten Brothers out for a peek at their investment.

Nicky, stepping from the motor, felt sick. His hand rested on the bonnet's silver sheen. If he could grab the moon he might be saved. 'Fuck this, Tone. It's black as Ridley Road.' Salt bit his scar. The gross lack of amenities was a scandal. Indefinite mud – without a flash of neon to protect your brogues. Even the sky was unsteady, clouds on the charge, like a flock of decapitated sheep. Animals yelped and barked. They were killing each other out there. You could hear them chewing flesh, crunching small bones. Leave the countryside to shirtlifting poets.

Wystan. 'A valley full of thieves and wounded bears.' Too right, my son. Eastchurch, the prison complex on Sheppey, brought back times better forgotten. Chaps together, sunbathing on the sward, after a heavy workout, not a care, giving Logical Positivism a bit of a bash.

Danny leant on the horn, East End fashion, doorbells were for toffs. He brought Helen, backlit, to the doorway, a towel around her neck.

'Monster news, girls. We've got the date and we've got the place.' Tarten, fronting it, reached for Helen's arm. Post-Don King, all serious promoters should sweat like Turks and rap in broken rhyme. He whistled low, impressed by Helen's muscle tone.

'Prime, darlin'. You're mean, clean, ready to be seen. And the mazooma's rolling in. We've named the day to make our play. Week Thursday: no more jaw, the war on the shore. The place with the pow-er, I – O – G. Reach that beach, Isle of Grain.'

Helen blocked the clown. No way was Tarten coming into the house. She felt that edginess that fighters are supposed to feel: male PMT – with horns. She'd drop him if he took another step. A veteran of inter-personal bother, Nicky caught the whiff of risk, and backed away. Flicked up his collar to hide the loss of face.

'Yeah. Mega. Right.' Back to the motor. One final throwaway. 'By-the-by, darlin'', your original opponent has had to let her opportunity go. Truth is, the bird we pencilled in has done a runner. Bottled it. Up the spout. Five months gone by a darkie. A useful welter Georgie Francis was keeping an eye on, as it happens. Management's still game. They'd put her in. But the punters won't wear it. Family men, know what I mean? So your mate gets her shot, the big girl. From undercard to headliner, don't thank me. Gonna be a cracker, the fancy all agree.'

No room to turn. Too dark to see anything beyond the track. The farmhouse door had slammed and the lights gone out. The silence of the sea. Egypt didn't dare to scratch the Merc. He'd have to reverse all the way to the blacktop.

Time's arrow: beams sweeping over events they'd already lived through. Had Nicky reached the house? Was it over? The landscape wouldn't behave itself, settle down, when Danny Egypt was not allowed to talk.

FIFTEEN

Ian Askead and Danny Egypt had, between them, fixed the boat. Sileen would have to take it on trust. Some deracinated hippie out of the Isle of Dogs, suckered in silt, and coming up for the third time: he was double-anchored fifty yards out from the Upnor Marina, windward of the power station. A nest of resin smugglers, pleasure boats with testosterone punch; rummies on the hard, ex-merchant navy salts with commendations in bullshit – bowlegged from pitching decks and oilskin sodomy in a force nine gale. They were, essentially, out of it, non-players, talking up the good times. Askead's man was, by repute, the most desperate of the bunch.

A runner – by water. Askead was wary of the substance. Water was hard times, the poser's whisky. (Auld wifies had been known to clean their teeth in the stuff, which explained the state of Scottish dental hygiene.)

When Egypt took him into the caravan to resuscitate the skipper, they levered a window to dilute the fug – saw nothing seaside but sloppy fields of muck left when the river drained away. Sand in solution, slime crescents, tyres. Take a breath. Swaying masts, creaking cranes, the percussion of all those loose bits hanging from poles. Mock voyages, abandoned forts, navigation lights chanced by wrecking gangs. A prime site for those who ship out in rum bottles. Who wrap their meat puddings in outdated charts. He was up for it, the sozzled wreck. 'No problem, man.' A oncer in the hand. Or half of that. Half of half. A can of red diesel and a spliff.

Static Sileen was beginning to see daylight. Upstream to Tilbury, then ship out to somewhere hyper-fictional, where Nicky Tarten would be deleted by the PC junta. San Francisco, Montreal. A bucketshop Polish packet. All he had to do was talk to the girls, explain the fix.

'Now,' Helen said. 'Let's leave now. Why wait?'

'What do we use for cash?' Sileen was playing it steady, weighing the pros and cons. 'We're charity cases, us. Parasites on parasites.'

He hadn't brought himself to let her in on the game plan, the grand strategy. A couple of brisk rounds, then the dive. The sky was portentous: star beams winked, recalling other walks, deeper, more intimate silences.

They had eaten surprisingly well. A special night, the last before the weigh-in, the battle. Helen wanted him to talk her out of it. Fitness was addictive. Unless they kept on walking, away from the farmhouse, the island of light, down towards the sea, she would have to take it to the finish, perform.

The sense of well-being was a snare: candles, fire, communal meal. Askead had cobbled together some quite acceptable nosh. Sileen waited patiently for the usual aftertaste – cramps, sweats. He was disappointed. The short order whizz had done a good job. That in itself was ominous. The relish with which the dwarf bunged vegetables into the pot, hacked at aromatic spices, peppered meat with ash, swabbed, macerated. Tested the bubbling solution until he reeled. Rich gravy stayed on Sileen's lips. The dozen bottles of plonk that Nicky Tarten sent over.

She took his arm: an Edith Wharton countess. His hand lifted the brush of hair from her neck, touched a vein. They looked right together. In the dark. But the suggestion holds: she is supporting him, fetching him home. Sileen's still weak. They have nothing to say. She likes the phosphorescence of his new black suit, the green of it. Egypt had scavenged the outfit from a Sheerness ragshop, still warm from an unexpected aneurysm. Funeral kit the installment-payer never got to use (even at his own). Pity about the size. But it gave Sileen a certain style. Electro-plated: long socks, short legs. A Liverpudlian assault comic. The dark glasses he'd found in the comb-pocket were a Mephisophelean touch. That was his charm, lack of taste, wear what you find.

Helen squeezed. He didn't know what she meant. There were horns on his cap. The nature of their relationship was secret. They would never be an item.

His shrivelled weight: she could carry him in her arms, the old warmth was still there, tested and true, inexplicable tenderness. Of all the myriad human possibilities, potential couplings, this one, by some spin of the dice, was hers. He knew it, played upon it, felt it himself. The best cons are the ones that are true. He had betrayed her before, was betraying her now, and would again.

Without premeditation, he led her around the house to the place where the car was parked. If they could not escape, they might dream of it. Black enough: he reached for her hand. Egypt's voice, tight with hysteria, climbed from an open window – the chemically aroused rush of it. Demented humour from an execution shed: a helium high to precede the cyanide cough. 'Rubrics of assumed servility . . . hawhaw . . . Can't lose, Tarten . . . haw . . . the bordello he operated in Belfast for Bernie Silver, suckering the Micks *and* Special Branch . . . haw . . . Vatican plum that turns to a furball in your mouth . . . hawhawhaw.'

Sileen opened the heavy door of the Mercedes and helped Helen in. Private space invaded. Hands on the wheel make the cripple an interrogator of instruments. The urge to lick Havanas. Shoot Verdi tapes. Witness silk. Plunge syrettes of morphine tartrate into milkwhite thighs.

'I can't.' She picked up on the game. 'Don't make me.'

She was taking her stand before he could open his campaign, outline his brilliant, face-saving notion. His curtain speech. 'I don't *have* to say it aloud. You know. You've always known. I care. Deeply. And I've thought of a way out. For you. For both of us.'

The smell of money disguised as leather, treachery, cologne. They sank into it – Tarten's venal affairs. The moon smoking to cocktail ice. The black engine of Europe. A tinted windscreen turning into cinema. Fog, shaken from the damp pelts of cattle, closed over them in a conspiratorial hug.

I'm one of nature's celibates, Sileen decided, a solitary. Why has this woman invaded my life? He didn't want her thinking for him, modifying his worst instincts, making him appear half-human. He couldn't – get enough. He had to be with her every waking moment. Sharing her risk, the challenge. Going into the ring with Andi.

'Helen?' A mistake. He *never* used her name. She'd be alerted now. He'd have to wait.

Night sounds, distance. Confused information. Copses and clumps in the tilted fields. She wanted him to be quiet. Freshwater streams: the trickle and gush, weeks of rain, puddles extending to ponds, ponds to lakes – nothing to keep the sea out.

He kissed her. Good move: affectionate desire. Invoking in its originality, previous assaults. Doing it, thinking about doing it. He gentled, probed. Controlled spontaneity. They could speak later. Not now, hearts in mouths. Blueness outside. The car invaded by rivers of mist.

He wanted this, more than the scam. More than Ireland, escape. This was all there was: glass, steel, rubber, chrome. Her breath, her scent, the stub of Tarten's cigar. More even than the solution of the tower.

Helen, laughing, followed Sileen into the back seat. She helped him, pulling, twisting, freeing the prosthetic limb. The act teetered on the edge of farce: they conspired. Then she was over him, her tongue, doing what he wanted her to do.

Partly undressed, they rested – undecided. The initiative faltered. Behind them: the winking lights of the farmhouse, Egypt's rock show salvage, smeared the rear window. Back projection. The illusion of movement: *Pierrot le Fou*. Sentiment without the Eastmancolor. A longer, bleaker night, this. A studio cradle. Grips rocking the chassis. *On the Waterfront*. Feel the car move, the sea under it. Feel the car shudder.

Shivering, Helen has wrapped Tarten's camelhair around her shoulders; collar turned up, playing the wrong part. She's not Rod Steiger, not the fixer, the mob's mouthpiece. She's too tall, with too much hair. She can't be a gangster – she hasn't got a brother. Sileen's confused. He's the one who should be persuading *her* to take a dive in the Garden. Not her night. They slide, both of them, eyeless, into the black river.

'Not your night, kid.' He can't do it, can't get the lines out. They've been said too often. Sileen's dead already, a marionette on a meat hook. A stiff with a hat instead of a face. She's carrying him. The victim's on top.

Licking, sucking, wild for, shamed for herself. Going alone while he watches. Watching him. He raises her sweatshirt, head between her breasts, tasting the sweet almond of her nipples. The musk of her stubble, the light fleece. This is the answer. He was panting, gasping at the limited air. Exhaust her, drink her dry. Again. Sacrifice himself utterly. Wear her out. Rubber legs, belly like water. Gorge himself, leave the rest to market forces. To Andi Kuschka. Andi is bigger, stronger, madder. She's got the weight, the reach, the chin. Do it this way. Bring Helen down – with love.

Nicky's suspension worked a treat; the motor didn't buck, it sighed –

as Sileen shook his mistress out of her leggings. The car was his pander. That's what you paid for. Top dollar hide to absorb all secretions. He rolled down the short socks and chucked them out of the window. Power play electrics. Her feet were gamey, flavoursome. He nuzzled the curd from between her toes. He massaged, smoothed the delicate arch of her foot. She liked it. Told him so. He moved on: sampling with rapid vertical strokes, through the gauzy material; then the meat itself, her labial trim, thick as gristle. They feasted. He. She. Those cries.

Outside, spreading the coat, he lifted her onto the bonnet – her knickers bowling away down the path towards the marshes. There was rain in the air. He would give the limo a thorough seeing to. Her knees were raised. It wasn't easy, she helped him to find the best position. He plunged, reared. His good leg buckled under him. They fell onto the ground. It was cold, wet, stony. They rearranged themselves, continued.

Sileen was in so deep that he had no connection with the act. The house in darkness. Helen was his entire landscape. A weakness – a thinning in the sky over Sheerness. A pale inevitability they strove, with all their power, calling out, to reverse.

SIXTEEN

The cream. The fancy in their pomp. What a mob! You couldn't rent them. All the chat, out in the weather, concerned Leonard McLean, the 'Mean Machine', the Guv'nor. ('Appalling exterior,' stated his own counsel, David Whitehouse.) Len had drawn eighteen months for some over-enthusiastic bouncing: his job, his wages – what was he supposed to do if some headcase from Coketown strips to the buff on the dance floor? Dead liberty. One of our own. Take the scrap with the Mad Gypsy, after he nutted Len. Spark out. Forty-five minutes on the slab. The quack thought it was a coldstore job, not unlimited rehab in the London. Hard as nails, Lenny. Harder: pig iron, rods in concrete. Big kid at heart. Always had his hand in his pocket. Never leave one of the old girls with an empty glass. Charity? They'd have closed down the Bethnal Green Kiddies' Hospital years ago without him. Cancer? He practically invented it. A diamond. Ask any of the lads down the Freddie Mills. Soft as shit – till you crossed him. Liberty takers, he couldn't abide them.

Faces. Motors. Threads. A genuine hum in the car park. The Isle of Grain had seen nothing like it since Dunkirk. More a showroom, a dream forecourt, than a paddock at the sea's edge. Salt'll play havoc with the paintwork. Rollers, Beamers, Mercs. White men's transport. And plenty of the flashier transatlantic cousins: fenders, upholstery. Thickets of aerials. Latest odds yelled into the mobiles. Plantations of rubber, Amazonia deforested, to mould these cross-plys. The alloy, the chrome – blinding, John.

They must have decanted Hoxton, called time in every Camberwell drinker, shuttered the Shepherd's Bush betting-shops. Clubs were deserted in Catford, ranks of cards went unpunched in Dagenham. Stag night, ladies' night, invitation only. Zapata moustaches dripping with

Bailey's, the girls. Blokes with enough gold in their mouths to tear up the national debt. Mink, camel, stoat, leopard – they coathangered the lot. No sex discrimination. The event of the season, definitely.

Ian Askead, fag in mouth, traditional jobsworth, moved along them, collecting tithes. 'Yes, sir no sir. Lefthand down, guv. A long one on the Wapping Wildcat.' Tickets, pink slips, high fives. Something in the pocket of his labcoat for every eventuality. Dutifully, he explained the last minute change of venue – keep the Old Bill on the hop – from the refinery to the Grain Tower. (He forgot to mention that the tower was a good half-mile out to sea). Much more exclusive. Preservation order. And the tide was right. If they hurried they might catch a glimpse of the car ferry leaving Sheerness for Vlissingen. Worth getting their feet wet. Miles of wrinkled mud and a big boat sliding across the rim of it – no water to be seen, a mirage.

Twilight: a chaos of headlights, horns, brake-lights, curlews, rooks. Askead's labcoat came into its own. He could have passed for a Walthamstow dog handler. A changeling, he flitted everywhere, deft as moss in the cracks of paving stones. He winked. He nudged. He worried the stragglers down the ramp to the shore.

Something of a challenge, the glycerine mouth of the Medway, for the crocodile-skin slip-ons, the heels that had you tripping like Nureyev. The foxes, the spunky redheads, they dug in their spikes: they weren't going to paddle along a slithering green causeway to no bleeding tower. It was fathoms out, duty free, see Calais from the balcony. The atmosphere took a turn for the worse. But Nicky Tarten, shrewd Nick, was ahead of the game. He had a consignment of rubber boots spread on the hard – fishermen's waders, overshoes, Cotswold green wellies. The cigars were mollified. The minks shrugged. Kvetching, they waddled into the sea-fret.

Tarten was waiting for them on the ruined deck. He loved it, the way they squealed and squelched – the rows, the rucks, the bother. The tide closing in behind them, cutting off their escape. His own kingdom, the Tower of Grain. 'So down the phallic stairway come with rage.' *Yesterday's Sailors*. The old songs were the best. What a venue! Eat your heart out, Barry Hearn. They'd swallow anything, the ones who made it before he locked the doors. The rest could swim.

Rubbish had been cleared, the floors swept and sanded. Limited seating on oil drums for the lame, the shrapnel-couriers. The balcony for heavyweights and connected families. The groundlings could stand and like it. Generator installed. Night-shoot lighting: pups, brutes, floods to knock Wellington bombers out of the sky. A pleasure palace. An ocean queen. A real pearl in a silicon sea.

Punters secure – tobacco fug marries mist – Nicky proudly announces the card. Cash changes hands. Bundles of it. Shaggy fingers goitred in gold. The reek of diesel cologne. Blue smoke-cones climbing back into arc lights. Galleries packed, flashy with tom. You could look down through the tower, a hollow cake. Weaving spots manhandled by doped-out roadies. Paroled maniacs choke the ring. Hired muscle, led by Anthony Tarten, clear a path for the participants. Nicky, aloft, white tuxedo, black silk T-shirt, climaxes his mike.

First up, nothing special, a couple of dogs ripping the fur from a black bear – an Albanian import with no pedigree. Bruno, muzzled, chained, has only his claws. Goes against the spirit of fair play. They don't like it, the animal lovers. They think it's Anthony in a hair suit. The creature is so clumsy. He backhands one of the mastiffs, the other hangs from his throat. Blood-spit everywhere. The legs of the ladies. The white jackets. One dog, his back broken, spun in the sawdust, frantically chasing a tail that was no longer there. They began to see the funny side of it. They hooted. Knockabout. Right then. The crossbreed, its ribs a cayenne takeaway, leapt at the bear's opened neck, locked on – while the maddened beast scooped out its entrails.

Sileen, Helen, Andi – in the boat – have different excuses for nausea. Waiting on the tide, they can hear the bearpit celebrations. Hear them and imagine them, the settling of wagers. Dogs screaming like children.

Navigation lamps sponsor an oily redness in the channel. The Grain Tower begins to float. There's still time. Danny Egypt's pilot, the self-incriminating moustache, could run them to the Essex shore – Southend, Canvey, Purfleet (sanctuary at Dracula's abbey). But they knew he wouldn't, they wouldn't let him. The tower was the end of England, the right symbol.

A disused lighthouse alongside the power station – torchbeams from that direction, high culture invective: the amphetamine Weltanschauung of Egypt bluing the slipway. A jangle of buckets. Danny as their cornerman? A preview of the sounds heard by concussed boxers.

Muscat. Sombre, dignified, arm in sling. 'Girls.'

The old lion tries to pump it, the right stuff. He's not sure about water, but darkness has always been his hood. Water excuses some criminal tailoring. Case proved by the freak untying the painter, poling them out. The current catches the stubby hull, they spin. Felix crosses himself. The women sit, silent, in the stern. Egypt and the bad moustache argue over the outboard, exchanging recipes for disaster.

The ruin loomed out of the fog. A barnacled Alcatraz of insecure platforms, ladders, stairs – with a single jutting periscope. Sileen felt his feet on the slippery concrete, the spiral ascent. He anticipated, jumped ahead: strange paddling steps, in expectation of the light.

Must go on, important. Rising from the silt, the double of his dream tower – before it was X-rayed. This wind. Can't fit the words together. Missing fingers, he bites them. Pain to bring back the cause of pain, memory. Swing the wheel, captain. Give up this story.

The star dressing-room: a windowless corridor. Muscat supervised the bandaging of hands. Mummy priest, master of oils, he'd never seen such puny mitts. Bone pencils – with painted nails. He was game, but he was on another loser. He felt it in his liniment. The flash bird on a bench, face down, while Egypt slapped on the rub. She should be on her toes, working up a decent sweat.

Advice? What was it his trainer used to say? 'Breathe hard, Felix. Make it look good for a couple of rounds. Puff when you punch. Thumb your snot in your opponent's eye. Take your fall near the ropes. Give the other bugger a good shlep to the neutral corner. Wear him down that way.'

Nicky Tarten pokes his head around the door to wish them luck (and palm Muscat the pills). Helen, in a hooded sweatsuit, clipping shadows, tells him to get lost. Andi matches her – flicking at her flickering self, the wall picture Plato mistook for an ideal form. Muscat and Egypt were next to go. The women wanted no part of them. Alone, they skipped and stretched; rested, fixed their costumes, checked their faces, their hair: each acting as the other's glass. They hadn't decided what they would do when the bell went.

A diamond-glass dome. In the lamproom of the lighthouse, Commander Klaw fiddled with a long-focus lens: camera as telescope. Old gears creaked and ground. He felt that the building's iron stem was fixed, the cockpit revolving, continually, around it. Sound reinforced the illusion of a sea cottage; a whitewashed space in which a man, in the gentle decline of nature, could meditate upon his approaching end. The wind, the waves, the fleeting sky.

'Sit on my face, bitch.'

The girl from the motor-pool didn't know where to put herself. Her skirt was too tight. Power is no aphrodisiac when the font of it gasps like a punctured goat. 'Sit on my face.'

Monkey Klaw, reading the headlines of her shock, rephrased. 'Tricky case, miss. Been watching these buggers for months.'

Offshore ops, he could do without them – liaison with the dreaded C & E. Customs and Excise. Crappy excuses, more like. Play-it-by-the-book wallahs, TV friendly. He'd much rather be over there, in the big tower, the thick of it. Mingling with the great unwashed. Incognito. A footsoldier of the Lodge, pressing flesh, while a bunch of dysfunctional lags club each other into premature senility. Bare-knuckle heavies, toe to toe, sledgehammering their other selves, bleeding like pigs, hurling their heads into a welcome fugue of fists. The claret! The honest sweat!

I was there, Harringay, ringside, the first Mills/Lesnevich scrap. Freddie sleepwalking for six rounds while the Yank sculpted him, chipped granite. No attempt at defence – you had to admire them, those dinosaurs. No namby-pamby medics standing by. The drum of bone on bone, elbows sounding ribs. Corkscrew hook to the kidneys, trailing thumb in the eye. Heads down like rutting stags. They were a different species, men. Pain? They didn't know what the word meant. Tear off an ear? They'd thank you for it, slip it down their shorts and carry on.

He was blue as the Bay of Angels. His tongue was out. The girl held the coffee beaker to his lips. She knew she was in for a night of it. Klaw reeled in erotic empathy. The dome of the lighthouse was another ring, the acorn head of a monster prick. Condensation. Married breaths. He'd done a bit in his day. They all had, the high fliers – Nipper Read and his trophy cabinet. No ghosted biography would have a prayer without the syndicated shot: arms folded, chest shaved, statuettes, poster from the Met Championships at Manor Place Baths. Soak up your punishment without complaint. Monkey suits, regalia in briefcase. Pain disperses through the system like the soft plum rush of heroin. Call it pleasure. Listen to its voice.

Through the hooting marine dark, Klaw's men – mud fetishists, crawling shrubs – move gracefully, silently. Like acid rain. A virus put to sleep for seven years. Nocturnal emissions of the Secret State. They slide beneath the storage tanks. Log the number-plates of the cars. Dig in the sand.

The Commander's grip trembles on the focus ring. The Grain Tower shivers. Don't breathe and he's over there. (Live sound wired to a shell in his ear.) He'll watch the girls go at it, hammer and tongs. Topless wildcats – scratching, spitting, pulling hair. Call it duty, defence of realm. Then whistle up the cavalry, snatch the survivors, inform Paddington Green. Squeeze the trigger. Tuktuktuk! Hold the front page: TERROR TITS AMOK. A night editor's dream conjunction that would make his name.

SEVENTEEN

Nicholas Tarten, breaking off from talking odds, glanced up, out of the roofless tower, at the sky. History happened too fast when there was no-one around to write it up. Low fog shot off before you knew it was there, clouds went on the trot to reveal fixed stars – sharp as the studs in a gladiator's posing pouch. He noted the conjunctions, accepted his fate. Scorpio rising. Heaven after heaven, as the old boys said, like lifting the lid on a wormy cheese. The heavy money was riding on the dyke, whatsername, Andi. Fiscal malpractice was urgently required: suitcases of Nigerian liquidity to feed a Soviet drought. One of the cows would have to take a spectacular fall.

'Felix, my son, looking good.' Tarten's lies were threats. He pinched the Maltese pimp's waxy cheek. Lenin had more life. Felix, in reflex, obliged with a diluted account of the Glare. Nicky feinted an evil jab. Muscat blocked it with his plastered forearm. They grinned – stretching gortex flesh that promised to tear.

'Felix!'

'Nicky!'

'Felix. You brought her on beautiful, the gel. Mouse on wheels.'

'She won't let you down, Nicky.'

'She better not.'

'No chance.'

'Smart money's on the slag.'

'No chance.'

'You sure? What you heard, Felix? You used to read meat lovely, bummaree.'

'Nicky. No chance. Ain't got the moves. Never go the distance, her.'

'Swear?'

'My life.'

'You said it, Felix. Right?'

'My bollocks, the brunette. All bottle, Nicky.'

'Prime. You done a good job. I was right to trust you, son. You never was a grass.'

Reaches out to pump Muscat's hand, the smiling Judas. Inside the sling: agony. Stiff fingers clamped. Not a sign. Stand-up villain. Old school (Queensbridge Road Secondary: nine lifers, two of the top lorry hi-jackers – plus, on the sporting side, Ron 'Chopper' Harris, and a bloke who brushed feathers for Prince Monolulu.) Muscat a wrong 'un? Leave it out.

A low, admiring rumble (like anticipating punters in the queue of a Chinese takeaway) at the first sight of the girls. They didn't half look tasty. The daughters you never had. Roadies (doing a foreigner) sweated to tosh their spots, follow the headliners down towards the ring. Simultaneous entry. Shimmering in white, swimming through the navy darkness like twin spermatozoa. No precedence, no previous form. Sisterhood. Goy princesses, live females – hair to shoulders, legs you'd have to imagine. Catching the debased light on white satin and tossing it back. Shields of purity. Angel dust glittering in their perms.

Silence at the eye of the storm. Then the howls, the stamps, approbation like instant regicide. A bearpit. It *is* a bearpit. They're sweeping blood and dung. Money sweating in their paws. Whack whack. My score to your pony on the blonde. Half a ton to a oncer on the gash. Anybody here speak English? Done! Monkey upfront says inside three rounds. The business. Top of the card.

The Commander's hand was out for a refill, a hot cup: he couldn't take his eye from the camera. The moon – its virgin path across the black water. Foreshortened intimacy. His driver, cap off, entering, despite herself, into the atmosphere of collusion and permitted sadism, gripped it – a tacit squeeze of sympathy. They had blooded themselves on slapstick, tested the limits of their humanity by watching the red stuff gush into the runnels. You had to admire the undercard, bouncers who had done most of their bouncing full-frontal – with their faces. How did they stay on their feet? Cillick-Klaw was proud to be one of them, the same species, male. On borrowed courage, he manipulated the driver's glove into his lap.

———

The costumes – Nicky had done a bit of work here – were suggestive of clubland, blue filter, benzedrine jazz. Rome, Hollywood, an upmarket roadhouse in Braintree. Gold dust powdering the waves of Helen's hair: dandruff from King Midas. Sparkling red stars on the blonde – as if she'd done her backcombing with a cutthroat razor. Beams crossed, to trap them, transforming women into holograms. After the shambles of the preliminary bouts the punters couldn't believe this: video quotations floating through the awed darkness. Anklelength, silk-finish satinette, wide lapel trenchcoats. Fedoras cheekily tilted over one eye. Molls *and* gunsels at the same time, semiotic confusion. Super-hero colours (from DC Comics) for their boots: Helen in scarlet, Andi in blue. The event was rapidly becoming its own retrospective. Virtual Reality is so much sharper than the other kind – the hurtful sharpness of assembly line Coke cans. Tarten's ring was the empty frame of a Pop Art canvas awaiting its apotheosis as silkscreen sentiment. (The audience would know, by colour balance, which champion to support.)

The girls ducked through the ropes to an overscored aria from the Fat Man.

Sileen, in negotiation with Egypt, out on the water, standing off, heard it – the Roman intro, louder than it was, amplified by the peculiar acoustics of the Grain Tower, its funnels, hollows, decks. One third of his winnings, Toddy offered. Straight in the pocket. No questions asked. 'Make that fifty percent': the counter. Don't forget the boatman, he needs his cut, his little drink. (Through the nose, Sileen reckoned.) Good thing he'd laid down his bet with Muscat months ago, the odds were tightening – despite Tarten's attempts to talk up Andi's pedigree, the killer punch she carried. She'd got no form. He'd have to close a premature book.

Sileen liked it outside, the uncertain status, tied to a slimy beam beneath the building, rocking gently in the gloom, hearing events upstairs as a thunder of inaccurate and conflicting reports. The night was everything he desired: the psycho dramas the tower provoked. But Danny Egypt wouldn't button it. He wanted to see action from the frontline, the ringside; synchronize his monologue with the dancing feet of women. Sileen would be forced to shadow the bagman, safeguard his investment.

Klaw's boys, his khaki minstrels, on their bellies, ducking among silos, wading through creeks, sealed off the Isle of Grain. Roadblocks at Allhallows, Cuckold's Green, Middle Stoke. Rubber dinghies sweeping the river mouth. The refineries secured. Men with nightsights scuttling up ladders. Kayaks closing on the tower. Hairtrigger stuff. Gummy jockstraps. Snuff previews. Kill pulses. Over-rehearsed mayhem.

The chief spook rode their excitement: guided from on high, issued instructions – closed his legs to retain the tentative warmth in his driver's hand. 'Blow me!' Andi and Helen, the female targets, were safely located. Askead with sponge and bucket. 'Blow me if I haven't lost him.' The men were ordered to tread water until the cripple was accounted for: laser crosshairs on his breast, marked with scarlet like an adulterer.

'Do it!'

There he is – battling his way down through the thick of the crowd. It's standing room only, but Danny Egypt's nasal whine, his ninety degree elbows, clear a route. Sileen sees Helen – at the very moment when Klaw sees him. From the rackety galleries, the rabble, looking into a smoky pit without the Commander's privileged magnification, can barely make out the bright dolls at the centre of a seething square. The chant: 'Get 'em off, get 'em off, get 'em off.'

Nicholas Tarten entrusts the bag to his brother while he climbs into the ring to make his announcement. Anthony, it's obvious, is holding the float, cash money, the grubby rolls. Nicky's hair takes the full beam, longer these days, greased like a melted LP. Arms aloft, palms open, he tries to silence the mob. 'Get 'em off, get 'em off.' Helen, who has tried her hat on Muscat's head, shifts her weight, fretfully, from foot to foot, while the old pimp growls his instructions.

'Get 'em off.'

It's the sight of the gloves – fists cased in soft-shell crabs – that incenses the customers. They haven't muddied their loafers to eyeball a beauty pageant. Nakedness, shit, death: they want combat. The mood is ugly. Nicky's never let them down before: pit bulls, eight hour epics, boilers with plenty of meat on the bone arsedeep in sirloin. 'Get 'em off.'

The dwarf Askead, riot's medium, saved Tarten's skin – bouncing through the ropes and tugging at Andi's wrap. (What an opportunity!) Muscat, one-handed, does his best for Helen. The racket dies so suddenly that the spooks in the channel can hear the rayon slither of the coats sliding from their shoulders. The roadies take their cue and dim the house-lights. Twin spots pick out the performers, the warrior queens.

A fusillade of vestas, Dunhills, round-the-neck-on-a-string blow-lamps: face fire. Photo-flashes at the throat. Dozens of high contrast portraits of lust and greed. Nose hair, the black pinholes of incipient beard – seborrhea. Pig eyes shuttering as small flares scorch dry tobacco tubes. The white women – pure as plastic. A smoke salute. Like the election of a Pope. A curtain of bad breath separates the mob from their prey.

Now syrups of sentiment drip on the spectacle. 'Good kids. Nieces. Brave salts.' They've all got one somewhere, hidden away, a bridesmaid in a golden frame. Heads down, they know the form, shaggy knuckles brushing tears from arctic eyes. Then gob it up, spit green, on with the show.

Anthony Tarten uses this reverential interlude to work his way out of the scrum, bag bundled under arm. Retreat – before one of the mares asks for her wedge. Sileen has him clocked.

Wondrous hair, hair you could eat, saponaceous, shoulder length, fissile with conditioners – even the women in the crowd grew horny at the sight of it. The hair dropped off. Cancer fear! Chemotherapy sob stories in the tabloids: a con. Wigs, like squashed cats, handed to the seconds. Heads shaven. Brides of the Hasidim. Bad. And worse to come. The nakedness, so much admired, was in the mind's eye, pornographic jolts summoned from elsewhere – one-night hotels, glossy pages blowing across the park. They thought, when the spots first hit the girls, and their poor hearts absorbed the shock, that they were honouring avatars of the New, championettes of austere narcissism – like Lisa Lyons (who they did not know) photographed by Robert Mapplethorpe. Full body drag. They fancied it, without having read up on the theory. The 'pose' as a gender challenge. A chick invaded from *inside* by a bloke, her animus. Imagine this: a *white* Eubank with perfectly formed (good as silicon) tits, gold hoops in the ear. *Health & Efficiency* with muscle tone.

Confusion made the crowd feel good. Something to talk about over a couple of drinks. But not this, Tarten's stroke. Body stockings, poxy gloves. Hair like chicken squit on a free-range egg. Heads like armpits, after the Ladyshave. The bastard done 'em for a oncer on the door. They wanted the full muff for that investment. Muff *and* muscle. Hair in all the places you'd expect, mounds of it. Cheeky, flocculent: the oakum of the unwashed. For what they'd laid out – petrol, bar snack, outfit for the bird – they might as well have run down Turnmills for a wife-swopping session (if they could borrow a wife). A choker! Brass neck. These tarts fronting it in lycra. Like cyclists – lesbos, freaks.

Gloves kiss. The usual warnings issued. Tarten decides to let it run. Give the women their head. Find Anthony and skip while the fancy are still in shock. But no more amateurs, not never. No pick-ups. Support the open market: he'll book direct from Hamburg in the future. The crowd are enjoying the first rush in their own style – stamping, baying, flicking lighted cigarettes. A disaster can be as good as a toe-to-toe affair. Keep them occupied while Nicky gets away.

One last attempt to make the girls see reason and shed their vests and he dives through the ropes into the belly of the lynch mob. Pandemonium. Factions splitting like rogue cells. Suspect tissue contaminated by noise. 'Kill kill.' They whip out fetish objects of their own desire: ivory-handled razors, flick-knives, Milanese coshes, tampon-shaped canisters of Mace (designed to look like vaginal deodorants). That's for the sophisticates from the Epping Forest fringe. The faces from south of the river, in shiny demob suits, ties jerked loose, scenic-railway scars, still favour traditional scrapyard weaponry – tyre leavers, screwdrivers filed to a point, claw hammers. Nudging and sniffing, they work foul air for over-assertive androgens. A few flash gits (Old Kent Road chapter) are tooled up, spoiling the hang of good cloth with a shooter's bulge. Something extra down the Y-fronts.

All it needed was a word, an unlucky inference, a clash of heads. Disrespect. The referee has wisely stayed out of it, pulled on a gaberdine to hide his dicky. The timekeeper's bell is part of the general din. Passionate intensity among the convicted. The minder cannot hear the minded. *Spiritus Mundi.* Images of the dance. Dream-flickers on the wall. The woman in white. Her black double. How to tell them apart? Overhead brute-lights splintering their shadows like blades of a fan. They scuffle and break. They are more evenly matched than it first appeared. The one in white was perhaps the one with the dark wig – but which was that? She's slimmer, but taller. 5′10″ against 5′9″. (It could be the other way about.) Nothing in it. Similar reaches. Not a lot, contrary to rumour, in the weight. Black's slimmed down, White has bulked up through diet and hard training.

They didn't fight like men, these novices. Their blows refused to challenge gravity, erupt – in hate – from the earth's iron core. They stung in flurries; rapid, but random, combinations. Men come together to save face by remodelling whatever is put in front of them: carving prominent brows with a trailing lace, puffing eyes, splitting lips. Enemies of classicism, they collaborate to provoke a coma state, propel the nasal bone, bridge and root, into the brain-jelly. Between collisions, they pose and posture, drip sweat; stand off, trumpet, beat their chests. The ring is territory to be dominated. Their rival an impostor – a cuckoo in the nest. Kill or be cuckolded. Easy as that.

Helen and Andi were different. They swarmed, spent their energy, fell back. They swayed from the hips. Their punches were all arm. No meaningful hurt. No genetic resentment. No fear. It was fast, furious, but lacked the stench of paranoia: that they should be exposed, publically unmanned. The faces in the dark, they hated it. They screamed for blood.

Slow handclaps, dog impersonations. The Thamesmead boys suggest rape, a doubleheaded gangbang, as a viable alternative, a sparky way to round off a damp night. Things are so sad that a heavy punter with a restricted view happens to notice Nicky Tarten's premature exit. The howl goes up: 'Tarten's doing a runner!'

They'll have him. They'll tear him apart. Nicky glossolals into his mobile, ordering the sparks to kill all lights. Impossible to hear anything in this din. Segments of the mob close on Tarten. Sileen, still gumshoeing Anthony, waits by the door, snatches the bag, as it's offered to big brother. He shouts Helen's name (a gesture). Then he's gone.

Monkey Klaw, choppered in, has a god's eye view. The solitary witness. The rest are in chaos, trapped between the disappearing cash and the shameful event in the ring. Nobody has yet been punched out, no arm lifted in the air. They were agitated, disturbed. It was like the dream of playing the Palladium without a songsheet. Or being caught in bed with another man. Bumping into one another, they didn't know where to look.

Out on the gantry, tasting the night, and viewing everything that happened beneath him, Klaw achieved a granite calm. Life through the end of a green bottle. The ring had become his private monitor, pretty homunculi dancing to his tune: such order, such delicacy! The slips and dodges, the subtleties of the rope. Andi was the aggressor now – while Helen played her part by inducing that aggression, decorating it, pastiching its excesses. She counterpunched, ducked under awkward lunges, teased ribs. The bigger girl, the one in black, was tiring. Who wouldn't at this pace – with no breaks between rounds? White was raining in punches. Too many and too wild. Leaving herself open to a tasty hook. She staggers. Nearly brings up her lunch. Her legs have gone.

Klaw was mesmerized. Too bad his orders couldn't be revoked. The dogs were already off the leash. Undercover thugs were cracking skulls with baseball bats. Veterans of Wapping adept at rescuing bricks from anoraks. The world's upsidedown when gangsters can't trust the coppers that they've pensioned for years.

Rival interest groups didn't see it that way, not altogether. They were hot to ruck: brass-knuckles, shivs, lengths of chain. Gear unrecorded since the Battle of Lewes, racecourse memorabilia. Iron bars dressed in period newspaper. Rusty gravy obscuring the starting prices. Clots of hair. A column of freshly-minted sovs hidden in a fist. A prostitute's stocking ballasted with sand. Go down and you were dead. Boats striped by Vorticist scars. Lungs punctured, spurting arteries. Teams stuck together, solidarity by district and betting-shop. Pubs went in mob-handed – gassy with agg. A race riot with no obvious target. Who to hit? They were all immigrants once, city scum on a Paddy bash. A rerun of the Albert Dimes/Jack Spot do. Two nutters and a single potato knife. No way to treat a fifty-guinea suit – in days when a guinea knew his place.

The ring was a refuge, a pool of calm. The ropes were sacrosanct. The women, like automatons, boxed on. Their conflict, unobserved, was a ritual to pleasure the stars. Helen *must* sustain consciousness – till Andi punches herself out. Klaw willed her to survive, prolong the stern debate. He alone appreciates that everything – Eros, Thanatos, promotion prospects – depends on the outcome of this scrap. A moth dying in Tibet causes cyclones in the Florida Keys. A fork sliding from the table of a pizza parlour in Northampton predicts an earthquake in Anatolia. Andi, putting Helen down, will plunge the universe into ten thousand nights of unfathomed evil.

Swollen glove-lips: Klaw rides in the scarlet of Andi's mutated hands – Sileenlike, fingerless. He follows them in, as they pound against Helen's undefended head. Andi is so intimately there, her previous identity forgotten. Everything she's seen and heard, the streets, the walks, her Whitechapel voyeurs, the lanes and courts of deleted Templar privilege.

At night the ancient City is deserted – and eerie. Exploring its shadowy back streets and dimly lit alleys we might be in a medieval citadel, in overpowering stone. The very street names – Aldersgate, Cloth Fair, Charterhouse, Threadneedle – take us far back. We're alone . . . or are we?

Blood, the colour of fresh liver, flows from Helen's mouth. She falls back on the ropes. Andi's gloves are polished with the dead sperm of St Anne's Court masturbators. Klaw has laced himself to her wrist. The clubland faces, the johns. Cars full of smoke. Repeating rifles from amusement arcades. Incognito royals in dark glasses on the stairs. Negatives destroyed: Stephen Ward. Whispers, rumours, lies. The coke. Rum and pep sticking to her teeth. Eyes blank. Touch like a lover's hand in the dark. Taking the range. The full weight of Andi's shots, sponsored by Monkey Klaw, jerks Helen's head, eliminates landscape memory.

Dawn in the city. Bridges over the river. Street markets. What has this to do with her? Helen searching for a site in which to locate herself. Small mad birds in the plane trees on the south side of Arnold Circus, their shrill din. Claws of horn scratching at her missing hair. Parks that refuse to hold their focus. A few tumbled headstones. 'Thirty years in domestic service.' Municipal gardens with their own dreams. The stones dream her, dream Helen – that name.

Andi is overcommitted, vulnerable. Helen, absorbing the latent power in her few yards of imagined earth, forces her back with orthodox lefts. Klaw loses faith. He hoped that White was finished. Now she's driving his fancy across the ring. Left, left, left: softening her for the short hook. 'Kill,' he yells. 'kill the bitch.'

His voice, breaking up, echoes around the pipes and storage tanks of the Medway refineries. Reverberations from a score of handsets. 'Ki-lll.' Pre-planned outrages to keep outrage at bay. Detonations the Taigs would be proud to claim. Steep fires that will burn for weeks. The shoreline blazes – thick black columns of victorious news.

The paramilitaries already in the Grain Tower have driven a firm wedge into the riot, reached the ring. Klaw begs them to hold back until the outcome of the fight is known. Talk to yourself, Monkey: they can *taste* arrest, helicopter interrogations, heads in sacks. Better than wages, better than sex.

Sileen arrives before them, pulling at Helen, tugging her back. Klaw fights his way along the gantry to the big spotlight. Helen held from behind. Andi drops her hands. The women embrace – talking to each other, rubbing cheeks. Klaw has the trio in his beam. Lesser lights are sparking, failing, spitting out: the generator giving up the ghost.

Her coat retrieved from Muscat. Excited despite himself, clapping her on the back. Sileen: the loot. Vanishing into the crowd. Klaw follows them. Then the generator blows (as per instructions) – his commands are mere noise. 'Open the ducts. Secure the boats. Destabilize the worst case scenario.' Nonsense phrases like the last words of Dutch Schultz.

Danny Egypt hands Helen down. The pilot has the outboard fired, idling in neutral, as Sileen stuffs his parka with banknotes. Egypt and his mucker are totally ripped. They make beagles look abstemious. The cabin smells like Amsterdam. 'Hey, guys – Wagnerian overkill. The fucking sea's on fire!'

They swing away from the tower on a steepling curve. Expletives justified. The thwack of a chopper coming in low. Waves from the downdraught break over the bows. Egypt chanting like a Hinayana cantor. A cone of fierce light sweeping the water. The helicopter hovering to winch up Klaw.

They bucked towards the navigation light on Garrison Point, doubled back, slalomed, headed for the deepwater channel, feinting at a Sheppey landfall; then opened her up, full throttle, played chicken with the treacherous shallows of the Roas Bank, and foamed for the open sea. The pilot could run this script with his eyes shut: to prove it, he did.

Helen shivered, salt stung her tight face. Her costume was ridiculous. She shifted closer against Sileen, who hugged the beating pulse of money to his heart. Having it, he loved it less: too many options. Life was sweeter when it pinched. Escape or suicide? He didn't care. Gently, he unlaced Helen's boxing gloves, dropped them over the side. The Grain Tower, lit from above, was a ruin that had outlived its time.

He watched it grow smaller as the boat turned back, upstream. A running swell. No orders had been given. The pilot, uniquely, seemed to know what he was doing. The straining outboard was the only sound. Helen turned his face. He submitted – looked her in the eye. They could never return to a London that wasn't there.

EIGHTEEN

Moonlight on Tilbury and all its ghosts. The S.S. Demeter hugging the Essex shore. At the rail, side by side, the man and the woman. Rootless couples, according to tradition, slide sternwards, to fetch up flapping against the view, the drag of landloss, like a white silk scarf: saying nothing. A cameo of alienation, they wait for the cold to cut through thin clothing. Wait for a surfeit of melancholy to excuse that first drink. Wait to turn in.

What they were leaving behind was flat, bleak, exploited – familiar. They could perceive, though they scarcely troubled to do so, little distinction between the Coryton oil refineries and the caravans of Canvey Island. Toxic leisure parks. A broad band of churned white water foamed and curdled behind them, fretting the sleek river in a visible skidtrack: the blade of a doublehanded saw.

They were removed from everything they knew. Their friends, who had been their lives, the way they defined themselves, abandoned. Betrayed. They were lashed close together in the self-serving conspiracy of love. The past, which had been so fiercely amputated, was now the most intimate element in their present condition: a cinemascope optimism, filtered with dolour.

The strangeness of the money – Sileen's pockets were stuffed with it. Fives, tens, fifties, large ones with white wrappers. He gave up counting after the eight thousand mark. It bulked him, granted him an undeserved gangland gravitas. Helen leant her cropped head on his shoulder. He had absorbed, through theft, some measure of Nicholas Tarten's virtue. His cock went hard at the thought of it, hard but uninsistent.

Time to rest, let go, enter into this new, collaborative existence – to sustain and depend upon another human being, a female. Sileen's furies,

Helen's sense of parade, her courage, firmly laid aside. It wasn't right. Voyages didn't count. They were the exception. Sea captains, however drunk, sadistic, insane, were entitled to perform ceremonies. The sea was an out-take, time in its liquid form – if this *was* sea, this latex soup through which they were barging. Dissolved landfill, the colour of old corsets. They must by now be cruising over the grounds where the city's sewage, its worthless residue, is dumped. A cacophony of gulls. They would have to turn aside, make the decision, go down.

Getting aboard had been a dream (backhanders, absence of luggage); getting shot of Egypt and the pilot – that was the stunt. At the finish, they managed to forcibly detour the pair to the World's End pub, cash in their fists. A private party was in full swing and they were ideal guests – rambling, incomprehensible, liquid.

Helen and Sileen slipped aboard the liner. That presented no difficulty, not the way they were dressed. This was evidently a *Narrenschiff*, a Ship of Fools, drifting through alternate worlds, memory odysseys. The decks were awash with determinedly local aliens, anoraks concealing mutant flesh – primitive gills, supernumerary mouths ridged in plasticene. The anoraks themselves were a sort of skin: lettuce water, over-macerated cabbage stalks. Freakishness was the norm. A normalcy of Asps with carrier-bags on otherwise deserted underground platforms, returning alone from allnight monster-flick retrospectives. The normalcy of those who grow up nervous, feeding upon their own bodily excretions. (The ones who don't turn into Howard Hughes.) The normalcy of deep-text colonists, pod people, copycat androids waiting in dormitory towns for the Venusian transfer.

They were all in character, the geeks. Who then did Helen and Sileen represent? Were sleepers from unpublished fictions allowed? Could they fake it as the genre stereotypes they *might* become – if their bad luck held? The card-carrying conference junkies were a strictly non-judgemental crowd, good sports (smashed, hyper, or punctured at the neck). Libertarians in bad clothes. Weekend werewolves in vivid mufti. A coven of benign necrophiles in surplus military wool. Sileen, his ink suit, cobweb shirt, skullcap shading a snake-egg bonce, was certainly one of them. A character they couldn't quite place. New Wave in the oldest way. Ex-Futurist: an alchemized retread. Some Nova-Elizabethan thug. Dig that abbreviated hand!

Helen could have come from *Blade Runner*, a replicant. She had that sheen. The Daryl Hannah or Brigitte Nielsen type? Hardly. But steroid-sculpted and wearing some very authentic bruises. More TV than movie, this girl. A series that never outgrew its pilot.

Why would the chick stay with such an obviously unreconstructed wife-beater – if it wasn't contractual? That's easy, check out the other bondings. The gimp's deformity emphasized her startling beauty, the pleasure the eye took in her swift movements. The sweep of her long white coat, his squat black mess. Such couplings were commonplace. Women came along for the ride, some of them even brought the kids. Women ran the thing, masterful types with clipboards. Women obviously performed. Independence seemed to be expected. How quaint! They'd finally found a place where they fitted in – wondering what it was going to cost?

If Sileen was not exactly in a joining mood, he wasn't about to draw attention to himself by refusing to accept a lapel badge: FLEXICON. A caucus of weirdos, sanctioned out-patients who cheerfully asserted their singularity by electing to belong. More ponytails than the Horse of the Year show. A gymkhana of talking heads. Sileen allowed one of the clipboards to encumber him with a carrier-bag – lists of lectures, signing sessions, membership roles, arcane and impenetrable jokes. He might have understood it if they'd blundered into a Holiday Inn on lodge night, or hazarded an out-of-season fire risk in Harrogate – one of those dark cliffs that make the dump in *The Shining* look homey and welcoming.

Attending an sf convention on a Polish cruise-boat didn't faze Helen. She had not yet emerged from that earlier dream: physical confrontation, gang glamour, dialogue that came in speech bubbles. Pushing through the fancydress crowds – their intense, one on one, conversations (picked up, mid-sentence, where they'd broken off the year before) – she flinched, suffered replays of absurdist chats in openplan offices (watching watchers, telephones, fax machines). The restless world of achievers, neuroblasts.

Flexicon was not like that: a celebration. Writers, publishers, bookdealers, agents – and, above all, fans. Fans? Too mild a word. Rabids. Enthusiasts with foam round their mouths (constantly recharged ice-buckets of Sol 'Especial'). Hell's legionnaires: they crawled aboard in their hundreds. Flashbulbs exploded in Helen's face. She has to be the new Name – cyberpunk dominatrix, cultivator of Southern

Gothic vines, slipstreaming succubus. They mobbed her, motormouths delighted to discover their name was Legion.

This was a ship liable to sink under the weight of embarking rats. They marked out the deck space with their sleeping bags and family-size thermoses. They commandeered lifeboats (smart move). The heavy metal lads rushed the bar and stayed there, chucking their empties over the side, vigorously debating Robinsonades and Fraudulent Utopias. Graphic novelists in expensive leather jackets entertained wizards of the photocopier by converting their royalty cheques into Irish malt whiskey. They had found their Sargasso Sea. They'd be propping each other up when the first tentacles of fungus plague slid over the rails to suck their spines.

They couldn't avoid the rumours. Iain Banks was aboard. A cultivated and sardonic beard was signing a raft of space operas with a good grace, flourishing the vestigial initial. Iain *M.* Banks. These were serious readers, readers of voracious habit. (If this liner hits a berg, they might as well put up the shutters at The Forbidden Planet.) The price of a paperback gave them a piece of the author's soul. One of the vultures had perhaps leafed through Sileen's lost *roman*. It wasn't impossible. The title might be lodged somewhere as a footnote in the Encyclopedia: 'a minor fabulation.' All this good fellowship was making Todd uneasy – the buzz of expectation, the hovering publicity women in their insect house maquillage.

What's on the card? Sileen checked his programme. First up – who else? – the rent-a-Dee of the basket-weaving set, Doc Hinton. The author of *The Astonishment of Alfred, Lord Tennyson: Some Paradoxes in Arthurian Teleportation Myths* was offering his Michael Moorcock shtick. Running time? Two or three days. Min. *Engines of Entropy: the Triumph of the Protean Imagination in Millennial Notting Hill*. As homage to the master he would deliver his lecture in serial form, different voices, contradictory slides (backing by Hawkwind, Mighty Baby, and Savoy Wars). Off-prints had been prepared and were already on sale in the book cabin, each one signed in the name of a famous author (deceased).

A compulsory nightmare! Hinton's charmless voice on the PA: a wild hypothesis linking Ireland with Mexico as 'states of death'. Permanent revolution, fermented grain, dead heroes tied to horses' backs. The dominant mode in Hibernian literature, Hinton stated, was the posthumous: postmortem reveries, thunderflashes of consciousness as the lights went out. It could have been a persuasive argument in another mouth. Flann O'Brien's *The Third Policeman*, his Dalkey Joyce paroled from the grave. Beckett's cylinders lodged in purgatorial bogs. John Banville's islands and Francis Stuart's one-street towns. Death was the passport, the only gate. Ireland was blessed with light, reborn too often, that previewed heaven – as malleable, perverse, and miles away. Her landscape made stiffs feel at home. Turf, bone, rock. Candles of hermit saints glowering through fine, wet mists – mountain-shrouding clouds. The meteorological rhetoric to gestate bombs. Grottoes so other-worldly and sublime they had to be blasphemed as martyrs' shrines.

If nothing else, Hinton's keynote speech gave them the clue, they understood why the ship was starting to pitch and roll – trawlnets of ancestors. It could be worse: crossing the bar, a double in each hand. A spectral Margate off the starboard beam, the Channel to come. The Irish Sea. City of Cork. ETA? Negotiable.

They had to go below to escape the attentions of the surging fellaheen. The passageways were Baltic in their tilt; grey rubber underfoot, dim lights above. One corridor, repeated, stood for them all: Polanski's *Bitter Moon*. Celebrity authors had split into breakaway cabals for private parties, shepherded by fragrant girls with surprise champagne. Names that were names, they meant nothing to Sileen. Neil Gaiman, Kim Newman, Alan Moore. A hair retrospective the bald gimp barged rudely aside. Afficionados, the ones who had evolved beyond speech, were charging the ballroom to catch the first appearance of John Clute. You didn't have to understand him to dig his style (Clute on the toot): neologisms at pace, a hank of dignity for the ghetto of pulp. 'Significance' in pre-sawdust paperbacks. Hardcore bites back. You can never learn enough about Philip K. Dick.

Nerds in Spock ears (their own) were tumbling out of lifts, sneering at milder citizens in *Prisoner* drag, bikers in Viking helmets and dangly bits, biro tattoos. Sileen flashed cash at a steward – real or masquerade? – and copped a cabin key. He helped Helen to step over squatters, corridor creeps, drunks who had decided to untank, get the seasickness thing out of the way, before they rounded Dover Castle. Dead fingers plucked at Sileen's hem. 'It's you!' They know everything, these closet libricides. Never had so many people told him with such relish that they hadn't read his book.

They lay, her knees drawn up, on the narrow bunk, listening to the muffled percussion of the ship's engines. Eyes open in the curious dark, they tried to remember how sleep worked. The porthole was cold with night and fog, a slushing of waves on the other side. Rock bands competed to savage fossil favourites and the ventilation system pounded in revenge. Iron doors slammed on the revels of a drunken crew. Sileen's neck was warmed by Helen's breath, a snuffly draw. In the old days, her snores acted like a drench on his fears, putting him out. His dreams fed on her rhythms, rapid-eye-movements he could borrow. Sleeping without her was impossible.

Her arm gripped him so fiercely that he couldn't twist or turn. He was fearful of the small noises in her throat, the horrors she was straining to absolve. Sweat soaked the coarse sheet. The hours were the longest he had ever known. (It was always 3.33 on the digital clock.) Desperate to free himself, escape her heat, but unwilling to wake her, he raced through lists of school-mates who were dead, the streets that filled the V between the Whitechapel and the Commercial Roads, the number of words to be extracted from LYSSOPHOBIA. Blacking-out for the odd moment, he woke to a scream of laughter or a dropped tray. The night condensed in subjective time. Helen did not stir.

It had to be morning, the partying had stopped. Sileen shook himself free of his woman, the knotted sheet, and rolled from the bunk, bellowing for a steward. While he waited, he cleared the porthole with an elbow – checked for icebergs. Zero visibility, a pitching sea. The porthole, glazed with frost, was an emphyssemiac's shaving-mirror: all cloud and spit. Not fouled enough to hide a surly Pole in blanco'd messjacket, scowling from the doorway – and prepared, for a consideration, to fetch coffee, chicken sandwiches, whisky. Sniffy at being denied the chance to dispense poppers and marital aids.

Helen, who had slept in her leotard, undressed and tried the shower. Amazingly, it worked. Water as hot as she could bear. Scour it, scrape it off – The Isle of Grain, Muscat, Hackney's fish-phosphor skies – while Sileen negotiates for women's clothes. It took some epic mime to make the Pole understand he did not want them for his own use. 'Me not fairy, savvy?' The man swore he'd return when he'd finished his rounds, mixing and matching whatever he could thieve from the other cabins.

The food was good – they'd taken the feathers off, and some of the scales. Hard to tell where the bread stopped and the chicken began.

Whisky washed the softened paste from the crevices of Sileen's teeth, thawed the chips. Coffee drowned the feebler bugs. He felt as if he'd bitten into a thermometer. His stomach strained to accommodate the boisterous gas. He lay back on foam pillows and enjoyed the diuretic fluting of the shower. The glass tipped in his hand. He dozed. Sky swallowed sea. Helen, steaming, crawled in beside him: lifted his head onto her lap, stroked his temples.

There was no dodging it – awake, dressed, revived – they'd have to take a turn around the deck, make plans for a new life after disembarkation. The corridors were deserted, the tranquil light of a winter aquarium. Like passing directly into the mind-set of a schizo surveillance monitor. Impossible to tell if it was night or day. They staggered, reached out for the walls, adjusted to the roll of the boat.

Dragging down some slithery stairs to the deck where they thought they remembered seeing the purser's office (they were wrong), Sileen snatched at the reflection, in a framed photograph of the ship, of a man he took for his former cellmate, Royboy. Royboy in a grey wig. An eighteenth century Royboy – coffee-house rakehell, armed with a sword, primed for affray. The cripple spun on his fixed heel, frightening Helen with the fury of the movement.

Nothing: more stairs, more empty corridors. A ghost vessel. Even the bar with the brochure view (sleet beading the observation windows) had been abandoned. They were tired, they sat on stools. Glasses with two or three good swallows left in them, holocaust ashtrays with smouldering butts. The clink of bottles afloat in silver buckets: Mexican imports with a golden sun, radiant beams, scarlet lettering. They didn't feel like drinking. Sileen was strung out in an anaclitic depression. He picked at one of the labels, shredded it, wadded the strips into a ball, flicked them against the rim of the ashtray. The sea was not big enough to realize his sense of desolation.

Sometimes, in my dreams, I see that enormous pit, surrounded, as it is, on all sides by wild trees and bushes. And the noise of the water rises upwards, and blends - in my sleep - with other and lower noises; while, over all, hangs the eternal shroud of spray.

That graveyard voice! Sileen on his feet. The Demeter was one of William Hope Hodgson's interdimensional ships, a ship filled with voices that never were. Unfinished: the morbid ventriloquism of dead authors who cannot lay aside their pens. The words of that mad book – written or unwritten – chambered his head; different chapters, different hospital rooms. Limestone pavements folding under stress. The field of X-rays he can't forget: not worth the effort of erasure – too rough to plough, more stone than earth. Coarse grass that would split a beast's mouth. Thistles, storms.

The voice was everywhere, broadcast throughout the ship: a recording. Sileen would run it down, destroy it – and all of Hodgson's pernicious weeds. He'd heard those sneers too often, the unemphatic drone of the psychopath. Drage-Bell! Drage-Bell was aboard. Drage-Bell revealed at last in his true form – a kraken, a many-tentacled, wounded, crawling destroyer from the deeps. A lantern of acid tongues: Bell had given Flexicon's tame vamps their finest show, devoured them all. Cannibalized by metaphors. Deck planks shone with his slime. Sileen could track the monster's progress through the Ship of Death. It was as easy as following underfloor exit lights in a crashed Boeing – to a wing that isn't there.

The door to the ballroom had to be forced by Sileen's shouldercharge, all heads turned. The audience: lead-white faces of travestied black men. Snail-silver lipstick and a pinch of rouge to enliven the trench pallor. China dolls: prominent eyebrows, teeth like piano keys. Geometric shadows from the brims of tin helmets (no longer present). Paste eyes. Uniform ranks of chairs. A mute regiment of smoking Tommies – their exogenous parts fractured by gradients of shock, repeating concussions. The smoke was the smoke of battle: shellholes, doused by night rain, continued to flare. Heavy cloth still burning on bodies caught in the wire. The stink of men in tunnels: nitrocellulose, sour excrement, shag.

Annoyed by the interruption, the fans, dutifully playing their part, stared, challenged Sileen, threatened to toss him out. The lecturer waited in front of his screen, tapping his stick like an acting captain. Drage-Bell.

Sileen held his preposterous pose, back against the door, arms outstretched. Helen had not followed him. She stayed at the bar, staring out to sea, her profile pitched above the waves.

Drage-Bell rapped his cane on the lectern, a fresh slide was projected. Sileen flinched. This was unexpected, not the heroic landscape witnessed in Simon Undark's Cambridge room, or seas that would offer no relief from the element that surrounded them now, fathomless developing fluid. Fall down and be absolved. How soothing it would be to endure Hodgson's own lectures, *A Sailor and His Camera* and *Through the Heart of a Cyclone*, the relentless procession of images – like an advancing spiral depression.

But Bell was playing another game. This slide belonged in the hospital, in Sileen's basement file. It took its place in a sequence of accidents, then faded away. Wild gardens, stone field, mushroom tower. Bell gave it a title: *Figure Falling from a Horse* by Wyndham Lewis, English School. Executed during the 'wilderness years in Canada', an obsession the poet/painter was never to be delivered from. Lewis's 'stalking horse . . . eyes full of mockery and madness' was also Hodgson's steed – that was Bell's point. A stallion of the apocalypse resistant to riders. In training for the First War, a Lieutenant in the Royal Field Artillery (Lewis was in the Artillery too: 'arrival at "the Front" for us was not unlike arrival at a big Boxing Match, or at a Blackshirt Rally at Olympia'); overage, he was badly thrown from his horse, jaw smashed, shaken, concussed – discharged. He drew on all his knowledge of the body's mechanics to rebuild his strength; recover, re-enlist. If he came through he would report a homecoming of horror that would confirm the legitimacy of his earlier prophetic visions.

Retaining the Lewis slide, Bell read, pianissimo, Hodgson's famous letter to his mother from the trenches. 'The sun was pretty low as I came back, and far off across that desolation, here and there they showed – just formless, squarish, cornerless masses erected by man against the infernal Storm that sweeps for ever, night and day, day and night, across that most atrocious Plain of Destruction. My God! talk about a Lost World – talk about the END of the World . . . it is all here . . . And the infinite, monstrous, dreadful pathos of the things one sees – the great shell-hole with over thirty crosses sticking in it; some just out of the water – and the dead below them, submerged . . . If I live and come out of this . . . what a book I shall write if my old "ability" with the pen has not forsaken me.'

Why didn't he move on? The borderland, the wire. Why must he blather until the chimney of the projector begins to smoke? Tears in Sileen's eyes. He couldn't face this black causeway any more: the falling, fallen man whose legs were crushed beneath the horse's monumental bulk. Bell was, despite the funerary drone, a forceful lecturer: his provocations came into their own, the insolent leaps – rehearsed to the final parenthesis and recited with the freshness of a free-flowing improvisation. Sileen didn't want to know who or why or when. Only *where* mattered now.

The 'Shamanism of Intent' Bell called it, the phallocentric way male novelists, such as Hodgson, develop their own force-fields, pressing innocent civilians into adopting the characteristics of their fictional prototypes. A very dodgy form of predestination. Writers, he asserted, were incapable of disinterested observation. They fudged, feuded, formulated a self-serving description of the world – then feigned surprise when the world obliged. Hodgson, fretted by all the usual imperatives, envisioned dying star systems, houses with mephitic plumbing, the extinction of hope. Then lived out what he saw, imploded under the startling dynamics of his own oracular charge.

Bell said no more, he whistled, tried to hum – beat time on the lectern with his cane. The sweating operative struggled to keep pace. Hope Hodgson's fifty-three glass slides shuttled in a speeding cycle: antlers of white lightning, thundercaps, schools of whales. The markers of Sileen's nightmare returned, and with them the pain. He leant against the door, viced his throbbing head. Frozen seascapes inhibited the flow of blood.

The projector was clicking with a plausible beat. The operative left it to its own devices; took Sileen by the arm, led him outside. 'A breath of air, old man.' In the open – caddied by a Force Nine gale. Like climbing from a marble bath with soapy feet. The ship was stone. Sileen clung to the rail. The sea refused to support this intolerable weight: one moment St Peter's and the next a cork. Waves enveloped the bows, washed the decks clean. Spray lashed Sileen's face as he countered the lurch.

'Steady in the ranks. On the count of five.' A horsehair wig pricked his cheek. It *was* Royboy. Royboy in waistcoat, cutaway jacket, stock. Tight grey curls – with the beret on top. Royboy with an 'Emanuel Swedenborg' badge in his lapel. 'Ruddy Captain's bright idea, camouflage. Never run across the feller myself. Johnny Foreigner, probably a Kraut.'

Royboy twisted Sileen's arm, apologetically, behind his back; forcing him to look into the chasm, the water's black rush. The cripple was willing, the time was right. He couldn't think of a better way out of his present fix. Hadn't Swedenborg said that spirits possess the memory of those who make contact with them – until those memories become eternally their own? Was he still the man he thought he was, or was he the invader from the other side?

The fingers of his good hand were being forced open and something hard pressed into them. 'A going-away present, old and quite valuable,' Royboy said. 'The kind the Incas appreciated, an animal familiar to do the heavy work – a panther's head.'

This wasn't how it should happen. No panthers in the Hodgson script. But Royboy was stronger than he appeared; the training hadn't been entirely wasted, the vineyard years. Sileen's ulna was about to crack when Helen brought the bottle down on the bravo's head.

'Oh, I say!' Royboy didn't drop to his knees, fold in the accepted way. The wig absorbed the force of the blow. A Pleiadic lightshow, bad moment – no worse than tumbling pissed downstairs, when some bugger's moved the Gents. But Sileen was able to disengage, slam a fist into Royboy's prominent Adam's apple. A literal choker. He locked an arm around the undernourished hitman's neck and pummelled him until he slumped. He considered using the broken bottle to carve a zodiac in Royboy's face; thought better of it, he couldn't improve upon a definitive ruin. He returned the baked-clay votive figure to the chancer's paw – tried, with Helen's help, to heave him over the side.

Barely conscious, Royboy hooked his spare hand onto the rail. Sileen, growling, knelt to bite. The sea reached up and Royboy took his dive: eyes open wide, arm raised, a kind of wave. Grinning, he peddled up a rope ladder that wasn't there – went under at the double, vanished from sight. A decent military send-off: no punchline codicil left on the wind. Helen was hauling herself, foot by foot, back towards the lights of the filling bar. A warm wig muffing Sileen's fingerless hand.

BOOK FOUR

THE BORDERLAND

*. . . the standard warning from Sendero. You don't
disappear, you reappear, dead.*

Edward Dorn, *Way West*

ONE

Atlanti Hotel, Kilkee, Co. Clare, Republic of Ireland

Dear Andi,

The absent 'c' sums it up perfectly: a cinemascope resort that fell off the back of Europe. Lenten curfew as the big attraction. Small wonder the statues decided to walk. Women would have more chance in a seminary (if they don't mind unlaved armpits and canting confessions with the post-coital chocolate).

You used to ask me why I left, remember? Provincial Ireland is morning sickness without the pregnancy, a pre-natal depression that only lifts when I walk, early, out of the hotel and down to the deserted strand, before breakfast (oink, oink, and more oink) – before Sileen can be bothered to rouse himself. Kilkee is the limbo chosen for our retreat.

Andi, I've never seen such skies. What a setting for a chaste honeymoon (three single beds in every room)! Perhaps that's why Charlotte Brontë came here – a respite from lusting after pompous Belgians. Weather unadorned.

There's nobody else around. The old growler and me – it works. He's behaving with previously unsuspected tenderness; he notices what I'm wearing, and even replies, on occasion to things I've said. It's beginning to worry me, love. It's all so easy when you have cash. We had no trouble persuading them to open up – Atlantic City run by a Jansenist mob, no action after dark. The heaviest betting is on when it will start to rain. The owner (yellow waistcoat, carpet slippers, ginger wig) is doing so well out of us he's thinking of buying a Revolutionary pedigree and joining Fianna Fáil.

Tea bread and butter with every meal, it floods back. The way the girl stares as she serves, in that vast, empty dining room. We're the talk of the town, the cabaret. She answers questions you asked a week ago – such as: 'when do we get water out of the taps instead of untreated mud?'

We might stay for the winter if this Irish skyscraper (three floors) doesn't fall

429

down. TV sets in all the bedrooms, but no electricity. 'The time of year, the storms.' Picture windows weakened by persistent rain. Drive-in facilities for tractors. Out of season in a land where the seasons are too bored to change. The hotel survives on its Valentine weekend frolics – old farmers decant from the hills to find some skivvy stupid enough to fill the dead ma's shoes.

A broad, sandy beach, as long as childhood, mirror-bright at the sea's edge, glistening with blue sky tributaries, firm as a bowling green – no filth, no ice-cream wrappers, no people. Sea the colour of a gin bottle, a perpetual ledge of white breakers across the mouth of the bay. Cirri in entangled sheaves, spouting, streaking into tufts and foamy bands: spectacular news. Nothing gets in the way. I couldn't begin to delineate the speed of the changes. At a distance, where we are, on the north side of the town – a low, dark curve – the huddle of small businesses, failing or failed, sustains an unexpected and quite exotic beauty. Ephemeral, but lasting. I'd like to stay here forever and almost certainly will, Sileen shows no sign of being ready to move on.

How did we find the place? It's all so complicated, darling. The fight, the escape on the boat, I don't understand any of it – but I'm still sore, you brute! I know I must have been mad to agree, get caught up in another of Sileen's manic charges. He decided to hire a car. (Cork City this was. It meant hassling out to the airport. Fat American priests scoffing pie and mash in the Bewlay's concession, arguing over the change.)

Vertical rain – from the ground up. He made me drive. (I wouldn't have let him anyway, he was shaking so much, a whiskey bottle in each pocket to keep him straight.) Any direction, including backwards, to get us out of town. Nothing's changed since I was rehearsing dirty weekends with Taylor in the early Sixties – bigger subsidies to waste, service industries in unconverted barns, museum-quality signs for operations that died before the war. A 55 mph speed limit everybody ignores, careering at roundabouts like sheep at a pen.

All the glamour of the East German steel corridor, then the bungalows begin. Dream territory for window-cleaners with vertigo. Sileen announced that we were heading for West Cork. He couldn't say where exactly – but he thought we might hide out for a while, take a breather with good old Sammy Taylor. Taylor! I nearly put us in the ditch – no way, José! I couldn't do it, Andi. Seeing Taylor again would be like going back to suspender belts, flytrap eyelashes, ironed hair.

I swung over – trucks steaming straight at me, headlights on full beam – and refused to carry on. Sileen got out, slammed the door, took off across the fields. 'That'll sort him out,' I thought. Up to his knees in it (raining every day since October). Starting to get dark. I waited. You know how stubborn he is – a mule is conciliatory by comparison. Oh shit, I had to stop the bastard before he marched back into the arms of Special Branch.

It absolutely destroyed my lovely black-strap jodhpur boots, new that morning. You're not meant to go riding in the things. I was wild enough to slap his stupid face. He found one of his ruins. Of course. Overgrown, a castle of thorns. Just what he loves – rain pissing down, clouds of white dust from a quarry on the far side, sinister sheds. He's standing there, hands in pocket, sulking like a little lad, and trying to look as if the whole mess is curiously significant. He'd planned it all along. The locals use this spill of heritage as somewhere to dump their cars. (You couldn't print enough money to make me open one of the boots!)

He talked, shmoozed, bullshitted – stroked my neck. I didn't listen to the words. Believe it or not, Andi, I was interested by now, I wanted to know what had happened to Taylor. (We like to think they go to pieces without us, waste away.) What is it about me? What's my attraction for these gonzo apes? Sileen/Taylor, quite a choice, isn't it?

There's not much to tell about the rest of the drive – windscreen wipers on the blink, road like a river; then, at dusk, convoys of locals operating with one headlamp between the whole pack. Whenever I spoke, Sileen just said, 'Keep going.' He's sure we'll find Taylor, out there, where the land gives up.

Eventually, we surfed the warp, reached Bantry Bay: the sea running alongside like a friendly dog. Glengarriff, Castletown Bearhaven – and on. He's convinced himself that Taylor's letters are friendly in intent, the standard macho banter between sweathouse buddies (combat dodgers). Taylor's always been good for food. A great guy, apparently, beneath the hallucinogenic froth. They went out together once in Carlow or Limerick, one of their scouting trips for an excommunicated printer willing to risk American Express, and some poor sod in a plastic tablecloth restaurant asked Taylor how he'd like his steak.

'Ah, just warmed through now, Seamus. Understand? Have the beast trot up and down the paddock a couple of times, to raise the temperature of the blood, then bring me a sharp fork.'

Taylor's threats are nothing, a courtesy, a bonding ploy. Sammy's an artist where feuding is concerned.

Total darkness. Darker than the womb. So Sileen decides to throw open the windows, 'taste the night'. Nothing to distinguish roads from fields. A steady mizzle skimming off the waves. Horseshoe bends. Pathetic windblown signs for *vegan pottery or handwoven clogs. Asparagus farms washed into the sea. The natives have retired to the city, given the land away, at a price, to counter-culture refugees – who have staked their children's future on the prevailing winds, an oilskin tepee to shelter them from the inevitable nuclear storm.*

Sileen, sticking his head out, perseveres with the most annoying chant. 'They sent for a Taylor to measure – him.' His bottle of Bushmills was almost drained. He had me singing. Andi, love, he tried it on! He picks his times to show affection. It was all I could do to keep the car on the road.

But we made it – three houses, a phonebox, and a pointer to 'The Cod's Head' which had fallen off the wall. Sileen galumphed out to try his blarney, to ask after 'The American'. Half the East Village could be bivouacked here – Hollywood rejects passing themselves off as blacklisted screenwriters, Ginger Man dropouts from TCD, folk-rock superstars who'd lost it to Scientology.

The mis-directions Sileen tried to translate back to me made no sense – other than getting us rapidly out of town and out of sight. Some nonsense about stopping at the yellow and black wall, to look over the headland for a distant light 'you couldn't miss at all'.

The mizzle was the most efficient shower unit west of Swansea. There was nothing to be seen. We clung to the famous wall, and to each other, while we launched the second battle. Magic, Andi! Completely lost, drenched to the skin, drunk on the cliffs in a gale, the Atlantic roaring beneath us like a coven of spoiled poets in McDaid's. Incontinent with laughter.

A huge car, no headlights, driver holding a torch out of the window, skidded to a stop, a foot shy of the wall. 'You'd see it a picture, sure you would, any other night. 'Tis the fecking mist, so it is. Better you follow me now.'

And away we chased. The man took the bends one-handed, his torch arm dangling limply out. He drove like a rally ace – by memory. I had trouble hanging on, sliding blind into lethal curves. We were hysterical by the time he stopped.

'Carry you on, girl, far as she'll go.' The message is unchanged. Avoid the boreen. Keep watch for a light. We bounced over pebbles and wet slag, scratched the paintwork on stone walls. A velvet darkness – like the inside of a whale. We gave it up only when the wheels touched water. Decided to stay put, sleep it off.

Who knows how much later? Horribly stiff, windows misted over. I opened the door. Andi – the light! A heavy sky, cloud obscuring low, sharp hills, beams breaking through like . . . I don't know, a gift, an intervention we shouldn't ignore. Revelation. Stunning, when it plays against stone walls, blotchy turf, porridge-coated rocks. (Now I understand where Taylor gets his adjectives from!) A fishbone greyness, centuries of gull shit dried to prison emulsion. The fields actually more slate than grass. A quarry landscape blessed by showers of liquid light, storms backing off: a narrow, secret cove.

I'd seen the photographs that Taylor had sent – in his pomp, his mania, when he was dynamiting the hillside, bringing in earth-movers. We'd found the right place, no question. Now there was Taylor, his guns and dogs, to confront.

Sileen stretched, yawned, kissed me, said it was all working out. He described the special quality of the light as the 'absence of surveillance'. For the first time in months, the cameras were switched off. Nobody was watching, nobody cared. Light travelled too fast for description, it 'distilled the truth', showcasing ochres, muddy browns. A soft morning, with barely enough rain in it to bruise your eye shadow.

We left the car with its front wheels on the beach, and walked up the track to where we knew we'd find Taylor and his pigs. A line of brightly painted cottages built to justify a commissioned portrait (they belonged on the windward side of the Arctic Circle). Sponsored exile. Property. Land. If he met us with a blunderbuss, it wouldn't matter. He'd earned that right, living here. Caretaking such prodigious desolation.

Sileen kept fingering patches of moss. Muttering about the thousands of years it took to evolve such exquisite form and texture – crumbling the wads between his fingers. Edgy. Stone walls built by anonymous virtuosi to look as if they'd grown overnight. Drowned fields with rocks surfacing like a school of limestone seals. Trickling brown streams, water running off the hillside.

This can't be right. At the head of the boreen, backed under a beetling crag of rock – the burnt-out shell of a positively Cromwellian ruin. There must be some mistake. I found myself, for the first time in years, calling Taylor's name. The slates had been carried off, the windows smashed. An untouched peat stack was grown over with grass. All the flat ground was churned to cloacal mud by the hooves of vanished free-range beasts. The sorry remnants of a French tincan car.

Sileen, wading heroically through the slop, discovered a faded poster nailed to what had once been a door.

GIVE UP ART SAVE THE STARVING. Seeing and creating an image are the same activity. Everything that is learned is alien. Fictions occupy our minds: we escape into art. Take your desires for reality. To continue to produce art is to addict our selves to our own repressions: the refusal to create is the only alternative left to those who wish to change the world. Give up art. Save the starving.

Taylor's testament.

We had to accept it, Sammy was gone. He'd done a bunk, taken off to another bolthole of equivalent charm – a timeshare apartment in Sarajevo. Or else: they'd finally caught up with him, torched the Antichrist in his lair. Look on the bright side, he might be living wild in the hills? He'd like that, aboriginal authenticity. Anything would be better than a return to the low budget, mini series Kennedy Camelot of the USA.

The story was hidden here – in the landscape – if we could discover it. 'A view is a window on the real data.' The conspiracy of light had to be paid for. Taylor's invasion was a form of suicide. (To tell the truth, Andi, I was relieved. Seeing Taylor would undo the past by making it true. Touching his hand would turn me to dust.)

Sileen took it very badly. He kept us there for hours, sifting through the cairns of brick. He would hold up some scrap of cloth for me to identify. 'Did Taylor ever wear this?' But whoever picked up the contract cleared everything of value. We found nothing more exciting than a tube of rust shaped like an iron telescope, a bicycle pump affair.

Sileen, moody, handled it like treasure trove. He always has to be the one who knows the answer. A story he'd heard in the hospital, conscripts (defaulters) ordered to kill a shed of squawking pigs with mallets. A test. A punishment. The awful Royboy gave him the gloating details. And that's what Sileen reckoned this thing was: a stungun for slaughtering complacent porkers. He carried it under his arm as we shuffled back to the car. The geology shrugged. It was a challenge now, an affront.

I hid from Sileen the item I dug out from behind the ashes in the grate. A horridly damp and bog-smelling notebook, bound in waxed yellow cloth. The thing is, Andi, it's exactly like one of Sileen's. Like the notebook he left in our room in Sly Street when he walked to Oxford. There's a red seal – which I haven't broken yet. I'm frightened, I admit it, a stupid sense of taboo. The seal has an 'H' or 'T' imprinted in it. (Taylor?)

The car was high and dry. The engine started first time. Sileen was sitting awkwardly, leg thrown out, on the anthracite beach. He wouldn't move. Against the zinc blue pebbles, the bedding of volcanic slag, he looked almost . . . healthy, fit. Heartbreakingly brave. My instinct was to drive away, leave him as part of this, petrified.

434

I couldn't do it. I had to fetch him. Andi, it was vile. He was staring at a hairless, stinking bladder – dried-out, abraded, pink. With tiny, shrivelled infant's hands. A sea pig, washed up. There were more, five or six of them, in varying stages of decay. Rotten, puffed with gas. Heads hacked off. A hose of gristle poking through the gaping neck. Barnacled: a pale salmon colour, flecked with violet growths. Like a rock that had turned to soap.

We didn't stop, kept our eyes on the road, until we reached the ferry, the sun going down, across the Shannon. Smoking, stubbing out half-smoked cigarettes, we began to catch up with ourselves. We read about Kilkee on a board at the pierhead.

Don't write back, darling, we'll be gone by the time your letter arrives. (If this ever reaches you! If you're not with O'Hagan, on the run. Or topping the bill at the York Hall.) Must stop – Sileen would kill me if he knew I was telling anyone *that we're still alive.*

Love to Sofya,
Hugs & Kisses,

Helen

TWO

O'Looney's Lounge (The Promenade, Lahinch) proved chimerical: as did the promise of SURF/ SEAFOOD/ SAND. Spurn roadside alliteration. A useful lesson learnt – the bars with the biggest signboards are entirely defunct; cashflow (and energy) exhausted by the publicity campaign. The fugitives, on their third circuit of the hibernating town, found another place in which to sip their stout in silence.

The sitting clients – boots, cattle coats – kept their eyes on the football, swift and skilled in its anarchy. Helen took the window seat, to check the street: a three-legged dog, forerunner of a circus that will never arrive. The draught melancholy of formless afternoons.

Sileen didn't like the way the other drinkers, solitary men, slid from their stools, and out. The child behind the bar took down the evidence of their orders in a yellow pad, then fled to a back room (to make his call?) – leaving their pints to drain like slow wounds. Pietistic military posters on the wall, and a bleak succession of landscapes doubled with the hurling round-up, led them to think they had picked the wrong pub.

Back on the road, Helen couldn't get a destination out of Sileen. 'Carry on.' She was happy to let the black runway unwind: the sea bordering flooded fields, telegraph poles, huge skies. Sometimes he told her to stop and let him out. He behaved like a man with a camera and a commission of some kind.

He crouched to analyse undistinguished lanes: compositions where soft cloud mattresses compressed the light into a narrow band, a scrape of distant blue. Clumps of hedges, tapering, dense with thorns. Puddles. Sand and grit recently spread to keep muddy tracks in use.

He sighed, a disappointed location scout. What more did he want? What could it matter if he absorbed all the visible information, put skin on his soul? Sometimes, with a snort, he was straight back on his feet;

sometimes he waited, hands on knees, for hours. Helen was content. The car. Sileen had never been a chatterbox. Now she felt he couldn't carry on without her. He lusted after her biography, the places that she knew. He relied on her to name stones and flowers, the density of animal skulls, the families of stars.

He wanted the traces of Taylor left on her skin.

At one estuary, a lull in the rain, they watched cattle swim across the bay, and emerge by the ruins of an abbey. Nothing was said.

Premature spurts of twilight jacked up the cloudbase by a few inches, exciting Sileen. The White Strand: a crescent of broken stones, tacky with gutted fish, gardens of seaweed, powdered cement. A watchtower where fishermen kept their tackle, another on the horizon. He held up a stick, made measurements, groaned. They had to drive around the bay – at once.

One of Sileen's happier inspirations, this marine graveyard. An unusual kind: beehives, hat-houses made from slate, ghost traps (better built than anything they'd passed on the N67). Houses uniformly drained of colour and display, windows like tiny blackboards. Gritty sand stung their ankles and scoured the scaled-down streets. Lilliputian: as if death, like dry cleaning, was a process of shrinkage. The shadows of the drowned. The Spaniards of the Armada whose bodies had been cast upon these rocky shores, or slaughtered in the surf by Sir Turlough O'Brien's men.

Wonderful. But not what Sileen was looking for. Limestone in grass, chlorophyll in granite, not a flower to be found. Sileen dragged Helen through the enclosure like a Hackney Council Tax assessor on the run.

They were getting closer to it, but they didn't know what it was.

Ennistymon, they loved. Cruising downhill, foot off the pedal for a marzipan church. Sandblasted communicants, spit-washed, polished necks, in huddles, waiting to cross the road. Angular with unease, they were caught between the recollection of sin and rehearsed confession: petty crimes to bore the priest.

Helen pulled on the handbrake, almost asked Sileen to take her in. She quite fancied the idea of candles, headscarves, bread and wine. Getting East London off her chest. They stayed until the last mass-goer was safely inside. A pair of large brown shoes had been left in the road, a stride apart. One of the faithful must have levitated to bless their journey. An El Greco apotheosis in a greasy tweed cap hung with flies.

Driving through, they discovered that each town is defined by the special quality of the holy idiot who props up the strategic corner, near the bus stop and chippy, his back against the wall. Take him away and the street goes down like a pack of cards. The brickwork behind him is scorched with the afterblast shadow found at Hiroshima, the pitch of his absent concentration is so intense. Out early for a newspaper, or returning late from the pub, you'll see him parading his badge of caste, a spectacular goitre or a hole instead of a nose.

Long, narrow streets, hills beyond: Sileen checked out Medical Halls, windows of bootlaces and Pompeian bread. He insisted on breaking the comfortably patronizing drift of Helen's mood by telling her one of Drage-Bell's worst shoe stories. Every time the boys from the Branch kick down a rooming-house door in Kilburn, Bell said, they check for shoeboxes. Never fails. Collar a bomber and you'll find a cardboard box full of dried shit. The first rule of engagement: locate the turd. Female terrorists – German, Dutch, locals corrupted by foreign habits – inevitably keep a lukewarm dildo close at hand.

That did it, they pushed on. A bag of soda bread and a brick of red cheese. He admitted it was a quest. He'd identify the place when he saw it, and not until. Based on a book. The author's father had been rector at Ardrahan. The book started there. Something for Helen to think about.

Meanwhile, she corrected his pronunciation. 'Ard-ra-han.'

What Sileen did not confess was that another car was on their tail, had been all day – that's why he'd pulled them out of Kilkee in such a paddy. Noises in the next room, a glint of sunlight splintering their window when they walked back from the beach. A hunchbacked shadow preceding them through the graveyard of the drowned. Sileen thought at first it might be the statue of the uniformed Republican with the gun. He moved fast to try and confront the joker: a sawn-off barrel poking like a cannon from the cat-sized door.

Every move they made confirmed somebody else's research. The thing followed them by staying ahead. It knew where they were going and could afford to let them sweat. The brown shoes in the road. The human buttress with his cap over his eyes. A face Sileen saw reflected among the cartwheels of soda bread – Taylor. Taylor had drawn them into his own territory. Now he could pick his kill.

A sign for Yeats's Tower took them off the N18. Helen was tiring. One last stop and they'd find a pub. It was only a mile or so. A mile across a lake. The road was flooded, island copses in esturine fields – plenty of cover. Bandit country. Crows. Peaty water lapping hedge to hedge.

Hedges thick as hides. The evening lane was the perfect ambush ground.

There was no choice, the tower had to be checked out. W. B. Yeats and Arthur Symons on the tramp through the West, struggling in the footsteps of Tonnison and Berreggnog, fellow members of the Rhymers Club. 'The Door of Death is near / And what waits behind the door.' Proving a dream in a dream, a poem anxious for completion.

It chimed too well with Hodgson's account: the initiate in seclusion with his wife. The poet of *When Helen Lived*, *The Tower*, *The Winding Stair*. ('I'll name the friends that cannot sup with us.') W. B. Yeats and W. H. Hodgson: visionaries on either side of that cataclysmic whirlpool, the Great War. Hodgson writing to hold back (welcome) what was to come, and Yeats stepping grandly forward to rebuild whatever vanished at his touch. The occult telegraph (automatic writing, tapping the dead) creates its own borderland. The poet's achievement was to rescue the divine imago from the cosmological chaos Hodgson's genius glimpsed – but could not synthesize.

Poetry outranks prose.

The piling upward of the Battlements of Evening. The topskin of the pond ruffled as Sileen set himself to paddle through. Helen, staying in the car, dozed at the wheel. Had this culture detour sickened Taylor, thrown him off? Or was he out there, already in the tower, taking aim from a ditch? Sammy Taylor and Todd Sileen, like Yeats and Hodgson, separated by an expanse of shallow black water.

The square tower was too domesticated for Sileen, unworthy of inclusion, wrong. Ivy rusticating a habitable keep. A study centre fated to demystify what it preached. The cripple beat the bounds and turned back. Not enough chiaroscuro for Taylor to cull him there.

Alternating beds of santolina and lavender: Helen walks through a Jacobean garden, close to the Thames. Her heavy dress sweeping the gravel, proud bosom exposed. 'Send me your dreams.' Blindfolded, she steers by smell, dizzy with spiky oils.

The pursuit is over. Pay off the boatman, but do not let the craft go. A man to meet – the arbour, the level lawns. Cries of wild beasts from the wilderness on the other side of the high wall. Box-hedges trimmed to a severe geometry, an open maze through which she runs. An assignation with a lover she does not know: fearing his claws, the diamond in his teeth, the blue silk waistcoat that marks so easily when she falls into his embrace.

Breath hot as a feeding hawk, he leads her to a bench. An alcove. The turrets and twisted chimneys of the house. Grass soft beneath her slippered feet. He unlaces the blindfold, forbidding her to look at his face. Draws her fingers upwards to his mouth. Lips dry as paper. She searches for a pulse. Gasping, she forces them open, gropes inside. A sudden thing of fur, armed with teeth. His tongue: a live mouse.

Slowly, he raises her skirt, sets the rodent on her trembling thigh. 'It's edible,' he warns. 'And stuffed with myrrh. Don't move a muscle. Let it run.'

Shivering and spaniel-wet, he shook her, demanding, as men do, a towel. Sileen back from his futile quest. Helen turned the heating up, reversed towards the road, hoping she didn't have to explain the loss of his trousers.

A sinking sun and a long straight road, glittering like a midnight canal. North towards Galway, hot water hotels. Nothing worth the insult lay ahead, no revenger dogged their tail. Off to the side, blocking each tributary, would be a man in a roped potato sack, using his bicycle to keep himself upright. A crutch on wheels: Sileen had been crippled in the wrong country.

Now Ardrahan. Where it is always 'the previous night'. Primal darkness holding off just long enough for them to enjoy a frisson of precognition. Fear the Placebo, not the bowel-emptying kind. A scatter of houses (post-office, pub) sticking dourly to the cross-roads. The *Bord Fáilte* version of Rennes-le-Château.

Why here? The elements are shifty in the Celtic gloom. Jimmy Burke's 'Thatch Barn' (larger and livelier on the hoarding than the place itself) does its best to hide the minor earthwork in the field, the jigsawed remnant of a wall. A customized nudge at the Gothic abandoned from lack of interest. Some sheep that fail to bleat.

So risk the church: rat grey, squat, ugly as a concrete boot. Ordered from a cut-price catalogue, not designed. One man, standing on another's shoulders, could stick his head out of the blunt tower. A place for burning things.

The gravestones suffered from Dutch Elm disease. Sileen stepped daintily over the untended grass, not wanting to crush the faces of the dead. All present: tump, church, pre-war railway station at the end of the lane, distant hills. What to make of it? Sleep and try again.

Hodgson had the advantage. He wrote his book in Wales.

THREE

Jaunting cars were out of season, they arrived at the cross-roads on the back of a cart. After Ardrahan they stuck by the book. No more self-drive, no more luggage. Slowly, hanging on to the feed sacks, they yielded to landscape, climbed. Stone walls replaced the coarse hedges. Somewhere, without noticing it, they breached the borderline between shale and carboniferous limestone.

It had been Helen's idea, a good one, to bathe in the chalybeate springs (sulphur and iodine); a radioactive purge to return Sileen to the purity of his original vision. Exposed, high enough on the back of the cart to appreciate the accumulations of glacial debris, they listened for the chatter of underground streams, holy wells, curses and cures. They sloughed off the flakes of old skin.

The land they were invading was bleak, sharply defined, a geological plate set to record the slightest tremor of alien intelligence. Sileen knew that he must lay aside his strategies of survival, the tricks and fabulations that had brought him to the place where dreams effortlessly defied the spirals of time. He understood that the forced scenario of the X-ray cellar was fractured, cut to suit the inadequacy of its audience. One man. Todd Sileen.

He told the driver to stop, and paid him, without counting the notes, all that he had in his pocket. They sat at the roadside, watching, until the cart was out of sight, lurching back to Corofin. Then they were free to look openly at Leamaneh Castle, the House on the Borderland. A fortified manor built around a fifteenth century tower. The damaged redoubt of the Tanaiste (the Expected One).

It was the picture Sileen had carried for months, the paperback. The perfectly weighted displacement of terror and respect, functional defence compromised by a brutal elegance. Roofless, poultices of lichen feeding the hungry stonework: copper dipped in acid. The tower, with its arrow slits, was the depository of meaning; the manor house an unconvincing addendum. The tower incubated darkness, while the house was a screen through which light was graded. Built to be a ruin, Leamaneh did not adulterate Sileen's purpose.

He had been wrong from the start. His project was as loopy as Taylor's – cod's head soup and thirdhand imagery. There was no 'House on the Borderland'. A condition had been described, a pathology, *not* a specific location. The forty mile circumference around Ardrahan would throw up dozens of potential dustwrappers, proposals for graphic novels. Finding the house solved nothing, it stranded them on a bone plateau of winds and voices. Difficult to accept, but William Hope Hodgson practised a form known as fiction.

Sileen pulled Helen away. No point in exploring the home farm for traces of wilderness gardens. They set off, walking fast, into the rocky uplands.

Cobs of damp air rolled off the hills, lifted from the green cobalt crust. Helen was delighted with the design of the walls, vertically stacked stones, forcing the sky through in a savage calligraphy. She wanted to stop, peer into the fields, but Sileen was remorseless. There was someone ahead of them on the road; the next corner, the next rise, would reveal them.

The scream of fat winds forced into their boreholes.

A steady ascent into the silence of the rocks. Helen felt it, she had to rest. She'd been here before, with girl friends, out of Dublin. Flowers, Alpine-Arctic and Mediterranean – mountain avens, blue spring gentians. Now the grey shield was lifeless, fissured. Shallow, earth-filled grykes were hidden in the mist. She wanted to search out the orchids and primroses.

Sileen left her. He limped on, determined to confront his man.

A few goats cropping on the far side of the wall – that's what it sounded like. Meteorite hollows. A glaccio-karstic desert. Underground water, hidden lakes and black rivers; salt rain attacking the porous rock. Unseen processes: dentritic patterns, echoing caves. 'No wood to hang a man, no water to drown him, no earth to bury him in.' The Burren.

Sileen was calling for her. Alone, the stupidity of it struck him – flogging his paranoia across this wilderness. Even Taylor, mad as malaria, would have more sense. It was hard to tell if the heaps of loose stone were walls that had collapsed, or another thing the walls were evolving towards. Entire villages had been lost to thorn. Burial mounds were promoted as the hermitages of saints who fed for years on their own dung. This story was better left untold. One field was as good as the next. There was too much of it. The epic starts wherever you bruise your foot.

It was so cold they had to pick a site that would take them out of the wind. A lake in the valley below. A horseshoe of tumbled boulders, erratics left by the ice. Teeth in a megalithic plum. Chaos as the grand design. Wedge tombs, shepherds' huts. They clambered over the outer rim and came within an enclosure of broken slabs. A killeen, Helen claimed, a burial place for unbaptized children. How small the memorials were! No names, no dates. A mushroom paste to erase all futile inscriptions. Something moved, a scrabbling in the undergrowth. A feral goat, a dog.

A shadow escaping from the menhir. Sileen was away. 'It's Taylor. I've got him now.' Walls to hurdle. Angry shouts: distant, then close to Helen, near the road. Precipitation drifting like steam from heated stones. She lost them both.

An open field, easy running, falling, sliding down to a lake as black as melted film. No cover for Taylor. He must be on the other side, climbing. Sileen's dream?

It took so long, working his way around the water, the soft ground. Taylor crossing the hill in the shadow of a cloud. A blanket of stone: crushed, flinty. No dream, Sileen turned an ankle. The wrong leg hurt. There were cracks in the crust shaped to trap a foot. He crawled, clawing at ash, clinker in nails.

Taylor must be drumming the scree with his boots, hiding himself inside the column of his own dust. Sileen forced himself to anticipate, secure the ledge the maniac was aiming for. But standing in a corkscrew wind is hard. He managed it, long enough for a rapid-scan orientation. He was penned in a steep triangle of dry stone walls. At worst, the X-rays were confirmed. Only his interpretation of them was flawed: the borderland as a political metaphor, a pompous newsreel. Donegal/Tyrone: fences, observation towers, surveillance. Nothing of the kind. This landscape was biblical, a high place temptation enscored by martyrdom.

Sunlight broke through the hanging clouds, a quiver of beams over

Slievecarran, the sacred mountain. Helen sat on a stone slab and took from her pocket the notebook she'd found among the rubble of Taylor's cottage. The red seal – she broke it with her fingernail. Nothing happened. The sky didn't drain away. No bolt of retribution poked her in the eye. But still she would not look at what Sileen had written. She *knew* it was his work. Why had he sent it to Taylor of all people, a man who repudiated the imagination? Had Taylor, meditating revenge, bribed some lowlife to steal the book?

Reading it would destroy the trust they had developed over years, she understood that. The loving indifference. Picking his pockets, or sleeping with other men, was one thing – this was serious. Like badmouthing Joseph Conrad. Too late to withdraw. The pages were damp, stuck together, words laid out in blocks like logarithms. Sileen's script was quaint but legible, secretive, barely punctuated: automatic writing transcribed by a speed freak. The paper felt like clay.

She'd have to hurry, before he gave up chasing shadows, came back. He'd find a different woman waiting.

ISCARIOT HACKNEY (OR, THE NIGHTSTALKER) A CHECKLIST

Allcroft, A. Hardiman. *Earthworks of England*. 1908.

Artaud, Antonin. *The Death of Satan & Other Mystical Writings*. 1974.

Bachelard, Gaston. *The Poetics of Reverie*. Boston, 1969.

Baron, Alexander. *The Lowlife*. 1963. (With ownership signature of Harry H. Corbett.)

Barrett, Francis. *The Magus, or Celestial Intelligencer*. 1801.

Blakesley, Stephen. *A Case for the Cardinal*. 1946.

Blakesley. *The Cardinal and the Corpse*. 1947.

Blakesley. *The Bloom of Death*. 1954.

Blayre, Christopher (Edward Heron-Allen). *Some Women of the University*. 1932.

Bossy, John. *Giordano Bruno and the Embassy Affair*. 1991.

Bousset, W./Keane, A.H. *The Antichrist Legend*. 1896.

Brownell, Morris R. *Alexander Pope's Villa*. 1980.

Budge, E.A. Wallis. *The Liturgy of Funerary Offerings (The Egyptian Texts with English Translations)*. 1909. (With bookplate of photographer/initiate Alvin Langdon Coburn.)

Buxton, Edward North. *Epping Forest*. 1905. With maps.

Cardinal, Roger. *The Landscape Vision of Paul Nash*. 1989.

Carr, Gordon. *The Angry Brigade*. 1975.

Castaneda, Carlos. *The Art of Dreaming*. New York, 1993.

Caulfield, Catherine. *Multiple Exposures (Chronicles of the Radiation Age)*. 1989.

Céline, L-F. *Journey to the End of the Night*. 1934.

Céline. *Guignol's Band*. New York, 1954.

Chandler, T.J. *The Climate of London*. 1965.

Cohen, Joseph. *Journey to the Trenches (The Life of Isaac Rosenberg)*. 1975.

Conrad, Joseph. *Nostromo (A Tale of the Seaboard)*. 1904.

Daunton, Claire (ed.). *The London Hospital Illustrated (250 Years)*. 1990.

Day, George E. *Productive Swine Husbandry*. Chicago, 1913.

Dobson, Anita. *My EastEnd*. 1987.

Dunne, J.W. *Nothing Dies*. 1940.

Eliade, Mircea. *The Forge and the Crucible*. 1962.

Gibbs, Denis. *Emblems, Tokens and Tickets of the London Hospital*. 1985.

Gilbert, Bob. *The Green London Way*. 1991.

Gordon, E.O. *Prehistoric London, Its Mounds and Circles*. 1925.

Graves, Robert. *The White Goddess (A Historical Grammar of Poetic Myth)*. 1948.

Hancox, Joy. *The Byrom Collection (Renaissance Thought, the Royal Society and the Building of the Globe Theatre)*. 1992.

Harrison, Michael. *London Beneath the Pavements*. 1961.

Hauser, Thomas. *The Black Lights (Inside the World of Professional Boxing)*. 1987.

Haynes, Alan. *Invisible Power (The Elizabethan Secret Services 1570–1603)*. 1992.

Hinton, Brian. *Nights in Wight Satin (An Illustrated History of the Isle of Wight Pop Festivals)*. 1990.

Hinton. *Immortal Faces (Julia Margaret Cameron on the Isle of Wight)*. 1992.

Hinton, James. *The Mystery of Pain (A Book for the Sorrowful)*. n.d.

Hodgson, William Hope. *The Boats of the 'Glen Carrig'*. 1907.

Hodgson. *The House on the Borderland (From the Manuscript, discovered in 1877 by Messrs. Tonnison and Berreggnog, in the Ruins that lie to the south of the Village of Kraighten, in the West of Ireland. Set out here, with Notes)*. 1908.

Hodgson. *Alcoyne the Star Cannibal*. n.d. (Unpublished manuscript, possibly spurious. Private Collection, Vancouver. 1908/1991?)

Hodgson. *The Ghost Pirates*. 1909.

Hodgson. *The Night Land*. 1912.

Hodgson. *Carnacki the Ghost-Finder*. 1913.

(Hodgson) Bell, Ian (ed.). *William Hope Hodgson: Voyages & Visions*. 1987. (With, loosely inserted, provenance unknown, 3 colour polaroids, front and rear view, Hodgson's house. 'Glaneifion', Borth, Cardiganshire.)

Holmes, Richard. *Dr Johnson & Mr Savage*. 1993.

Hopkin, Alannah. *A Joke Goes a Long Way in the Country*. 1982.

Hopkin. *The Out-Haul*. 1985.

Houghton, Henry D. *The New World Coming!* Toronto, 1930.

Howard, Luke. *The Climate of London (Observations 1806–1830)*. Revised & enlarged. 2nd edn, 3 vols, 1833.

Howard. *Barometrographia*. 1847.

Hutchinson, W.W. *London Past and Present (With a Chapter on the Future in London by Ford Madox Hueffer)*. 1909.

Jefferies, Richard. *After London, or Wild England*. 1885.

Josten, Charles. *Elias Ashmole (1617–1692). His Autobiographical & Historical Notes, his Correspondence, & other Contemporary Sources relating to his Life & Work*. 5 vols, Oxford, 1966.

Kees, Weldon. *Collected Poems*. 1993.

Kersh, Gerald. *Night and the City*. 1938.

Lambrianou, Tony (Carol Clerk). *Inside the Firm (the Untold Story of the Krays' Reign of Terror)*. 1991.

Lewis, Wyndham. *Blasting and Bombadiering (Autobiography 1914–1926)*. 1937.

Litvinoff, Emanuel. *The Lost Europeans*. 1960.

Lodwick, John. *Peal of Ordnance*. 1947.

Lowes, Tony. *Lull's Device*. Co. Cork, Ireland, 1984. ('Traditionally used to stimulate discussions among circles of friends gathered together for spiritual and self improvement.')

Miller, Hamish/Broadhurst, Paul. *The Sun & the Serpent (An Investigation into Earth Energies by tracking one of the world's most famous Ley Lines)*. Launceston, 1989.

Morris, E.W. *A History of the London Hospital*. 1910.

Morris, Leon. *Apocalyptic*. 1972.

Morrison, Arthur. *Tales of Mean Streets*. 1894.

Morrison. *To London Town*. 1899.

Murray, Geoffrey. *The Gentle Art of Walking*. 1939.

Needham, Joseph. *Time, the Refreshing River*. 1943.

Nicholas, Barton. *The Lost Rivers of London*. Revised, 1992.

Nicholl, Charles. *The Chemical Theatre*. 1980.

Nicholl. *The Reckoning (The Murder of Christopher Marlowe)*. 1992.

Nuttall, Jeff. *Bomb Culture*. 1968. (See Latham, John. Pps 127, 154, 159, 190, 212, 225–26, 232, 234, 239.)

O'Brien, Flann. *An Béal Bocht*. Dublin, 1941.

O'Brien. *The Third Policeman*. 1967.

Owen, Walter. *The Cross of Carl*. 1931.

Pennick, Nigel. *The Mysteries of King's College Chapel*. Cambridge, 1974.

Petit, Christopher. *Robinson*. 1993.

Philip, Brother. *Secret of the Andes*. 1961.

Pitt-Rivers, George. *The Riddle of the 'Labarum' (and the Origin of Christian Symbols)*. 1966.

Prynne, J.H. *The Oval Window*. Cambridge, 1983.

Raymond, Derek. *He Died With His Eyes Open*. 1984.

Raymond. *The Devil's Home on Leave*. 1984.

Raymond. *How the Dead Live*. 1986.

Redgrove, Peter. *The Black Goddess and the Sixth Sense*. 1987.

Riley, Denise. *Mop Mop Georgette*. Cambridge, 1993.

Roberts, Marie. *British Poets and Secret Societies*. 1986.

Rohmer, Sax. *The Dream-Detective*. 1920.

Rorschach, Kimerly. *The Early Georgian Landscape Garden*. New Haven, 1983.

Rosendorfer, Herbert. *The Architect of Ruins*. Zurich, 1969.

Sacks, Oliver. *A Leg to Stand On*. 1984.

Scholl, William. *Dictionary of the Foot*. Chicago, 1918.

Sheldrake, Rupert. *The Presence of the Past*. 1988.

Sinclair, Arthur. *In Tropical Lands (Recent Travels to the Sources of the Amazon, the West Indian Islands, and Ceylon)*. Aberdeen, 1895.

Story, Jack Trevor. *Up River*. 1979.

Story. *Dwarf Goes to Oxford*. 1987.

(Story) Darwent Brian. *Romantic Egotist (an Unauthorised Biography of Jack Trevor Story)*. 1993.

Swedenborg, Emanuel. *Arcana Caelestia*. 12 vols, 1863.

Swedenborg. *Miracles and Signs (and that they are not expected at this time when the end of the age is near)*. Ed. P.H. Johnson. 1943.

Swedenborg. *Death and After*. Selected by Richard Walton Kenyon. Revised, 1984.

(Swedenborg) Dingle, Herbert. *Swedenborg as a Physical Scientist*. 1938.

Van den Bergh, Tony. *Who Killed Freddie Mills?* 1991.

Waite, A.E. *The Alchemical Writings of Edward Kelly (The Englishman's Two Excellent Treatises on the Philosopher's Stone, together with the Theatre of Terrestrial Astronomy)*. 1893.

Whitehouse, T.H. *Ezekiel's Temple & Sacrifices (A Prophetical Enigma & its Solution)*. 1951.

Yates, Frances A. *Giordano Bruno and the Hermetic Tradition*. 1964.

Yates. *The Art of Memory*. 1966.

Yates. *The Occult Philosophy in the Elizabethan Age*. 1979.

Yeats, W.B. *Rosa Alchemica, The Tables of the Law* and *The Adoration of the Magi*. 1897.

Yeats. *Collected Poems*. 1933.

Zajonc, Arthur. *Catching the Light (The Entwined History of Light and Mind)*. 1993.

Zangwill, Israel. *Dreamers of the Ghetto*. 1898.

Zimmer, Heinrich. *The King and the Corpse (Tales of the Soul's Conquest of Evil)*. Washington, D.C., 1948.

She slammed it shut; pressing her hands together in the clap of prayer, trapping a wafer of light. Another of Sileen's aborted projects. She flung the notebook into the brambles, where it hung like a false hint of spring.

'Quite right. Why labour on when the bibliography is so much more interesting than the book? A decent man abandons fiction at that point. Finds a proper occupation.'

She hadn't heard the prowler sponging up on his desert creepers – probably because he'd arrived first. He was the shadow of the standing stone, the wrecker of colour balance on the monochrome veldt. How had she failed to notice that suit – the green of watch-hands that glow in the dark complementing a cranberry nose? The cancelled smile of a near-gentleman who said he'd give his eye teeth for an introduction, then did.

His merciless courtesy put her at her ease. His conversation was as soothing as a weather report. Nothing ever felt more comfortable than sitting on a rock in Ireland, listening to a stranger who displayed the dress sense of an ex-monk let loose in the Portobello Road under the tutelage of Screaming Lord Sutch.

He offered her his flask, extemporizing while she drank – coughed lightly to condone her hiccups. He helped her climb on to the cairn that stood at the centre of the field, so that she might see for herself what he was too subtle to point out: the complex system of stones set down, or dug out, with random precision in the shape of a gigantic footprint. A print worn deep into the bedrock. A print enclosing hut circles, cists, burial mounds.

'Now,' he said, 'as you'll notice, the present particular asserts itself in such a way that past and future are divorced. A point in space, defined by one sharp perfect landscape in the mind, holds its focus for a second and then fails. And will not, ever, be quite so sharp again. The lake below us is a crater filled from the discharge of a subterranean cavern the natives know as "The Cave of Brazen Horses". Forgive the inadequacy of my translation.'

Either I am two people or somebody else.

Sileen scratched like a cat in a tree. Taylor was slowing – how could he climb with a shotgun tucked under his arm? Standing upright was out of the question on such a slope. The scree shifted like a conveyor-belt. Even when Sileen got himself moving, it was backwards; he lost all he'd gained, dropped the pebble he intended to fling. One clear throw would bring Taylor down. He must get in closer for a quick kill. The rest was hogwash: pits, porkers, planets. Too tame. Blood sacrifice would restore his capacity for invention. Squeeze sap from the barren stones.

Clumps of yellow things grew in black earth veins, promoting a buttery thirst. Reach the summit, then look for a milk sea. He zigzagged in terse diagonals, leaving a confused trail of dust. Blind, he pushed through the curtain of permanent mist. Better. Much better: hopeless, insane. Weird outcrops announced themselves by other means. Climbing by touch, Sileen was not sure if he was going up or across. He expected, with each short step, a chasm or a swallowhole. Taylor's manic laughter fracturing the limestone drape.

Trying to haul himself up, he found that he could. The mist hid him from spies in the valley below. A tower was waiting – just for him. Nothing like the concrete atrocity of his dreams, no jutting platforms, mesh of protective wire – smooth as a wooden pepper-grinder. One of those Round Towers that were never lived in, supposed refuges in time of war. But who'd fall for that simplistic explanation? They'd treat you like an indoor bonfire. Meaty smoke from a black chimney. These things, with their queer conical lids, were bred not built. On off-shore islands where women were forbidden.

Sammy Taylor had made his first mistake. He was inside. Nowhere to go.

'Who can distinguish darkness from the soul?' Sileen, calm now, stood waiting for the spiral stairs to take form. Wind hissed like a pressure-hose in the arrow slits. *I want it*. Like the chanting of pinhead priests who calibrate the stars. *I'll pay the price*. Star-acid scoured colour from the rocks.

He rested, listened for Taylor, up there, under the steep hood, meditating on a platform of bricks. But the American adventurer was too canny to breathe. He knew it was over and was preparing himself.

Sileen counted the steps, sang out: 'They sent for a Taylor to measure – him.' Faster and faster in the narrowing bore, fierce in concentration, until predator and prey share a single heart. Soon he would know.

A bird's claw scratching on parchment. Taylor was trying to write, the last word, ensure that *his* account was the one found by the archivists.

Who would dare to move first? Who had the more convincing synopsis? Who could quote Hodgson, line for line? It was almost his: the fusion. Writer, character, writer. The visionary's instant of annihilation and ecstasy.

This was all that we could learn. Of the author of the MS., who he was, and whence he came, we shall never know.

A traitor wind. The tower: a stone flute. Sileen risks his hand on the ancient oak door, and, as it creaks, alive and dead, is doubly blessed. 'What matter if I live it all once more?' He would be sure – *sure* – of the secret of Hodgson's recluse. Was all the study, the suffering, worthy of the wisdom gained? Sileen, advancing, was not the hermit, the seeker trapped in his cell, *he was the thing on the stairs*. The Tanaiste. The web-foot beast.

Taylor's blast, both barrels, ripped him open. He tried to tuck his shirt back in, but his hands went through. After the hush, the vacuuming of incidental sound, a scalding breeze rushed through the chamber, from below, the magnetic core. Sileen stepped into the flood of images that engulfed the tower. He saw what he wanted: the Burren cobbled over. It looked like London. The lights of a public-house. A roebuck carved in frost. Arms clasped, they drowned in air, both of them. Alone.

Voluntary amnesia: a new sky on a blue canvas blind. The man was pleased with himself, deservedly so. He'd found what he wanted, confirmed what he knew. The landscape could be returned to his study, put away. Helen couldn't see much point in that. What did it leave to do with the rest of your life?

Nice hands though. Unlike Sileen, he managed to keep them still when he talked. A story she didn't need to hear.

It had been foretold, at his birth, that a man of this country would be killed by lightning. He grew up with the comfort of that knowledge overriding lesser torments. Fear of lightning defined him. He kept to his house, refusing to take his share in the tending of the animals. Orphaned, celibate, he lived that way for years – until, during one particularly savage storm, skies black as the pit, the man cowering in the straw, a thief broke in and stole his clothes, his boots.

Now, at last, anger overcame fear. Hot with spite, he pursued the rogue, and, catching him in a field, in the enjoyment of the boots, smashed open his head with a convenient rock – to recover the sodden rags. In that moment his phobia was conquered.

But the act of revenge had been witnessed by a child, a girl. The other villagers, having no reason to hold him in affection, judged the man and condemned him to death. He was stoned in the very place where his fear had been lost. The prophecy, as always, being fulfilled. Lightning, the fear of it, was his destroyer.

The storyteller bowed to pick Sileen's notebook from the bush, hand it to Helen. He was too polite to walk away. They sat, talking, in the field. Drinking from the flask. The sun moved round the hills. He knew about Sileen, the quest. Of course he did. Knew things her lover had refused to explain. All this time the lame fool had been chasing a manuscript! Perhaps he knew Taylor?

'Oh, certainly, yes. A desultory correspondent, useful for ferreting in Irish libraries, faxing maps. Sammy was a writer by conviction, not ability. One who survived, I'm sorry to say, by minor feats of mediumship, literary impersonation, fraud. Contriving sequels which, for good historical reasons, never existed.'

'*Was*? He's dead?'

'Quite. Years ago. Late Seventies? Some little local difficulty, Art Wars. The Mung Beans Mafia burnt down his house.'

'But – we've been getting letters from him, Sileen has. Who *are* you anyway?'

His hand.

'Undark. Lachrimae Christi. Cambridge.'

'The bastard was sending letters to himself!'

'Very probably. Excellent therapy for a writer's block.'

That seemed to finish it. The imprint of a foot on a table of rock. Unbaptized children: a nest of bones. A lake that could be sucked back into the ground at any time. She wanted to return the favour, give him a name.

'I'm Helen.'

'Helen.'

No question mark. His eyebrows. The understudy of a smile. It hung over her like a cloud cut from tin. His interest was genuine, but detached.

A bird hopping over prison grass. The outline of a demolished church. Whitechapel. Mary Matfellon. She had always kept to the path, walked quickly through.

HELEN REDPATH. Thirty Years A Servant.

'Redpath,' she said. And it was true.

The bird settled briefly on the curve of the gravestone – swooped, righted itself, skipped erratically away. A lapwing.

AUTHOR'S NOTE

Wishing somehow to authenticate the fanciful notion of a triangulation between the earthworks of Cambridge, Whitechapel, and Oxford, I invited three friends, who had associations with those places, to rise before dawn on the shortest day of winter, 1992, to make a brief report — in whatever form they chose — on the advent of light.

My thanks to them. The book would otherwise be incomplete.

LAURENCE BICKNELL. REED MAN & CAMBRIDGE. *Castle Mound /*
Shortest Day

dream in the North of the large lakes / flooded areas of rings
I decide to swim round /some metal object with me, dropped in first lake . . .
I am asking whether people make the rounds of the group of stone circles
to celebrate
the round of the seasons   (knowing the answer is YES)

leaving my Parents home at 4 o'clock
Across Fen Causeway / layers of clothing / starry
then clouding in / thoughts arising / Along the Backs
the ditch / childhood / stones not indigenous

The Tor had emptied itself long before my feet; standing within the dispersed mountain offered no comfort against the freezing dark.
In a ticking chant I circled the late dolmen, a fulcrum between history and invention: a mechanical mantra recreating the solid air.
The crescent's rise above this stone heart suggested a height for the new mound, a congealed mound of activated space and ghost-imagery.

BRIAN CATLING. CASTLE MOUND, OXFORD

The creosoted string has given its black smell to the knife and the small light of the torch that I carried with me to the shuffled spiral of the mound, a vagrant Silbury, coining no pilgrimage and claiming no pulse other than its own astonishing invisibility.

This is my site to dawn, any idea of the others contacting me along straight lines of intention is erased by the slumped centrifuge of the place. The brittle triangulation of our mutual awareness is strained and given up against now.

It is impossible to tell if the cold is forging the darkness outside or brutalising it into existence inside this hump of loosely mangered earth, spiking it out in bladed frost so that I slip wither tongue between its anemone fringe of iced black green. The city, the horizon and the sky oceaned in a myriad of shades, collapsing distance, black slutted with all colour, so that it patches a rag worn scarfing on to sight, an ink cezanne quilt squided and flint slivered to the straining eye.

There is no sense of direction up here, in this forgotten corner of this most memorised city, the sun could rise in any direction. Below the flood knotted rivers howl and pack against the draining roads and iron spoor of railways. At bleating dawn they will begin to vacantly tip arrival here, outside all the city walls.

But at this hour the only movement is upwards, the city steams off its heat from empty offices full of curdled dreams, rising up from the prison and the college, plumes of white fleeing to the icy stars. This fence of exhalation is satellite to the nub of shadow on which I stand. The root bones of cold filling my shoes, snuggling clay into my blood, an embrocation of sleep and futility that disconnects the heart and the senses from perception.

To invent gravity and grip purpose I walk a continual wheel along the crown of the mound, the stiff frozen grass cracking under the stumbling insistence of the circulatory mantra.

Without design or expression I have drawn a dark ring on the white dome of frost. The trampled perimeter has attracted the sun. Hours have been eaten by repetition, the feast giving energy to quietly open the vision and leave the husk of intension to fade in the first accent of morning wind. Now I can approach the centre.

Men were hanged here. Spilling out over the oxpens, twisting, wringing out over the mound, draining into the cup of its hidden interior a flailing tongue to this mournful bell of earth.

I enter the gate before light or warmth has touched its frozen padlock, a steel heart burning a bruise in my hand. The irregular stone stairs lead down into the nightcore of the hill, stopping and turning to the right is a circular room brimmed with stone to listen and nest water.

A well at the centre falls even further, its wide mouth hooked into the chamber by a girdle of iron. Above passing and floating is a canopy of fluted stone, its intimate dome being sentinel, sternly caressing some inner property of this nocturnal shrine. The darkness sucks against the flimsy of the torch, I turn it off. The sublime and for the first time warm dark enfolds and walks through me, all the ideas and motivation are snuffed, the wick's gentle smoking in the draughtless enclosure of my head, echoing the dome quietly without image. Absolute peace, the body dissolving. I have entered a model, a simple and almost forgotten construct. This knowledge walks me out and back to the road of my sleep.

The white dream
the necessity to invent a crude and angry machine. The bed has suffered me this, shrouding out the iron frozen night, sense vengefully giving reason to bliss.

Returning in equivalent light, I erect the night halo by temperature change. The rising sun giving heat difference to the unseen first stage platform. Standing in the hanging place I unwind the cord. Twisting the tarry burn into furrows and scars of my labouring heart, I have to wrench this engine alive and gun it into an inner vertical direction, tugging the choke to chant. The dark halo rises, the ground heat lifting the crushed circle into light. While the negatives shimmer in transfusion I rip the greasy rope, the pain storm hushes the inversion to a slow inch, the string falling to nuzzle worm-like down into the wet soil, tiny circle pluming around the puckered dive. The halo is now invisible and stationary at the height of the previous hanged men, the string has centred down and scratches at the outside socket of the stone room. It has grown a nail or claw or egg-tooth to splinter and write inside the sanctum, it is embedding a line in sympathy inside the well, luminous and turning. The hollow of its passage above awaits some drizzle from me, perhaps the tapped and acrid nectar from my spine which has already begun to rotate in sympathy with the well light and spinning sound above.

The waking will vapour a different road back, a different excuse to submerge and clasp the place, another fiction hook cast to hold on.